Alan M. Kent was born in the i  all, and graduated from the Unive ist, dramatist, poet and a literary sch<del></del> *ies* won the Holyer an Gof Prize fo<del></del> e- winning plays and acclaimed vol<del></del> *of Truth*. He has been the recipient <del></del> ...ptwriting Award, the Charles Lee Prize and a Bristol Old <del></del> Open Season Playwriting Award. His stage adaptation of the children's picture book, *The Mousehole Cat* has toured internationally. As well as his non-fiction writing, he has edited several collections of Cornish and Anglo-Cornish Literature. He is the series editor of *Lesser Used Languages of Europe*, and joint series editor of *Cornish and Celtic Alternatives* and *Corpus Textuum Cornicorum*.

BY THE SAME AUTHOR

A SELECT BIBLIOGRAPHY

FICTION
Clay
Dreaming in Cornish
Proper Job, Charlie Curnow!
Electric Pastyland
The Cult of Relics
Voodoo Pilchard
Voog's Ocean
Dan Daddow's Cornish Comicalities
Turning Serpentine

DRAMA
Ordinalia: The Cornish Mystery Play Cycle
Nativitas Christi
Oogly es Sin
The Tin Violin
Surfing Tommies
A Mere Interlude
Bewnans Peran
National Minority
The Incredible Balti-Celtic Carpet Ride

POETRY
Grunge
Out of the Ordinalia
The Hensbarrow Homilies
Love and Seaweed
Assassin of Grammar
Stannary Parliament
Druid Offsetting
The Hope of Place: Selected Poems in English 1990-2010
Interim Nation
The Mouth of Truth

NON-FICTION
The Literature of Cornwall: Continuity, Identity, Difference
Pulp Methodism: The Lives and Literature of Silas, Joseph and Salome Hocking
Cousin Jack's Mouth-Organ: Travels in Cornish America
The Theatre of Cornwall: Space, Place, Performance
Celtic Cornwall: Nation, Tradition, Invention
The Festivals of Cornwall: Ritual, Revival, Re-invention

AS EDITOR/CO-EDITOR
Voices from West Barbary: An Anthology of Anglo-Cornish Poetry 1549-1928
Looking at the Mermaid: A Reader in Cornish Literature
Inside Merlin's Cave: A Cornish Arthurian Reader
The Dreamt Sea: An Anthology of Anglo-Cornish Poetry 1928-2004
Wave Hub: New Poetry from Cornwall
The Charter Fragment and Pascon Agan Arluth

SAFFRON-BUN
CHAPEL

First published in Great Britain in 2022
Copyright © Alan M. Kent 2022

Alan M. Kent has asserted his right under the Copyright, Designs
and Patents Act 1988 to be identified as the author of the work.

Cover design and illustration: Lorraine Inglis

British Library Cataloguing-in-Publication Data
A CIP record for this title is available from the British Library

ISBN 978 1 906551 48 3

RYELANDS
Halsgrove House,
Ryelands Business Park,
Bagley Road, Wellington, Somerset TA21 9PZ
Tel: 01823 653777   Fax: 01823 216796
email: sales@halsgrove.com

www.halsgrove.com

Part of the Halsgrove group of companies
Information on all Halsgrove titles is available at: www.halsgrove.com

Printed and bound in India by Parksons Graphics

SAFFRON-BUN CHAPEL

CHAPEL

An Industrial Fairy Tale

Alan M. Kent

ryelands

"Our eyes are sentinels unto our judgements,
And should give certain judgement what they see;
But they are rash sometimes, and tell us wonders
Of common things, which when our judgments find,
They can then check the eyes, and call them blind."

Thomas Middleton and William Rowley,
The Changeling, 1622

'The intense ignorance which existed in many of
the districts visited by me, at the period named, has
been almost dispelled by the civilising effects of
Wesleyanism. Consequently, when a scrofulus child
is found in a family, we no longer hear of its being
a changeling; but within a very short period, I have
heard it said that such afflicted children had been
"ill-wished."

Robert Hunt, *The Drolls, Traditions and Superstitions
of Old Cornwall*, 1881

Callin' un 'ome

Some things never change.

Aaaaahh!

An h'aromatic and slightly h'astringent fragrance greeted her upon her entry. Es – it was a door that she dearly wanted to open. Such a smell had been tempting her for a while now, ever since her arrival. She plunged in, almost without thinking. It had been a long wait. She was quickly offered one and opened her mouth wide. Already salivating – automatically, and out of habit – her teeth bit into it. She felt them slice through the spongy mass of it, sprinkled with the hardness, the lastingness of blackened, juicy currants – and still a little hot in the middle. Whoops. Be careful now. She needed to be sure it did not burn her tongue. It felt good though: warm and moist. Oven-fresh. Zactly what wuz needed. It tasted of home. Yes, she could recall it. That taste. She felt all of the gentle love and kneading that had gone into it here.

Somewhere, back in time, she had a picture of the heel of her grandmother's hand pressing, forcing it out, turning an idea into reality. Then there was the flour-dusted surface: the folding over until it became elastic and stretchy. Rotating and proofing. Then, the portioning. Mounds were placed as granite tors upon the greaseproof paper. Piles like the *radgell* rock scree found on the road from Botallack to Zennor. It all reminded her of her childhood. Aw es – that was the way of things back then. There were memories of Sunday-afternoon teas at her grandparents – or, until recently at least (when it had started to fray and not be passed on, like it was meant), a festive tea-treat in the village.

The revel buns were always the size of cow-pats; they were as big as your head. They lasted for days afterwards. The rest you'd save for crowst that week. 'Eave on a spoonful of clotted cream if it dried up a bit. That'll sort ee out. Somewhere, close to the food table, the crazy cyclical twists and turns of the dance of a snail creep. The hazy face of the reluctant boy she was put to dance with: his frothing, oscillating gob still chewing the remnants of the sweetened roll, and its scattered dried fruit. In the distance, the wheeze of an accordion; the jaunty scrape of a violin. Simple pleasures. Es. There was the tay, and then there was the treat. For devilment, she'd give un a kiss.

With it, came sounds and voices. Pieces of dialect. Older words too. All those endearing (but equally annoying) habits of both tongue and lip that marked them out as different. The musicality of ut. The rhythm of aspirated vowels. The understated dry humour of them. Their capacity for archaisms. The comical gravity: sense always twisted with a pretend solemn air. Their stories and their tales. Unconscious drollery. The folklore. And spicy innuendo, even found here now from some of the men present – boys still with a twinkle in their eyes. She'd still kept her looks, she thought. To think of it! An' they s'paused to be Methodists too!

She felt both tongue and taste. It hit the minute receptors on her tongue, and she felt it all in the back of her throat. A sensation like no other. It was a taste that had travelled far and wide with her. It had helped her to negotiate her passage around the earth. It was both her stars and sextant, a fixed point on her horizon. Familiar, even in places dark, hot and muggy – when there was no air, when mid-continental summers like these, brought no breeze from the west – and all you wished for was to stand next to the cooling ocean, back home. There, you could see mines on the very edges of cliffs; not like the one here, bizarrely located in the middle of the forest up on the high fell.

Before indulging again, she looked carefully at it. Longingly. Lovingly. Es. Es. Everywhere around her, inside the once-white chapel – a yellowing. Sepia-tinged photographs. Founders. Congregations. Rolls of Honour. Organ funds. Fresh paint now, where until lately, leaf fronds unfurled and reigned. Even trees in here they had said. Then, another bite. More stamens of power. Dear as. Threads and seasoning. Dots of those bleddy currants. Like bullets they were. She saw the bobs of heads. Short back and sides and those ' taches that all men seemed to wear back then. Four walls keeping everything in. A bewdie planchen floor of amber dough though. That golden top of a roof, tiled good and proper. Almost like that from Delabole, or that's what they'd have you think. In truth, they were grey, timbered shingles. From those, fell tiny crumbs. Maybe if she listened close enough – hard enough – there'd be a sound to it: an unveiling of flavour and culture, just audible. If you pressed it, it would creak. Some old, you. You enjoyed the feel of it in your hand. It was comforting both in taste and touch. Golden. Priceless. Tradition: the shared practice of her people. And the food of a nation: its beating heart – what lined its stomach, what it threw deep down its clunker and into its belly.

And then, when magically she proceeded down the aisle as guest of honour to give her speech, she realised that none of it was edible. Not at all. She'd been hallucinating. Gah! She'd been deceived. Someone had made a play – a sleight of hand. It wasn't even a cake. Sadly, it wasn't truly a bun either; at least no bun that she'd ever come across before. Something had led her astray. Was it her instinct – or just pure imagination? Magic even? The magic was reflected in the orange- and black-winged butterflies that had somehow got inside, and now danced in the windows. Because of their colour, apparently people here called them Tigers.

Maybe this dark and thundery Michigan summer had affected her: easy, up here on the Keweenaw, on the Upper Peninsula; this far from everything, this isolated. She looked around her once more. She was inside. It was her jet-lagged mind had made it something else. The box that was the building had momentarily been a line of edible treats. In reality, it had pews: hard, inedible pews. It had black Hymnals; the paper leaves of which would be flavourless. They'd be inky tart. She noted the grand yet sour pulpit, once the source of promulgation, of reflection and of God's love. The high ceiling rose, though beautifully crafted of plaster, would be bland and insipid if ever licked.

She then realised that yes, she was caught in its airless surround. It was, in fact, a chapel and, over time, it had been given a name. Or maybe, she thought, as her senses danced at such smells and odours from the past, it had named itself. And then she realised, it had become itself in a way by some kind of odd parthenogenesis, created without the need for a pairing. Yes. That was what it was. She looked up at the interior yellowed walls, ingested the smell that only old America has (a mould produced by heat and dryness, not like at home by damp and cold) and only then, did she realise what she had entered. This was immaculate conception and it had lost its earlier name somewhere in the mists of time. It had no other name now, apart from the lugubrious 'Saffron-Bun Chapel'. Unlike most other people, places and things now, unusually, it looked like it fully knew its place in the world: at no odds with the present and at peace with its past. So there ' twas. Despite it being a chapel then, something still told you to bite into it – and to her, it tasted bleddy 'andsome.

1

Some pair they wuz. Damme. There was the good one. And then, there was the other one. Right mucker-outters, this pair of Cousin Jacks were. Pards for life. The good one's name was Francis Nankervis, and he was aged but twenty-four. And the other one wuz his brother – Justin Nankervis – a year younger, at twenty-three. By the look obm traipsing through the dark forest in the summer of 1900, you cudn' tell them apart. They had a Cornish look to them. What the hell tha' wuz, you cudn' rightly say, but you knew it if you saw it. Somethun' about the way they carried themselves. Somethun' about their gait and strong upper torsos, something to do with the determination in their eyes to make a better life for themselves. Something ancient in them too: primitive, like they was another species of humanity; one that had either not evolved as much, or had evolved further. Whatever it wuz, it brewed inside of them. It made the air sultry.

This pair of bewdies were walking in the high fells, amongst woods so deep and expansive that light got sucked away from them at every inhalation of air. It was fairy-tale dark, like the woods once were in the old country, before half of that timber got cut down and now propped up the levels and shafts of innumerable mines. Here was virgin forest, and they were walking where no one had walked before. There could be anything out there: piskies, buccas, unicorns, and scary wood-beasts no one had thought to name. It was untouched. It was pristine. It felt like there were no seasons. Or rather that the four seasons came all at once. In one hour, there could be a spring wind, summer sun, fall rain and winter snow. It was like that here on the Keweenaw. It was a separate world: its own kingdom. Like Cornwall, it had its own rules, and it wuz charged with myth.

Justin, though squatter, moved better than Francis through the forest. He spread like pump oil, or maybe even quicksilver, quickly sizing up every bush or hillock. He had a nose fur copper ore – that was true enough. He could sense it: feel it in his bones. He'd always been that way, ever since they'd been boys. Francis was taller, slower, more cautious and observant, like a shy wild animal testing for predators. He never relied on his nose alone. His faith was in science, in assaying and testing. That's why he kept a mobile boxed-kit of chemicals and test tubes on his back. He knew its importance. Unlike his more wayward brother, he'd taken to attending evening classes in Metallurgy at Camborne School of Mines. He wanted certainty. But there wudn' much of it out here. In fact, it was surely lacking. The place constantly shifted and changed position. A man could think it one way but he'd be dumb to do so, for in a blink of an eye, it would change again. Mining landscapes are always like that. They are shifting sands.

Es – and accompanying them (as ever) were their loyal Knockies. Effectively, the brothers were their masters. You cudn' see their Knockies but they wuz there. They weren't folklore. They were real. If anyone tells you anything different, then they'm a head-case. They awnly shaw themselves when they want to because that's the way they are. It's always been that way. Knockies are mining spirits, and go deep down in any hole in the ground in the world and you'll find them. See, they dun' stay put. They travel. They migrate. They move. Just like humans. The good one had a naughty Knockie named Gourgy. Gourgy was a name from the Cornish language and it meant 'mad dog' and that was right enough because that was what he was like. A mad one, and queer enough with ut. All the Knockies back home thought so.

The other one had a sensible Knockie named Luk, and that was a name that wasn't anything special. It just meant a combination of Luke and Luck. And the way it was, the Knockie looked after his miner, and the miner looked after his Knockie. So every so often, back home, after crowst, each miner would toss a knub-end of pasty, or a small passel of saffron bun, on the level floor for his Knockie to eat; and in syncopation (at some later hour), his Knockie would knock on the walls of the stope to foretell of a rock fall, so as to keep their miner guardian safe. Either tha', or they'd hear ov a knocking and get everyone out of ut before a collapse. And that was the way things were back home in Cornwall, since, so it was said, the Phoenicians came and first traded tin. Es. So 'twas.

Some said the Knockies were the spirits of dead miners who'd gone on before, and others said they were just stupid goblins of the ground, but whatever they were, 'twas best to keep um on side and to keep them close. That way, they would warn a man of a giving-away or a cave-in. Sometimes too, they were practical jokers, and spent their time hiding tools and hindering work, but that was all part of ut. No one minded. Na. 'Twas the way 'twas. Over millennia Knockies had evolved to not be very tall (well you wudn' want to evolve too much, if you lived underground). They wuz two-foot tall, and had disproportionately large heads, long arms and saggy, wrinkled skin (fur lack of sunlight). Most of um had long white whiskers, and thick sideburns, for they were old; and over time, they'd come to dress like miners, with felt 'tull' hats and candles, and carried pick-axes to help them do whatever they did. They tended to wear loincloths and waistcoats. Buggers they could be, but no one wanted to be in a mine without them. There wuz thousands of um back home, but hundreds of um had travelled to the new world, and got on boats to America, or what they called 'Merky'. Good luck to um. They were only doing the same thing that their humans were. What did ee expect? Did ee think they'd just stay behind?

What happened wuz simple enough. It dun't merit much telling, not like the rest of this yarn. Naw, indeed. The two men and their Knockies had arrived by ship to New York. For a week, they had stayed in the city, residing at Sid Blake's place on 23rd Street. The place, 'The Cornish Arms', was a hovel, and always stank of stale beer, tobacco and piss, but it was famous enough amongst migrating miners for all those who arrived to go there. The grapevine told them to board there, so they did. There could be found communion and safety in one's own people; like this vast land was not as frightening as it seemed. In Blake's place you could hear the old accent. 'Twas a kind of home from home. Better at least than in the cramped steerage on board the ship from Bristol with only a stinking mattress, bowl, knife, fork and spoon.

And before that, the long train ride up the peninsula to the port on the River Avon. Hundreds of Cornish there ready to come out. Lined up on the railway platform at Redruth they wuz. Swarming with them 'twas. Rats leaving a sinking ship perhaps? This was the way of things. Every bugger had someone abroad. It seemed the natural way of the world. As fer the crossing, they just grinned and bore it. That was all they could do. Like most Cornish from the interior, they wudn' much good on the ocean. All they and their Knockies could do was just settle in steerage in the best way they could, a-playing cards and dominoes. 'Twas hard to sleep though when the vessel was creaking like a stuck boar and rocking like a steel logan stone.

After finding their feet in New York they resolved to make ut to the copper mining country in Michigan; a decision, like some are, made on a whim or the turn of a card. That in itself was a trip and a half. Fust, there was the greasy railroad to Buffalo. In the port there, they searched for a vessel to take them through Lake Erie and on into Huron, up past Detroit. Sortin' through the lakers and salties (thaas the lake ships and the ocean-going vessels) took another week: discovering the moast efficient vessel that would take them all the way up into Superior. A couple of weeks was spent on that bugger by the time it had put into every port along the way. The crew, led by a man named Nathaniel, were in no hurry, but this foursome were. Both Francis and Justin got bored with cleaning up the daily Knockie sick.

Heading true north they were then: around the chink of Manitoulin Island and putting in for a stop at Little Current. More miners now: Germans and Poles, and Norwegians and Finns; Swedes and Italians. Irish too. New names. Unpronounceable names, and all of them with their mine creatures as well: Kobolds and Menninkäinen. A lot of ethnic tension there, it is not worth discussing here. Rogues, the lot of them. The odd Leprechaun maybe. No skills they buggers: just there for the crack. Then, upwards and on into Whitefish Bay. Es. That's when they saw the expanse of Superior. They knew they were getting close now.

Both the Knockies and they went out on the deck every day taking it all in. At Marquette they paused to load on more coal, but then, the next day, the laker took them around the top of the peninsula. They were at the Keweenaw proper now. The fabled destination. They'd heard it spoke of enough back home at chapel and in the kiddleywinks. Now a bit of that was coming true, and manifesting itself in front of them. They couldn't see it, nor even hear it, but the Knockies were yipping up good and proper, and dancing on the decks, for they too, could sense it. The way they did ut wuz to lay down their pick-axes, into a cross, and nimbly dance around them. That was one of their favourite pastimes down in the caves and galleries of the mines. Others of their kind were already out there making a new life for themselves. Oh, the ingenuity of the Knockies! Ut never let up.

The Bay brought the peninsula into their sight and supposedly, it was about the same length at their homeland. Lower to the shore though. No threatening cliffs, nor gaping zawns. Na. Here the land was lower, more peaceable: a run of trees down to the shoreline and all along the coast, an expanse of ancient black water that looked like it was freshly broken through with the laker's prow. This was it then. The dream was becoming reality. And in the distance, rising up from the shoreline were the mountains and fells, great slabs of land that surely contained what they were looking for. They could taste the ore in the palms of their hands: smell it emanating from the lined sworls on their fingertips.

There wuz a foreboding to the party though, because all of them knew that this was the landscape that would either make them or break them. So they rounded the northernmost tip of it, and the laker dropped anchor. From thereon, it was rowing boats into the inlet that was to become known later as Eagle Harbour. But then, it was a nothingness, a mere trading post, with not much going for it. So they got their gear unloaded: a few belongings and their lucky tools; tools that they hoped would set them on the right place. These picks, shovels and dabbers see, were Knockie-blessed and that's why they'd brought them. 'Twudn' no good to upset your own Knockie with new gear. They wuz to be looked after – and respected. Get that, do ee? It's important. You'll come to see how.

Once they'd all got their bearings, well, then ut wuz three months mucking, in the established and famed Cliff Mine. No rules here like back home. No tutwork nor tribute. Instead, just what was offered. Both brothers and both Knockies worked as hard as they could during this time, to earn a bit, to put some back, to have enough money to go prospecting. See, working for someone else wudn' their aim at all. Na. Not really see. They wanted their own bal; their own claim – to be adventurers. Es. Create a legacy. Something to pass on. Here, they'd both become Cap'ns. That was what the continent of 'Merky' was all about: re-writing the order – turning things upside-down.

They'd had time to weigh it up. They'd nawticed the landscape. They knew where the runs of copper were. They knawed more than most, but they didn' reveal ut. These two brothers had something about them. There was something unusual in them. They were special. So they gabbered on at crowst time with the rest of them, but they asked the right questions. They listened to the folklore. They heard tell of the way the levels were going: where 'twas productive and where 'twudn'. They heard the established boys who had the nawse for it and could smell the ground, and knawed where to dig. And they didn' say much about their own plans: they just touched pipe, listened and absorbed. And they told their Knockies to do the same thing in the levels and beside the trammers coming out. In this way, they came to know the mountain behind them. They understood its make-up and what lay beneath the pine cones and leaf litter. Like the great trees, they spread their roots and came to know the land.

In the end though, they made a decision to leave the Cliff Mine. They gave up their places in the sweaty bunkhouse, handed in their notice to Trevorrow the Cap'n (you'll hear more of ee soon enough). They noted his disappointment, for they were good workers, these two brothers. They didn' mind grafting and everyone knew that. Es – the Cap'n wuz sad to lose them and when he asked them where they were heading for, they just said they were moving on: moving on as if they saw their fortune further to the West, or beyond maybe the Mississippi. Maybe he thought they'd go below to Detroit, or maybe even further north, into Canada, but nonetheless, they picked up their last earnings at payday and left.

And the Knockies did the same thing, and explained their position to the Overseeing Knockie. But Knockies aren't as good as humans as keeping up a lie, and the Overseer knawed in his heart that they pair of Knockies (Gourgy and Luk, as they were called) wudn' quite giving the full story. Them two seemed like they were one rutabaga short of a pasty and tha' wuz for sure. Still, the Overseer knew that in good time another laker would put into the harbour and up the shore would walk more wide-eyed migrant Knockies with their human companions. And this was how it went on.

So now as we join them 'twas day two of their traipsing and tramping, and on their backs they carried their prospecting gear, and it being summer (the middle of June), there wudn' much of a need for a tent. A blanket would do but they knew well enough that they'd swapped the comfort of the bunkhouse for the hardness of the forest floor. All the while, crows and blue jays chittering on, and in the early twilight, there wuz the flittering ov orange-and-black butterflies. Lovely they wuz, to see. And although neither of this pair said it, they were worried-up good and proper as to whether they'd made the right move. They hoped it would be temporary. And so they went on like this, not saying much to each other (much like half the silent and brooding Cornish male population); not even saying much to their jabbering Knockies who ran along beside them; frightening birds, and causing foxes and bears to scatter. Wolves too, more than likely. And when there were no animals or birds to tease, they'd snap twigs or for a laugh, get insects and the butterflies to fly in the faces of their controlling miners. See, a bored Knockie wudn' a good Knockie. They'd do well to remember that.

The problem was that the dark, foreboding forest went on forever. None of it was mapped. None of it was known. Aside from their footsteps and their voices, there was no sound: and the silence went on for miles. Sometimes, in the vast concave of the hills, both of their voices would echo. Occasionally, they'd come across a clearing, or a lake, waterfalls and rivulets which all needed negotiating. Francis kept a map of their trail. He tried to sketch the general route of where they'd been. It went over Justin. He wudn' so bothered at that. Instead, he wondered about what they'd eat that night and when they'd rest again. When Francis stepped up the pace, Justin always pleaded for him to hold back a bit and think kindly of the Knockies travelling with them, and their small legs. In reality though, there was only one person Justin was thinking about – and that was hisself. Thaas who he was, and he wudn' be changed fur love nor money.

In these woods, the darkness was crushing. At first, when you entered the next patch of forest the light was retained; and it still filtered in through the tall trunks of the trees on the edge but as you waded in further, successive trunks blocked out any illumination, and gradually they formed a stockade into which you stumbled. There were the occasional patches of light shining, where by chance and nature, the canopy parted.

These were old trees. They carried wisdom and both of the brothers knew that. That didn' stop them from eyeing them up as good lumber: for ceilings and pit props underground, for the making of winzes and solars, for long-term building of cabins (Cornishmen could only see wood that way). And then, from that, shops and saloons, a smithy and a telegraph office: the trappings of civilization. Maybe even a chapel, for both of these brothers were brought up Methodist, even if one wudn' much enamoured ov ut and hadn' allays followed ut like ee should. Es – they cudn' help but nawtice ut. One day, this would be useful. This would help make them. This would help make this new 'Merky'; this new Cornwall that they had always dreamed of.

They were climbing. It was hard going. The mountain got steep. The fells took longer to reach. This wudn' no Carn Brea though. They got so high that in patches in the forest they could look right out over Lake Superior. At such moments, they understood the vastness of things, and wondered again, if they were mad – what people back home would say wuz 'properly mazed'. But neither of them said it. They may be a lot of things this pair but neither of them were prepared to let their dream go. Their limbs ached and they were bored of lugging their heavy backpacks (full of prospecting gear) up the mountain. But they weren't for quitting – neither of them, and even though they hated each moment of it, they stuck with ut. Ut was how their nation operated: they stuck with it, even though you didn' care much fur ut. Both of their Knockies wuz cussing bad too, but there wudn' nothing they could do about ut. That was the way 'twas back then in this time. Everyone knew the order of things. Knockies cussed. You just didn' listen. Any preacher worth his weight would tell ee that.

On the mountain (in no way yet was it 'Copper Mountain'; that's to come), it was hard to tell the time of day. In the belly of the forest the grim twilight did not change, and it was hard to see the passage of the sun overhead. A routine soon became established of rising early, before dawn, and setting off when it was still cool. The Knockies didn' care for it much. They liked to lie-on a good deal, and grumbled and moaned when they were awakened, and could smell their insufferable humans brewing coffee. There had been worse hardships they knew (stuck in a stope on the twenty-third fathom back home after a joist buckled and having to go without crowst fur a week) but like the people of their nation, they liked to moan on just a little too much and a little too often. And for breakfast, there really wudn' much on offer; biscuits would have to do, and when their miners tossed away a corner for them, they found themselves having to compete with the crows and blue jays that had been following them for the past few days. Noisy birds they were, and aggressive too. Gourgy and Luk had to fight hard for their sustenance. Gourgy was always the crafty one. Luk moved slower and had to hope that Gourgy would share his.

Later, on the third day, there was a steep incline that neither of the pair of Knockies liked very much; and they set to, forcibly moaning about how bad things had become, and it even went from bad to worse, with them rejecting any dinner time offering of biscuits to them questioning the miners in whiny voices as to why there wudn' no pasty crust, no hobbin, and most importantly, any saffron bun. And both the good one and the other one tried to explain why there wudn' anything nice to eat, but despite this, the Knockies didn' like ut much.

Very aware that in the middle of the forest of the Keweenaw they could do without a mutiny of this kind, eventually the two mining brothers placated them and promised wonderful offerings in the near future, just as soon as they'd make their claim. And it had to be said that Justin sided with the Knockies in this matter. Francis did his best to encourage all three, and told them that very soon, they'd make their strike. He could sense it coming, and even Justin said he could feel it in his bones. Gah! the Knockies went, but it wudn' like anyone wuz goin' to the pantry for they out here. They had to put up with it and so they walked sullenly, stomping upwards with their hands in their pockets.

This had all come to a head of late, and that was why Francis was so glad to find what he felt to be mineral-bearing ground. It wuz Justin who nawticed ut first though: mineral-bearing ground always gave rise to little lights jumping in the air. And he wuz swearing that he saw them, what his people called 'Jack O'Lanterns'. Get those, and as sure as eggs wuz eggs, there'd be ore there.

"Lights dancing." said Justin. "Over there look."

Back home it would be near the furze bushes, but here 'twuz beside the undergrowth on the edge of a clearing.

"Lanterns. I'n see them."

They had followed this run of copper up from the Cliff Mine, and as he and his brother had expected, here it came to the surface in greater quantities. They needed to assay it, and after Francis had got out his small assaying kit, made the necessary chemical tests – and then they could mark the run of it – they realised that this might be it. This was what they had been looking for. Now they could tentatively call it 'Copper Mountain' because in the mounds of rock that emerged from the floor of the forest they could see the traces of the mineral: sometimes blue, sometimes dusty orange if oxidised, but it was definitely there. Justin instantly scrawled out their names on a length of wood with his knife, and mounted it on the top of a sturdy stick. This signified their claim. It was what determined it as theirs. No one could remove the sign and no one could put in a counter-claim. That broke every miner's code.

Mining is never certain though. One day you can be joyous; the next day not so much so, and maybe that would be the case here too; but at least there was something here, and a diggings looked possible. All that hope that had manifested itself back home, and on the Atlantic crossing, the patient wait on the laker, and the mucking and tramming, had now paid off.

"What ee goin' t'do then boy?" Francis felt Gourgy ask.

He was a nosey one, that Gourgy.

"Put in a winze, I d'reckon," said Luk, who usually had sense enough to see a job through and what was required.

"My thoughts zactly," said Francis.

"Initial shaft then?" asked Justin. "Bewdie. Crack on."

So the four of them dug – and dug hard. They used shovels and pick-axes and dabbers to scrape back the soil precisely where the lights danced. For them, digging like this was as natural as the circle of day and night. They had the arms for it, and they had the muscular torso for it. It was in their blood. So they swung and shovelled, shovelled and swung. The Knockies did what they could, but mostly, they sat and watched. They pretended they were checking for any small rock falls, collapses and any dangerous rises (like hell!) that might come in over their heads. Mostly though, they sat admiring the view out over Lake Superior and whistling some good old Cornish tunes to themselves for their amusement.

And as they dug, the light began to fade. They went deeper into the hole, but above them, up in the sky, the moon and the stars rose. Eventually, Francis saw something shimmering that looked like a blindingly large lump of pure copper ore. It was about twice the size of his fist.

"'Eave that piece out," he said to his brother, and Justin did just that. He scratched and he dug, then he stuck his fingers around the mass, and tried to ease it out. After a slight struggle, it came out of the ground. These were experienced hands see, and they knew how to make the earth work for them. When the ore had been obtained, the two brothers clamboured out of the hole. They stood back from it closer to the dense forest. The assaying kit quickly confirmed it was copper, and now in their hands they held a lump of it. They smiled at each other. All that effort, just for this. The Jack O'Lanterns had been right. The folklore was true. The magic worked.

And there was no denying it. They passed the lump of ore between them like a rugby ball, and they knew the weight of it. They knew what they had. All looked good high on the mountain, this newly-named Copper Mountain; and then, as the ore passed back to Justin and he turned it on the palm of his hand, from out of the darkness, from the edge of the trees, darted a hand. It was a strong, muscular hand that grabbed Justin's wrist tightly and would not let go. The fingers on its hand snaked around his bones and began putting pressure on his arm and hand. The two Knockies audibly hissed at the limb, with Gourgy jumping up onto the arm itself, and prodding it with his pick-axe, probably no more than light pin-pricks to he whose body was attached to the arm. In the end, despite Gourgy's efforts, this new crushing hand forced Justin to drop the ore. It landed with a thud on the ground, narrowly missing Luk's head and so he shook his fist at the perpetrator. Only when the ore was on the ground did the aggressor let go.

"Never count your chickens," voiced Luk, and he was right because standing fiercely over them was a statuesque, male Indian, who'd probably been tracking this noisy Cornish crew for days, and looked on them with derision and anger. Justin and Francis knew why: the Knockies moved through the forest like bulls in a china shop.

"Whaas on Sos?" went Gourgy to the mighty warrior.

Sos was the Cornish word for friend but mehty the Indian wudn about to knaw that, wuz a?

The four of them knew that some serious negotiations were now to be in order. And damme it, if Gourgy and Luk weren't even then, in the face of this giant, still talking about what they might have for their supper.

2

"Cen't ee plead Stannator's rights?" was the only thing the brother called Justin could offer up.

He was drawing on the ancient mining laws of Cornwall, but he hadn't really thought through the fact that they were in the New World. None of that jurisdiction applied here.

"I dun't think thaas goin' to work, do you boy?" replied Francis, raising an eyebrow. "Whaas' a want?"

"An apology perhaps? Maybe he dun't want no more mining here. Maybe the ground here is sacred."

"I know, but this idn' no one's land here, is ut?" said Justin.

"I think you've got that wrong. I mean, the whole of 'Merky' is Indian land by rights, idn' ut? We'm just interlopers really, ent us? Fly-by-nighters who've just waltzed in. "

By now, the Indian gentleman was just staring at them. He was breathing deeply. His dark, locked hair fell over his face. 'Twas hard to tell the age ov un. Gourgy reckoned he wuz in his mid-twenties but Luk reckoned he wuz older. They seemed to age differently somehow.

"I dun't like the look obm," said Luk nervously in a whisper.

"Nor me," said Gourgy, quietly gazing at un. "He d'look fierce as a buckrat. My pick-axe didn' even make a dent on his arm. He's got tougher skin than us two."

Bugger. This wudn' naw easy situation.

"What tribe did Trevorrow say they wuz up here on the Upper Peninsula? He mentioned the Injuns once or twice, didn' a?"

"Objibwe, I think," said Francis, and when he said it, it was hard to get it out from his tongue through his teeth to the outside world.

"I didn' think anyone lived up here. This far up, I mean," pondered Justin.

"I wonder how the Cliff Mine began. I mean, they'd have to have negotiated too, wudn' they?"

"No one seemed to knaw. Boys there just carried on like it had always been there. Trade, I expect, said Justin. "We need to trade somethun' with him. Then he might let we crack on."

"The problem with you fools," observed Luk logically, "is that you ebm got anything to trade with? Didn' you think of that when you traipsed up here?"

Francis and Justin reckoned they had already worked that out.

"We could trade our pair of interfering Knockies," Justin went. "They probably ebm got Knockies – and might relish some. For eating."

"Sos, are you insane?" shouted Gourgy, giving the rock next to him a resounding kick which echoed across the valley. "Dun't be such a tuss."

Luk said to his miner, "I can't even believe you said that, after all I've done for you... and me and poor Gourgy there, traded as a bargain. Dun't we mean any more to you than that? There we were, thinking we was special."

"Well done," said Francis. "Now you've upset them two. Don't worry boys. We ent about to trade you. You'm too important. You'm one bit of lore we ent about to get rid of any time soon. You'm too important to we."

Both the Knockies collapsed on the ground in sheer relief that they were not going to be part of some bargain. A string of ripe old curses came out of the mouth of Gourgy. Ee cudn' help ut. Bad words were his thing. Methodism had broadly passed un by, even though he'd seen ut all come 'n' go.

"They're right. That is our problem though brother," said Francis. "We've nothing to trade..."

"How about we make him a share-owner?" thought Justin. "You knaw, so he owns a third... Another a'venturer like we. "

"Hear yourself," said Francis. "He already owns the land. I didn' think anyone would even be bothered about our small diggings up here."

"Well," said Justin. "Either way, we need to gibm somethun. Try talking to him... You'll do ut better than I will."

"Ee idn' goin' to understand we now, is a?"

All kinds of issues compounded this negotiation process. For one thing, both brothers were exhausted from their day's walk and labouring. For another, the gentleman (however old ee wuz) did not speak English, and they were not fluent in the language of the Objibwe. Another difficulty was the fact that it was dark, and time for some shut-eye. However, looking at the gentleman, it seemed he had no interest in resting and still peered menacingly above their workings, scanning the broken mess of soil and rock from side to side (something that no one would look at twice in Cornwall: but here looked like an explosive artillery shell had landed).

"I knawed this was a mistake," said Justin in resignation. "We should have just stayed at the Cliff Mine. Maybe partnered up with some other party. Then we'd have been set fair."

"Now, don't be getting jittery on me," said Francis. "There's always a way through. You know that from home. Listen. Light a fire... Get some sticks and fallen branches and put light to ut. Use one of the lucifers we're carrying..."

"Thought you'd never say," said Luk.

"Es," said Gourgy. "I'm freezing. It's getting cold. I'll get frostbite on me bezants."

"I need to see his face," said Francis.

All of them pitched in and gathered a fair mound of wood, which could be lit. Justin erected a pyramidal frame over the fire from which to hold a billy-can, and gathered some water from a nearby stream, steeply running down the side of the mountain. And then, from his backpack, he stirred in a packet of some processed beef stew.

"Is that all you got?" asked Gourgy, looking a bit mazed.

"'Tis, as it happens," replied Justin.

"That idn' goin' to fill our bellies any," said Luk, perhaps stating the obvious in only the way that Cornish Knockies can.

"That's not the point," noted Justin. "'Tis our big fella here we'm trying to attract, and sit down with us by the fire. T'shaw him we're friendly like."

The fire got lit and a bit ov a stew was boiled up. Initially, the gentleman seemed puzzled at their actions, but then gradually took more interest in their cooking. Perhaps the smell of it tingled the insides of his nostrils. Fur zertain, 'twudn' naw pasty shop from back home, but nonetheless, the smell seemed t'loosen his strings a little. They felt his sinews relax. Rite on then.

Es. They all knew that the packet of preserved beef stew had been carried all the way from back home, and it was so unattractive that so far, none of their party had seen fit to use it. Now though, far up a mountain, it was finding a purpose. Justin ladled out a small cup of the stew to the youngish gentleman, and held it up for him to partake of, gesturing for him to come and join them around the fire. Es. This was the way of things: sometimes apparent enemies can turn out to be friends. And the converse. You'll see that soon enough. Es.

When the gentleman moved to sit down next to them, all four of the party marvelled at his size. They noticed the long slope of his forehead, his angled nose and square jaw; then there was his long black hair, clumped into locks, a style none of them had seen before. Gourgy made a squawk and flinched nervously away from the decorated tomahawk he was carrying in his belt. The strange thing was that, by now, all of them were not just thinking about this individual. Naw. They were thinking of the rest of his community. That would really be ut, if all of they turned up here. All them were worried about being scalped. Well, anyone would be. It was what you heard about the Indian Wars. It was the talk of things on the lakers. It put newbies and green-applers in their place. Ut kept um on edge.

Justin passed the gentleman the cup of beef stew and then all four of them gestured a cheers to him, then supped at the hot fluid and its meat. The Knockies greedily drank down their portion and were soon pleading for more, but the gentleman seemed to savour the taste a little longer. Despite it being summer, he also seemed to appreciate the warmth of the fire. It got chilly this far up the mountain, in spite of the season. It meant togetherness: that they were one and the same. Maybe this party and he were not so different after all. They could see his pleasure at the taste of the stew. They watched his countenance change. Small steps then. Small positive steps.

At this, Francis decided to introduce each of them to him. 'Twudn' naw point in dealing with their surname and telling un that it meant 'Valley of the Stags'. No point in that at all. And then there wuz the Knockies. They had superhuman surnames that went on forever, and included every father figure in their lines going all the bleddy way back to Corineus. And so that wudn' necessary either. 'Twas best to keep ut simple. He pointed to himself, labelling himself with his first name and then slowly went around the circle, issuing forth the other's names. When it got to the gentleman, they were all hoping he'd pick up on this and perhaps offer them his name, but when the task reached him there was actually only silence. Francis tried again, but again, there was no response. And because they were cheeky buggers, these Knockies slapped their foreheads because they knew this was not going the way it needed to.

"This is worse than speaking t'someone from Devon," observed Gourgy laughing loudly. "We got steam-powered engines, and they'm just emerging from the primordial soup."

"You'm right there," said Luk. "What we got here is similar. There is a real communication barrier."

Francis scowled at them. It wudn' like he didn' know that. All of them realised that they needed to be patient. Perhaps in daylight there would be better ways of trying to explain what they were doing. The Knockies were yawning and, tell the truth, so were Justin and Francis. No one wanted to fall asleep with the gentleman still in their company. They all feared that they'd be robbed and their throats slit, or they'd wake up in the morning with a tomahawk embedded in their backs. But it didn' happen like that, oh no. Not yet at least.

In the end, Luk fell sleep onto Gourgy, and Gourgy fell asleep on Francis and Francis fell asleep on Justin, and so they all toppled over like dominoes. And above them in the clearest sky they had seen for some time, the stars came out and shone at them. Out comed a bright moon too. But the gentleman kept stock still, and upright, and the last thing that came into Justin's head as he leaned over, was the fact that this warrior was meditating and absorbing the world around him. Es. Some boy, ee wuz. Mean-looking – but some boy still – young perhaps in his form, but old an' wise in his mind.

And when dawn came over the east, Francis's head was still on the ground. The camp-fire had burnt down to a set of greying embers. The sun was travelling up his spine to warm up the back of his stiff neck. Ut wasn't the light that had woken him though. Instead, it was a sound that he had heard almost all of his life. Ut wuz the sound of someone digging. Every so often there was a pause, and then, while the digger swapped instruments, next could be heard the hike and push of a pick into solid ground: the thud and scrunch as it first hit soft earth and then the clang and clink as it made contact with rock. Between sensing this noise, he noted that the gentleman was not where he had left him last night. He also noted that the other three were already up and stood on the edge of the diggings they had begun yesterday. Still on the ground, he observed every so often, the vast energetic swing of that pick-axe into the air, and then down again into the earth. With ut, came a groan at the difficulty of the activity. He was sat up by the time that the sound momentarily paused. It was like some treasure had been found.

He watched the edge of where the sink had gone down into the earth and then observed two hands placing several lumps of rock onto the remaining ground. Only they weren't just pieces of rock; they were, in fact, very fine examples of copper ore. They shone at him, and judging by this brief look at them, they were clearly of a better grade even than the first nugget they had found yesterday.

"Ee's a better miner than you Justin," said Gourgy.

"Es. Like a geht machine," observed Luk.

Now, Francis understood what was goin' on. The gentleman was imitating their practice and was seeing what he too could extract from the ground.

"You seen these?" asked Justin, and with a twist of his head directed his question at Francis. "The size of the lode is massive. Easy pickings..."

The gentleman then said something in his own language, and all of them were silenced. Justin gestured for him to speak and he did, but again, it sounded as mad and as downright crazy as ef from some of the fishermen down Newlyn. The important point though was that the gentleman was smiling at them, pleased with his accomplishments, and that the four of them were smiling back. Now things were on another level. They'd taken an unexpected turn, which is most often the way. Gourgy began clapping the gentleman for his achievements and Luk joined in with a whistle and, as was his way, a bit of a skipping dance.

The new finds made Francis jump straight up and stride across the camp-site to where the hole had been dug. Since they'd looked at the venture last night, the width and depth of the shaft had increased greatly. This boy knew how to work, fur zertain. And just to the north of him was a great pile of tailings and waste that he'd shovelled there. Bewdie. The gentleman took pleasure from seeing Francis pick up one of the ore samples and hold it high up to the sun, so that he could inspect its quality.

"Whaas ut like Sos?" asked an eager Justin, darting around him.

"Top quality," said Francis. "Better than down the Cliff Mine... Looks to me like a much higher grade."

Francis lowered the ore sample and looked down at the gentleman. The two of them beamed smiles to each other. Francis clenched his fist and made a 'thumbs-up sign' to try to tell the gentleman how pleased they were with what he had found. Mehty the Indian nodded, and made a gesture seemingly to express his enjoyment of what he was doing. Despite the language barrier, everyone knew the difficulty. They were a long way from Eagle Harbour. The other major town, Calumet, was a good way down the peninsula from where they were. The problem now would be getting enough gear and manpower up here to work the find. But as was the way with mining, ut didn' stop any Cousin Jack in their stride. After all, they were used to travelling half-way round the world, and to mining the most difficult terrain going, if only to find a worthwhile lode. It was fixed in their minds: if you could get there, then it could be mined. This glee momentarily ran through the four of them.

Then Gourgy said, "What about mehty though?"

They all turned back to the gentleman, who was somewhat alarmingly now, still smiling at them. At this moment he was pointing at something on his own body. They peered at him and got in close: closer in fact, than some wanted. He was pointing at his necklace and the metal decoration on his clothing. And then Justin realised what he was showing them: they were beads of copper.

"His people have done this before," said Francis. "They know metal. They d'knaw how to work ut. The Cornish cen't think themselves the only miners and smelters in the world. This proves ut. Bet they've been extracting it from the ground just as long as we have..."

Nonetheless, Luk was pointing from the decorative metal in his necklace and clothing back to the lump of ore.

Luk clamboured onto him and peered closely at the bead.

"Nice," he went. "Decorated too..."

And at this, the gentleman nodded. Now, they were getting somewhere. Ut wuz interesting with the gentleman. Unlike most other non-Cornish, he could see the Knockies. When Francis next tried to communicate with him by scratching symbols in the earth, he was able to draw them. They expected him to just see two people, but no, he accurately drew the two brothers and standing next to them their two Knockies, depicted about a third of the size of a normal human.

"Ee've captured you good and proper Gourgy," offered Luk. "Even your bandy legs and hunched back..."

And then, of course, they got to thinking about why this was. And for a while, no one spoke because they were thinking so hard about ut. And then, at last, Justin said ut.

"They're a spiritual people," he went. "Just like the Cornish. Very superstitious. They see things others can't see. The spirit world. Like we do..."

There wuz definitely something in what he said.

"Aw yeah," said Gourgy sarcastically. "The Cornish love the spiritual nature of the landscape so much... Thaas why they have dug up and destroyed most ov their world back home."

He did have a point but right then, nobody wanted to hear ov ut. So that shut un up for a bit, which wuz always a good thing.

"Try to show him that he'll make a profit out of the mine," argued Luk. "Try and draw it for him to see."

Again, Francis took a stick and cleared the earth of leaves and pine needles. Then he tried to draw the development of the mine, and what the gentleman could expect to receive in return. The problem was he seemed to have no real concept of wealth. And when Francis tried again, he came once more to a standstill when he tried to illustrate how the gentleman and his family or people could benefit.

"Yeah, well," said Luk with his arms folded. "Most times, the Cornish take what they want and then bugger off when a mine gets too deep and too expensive to work. They allays leave someone else to clear up their dirty work, and that cen't go on forever."

Justin and Francis knawed he was right, but 'twudn' the time now to have a philosophical debate about the boom and bust nature of mining. You had to make hay (or mine copper) whilst the sun shone. And that was the attitude that had nurtured an entire people.

"Maybe he'll be alright with it," suggested Justin. "I mean, ee's smiling a lot more now."

"I dun't knaw," said Francis. "I knew we might have to negotiate rights but I didn' knaw it would be this difficult..."

They both knew that the development of any mining in this particular location would change the mountain-side here forever. They'd need to drive a road or a tramway up from the harbour, and then there was the whole business of getting equipment up this far to the fell they were currently in. Mind you, some sturdy horses or ponies and a dray or two would be helpful, and once people knew ov ut, then they would come. In silence, they both jointly imagined some future moment back home when the news arrived that some new mine had been discovered on Copper Mountain and that there was plenty of work out there. That was the sort of news Cornwall longed for.

Justin was seeing the newspaper headline back home: "Nankervis boys make claim in Michigan". Meanwhile, Francis was seeing the look on some mine owners' faces that there would now be even more global competition. Forgetting that, he took out the maps he had sketched of their route up the mountain. He showed the gentleman to where he felt the lode ran. Then he tried to say that they wanted him to accompany them back down to the community around the Cliff Mine. There at least, they might be able to translate one another and negotiate a deal.

Now as to whether the gentleman actually understood or not, was hard to tell, but he seemed to do a lot of affirmative grunting. For now, that had to be good enough. Maybe this negotiation might in the near future, be the end of things with this particular individual but in fact, as we shall see, that was not the way it panned out at all. Sometimes, what is hoped for never materialises, and instead, something else, something much more random and luminous comes and takes its place, and so it was here with this tiny moment in the history of the earth.

The Knockies were more relaxed now, and they kept chittering on to the gentleman asking if there were any nice Indian lady spirits who might want some male company. He didn' knaw zactly what they wuz saying but somehow he got the gist of it, if you will. And in this time, Francis and Justin gathered up a couple of the best ore samples they could, and loaded them into their backpacks.

Before that, they checked that the important claim sign was still standing, and then, as was the way of the Cornish in prospecting, they bounded the enclosure of the mine, half a mile in each direction from where the claim sign had been hammered into the ground. They didn' need to measure anything: the Knockies had this in-built way of knawing distances overground and underground, so all that became quickly sorted, and at this, both Justin and Francis were glad they'd brought their companions. Annoying though they were, they were damned useful sometimes. Aw es. The claim seemed sorted now. It was their territorial marking on the lone mountain, and it stood there, lonesome, waiting for them to return.

And at this point, nawbody knawed what would grow from it and what ut would become, nor what ut would yield. Then, it was just a small mark on a map, but God in his wisdom, and all the other small and spiritual people of the world, had plans for it: big plans as you will see. And that's the way they all liked to think of it, as they walked back down the mountain. The gentleman was leading, and from him now exuded beams of light, which reflected off the copper beads of his clothing. He was sure of foot, and found a way down that avoided the pitfalls and ravines that Francis and Justin had negotiated on the way up. Francis was sketching this way down, and remembering the landscape, for he hoped that very soon, they'd be coming up this way, and perhaps driving a track-way through.

Meanwhile, his brother was wondering what all of this would bring, and whether it would make them rich. He was thinking of money in his pocket, and then (though he really shouldn') of gambling, drink and especially women, for that was how he was. Francis kept his thoughts to himself, but dreamed of freedom and a re-start: a new way of going on. They two little spindly buggers were yipping on to each other ten to the dozen goin' on about this and that, and things that didn' really matter. But sure enough, they were sharing dreams and thinking they'd gone up in the world. They was talking about what it would be like to be mine overseers, with Luk wanting to be the Grass Cap'n (organising the stamps, the launders and the buddles) and Gourgy wishing to be underground, right in there with the slimes and safety fuses.

In all, they were a good pair, but much as things were goin' on smoothly now, 'twudn' always going to be that way. Es. Ut was 'One and all' with the Cornish (which sounded a'right) but every bugger cudn' wait to stab someone else in the back. That wuz the trouble with um: they cudn' bear to see someone being more successful than they were, and that, my bewdies, as this tale might well show, is always a recipe for disaster.

3

Es. Proper. These bright pair wuz feeling good about themselves when they got back down the dark mountain – the mountain they were now properly calling Copper Mountain (see how this landscape gets so easily changed and altered all the time. See how it is constantly in transition). They kept on pointing to it and turning back to give it admiring glances. Puffed up they were, like bladders of lard. Proud as peacocks. And when they finally reached the outskirts of the Cliff Mine on the lowland, they realised they might need a bit of help to try to translate their intentions to the gentleman who was silently padding along, and walking side-by-side with them, and to fully have the ore tested to see if it was what they thought it was. Right there and then, they had no doubts. They knawed the look ov ut. So they wuz whistling and singing. And they and the Knockies made quite a chorus. Quite an entrance you might say.

They fully knew the ramifications of ut. Ef every boy found out that there wuz a new strike up there in the fells, then they'd swiftly down tools at the Cliff Mine and like a shot, start heading up there themselves. A great swarm of them, there would be. Then again, they themselves needed enough labour and equipment to get up there in order to make sure they gave the enterprise a good go. Boath of them had thought it might be some small find, but clearly, there was more potential than that. The Cliff Mine had been a profitable one but was getting deeper and more difficult all the time. Depth meant water and more water meant bigger pumps, more expensive pumps (getting a message back to Harvey's of Hayle to have new ones made and shipped over – and costly all of that): more time dealing with that than actually working through the lodes. With mining, this wuz allays the way. You cudn' odds ut. But this find on the mountain – maybe that would change all of that. Maybe it wuz their bit of luck. Finally, the wheel of fortune turned their way. It had been a long time coming.

The little Knockies had grumbled and moaned all the way back down the mountain to the camp beside the Cliff Mine. As they approached the camp, they moaned a little less, seeing the familiarity of the place. Knockies were like that see. Actually, they didn' much like change or disruption – and they were soon scampering about, asking others who were lazing around the collar of the mine, what wuz on, and whether there was any good grub going. That wuz the way of their people see. Always, their minds on their bellies – and to be honest, not much else. Instinct 'twas – born of aeons in the muck and darkness of tunnels. But then, the miners had to hand it to them. That's what you wanted in a Knockie. You needed them to be familiar with all of the cracks and the heaving props, the pinch points and the shaky adits. Their familiarity with the layout underground wuz what might save your life.

Because they walked back into the camp with an Indian gentleman, everyone took notice of their arrival. Indians, well, they all knew they were out there. Everyone spoke about them as if they were some malevolent force beyond the forest, but here this pair were: walking bold as brass with an Indian fella back inta' the camp again. All of them had said that they thought they pair had jacked ut all in and were off out west, but by the look of ut now, this wudn' the case at all. So when Francis and Justin made their way through the gates with their companion, everyone grass end of the mine, had a geek at them. Crowst stopped being eaten. Pasty pails were dropped and tobacco stopped being stuffed into clay pipes. Several put their hands to their suspenders and watched. Time stood still.

"They pair again," wuz what wuz said. And some spat and some swallowed, but everyone had to admit the two brothers had some sense about them. They wudn' nawbody's fools.

Everyone wondered what this pair wanted. And, as was the way, like back home, it only took one conversation, one tiny share of this information, and within seconds, 'twas known over the stamps, in the count-house, up on the sluices and launders, and in the back ov the carpenter's shop. A few minutes later, 'twas known on the bottom-most levels of the mine that that pair had strolled in. And the trammers all said they had ideas above their station, and that they'd probably fail at the first hurdle, even getting s'far as Calumet. Es. That would be it. And thaas because none of um expected much of this pair. Jealousy moast ov ut, fur the Cornish were a very jealous nation: always jealous of they next door, always thinking the grass was greener somewhere else. You get that from always living on a sticky-outy piece of peninsula.

Either way, the pair were goin' for ut like a skeiner, matched by mehty behind them who they didn' much like the look ov. But they wuz still polite to all who seen um, giving the occasional 'Yew!' or 'Alright Sos?' to each of the Cornishmen who saw them. And like it is with all Cussies around the world, they gave a respectful 'Yew!' or 'Alright?' back to them. They were men on a mission by the look ov ut, and they by-passed the count-house completely. And all the while the face on that Indian: well, you wudn' want t' see that in the darkness down the sixtieth fathom back Botallack. No way. His fearsome face was worse than the sound of the boulders at the bottom of the sea rolling around above your head. An' his hair – all in locks yew – see the state ov un.

"Goin' to see Skewsy, ent um?" one Jacker observed.

And that wudn' a bad call. He'd noted their direction of travel, the two pards, their two Knockies and the Indian boy.

And even before that Cussie had observed that, Skews was standing on the porch of his Assaying Office watching them tramp up towards him. Samuel Skews was a crotchety bugger, better off as a wheeler-dealer than he wuz as a Mine Assayer. Ee didn' want to be in Michigan t'all. He didn' like the climate one bit (the winters were a sore point with un), and he'd awnly come because when the mines over Rinsey went all t'lerraps, he had no choice. He had a passel of daughters back 'ome apparently, and so he'd signed the contract. He had a wisht, drawn face, and looked like ee never got enough sleep. There were black circles around his eyes, like he was one of they tumbling bears from over China way. And he was hunched too. His profession had made un that way. Hours sat over a desk and scales, determining the proportions of metals. He was all sampling, fusion and cupellaton. And then after that, he'd be weighing and parting, and then weighing again. All numbers and calculations ee wuz.

Mines needed someone like him, but he talked a damme good show – a pretence of activity. Half the time, the tuss did nothing: pretending to be monitoring the output. In fact, he liked to lord it about a bit. Walking round like ee owned the plaace – which he didn'. Makin' a point of ensuring his clawthes didn' get too dirty, so as to show they he wuz above um, and talkin' all cut up like he wudn' from the same stock and people. Everyone had to admit ut though: sometimes you needed his skills. Nawbody else could do ut. Francis had some limited knowledge – some skills in assaying – but no one could give the ore the seal of approval like he could. His word wuz enough to secure regular lakers coming up from Detroit, an' the loading of that ore in their vast holds. Es. That wuz the way ov things. That wuz the way money wuz made. So you had to put up widn'. If aggrandising un wuz the thing he wanted, well, then you had t'do ov ut.

"Look out. Look out. 'Ere they are. What do you baissly buggers want?" wuz the fust thing he said, all keenly like.

"Good to see you again' an' all," went Justin.

"Thought you'd had enough of ut up here. Last I heard you pair was heading out West. Californi-ay an' tha'."

"'Twudn' quite like tha'," said Francis. "We ended up changing our plans..."

That wuz a lie. And the two Knockies knew ut. Ut had been the plan all along. There wudn' ever goin' t'be naw trek out West. Who'd want t'do tha' anyway? 'Twas a brave an' knackerin' journey tha', an' they'd come far 'nuff already. Over the Rocky Mountains maybe – or down the length of the mosquito-ridden Mississippi and then crossing via Mexico. No thanks.

"'Ow come then?"

Skews stretched the posture of his back, to ease the pain in it. He made a noise which might have been a small fart.

"Got some samples fur ee to test..."

Skews raised a nervous eyebrow, catching momentarily sight of the intensity of the look of the Indian. The brothers could see that it unnerved him.

"Dun't worry about him," said Justin. "Ee wun't do ee no harm. He's with us."

Skews nodded nervously.

Wha'f ee got then?" Skews asked. "You best come in to my establishment."

Establishment? Who wuz a kiddin'? 'Twas the mine assay 'ouse and nawthun' more.

The five of them entered. To call ut some kind of laboratory would be a vast exaggeration of what actually wuz on offer. Like everything on the Keweenaw, material things were hard to get hold of, because everything had to be brought in by ship or overland by 'oss and cart. Nonetheless, the Office had some of the characteristics of what you'd expect to see at home – in any mine back home: scales and weights, rows of test-tubes, benches on which were geht jars an' funnels, and then solutions of rock undergoing some analysis, contained in further apparatus. Against the back wall, was a run of different coloured chemicals that looked expensive and probably had been difficult to get out there. Beyond that though, it was just a regular slapped-up timber and shingle dwelling that might be found at any diggings across 'Merky'. Skews might be a tusser but he was definitely the tusser they needed.

"You expecting this on company time?" asked Skews. "I mean..."

"Na," said Francis. "We know we're not employees here no more. We'll pay fur ut under our own steam. Our money's as good as the Mine's no doubt?"

"It's pricey," offered Skews. "A full assay idn' cheap."

A low-paid man would be on fifteen dollars a month at the mine; experienced men like Justin and Francis up to fifty. This would be all of one of their collective wages.

"We knaw that."

He nodded at the verbal contract.

"You'd better show me what you got then."

Justin removed the rucksack from his back and placed it onto the planchen floor. He untied his sleeping mat from the top of the sack and reached inside. During all of this, the Knockies were behaving remarkably well. Francis had pre-warned them not to touch anything or there'd be hell to pay – and certainly no decent crowst later. After delving into the sack, Justin came back up holding two ore samples in his left and right hands. Ee placed them silently onto the counter, behind which Skews was now standing.

"See they samples," said Gourgy. "I bet they'll make his hair stand on end."

"Reckon so," said Luk.

"Copper?" questioned Skews, though he didn' really need to. He already recognised the sample and what it contained. He could smell ut. All assayers could. Besides, on the Keweenaw, all that was sought was either copper or iron.

He leaned in to form a more comfortable position over the sample and prodded both spheres of ore with his forefinger. He scratched the surface with his index fingernail.

"Where'd'ee find this then?"

"Can't say fur now," said Justin, which was precisely the answer Skewsy expected.

"Looks somewhat similar to what we got here at the Cliff... Now, 'tidn' from here, is ut?"

"Na..."

"Similar colour and texture though... so nearby then?"

"Better though, idn' ut?" stated Francis confidently.

Skews did not answer. He kept counsel. This was a good sign.

"You'd... ah... best leave ut with me... I need to run a few tests. Apply some heat to ut. Best get the furnace out back fired up – and see what we'n do."

"How long?" asked Justin.

Skews gave both him and his brother a look.

"As long as it takes."

"Shall we come back later?"

"Best let me find you... Where will you be staying?"

They'd not yet fully contemplated this. In the forest, it had seemed fine to sleep around a camp-fire. Back down here, it was different. There was the Indian gentleman to think of too. Whether he needed accommodating was a mute question. Prior to his grasping hand emerging out of the edge of the forest, presumably he'd been sleeping rough in the woods, covering himself with ferns and lichen-clad branches. It probably wudn' be the best thing to ask for a night in the bunkhouse again; there, they would be subject to a great deal of questioning. Skews appreciated the dilemma.

"There's always the *regular* accommodation in town," he suggested. "You know..."

They did know. Town was hardly the word for it. But es, some kind of development had grown around the mine. Town wudn' zactly what most people would call ut though. Shanty-town wuz more like ut: just a scattered set of buildings which had haphazardly mushroomed next to the camp. They knawed some ov the places they were talking about, and one in particular. They wudn' great, but at the moment, they were beggars and they could not afford to be choosers.

By the tone in which Skews spoke, there was probably only one place that would be appropriate and that was the so-called Cliff Hotel. The place had a bit ov a reputation. 'Bit' probably ent the right word, alright? There were girls. Ladies of the night, so to speak. Es. Clean ones. That wuz the way ov ut. As sure as eggs wuz eggs, once an operation succeeded (however distant it was from the rest of civilization, soon, the pleasures of the flesh would arrive). The maids were somehow always named Anna or Mitzee, and tell ee what, it felt like they'd never been Sunday School in their life. As much as miners laboured, they always needed places to spend their money. And at the Cliff Hotel could be found perfume, stockings, and well... a bit of female company. There wuz plenty of lonesome buggers who were partial to ut. Let's be honest: ut wudn' like everything earned was sent back in letters home. Get away with ee, if you thought otherwise. If there wuz one thing the Cornish were, 'twas expert liars.

From the tone of the conversation, the two Knockies had picked up on this already.

"Luk, looks like we'm off Cliff Hotel," commented Gourgy. "Right on."

"And Sos, you knaw what that means..." said his pard.

"Girls?"

"Yeah. 'Course there'll be maids," said Luk. "But also, decent food boy. Caake. Taa. Pasties maybe. Buns. I'n taste the *seffren* already. "

They knawed the strands of gold came on the lakers every fortnight. Currants and dried fruit too. Sometimes, if they could get ut – even orange peel. They were made regular for all the Cussies who wolfed them down in their droves. As soon as they were out the oven, they were scoffed.

And at this, perhaps all the suffering of climbing up and down the mountain seemed worth ut. They looked at their humans, who were still conversing with Skews. They gave a nod to each other. Neither of them liked Skews. That wuz it with Knockies see – they were good judges of character. But when they turned around to leave the Assay Office, there wuz the geht, tall, lock-haired Indian again, who wuz looking down on them. They still didn' quite knaw what t' make obm. Ee was like some Gogmagog or Trebiggan. They wudn' the only ones. Everyone else felt the same way. But his story ent finished yet and neither is the tale of this pair and their mine spirits.

When Justin and Francis came outside, they were arguing. Nawthun' new there.

"Jeez Frank, thaas a helleva lot ov money t'pay un," said Justin. "We ebm got ut to give."

"Es," said Francis, "but unless we get confirmation of the quality of the copper we ebm got nawthun'. That assay means everything to we. If Skewsy comes back to we with a good result, then we'm made. We'n work a deal then."

"True enough, but the cost ov ut have near wiped we out. A whole month's wages. What about provisions and gear? How the hell will us do ut? The whole idea wuz to save some after our time in the Cliff Mine – and now look at us. Broke again. 'Tis nearnly as bad as being back home."

Justin's face wuz turnin' from exasperation to desperation. That wuz the way ov ee sometimes. He wuz always a glass half-empty. Maybe you'd say he wuz a realist. And it wuz true that compared to him, the other one – that Francis, well, he was always the dreamer. Ee had his head in the clouds a bit, but his glass wuz allays half-full. When they worked best, they wuz a good combination, but when they wuz at war (like now) then there wuz 'ell up you. An' saying tha', the way they carried on sometimes wuz more like they wuz sworn enemies than decent brothers to each other. Es. This was one of they moments, and like as always, the Knockies just let un get on with ut until ut got settled. Fur now, because ov all the 'ell up, they wuz forced just t'skim stones across a muddy tailing pond fur jerks.

"How come you always control the purse strings anyway?" asked Justin, giving his brother a good shove.

"You know why Sos," offered Francis sardonically. "Remember down Penzance, do ee?"

"Thought you'd bring that up again. Always your way, idn' ut?"

"Tidn' like tha."

"Idn' ut?"

And by now, the veins on Justin's neck had become sinuous, as if he turned into some geht bear. And at any moment, it looked like he was ready to batter his brother in a moment of fisticuffs. Didn' you knaw that about these pair? They'd have set-tos like this sometimes. Right scrappers they were. Celtic blood see. Ut always comes to rise. They get riled quickly. Anymore and the Knockies knew that a first punch would be thrown. Then a few more would slam in and then it would be back like ut used ot be – and then they'd have t'wrassle ut out.

Justin was already framing up fur a fight but Francis wuz still trying to talk his way out of ut. In the end, it was the Indian gentleman who stepped in. How ee did ut prop'ly amazed Luk and Gourgy. He just silently stepped in between them and stood there like a wall, with each of them unable to penetrate through to the other. Neither of them zactly wanted to commence any pugilism with the gentleman, for it looked like he might knock them out with a single punch, and so they eased back from conflict and stopped hurling abuse at other. Finally, this capitulation came out from the boy Justin.

"Hold fire. You'm right. The assaying is the key. It's essential you. Without that, we ebm got nawthun.'"

Still breathing heavily, Francis responded with, "We'll get through boy. Dun't ee worry. I knaw 'tidn' lookin' great now, but mark my words: one day, that Skewsy will be under our control. Fur now, he may be full ov his own self-importance, dressed up like a 'oss marine... but some day soon, I tell ee, we'll have more money than an 'oss can shit."

He put his hand over his brother's shoulder, and tried to reassure him.

And that wuz a very Cornish thing of Francis to say, for his people were honest that way, and when somethun' needed saying they said it directly, with no airs or graces. Es. Direct they were. A spade was called a spade. And maybe that was a good thing and maybe it was not such a good thing. But you cudn' alter ut. 'Twas too ingrained in they to change now.

And then the two brothers shook hands. They were firm again: like nothing on earth could prise them apart. There were old stratas there – deep layers. That was true. But always they could put down somethun' tasty on top. That seemed to please the Indian for although he said nothing, he seemed to smile a bit. And as you knaw, keepin' he sweet wuz important. They both looked at un, and realised that they still needed to talk to the bugger. This silence cudn' carry on the way it had dun.

4

'Andsome you. It wuz true that with Knockies, you didn' want to think much about their biology. In point of fact, you never did. 'Twas fur the best. 'Twudn' worth the trauma. Naw. But there, the pair of them were, flirting with some of the purty maids in the Cliff Hotel; they with the heavy make-up and silk gowns, purposely exposing their boobage to show what was on offer. Well, by rights, none of them wuz zactly maids now, wuz um? 'Twud be fair to say they had a fair bit of mileage on um. But then again, so had moast of the boys in here as well, an' they wuz s'paused t'all be Methodists. Ut wuz the way of ut this far up, this far from Detroit. The Keweenaw was the edge of the known world. 'Twas best to accept ut that way. Who needed chapel anyway?

They maids clearly cudn't see the Knockies nor any of the others of their kind that were scampering around in the bar that early evening. They just sensed something present: the occasional flirtatious rush past them, a tickle here, and then a tiny touch there. Whatever these things were that were inside the bar, they liked them. They made them feel like goddesses once more, which wuz a good thing when you looked outside at the pulverised tip that was the Cliff Mine's shantytown. Everywhere, stent and tailings. Nearby, polluted shallows and slimes. This wudn' no American Dream.

What attracted the Knockies to the ladies wuz that they lived in a very male world all the time, and aside from a few bal-maidens (moast of whom resembled pack-horses), there was not much feminine contact. The issue as to whether there was actually somewhere a female set of Knockies which would then enable procreation of their species was one that had been raised several times by countless generations of enquiring miners, but the Knockies never gave a direct answer on ut. Ut wuz taboo. Perhaps therefore deep underground there was a whole female society of these creatures that humans were not allowed to see. Otherwise, how else did they reproduce? At the moment, 'twas best to let Luk and Gourgy just get on with ut, and get some kind of satisfaction. For zertain they were up in the maid's bedrooms makin' havoc. What the hell wuz goin' on up there? You could near 'nuff feel the walls shakin'.

"Alright if...?" Justin had asked the bar manager if the young Indian gentleman could come inside with them.

"Friendly is a?" he'd asked. "If he's friendly then 'tis fine, but otherwise, the forest's that way."

Nice. He pointed up into the hills.

"Ee's friendly enough," said Francis to the sneering manager. "Dun' ee worry."

"He brings peace," offered Justin.

"Just dun't want un putting off other drinkers... thaas all."

Jeez, both Justin and Francis thought to themselves. This was supposed to be the twentieth century. In 'Merky' a man should be able to walk into a bar with an Indian, shouldn' a now? Whatever wuz wrong with people?

"So, whaas the plan then?" asked Justin.

"The plan's easy. We just wait here. Kick back a bit."

"How come?"

"You'll see Sos. Skewsy'll be here. I guarantee it. 'Tis close of business soon for the day core so he'll be here. Ee wun't be able t'resist, not after he works out the quality of that ore. Ee'll be puzzling over where we got ut."

They ordered a round of whiskey, and Francis slid one of the glasses over to the gentleman. He seemed to understand what it was and smiled. The bugger drank ut down in one go though and put the glass back on the table.

"Better get un another..." said Francis.

"Rite on..."

The barman poured another shot and Justin once again pushed it across to the Indian. This time though, he perhaps realised to take his time over the shot, and he sipped it more gently. Francis and Justin had a kind of telepathy between them. When you are brothers, it comes natural. Sometimes, it is not in what is said, but what is not said. It comes in physical symbols too – slight movements, the twitching of an arm, and the particular dart and fix of one's eyes. The plan, in a way, had morphed and changed.

Before now, they'd set out for Copper Mountain and they'd reckoned on the pair of them sharing the profits from any strike fifty-fifty. But then when the Indian gentleman became involved, it looked like they needed to treat ee right too. Es. Moast boys might have fobbed them off with a few provisions and taken hold of the land without asking, but that wudn' this pair's way t'all see. They wanted t'do ut proper. So with that, mehty the Indian would need to be a shareholder too. Now it was going to a thirty-three and third percent of the total profit. But then they knew that they also needed to build in Skewsy because without ee, they'd have no way of assaying the copper and no way into the shipping ov ut down through the Great Lakes. So in truth, 'twas looking more like twenty-five percent each. The Knockies had come to the same conclusion. Overall, that wudn' a bad outcome. Worse things might have happened.

But all that went t'grass as soon as Skewsy entered, because stroathing and striding in alongside un was old John Trevorrow, the Cliff Mine Cap'n. Johnny Trevorrow was all dressed up in his usual Cap'n clobber: pressed black suit with a bowler hat, a waistcoat trying to disguise his girth. In his waistcoat pocket, a gold watch ready to mark time, for when he needed to pause and contemplate how a lode should be worked. Cap'ns like ee allays took sharp intakes of breath, just to make ee think they knawed what they wuz doin'. It wuz a way of showing their status, and indeed, 'twas true that they were to be respected, fur the Cap'n always ruled any Cornish mine, and there wuz no way ever that that wuz goin' to be contested. Even Mrs Cap'n Trevorrow, who nawbody see'd much, was called Mrs Cap'n.

"Shit," went Justin. "Wha d'fuck d'ee want?"

"Ah no," said Francis.

"Knew we'd find you in here," said Skewsy with an air of satisfaction. "I hope you don't mind. I've brought Cap'n along with me. You'll soon see why."

"Whiskies?" offered Justin.

"One with water please," said Skews.

"Mine too," offered Trevorrow.

"Boys, good to see you again," said Trevorrow offering his spade of a hand out for both of the brothers to shake. Interesting move that, considering what he'd probably learnt of them in the past few hours. Fust, he'd have been raging at them two making a strike so close by, but then maybe he needed to contemplate ut a bit more. Maybe this pair wudn' the daft, half-scraped carrots he first thought they were. And then surprisingly in all this *bonhomie*, Trevorrow turned to see the Indian gentleman, and no one knew how that wuz going to go. But then, of all the surprises in the world, ut turned out Trevorrow knawed un. The Indian gentleman did something with his hands then – putting their palms together, and Trevorrow did the same, like he knew what wuz on with un all along. Had they been talking then?

"You know him?" asked Francis, curious.

"'Course," said Trevorrow taking a sip of his whiskey, and adding some water to dilute it. "This is Nimkii. His name means 'thunder'."

That made sense. His face was often like thunder. When Trevorrow said his name, Nimkii smiled in a way that he previously had not.

"How do you know him then?" asked Justin.

"Oh well. When I fust came in here, there were some negotiations to be had. That's when I met Nimkii and his people. We managed to find a way through after that. My predecessor introduced him to me. Young he is, but he've been a man fur a goodly while. You ent long a boy in his culture you. "

"So you can communicate in his language then?"

"No. Not quite. I've worked out a way of getting things across to un. Symbols and drawings mainly. He'll understand. This is an intelligent man sat next to you gentlemen. I've met with un a fair few times over the years."

"We tried," said Francis. "But we didn' seem to find a way of getting through..."

"Let me handle that," said Trevorrow confidently, and then, momentarily, he changed his tone.

"So you pair had your own plans then? Bit cheeky, wudn' ut?"

"'Twudn' really like that..." noted Francis.

"We had a dream out here see," went Justin.

"Like everyone," offered Trevorrow. "I knaw. I knaw. I'd be the same if I wuz you. This is a land of opportunity. I get ut. You have to do what you have to do..."

"So why are you here then?" asked Justin more directly.

"Well," said Trevorrow, sizing it all up and shifting his sweaty bottom on the seat he was on, "I think we and you might need each other. Let me hand over to Mr Skews. Hear ov what ee got t'say."

Skews nervously pulled a set of notes and diagrams from the briefcase he was carrying. Then he slowly and eruditely took his glasses out of their case and put them on, bending the thin wire around his ears on both sides.

"Here's your assay report," he went. "I think you'll find all in order."

Justin picked ut up and gaked over ut. Justin cudn' read much an' what he saw wudn' like anything he wanted to see. He gave up and passed the documentation on to his brother.

"These the mineral percentages?" he asked.

"Yes."

"Is this right? It d'say here nearly ninety percent..."

"On one of them, yes. The other's kicking around seventy..."

"That's good, isn't it?"

"Very good," said Skewsy. "In fact, it's excellent, Mr Trevorrow..."

He made a gesture for Trevorrow to continue the conversation.

"They are the highest percentages we've found here on the Keweenaw. We think too, in the whole of the Upper Peninsula opened up so far. Gentlemen, congratulations. You have quite a find there. Tell me – and let's get down to brass tacks. What are you proposing to do with you claim?"

"Mine ut," said Justin.

"Es," said Francis. "Get up there an' start opening it up."

"What, with a whim?"

"To begin with, es... Grow ut natural-like," said Justin. "Like back 'ome."

Trevorrow shook his head.

"Na. Na. Na. That idn' the best way t'do ut now," he argued. "What you'll end up with is chaos. 'Twill end up looking like old men's workings. No order to ut. No system. Suppawse you'll take the eyes of ut, and then move on? That your plan, is ut?"

Neither Justin and Francis wanted to answer that. In truth, they hadn' got any further than thinking about the ore's quality. They were *that* organised.

"What you boys need is a planned h'operation, and here we might be able to help one another out. Every bugger up here knaws that Cliff idn' going to last forever. 'Tis goin' to soon go scat fur zertain. You knaw yerselves 'tis in the country. The best of ut wuz in the last century. Es. Es. There's more ore in there, but tis gettin' harder to get out. It won't be long afore the company sees this and they'll pull out. I reckon this new find, well, if it's up on the mountain might be easier. Less water see ... you dun't have the same issues with ut. That a map ov ut, is ut? "

Trevorrow gestured for Francis to show him his directions, and where the stake was located.

"I think I d'knaw the place where you'm talking about."

"What you proposing then Cap'n?"

"We each have a stake in ut. Like back home. I'n get you the boys and men to work the ground. I'n get gear in there. Mr Skews can do a survey and we can map it. Design the h'operation to most efficiently follow the lodes. You got ore there that's ninety percent. That's huge. Even the best of Cliff is only pulling in the upper fifties. You mine less but you get more ore. The thing is, whether you like ut or not, you pair of idiots need me – and you need Mr Skews here too. You might not like ut but you presently ebm got the wherewithal to make it happen. We have. And we're the same if I'm honest. Me and Sam here, we need you. There's plenty of good miners who need you too right now. Otherwise the Upper Peninsula's going to become a desert."

"A ghost town – if people left?"

"Exactly. The people got dreams see," continued Trevorrow. "They want shoppin' s'good as Falmouth or Truro, an' they want parks an' avenues like there is in Detroit. They want large houses: not the granite terraces we got back home, but proper houses – with gardens. They want chapels, churches and summer parades ."

The way 'twas goin' boath Francis and Justin could see the logic in what wuz being said. They knew Trevorrow could make it happen far quicker. The boy also knew his captaincy at the Cliff Mine would soon be coming to an end. There was still Nimkii though.

"Twenty percent shares each then," negotiated Francis. "Split five ways: me, Justin, Cap'n, Mr Skews and Nimkii."

"That's right," said Mr Skews. "That alright with you Mr Trevorrow?"

"Fine by me."

There was one individual who'd so far, had no input into this contract. That was Nimkii himself, but perhaps from the present gathering maybe he was starting to get a feel of what was going on.

"You got a pen Samuel?" asked Trevorrow. "Let me sit a while with Mr Nimkii here and I'll explain to him what is being proposed. He responds well to illustration. You know, like they there Egyptian hieroglyphs... Well, so as I've found, 'tis a bit like that."

"Watch un," said Francis covertly to Justin. "I dun't want Trevorrow cutting no side deal and diddling Nimkii out of his percentage."

Skews passed over a pen and a sheet of paper. Trevorrow and Nimkii moved to another table, and Justin observed.

"What about contracts?" asked Francis.

"I've taken the liberty of having some drawn up already... if you would like to look over them. I don't wish to rush you Mr Nankervis but our need is to get started soon on this operation... If you and your brother sign today then whilst the laker is in, I can get word to the processors and manufacturers in Detroit. The smelters are crying out for quality copper they are. We should strike while the iron is hot so to speak."

Skews pushed a set of contracts his way. Francis glanced at them.

"I've... a... kept them as Cornish as possible. There won't be anything too different in there. Rest assured, I think mining law in American is going to be based on Cornish mining law anyway."

Whilst Skewsy spoke, Francis made sure he kept an eye on what was being negotiated between Trevorrow and Nimkii. Could his brother be trusted to get a grip on what was being said? He didn' knaw, but he had to hope. Twenty percent was being mentioned a lot. And from Nimkii only came what appeared to be guttural sounds of approval. Eventually, there was a shaking of hands between the three of them. Trevorrow, Nimkii and Justin then came back to the main table.

"Settled?" Skews asked.

"Settled," said Trevorrow. "Nimkii and his people are happy that we may mine there..."

"What about limits?" asked Francis. "How long can we go on for? What size can we go to?"

Skews gave the Cornishman a look. Now we were getting it. This was how exploitative business overseas was done. This was the British Empire at work – or at least the Cornish end of it.

"They don't mind," said Trevorrow shrugging nonchalantly . "The important thing is that they are paid regularly for all the ore mined. They'll just want their share. Their cut of things."

It didn' sound right. If this deal wuz being negotiated at home, those sorts of questions would need answering and laying out on the table.

"What happens when mining ends?" asked Francis.

"Y'knaw... like it always is. Nature recovers and claws back the territory. Regains what it has lost. Like all the abandoned bals back home."

"Is Nimkii's land there spiritual in any way?"

This seemed an odd question to ask.

Skews and Trevorrow never, in a million lifetimes, expected that.

"How do you mean?" asked Skews, puzzled.

"You knaw... As a people they are very connected to the landscape... to the animals in it. I mean, the harmony of it all."

No one knew what to say. Francis wuz sounding like some philosopher from Switzerland, who had quaint romantic ideas on how the world should be.

"You mean witchcraft like?" asked Trevorrow. "Is tha' what you mean? Frighted if there'll be revenge on us."

"I mean whether 'tis sacred... special in some way. I mean, that was what a lot of the Indian Wars were all about. It wuz in the papers."

"I dun't think we need be worried about that," offered Skews, stifling a cough to show the insignificance of the concern. "A truce wuz signed here a long time ago."

But Francis wasn't listening.

"Ask him. Please."

The intensity of the way Francis asked this, suggested that it was very important to him. Now amongst this gathering in the Cliff Hotel, only Justin knew why he'd asked that question. There had been things that had happened in the past that did not need to be unearthed again here. But happen they did, and that's why Francis asked.

"I'll try to ask," said Trevorrow, noting Francis' genuine concern.

This time, Francis watched as Trevorrow drew the mountain once more and then sketched in what looked like a bear and an eagle. He used stick men to indicate a kind of tomb. Then Trevorrow gesticulated between the two images. Nimkii seemed to pick up on what Trevorrow was asking and then shook his head vigorously.

"No," interpreted Trevorrow. "Nothing sacred up there. Just forest..."

And at this, Francis wondered if the forest itself was sacred enough on its own but he did not say anything. His brother knew what he was thinking though. It was the way of things between them. Still, nobody wuz about to upset this deal, were they? This proposed mine could make them all very rich. Who wanted to destroy that? Not Justin – and not Francis. This wuz something they had imagined endlessly when on board the ship crossing the Atlantic. All the time maybe ut wuz feeling a bit like they had stumbled into a fairy tale though, and that absurdly, they were its central characters. And maybe any time soon, a giant, a witch or a wolf might deceive them – or worse still, consume them, and spit out their bones. But there wuz no other way. They had to go with ut because they both knew that the alternative to this wuz passage back to Cornwall, and turning up in the parish broken and empty-handed. So when the furry happened, everyone dancing through could label them failures and not couple with them.

This wuz not the best of a bad deal. This, in fact, wuz the best deal they could put together at this point in time. They'd contemplated all other actions, and much as they didn' really want Trevorrow getting his teeth stuck in, both admitted that he wuz an experienced Cap'n. He brought something to the table. The contracts got signed by the five shareholders. In that swish of a pen they'd formed 'The Keweenaw Copper Company' and things now looked set. Back home such deals took months to arrange but the bewdie of it here wuz that you could dispense with formality. On the mining frontier, things went faster. And when the ink dried, toasts were made and everyone present drank a little more than they should, even Nimkii. But as it grew dark outside, Nimkii made it clear that it was time for him to leave.

"We don't mind paying for a room for him," said Francis. "We booked ours, but wasn't sure about him."

"Dun't ee worry 'bout that. Most Ojibwe are happier sleeping under the stars than in the confines of a hotel. Let un go. He's resilient."

"Where's a off?"

"To the forest."

"What? We doan't even know where he lives."

"No need," said Trevorrow. "He'll find us when he needs to."

"Is that how he found us?"

"He'll have tracked you for days. They reckon they have a sense for it. Ojibwe have always had to cross vast land. They have a way of honing in on what is important. The slightest movements. He told me once he can hear the earth..."

"Like when we dug the hole..." stated Justin.

"Zactly."

"He can see our Knockies too," asserted Francis.

"Es," said Trevorrow. "Not many people can. But Indians. They'n see them. It's like they'm looking closer. They see a world beyond this one. Funny, idn' ut?"

By now, boath Trevorrow and Skews were ready to return to the camp, and to their lodgings there. They had enough ale and whiskey in them, but then, fur a change, there'd been something to celebrate.

"You pair dun good," Trevorrow belched. "Proper job, both of ee. Mining's set here for a while now. Once word d'get out, then boom, every bugger in the world'll want to get here. Come on Mr Skews, let us get back and allow these fine gentlemen to enjoy their evening here. I see your Knockies are already at it... There's a nice mulatto maid here usually that I wudn mind nestling inta' – and thaas fur zertain..."

He stopped speaking. He realised that as a pillar of the community he was not really to mention such matters. But still a man he wuz and Mrs Cap'n didn' appear to be offering un much in the way of charm or comfort.

Both brothers followed him out, wincing at the sight of Luk and Gourgy cavorting in a suggestive dance with the maids of the hotel.

"Goodnight to you both, fellow shareholders...!"

With that announcement Trevorrow nearly fell over, but Skews was there to steady him.

Es. Things were moving forward now brave n' fast. But then. that's what everyone wants. Nobody needs prevarication or procrastination. People d'say the Cornish are all about the concept of dreckly but that idn' right t'all. When they want to move, they'll move – quicker than duckshit, and thaas a fact.

"Look brother, I'm goin' over with Luk and Gourgy. They know how to party. We'll dance the night away..."

And that's what Justin did because that wuz who he wuz. And Francis sat at the bar contemplating everything. That wuz his way of doing things. With that, he settled down to contemplate this deal. He spent a few moments thinking over everything that had happened. And then from the bar, Francis noted the slight noise of a new family come into the hotel lobby. From what he could see, there was a bearded man and his wife, two daughters and a chield. Judging from Skews' wish to hurriedly get an order in to the laker captain to take that back down to Detroit, the family that stood before him had obviously just come in on the northwards journey of the current boat. He knew the turnaround was quick. He hoped that Skews could make it.

Their faces betrayed the same signs of exhaustion that he and his brother had felt when they'd finally arrived on the Keweenaw. Obviously Cornish (he recognised the cut of their cloth in the Cornish style, but also their faces, which had that look of grim darkness to them), they would have endured the same journey perhaps as he had done some months ago. What brought them here was unclear at this point. The man was obviously not a miner, and the woman no bal-maid. Pin-tailed she wuz, with narra' hips. The girls had an educated look to them that wudn' much seen up here. This hotel wudn' perhaps their normal choice of accommodation, but considering that was pretty much all there was, perhaps they had no choice.

Francis tried to overhear their conversation but the woman said little and the man spoke in a low, deep voice that was now drowned out by the noise and dancing in the bar. He did pick up on the fact that a telegram had been sent on, and that the hotel had had confirmation of their reservations. Once they'd signed the register, the family began to load in their possessions. Francis and his brother travelled relatively light, but not this group. The father had taken the trouble to hire a horse and cart from the harbour up to the hotel, and now a boy was helping them in with what looked like heavy trunks and suitcases. Es. They wudn' here temporarily – that wuz fur sure. This wuz kit and caboodle.

No doubt now, they'd just be glad of clean sheets and comfortable beds. The lakers wudn' no place fur a family like this. The Upper Peninsula tended to be a single man's world. Maybe they'd come to realise that soon enough when they might discover that the 'hotel' they were staying in was actually a den of inequity. Curious, he noted the man and his daughters paused to look into the bar, but Francis being of a shy type anyway, kept his head down and looked at the bar instead. No one else bothered to gake at them. They were probably just coming through – making their way to Calumet or perhaps even Houghton. They looked right fur ut.

At that moment, they piqued Francis' interest, but in the seconds following, he forgot about them again. His contemplative mood wuz broken by the arrival of his brother, who by now was in good spirits. The Knockies and he had already quickly been knocking back shots and they were ready to take their good luck to another level. He wudn' meant to be doin' tha' you.

"Shallus play the carding tables?" asked Justin, clearly forgetting his commitment to teetotalism.

"Es. We'm on a run of luck. May as well see it through..." offered the slurred voice of Gourgy, which in no way, was very helpful. "A deal has been signed on our new mining h'enterprise."

"You knaw you want to," offered Luk.

"I dun't think that d'work with blackjack, do ut?"

"Alright," said his brother. "Poker then... or perhaps the roulette tables..."

"You knaw you'd be best off not touching they," went Francis, trying not to engage them in further conversation. "Best if we all went t'bed I reckon, and then wake up in the morning with a clear head."

All they three made disapproving faces.

"Killjoy," said Gourgy.

"I thought you might have had more sense," he said to Luk, who generally was the more sensible of the pair of mine spirits.

For once, that left Luk a bit tongue-tied and he didn' rightly knaw how to respond. It burst his bubble a bit, but nonetheless, the other pair were as crazy as ever. This wuz it see. This wuz who they were.

"Well, I'm going up," Francis said, downing the last of his drink. "I'll see you crew at breakfast."

He knew that whatever he said to Justin and Gourgy it wudn' make naw difference. Fur they the night wuz still young. And yes, Francis understood it. He understood why they needed to let go a bit – the last few months had been hard-going. But his brother? Tha' disappointed un.

"You coming?" he said to Luk.

Luk wudn' sure what to do. He was Justin's Knockie really and by rights, he was the right bread to his butter. Luk was glancing this way and that, unsure how to proceed. But Francis was now outside of the bar and standing in the lobby about to go up the stairs. He didn' look back at the others. They'd do what they needed to do.

"This time," he shouted back to them, "dun't expect me to fix it."

And then Luk remembered what had happened before, and as Francis climbed the staircase, he found the crumpled mine spirit walking next to him.

"You made the right choice boy," said Francis to him.

"Have I?" asked Luk.

"Reckon so."

Ut didn' take Francis long to get changed for bed. By the time he was ready to sleep, the bed that they'd made for their Knockies in one of the drawers of the chest opposite contained the fragile and exhausted body of Luk. He was already asleep and snoring loudly. As he tried to get off, Francis attempted to forget about the carnage going on below them. That was the way of ut, if you were pards though. 'Twas like a proper marriage, and you had to tolerate a lot. A bit of give n' take, as they say. After tha', the boy Francis fell asleep and dreamt about walls of gems and canopies of copper.

5

There wuz a maid who worked in the Cliff Hotel who went by the name of Rosie Koskinen, and she wuz some beauty. She wuz a looker definitely, but at the same time, she wuz feisty like there wudn' naw tomorra'. There wuz somethun' about she. 'Course, the way things were: Justin and Gourgy made a beeline fer she, and she made a beeline for they. All this happened, while sensible Francis and little Luk slept upstairs. Snoring deep they were by now, as if under a spell, which in a way they were. Now, you'n see the difference between these two brothers who'd travelled all this way. And this was partially how Justin had found hisself in a heap ov trouble before. But we shen't go inta' all tha' now – least ways not yet.

Anyone could see ut in the smoky haze of the bar. Justin and Gourgy wuz out to party. They both wanted t'celebrate their strike and the deal they'd made. Some made-up Justin wuz, now that he was a proper shareholder in a mine. 'Twudn' be like this back home. Chance of owning a bal like this would never have comed his way; not in a million lifetimes. And Gourgy, well, he was made-up too, fer it meant stability, and Knockies like that. Tay an' cake an' buns – regular-like. Naw more wanderin' the hills and the gulleys like it was back home for a goodly while – too long a while. This place could be somewhere t'settle. So that was the way 'twuz and the reason why these pair were knocking back the liquor. And see, men and Knockies with a goodly amount of liquor on board, can be spot a mile away by maids like Rosie.

She wuz dark-haired see. Voluptuous. Curvy, the way that Justin liked women. She had red lipstick on that no maid back Cornwall would ever paint on her lips. Ut wuz a kind of exciting exotica you never got down Morvah or Pendeen. Rosie wudn' Cornish. Oh no, by Gar. She wudn' act the way she wuz if she wuz. She wuz a migrant too. Maybe she wuz German. There wuz that accent about her. Maybe not German. Maybe Polish perhaps. A lot of them were up here. There wuz a lot of Polish who worked the mines. It wud make sense if she wuz. Justin asked her, but she wudn't reveal much, least not first off. Well, we'm all like that, b'aint us? An' women, well, they liked to keep an air of mystery about them. That wuz it with girls see. She knew it. He knawed ov ut. The moment all the mystery's gone, you'n forget ut. Thaas when you'n lose everything. Always keep a bit of mystery about ee. Thaas the best way.

"You a Cussie then?" she asked, drawing up cosy-like to Justin at the bar.

Gourgy was next to him, slouched on a bar seat to the right of him.

"You'm in there boy," Gourgy whispered.

She knew he wuz a Cussie. He wuz wearing their uniform: hobnailers, corduroy trousers and a waistcoat. All the stupid saffron-munchin' Cornish looked the same.

"I dun't need t'answer that now do I?" replied Justin. "Who might you be?"

"They call me Rosie..."

"Do they now?"

"You looking fur some company, my *pupu*?"

Gourgy nearly fell off his seat at that.

"'Course you are, you stupid bugger. Tell her. Go on," he said, offering advice.

"Might be," offered Justin.

Gourgy held his hand to his head in despair.

"She's gorgeous," Gourgy went. "I'd bite her hand off. I'd gorge on a lot else too. I'd begin with her toes and work my way up."

He probably would, knawing ee.

"I'm playing it cool," he said to the mine sprite.

"Tool," replied Gourgy and carried on drinking.

"You with someone *pupu*?" Rosie asked.

"No... no... My brother wuz here earlier but he's gone to bed now..."

"I saw. Looks like you and he had a big meeting."

"Well, yes. We two, and the Indian fella..."

"...And Trevorrow and Skews... We know them here. Anything important?"

Now, if Justin had any sense to un, he'd say 'twas somethun small and negligible but he being he, he cudn' leave ut at that. Gourgy did warn un but Justin cudn' help but be the big 'I am' and tell her 'bout what wuz goin' on.

"We signed a deal on a new strike..."

"A strike?"

By now, Justin, with a wave, had silently called the bar manager over and ordered a bourbon for Rosie. He could tell it wuz what she was drinking. And at the word 'strike' this Rosie sidled a little closer to Justin, and put her hand on his shoulder. And well, fer Justin that felt nice, but he shushed her when she loudly called out the strike in the way she did. He didn' want to, mind. He could sense her perfume. He could smell her hair and see the powder on her soft face, and it felt wondrous. And because of that, he opened his gob a bit further, even if by now he wuz just whispering it, perhaps taking a bit more leave of his senses.

"Up on the mountain. A goodly way from here now but 'tis a rich find. Good quality copper... Better than at the Cliff Mine..."

"Better than Cliff, eh? Well you must be very pleased... now... What's your name again?"

"Justin," he said. "Justin Nankervis."

She hadn't actually asked for his name before but she wuz good at making the conversation flow. These were the tools of her trade. His surname didn' matter. In her experience, usually, it never did.

"You on your lonesome now then Justin?"

"Well..." Justin answered. "Kind've..."

"Thanks very much," said Gourgy, who'd by now resigned himself to the fact that he wuz having to watch all this sweet talk and be utterly ignored.

"You know, the Cussies always say they travel with their spirits... is that right? Sometimes we can feel them. The girls and I. We can sense something there when they are in. You travel with creatures don't you?"

"Na... It's just us," said Justin. "Dun't listen to that tripe. It's just folklore..."

At that, Justin felt himself being kicked hard in the thigh by Gourgy. He'd go for his bollocks if he could. It didn't do t disrespect Knockies in this way.

"Folk creature denier," he shouted. "*Pupu!*"

Gourgy sulked. He knew humans could be geht tusses sometimes. They denied the truth every time. And this time, it looked like Justin wuz denying it, just so this new ladyfriend of his wudn' think he was crazy.

"So, you hoping to make some fine money out of that strike?"

"Maybe," said Justin. "If the run of the seams is with us..."

"And what if it isn't?"

"Move on, I s'pause... or head back home..."

"I see... These mines bring us all here, yes?"

"Es," said Justin. "And where's home fur you?"

"Ha... Here, now. I never had a home *pupu*... not like you... I came with my family to New York a long time ago, when I was a girl... and gradually we made our way west. And then northward, to here..."

The way she said 'here' sounded like it was the last place on earth she wanted to be.

"But where are you from originally?"

"Finland..."

In Justin's mind that sounded a long way away. She'd come further and for longer than him. For any Cornishman, 'Merky' was absolutely the next parish after Land's End. Fur she, this wuz something different.

"The winter's here do make me feel at home though," she said. "I thought America would be deserts and sun... but up here, there is none of that. Just cold – and trees. Endless trees. Like what I remember when I was little."

Her words seemed to give her the cue to nuzzle in even more closely to Justin, who by now, was warming to her. As was the way up here, they were two lonely souls wanting comfort and needing touch, a touch you didn' get from pines or ice.

"Oh. Get a room," Gourgy said below his pasty breath. He wuz starting to get restless. He needed comfort too but it wudn' like there wuz any female spirit creatures in here to offer him any. The place wuz just filled with Jackers and their Knockies, who all seemed to be kept on quite a tight leash. You know this Gourgy by now. He wuz Francis' Knockie, but well, Francis wudn' here, wuz a? By his reckoning, he cud do what he liked.

Justin was sensing this, and needed to deal widn'.

"Excuse me for a moment ma'am," he said, and dragged the Knockie out of the bar to the stinking urinals at the rear of the establishment.

"You want to mess up my date?"

"She ent no date," went Gourgy calmly. "She's just paid by the hour... and you'll be slipping her some money soon enough. Never learn, do you?"

"Keep your comments to yourself. If you don't like ut, then bugger off. I don't care what you think. If she wuz kindly to you, you'd be in there like a shot..."

Gourgy hissed at him, and with some difficulty levered himself up in the air so he could reach the urinal. Then he took a long, steaming piss.

"Ahhhh..."

"I know you Gourgy," said Justin. "Remember that... What have you got to worry about? I'm buying your bourbon and you're drinkin' it like there's no tomorra."

"I'm bored," said Gourgy. "I ebm got no one to play with. No one to make mischief with."

"There are other Knockies in there. I've seen them. Go hang out with them. Put the world to rights. "

Gourgy launched into a rage of disparaging comments about all of them. According to him, they were all mummy's boys who didn' have a clue how to act when in a bar.

"You go back to she," Gourgy said. "I'm going on the card tables. Do whatever you want..."

"You haven't got any money," stated Justin.

"'Course I have," said Gourgy. "And normally, you'd be right in there with me... Comus on you, tell me now. Whaas become of the real Justin, eh?"

That wuz an incendiary comment which was why the little, pugnacious Knockie made ut.

"You've got boring since you've been over here..." the Knockie added, just to rub salt into the wound.

Justin looked at himself in the mirror on the wall in the toilet. He noted what he'd become. Knockies allays had a way of making you see yourself in a new way.

"Alright," said Justin. "One or two hands..."

"Rite on." said Gourgy, smiling. "I knew the old Justin was lurking there on the inside."

"She comes too?"

"Rosie?"

"Alright. S'long as we can have a bit of a flutter... A decent game like."

Knockies were, of course, keen on cards. At many a halt underground for some reason or another – the pause for a fuse or the wait for some new piece of gear to come down – a miner would get out an old elastic-band-bound pack of cards. Knockies learnt every trick in the book. They were good at poker faces too. You cudn' penetrate their thinking. They'd dunk their hard, resin-coated felt 'tull' hats down over their eyes, and not make a move.

"I reckon there might be some money to be 'ad out there on they tables. I've been watching. There idn' anyone a bit tasty. No players. Not like you Jus..."

And because Justin wuz who he wuz, he cudn' resist but go along with what this Knockie said. Bugger boring Francis and bugger boring Luk.

"Come on pard!" went Gourgy a little more enthusiastically.

They washed and rinsed their hands, and then went back inside to the bar.

"Rosie, do you fancy some time at the tables?" asked Justin.

He gestured towards the poker and blackjack games. A thread of guilt found its way up from his stomach and into his throat. He did his best to ignore it though.

"Why, I thought you'd never ask," joked Rosie. "You sense that?"

"What?"

"I dunno. Something then. I felt it."

Justin scowled at Gourgy who'd briefly placed one of his hands on Rosie's pert bottom.

"Dun't ee worry," said Gourgy. "She thought it was you... and she likes you... so we win all round."

The thing nawbody had said yet, wuz that this Justin, well, he'd had a bit of a problem after some gambling at home. So much so, he'd had to rely on his brother to bail un out. Not just once, but several times. And as much as Francis had tried to steer un down the path of Methodism and get him to go to chapel each week (where successive preachers spoke against the sins of gambling and drink), he didn' much care fur ut. Allays the same, ut wuz. He'd needed help to pay off some debt and swore blind he'd go back chapel and take on board all that wuz said, but he could awnly keep it goin' a fortnight a'fore he'd lapse again.

But maybe that was a time ago, a continent ago, an ocean ago. Maybe here in 'Merky' it would be alright. Luck was widn'. And that's how Justin approached the tables that night. Luck had come to him in the form of the strike, and luck had come to him too, in the form of the deal he'd made with the other shareholders. In this moment, he was glad that his brother was not there for he knew what would happen if he was. He knew he'd be dragged away.

He'd been starkly reminded of who he was, and right now, he did not care for that. Right now, he wanted to at least think he was successful, and had money to burn: that he could afford this girl Rosie. She wuz certainly getting looks. She wuz a catch, fer zertain. They were other men who liked she, and well, Justin didn' want to see that. And in his mind, he wanted people back home to see un, even though they cudn': especially they who'd written un off; they who said he'd never make anything of hisself.

The draw wuz there though. Right there in front of un – the green baize of the tables.

Temptation.

The belief that you could make something out of nothing.

It cudn' be odds. It wuz the way of things.

Now he had supporters in the form of Rosie and Gourgy. Well, the Knockie never needed much encouraging. But she, wuz different. Of course, that was the aim of the girls who worked there: to get the men (miners or laker hands) on the tables, where they'd always put down a bit too much, go that little bit further than they should, blow all of their earnings in one moment of madness. And they'd have to live like a pauper until payday again. Go much beyond that, and they'd have the shirt off your back. You wudn' ever be able to go back inside the Cliff Hotel, and there wuz plenty like that: men who were stuck in Eagle Harbour and men who wudn' ever venture outside the camp. Some men moved on to Calumet because they knawed their faces weren't welcome here. At least in 'Merky' you had a second-chance. If you cocked up somewhere, well, there was always another mining town you could move to. This was not like Cornwall: one bad decision and there – Gah! – you were labelled fer life. Small mindsets see. No way of looking beyond the Tamar. But here – something different.

And loaded with bourbon, and loaded with the cool prestige that owning a mine brought, Justin thought he could be someone: a player see.

And fair dues to him, for when the boy sat at one of the poker tables, he won a fair old set of games. He wuz in touch with the cards and the game flowed his way. All gamblers know how that goes. So he was betting according to the rank he believed his cards were. And with Gourgy peering over his shoulder and giving him the run down, they made some smart moves. Es. Rite on. And when the other players called their cards, well, they couldn't raise nothing. But every time Justin could raise his. Come showdown, Justin always took the pot! And he wuz doin well, this Cussie. He was showing the other players how skilled he was at this game. Cunning he was and between him and Gourgy, they were employing every ounce of probability, game play and psychology. Their bluffs worked each time, which wudn' always the case back home, but seemed to work fine here.

Now in these first few games, everyone was playing for cents only but gradually, the dollar bills went down. And that's when things got more serious, and when the values of those bills went up exponentially, well, that's when the other games stopped being played, and people took interest in this one. Now this Cussie named Justin, it looked like ee wudn' a bad player everyone said, because he wuz taking in a good bit of money, which he was handing over to Rosie. And Justin – he delivered flush after flush, and if that wudn' forthcoming then he went for four of a kind. Es. He wuz getting some good cards on the initial deals wuz this Justin. He kept a good face on him did this Cornish boy, so others wudn' suspect anything. Gradually, they comed to see that he wuz a bit of a player, and they jacked their cards in. They knawed when they wuz beat. They knew the run of luck wudn' with them that night and that it wuz with this darned Cussie. In short, he took the pot again and again.

Normally now, Justin would think himself invincible and have carried on playing. In the past, that wuz where all his problems had started. But maybe this boy had learnt, like we all do. And when he'd amassed a goodly amount of money, he stopped. He knew how to now, and it took some doing on his behalf, because no gambler wants to quit, especially where there are other hands, and men get lapse with beer and bluffs, but quit he did. So fair play to this Justin. Even Gourgy, who delighted in the game, admired how he'd played ut, how he'd kept his head and not run with his heart. Es. So some profit wuz made there.

"How much?" asked Gourgy.

"I reckon at least six months worth of mine wages."

Fur a change, the boy'd done a'right: a goodly amount of cash most of which Rosie gave back to him, and a bit of which he let her have because she'd been his good luck that night. You know how 'tis with men and women sometime; daggun' fer a kind of love ov sorts, fer in truth, Justin didn' want the night to end like that. Aw naw. Not when there wuz more pleasure to be had.

"You coming up *pupu*?" Rosie asked in that Finnish accent, which drove this miner a bit mad and made his loins tingle.

That night, no one knew where Gourgy slept, but after a negotiation, Justin found himself in the boudoir of Rosie the Finn. Anyone observing might have thought this was brutal and unloving but it was not like that at all. Na. Instead, it was the coming together of two desperately lonely people whose lives were holding on to hope by way of a thin thread. And when Justin felt Rosie's naked body in her bed, he dreamed not of shafts and levels, of seams and stopes of copper, but instead, of fairy tales, still not quite realising that he himself had stepped into one. And that Rosie – 'andsome as she was – liked how this Cussie held her, and kept her company. They entwined around each other in the dark – seeking sweet new ores.

Back in the camp, Cap'n Trevorrow took off his bowler hat, hung up his suit and bedded down for the night. He'd earlier made a cup taa on the slab and shoved the remnants of some stale saffron cake made by Mrs Cap'n down his gullet. Mrs Cap'n snored and had her back to him. Skews tried to do the same but could not sleep. His acute loneliness and the beat of money kept his heart awake.

Some distance away, that Nimkii bedded down on the forest floor: a forest that was about to be upturned and broken.

That Gourgy, well, no one knew where he wuz. And perhaps that wuz a good thing.

6

Labels don't always fit, as we shall come to learn in this lowly hearthside tale. Es you. Sometimes things are thought to be one thing and turn out to be something different. Thus, in what might or might not best be called the dining room of the Cliff Hotel, Francis and Luk were sat opposite each other in an east-facing winda' alcove, indulging in a breakfast of coffee, eggs, bacon and hog's pudding, delivered in and on enamel mugs and plates. Apparently, the hog's pudding wuz made down in Detroit and wuz shipped up here for all the Cussies to gorge on.

Dining room wudn' quite the word fur ut. It wuz actually just a somewhat poky room in the northern end of the hotel where guests could be served food without the unnecessary distractions of liquor and poker. An' for Methodists, tha' wuz precisely wha' wuz needed. Any of they who comed in on a laker would have to put up with the evils on offer, fur the sake of the accommodation. Cobwebs though, raged in a ceiling that was too high to clean and the floor planchen creaked whenever the waitress came in and out. Es – it sounded like an old solar platform above a sump, down in the fifty-first fathom, less of a hotel and more of a low kiddleywink.

They had both slept well (with Francis dreaming of vast mounds of shimmering copper and Luk mumbling a few lines or so of the song 'Trelawny') though the former had been awoken by the dawn's sun streaming through the thin hessian curtains of their room, a sun that could be seen this time of the morning illuminating the dark waters of Lake Superior, just to the north-east of them. Dark was the lake you, and dark were the mountains. That should tell ee somethun' 'bout this place.

Suddenly, fur Francis, their adventure was reaching culmination. An hour or so before, when he awoke, he swung his muscular legs out of the bed and yawned. Then, with satisfaction, he scratched his crotch and felt the roughness of his beard. In his mind he reflected on yesterday's momentous events and smiled to himself at what they had achieved. Es. If nawthun' comed out the ground, he could be dead an' buried and be happy that he'd make it to the rank of shareholder. He was truly an Adventurer in Mining. These labels delighted him.

There were presently more practical matters to be dealt with however. He'd requested some hot water for the morning at around half-past seven, and at that time, there was a knock at the door. Outside, had been left a bowl of boiling water and a towel. He carefully brought it in and placed it before the mirror. From his bag he took his razor and some shaving cream and began the process of scraping away several days' beard growth. Whilst he was shaving – at the dip of the razor in and out of the hot water – Luk opened his eyes and stared over at him. Francis knew what he would say.

"Es ut morning already? I'm hungry. When's breakfast?"

When they had relocated downstairs, a jolt of reality hit him as he poured out another cupful of steaming coffee. What had they taken on here? Could they actually transform that acre or so of their strike in those deep, dark woods into an advanced mining operation – one to rival the big producers at home, and here in 'Merky'? What would become of ut over the next decade and the rest of the now unfurling twentieth century? How would it truly be when he was dead and buried? He realised he needed the coffee to steady him. Luk, on the other hand, seemed more confident, jabbering on to himself and now tearing into a delicious hunk of hog's pudding. Ut was cooked just the way he liked it. The hotel wuz used to the tastes of miners from old Europe. Discs of white hog's pudding wuz exactly what the Cornish liked of a morning – and their ravenous Knockies too.

Something else unnerved Francis. He couldn't precisely work out why, but in the far corner of the dining room, the respectable family that had arrived last night, had ventured into the space, and were now being attended to by the waitress. He could not get a better look at who they were and, in staring at them he tried to work out what had brought them here. He noted that they ordered the same breakfast as he had done, which stamped them out again as being Cornish, and when he heard them speak he noted the soft, western tones to their voices. Certainly though, they were a class or two above him. The cut of the gentleman's suit, the precise turn-ups on his trousers and crisp collars he wore marked them out that way, as did the girls' floor-length dresses and petticoats; their pristine blouses, tied by ribbons at the neck. He noted too the neat way they wore their hair – pinned into a bun.

The father in the group had a generous spade of a beard of the kind that gentlemen of his class felt fashionable. It had once been fully black but now carried a dominating grey colour as if he had already experienced some of the pain and rigours of life. The two girls with him (obviously his daughters) were in transition from being girls to women. One was older – possibly in her early twenties already; the other younger, still carrying the retention of childlike features, and was not yet as tall as her sister. They sat with their backs to Francis, so he could not fully see their faces, and these two young women, as all women did in this time, kept their faces downward, not wishing to draw attention to themselves (especially in the tumultuous male landscape of a mining camp). But attention they were gaining. The thin-faced mother was more talkative, more commanding of the situation, checking that all of them had what they needed, and also serving the infant with its needs. He worked out that the baby wudn' a chield. It wuz a boy – his name being James.

Maybe this family group unnerved him because they felt like a return to civilisation once more. The mother fussing over her family brought an air of domesticity to the wilderness that they all found themselves in. She reminded him of his own mother, and so both comforted and repelled Francis for it somehow seemed so out of place. He observed how they poured their tea, how they ate their food (certainly not in the style of him, with just one fork, but correctly using the full set of cutlery) and how they did their best to draw little attention to themselves. Maybe Francis considered, this was their last dose of civilisation and that they were anticipating what was to be experienced further on in their journey. This temporary comfort might be as good as it got in this part of 'Merky'.

"A'right there? You... ah... just come in last night?" he questioned across the room, half-shouting and projecting his voice.

At first, they took no notice of him, so he tried again; this time, more loudly.

"You just come in last night?"

This time the father caught his question and realised it was for him to answer.

"Morning," he said, "Yes – we arrived yesterday. A long trip up from Detroit... Felt like an eternity on that laker. Glad to be on dry land again. An interminable voyage!"

His answer was convivial and the gentleman seemed glad of the conversation.

"I'm Francis. Francis Nankervis..." said the miner.

"George Jewell," said the gentleman, probably about to introduce the rest of his family, but this was not possible because Francis interrupted him. He did however manage to get out the name of his wife.

"This is my dear wife Clara, and these are..."

"You staying here, or moving on?"

This time, the gentleman put down his cutlery to give a more considered response.

"I... have accepted a post here. On the Keweenaw... as a doctor. Brought the family with me, as you can see..."

"You Cornish?"

"Of course. Aren't we all out here?" remarked the doctor smiling. "We're from Bodmin originally. We both grew up there."

Now it was making sense. Posh see. Bodmin. A better-most class of people.

"A medical doctor? For the mines?"

"Well yes... I'm a qualified surgeon... The idea is to build a practice over here. Plenty of business is expected I believe."

"What ee mean?"

"Well, Cornish miners and every other kind of miner coming over here from what I gather. Stands to rights... Cornwall's dead right now. Not much work for mine surgeons. And you know, we Cornish... we are tryers... always have been... always will be."

"You're not wrong there," said Francis. "All the world's looking to the Keweenaw to make or break them... And good that the Cornish are in here from the start of ut."

There was a slight pause as they both contemplated this.

"And you sir? Are you a mining gentleman by profession?"

"Certainly am," said Francis. "An Adventurer. I own a mine, up on the mountain. Good quality copper. About to open her up..."

"Splendid... And you will do this on your own?"

"Aw naw. With my brother. We've other shareholders too... But 'tis a brave an' keenly lode so we'm hopeful."

"Good..." the doctor managed to say.

He seemed to be contemplating the fact that the opening of another mine in this part of Michigan might give him good reason to remain in these parts. If this mine did become something, then his professional skills would very much be needed.

Their conversation was curtailed by the arrival of Justin.

"My brother Justin," Francis mumbled, though in a way, Francis was not keen to make too much of an introduction to them of his sibling. He was still unsure what adventures he had succumbed to during the night, or what amount of alcohol was still slushing around inside of him. He didn' want him to blabber anything stupid.

Purely perhaps from the outward look of him, the doctor and his family went back into their own world again. Justin had seemingly been thrown together this morning: his shirt tail was out, and his boot laces were undone. His waistcoat was unbuttoned. His hair looked as if he had been dragged backwards through a furze-bush. Given the situation with his laces, he almost tripped and fell as he entered the dining room. It was easy to tell that the bright morning sunshine wuz hurting his eyes. He gave a brief glance over to the other diners and gave a knowing nod to Francis and Luk.

"You alright meht?" asked Francis.

"Yep. Proper," was his brother's response.

"Good night wuz ut?"

Justin smiled broadly. He didn' need to say anything else.

They paused and thought through the possibilities.

"I take it you... ah..."

"Certainly did."

"Y' dirty bugger," whispered Francis.

"Wuz ut nice?" asked Luk – ever curious about such matters. "Did she – ?"

But before Luk could say any more, his mouth was covered over by Francis' censoring left hand.

Justin sat down beside the pair. He looked rough when seen close up. He was unshaven and his eyes still had sleep in them.

"Have you looked in a mirror this morning?" asked Francis.

"What ee mean?"

"You just look like you've been through the wars a bit... That Rosie, wuz ut?"

"She's a fair maid that one," he said in response. "Knaws what end of a spade t'grab onto!"

"So... you... and she, yeah?"

"Maybe," said Justin teasing them a little, and then he paused that conversation, asking. "Who are they then?"

He pointed covertly to the family across the room.

"He's a mine's doctor. Man by the name of George Jewell. From Bodmin," Francis whispered.

By now, the waitress had come over to Justin and asked for his order. She needed his room number which he'd forgotten. Francis had to give it to her: it was fourteen.

"The eggs and bacon are good," noted Francis.

"Nice hog's pudding too," said Luk, hopeful of a drop more.

But Justin looked like none of that appealed. Maybe his stomach was still full of storms from last night's drinking. He had got through a brae bit.

"I'll just take some coffee and some bread and butter please..." asked Justin. "Maybe some jam too, if you've got any?"

His order got noted on the waitress's pad, and she soon brought over a fresh pot of coffee.

"There you go," she said.

Justin mumbled a thank you.

"So wuz that all you did last night then?" asked Francis.

"No," said Justin, "Not zactly."

He spoke those words curtly; knowing that Luk and Francis would know precisely what he meant.

Francis gave his legs a kick under the table.

"You didn'? Aw, Please tell me you didn'..."

"You should have stayed widn," offered Luk, which frankly, wuz unhelpful.

"I might have had a bit of a flutter..."

Francis seethed, but he controlled his anger, not wishing to upset the Jewell family opposite.

"Never let ut alone can ee boy?" went Luk, which again, wudn' a very helpful thing to say.

Ut looked at that moment like a chapel wuz needed out of nowhere to put un back in the right moral direction. Prob'ly, the Jewells were wishing fur tha' too. The style of their clothing made um look very Methodist.

"I reckon you'll feel a bit different this time," said Justin whose bread, butter and jam, had by now, appeared.

"'Ow come?"

"I never lost a game. The cards were on my side. The poker paid out all night. In my pocket here, I got enough money to set we up good and proper up the mine."

"How much?"

"Six months wages – near 'nuff."

"You're kidding?"

"Not bad," said Luk. "You ent no ordinary fool, are ee?"

"Show us," demanded Francis.

"What? Here? – in the dining room?"

"Yeah... Prove that you're telling the truth."

Justin looked about him. Now the farce would come out. He'd bullshit them like this always.

Then he made his back rigid and extended out his legs so he could reach deep into his pocket. On the table he placed a wedge of dollar bills that confirmed what he had said was true.

"You made this off the tables?"

"Yeah. A lucky night, eh? One we needed I reckon – considering how much we spent on all that assaying."

"Bewdie," said Luk. "We'm set now. Proper grub."

"Fur the mine?" asked Francis.

"Fur zertain," said Justin.

Francis smiled at his brother. The boy could be a tusser – that wuz fur sure, but then sometimes, out of the blue, he'd do something that wuz so magical, so crazily absurd, that you could barely believe it had happened at all. And this wuz one of they moments again. And that is the way 'tis sometimes in life. It can turn on the spin of a dice or a quick turn of a card. This time, fortunately, ut had worked out alright. Francis knew the risk though. His mind had raced and made several calculations: several projections about how Justin's habits might cause the ruination of they. Es, he cudn' help but do ut.

"Don't do it again boy," he said. "Realise your luck when you've got ut and dun't push ut."

"Dun' ee worry brother," responded Justin. "I d'knaw me limits better now."

He rammed a large hunk of bread, butter and jam into his mouth and gave it a good chew.

Between his forthright chewing, he managed to say, "Once we're done here, then let's get ourselves up to see Trevorrow and get started. We need to get provisions from the store. Maybe see if we'n buy a 'oss and dray too. Get we up the mountain again. "

"What about that Rosie?" questioned Francis.

"Well, she idn' nawthun'..." he said back. "You knaw how 'tis..."

"Really?"

"Really," Justin confirmed.

See, ef this Justin had anything about him, he'd have asked that Rosie to go with un, but he wuz a fool, this boy, and despite how close they had been that night, he'd reckoned on her not giving un the time ov the day, because in the clear light of the morning, he wuz nawthun' but another customer. And she too, had realised that he and she might have something there but that he probably wudn' interested, and so in the morning, he'd left her sleeping and didn' even say goodbye. How wuz tha', eh? Tha' wuz how men an' women are sometimes: stupid, because of pride, of saving face. But that wudn' the end of Rosie in his story. Aw no. That's because our past often comes to bite us when we're not looking fur ut – and es, bite ut did. But that is fur later on, not now. Leastways Justin knawed he had to leave her fur now, because there was a job to be done. He and his brother needed to get back up the mountain again.

Now, there are only two speeds for opening a mine: slow and very slow. The energy and resolve required is immense. The money that Justin had earned from poker would go a long way in getting and gaining the pair moast of the major provisions they needed to start opening up the shaft on the mountain. Plans would need to be made. They needed to survey it properly and make good decisions about the levels put in and the seams of ore they'd be chasing. Maybe this boy Justin wudn' quite the fool that everyone first thought, eh? Maybe there wuz more to un than you would think.

They went upstairs to get their provisions, tools and backpacks, and then came back down to the hotel's reception. It was Justin who settled their tab. A lot went on in those few moments. Unseen by Justin, Rosie looked down at him from the top of the stairs. Luk caught her looking and gave Francis a nudge. Her face was hard to read, but it perhaps looked like she'd caught a salmon in a river, and was now throwing it back again. She looked for a while, and then disappeared from the rail overlooking the stairwell. You cudn' tell if she wuz disappointed or disapproving. That wuz the way of women sometimes. You cudn' make them out. He'd learnt that ut wuz best not to interfere either.

From out of the dining room, now came the doctor and his family with whom Francis had talked earlier. This time Francis got a better look at the girls' faces as they walked past them. He could not help but note the form and figure of the elder daughter, who despite trying hard to look down and not be noticed, momentarily caught Francis looking at her.

"Gentlemen," said the doctor, giving them a nod as he put out his hand to allow his family to pass through.

At least, now, Justin had tucked in his shirt and tied up his bootlaces.

"You all have a good day now," said Francis, which came out of his mouth in the weirdest way possible. It sounded as if his old language had been left behind in Cornwall, and that something else had climbed inside his mouth, perhaps from the recesses of Detroit or New York. Still that didn' matter. At least, it had made the elder daughter smile. He could see her blushes as she turned left towards the staircase. She had an elfin face, thin and long with wide eyes and long lashes. Her skin was as white as Gwithian sands, smooth like when the tide was out. The lines of her form appealed to him, in ways that he had never contemplated before. In point of fact, he realised that she wuz only a few years younger than ee.

And in that moment, maybe he knew somehow he'd have to see that girl again. Where and when he had no idea, and ut certainly would not have done to have asked anything else about their plans, or even have struck up a conversation with other members of this Doctor Jewell's family. However, something happened then which happens to all young men with ambition in their hearts. Es. Somehow it gets superseded. It alters. Maybe this wuz the first time with this Francis. Maybe too, this young woman might be seeking a husband.

Then, just as he thought he'd lost sight of her, the elder girl he was watching but not watching accidentally collided with the younger daughter, as they climbed the staircase. Maybe she was watching him too and not looking where she was going.

"Becca!" the younger sister shouted, annoyed at the incident.

So Francis had her name now. She was Rebecca Jewell, and she was from Bodmin.

Bewdie. Rite on. They had full bellies. The sun was shining. They had money. All they had to do now was go and open up a mine. Francis felt something new that morning, and his brother felt something old – a feeling of satisfaction that he had not had in a while.

But then they suddenly and overwhelmingly came to a collective realisation. They all stood stock still on the steps of the hotel. They realised that they couldn't do anything yet. The three of them looked at each other. At once, all of them asked the very same question: "Where the 'ell's Gourgy gone to?"

7

Buzzed on plenty of shots of hard bourbon and a confident feeling of pride that his poker advice to the boy Justin had paid off, Gourgy had been in no mood to let the night's partying end there, at the precise moment in which he saw his temporary pard negotiating a pleasurable night in the sack with the sumptuous Finnish warmth of Rosie. All this, he considered. Es – there's no point in splitting hairs – Knockies have needs too, he told himself, and that is why he covertly left the bar, and found himself sat outside in the cool Upper Peninsula air of this summer night. He positioned himself on the hotel's main steps and touched pipe with an end bit of tobacco.

Ut made un taissy as a snake that he cudn' get naw action. He wuz imagining much, but the idea of a kinky threesome upstairs did not exactly appeal to him. Knowing that moast decent (by that he meant good-looking ones, not respectable) Knockie women were still back in Cornwall wuz not helpful either. Even then, they required finding and courting in the very deepest recesses of the mine (you did that out ov duty to the species rather than for any kind of sexual pleasure). No, that would not do, but undoubtedly, he wanted to cavort with other like-minded and fun spirits – and maybe flirt a little. Maybe there wuz a certain exotica to be had out here. He had to try at least. He wuz abroad. Who wuz there to stop un? This wudn' like back home where chapel onlookers could follow your every move an' if they didn' care for you, then report ee to the preacher.

He knew himself though – all Knockies did – that chatting up other sprites wudn' easy. He knew what he wuz working with, and 'twudn' nawthun' special. To the untrained eye, they might all be cute, playful and fast as lightning in their movements which allowed them to get away with much in the company of individuals such as that Rosie. But when others could see him, well, then 'twas a hard sell. On the crossing over, ee'd leaned over the deck and chatted up several passing mermaids and kelpies; only for them to dismiss his appearance. Half-heartedly, he pinched his wrinkled, baggy skin. The fundamental problem with Knockies wuz that they were born to look old. He knew the effect of this. Moast spirits wanted physically vibrant and virile companions, not the bag of seed potatoes that he sometimes looked like. It was perhaps the reason why they acquired such charm and verbal dexterity – to talk their way out of any situation. Let's face it though: they had nothing else much on their side. At least all those lazy and whining ginger-bearded bunch of Leprechauns (who accompanied some ov the Irish labourers) had a pot of gold at the end of their rainbows.

Gourgy considered the momentous events of the last few days. Perhaps this pair that he and Luk had been assigned to all those years ago might, for once, do something extraordinary. And in that possibility, he felt contented, for he knew that humans had to lead such things. No Knockie could do it. All they had to do wuz protect. That wuz the deal, a pact made long ago when humans built quoits and stone circles, when the mines first got opened, and when behind every hedge and stile in Cornwall there lay a magical being: fairy, spriggan, piskie or brownie. 'Course, Gourgy knew of their decline. Everyone did. It wuz an extinction event really. Industry had a lot to do with it. Whilst the Knockies revelled in it, other creatures were less keen, so they shrunk in numbers and disappeared. There were still pockets though, and then recoveries –

where mines were abandoned and those kinds of creatures moved back in. But towns were no good, naw. They pushed them all to the fringes, almost to the very tips and edges of the peninsula. Humans needed to be careful, or else they'd lose them all. They'd become legends; the domain of folktales alone. And what use wuz tha' t'anyone?

After touching pipe fur a bit, contemplating all of this, he stood up and stretched his body. He knocked the used tobacco out of the pipe onto the ground. Gourgy had an active mind, and wuz in naw mood for sleep. Of Luk and him, ee wuz often the restless one. He couldn't put it down to anything particular: ee just seemed to need less sleep than other Knockies, and it certainly wudn' a case of him sleeping on the job either. All the time when they were belaw ground, he allays kept a watchful eye on the rock above, a keen ear on tremors and cracks. All he could hear now though were the occasional giggles and high-pitched pretend laughter of girls from the upstairs windas of the hotel and the ripe songs of men stepping out of the hotel, and heading back to the camp at Cliff Mine. They were Cornishmen – but drunken – even they couldn't see him in the darkness. He had to dodge their thick boots.

Gourgy had an itch that he couldn't scratch and struggled as to where to look for a solution. There were, he knew only three options: he could go back to the camp and try and find some fun. The move was an unlikely solution because he knew there would be little feminine company there. Any bal-maidens tended to keep themselves to themselves down in the town, knowing the wicked ways of lonesome men, and besides that, t'him, those women were more male than female in appearance moast days. Inter-species sex ee could take at times, but not tonight. Ee didn' want t'get labelled over here as some kind of deviant incubus.

Then there was the lake itself, down there below. Even in the summer blackness, this far north, the light never completely disappeared and the water of the vast expanse shone brightly. Surely down there, were water nymphs, selkies and nereids? Maybe some attractive limnades – or even a sexy nyx? Perhaps a morgen, even though they were meant to be the spirits of the drowned who'd somehow shifted into female form? Hell, he'd even take on a Siren, but when he contemplated ut a little more, ee thought not. Perhaps that might push things too far. He'd heard tales of those back 'ome who'd got involved and it didn' end well. And even then, he knew such beings from home, but what were they like out here? Fur zertain, they'd have different names and maybe different attributes. But ee'd heard the stories too. The laker deck-hands talked much about lake monsters; and said that out there were huge beasts – the size of the Loch Ness Monster – who could devour you in an instant, regardless of the fact that you might be a magical creature, and supposedly had union rights.

Na. The lake had appeal then, but naturally Knockies veered away from water. In the fathoms belaw, it was in their minds to keep the wet out, to not let it tumble into confined spaces, and so at this point he rejected it. He was, in fact, finding himself wandering up an old lumbering track into the dark forest that looked down on the mining settlement and its harbour. Knockies had exceptional vision. Their eyes matched that of cats and birds of prey rather than squinting gnomes and bespectacled piskies. That had been born of thousands of years of working in the darkness belaw. Their eyes had evolved into having highly detailed receptors that saw things that the human eye could never observe. That again, wuz one of the reasons, human miners needed a Knockie on-side.

He saw himself going no further than the lower slopes. There, he had noticed previously that there was a layer of meadowland which seemed to wrap itself around the skirt of Copper Mountain, and smelt glorious. Even in the night-time, it would still hum with bees and be the fragrances he somehow craved. To get there, he would have to negotiate his way through the first band of forest that clung to the slopes just above the settlement. Some of the forest had been trimmed back already: with logging already taking place for construction and, of course, for props underground. Mining consumed wood like there was naw tomorra', and any mine owner knew that access to good, strong wood wuz essential. Without ut, any operation underground would collapse. And now, a little breathless as ee climbed, ee hoped that the scything of the forest would not be a curse on him or his human pards, and that the land would understand, and yield.

Forest sprites, ee knew rather less about. They were very shy in Cornwall due to the lack of indigenous forest, but with his eyesight he knew they were about. He could feel them watching. He knew too, the vibration of his chest cavity and the heavy, panting breaths he took as he climbed, which wuz bound to wake them. Usually, these were the dryads and tree fairies. They were the ones who governed ritual and devotion, and in these wilds, presumably their practice remained relatively untouched; he suspected that only the native people of this region were able to commune with them. The dryads and tree fairies he liked because they were often gracefully elfin in appearance, with thin, sensual bodies that were the female kind that Gourgy liked. Plus, although there was the smell of earth-mould, it was still preferable to the fishy, moss-water smell of rivers and lakes. As they had observed at their new strike a day or so ago, forest sprites often showed themselves in circling lights to begin with – darting in and out of the tree trunks and branches. But fireflies they were not.

He knew that he wuz stumbling through their sacred groves, but he had to do it. He needed to know what wuz out there, and how he might communicate with them. Like Cornwall, everything here was very old. That didn' mean just a couple of centuries ago. Oh naw. It meant thousands of years old, so old that it had all been laid out in time immemorial, and that the landscape had been formed when the gods and goddesses of old had first walked the earth. They had provided for the Cornish in terms of the mineral resources beneath their feet, and here too, so it seemed, the earth would hold similar riches.

"Anyone here?" he said. "Halloo. I'm Gourgy... not long in from Cornwall. Just come to say hello – thaas all. I've come up from the hotel... looking for a bit of company... yap an' a cup tay?"

His voice echoed through the trunks and spun up the mountain to the meadow he was questing towards. The meadow wuz a longer distance than ee thought.

As yet, no one answered him. Forest sprites are like that. They spend a good while watching and testing before they reveal themselves out of the mosses and lichens, the leaf litter and fallen strips of bark. Gourgy understood tha'. Ee could see the energy of this forest. Although ee did not say it to himself then, or even mention it to his humans later, ee wondered about its destruction. For Gourgy, although crazy and mad, knew quite a lot about the world. He knew when things were right and when they were wrong – even though he himself wuz not always so good at adhering to that rule. And when he thought about it, he stepped more softly, and listened a little more.

This far up, he could now see the settlement below. Before, the air had carried still the air of talk and song: about Jackers putting the world to right, and being hopeful (as ever) of a keen lode in the morning, but now it was still. This was the time of forest sprites, Gourgy noted to himself. He could tell because now fairy rings of mushrooms dotted the floor of the forest. That wuz always a sign. Everyone knew that – even the daft humans. They wove in between pieces of fallen wood, rock and leaves, and showed the world that this place held a long memory. Caps of toadstools unfolded and spores got released: sentient travellers over the forest floor.

Puffed out, he sat down next to a great tree that seemed to spread out not just across this forest, but the whole of the world. He was connecting with it all again. He knew how with its branches reaching up into the sky, and its roots threading deep into the earth such trees were the connection between three places: the underworld (which he knew fairly well), the earth itself and Heaven above. Ee did not truly know if that Heaven above really existed, but the Methodist humans seemed to go on about ut enough fur it to be real, and so he supposed it wuz. What this forest and its trees did though wuz to unite what wuz below with what was above, and what ee wuz doin' right now. And right now, ee wuz sorely wishing for a bit of crowst to gnaw on, because the evening's alcohol had worn off, and ee wuz feeling brave an' hungry.

In his mind, he wished for a nub of saffron bun. Ee craved the fruit and the spice. If fresh-baked, the spongy feel of the bun itself, so satisfying to the stomach. And if there wuz some going, then a little dollop of clotted cream on top. Es – the perfect combination with the bun and its fruit. Oh, he could dream plenty this Knockie. Ut wudn' comin' anywhere near un this night, and in his loneliness and his hunger, he began to bitterly regret his climb up here. He wished he was back down in the hotel, in the warm bed in the chest of drawers that Francis had prepared fur un. He wished now he could hear the deep snores of his bud Luk, and the occasional pungent fart from him. All that seemed very comforting. He still had a craving for the taste of saffron bun in his mouth and ee cudn' get rid of it.

"Bugger," he said to hisself. "What I want, I cen't have."

Idn' that always the way? Es.

And maybe the forest heard him. And maybe it didn'. Es. Nawbody could tell. Nawbody else wuz there.

But the alcohol and the night air wuz soon inducing him to sleep. And although he had no food, he put his hand on his belly, and hoped the weight of his limb would feel like a goodly bit of stodgy bun and cake in his stomach. He wuz drifting off, this Gourgy, into the zone of sleep. At fust, he didn' want it and tried to resist it. He kept looking out over the canopy of trees below and saw the settlement nibbling away at the land all the way down to the sea. Ee could see the moon high in the air; the same moon that later would spread its way across the beaches and coves of Cornwall, and all its now stagnant chimley stacks, stamp-houses and arsenic flumes.

On the lake were flashes of light – but they weren't water sprites or limnades. No, they were the lights of the lakers and fishermen out on Superior. The last thing he could remember noticing were the huge trees immediately around him where he lay. In his hallucinatory stupor, they appeared as giants walking towards him: one leg behind the other, pulling all of the rest of them towards him, noticing this strange new creature going to sleep in their forest. The way their trunks twisted and rose gave rise to him seeing the flanks and thighs of these elemental beings walking towards him, inquisitive faces high up in their canopies and upper branches; leaves and needles daring to touch this lone figure and find out what he was made of.

For Gourgy, who was nodding off, the roots emerging from the ground were these giant's toes flexing and moving in the soil. The force of that energy wuz unstoppable on this Gourgy who was mouthing something that could not be heard by these curious sprites of this forest, but wuz sometimes wistful and sometimes sad. Besides the giants, now other sprites lifted their heads up from the ground. In fact, the whole of the forest was crammed with them. Their heads were made of moss-covered boulders and their straggly hair, weeds and flowers that grew out from the layers of peat. Sprites popped their heads up and brushed off tiny pine needles. Everywhere, the earth shifted and groaned at their release.

These sprites and giants however, were not ferocious or evil. Aw naw. In fact, they were full of kindness. They heard his cries and realised he wuz hungry and so they set upon gathering fruits for him. At first, they had remained hidden. This little figure, this wrinkled little being who they found had wandered into the forest looked like nothing they had seen before. Several metamorphosised from being darting lights into sprites who ran into bushes and pulled edible mayhaws and persimmons from them. Elderberries and wood strawberries they also brought to him and were laid on a plate of leaves before him. It was a banquet like no other. From the bogs below they brought up cranberries and from the low bush ground, fresh blueberries. Were they in season, they'd have offered blackberries and cherries too but at least this meal would provide this unusual fellow with sustenance, and when he woke, he would have enough strength hopefully to make his way back down the mountain.

So in unison, the beings watched him doze, and those who had not collected food, wove from lichen and fern, a comforting blanket to put over him, for when that moment of the night came, which was always the coldest – the moment just before dawn when the body is at its loneliest. Although he'd told them his name, they still wondered about him: wondered why ee looked so old and wrinkly, wondered why his clawthes were stained with the earth and copper, and why upon his back was strapped a strange tool: a pick-axe. His form puzzled them so much that they called upon the Moon Goddess to observe.

Now the Moon Goddess happened to have the name Yolkai and she was as powerful as all the standing stones in Cornwall that pointed up to the firmament and traced the movements of the planets and the stars. She would put all of that into Gourgy's head and more. She had ways of doing that which she had perfected over millennia. She was very beautiful, this Yolkai, and never aged. She controlled much and saw much. She understood the tides – and she understood flow and retreat. She knew all the ways of women, but knew too, the ways of men. She was wise, and this was the reason the forest sprites called upon her. Ut was also why the water sprites relied upon her too. She was no new god, not like this Methodist God, that god of chapels and preaching pits. Na. She was ancient but kept her beauty in the way that any man might wish of his wife. This Yolkai see, was married to the earth.

When the Moon Goddess came – and she came within an instant of hearing her name being called by her people – she lifted her illumination from the lake and brought it to this clearing in the low forest. She carried the moon as it if were a lantern and shone it wherever it was needed.

And all those gathered asked of her, "What is he?"

She could see him now and answered with, "A Knockie of the mines."

So then, they knew and they thought him sweet and old. They knew not that he was lecherous and craved the fragrance of the beautiful sprites that now hovered above him and left trails of perfume to tingle his nose when he awoke.

"Leave him be," said the Moon Goddess. "We must find out why he comes and what he brings..."

And in saying that, the Moon Goddess Yolkai swirled her light around him. She parted the clouds and let in a bright incandescent spell that became dreams in Gourgy's mind. And she let the dream work its magic – for old magic it was – that was to work its way into this Knockie's life, and all those that he cared for. Gourgy saw so much in his dream that had he written it all down, there would be no point in telling this tale, for the dream covered it all. But when ee awoke – and the forest wuz still and silent, and neither the lichens nor the ferns moved, and the roots of the geht trees were just that – trees – he perhaps should have tried to remember what he'd dreamt. But like all dreams they are so vivid when we have them, and then, in the few moments after we wake, they are lost, like grains of fine copper ore cast on the level floor. And in the air there was that appealing perfume he'd craved from the meadow, so wondrous and sensual, that it made his todger twiggle.

Now, there is a lot still to say about Knockies and their ways but one thing sometimes happens to them, and happen here to Gourgy ut did. When they are dreaming or meditating, and receiving pleasurable thoughts, their skin colour changes, and in the past few minutes (when Yolkai had foretold of the future) ee had shifted from his normal brown-grey, to yellow, to green-yellow, and then to blue. He woke to see that change: the green-yellow to a blue tone and, on seeing it, he made a slight jump, as if he no longer knawed who ee wuz. For all Knockies know that if their skin turns black, then that is one way of noting imminent and life-threatening danger. Blue wudn' a colour he turned very often, even when partaking of the most delicious saffron bun, so ee wuz surprised to see his skin transform and alter like some kind of underground chameleon. But this wuz how 'twas. Nothing could alter it. It wuz what the gods had intended. Now, Knockies can turn purple too, but perhaps that's best left to later.

So this Gourgy – some boy that ee wuz – woke to find daylight, and before him a meal of bright berries and forest fruits. And at this, his skin turned back to its usual brown-grey. Both sharp and sour, and sweet and tasty the berries and fruits were, which should have told him much, but instead, ee urgently placed them onto his tongue to satisfy his hunger. In his mouth though, they formed into the perfect flavour: a taste not too tart nor too sickly sweet, and so they were soon devoured and found their way deep inta' his belly. So too had the forest sprites left him a wooden cup of water: the stump of an old mossy tree in which had collected the morning's dew. And that dew tasted as refreshing and cool as any drink that could be bought back in the bar ov the hotel.

Wiping his mouth and giving a slight belch at the large quantity of forest fruit he had consumed, Gourgy looked around him and once again, tried to tell the magical from the real. But sometimes, ee could not – and this was one of those times. He realised ee had acted some silly, coming all the way up here, in search, well, in search of company, or rather, femininity. He realised he had found it – but perhaps not in the way ee had anticipated. He'd had in mind a bit ov a bunk up but what he got was insight into another world. So he started walking, for he knew that down below, they'd be waking and wondering where he wuz and what he'd been up to. But ee resolved not to say too much, for if he told them about the forest sprites and the dream that the Moon Goddess Yolkai had supplied him with, they might legitimately think him mad, and set un on a boat back to Bristol, or more likely just toss him out with the attle.

So he would be circumspect, and careful. Ee wudn' tell the truth of what had happened to un, but maybe that wudn' the right decision. We shall see. Maybe if he'd said something, then perhaps some other things might not have happened. But es, it's always easy to look back in the mirror and say what we'd do different after an event. This wuz it with this Gourgy, and as ee strolled back down the geht mountain, and the warm sun rose in the east, he contemplated whether the whole thing had been a deceptive dream, and that, in fact, the food and the drink, and the woven blanket had been placed there not by kindly forest sprites, but instead, by that Nimkii. Put ut this way: he didn' really believe that but, well, this Gourgy, he *wanted* to believe ut. Aw es. That version ov events suited un – an' sometimes, thaas the way ov people. Actually, they dun't want t'knaw the truth. They got their mind set and nawthun'll move um. An' awnly when they d'hear the truth do their mouths fall abroad. Whatever way it worked out, Gourgy knew this Moon Goddess would be watchin' um all, like a hawk. Ee kept checking his skin that morning, to make sure that ut wudn' changing colour no more.

8

On the vast expanse of the North-American mining frontier (and indeed, this tiny kibble of ut) everything took time. Nothun' comed easy. Ef something was needed, then you either had to buy ut or make ut yourself. Because of this, any attempt to forge a new settlement, or to make a new community wudn' anything instant. Perhaps then, this Justin and this Francis were naïve about what wuz required for their story to succeed over the next few months; and throughout the whole of the Fall, it wuz reckoned to perhaps be one of struggle and difficulty. The reason for this wuz obvious. Where they had made their strike, on the side of a mountain, and in the middle of a vast forest, ut wuz a location on the fell to which everything had to first be transported. If Justin or Francis paused to really think about what they intended to do, they would prob'ly have not gone down the path they did. But humans wun't ever be told. Es. Tha' is the way of things. They are obstinate. But in them too, wuz an admirable determination. It was a determination that had kept the Cornish race going for thousands of years: the mindset wuz that if there was valuable stuff in the earth then all you had to do wuz dig ut out. You awnly had to reach your hand in.

It wudn' like the mine at New Diggings (as it was soon named) became a copper-mining complex overnight. It was rathermore, at first, like a slow procession of ants who gradually colonised the hillside, and by gentle attrition and attention to detail, made good progress in achieving their objective. The first task had been to clear a decent pathway up from the shore-line settlement to the strike. The route got surveyed first of all by Skews, and some of the Cliff Mine h'engineerin'-brained boys were tasked with finding the most efficient route. Obviously, the gentler the gradient then the better, but they also negotiated the best way they could find over the many streams and rivers, not to mention the belligerent crevices and ravines in the mountainside. More trees were felled, allowing for a ready stock of lumber, but at the same time, that process wuz costly and time-consuming; so again, a route wuz chosen along the limits of the denser parts of the forest where there were then less trees to fell.

The lumbering ov the wood wudn' the greatest problem. What wuz primarily difficult were the stumps of any felled trees, which meant extra labour. Some were left *in situ* where the lumber had been cut down, but in other places, these stumps required removal to allow the wheels of carts, trolleys and drays to pass through. Considerable labour wuz put into this, and carefully, wily Trevorrow had gradually manipulated labour in the old Cliff Mine so that more and more of it wuz spent opening up this new resource. Because of this, word spread like wildfire as to what wuz happening: it soon became clear that the Cliff Mine wuz declining, so entering a period of its last working days, and new energy wuz being put into the New Diggings high on the mountain. But nothing official wuz being said: not yet at least. See, these were the absolute, non-negotiable rules with a new strike. If it had been demarked by someone, no one had the steel balls enough to go in there and contest it – and no one did. These were men of honour, these Cornish. Stealing another pard's strike was as grave a sin as any Cornishman could do. Ut guaranteed ee a special place in 'Ell.

In all this though, no one considered consulting the forest sprites. No one had talked to them since Gourgy's dreamtime. They'd had to flee from certain gulleys and groves when the road-building came through. They'd abandoned their homes and their territories around individual trees and moved further up the mountain-side. Streams of them could be seen (ef you had that kind of sight): confused refugees forced to march through the forest. Where were men like Nimkii now? They thought he was their protector, but right then, viewing this caravan of sprites on the move, they wondered if he had sold them out? Was he still on their side? And what about that Gourgy? Surely he was like them. They craved more dialogue with him but it was never forthcoming. Maybe what the Moon Goddess had done had put him off them: all that wrinkly skin, changing colour.

Change wuz coming from these two exploratory pards. Change too, could be felt in the air though: that what had been reasonably permanent for the past two decades on the tip of the Keweenaw was about to alter markedly. Those who owned or had built properties down at Eagle Harbour, or who had developed the settlement close to the Cliff Mine were now reviewing their options carefully. Was it best to stay put and retain their business here? Or, in the long term, wuz it better to move up the vast mountain with what wuz perceived to be everything else and everybody else?

It wudn' naw easy decision. There wuz lots to weigh up. Whatever happened, there wuz the need to retain the harbour because that was still the likely way the ore would be leaving the Upper Peninsula. No one was going to drag it miles back down to the base of the peninsula and trade it at Calumet. The road that ran past the by-now old camp, twisted and turned its way across the untouched wilderness down to Calumet and then on to Houghton itself, and communication with those places would still be needed. That seemed to be going away from Detroit, and as Detroit was where the copper was most needed, any new trading hub in that direction seemed illogical.

Maybe the hotel should stay where it wuz. It felt like there would be enough passing trade once this place on what they were calling Copper Mountain was opened up. Those down at the harbour were already reviewing their facilities: were the present jetties sufficient to handle the trade? Could they cope with the projected amount of ore? For the whole community there was much to consider. This wuz how an individual hole in the ground can change things. This was how landscapes got changed – and how magic got used.

At this moment of transition, many letters got written. Men who had not sent a message, note or money home for years knawed that they had to write back and tell their almost-forgotten family that they were moving. They did that in their droves. But another group wrote back and explained that a new opportunity was opening up. Some letters went down to the oven glove mitten of the Lower Peninsula, and some went down to the iron mines of Minnesota and Wisconsin. Others went out to Colorado, Nevada and California. Several made it back home and soon, the old mining towns of Cornwall were awash with the news of a new mine opening on the Keweenaw: the 'richest ever' so the newspaper headlines went.

But that wuz always the way with the rags – they liked to sensationalise everything. The thing wuz that although Justin and Francis didn' necessarily need that kind of publicity for their operation, people at home did need ut. See there, compared to the Keweenaw, copper and tin were in the doldrums, so any news like that felt that at least somewhere on the globe, some Cornish boys were doing alright. That made sense and ut made the people content. Ut gived um hope an' feyth. And exploits like this overseas

– well, that and Methodism – kept the Cornish sedate. Anything different and they'd be rebelling again like in previous times, and to be honest, no bugger wanted that now.

And everyone knawed how 'twas goin' t'go. Somehow, the migrating hoards of miners would end up here, dragging along with them the bastard offspring of other nations too. Es. And particular skills and jobs would be enquired about by those doing the hiring, and when those offspring were asked if they might be able to do a particular job, they might have to decline it because they did not feel competent enough to do it, but if ever that same question were asked of the Cornish, then they'd probably leap at the chance (whether they were technically capable ov ut or not), and if they really knew they couldn', then they'd always be minded of some cousin who could, and would report for duty in the next days or so. And in this way, these mining ancient Britons gained their overseas nickname of being labelled 'Cousin Jacks' – or, as they called them here, 'Cussies' or 'Jackers'. If someone couldn' do ut then their Cousin Jack would. All over the world, this was how the Cornish built their reputation in the business, of firstly, being reliable and ready for anything, but secondly, of knawing somebody who could fill in. There wuz always another Cussie who'd step up to the plate, who knew how to set up a drill or quickly repair a pump.

As for the hole in the ground, well, once Gourgy had been located that summer morning (ee didn' rightly say where ee'd been all night but ee comed back ashen white), the four of them had been up to see Trevorrow. You'n picture ut: now Trevorrow felt these four wuz goin' to be eternally in his debt, particularly for the mining gear they needed to get up there. But it didn' go down like that t'all. An' tha' wuz because Justin wuz able to produce a wedge of dollars out of his trouser pocket and slap that down on the table. That amount of money wuz able to pay for the whole damn lot. And considering the forthcoming closure of Cliff Mine, they were able to negotiate a good deal on a couple of 'osses and carts to load everything onto. Their plan was to strike camp with a couple of tents, but over the forthcoming autumnal months, to perhaps see if some permanent cabins and bunkhouses could be built up there. They realised that winter wuz coming and they needed to be prepared. Ut wudn' like they wanted to be traipsing down and back off the mountain all the while.

"Where you been to? Where'd did ee get that lot?" asked Trevorrow. His faace was a picture.

That boy maybe had other plans – an' they needed to be careful obm. Indenture wuz a terrible thing (they'd knawed ov ut back home), and this would be how he might one day lever control. Na. 'Twas like Francis said. They'd pay as they went. Trevorrow wudn' have anything on this pair. But no way wuz they about to hand over all their money. Aw naw. They kept some back, for an emergency. You cudn' ever tell how things would pan out, and a fund like this might one day be valuable for somethun' or other – fur when enchantments ended.

"You buggers ent daft, are ee?" went the Cap'n.

And maybe ee wuz right – because they wudn' daft.

So they and their Knockies got to load provisions on 'osses and asses, and prepare for their time up in the forest. All the while, the dark forest looked down on them in those August days. And when it was thundery in the afternoons, ut looked angry and dangerous. On some mornings of late, ut could not be seen. An early morning fog wrapped itself around the trunks of the trees. The Finnish miners all said that when the weather wuz like that up there ut wuz because 'the gnomes were brewing beer' – a point that Luk and Gourgy seemed to take especial nawtice ov.

Word got around. Es. All this energy never went unnawticed. And maybe at this, Justin and Francis were overnight somehow magically turned into Cap'ns. Someone had cast a spell. Someone had definitely waved a wand. They knew this because one kettle boy (by the name of Snell) who'd worked at Cliff addressed Justin in just that way when he'd helped them load tools into one of the packs to be carried up. And when Justin heard it, it didn' sound right. The boy Snell's words stopped him in his tracks: ee wudn' that, wuz a? Suddenly, it seemed, so he wuz. This is the way that things can sometimes change: es, this pair of mucker-outters, these two pards, could now stand tall as full Cap'ns of their own enterprise.

"Just dun't get cocky," said Francis.

An' ee wuz right.

Along with the other shareholders in this enterprise then (which were Trevorrow himself, and Skewsy of course, and somewhere – the ethereal Nimkii) began the process of making this dig into something great. There had been no word from Nimkii but frankly, no one expected there to be, not at this stage of the operations. Skewsy himself had already set out from the Cliff Mine and had a gang of men to order about. He didn' really need them. He just liked them there to say things at and shout out orders. He was full of his self-importance, that boy. He wuz travelling in some style, with an expensive tent and enough food and provisions to last for a while. The temptation was to poke fun at un an' his needs within the forest, but ut was best not to – because Skewsy was still the man to have on side, surveying the ground. He would be the one who would best map the area, and he spent the next month or so testing boreholes all over the clearing where the mine camp would eventually come to mushroom. Oh, how things were opening up! How the landscape was altering before them! What fortune!

Sampling, apparently, was the key: that would tell him which way the lode was running. He'd have several rock cores brought up from underground and try to provide a diagram of what they were working with. This was so different compared to how Justin and Francis thought it might go. They perhaps had some romantic notion of them alone in the woods, working like old streamers with a Long Tom and aiming to find as much metal as they could before settling down to a campfire meal. But naw, that wudn' the case at all. It became clear that setting up the mine needed to be a military operation.

"I'll see you pair up there," Skews had shouted back to them as he left. By now, a route to the new mine had been pretty much established, and as things grew, they knew that very soon the route would turn into a path, the path would turn into a track and one day the track would turn into a road. This was the way of things. This was how all humans claim and alter the world. Roads bring success but they also bring ruin. But no one here was talking about ideas or ethics. No one was considering what they were doing with the earth. And the Cornish were like that. They had always been like that. Home, they'd always shat in their own backyard: anything to get something valuable out of the earth, no matter what mess they left afterwards.

Sadly, here too, ut wuz the same. And did anyone say anything – or even think about that? Na. You couldn' hear it. Back in this time, men and women had more to do than think of how they were decimating the natural world. Wha' they worried about was gaining a dollar or two, and putting some food on the table. It was about that alone. And perhaps it will be until someone takes stock, until someone says, "Are you sure you want to do that?" But this was the Cornish mindset see – an' there wudn' naw stoppin' ov ut. 'Twas resolute – allays.

Where the Cornish led, other nations followed. Some people 'ummed' and some people 'aahed', but in the end they could see the Cliff Mine receding around them. Galleries were left uncleared. Water built up in the lowest ones, where Lake Superior reclaimed them. The work transferred from getting ore out of the old mine into setting up the new one. It didn' matter where you went in the world: 'Stralia, India, South Africky or Merky, the Cornish always led the way. It was like they had a sense of the ground and could feel the earth talking to them. They were the h'engineers though: the planners, and the management. They were the best at working the stopes. What they said went, because ef you didn' follow ut you'd end up digging fur nawthun' or flat on yer ass from a rock fall. So the Cornish had that level of respect. The other nations – the Finns and the Swedes, the Germans and the Polish, the Irish and the English – followed their lead. Soon, an army of these workers (of every profession you might think of) were breaking camp and following the train of others heading up the mountain.

The view of it scared Francis when he observed how quickly this transhumance happened. He understood the fickleness of their trade, and how soon one space could be abandoned for another. This scared him to the core of his bones, but also brought about another deeper fear inside him that this wuz his responsibility. If the mine failed, if riches were not found in the way they thought, then this group would be sorely disappointed, and blame him and his brother. Such wuz the endeavour that if this mine did not reach its full potential, then the whole of the Keweenaw might be abandoned. What then? Where then? There were places in Cornwall like that, which once they'd been raided, were then cast aside. Care would be needed, he realised.

It was Luk who picked up on his fears.

"You worry too much Sos." he said. "'Tidn' your fault they'm all traipsing up to your place. They knaw what mining is like. It's hard work es. But sometimes, 'tis luck. There ent nawthun' you'n do 'bout that."

And Francis at that moment, thought he wuz right. It wuz by luck and chance that they'd prospected that site anyway. It was by luck and chance that Justin had won that money. But sometimes the world is not all about that. It is sometimes not what it seems: there are falls and runs, slopes and gunnies that can trip you up and make you plunge into the darkness. Sometimes too, things happen in reaction to other things that happened long ago – or will happen a long time in the future. Maybe there wuz some of that here too, but neither Francis nor Justin cared to think about that. Es. This wuz their tale fur now.

Trevorrow had set forth the lumberers and they were ploughing on. High in the dells and beyond the meadows could be heard the sustained chop-chop of axes into old wood. In the long runs of silence, for the first time could be heard the push and pull of bow saws opening up the pathway to the new venture. There was no time for sentimentality. They knew that Fall was coming and that the mine needed to be functional by then. If not then an awful lot of men and women were going to discover that this year's Upper Peninsula winter wuz much harder than the previous one.

In all this activity, Gourgy had remained relatively quiet. He seemed distracted from all the activity of the mine, only briefly saluting a few of his own species as they made their way into the light from two decades of darkness. They too, had gathered everything they owned, knowing that if their humans moved, then they had to as well. Even the most elderly of Knockies were making their way up the slippery ladders and platforms, or making their way out from long-forgotten adits. There were too many ee thought. There were masses of them. Their croaking voices and laughter would scare the forest sprites. Knockies were always the most confident of all magical creatures.

Ee felt sorry for them, and maybe lamented what wuz transpiring. Ee told no one of his feelings though. After all, ee had a front to keep up. Every Knockie in the mine knew him well and respected his opinions. Moast often that Gourgy spoke sense when others came out with twaddle, wuz the standard view ov un. Ut wudn' do to let tha' slip. He still mouthed "Yew!" and "Yo!" to those who came out though. Some he'd not seen for a while, and the other nation's mining creatures left their posts too, to join the oscillating ragged-ass parade up the mountain. In the end though, when the essentials were packed, he joined his pards on the upwards excursion.

In those few days, no one much nawticed the arrival of Doctor George Jewell to the Cliff Mine camp. A man like him would normally have been given considerable attention: his clawthing gave off the smell of money, and so a volley of volunteers would be there to carry his bags or help in any way possible, all for a cent tip or the possibility of working with un again sometime soon. They'd have nawticed even more the arrival of Jewell with his two daughters: the one that you knaw by now, named Rebecca, and the other that you do not, the one that they had decided to call Mabel.

Rebecca had not much of an interest in the mine, but knawed tha' given her age, she needed to find some work in this new community, Mabel, was too young to yet be working, but as opposed to her older sister, found great interest in the procession of humanity that was making its way up the lower slopes of the mountain. In her eyes, it looked positively Biblical, and were her eyes deceiving her – or were there little creatures walking alongside the miners? When she looked again they seemed to disappear, but yes, they'd been there – she knawed ut. This new land deceived her on a regular basis and so here again. Both saw the immensity of the process, all of it determined by these two pards who everyone seemed to speak of: Justin and Francis.

So here wuz this Jewell and his two daughters, seeing – in Cornish parlance – wozzon. His wife – the one whose name no one knew, but was, in fact, named Clara – was still back at the hotel looking after their baby boy. She'd got into conversation about life here, with that Finnish girl named Rosie, and that Rosie – she was intrigued at where they'd come from and what they were doing, and so gossiping in the way that women often do, this Clara learnt much: particularly about this miner who went by the name of Justin Nankervis, who with his brother Francis, was now leading, like a geht Old Testament Prophet, this geht excursion up the hillside. Not the full truth wuz said about how they knew each other, but Rosie offered this doctor's wife enough information that would be useful. What maybe anyone didn' know was how much this Clara disliked this world they had moved to (for she never said) and how she feared for her daughters and her son here. And that Rosie, well, she said she fully understood that. She'd had hard decisions to make herself – about sex, and survival.

But at the mine Doctor Jewell was wishing to speak to Trevorrow to seek what wuz on. It took a while for him to gain his attention because at this point in time, the Cap'n wuz a busy man: trying to negotiate the shut-down of Cliff, and the opening up of the new mine on the hill. But through persistence and patience, the doctor tracked him down. He found him drinking tay and munching on a saffron bun in the grass-side crowst hut.

"Cap'n Trevorrow? I wonder if I might have a word..."

Trevorrow stood and momentarily paused from his eating and drinking to direct some more boxes of fuses out of the camp.

"Keep em dry, mind," he managed to mouth.

Crumbs of saffron bun fell onto his collar. Trevorrow said nothing much at first (ee wuz like tha', sizing ov un up) but spent a few seconds looking at this well-dressed gentleman who stood before him. He acknowledged the presence of his two daughters too. Finally, he responded.

"How can I help?"

The moment Trevorrow said those words they came out in precisely the way he didn' want them too. It sounded like he was annoyed at the intrusion into his already busy day. Jewell instantly picked up on the tone, and knew he had to strike quick. This wuz clearly a man who everyone wanted a piece of.

"The mining company requested a surgeon. They should have had word about my arrival. Doctor George Jewell. These are my daughters: Rebecca and Mabel."

Jewell looked at un straight up.

"We're in the middle of moving operations..."

"Yes, Quite. I see what's going on. But your request?"

"How long ago was that put in?"

"Some time ago. It was received by an agent in Cornwall who appointed me. They said you'd be expecting me..."

"That were over a year ago," said Trevorrow, "when we seemed to have a small series of accidents."

"And how are things now?"

"Safer..."

"But the Cliff Mine is closing? I mean, by the look of it."

"In a few weeks. I'll be honest with ee Doc, there en't naw need fur ee here no more... Not really."

"But we've come an extraordinarily long way..."

"I knaw tha'. We all have. But we'm a year on boy. I got t'be honest with ee. We expected ee in a fortnight. Not a year later."

This was sometimes the slaw way ov communication overseas. Jewell shuffled on his feet. He had to think quickly for the preservation of his family and his career.

"The new mine? Will you be requiring a surgeon?"

"Perhaps," said Trevorrow. "But nawthun's open yet. You'd be as well to set up there though – as down here, for there won't be much trade down here any longer, and es, if the mine proceeds, then maybe they'll be a-wanting a surgeon."

"Good... I see. I mean, I would be happy to accept the post... to be appointed at the new mine then... and pick up other work in the community."

"Good luck with tha'," said Trevorrow gruffly. "There's nawthun' there yet. 'Tis just a hole in the woods..."

"But given time?"

"Well, you might see something emerge," offered Trevorrow. "'Tis like everything else Doc. When you get some ore out, people'll need ee."

Jewell eyed the route up the mountain.

"Are there any carriages?"

"Not yet, my bewdie," said the Cap'n, "but there soon will be..."

"We'll take our chances up there then."

The Doc obviously did not want to cross the Lakes again and neither did he seem ready for a land trip down to Calumet.

"Are there any houses up there?"

"Not at the moment. What's there now – is a tented camp... but if you'd like a house or cabin built, we'n make it happen... I'n get the chippies right on ut if you got the cash t'front ut."

"Please," said Doctor Jewell. "I'll get specifications to you... a consulting room etcetera... Somewhere for operations to take place in."

Trevorrow got to thinking. He supped down the last of his tay and threw the end of the bun away to the corner. Force of habit. There wuz enough in the current miner's fund to probably sort out a surgeon.

"I'll tell ee what Doc. Seeing as you've come to me ere, we'll sort half your wages... but the rest you'll have to gain by general practice. Thaas the best I'n offer really. See a year's a long time in the business of gaining ore from the ground. A lot changes..."

Realising that out here no immediate better offer was about to come the way of the Doctor, he released his hand and shook that of the extended paw of Trevorrow. His educated hand felt the hard skin of the Cornish shovel that was the Cap'n's hand. This maybe wudn' ideal and he'd have to put the idea to Clara back at the hotel, which might be difficult, for he was starting to sense how she felt. However, now they had a way forward. Now they could integrate and begin a new life. He peered up at the hill, which was illuminated by the early afternoon sun. The fog caused by the gnomes and their brewing of beer, had lifted. The agenda of all those striving up the mountain wuz about prospecting: either for ore, or for a better future, or even a mixture of the two. The mass of humanity and the entire Knockie population that were making their way through the dark forest to the strike were about to be joined by the Jewell family.

In mining, whether underground or overground, you keep your eye on everything that moves. That is often the difference between life and death. But in this moment, the two pards and their Knockies who were climbing, perhaps should have looked back to see wozzon below. Es. One day maybe, they would wonder about this moment, and question why they hadn't seen things as they truly were, and why things ended up the way they did. But tha' is the way of our species and all our stories. We never know which way ut will wander. We never ever know which lode we will follow or why.

9

The mountain then, got scat t'lerrups. By good hap, there were a brae many people up there now. Ut wuz hard to say precisely how many days ut took to really start developing the operation. With the earliest phase of the mine, two relatively small shafts had been sunk. This was standard practice fur Cussies opening somewhere up. One shaft tended to carry the winze. This wuz a rotating axle that was turned. It crossed the entirety of the shaft and allowed buckets, or what the Cornish called *kibbles*, to be lifted up and down. In the morning core (or shift), men went down one at a time in the kibbles as well. They were hefty enough. To begin with, the winzes were worked by a couple of boys, but when the depths got greater usually mules were employed to do the same work, transferring their horizontal energy into vertical movement.

This was a core part of the early focus at New Diggings and ut wuz Justin and Francis who oversaw this part of the operation. Daily, about fifteen men were transported down to the first level and they were gradually working into a cave-like space where some of the early ore could be found. These were rich pickings and the ground relatively soft, so once broken into nuggets, the boys loaded these into the kibbles to be lifted skywards. According to Skews, the idea wuz that Shaft One would become the main shaft of the mine, and it wuz with that that they would eventually drive down through the mountain.

Shaft Two was being supervised by Trevorrow, and its purpose was different. It was being driven vertically as well, but as yet, naw ore was being taken out. Ut wuz purely for ventilation, the idea being that once the gallery beneath had been met from both sides, this would create airflow underground. Such air wuz allays necessary in the mines back home, and was even more urgent here, where the air was still and muggy, and sometimes conditions underground claustrophobic. There wuz a goodly amount of waste attle to be removed here, because what wuz needed first of all wuz access. In taking out the generous space in the first level, several pards were employed on various stopes. Once each stope wuz worked back, then they retraced their steps back to near the shaft and went in again. This was like the old tributing of the past, and it wuz here that any Cap'n employed their best miners.

Those of lesser ability or experience were nearer the shaft itself doing tutwork: breaking up what had been mined and filling the kibbles. It was the same in Shaft Two. If there was any decent ore in those kibbles, they'd find ut up on the surface when it went t'grass. The key thing was to break through so that the two parts of the mine met. After that, you could go any way that you wanted. Fust of all, of course, you would probably drive out horizontally on this level – that wuz, of course, if the ground permitted ut. Another important factor wuz keeping the flooring level, or at least if there was a slope, to make ut dip like the run of the rocks or even the mountain itself. That way, any water would drain out more easily.

'Course, when they were working this place 'twuz in the middle of August: perhaps the driest season of the lot on the Keweenaw. The rains and water tables could only perhaps fully be understood in the winter and spring but at least right now, this wudn' an issue that they had to face. Ut wuz awnly going down through the fathoms that brought such difficulties, like in all the bigger enterprises back home. Skews wuz pleased enough with how ut wuz goin'. Already, some ores had been taken down by cart to the harbour to be transported to Detroit. He wuz aware though that after about a month, some derricks and head frames would need to be positioned above the shafts. Considering the kibbles coming up and the quantity of men going down, what wuz needed wuz a bit more serious kind of h'engineering. A bucket on a rope wudn' zactly the safest mechanism either, not fur the depths they wanted to work at. But it wud come. Es. It all wud come.

Amongst the first in had been the Knockies, each obviously following his miner, and making sure things were safe down there. Moast agreed it wuz looking good: a darn sight safer than what wuz goin' on at the Cliff Mine. There were certainly less grumbles from they. Well, they wuz back in their natural environment, wudn' um? Generally, the rule wuz that if the Knockies were happy then the mine ran smoothly. If they didn' care fur somethun' they'd soon let the management know. That wuz when accidents occurred. So far, so good then.

The next level of expertise needed wuz the timbering boys. They had usefully amassed a good load of wood by now. The clearage of the track up to the mine had provided them with a ready supply, and over the past week, that core of men had been shaping the wood into planks and lengths to get down underground. Moast miners over the globe have a way of doing things, but the way these Cussies worked was usually to get the verticals in fust. They were shaped to be heavy, squared-off bulwarks of wood that ran from the floor of the level to the ceiling.

Their purpose wuz two-fold: to help hold up the ceiling, but also then to reinforce the walls. The latter was completed by forcing unshaped lengths of still rounded wood in-between these uprights and the rock behind them. Usually, these lengths were shaped just longer than the uprights so they fell neatly in behind them. Any miner or Knockie felt better once they'd gone in. Ut was some force against the pressure of the ground. Good timberers were worth their weight in gold. Although the Cussies were skilled at ut, ut had t'be said that some of the best of their profession comed from Finland and Sweden. They knew how to work wood did they boys. Pine and spruce they always worked well, knowing their vagaries – the sap and the knots.

The final job was timbering the ceiling. This meant connecting larger runs of wood to the uprights and seeing if they could at least bear some of the weight. Justin and Francis both knawed tha' when it comed down to ut, if a cave-in wanted to happen, then ut would. Naw amount of timber on the earth could stop the ground from moving ef ut wanted to. But, the point wuz this: runs of ceiling timber would at least give pards a little more time to get out and be safe. That wuz the point of ut. So in this earliest phase of the mine, often they were called down to inspect the timbering. They never had any complaints.

"You happy?" they'd ask their Knockies.

"Es. Proper job," their Knockies would say back to them,

And if that happened – if they gave ut their blessing – then you knawed 'twas good.

Es. So this wuz the way this mine wuz opened up. Daily, you could see it expanding underground, and daily too, you could see the surface work pick up and develop. More timbering. More washing. More processing. More stamping. More cobbing houses. More loading. Es. 'Twas as you'd want ut, ef you wuz Cap'n. The mine wuz beginning to turn a profit. Money went into the brothers' back-pockets.

Up there, landscapes changed easily. One minute there wuz moss and lichen that seemed centuries old, binding time to rock and stone, and the next it became a throughway or a drang. On that throughway up to the mine in the now not so dark forest, rode George Jewell and his family. They obviously weren't going to walk their way up to the workings. Aw naw. Instead, they were riding on the back of a rickety, canvas-covered wagon, and in another behind them, were their trunks and possessions. None of his family party really understood what they were heading for; least of all his two daughters. His son James sat mewling on the lap of his wife Clara, who was even less keen to come up all this way, seemingly into the remote wildness of the landscape.

See, she wuz one, who it turned out, hated the isolation. She craved company and community and that was going to be difficult to find for a while. When her husband had told her about what his contract would entail she wudn' very pleased, and as wuz the way with women sometimes, she kept counsel and did not have a lot t'say to her fool of a husband. The prospect of living in tented accommodation for the foreseeable future did not exactly thrill her either. All of this wuz not part of the bargain. In her mind, this chaos wuz not something she had signed up for; nor for her family to experience. George Jewell knew, by now, the mood she wuz in. But he was aware of the few choices he had. He blamed the agent for being too slow in getting him over here. He blamed chance that the Cliff Mine wuz worked out and now closing, but he also blamed fortune, for somewhere in the deepest recesses of his heart, he thought that eventually – and over time – this new venture might work out. He believed he'd met the two Cornishmen already, whilst breakfasting in the hotel.

The Doctor had brought his family up in the ways of Methodism, and he wuz keen too, to impose that sense of order and progress on the developing camp. Back home, a man of his class might well have been seen as an Anglican, but no, not him. He'd knew the way that Wesley's faith had brought stability to Cornwall, and he was also aware of the Temperance values of the church. In his time as a doctor, he had seen the degenerative effects of alcohol, and for many, Temperance was one way out of it. A stalwart of his local Wesleyan Chapel back home, he hoped that maybe he and his family could found another over here. There might even be many men and women over here that would be receptive to its values. He'd enquired at the hotel as to whether there wuz a local chapel, and wuz politely told there wuz none.

Certainly this travel into the wildness reinforced his belief in the redemptive power of Christ. As the wagon trundled along he noted both the beauty of the landscape they were invading, but also something stranger, something darker and malevolent that seemed to lurk in the gaps between the tree roots, and even seemed to spring up from the soil. He was glad he wuz with his family, for he realised that being alone in these prehistoric, near-gothic forests would be enough to drive a man mad. He wuz glad he had his Bible close to hand, in his doctor's bag. About this sensation he said little, and instead, smiled paternally at his two daughters, and leaned in next to his wife so as to comfort his son's gentle crying. Oh yes, that paternal gaze was important to this man. He knew his wife's fears, and he tried to reassure her.

The shudder of the wagon's wheels over the newly-released ground had a different effect on the two girls travelling next to him. The younger one, Mabel, devoted her time to reading. Throughout their journey across the globe she liked to indulge in fairy stories and fantasy tales to take her mind off the boredom of travel. These distracted her from the reality of what they were enduring. Anyone watching would have said she was 'away with the fairies', and to an extent, that may well have been true. She was bright and literate though, and carried still that childish wonder of investigation about her. This was obviously the reason she thought she had seen small beings walking with the miners. They were her over-active imagination, yeah? Her father had told her so.

She disliked chapel because it interrupted her imaginary world. Indeed, the Bible always seemed quite grim and serious and she did not like that. She disliked the preachers back home who'd bang down their fist and rant their words about salvation. She hated the way raving spit left their mouths and coated their clothing. Maybe this Mabel had decided earlier on that religion wudn' fur her, but that idea had not been fully formed in her head yet. It was coming though, for this Mabel was going to have to grow up very quickly in this new community.

Her older sister, Rebecca, was more refined and less troublesome in many ways. She was more woman than girl, and took note of everything she saw. She realised the immense changes that not only they were enduring as a family, but also the whole transition that the world was enduring. But she did not embrace the superstition of the past, this Rebecca. Instead, this new century brought hope to her. It seemed a time where the oppression of women (like in her mother and grandmother's era) might be cut away and overturned. It felt like this new land might bring new opportunities and she wanted to be a part of that.

She was educated this young woman. Her regret was that she had not been allowed to proceed to medical college to train like her father (their emigration had denied her that, along with the still prevalent view that women were not to be trained in such a profession), and before they had left, she had declared that it was her intention to become a teacher. It was that career that she had in mind in this new world. Maybe what lay ahead in this forest wuz her classroom, a place where she could educate this community? There were young children, she'd noticed, as well as older boys and girls who'd probably not yet even learnt to read before knowing how to work a drill or cobbing hammer. About all of this, she said very little. She retained it in her heart though, and thought that only when opportunity arose, she would make good her plan.

Their small convoy had set off from the Cliff Mine camp before dawn, with the notion that they would arrive in daylight, allowing them and others sufficient time to set up their tents and make their accommodation viable. The August heat was still in the air, and at night few people needed sheets and blankets to sleep in. Doctor Jewell hoped that this forever-travelling family could adapt to this fresh challenge. He worried about the lack of toilets and washing facilities, but tried to cover this with his family by explaining how the whole thing was one huge, exciting adventure. It worked well enough on Mabel, a little less well on Rebecca, but not at all on his wife.

When their convoy pulled into the clearing of New Diggings he did not quite expect to see the visceral activity going on. A shanty town of tents and *ad-hoc* dwellings had already been constructed and men and women seemed to be working to establish all manner of different parts of the surface structure of the mine. Everything was in miniature so it seemed to him, but he soon picked up on where certain parts of the mine were planned, and where they would grow and evolve.

Unexpectedly, some design had gone into the planning of the community and the mine itself. He knew how chaotic these things could sometimes be, but here, there seemed already a sense of civic pride, and that people were building something bigger and better. Perhaps the lessons learnt from the shoreline community were going to be newly applied here. Even now, Doctor Jewell noted the marked-out streets and the early erection of latrines and wash-rooms. Launders of water were being directed from a lake further up the mountain. The ingenuity of it was fascinating to observe, but even more surprising was the fact that all of these people seemed so assured in the success of the venture when, so it seemed, such a small quantity of ore had been raised from the ground.

Trevorrow wuz there to greet their arrival: thumbs in both waistcoat pockets. With him stood another well-dressed gentleman, and two other men of similar appearance: both typical-looking Cussies. He recognised them instantly as being from the hotel. Barely noticeable were two Knockies too, whose names you well know. Doctor Jewell stepped down from the wagon.

"I'm liking your latrines and washrooms Cap'n Trevorrow. Most commendable – especially in the light of these days of cholera," was the first thing he said. He could not help but have his medical hat on.

"Doctor Jewell," introduced Trevorrow, "and his family... Doctor Jewell, as we discussed, will be acting as our mine surgeon, but also taking up practice here."

That wuz a laugh. Trevorrow had appointed him without any discussion with they. However, they did realise that such a man was necessary.

"This is my wife Clara and my son James. These two here are my daughters: Rebecca and Mabel."

Clara curtsied a little, but Rebecca stood and stared at them awkwardly. Mabel was already distracted by some wood pigeons who'd been disturbed.

"And these are my colleagues in this endeavour... yes. Mr Skews, our surveyor and assayer..."

Skews leaned in forcibly to shake the Doctor's hand. Knawing Skewsy, he was already sizing up how he might weasel his way into the Doctor's confidence.

"And here are the two gentlemen who we have to thank for this find... This is Mr Justin Nankervis and his brother Mr Francis Nankervis..."

"We've met already," interrupted Jewell. "We... ah.. sat together at the Cliff Hotel..."

"I see," said Trevorrow. "Of course..."

Skews looked the kind of man the Doctor was not surprised to meet. Such men existed back home in Cornwall but had also made themselves useful all over the world. In these brief seconds, he also came to understood how clearly Trevorrow seemed to be taking charge of operations. It had been right to have gone to him at the old mine. But these other two? Both looked a little incompetent (he'd seen the rough-looking one at breakfast, probably recovering from a night's whoring and drinking), perhaps only in their early twenties. Still a strike was a strike, a find a find, and maybe he might learn that there wuz more to they than met the eye. Despite his misgivings, the Doctor leaned forward to shake hands with each of the brothers.

"Much out of her then?" he asked.

By her, he meant the mine. Mines were allays female.

"The initial samples are good. We've a few ton up... but Mr Skews here has extensively mapped the seam and we're hoping to start working it proper these next few days..." said Justin.

All the while, these pair ov Knockies didn' have much to say: they were, however, a little more fascinated with the two daughters and the baby boy. Luk tickled the hands of small James and made him laugh, whilst Gourgy gently teased the daughters, throwing pieces of moss into their hair, which they thought came upon them from the wind coming up from the harbour below.

"We've got a good sense of how the land lies. If you see, the seam runs straight down to the shore where the old mine is. If we follow up and down, there should be enough deposits here for a very long time," offered Skewsy appearing sensible and thoughtful.

Further facts about the operations were discussed, with Justin taking the lead. Francis knew he must have come across to the Doctor as a fool, or as some kind of dullard but he genuinely knew not what to say. Maybe even, he couldn't speak presently or somehow lost his tongue. He'd been right about that older daughter of the Doctor's though: she was purty, and he couldn' help but stare. Her blushes told un that she nawticed un gaking at her and although Gourgy's actions annoyed him, at the same time, he watched her body turn in the shafts of light that were streaming through the tall trunks of the pines. There wuz somethun' about her that he admired. Maybe ut wuz her neck – or maybe it wuz the delicate curve ov her lower back. So he wuz distracted by her, this Francis, which wuz unusual, for as you know by now, normally he was the sensible one of these brothers: always had been.

"Aay?!" went Luk. "You'n put your tongue back in yer mouth now."

"What ee mean Sos?"

"She over there. Me and Gourgy knaw you like she."

This snapped Francis out of the vision. He knew he needed to say something constructive and welcoming to the Doctor.

"Doctor Jewell. If you have any suggestions to improve our mine's safety record, then please let me or my brother know."

"Well, I suppose at the moment, it's one hundred percent safe... but yes, I have some experience. Most mine surgeons know common complaints and injuries. Prevention is always better than cure. That offer is most welcome..."

Jewell nodded this response to Francis, whilst he tried to keep his eyes off Rebecca. The Cap'n had progressed to showing the Jewell family where he felt they might best be accommodated for now, and was already instructing some workers to set up their camp. Unknown to Francis, the maid Rebecca was not the only object of attention in this meeting. One pair of eyes also fell on the younger sister, Mabel, but as yet, nawbody knawed anything 'bout that, so 'tis hardly worth saying at this point. But like ut always does, 'twill come out at some point.

"Best get on then," went Trevorrow after he thought he'd sorted out the Doctor and his family.

But the Doctor's requests wudn' over yet.

"Cap'n Trevorrow, might I ask about worship?"

Cap'n paused in his steps back down to the mine's entrance.

"What ee mean?"

"Prayer. Today is Saturday. And I wondered what arrangements there were for Christian service for tomorrow – we being Wesleyans you see..."

This revelation came rather as a shock to all standing there from the mine. That they were Methodees wudn' knawn about, and t'be honest, not many had contemplated the need fur religion in the past, at the old mine.

"There are others here of our faith surely?" asked the Doctor. "I mean, this is a Cornish camp, is it not?"

Cap'n weighed ut up in the manner of old-style Cap'ns, with Justin and Francis almost taking notes.

"'Tidn' a thing we've done much of before t'be honest with ee, Doctor Jewell... Men out here... well, some d'feel that God left they behind a long time ago... There idn' much call fur ut."

"Or rather *they* left God behind perhaps?" interjected the Doctor.

"Maybe," said Trevorrow. "There ebm been naw cause fur a chapel afore now..."

"The men don't pray?" he questioned

"Well, they do. I d'knaw many who d'take a pocket Bible with um underground... and dare say. there's plenty of prayers made... but formal services here? Well, thaas a new thing, sure 'nuff."

"You've no objection then, if I offer service tomorrow then... a gathering at least... At home, I was a lay preacher. My father preached at Polperro where my family originate from."

"By all means," said Trevorrow. "Naw problem. We've naw chapel fur ee though..."

"That won't be a problem Cap'n Trevorrow. Not at all. We shall do it open air – *en plein air* – just as Mr Wesley once did."

"There's a rock upon the right-hand side there," offered Francis.

"Make a good pulpit," noted Skews, for he'd recently surveyed it. "Below is a kind of dip: an amphitheatre of sorts. It'd make a good meeting place."

"Follow yer nawse," said Justin. "You cen't miss ut."

"Wonderful," said Doctor Jewell. "That warms my heart. A new Gwennap!"

"We'll put word around," said Trevorrow. "I cen't guarantee how many will come mind. Aw, if you need anything else... let me or the boys here knaw..."

"I will sir," said Jewell.

This time, Trevorrow resoundingly hoped there would not be anything else he instantly required. Preachers were tiresome in his view. They always complicated things.

It wuz time for all of them to get back to operations at the mine itself, but still Francis turned behind to see if he could catch a further glance of this Rebecca. But she could not be glimpsed now because she was already assisting her mother, unloading items around the rear of the wagon. This other daughter though did not move: she just watched them walk down the hill to the mine entrance. At that point, she was now contemplating the fullness of the magical world she had accidentally been forced to step into.

"Didn' knaw we wuz getting a Reverend as well as a Surgeon," noted Gourgy to Luk.

"Es. Well, two fur the price of one is always good," replied Luk. "Nice maids them two. Frank's keen on the older one..."

"Obviously," said Gourgy. "She's tasty."

They carried on walking.

"And the other one? asked Luk.

Gourgy gave a sharp intake of breath and said. "Dunnaw about she. Somethun' about her. One of they humans that..."

He paused and said no more.

"What ee mean?"

"I dunnaw what I mean. She can sense things..."

"What kind of things?"

"Things."

"Things?"

"Es."

"How do ee knaw?"

"You dun't come across um very often... but I've lived long enough of a life to knaw... Mark my words."

Luk did. Ee always did. Ee wuz like that.

"You goin' to this temporary chapel tomorrow then?" he asked.

"What ee think?"

"I s'pause not."

"Correct," said Gourgy. "I ebm been chapel fur centuries and I ent about t'start now."

"What ee goin' t'do instead?"

"Go inta' the mine... have a gake at what ut's like inside... See what we've got. I reckon there might be more in there than Skews knaws about."

Luk knew that wudn' such a bad idea. Even though not much ov ut had really been opened up yet, Knockies had a way of squeezing through gaps and cracks that made house-mice look inflexible.

"You'm on," said Luk. "I dun't fancy chapel either. Boring, idn' ut?"

With that, the two of them got back down to the digging, having followed the four humans.

"Time fur a bite t'eat, edn ut?" went Gourgy.

"'Tis indeed," said Luk, "but naw pasties have been made up here yet and I had some bun earlier but there was naw saffron in ut you."

Gourgy spat.

"That idn' right. We need to make sure the Cap'n knaw thaas an issue."

"Coming in on the next laker apparently," said Luk knowingly.

But maybe this lack of nicies up here wuz to be expected – fur a while at least. Grumbling, both ov them went back to their protective duties. Perhaps there wuz room fur someone to plant a small crocus field.

For the next week or so, nothing but noise emerged from this black mark in the forest. Either came the sound of spades shovelling and picks axing, or the grunt and puff of men labouring and shouting at their tasks. Elsewhere, ut wuz the hammer-and-nails sounds of derricks or launders being erected, or the cracks of timber being sawn and split. There wuz even the thunder of wagons and carts, the rotating wheels of barrows and skips. The din of urgency dominated. The very earth groaned.

But that Sunday morning, at the Pulpit rock all of those sounds dissipated. To begin with, the natural nothingness of the forest returned. This was microscopic growth and tone: in the unfurlings of fronds, the twistings of lichens and the spurt of fungi – but as a few miners gathered for this service to be delivered by this lay preacher by the name of Jewell, a hum of polite conversation came over the natural arena in which they sat. They'd not necessarily come for the purposes of Christian conversion or edification, but somehow through the pure pleasure of doing something different: of the social nature of the gathering; to recognise now who wuz in this community and what it consisted of. Lay preachers sometimes had nice voices; they could lull a man to sleep in a way that he couldn't inside his tent or bunkhouse. Usually, even if much of the service wuz twaddle and tripe, or even hellfire and brimstone, they could take some message of hope away with um. Sometimes the words of the Bible gived ee fortitude underground, and fur that, they were allays thankful.

In moast frontier mining camps there wudn' a pile of married couples but those who were joined in this way perhaps felt here wuz some break from the monotony of union, and an ability to circulate and compare notes: to comment upon how this operation at New Diggings was going, and perhaps to also lament the loss of the old Cliff Mine. Many too, discussed the half-remembered ways from back home, and news they'd gained from relatives. Children too, could play and meet: tackers and toddlers were already tumbling their way down the slopes of the natural amphitheatre. Ferns got flattened and brambles cut back with pocket knives. And when this lay preacher spoke (apparently, the new mine surgeon too) it tapped into something in their make up; something that had been installed in them a long time ago, and which they had grown used to. Some could even smell the old mouldering chapels back home. They remembered holding hymnals. Dare say, if they were required to sing, they could remember a few hymns sung at Anniversaries and tea-treats.

At the top of the rock stepped forward a nervous Doctor George Jewell. His hair was a little uneven from the fact that he'd not yet obtained a mirror in which to comb and balm it, and perhaps if you had observed him in the hotel a week or so ago, you'd not have thought this was quite the same man, for his appearance was a little more ragged than he might have hoped. But still, the fact that he was a doctor impressed those who sat below, and a hush came over those sat there. To call ut a congregation would have been a great exaggeration of the numbers. Jewell steadied hisself on the ledge, because he knew that if he moved his feet any further, he might accidentally fall, and *that* would certainly not do.

"Ah... Good morning to you all. For those of you who do not know me, my name is George Jewell and I have taken up a position here as your doctor and surgeon to the mine. Like most of you, my family and I have come on a long journey to be here, and we hope and pray that this venture will profit and sustain us over time."

He gave a small cough and then continued.

"Today's service is very informal and although we have not the pews or walls of a chapel, I think you will agree that we have the wonder of this forest; a forest of God's creation, in which I come and preach to you today. But what we do here, is nothing new, for many of you know that our faithful leader John Wesley preached in the open air many times in his life: most famously of all of course, at Gwennap Pit, and maybe as you sit there this morning, you will remember that moment in history. Now, I come to you this morning to speak about all of our own personal journeys toward the Kingdom of God..."

Not quite listening the way that others were, stood these two brothers on the rim of the amphitheatre; not quite involved, but not quite uninvolved either. There wuz one thing fur sure: this boy Jewell spoke well. He'd already captured his audience's attention, and maybe there wuz some sense in what he wuz saying. Both Justin and

Francis had seen enough of Sunday School in their young lives to know the run and pattern of what he was about to say. It was like predicting a vein of copper in a gallery. You always knawed which way ut wuz goin'. Maybe there wuz somethun' comforting in what he wuz saying; some familiarity that ended that feeling of isolation, that they were working the very limits of the known world. Thaas wha' ut felt like at least.

Cap'n wuz there too. Ee didn' seem to be takin' too much nawtice of wha' wuz bein' said, but instead, just circled the arena nodding at men and women he knew, perhaps affirming that this moment of preaching' wuz a good thing, and this community might be a little more God-fearin' and abidin' than the last. He walked next to Mrs Cap'n – a woman knotted up, and all hunched over – a face s'angry 'twould make milk go off. Nevertheless she kept Cap'n fed good and proper. She was some cook that woman. Cap'n's approval on such matters as this gathering wuz important. In such a scenario, Justin and Francis viewed themselves still as lesser Cap'ns. They hadn' his experience. One day, they hoped fur his status though. Ut wuz surely only around the corner, once this plaace wuz fully operational.

Boy Skews wuz there too. Francis wuz trying to make out the expression on his face. Ut seemed almost tearful an' by the look obm, maybe he wuz recalling home services with his own family. Prob'ly like many Cornish overseas, ee wudn' recognise one of his children if they comed up and walked right past un. Ut had been that long perhaps since he'd been back. Maybe his missus had given up on un. Maybe his childurn too. He'd positioned hisself at the top of the round, just above where Jewell's family were sitting. Perhaps he wanted to be reminded. Usually, he fronted ut well, like moast men out here, but the word of the Lord always had a way ov touching a man's heart.

Jewell meanwhile, was continuing with his sermon, checking below to see who was still interested and whose attention he'd kept.

"I would like to discuss with you today the idea of the Way to the Kingdom of God. Now this was the seventh sermon of John Wesley. You'll see that the sermon is divided into two parts. The first part, I hope, defines the kingdom of God and the second part defines the way to the kingdom of God. I will read to you what Mr Wes-ley has to say about this."

He said Wes-ley like the preachers back home, splitting the two syllable parts of his name.

"Believe that this Jesus Christ came into the world to save sinners," Doctor Jewell continued, "and the kingdom of God is thine. By faith thou attainest the promise: 'He pardoneth and absolveth all that truly repent and unfeignedly believe His Holy Gospel.' As soon as ever God hath spoken to thy heart, 'Be of good cheer, thy sins are forgiven thee,' His kingdom comes; thou hast righteousness, and peace, and joy in the Holy Ghost."

There then followed a commentary on that, which Francis in particular spent little time listening to. Not only wuz he fixated with what they had somehow accidentally created here, but also again with the slender form of Rebecca. Now wuz not the time to speak to her, but sometime soon he'd find a way. And this Justin, his brother, knawed precisely what wuz going' on, and maybe he wuz stood there thinkin' about his awn more recent sins.

But perhaps 'twas good fur his brother to be thinking fondly ov this maid. Before, ee'd never given much over t'whistling at maids or chatting them up. That was unlike him though: he'd spent a lot of time at ut as a young man. Then again, ee wudn' sure as to how ee felt. If this maid got together with his brother, then tha' would split they apart – and es, that would be strange, for the bugger standing next to un wuz all ee really knew. Perhaps however, as the good preacher wuz now saying, 'twas all part of this bigger redemption ov humanity. Ee didn' knaw ut all quite then, but well, that wuz goin' to be a big thing in this boy's life. But let's not go there now, for here, ee wuz still young and full of zest for living. Like the preacher said, redemption wuz everything though. Redemption wuz all.

To those little sprites watching in the forest, if the topsy-turvy world of the mine workings and the settlement around them wudn' enough, then this new gathering drew them out further to see and listen to what wuz being said. At the chopping down of trees an' all the banging, digging and cutting, moast of their species had laid down in the earth or slept high in the surviving trees in order to escape human activity. Now, the dulcet tones of this preacher gentleman had brought them out of their nooks and hidey-holes in the forest to witness wha' wuz being said, and this strange belief tha' these human creatures had.

When they listened, it seemed platonic and friendly, had the air of being kind to one another for the benefit of the whole, but some, rightly, weren't sure ov tha'. Some of the forest creatures observed tha' they said one thing but often did another, and tha' their words were like the wind: temporal and fleeting. They looked around but there wudn' even no Knockies to ask about ut all. And that Gourgy, ee wudn' here either to explain things to them. From under moss and lichen, all they could do now wuz to listen, but when it got dark, they'd yell fur Yolkai the Moon Goddess and tell she what they'd witnessed. She'd knaw what to do. She always did.

Maybe too, from the forest, that Nimkii had picked up on the earth shaking. Maybe he'd felt the vibrations. Perhaps he wuz watching too. Trevorrow felt un there, he thought. Ee didn' say anything t'Mrs Cap'n though.

Come the end ov ut, the service delivered by Jewell had been very successful. It had established him now as a force of good at New Diggings, and rightly or wrongly, the miners and others felt they could place their faith in un. Here wuz a man who could help them physically with illness and injury, but also a boy who might assist with their faith too. Even a few miners from the other nations present had turned up to watch, and felt the depth of his message. He'd wanted to finish the service with some hymns but as there wuz no hymn books and no easily obtainable music (not even a portable harmonium), that idea would have to be scrapped. Some kettles of hot water had been brought up though, and from a few old bits of planchen 'eaved up on some legs, they poured out cups of strong taa. That wuz good because moast of the attendees were chackin' ov thirst by now.

Rite on then. Ut looked as if the New Diggings wuz t'have some input of religion. Naw one wuz goin' t'make a jig out ov tha' anymore.

Clara clapped for her husband but not many of the other women spoke to her. They noted her class, and perhaps felt they shouldn't just go up to her. This was a new land, where the rules of class should have been swept away, but instead, they sometimes just got transferred. Out there, in the forest, the sprites zoned in on her. They saw her isolation. And because they were kindly beings, they sympathised. But there wuz nothing they could do. Not now at least.

Such wuz the success of the morning's preaching tha' people stayed all afternoon and got to know one another. Maybe ut wuz needed because the past fortnight had solely been one of work and toil. What wuz the point of the seventh day unless you cud rest?

"Well done, Doctor Jewell," said Justin to the surgeon. "Bewdie bit ov preachin' that. Took me right back."

"Good, good," said Jewell back to him. "Thank you. I think you are building somewhere very special here... you... and your brother."

Perhaps having this here meant everyone felt a little more protected and a little safer. That wudn' necessarily because this place wuz different than Cornwall. Rathermore, it wuz because it was – in so many ways – zactly like ut. There were always shafts to fall down and rocks to crumble. So too, were there forms in the darkness; and occasionally, a malevolent lore in the land. Es.

Now, far down below all of this, as the sun set over this now strangely quiet landscape, a rusty laker pulled into the deep water outside of Eagle Harbour. Amongst the many items slung off it and placed into a rowing boat that would bring them into shore, was an order of desperately-needed spice – containing saffron (Gourgy wudn' the awnly bugger who needed ut) – an order that had to be signed for at the harbour office and rigidly guarded before it made its way inland, and hopefully up to this place, name ov New Diggings, that everyone wuz yipping on about.

But that wudn' the awnly valuable goods brought in that Sunday. Someone had also been carried a long way across the Atlantic, and she spoke differently than moast of the rest of them already there, and she wudn' about to put up with the shenanigans of any of these damned Cousin Jacks. Naw way – because she'd already come across they fools a'fore now. Tha' – and other things unspoken about for the moment – had made her wise. She wuz neither crone nor child, but her unlined face mapped something untold and as yet unwritten. It wuz fair t'say that she had her own darker spice about her: not the colour of saffron though, more the hue of coal. Put in mining terms, she was a choice ore indeed. And the sailors who'd ferried her up from Detroit knew it. Despite her many charms, they knew ut best t'leave she well alone.

10

Thaas obm see. The evolution of a settlement from a mining camp into a proper community is difficult to nawtice. Change is gradual, but in the slow run of the early days ov Fall, ut was still barely perceptible to those watching. Overnight – or as if by magic – a tent transitions into a shack, then that shack gets incorporated as a room within a larger house. Sometimes, shacks are fixed up and developed and sometimes they are demolished and something better is put in their place. Es. Always the place wuz shifting its shape. And in this manner, so the town sways and moves as if on the ocean, up and down, and from side to side. Pulleys and scaffold, shingles and thatch: the corners of cabins fixed with tongue and groove and half-lap. Doors and shutters were put in place. Still the prow of this land vessel drives on to further the settlement's sustainability: for the workings underground to deliver a profit, and for that profit to be distributed amongst the community. There'd be a fair price for fair work, the way ut should be. Here, there'd be no exploitation; no muscling in of weight or power, no grab at what was someone else's (unless you counted those sprites of the forest, and those peoples that had lived here for generations before).

Such development follows fashions. One dwelling inspires a host of others to emerge; and those national groups from the old world took their inspiration from designs back home. They made their dwellings the way their communities always had done. And so there were lessons to be learned from the Swedes and the Finns about how to build property that could survive long winters. Likewise, the Cornish knew how to make homes comfortable and furnished, with planchen and wallpaper. They liked stone and spent much time splitting boulders and levering them into place. They liked ut solid did these boys. Aspect too, was important to them. They always built their dwellings with a view, perhaps to assure them that even if they could no longer look out upon some iconic bay, there wuz at least something to see. Maybe – and some knew it to be true – the bay across Eagle Harbour wuz becoming iconic to they. Each day they knew Mount's Bay or Falmouth a little less, and knew the ways of Superior a little more.

No process in the uplands of this mountain was ever easy. Everything required prior planning. Materials needed ordering from suppliers to be transported up from Detroit. Ut sometimes seemed like no one would ever be truly settled, for there wuz always want of a new thing that had been forgotten about, or was now urgently required. Mrs Cap'n (she who normally didn' say much, and when she did, only moaned) wanted a decent range to cook on, so that had to be ordered. And she wudn' keen on naw stuff from Merky. Just outside of Buffalo, there wuz a firm that had Cornish owners, and so product was ordered from them. A host of griddles and kettles were obtained to keep the workers fed and watered. The wagons brought up coal, and soap, and detergent, and bleach.

When Justin and Francis moved from their own rough and ready tented accommodation, into something approaching a cottage, they ordered new beds and mattresses. They'd had enough of having of having to sleep on the floor, and it had been a long time since the straw-stuffed beds of the bunkhouse. Wily Skewsy knew all the suppliers and companies that could provide for people and already, he had employed a couple of associates to help him with the process of supplying the material needs and comforts for those at work in the settlement. He was amassing quite a trade as a sideline, and soon was the owner of one of the grandest dwellings on the mountain. If awnly his family could see un now. But then, did the bugger need ut? To moast, he seemed t'rattle round inside ov ut. You'd see un yipping up to the Doctor and his daughters, explaining what he intended. And that Mabel, she wuz full ov ut, she wuz. Ee always had time fur the girls; almost like he'd become their default uncle. Francis watched un pretty close.

The other grand dwelling being constructed was that for the Doctor and his family. His property was so designed that a dwelling house was bolted right on to his surgery, and when the surgery was all set, he began ordering all manner of preparations and instruments from suppliers in Detroit. He needed surgical tools and canisters of gas, in case of more serious operations. A whole laker arrived at Eagle Harbour with what Jewell needed. Medicines, cures and tablets were all heaved up the mountain and brought to New Diggings. He realised his responsibility and bought dental tools and equipment too. Well, who else would do ut? The miners often used the force of a whim to pull out any rotten teeth, and that wudn' do t'all.

So too, did the calm Doctor order decorations and furnishings for his wife to try and somehow alleviate the fact that they were living in a forest in the middle of nowhere. Posh drapes and utensils were requested, as were an expensive set of neo-classical sconces to hold the dwelling's candles. That made Mrs Jewell feel a bit better – but did ut save she in the long term? Naw. You'll soon see how. The regulation beds and mattresses were also all brought up the mountain from the harbour. Like moast women in the camp, she spent her days denying dirt, mould and fungi an entrance. Down in the mine, none of that mattered, but in the homesteads, it became essential to clean and protect.

There were other men who were less fussy about accommodation and the company had built them bunkhouses on the same lines of those found at the Cliff Mine, and so for them it was more like a home from home. Some men (who'd worked long in the mines and forgotten their precise ages) preferred the atmosphere of the bunkhouses to a move into domesticity. They knew that such living had been their life and to separate them from it now, would probably kill them. There was camaraderie in them that could be found nowhere else. They liked the smell of the indoor stove burning, the comforting pipe smoke and the late nights – telling drolls and stories about daft Cussies and their ways. In such surroundings the stories got embellished and enhanced from that they once were, but tha', wuz the point: ut wuz a factory of mirth and the tales were often lessons in safety for younger miners. Ut allays made Justin laugh because such wuz the dominance of their accents and narratives that even those working there from other European countries ended up speaking broad, just like Cousin Jacks. Nawbody cud help ut. Ut entered ee and didn' let ee go.

The laker vessels not only brought material goods to New Diggings: they also enabled a wider range of commodities to be obtained. For a while now, the camp had been living mainly on tinned goods, and there came a point where appetites wanted higher-quality food. No one wanted to twist open another tin. Fresh tastes were needed. Therefore, it was a grand day in the camp when finally; a box full of saffron had to be signed for. Skews wuz the man who put his signature on the drover's form denoting that the spice had been received – and that ut wuz in good order. But crocus corms too. Soon, there'd be a field where they could graw their own. No need ov runs ov spice then.

From that moment, baking could commence and it wudn' long a'fore every tent and shack in New Diggings had set up a board, oven and bowl, to make nicies. Oh es. They'd be consumed on the number one level belaw – and they'd be eaten in the timbering yards. Nub-ends would be tossed to the Knockies and all would be well. What wonders the laker vessels brought in! Ut made the work go better with that taste of 'ome inside your belly. Such food brought some satisfaction to the camp and always boasted morale. Ut set ee straight.

Then one morning, there wuz a surprise visitor-cum-migrant who moved inta' the camp. Just as the evenings were pulling in and the mornings were that bit darker before daylight came, a cart an' oss pulled into the camp, and sat on ut wuz none other than that Rosie Koskinen. Some knew who she wuz and heartily disapproved ov her ways. That wuz the women mainly. The men were wider eyed and keen, for many were sweet on she. She'd serviced plenty of them over the years alright, seen their flaccid penises and saggy asses. There wuz a view in some minds that she wuz better off left down below and tha' her type should stay there. She wudn' wanted up here, not with the way things were panning out – not fur example, accordin' to what this new lay preacher (the doctor fella) wuz saying about forming a new Christian community. She hardly fitted the bill, did she? – 'specially in they scant dresses she wore Es. Usually, you could near 'nuff see er nipples, she wore her corsets s'low. In this weather though, she was shawled up with a bonnet on, and ut looked like her move wuz permanent. She wuz never without her rouge though, and the way she waltzed in, she made sure everyone nawticed her entry. Like a queen she wuz.

Sometimes you can control things, and sometimes you cen't. And who wuz to control who now came into this community? Fur zertain, ut wudn' the bosses of the mine. Es, they'd had first say and selected those to be employed, but after tha', when the diggings were getting known all over the Keweenaw, who wuz t'stop anyone coming in and grabbing a piece of the action? Some might say like attracts like in the form of her, but others might argue for the free economy of 'Merky', and that the likes ov she wuz just as welcome here as anywhere else.

Someone gave her a wolf-whistle.

"Whaas brought you up here then?" one or two of the grass workers asked ov er. They was the boys working the stamps and cobbing away at the ore.

"I've come where the action is," she said in response in a flirty tone.

"Another hotel?"

"I don't think so. Just a saloon perhaps... somewhere for you lot to all go off to on a Saturday night."

Now when she said that, well, that ignited their interest, because 'twas a helleva' long stank off the mountain down to the Cliff Mine hotel. At least now, there might be a bit more 'h'entertainment', and once she wuz in place, then maybe other girls ov her persuasion would follow. Rite on. The camp would be all the better for her arrival. Maybe they'd missed her somehow, and maybe she wuz missing their trade. As wuz her prerogative, she didn' say too much else about that, though rightly as this tale will tell, there were other reasons fur her relocation.

Unbeknown to others, Rosie had written t'that Skews and asked him to reserve her a plot. He'd duly obliged and set her up bang in the middle where the main throughway in the camp had been driven. She nestled right in there amongst the other Cussies on that side of the street and made herself at home. A tent had been supplied but soon enough she wuz commissioning (by way of a loan from Skews) a new saloon. Many a Cussie smiled when they knawed that wuz goin' in. Bugger all the Methodeee stuff going on up near that rock, especially when you had somethun' like this. A saloon wuz more like ut. Who needed Mr Wes-ley when you had a pint of good ale?

'Course, word got round that this Missie Koskinen wuz now in town. An' sure 'nuff, down in the first gallery, word got down t' Justin, who wuz stoping back one of the final runs of rock to allow air in. Justin carried on scraping his pick-axe at the wall of rock, but a certain nervousness raged through him. Ee didn' knaw what ut would be like seeing her again – not after what happened between them – not after they'd... er... exchanged the life-affirming juice of sex. See, there wudn' naw other way of puttin' ut – fur tha' wuz what had passed between um.

"Knaw she, dun't ee?" went Luk, overhearing the news. "Best get over and sort ut out with she boy."

Luk's advice wuz sensible, so when his core ended he went up in the kibble. When he comed t'grass he knew he had to seek her out. Already, word had spread as to where she wuz setting up and what kind of building wuz planned. When he found her, she wuz making small talk with that Clara Jewell over where things were located. By the items in her basket, ut appeared as if Mrs Jewell had procured flour, sugar and currants for some baking. But Justin knew that this Rosie wudn' the kind ov girl to spend time at home baking saffron buns. Aw naw. She wuz something quite different. Mrs Jewell said hello to Justin, but sensed that her presence wasn't needed.

"Best get home," she said. "Making some buns for the Sunday service..."

"Didn' know there was a chapel," deadpanned Rosie.

"There isn't," said Justin. "They just meet. There's a bowl, a kind of amphitheatre... You'll have to go. I mean, you're such a regular attendee at chapel, aren't you?"

Rosie looked him up and down. She ignored his taunt.

"You seem to be doing alright fur yourself... I mean, that was a good night we had, wasn't it *pupu*, ah?"

Justin nawticed she still had the Finnish edge to her voice. He didn' answer. He was not sure whether he wanted to revisit that moment. In all honesty, what wuz embarrassing wuz that he could hardly remember what had happened, nor did ee knaw precisely what had passed between them.

"You never said goodbye in the morning."

"Didn' I?" said Justin smiling. "You got your payment though... so we'm sweet, yes?"

"I suppose when you put ut like that, then yes, we're sweet..."

Rosie glanced from side to side.

"Just thought that you were a bit special like..." Rosie said, closer to his face. "I was genuinely sad to see you go... I saw you having breakfast..."

"Es. Well... I'm sure there've been more since me who you've been keen on..." he offered, his voice still weaving out a heavy thread of sarcasm.

"Maybe," she said. "You've made it clear..."

"How d'ee mean?"

"Well, you dun't want anything to do with me up here – and that's fair enough... you being a Cap'n here and that... but it's a free country, ah? I can move here if I want to, can't I?"

"Es," said Justin. "Nawbody's stopping ee..."

"No."

Some time passed. Each awkwardly contemplated the new world they were in.

"Word is that Skewsy set ee up?"

"Yes. A loan..."

"Ee didn' say anything t'me about ut."

"Why would he, ah? Nothing to do with you, is it? It's a private arrangement between me and him..."

Justin didn' like the way she said 'private'. He didn' like the control this gave Skewsy over her. Aw naw. Ee wudn' keen t'all. That boy already seemed to be running the shop and the supplies to the settlement, as well as making his bit out of the share agreement.

"If you want my advice, you'll watch ee."

"Don't worry. I will."

"He's ah..." but he could not quite express what he felt about him. He wuz picturing him with Mabel: the way that she doted on him, the way he always gave her free sweets at the shop and asked about her books. Instead, he changed tack. He didn' want to think of Skews.

"You'll do well here, I d'reckon," said Justin, gritting his teeth.

"I reckon so," said Rosie, as confident as ever, her face beaming at him the way ut had done when he first met her.

Justin began to part from her.

"You stay safe Justin," Rosie said.

"You too," Justin replied.

He began to move some feet away, but his feet were seemingly sluggish.

"Can I ask you something though? Why did you move Rosie?" he asked. "I mean, there's still good trade down at the Harbour, idn' there? And I mean, those arriving and departing from here would have to pass by you, wudn' they?"

"True," she said. "This idn' all about you, by the way. No. It's changed of late."

"How come?"

"Maybe I don't want to say... I don't like to speak ill of people. You know, we Finns don't like to do it."

"Come on. Don't play games. It's me – Justin..."

"Let's just say, I don't much like the company of some of the more recent arrivals down there. They aren't like you and your brother."

Now they were getting somewhere. Now, she wuz being more honest.

"Well, tell me," he said, still frustrated. "We need to knaw about our neighbours below. What affects they, affects we..."

"That's the point," she said hissing. "They've been there a fortnight now... a right crew they are. A right rabble ov good-for-nothings."

"Who?"

"Some Irish."

"Irish? We've got them here already working. We get along fine with they boys. Really?"

"Yeah, come up to work the Upper Peninsula. Led by this woman... a right bitch she is... by the name of Maddy."

"Really?"

"Wrecked the hotel they have. An' you'd best tell Cap'n Trevorrow, they're working the old mine... picking out the last ov ut..."

"What difference does that make t'we?"

"None at all I suppose," said Rosie, "except that she's undercutting the price for your ore. She's got the lakers in the palm of her hand."

"Whaas her name again?"

"Maddy they call her. But so I gather, her full name is Madelaine O'Donahue. From County Cork she is: is it the Beara Peninsula, ah? You heard of it? Hard as nails she is, and with an evil heart – a black heart. Mad is her name, and mad she is in nature... You Cussies better watch yourselves."

Certain things now spun into place. Beara in Ireland was a copper mining area. Many a Cussie had headed out tha' way before now.

"I gotta' go," said Justin. "Honest, I ent angry with ee an' I ent takin' up with ee Rosie, but this is important."

An' just when things looked 'andsome, it turned out they wudn'. Bugger wha' had happened between Rosie and he a'fore now. Though he'd been frightened to see her, the news she brought wuz far more world-changing than anything he'd heard. Ut had knocked un skew whiff. Damme. Ut wuz going t'knock others back a bit too. Already, the watching forest sprites had deduced this information. It ud spread up through the lower slopes – from thicket to stone, and from stone to glade. This woman who'd arrived on the Keweenaw; Yolkai, the Moon Goddess needed to be told about her.

11

Cu, ut read. Cu. On the ragged poster pinned on the wall in Skews' Assaying 'Office', the chemical symbol for copper was found in the middle of the metals section of the Periodic table. To call Skews' place an office wudn' quite right, for the building they stood in wuz no more an Assaying Office proper than a hastily-erected shack. It wuz nowhere near as plush as the now abandoned domain that he had built down at the old Cliff Mine, but still, he'd had lots of his implements, desks and cupboards brought up. They all knew he had plans though. Skews always had plans.

The four of them in the room were fully aware of the significance of those two simple letters. It wuz what they spent their days searching for: this valuable metal that was soft and ductile, that wuz so malleable and useful that it wuz goin' to be needed in virtually every important product manufactured in this emerging century. Its uses spun out before them. Primarily, of course, it was an excellent conductor of heat and electricity but then it also had its essential and ancient function as an ingredient of various alloys. Put together with that other metal that the Cornish were fond of finding: tin, then the molten mixture created, formed bronze. All well and good wuz that, but the real beauty of copper was that it wuz almost directly usable and that meant it didn' require lengthy or costly periods of processing.

Their meeting that morning though, wuz about processing the fact that Justin had told them about the Irish raiders below, and to try and decide what they should do about ut. Their discussions were initially stuck on shifting sands, and moved first one way, and then another. A key difficulty was how to balance any action taken, with the Irish already working at New Diggings. The lot already engaged were reliable boys and many had worked with Trevorrow since day one. Ut wuz the way of operating all over the world: the Cornish organised, and the Irish dug out the attle. This symbiotic relationship had worked for a century or more. Upsetting that balance was not something they really wanted to do. Had there ever been any religious conflict on the Upper Peninsula, the Irish being Catholic – and the Cornish being Protestant and Methodist? There were subtle digs sometimes, but they were well-intentioned enough, made for comedy rather than hurt. It never got beyond a crowst-time joke or a passel of fun. Larks ut wuz only, but these new Irish, maybe they would upset the balance. Maybe they'd not like the way all that went on.

For sure as eggs wuz eggs, eventually they'd come here. Their arrival might upset things: change the balance. Es. But there wudn' anything the Cornish could do about ut. If they wanted t'set up an Irish camp next door, well, they could do ut. The Cornish could go and speak to Nimkii if they needed to. The second difficulty wuz the labour supply itself. The way the mine wuz going, certainly in the New Year, they'd need more labour. Unless boatloads of Jackers comed in (and they generally didn' arrive in the winter), they might get stuck fur manpower. In that scenario, the Irish would need to be employed. But at the moment, they were future decisions. The more urgent issue wuz about them filling their boots from the old mine, and undercutting their prices. That required swifter action, and this wuz the reason Francis had hastily organised this meeting.

On the small stove in Skews' shack, rattled a coffee pot, and despite their discussion already lasting an hour, more needed to be discussed.

"More coffee?" asked Skews.

Justin held out his enamel mug for more of the fresh liquid to be poured. Trevorrow took some too, but Francis declined. He wuz alert enough already at this worrying scenario.

"Just how much is there left in the Cliff?" he asked Trevorrow. "By tonnage?"

"Aw... A fair few hundred I 'spect. I mean, if they seek some of ut out, they might find a fair old whack in the deeper levels. But they'll have a dang of a job gettin' ov ut out. None of the lifts are working any more. And naw winzes could be fitted. Some ov it up top-side is probably easy pickings... but the rest... they'd need gear and expertise... The trams wuz gone anyway. Rusted out. Thaas why we left um."

"That's what worries me," interrupted Justin. "You boath knaw these ent no Johnny-come-latelys into the world of mining. If they're from the Beara like what Rosie said, they d'knaw copper, and they d'knaw how to get it out. We knaw boys who've worked Allihies and Berehaven. They ent no fools. In fact, they'll have learnt their trade off the Cornish."

This fact scared the company present.

"Should we go down and stop them? Bar the mine off to them..."

"Thaas very hard to do," said Trevorrow. "Lots of top-side air holes and adits – as well as all the level openings going in. The collar's sizeable too. 'Twud need some money and labour to seal ut up. 'Tis money I dun't reckon we have, do you?"

"Maybe we should seal ut," said Justin. "Seal ut up with they inside ov ut. See how they like that."

They all liked Justin's sentiments but knew the fantasy of that suggestion. This kind of ill-wishin' wudn' goin' t'work.

"Not sure we'n odds ut," said Trevorrow. "It've always been the way in mining. People d'think that once a place is shut-down then ore stops coming t'grass. 'Tidn' the way t'all. You knaw back home that once a place is abandoned, others gaw in like craws and feed off the carrion. 'Tis zactly like that out here."

"Chancers then?"

"Es. Chancers... but thaas the way ov ut. You d'knaw that where the Cornish lead, there's always some bugger in their slipstream..."

"Mr Skews, what about the buyers though? I mean, that undercutting surely idn' allowed, is ut?"

"This is business," went Skews cynically, trying to control a slight cough. "Anything's allowed. A man will do whatever he can to pay out a few less pennies for product, and thereby enhance his own profit..."

"But surely they knaw ut edn goin' t'last forever with they chancers?" asked Francis.

"True 'nuff. But they dun't think like that. Everything's a negotiation. If you'n get ut cheaper and tis good stuff, then why not? This is a market economy Mr Nankervis. The old allegiances people had back home – well, they're all gone out here."

"But the ore?" asked Justin. "It's inferior. You knaw the grading."

"Very well, I assure you, but that won't stop them in Detroit. They'll order what's cheapest..."

"A'right then... we get back to them," offered Francis. "You get back to them... See the lakers... get a message down. Write to them. Do what you need t'do. We'll have to undercut them..."

"What? And sell our copper below market value? You're mazed," went Justin brusquely, sticking his head out of the shack door, and tossing away the dregs of his coffee. He wuz still keeping an eye on the progress of Rosie's saloon.

No one said much. All of them were contemplating the idea.

"It'll mean we making a temporary loss," said Skews, "but if we play ut well, we'll end up dominating the market. The chancers wun't want to go any lower. It'll make their operation completely unviable."

"Could make we unviable too," spat Justin.

"I dun't reckon so," said Skews. "Not in the long term. I'll make some enquiries. I'll write and get word down to Detroit."

"Aren't we cutting off our nawse to spite our face?" continued Justin. "What ee think brother?"

"I dun't see as we got any other choice Sos. 'Tidn' like we can run um out ov town... Nawbody even knaw what they'm like. We ebm seen um yet. All we knaw is that they'm led by this women, O'Donahue, and she d'seem like a right pile of trouble."

"I d'reckon this might be our best solution," said Trevorrow, stretching his legs, and peering outside to the works below. "Mr Skews will make our offer and we shall see what that brings. It's my firm belief, they won't say no. Indeed, it may be purposeful on the part of the suppliers. They may be testing us to see our resolve. Once we dominate again, we'll be able to raise the price – and get back to where we are now."

"I cen't wait t'see this Irish bitch in the flesh," said Justin, "and look her in the eye."

"You ent the only one," said Trevorrow. "No doubt she'll show herself soon enough... From what I've heard, she wun't be able to resist comin' up here at some point."

Now Gourgy and Luk weren't privy to this conversation. The meeting wuz one of they naw-Knockies-allowed-kind-of-deal, but the pair were both well enough aware of the threat and the problem of being undercut. Being shafted in this way wuz something they'd seen a hundred times in their lives, for they knew that the whole business of mining was full ov back-biting, and difficult wheeling and dealing. Ut didn' surprise them that this wuz going on one bit. They realised the fate of the operation wuz now in the hands of Skews.

"You sure you want ee negotiating?" asked Luk to Francis.

"Why not? He's best placed to do ut..."

"Es. But you knaw what he's like, that boy..."

"How do ee mean?"

"Just keep an eye on un..."

Francis looked to Justin.

"What you pair saying?" asked Justin.

"Ee sometimes ent right in the head that boy. He's a bit mazed..."

This wuz new information but Gourgy and Luk were well ahead of them by now in going back to the shaft.

"Hang on. Dun't just walk off... What do ee knaw that we dun't?"

Gourgy and Luk stopped in their tracks. They looked to each other to see if they should reveal what they knew. Then, they nodded to each other.

"The forest says that he ent what ee seems..." said Gourgy.

"The forest?!" exclaimed Justin. "What ee mean? The Forest..."

"Ee's right," chipped in Luk. "The Forest do tell us things..."

"What? It speaks to you?"

"Es," said Luk. "We speak to ut nearnly every day..."

These Knockies were always full of surprises but this wuz a new one, even on Justin and Francis.

"You're kidding we? What? The trees speak, do they?"

"Not like that," said Luk. "There are... beings out there."

"Beings?"

"Yeah. You knaw. What we call *poble-vean* back home," explained Luk.

"Little people?" asked Justin.

"Es. Thaas ut," said Gourgy. "They'm all over the place. Just like ut is in Cornwall..."

"Right," said Justin, with his usual cynicism.

"I's true," said Luk.

Justin and Francis still thought it could be a ruse. They were good wind-up merchants these pair. They allys had been.

"What they say then? About Skewsy."

"Just watch un," said Luk. "They say ee idn' what ee says ee is. Somethun' about un idn' right."

"We knaw tha' though," said Justin. "We knaw he's slippery as an eel. A duplicitous bugger, sure 'nuff. Always has been. There's naw way he'll pull the wool over our eyes though – not with the profit and income..."

"Maybe. But they said to we to keep an eye on un. Thaas what we'm goin' to do and what you should too..."

"What – trust a bunch of little people!" scoffed Justin.

"You trust us, dun't ee? You should trust they too."

"Es," said Luk. "But dun't shoot the messengers, eh?"

Gourgy looked around un as if he'd suddenly realised the time and that this conversation needed to end. He instantly dropped all previous matters in the way that Knockies do sometimes.

"Crowst-time," he said. "And Mrs Cap'n d'make lovely saffron buns for anyone underground... I've heard tell she be plantin' up her awn crocus field."

"Time t'go," said Luk.

And they did. Above ground, Knockies moved at the speed of light. There were shadows against the piles of attle and some unused kibbles – and then they were gone again. Francis looked out into the forest.

"What ee think?" he asked his brother.

"They'm mad, es, but perhaps there's somethun in ut."

"We'll keep tabs on un, like they said," stated Francis, "especially when it comes to the new deal he strikes."

"Not sure 'tis tha' they'm worried about though," observed Justin. "But es, he's one bugger we need to keep an eye on."

There were others too.

By the fern stumps, and behind moss-covered rocks, some small, liminal individuals first raised and then lowered their heads at this conversation. Es. By now, this wuz normal for Copper Mountain. What neither of these two Cussies realised wuz that they'd come to colonise this forest world, and to irredeemably change it. Naw one had asked they in the glades and groves; and as they watched, by now, they had come to a decision: a price needed t'be paid.

12

Harken to me wuz ee? Maybe you wuz – and maybe you wudn'. Es. You'd best listen good and proper though, fur the next week of work at the mine went on as usual, and then, well, ut all got scat t' scudmo one Friday evening. This would have been – aw – about the second week in October – when on the fust level the mine had branched out on two galleries and worked some 'andsome stopes. Out of the kibbles comed just the kind of ore that Skews had predicted. Not only that, but the deposits were precisely where he said they'd be. Es. Skewsy had nailed ut. The mine wuz opening up a bewdie, and a goodly amount wuz ending up on the surface. It was cobbed and stamped and 'eaved inta' long wagons t'pull down the hillside.

George Jewell wuz enjoying setting up his new surgery. He'd not had much to do yet: awnly a small cut from a saw, and then a three-year-old child with a cough. The rest of the time, he just moved around objects in his establishment to test their properties and where they were best suited. Sometimes, he moved them back to the original location he'd first placed them in: discovering that wuz best after all. He wuz anticipating more work though. He knew what the lower levels could bring; he knew that the closer men went to the core of the earth, often the greater their wounds and needs. This wuz the way of ov ut. Once you had drills and fuses, then look out.

For now, his Clara had temporarily stopped worrying about the isolation. He'd sometimes catch her gazing into the forest though: at the endless run of trees that covered the dark horizon as far as she could see.

"Come inside dear," he'd say, trying to be kindly, though instead the way the words came out sounded rather condescending. To be fair though, he'd already noted her obsession, and it scared him. It sometimes stopped him from sleeping.

"Perhaps more some baking this afternoon?" he suggested, producing from his coat pocket some threads of saffron gained from Mrs Cap'n.

Anything to distract her, he thought.

His son and daughters were doing rather better. Little James seemed to be thriving in the mountain atmosphere, whilst Rebecca and Mabel readily occupied themselves. Rebecca had come to him a few nights ago, and discussed with him in earnest the possibility of her becoming the community's teacher. Though no building had been erected, she had seemingly already organised outside classes. Parents had been contacted and they'd been asked if they thought a schoolhouse was a good idea. She'd taken it upon herself to obtain chalk and had asked one of the kindlier carpenters to make and paint a blackboard for her. Jewell was not surprised at her ingenuity. She had been this way since she was a child. There was much of him in her.

Sometimes, he had wondered why he could hear her pretending to have a teacher's voice outside his winda'. At first, he had thought she might have been playing a game with Mabel, but then he realised that actually, she was testing her own abilities and role-playing pedagogy. He told her he thought it would be a capital idea, and that he'd have a word with Trevorrow about commissioning a schoolhouse. An educated populace would be a good thing.

Mabel was Mabel. She had adapted well to the surrounds of the mine. It was she who explored a little wider into the forest than he would like, but certainly her knowledge of the landscape became very helpful. She soon knew all the rivers and the glades. She knew the deep pools and the groves, giving each of these locations her own names. She seemed to be processing this new world in this way. As no one else seemed to have named the detail of this landscape, he noted that the more she articulated her place-names and associations, the more they seemed to transcend to the rest of the camp. If he himself used those names from his daughter, then he noticed they took on even more status. In this sense, she almost had a God-like power in naming the land after her own frailties and concerns. Certainly, her reading meant that she saw story everywhere, and kept talking of fairies and pixies. She'd grow out of that soon enough.

He'd noticed that Mr Skews took some considerable degree of interest in her. Her names for everything seemed to make him laugh, and he one day confessed to the Doctor that Mabel reminded him of his own daughter, and that he loved to hear the fantastical ideas of children. He said that it gave him hope, though as they had talked, Jewell soon noted that in fact, Skews had not seen his children for ten years or so. The girls who he once doted upon (and who Mabel reminded him of) were therefore now grown women. Time passes, and as he was daily realising, his life had been spent too often over test-tubes and weights rather with people.

Whilst Jewell *tsk*ed-*tsk*ed at the saloon, this Justin and this Francis – the boys who, in essence, had made this place – were mozeying up through the main street. They had been working hard underground, stoping back one of the more productive galleries. Now that Rosie's wuz deemed to be open, and you have to remember, 'twudn' much more than a shack, and a bar with a door on ut, at least the town had a saloon. The Doctor had been hoping for a community of Temperance but that simply wudn' goin' t'happen. Besides, after an eight-hour shift, what you moast wanted wuz to settle and drink down a bottle ov cold beer or two. Rosie had the beer shipped into the harbour and then had ut carried up the mountain. Ut wuz imported in from a brewery down below based in Port Huron. 'Twas always a good day when the brewery delivery wuz made, and a very bad one when the bar went dry.

She wuz doin' good trade this Rosie, and of course, every bottle she sold, Skews made a profit. Ut had become a regular thing: the boys went down there and had some fun. As yet, there wudn' naw women in town, but Rosie had promised that would soon change: she had plans. As wuz usual, the Cornish boys liked to numb their heads with alcohol and at least feel like ut wuz back home (if they could even remember a time when they weren't here). When it got late, out would come the old Cornish songs, and wha' did ut matter if they got the lyrics wrong? Nawbody told they off. They even had their ways ov adopting the loveliest of songs into pieces of smutty innuendo. Well, you knaw how 'tis when men get together. This wuz a mining camp after all.

When Rosie opened her establishment, George Jewell had a hope that maybe in getting up on a Sunday a few miners might realise their sin and get over to the pulpit to hear the Sunday Service. That wudn' quite how ut worked out though. They might have had guilt in their bunkhouses and realise from their need to piss every whip and wan throughout the night, tha they'd drunk too much, but fur they, the day ov rest meant just tha': complete rest. Why should um go chapel and hear the same old claptrap when they could stay cosy in bed? Only when the beer churned a bit more readily in their stomach (and they had to be sick s'hound in the latrines) did they perhaps consider their actions. Some felt this way, but for others, more used to liquor, vomit wuz a kind of necessary professional hazard. It comed with the territory, so to speak.

Letters and messages had been written by Mr Skews but nothing had come back yet. Maybe the Irish below knew that somethun' wuz afoot – and maybe indeed, someone had talked; because that night in Rosie's saloon, a few different faces were in. Unbeknown to the forenoon and afternoon shifts, from the bottom of the mountain, a group of men and women had finally consigned themselves to trekking up the mountain. They were the new Irish: those rascals who'd squeezed their way into the old Cliff Mine and brought out whatever crumbs were left. Obviously, they'd learnt much from the harbour workers and those remaining in the old hotel. They'd come to know how the landscape had altered, and how the population had shifted from the coast all the way up this newly-named Copper Mountain. Rumours of it had been found down in the Lower Peninsula and they'd followed the span of their rainbow to here.

Just like the Cornish, they had much invested in America, and just the same, it was a land of opportunity. Why stay at home with peat and sheep shit when there wuz a better life to be had? And like the Cornish, they'd come off the tip of a land that poked into the great Atlantic ocean. And whilst the Cornish had come off the granitic trunk that poked south-west, the Irish too, had made their way here from one of the great peninsulas of the west of their country: in this case the lowest of them – the great Beara. And at a glance, they looked much the same as the Cornish: with their wide shirts and waistcoats, their boots, and that orange-blue stain of copper that could never quite be washed out. But they didn' speak the same, and you could hear that difference. And some of them too, carried words of the old language of Irish with them: a more ancient tongue than English, whose sounds and glottals now resonated through the mountain village. Of course, the Cornish had that too, but their old tongue was a little more distant, a little more buried in attle than the Irish, but still old words and rhythms poked up through, growing up like weeds.

This group were clever. Maybe their leader had told them to be. Es. She was a wild one, true 'nuff. Not many men would take she on. She had a quick mind fur zertain and she wuz ethereal. She could move between shadows, so it seemed, for she had snuck her way into Rosie's saloon, without the hostess even seeing her. They'd set up accommodation in a distant clearing, and then in pairs, subtlety moved into town to see what wuz there. She wanted reports back from everyone as to what they'd found, and what the layout wuz. What benefits could be gained? How might this place add to their cause? She commanded them without fear, did this woman. She had metal like no other.

That idn' how she came across though: instead she gave out a wiseness, a knowingness, and she carried all of the old ways about her, learnt from a long line of strong women just like her, who'd had to live on the periphery with not much more than rock or fish. She was someone who hadn't been granted a life like Rebecca Jewell but who had magicked one out of nothing. Es. That was ut. She was a conjuror. A sorceress. She readily knew it too. She knew her power. Nothing like saffron: instead, a dark spice – black and cruel to the very core. Es. A sylph she wuz. Horny with ut too mind. That wuz the thing. Even Justin would note ut.

She slipped in with her lieutenant, a hirsute man in his sixties by the name of

Flannery, a big fella with a reputation for wrestling and boxing. He wuz her protector – her bodyguard – and she paid him well. And this woman wuz half his age, perhaps even more, but she had power and command in her voice. Es. She had certain skills – maybe skills you cudn' learn from naw book or mining manual. Both he and she knew the Cornish. They'd suffered their exploitation on the Beara, and put up with their bastard ways for long enough. They knew their stinking pasty breaths, their want of Christian song in the lodes and those foolish clods – their Knockies, who trailed on behind them like the churls they were. Aw es. They and their crew had suffered at the hands of these Cornish and their predecessors back home in Ireland. And once they'd had their fill, they'd left the Atlantic coast on Beara a wasteland. She hated them for their exploitation but she also hated them for their jollity, and ability to always end up smiling. She had on an outer layer of armour that day, did this woman. This wuz partially why they'd gone inta' the Cliff and cut the price of copper. Revenge you might say. A kind of pay-back for these Cussies who thought they were cocks of the walk. They weren't that. They were just cocks – all of them.

Sneaky they were, this lot. That wudn' to say all the Irish were that way. Not at all, fur the Cornish had many companions in there who were Irish, and they loved them to their very cores. They worked together and lived together. But because the beer wuz going down and because ut wuz getting dark, nawbody much nawticed who wuz new in and who wuzn't. Initially, this Finn – Rosie, wuz pleased because it looked like her venture was being successful, but when she looked over in the corner an' saw that Maddy and Flannery, aw, well, her heart definitely skipped a beat. She knawed what this meant. Her crew had wormed their way in here. She'd half-expected ut of course, but maybe not quite so soon. Rosie wudn' naw wallflower. She was Finnish and she'd say what wuz on her mind. She went up to this Maddy and this Flannery.

"Hei. I thought I'd told you that you weren't welcome," she stated.

Maddy didn' move. Nor did this bear called Flannery.

"That was down there," he replied, barely glancing at this Rosie. "We're up here now."

"Same rules," said Rosie.

"Really?" went Maddy. "I doan't think so..."

Now this wudn' lookin' good, but elsewhere in the bar, 'twudn' looking a lot better either. See, beered-up these new Irish started to get a bit too loud. They overstepped the mark with their behaviour, and the Cornish, well, they wuz initially tolerant. Maybe this new lot in were Cousin O'Flynns – just off the boat – or some of the Irish who already worked at New Diggings, but somehow, ut didn' feel that way. Ut didn' feel right. What ut did feel like, as they heard their boasts and conversations, was that these were the buggers who'd muscled in down the Old Mine, and they were now in here, having another gake at what else might be on offer. Gradually, good nature and drunken camaraderie turned into something else.

How it happened wuz that people stopped drinking. And when they stopped drinking, they also stopped speaking an' tellun' ov the tale. A silence descended and in two peoples who normally cudn' keep their mouths shut that felt decidedly strange. And ut would be impossible to work out how the fisticuffs started but maybe it wuz one of these new Irish who boasted about how the way he put in fuses was better, or perhaps even 'twas an idiotic Cornishman who thought he knawed best with his

Methodism. Maybe there wuz multiple conversations like that and maybe some of it wuz truthful and some ov ut wudn', but the very fust ov ut that Justin and Francis knew wuz when the door of the saloon burst open and a body got scat out, travelling horizontally clean across the street. There wuz a pause an' then a cheer, and then from inside comed a brae old noise.

An' then there wudn' naw stoppin' of ut. Fists got 'eaved inta' faces and fingers got poked up nawses. Teeth got scat out and purple bruises were torn along the edges of knuckles. There wudn' much furniture inside but wha' there wuz was pretty much scat t'pieces in seconds. The glasses and bottles were next to get thrown – and shoved into people's necks and arms. Es. Soon there wuz a brae bit of blood on the planchen and out on the dirt in the street. There wuz plenty of cussing and plenty of swearing. Fuck. Neither Justin or Francis had seen anything like ut since they'd witnessed a brawl over a bal-maid back down St Just. Every bugger in there thought they had some moves and had to show them. In general, the Irish were better boxers, but the Cornish cud wrassle a man like no other. They could dodge a punch and easily grip a man 'til he wuz down on the floor: this wuz the old Cornish hug and the bastarding Irish would now feel the warmth of its welcome. The Irish wudn' no walkover mind. She'd made them that way: trained them for just such an occurrence.

Into this chaos walked Justin and Francis. They guessed that up in his house, the gentle Doctor Jewell would be appalled at what this town had become: oaths, cussing, swearing and fighting. But there wuz no oddsing ut now. The Cornish needed to fight back and prove their worth. The boy Francis strolled on in, and caught a kind of glimpse of recognition in the faces of this woman and her man. They almost looked like they'd been waiting for him to show up. The old boy name of Flannery wuz up on his feet and wuz 'eaving out some strong punches inta' Francis. They hurt, but he wuz giving some back too. He had good upper body strength did this Francis. Back and forth they went at ut, knocking, well, seven bells of shit out of each other, so much so, that the rest of the brawl began to stop. and they already fighting dropped their guards and watched this Francis and this Flannery goin' fur ut. Outside their battle went, right into the street, with them both getting sweatier and bloodier in the process.

"I'll be taking you down, y'bastard," Flannery kept saying.

"Come on then. Give it a go, y'tuss," Francis came back with.

Inside, the boy Justin went inta' a rage, as ee watched this bitch Maddy give Rosie a side kick that scat her flying. In protection, Justin launched at her, but she blocked him with her cloak, locking his arm so that she could turn him and push him to the floor. He wriggled out of the hold, but she comed at un again. The woman had an unnatural power, and when her hood wuz down, he nawticed something about her. She had a glint in her eye, an unusual look that he'd not seen before. He hated her, but there wuz something in her too that made un paradoxically like the control over un she had. That sensation shocked un plenty.

"I heard about you quare pair up here... you and your little operation... We've come from beyont a-looking fur two brothers. Two Cornish ."

She said the word Cornish with such hatred.

"Maybe you've found them?" said Justin as he tried to land another heavy punch on her.

But she had the greater skill: if not the weight and force, then certainly the leverage.

"So now," she said. "Tell me which one of those two fookin' Cornish arseholes are you?"

Justin didn' have time to respond.

Her iron gad of a fist clunked un one hard an' fast – and he felt himself staggering backwards into the wall of the saloon. Such was the force with which she'd hit him, that his form created an outline in the soft wood, cracking it in the shape of his upper body. He slipped down the wall. She folded her arms and stood over him. He realised that he was losing consciousness, but still felt the heavy and well-focused ram of her thick left boot into his bollocks.

She dusted down her cloak and put up the hood on it again.

Outside the punching being delivered back and forth between Francis and this Flannery had gone up a gear. Francis wuz now bleeding from a bad cut above his eye, and the iron-y red liquid ran down over his eye and cheek into his mouth. He could taste it on his tongue. The fight only stopped when Francis gathered up one huge motion of energy and scat Flannery flying. The only trouble wuz that he fell backwards from ut, and managed to lacerate himself on the prongs of a flailer that had been left outside one of the carpenter's shops. In slow and grim disbelief, two of the steel prongs entered his back and came glistening out through his stomach. Aw hell.

As he looked down in horror at what he'd done to hisself, everyone looked away. The plaace went stock still and the awnly person moving wuz Doctor Jewell, who at the noise in the street, had flung himself outside to see what he could do to make repair. Already though, repair ov the injury this man who wuz suffering didn' look very hopeful.

Both the Irish and the Cornish observed the face on this Maddy woman when she saw what had happened. 'Twas a picture.

Around the chaos looked on other creatures too, who'd been attracted to the noise. This wuz the closest they been into the camp, and at the final bloody end of the fight, they scurried to be unseen again.

Late to the party were Luk and Gourgy who'd just come up from belaw.

"Wozzon?" asked Luk looking over the remains of the melée.

"'Ell up by the look ov ut," stated Gourgy.

Ee wudn' far wrong.

13

We learn by our mistakes, dun't us? There wuz this whole fisticuffs thing and then there wuz over-running the forest, over-running the planet; in fact, over-running it all. But nawbody then could see ut. That wud only come later... when the chapel wuz built. Meanwhile, the Cornish stood on the left-hand side of the street, faces ashen and full of concern; the Irish to the right, with the same expressions. It was starting to rain slightly and the street was becoming muddy. Rivulets of water ran through the camp, and hit the boots of men who only a few minutes ago had been in combat. Each party looked to the other like they were varmints. The reality of the brawl now started to hit home to all of them. Fur two nations that usually had big gobs on um, no one said much. All they could do wuz to look at the bloody mess in front of them.

Fur Flannery, the options did not look too good. He wuz moaning and groaning, and any bruises or cuts they had on their hands or faces were soon put into perspective. Men twisted their jaws to alleviate the pain, and rubbed sore knuckles. Wha' the hell had this all been about? Perhaps it had been about territory. It was about the fact that the Cornish had established this place, and now these new Irish (not the boys already there working) were attempting to muscle in. But maybe there wuz more to it than that. Maybe there lurked in this Maddy and her men some latent inferiority; some sense that they'd been wronged in the past, and that they were here to reverse the order. None of that really mattered at the moment though.

The most urgent issue was to deal with this man named Flannery; and George Jewell, mining surgeon, instantly sensed where the need was. He'd already moved in front of the man and was assessing the best way to approach his injuries. In an instant, he knew that alleviating the man's pain was the most important thing he could do, and so reaching into his medical satchel, he grabbed a syringe and a small bottle from it. With the syringe he drew up some fluid from inside the glass and gave a quick check of the plunger to see that it was loaded. Then he moved to the upper arm of the man, who by now, was screaming in agony. His screams echoed around the darkness of the camp, and woke children in their beds. This wuz obviously a good dose of morphine to help remove the most repugnant aspects of how he was feeling – and to alleviate the pain. Clearly by now, he'd realised what had happened and saw the two spikes of metal poking out of the material of his shirt still covering his stomach. Jewell made a call for help and instructed the fetching of a stretcher from his surgery. Now both nations combined in their help for this man.

As all this happened, Francis was recovering from his own injury. He'd been on the floor, and the cut on his head was still raw. He now saw the grave danger the man he had fought wuz in. How had it come to this? Francis wuz in general a peaceful man; he didn' normally wish men harm in any way, and he shivered at the consequences of what he had done. If this man Flannery died, he would be unable to live with the guilt. Wuz history repeatin' ov itself? That said, ut was he who had started with him. He'd not wished him ill in any sense of the word. But the man had targeted him upon the instructions of the woman he was with.

By now, she was standing at the door of the saloon, but her face was not giving much away. The horror inflicted on her protector almost seemed part of a wider process, in which she almost knew, not everyone would make it. It seemed to him that the only thing that mattered to her wuz the survival of the fittest: she in particular. That said, her eyes were not on him, but on the way in which the other men were lifting an agonised Flannery off the spikes. Fortunately, they were not tipped, so in effect, the flesh of the man could be just slid off the metal. The sound of this made the men doing it wince in agony.

"Alright," said Jewell, "The sedation should start to work by now. Let's get him on the stretcher. Take him up to the surgery. I can better examine the injury up there."

With care, Flannery was man-handled onto the stretcher. He was a big man and others leaned in to help with his weight. Getting him down to the canvas of the stretcher was not easy. Everyone knew that his organs inside would be damaged. From the look of it and where the wounds were located, it would be his intestines and perhaps his kidneys. There'd certainly be some internal bleeding.

"I didn' mean to..." said Francis, realising the fate had inflicted. "You set him on me."

Those were the words he hissed at this woman Maddy. A protective guard of other Irish had formed around her. How did she command them so? They did it without her even saying a word, almost as if she had some kind of mind control over them. Her face was hidden within the hooded shawl that she wore, so it was still hard to detect any emotion.

"We know what you Cornish are like," she said. "We've seen it before and we'll see it again. All of you are plain thieves and fools... You've banjaxed me man there. "

This was unexpected. Despite the guard around her, Justin stood in front of her. He said nothing but just slowly shook his head. Francis hoped to God that they would not have another set-to. That was the last thing needed now. Francis could not see his brother's face but knew how penetrating his stare could be if he were angered.

"We'll see you bastarding Cussies gone from here soon enough. Just like back on the Beara, eh? Cowards, the lot of you. Crack on back to your holes in the earth."

Trevorrow, who had now arrived on the scene, had made his way to the front of this conflict and stood next to Justin. The Cap'n was ready to restrain him should her words ignite any more violence. But there was no need for his presence. Unbeknown to Francis, all the while, this Maddy had kept her eyes closed, so that the words from her mouth came out as a kind of incantation. The spell worked well on this Justin. Maybe it wuz because ov wha' he wuz like: a bit weak ov mind. There wuz a poetry about the way she spoke though and somehow, Francis sensed that wuz intriguing his brother.

When she finally opened her eyes at him, Francis perhaps did not realise it during this moment but something had clearly shifted inside his brother. There was no massive change to be noted there and then, but on reflection maybe ut wuz at this moment that the planets shifted into a new alignment. His biology and landscape reformed. His lack of response showed the alteration in his chemistry. She gave nothing away though. She'd had years of self-protection and she knew how to make a man feel useless, yet in her power.

"Come up to the surgery with us," said Trevorrow. "See what progress can be made. Doctor Jewell's a good man. He will do what he can."

"Very well," she said, and turned with her group to follow the direction the stretcher wuz being carried in.

The way she said that made her already sound like a Queen: someone that it would be hard to deny or resist. Perhaps that was why she'd levered this Flannery and other men into her service. She certainly had command of all – dominated them – and unknown to them, even those watching from the edges of the forest understood her power and fortitude. Like them, she was a real force of nature.

"Thank God you didn' have another go at her," said Francis coming up on his brother who was stood stock still.

"I wanted to," was Justin's response. "I mean, I really wanted to... but I couldn'."

This wuz one answer that Francis wuz not expecting. Justin usually led with his heart and not his brain. He punched first and asked questions later. That had brought him a lot of trouble back home. But now, somehow, he'd been placated.

"Why not?"

"Dun't knaw."

"What ee mean?"

"Somethun' told me not to... despite what she said about we."

Gourgy and Luk had gathered next to them by now, alongside Rosie, who'd already begun to assess the damage inflicted upon her newly-opened saloon.

"Ha. Watch her!" was Rosie's advice. "Mark her card... she's as deceptive as they come... so don't be fooled..."

Justin nodded but it seemed like he was only doing this in body and not in spirit. His mind seemed like ut had been stamped and cobbed over.

"I'll get you a drink," said Rosie, surveying the remnants of her bar.

There were enough bottles of whiskey still intact, for her to open one, and pour Justin a shot.

On the other side of the street, Francis gradually realised that a lone figure was watching him. She wore a bonnet to protect her from the rainy night-air and wore a long formal coat. Surprisingly, the figure was Rebecca Jewell. Francis gave her a look which allowed her to speak.

"My father said to come down and tend to you. The wound... on your head..."

Francis had forgotten about tha'. In watching the encounter between his brother and this Irish Queen, he had neglected his own state of affairs. When he felt his forehead he nawticed the cut and the fact that an ooze of blood still ran down over his face.

"Alright," Francis said. "I'm coming..."

"Best if you come up to the surgery with me... We can deal with you better up there Mr Nankervis..."

Francis knew he should go, but first, he had a word with the Knockies.

"Boys, see what you can find out about these Irish..."

"What ee mean?" asked Luk.

"Get to their camp. Follow them. The more information on them the better.. When you're not blabbing loudly, you pair can be pretty quiet... Use some stealth. They'll not nawtice you... Do whatever ut takes"

"We'll talk to our friends in the forest..." offered Gourgy.

"Talk to whoever you need to... but come back to me as soon as y'can."

The pair nodded. They knew the seriousness of what they were being asked to do. Francis looked to Rosie.

"You go with Rebecca" she suggested. "You need sorting out. I'll stay with this one."

By that, she meant his brother. Maybe that wuz a good thing, and that this Rosie at least somehow still seemed to care for him. The sad truth wuz though, that this Rosie wuz perhaps wasting her time, for Justin wudn' in no state to lie in a warm bed with she. In fact, all ov that had just got turned upside-down. Now you may think that there is no place further for this Rosie in this story but that is far from the truth. But this Francis could not think about that now. Instead, he walked away from the Knockies, her and his brother, into the care of this Rebecca.

"Who were you talking to?" she asked.

"Rosie and Justin," he replied.

"No... I am sure that there was someone else you addressed..."

"Really?"

"I thought so."

"No," said Francis firmly, but knawingly. "Nawbody else."

She gave a look to his wound. He stood still so that she could examine it. The dark wuz fully down now but he felt her hands touch his head. They were cool and soft despite the fact that the touch wuz momentary, and that an incessant drizzle was now falling.

"I can't see it very well here," she said. "I need some light, though come to think, the surgery's full at the moment. We can go into our home..."

"Really?"

"My father won't mind. He'll want to see you treated and he's too busy with the other gentleman."

"I'm a mess," said Francis. "In some state."

"Don't worry. It's only a little blood and mud."

"What happened anyway?" she asked. "A fight?"

The pair of them kept on walking up through the camp. Ahead, they could see a mass of people outside the surgery, waiting for news about the patient.

"Yeah... well more than a fight you might say. More like war..."

"A war?"

"A war of possession..."

"For the mountain... for the copper..."

"Yeah. Seems that way. It seems the Irish have bad memories of us Cornish in their land. Maybe thaas something we need to put right, though I'm not sure how. The woman who runs them – the Irish – she's going to be hard to break. Until then, it'll be havoc."

"And do you want to break her?"

"Not sure. She's an odd one though. She's got a lot of power."

"Women like that are hard to find," Rebecca noted. "Out here... even harder... This place... it's a male world really... I am sure a lot of women find it hard to fit in. I admire her."

"Do you fit in?" Francis asked.

She led him up the steps and opened the front door to the Doctor's dwelling.

"Sometimes," she said. "When my opinion is asked for..."

"Sit down," she said. "I'll just get some water and soap..."

Rebecca moved to the kitchen area and Francis observed the inside of the dwelling. Although there was no carpet and the walls were bare, already a few shelves had gone up with lots of books on them.

"And who *doesn't* ask for your opinion?"

"My father..." she shouted back in. "He thinks he always knows best when sometimes he doesn't – not out here at least... and especially with my mother..."

Lots of questions now entered Francis' head.

"What about your mother then?"

There came no response first off, but instead Francis gazed at some of the book titles. When Rebecca came back in, he tried once more.

"What about your mother?"

Rebecca brought the bowl of water over and rested it on a small table next to where he sat. She began to clean his wound by dabbing it with a cloth.

"She's not taken well to it here. The isolation I think. She was used to a busy social life... and now, well, now there is nothing. You know what it's like up here. Out here..."

"If she gives it a while, others will come... They always do."

"Maybe... but my father and I think time is of the essence with her."

"I see."

"I just want to add some iodine," she went.

"You've inherited a few of your father's skills I see."

She squeezed out excess water and blood, and then dabbed the dark orange liquid onto the wound.

"A few. You grow up with it... I thought maybe I'd train... but out here that seems impossible."

"Ow... that's sore."

"It hurts a bit I know... stings, doesn't it? But no, I have decided that out here I would like to be a schoolma'am."

"Really?"

"I think I may well be needed..."

"Maybe," said Francis.

He was thinking about the incursion of the Irish and how the camp might evolve.

"The children will need educating."

"Of course."

"There... Looks better now. We've got the blood off. It might need a couple of stitches. You alright with that?"

"You can do that?"

"Of course. It's one of the first things my father taught me. He had me practice on oranges..."

"Oranges?"

"Yes. Hang on... I'll need some kit from next door. Stay there."

Francis noted her form once more as she opened the front door. He realised he liked her company but figured that a woman of her status, of her education, would never be for him. He wuz literate yes, and he'd completed those metallurgical evening classes at the School of Mines, but even he had to admit that he was stepping into a new realm. She wuz too grand for him. Sometimes men have to realise that. It wuz best sometimes, because women of her rank and status would have needs and desires that he could possibly not provide for her. Es. Best let it go. If you're working-class Cornish, you were used t'that kind of disappointment.

By the time Rebecca had come back in. Francis had decided to look at their library of books.

"Got what I needed... Anything of interest?" she enquired.

"The fairy stories... Lots of them... Legends and so on..."

"My sister mainly. She likes that kind of thing... Always has done."

"But your father? He's a Methodist. I didn' think they liked that kind of thing very much... You know... the only correct story is the one about Christ..."

"Oh... He's not like that... I know some are, but he isn't... In fact, he sees the Christian message in just about everything... He's quite pantheistic."

"So he doesn't mind Mabel reading them?"

"Oh no...Quite the opposite in fact... He says Mr Wesley was very interested in them too..."

"I see. Interesting."

"Come. Never mind the books. Sit down again so I can sew you up. This will help it heal quicker. No chance of any infection then..."

Francis sat down once more and leaned into this young woman. He tilted his head and let her do what she needed to do.

"How is it next door?" Francis asked while she worked.

"My father was at work. I didn't want to interrupt him..."

"No news then..."

"No."

"You have to understand. I don't make a habit of doing such things... I feel awful about what I've done... Ouch."

"I know it'll hurt a bit... One's in... Just the other now."

He could see enough of the needle she was using not to look any further. This close however, he could also sense her breath and smell the perfume she wuz wearing.

"He can't die," said Francis. "Your father can't let that happen..."

"He'll do his best... Internal damage like that... Tricky though. It'll be hard to tell what's been damaged."

"I know," Francis nodded compliantly.

"Stay still for this next bit please... It's a little awkward..."

Francis tried to do what she said.

"I'm glad you're doing this," he offered.

"Why?"

"So we could talk..."

"Ha... really?"

"Yes," said Francis. "You're one of those interesting people that one takes notice of... There aren't many out there. You've noticed that."

"I don't think so."

"Well, I do."

"We'll have to disagree on that then... but there... that's sewn up nicely. You'll have a bit of a scar there... but better than a gaping wound, eh? Come see – in the mirror."

The household had a small mirror installed above the stove. It was nothing special or ornate but it allowed him to see what she'd done. She'd done a good job. One of the sconce candles lit up his face. He could see now how the wound would heal.

"A light bandage maybe? To protect it."

"Very well."

From the pantheon of items she had brought in from the surgery, she produced a thin bandage and began to wrap it around his head. In this, Francis now realised why they'd established a miner's cooperative fund. Such services as this were essential to the community. He understood his own ambition a little more now. Ut wuz all well and good to have such ambitions but ut brought with ut a degree of responsibility that he wuz only now becoming accustomed to.

"I didn' mean fur what happened to have happened. You knaw that, dun't ee Rebecca? I cen't have that fella die on me..."

"I know. I know you never intended it. Sometimes things d'happen Mr Nankervis... that we never want to happen. But happen they do. That is the way of the world..."

"A hateful, disappointing, disingenuous world..."

"Yes... it sometimes seems so..."

"Despite all that we try and do."

"Yes. Sadly. Despite all that we do to make the world a better place."

"You believe me then...?"

"I don't doubt you. I didn't see the fight between you and this man, but I know you are a good man. I can sense it."

"I need you to believe me."

"Why me – above others?"

Francis could not answer that directly. Not now at least.

Maybe she knew however, the pinprick he'd made upon her heart.

"I can tell. You'll come to understand I think, Miss Jewell," he said instead. "You know there is something special about you... ethereal even..."

"Ethereal?"

No one had ever thought of her in that way.

"Yes."

But their conversation could not continue.

Across the darkness of the rest of the room, a triangle of candlelight appeared, as one of the doors opened. Two feet plodded out and the form of a girl appeared. Her unkempt hair fell in tresses over her nightdress.

"Mabel. Go back to sleep. It's only Mr Nankervis and I. He's had a small accident – a cut on the head. There's nothing to worry about. Now, go back to sleep. Why are you up?"

"The forest was speaking to me," she said.

Rebecca gave Francis a puzzled look.

"The forest can't speak my love," said Rebecca. "Not to anyone."

"Well, it can – and it was," argued Mabel.

"It's just the wind and rain... Papa's had to open the surgery. It could be some noise from there..."

"No."

"Come on now. I'll tuck you in..." Rebecca said, hurrying to where her younger sister was standing.

"I'll just..." said Francis, gesturing that he was about to leave and discover what progress was being made next door.

Rebecca took the hand of Mabel and encouraged her to go back to sleep. At the same time, she gestured to Francis that it was fine for him to leave under his own steam. He went out into the night air realising that his wound had been fixed. With this Flannery however, such a solution would not be quite so simple. The Rebecca he had encountered that evening was much more than he had imagined but he was not certain if he should pursue her any further. There was the fact that Jewell was employed by the company and there wuz the added complexity of him being a lay preacher. With any potential courtship with Jewell's daughter, he would surely have to show the Doctor that he was a committed Methodist. He was not sure about his ability to do that. His fighting in the street and causing injuries to that Irishman in the way that he did would not exactly endear him to her father either.

And then this strange younger sister. What had she heard? How was she reading the world? Out there was just nothingness: miles upon miles of fell and forest. Unless... Now what wuz ut that Gourgy had said about his friends out there in the trees?

14

In this land high on the Keweenaw, so ut seemed, everything had the potential to be backsyfore. Es. Francis had gived ol' boy Flannery bell tink and naw mistake. The weather that morning wuz catchy and unsettled. By the time morning eased over the camp, a small body of belligerent Irish and Cornish stood outside of Jewell's small surgery hoping for some good news. However, a fair number had, by now, gone home: the Cornish to their humble shacks and bunkhouses, and the Irish to their newly-erected camp to the East.

Maddy O'Donahue still stood there though: seemingly as grim and determined as ever – waiting fur news on her man inside. Mrs Jewell, who had been woken at the same time as her husband the night before, brought around tay and saffron for anyone who remained, which served as a kind of improvised breakfast. It was food the Irish knew of, and ate only because there was nothing else going, rather than any great like of what wuz being offered. It was a different matter for the Cornish who saw the offering only as comfort food in times of distress or danger.

Apparently, the Doctor had come out earlier in the pre-dawn, and told the crowd gathered that he had determined that the wounds had only apparently punctured some places in Flannery's large intestine which was something of a relief. A urine sample had told him that the man's kidneys had not been damaged, because the fluid contained no blood. Yet still internal puncturing of the intestines was serious. Any digestible material which exited the internal injuries could get into the body's cavity and cause an infection. The wounds outside would probably heal swiftly but these were the least of his worries. A decision now had to be made as to whether the patient might be better served being transported by a laker down to a hospital in Port Huron or Detroit. That journey had to be balanced with the patient's overall health though: there was concern that he'd not make it tha' far.

The reality facing Jewell was that he could either decide to operate to try to repair any internal damage or he could hope and pray that this would naturally heal and that there would be no lasting consequences. Both seemed difficult choices. Although he did not state it overtly for the gathered audience, he barely thought he had enough equipment or experience to carry out an operation of such magnitude up here, in what was still effectively a kind of a shack. The gas supply of anaesthetic he had was hardly enough to keep Flannery under for the duration of such a procedure. However, the decision to send him down to Detroit also seemed impossible. Who, for example, would be able to look after him on board the laker? Probably, he himself could not go. Jewell was aware that this was his big first test as a surgeon, and that whatever decision he made would have lasting consequences. He'd informed the fearsome woman O'Donahue about the difficulties. This might have to be one situation where the Doctor put more of his feyth in God than in science.

At the moment, perhaps he was stalling for time. He'd set up a pump which gave Flannery regular doses of morphine to keep the pain at bay. This sedation also helped him to deal with the wounds. What he tried to do overnight was to try to predict more precisely what the two spikes had pierced inside of the man's body cavity. The deduction that the kidneys had not been touched was important; for up here on the

Keweenaw that factor would surely have meant swift decline – and likely death. In examining the man's torso, he was looking for swelling to see if there was any further internal hemorrhaging but at present, none could be found. In his mind, this was a good outcome, but there was no way he could be sure that there would not be any further problems. Once the man came off sedation, he might still be in terrible pain.

The saving of both Flannery and Doctor Jewell came in a most unexpected way, though, when the company's directors reflected on it after it had happened. The logic was complete, though maybe still somewhat mysterious. Certainly, it had little to do with either a Christian God or traditional science. How it transpired came to be first noticed by Justin and Francis. Justin had joined Francis outside of the surgery, standing there awkwardly with Rosie, though sensibly they'd kept a good distance off from this Maddy and her band. By night, as requested by their humans, Gourgy and Luk had entered the forest, and whilst there, they had spoken to the sprites of the forest. Now at this, Francis' ears naturally picked up, for according to Gourgy, the forest wuz full of a great row over what should be done.

Had such a noise really been heard by this Mabel? Francis did not look at her in the same way again once Gourgy had told him this. This child was clearly sensitive to the will of the forest. It had initially been some of the sprites' will to let this man, this Flannery die up here, but then others had suggested a fix: that they had the power to alter fate, and that maybe this should happen. The problem was that although the Cornish had seemingly fixed their relationship to the forest, the Irish had not: they'd mistakenly camped in one of their most sacred spaces.

That did not go down well, but a life for such a mistake? That seemed too harsh, even by their usual standards. But it had been Luk and Gourgy who had asked for their help, and in so doing thus began a cacophony of dialogue with the sprites of the earth, culminating in them drawing down the Moon Goddess Yolkai. Despite the transgressions of the Irish, Yolkai had agreed that sparing the man's life was the best way forward, and that it may well lead to a desirable outbreak of peace between the Cornish and the Irish. She agreed that in a situation such as this, this was the best solution. At this, those sprites who had been angered acquiesced, realising that maybe she had made a better decision; and at that, they'd set to work and performed the gathering of a remedy as required.

This was because the goddess Yolkai took her light, and poured it down upon distant Nimkii as a bowl of glowing energy. Now Nimkii was distant, far up towards the mountain heights, but had felt the dislocation, and knew he should travel back to New Diggings. Now he had instruction to proceed with lore and medicine. So the gathering was easy for him because the forest knew precisely what herbs and plants he would require. The sprites emerged from their hidey-holes, and stopped the cacophony and, instead of disagreement and disharmony, urgently found what was needed. To each species, a specific task was given. And as Nimkii made his way down the mountain towards the camp, they gave him what he needed. And this wuz precisely what Luk told Francis and Justin.

"Nimkii's coming," he said. "The forest has organized it. It knows what to do."

"The forest?"

"Es," said Gourgy. "The forest will save this Flannery bloak. Nimkii will do it. He will enact its will."

Es. Now all that sounded like a pile of bunkum to this Francis and this Justin, especially when just in the surgery wuz a fully-qualified doctor. However, they'd come to trust their Knockies in ways which they could not possibly describe to anyone else, and so, as bizarre as they knew it to be, they boath realised the truth in what wuz being spoken. No one knew better the natural world than Knockies.

"The deal," said Luk, "is that you should make peace with the Irish. Whatever ill was there from the past, it needs to be cast away. If that happens, then this man will recover..."

"I understand," said Francis and, as it had done several times before in his life, he let the magic do its work. But then again, he had to do so; for he had no other choice. And sometimes, when humans need events beyond normality, then that is just what is required. The job is to not think too much but instead, to just let nature take its course. Older people may call that fate, but Francis knew it to be more than that – as this tale will oft prove.

"We had a meeting," explained Luk, "in the forest near to the doctor's house. People came from all over."

By people, of course, he meant beings undetectable by moast; those who went in the shadows, or passed by the rustling leaves.

"The *poble bean*?" asked Justin.

"Es..."

"You were overheard," said Francis. "The doctor's daughter... Mabel..."

"Bugger. I told them to keep ut down. The wood sprites were giving it welly," said Gourgy. "They got naw volume control: thaas the problem..."

"But they're agreed?"

"Es," said Luk. "There's something about that Maddy too... They love her and they hate she... Apparently, her story ent what you think ut is..."

"How do you knaw?" questioned Justin. He asked because he knew exactly what they meant. He'd felt the very same thing himself.

"It's what we heard. It was what was discussed. You cen't odds ut. They pick up on stuff like that. Call yourself Cornish? You knaw that..."

"When will Nimkii be here then?" asked Francis.

"Cen't say. You knaw what he's like. He's the wind, idn a? 'Tidn' like he's on a core, es ut?"

"He'll be here when he's ready I reckon," said Luk. "When what the forest needs to gather has been gathered."

They were speaking weird these two Knockies of theirs. They weren't normally like this. Something must have happened. The order had altered.

"Ol' doctor idn' going to be very keen though, is a?" stated Justin. "I mean, he's going to be made redundant by a man carrying a bagful of mosses, mushrooms and some wood herbs..."

"He'll understand. He's desperate. He needs Flannery to recover as much as we do."

Justin gave a quick glance over to the party of Irish. No more had been said to this Maddy, but all of them noted the desperation on their faces and on hers.

Suddenly, the mountain seemed to be revealing all kinds of oddities and behaviours to its new residents. Just like them, it was full of secrets. And with that, the man Nimkii was there in the street. Nimkii had no weapons with him, but only a leather bag inta' which clearly the forest's healing plants had been collected. The Irish looked a-feared, worried what this man would do. They suspiciously eyed his lean form and strange, locked hair.

"It's okay," said Justin. "This is Nimkii. We know him, and he's here to help the doctor... with your Mr Flannery. Don't worry now. He's alright. He's got good intentions."

Awnly this kindly Rebecca wuz inside with her father, working on the patient. She had sensed her father's desperation; his feeling that he could do no more with conventional medicine. It was the more diplomatic Trevorrow who had accompanied Nimkii into the surgery. An hour went by before the door of the building opened outwards, and inta' the light stepped a standing Flannery, holding his side but awake and smiling. His colour had returned and from the way he was walking, it was clear that his injuries had been healed. There was recovery still needed yes, but now he'd live. Whatever concoction Nimkii had used had worked fast, and healed him the old way, older than both the Cornish and the Irish.

Trevorrow and Rebecca told them what had happened. Nimkii had gone in and made a compress of herbs and plants. These had been applied to all of the man's wounds. Once this was achieved, then Nimkii had passed healing stones and sticks over the man's torso, meditating and chanting over what he was doing. He got the doctor to remove the morphine drip and then took the man on some kind of shamanistic journey, which in his mind made him think he was flying above the mountain forest.

"I wudn' have believed ut, unless I saw ut with me own eyes," said the Cap'n. "The boy Flannery wuz talking all the while, telling us what he was seeing... he spoke as if he were an eagle,"

"It was incredible," said Rebecca. "I don't think my father has seen anything like it before now... He's learnt something new today. This land can teach him a lot..."

And then, when Nimkii emerged, everyone clapped. But he was a man, who as you know, knows not of fame or the modern concept of ego. He was a man who responded to what was necessary: who enacted upon the will of the forest. And so as silently as he entered, Nimkii left. In a thrice he was at the edge of the forest, and in another, he was lost between the dark tree trunks. Into the void of nature he disappeared once more.

Flannery wuz explaining to the Irish host what had transpired inside, and how remarkable his journey to recovery had been. He was showing them how the ingress and egress wounds were healing over.

This Maddy O'Donahue wuz now over to see the Cornish.

"Sure listen. I'll give y'that one," she said. "You're no sleeven in the way perhaps I had thought. I thought yer Indian would do it arseways but that's not the case at all. I'll work with you. Sure, let's look at it on the morra'..."

She even seemed to smile at this boy Justin.

"Es. We'll have a yap and see what can be done," he said.

She nodded a thank you and commanded her men to move away, taking the recovered Flannery back with them. He'd require some rest back in his tent.

"You played a blinder there," said Trevorrow. "How did you get hold of Nimkii? He's normally a bugger to track down..."

"We sent out some enquiries," offered Francis, pressing down on the heads of Luk and Gourgy.

"Nice work boys," said Trevorrow. "Saffron bun for you pair later on obviously."

That day was an extraordinary one but moast days of late, had been extraordinary in some way. This was only the start of things on Copper Mountain though, for magic would weave its way in and out in other forms too.

Inside the surgery, a shocked Doctor Jewell did not know what he had just witnessed. He would certainly have something to write up in his notes: maybe even contribute a piece to a journal in the future. He had tried to get Trevorrow to ask Nimkii what the compress was made of, but according to the Cap'n this shaman would not offer up its contents. Only one person in the forest knew and that wuz his daughter Mabel. She'd noted everything the forest said, but being the man he wuz, Jewell wudn' about to ask she now, wuz a?

Jewell wuz coming to the same conclusion as Justin and Francis: that this world he had accidentally stumbled upon was indeed a place of rapture and enchantment.

"My dear, I witnessed something extraordinary today," said Doctor Jewell to his wife Clara. "It was the most incredible moment of my entire medical career. I think I need to re-think everything I have ever learnt."

"Good," said Clara nonchalantly. "Amazing what there is here, isn't it?"

She didn' say it then, but something unnatural was pulling at her.

15

There ent naw use in pussivanting round with ut: any storyteller will tell ee tha'. See, there wuz pretty many things goin' on at once by this time. The mine opened up some more and the town around it grew. It is always the way of things. The miners went down a few fathoms and opened up a second level. They extended the ventilation shaft to meet it. The first winze got removed and a more sophisticated cage was put in that lowered miners – four at a time – into the earth. Again, they used mules and horses for energy but, by now, Skews had already put in an order for two steam engines to be imported directly from Cornwall: one would eventually work the cage; the other was to minimise the eventual incursion of water and to pump it to the surface. That order meant the mine wuz now a serious proposition. Such pumps required buildings: engine houses and shears, so that needed to be planned for.

The long track up the mountain from Eagle Harbour got widened. It became a road. People set to, building, developing and enhancing the world that they lived in. Piece-by-piece, and little-by-little, the former camp expanded. The hamlet became a village, and soon, the village began to look more like a town. People were appointed to be in charge of new roles. Particular individuals were enlisted to deal with sewerage; others made the streets better; there wuz even an attempt to install some gas lighting between the saloon and the surgery. Every time the people looked, there was something fresh to consider: some new element of modernity impinging on the ancient side of the mountain. The place became more like a Calumet or a Detroit every day.

The predicted size of the mine and its community grew. The distance from the mine to the edge of the forest expanded. Further areas of woodland were lumbered. Land started to be enclosed. People planted crops that they hoped might emerge in the spring. Women tended to crocus fields. No one mentioned any of this to Nimkii. Perhaps he knew – and perhaps he didn' want to know. Maybe he didn' care. Maybe it had gone beyond all expectations; the way it was with all white men – the way history had taught his people. And here were the pious Cornish once again, colonising the world for their love of precious metals.

At the outset, an accommodation had been agreed, but this now seemed temporal. With more people making their way there, the town had no choice but to expand. A few lakers full of new Cornish workers (inspired by newspaper stories back home) put in to the harbour below, and eventually, they made their long climb to the mine. Unavoidably, copper wuz some draw you. The forest suffered. It witnessed destruction on a scale unheard of. There was a kind of cleansing: a holocaust of sorts. Swathes of it were cut down and that scattered its population. One migration event caused another. Nobody asked the creatures and beings belonging there if they were alright. Nobody sought to check. But that is the way with lore and magic. Everyone assumes it will carry on forever. Nawbody realises how precious ut es, nor how ut needs protecting.

Although in places, the town had a semblance of order, in some areas still, there wuz barren ground, which had been partially dug over and, at one point, might have become a dwelling, an outfitters – or say, even a new blacksmiths; but these, in fact, got abandoned and were left in a sorry state. The biggest change derived from the opening up of the forest wuz the fact that the destruction of the upper canopy brought in more light. For the human populace, this light wuz most welcome for it seemed to alleviate their natural fear of the loneliness of the dark forest, but for others, it sent them scampering into gulleys and ravines, then caves and hollows, where the sun's rays were not so strong. At night, the moonlight of Yolkai lit these new spaces and made new shadows. Even when the town was supposed to be at rest, it was still noisy. The forest could not help but notice.

The wishes of Rebecca Jewell were followed in the late fall. A rectangular schoolhouse was opened, and she took charge of around fifteen pupils aged from four to eleven. The schoolhouse was nothing special, just a timber-built construction on the south-eastern side of the settlement, but it was enough to accommodate them in their learning. Pristine desks and chairs were shipped in to the harbour and loaded on wagons to take up the mountain. When they arrived, it felt like things were really moving forward. Until then, Miss Jewell – as everyone now seemed to call her – sat her pupils on home-made cushions on the floor. But the desks, well, they made it a proper educational establishment. There was ink and exercise books to match the blackboard and chalk. Lessons commenced at nine in the morning and finished at three. A pike-fenced area next to the building gave the children a small playground when pauses in their tuition were made. Their voices made for an aviary of sounds which replicated a memory of village schools from back home. Their yelps, laughter and shouts normalised everything.

Francis and his brother Justin were pleased about this. They realised that not only had they founded a mine and a copper company, but they'd also constructed a community. This Francis, of course, could not help but spend more of his free time with Miss Jewell, and it had been he who had laboured hard when not down the mine to help with the construction of the school. The wound on his head sealed over gradually, and weeks earlier, she had carefully removed the remnants of the stitches with tweezers and a pair of surgical scissors. The scar was not as bad as it could have been. In time, it would fade further and after another summer, it might not be noticeable at all. Their companionship did not go unnoticed in the settlement, least of all by her father, Doctor Jewell. He offered her counsel when she needed it, but knew her will. Rebecca was strong and she had her own mind as to how things should be done. In this world he had brought her to, who else, but this man Francis Nankervis was the best choice for her? He only wished her choice was a little more educated. The miner was bright he felt, but a little ragged around the edges.

It seemed that Justin had his eye on other prizes. He was still as committed to the mine, but he'd struck up a paradoxical kind of dialogue with this Maddy O'Donahue. Once the peace had been negotiated, the bulk of the Irish mucked in, and obtained positions in the mine. They were all hard workers and they actually brought a lot of experience with them too – skills learned on the Beara (maybe from the Cornish once out there); so they fitted in. There were no more brawls. Somehow they got the feeling that where they'd located their first encampment was not the best choice, and so gradually, these men and their Maddy also moved into the town, making up a greatly expanded Irish end to the community. This Maddy had noted that that particular part of the forest was not conducive to their well-being. She'd sensed it. Es. A presence. There wuz more to this Maddy than met the eye. You'll see more ov tha' soon 'nuff.

At first, Justin and she flung insults at each other but there wuz an obvious attraction between them too. Maybe it was a case of two individuals coming to love what they had first hated. But barbed they were, their comments and digs. This Maddy kept herself to herself too. She had command of her men, but she never had any other relationships, not so as Justin could see. There wuz no mention either of anyone at home, of some lost love back in Ireland. Initially, other women in the settlement thought that Maddy purely travelled with her men as their kind of chief bottle-washer, cleaner, and cook, but as time pressed forward, that was clearly not the case. Compared to them, she wuz much more a lady of leisure but she was also an astute business woman. Apparently, she took a cut of the men's wages which allowed her the lifestyle she had. Was she their agent or their true Cap'n? For all intents and purposes, she behaved as if she were a Cap'n. All the while, she kept her power over them, and from what people had seen, they did as they were told. Any compromise – and you were gone. No messing.

Everyone got to see more of her. Although the late fall winds made her dress in thicker clothes and hold her cape a little tighter around her frame, they could see her better and they noted her features. Her hair was fair, and she wore it long: not like the other women of the camp who always kept theirs neat in a bun or tied back. It curled down from her head onto her shoulders and reached down as far as her breasts. It was centre-parted but often held in place by a band of metal that she positioned across the top of her ears. The band of metal seemed to be made of copper itself, and held within it several jewels that some felt were real diamonds, rubies and emeralds, but which others argued were just pretentious costume pieces. No one asked her the truth. It was best not to. It was said that she had a mouth on her like the Devil hisself, and that she could swear like a trooper.

She wore long, calf-length black dresses that were held at the waist by a belt, and it was around these that she hung her shawl and cloak. These two items were pinned together over her heart. Although she sometimes wore a pair of intricately painted boots (it seemed to be the only pair she had), she often went without them and walked barefoot around the camp and into the forest. In reality, she did not walk, but instead, crept through, always as if on a mission towards some greater knowledge. Because of her ways and her sometimes scalding tongue, the other women, although outwardly polite to her, gave her distance. She was not their type. The one place she never entered again was Rosie's saloon, and so it was said, this Maddy made her own liquor. People speculated much over her origins: was she some kind of Irish Queen, or was she just a plain gypsy? Whatever they thought, it wuz clear she knew well the ways of working the mines. Many wuz the time she went down in the cage to see how work was progressing. It wuz then that she wore her decorated boots, washing them clean the moment she was back up t'grass.

Es. She wuz a piece of work this O'Donahue. And her blue eyes pierced through everything – perhaps even copper itself. Certainly her gaze had found its way into Justin, and he often gazed back. He'd not seen such a woman before, and despite how she treated him, he liked her for it. Perhaps she recognised the rascal in him and that she and he were of like minds, even despite their different heritage. Francis had less to do with her. There was something about her, he said, that didn' quite fit; that made him cautionary, despite her knawing the ground and knawing copper. He then understood though, why the Irish had been so successful initially in extracting ore from the old mine. She had a keen sense of it.

During this time, she also looked after old Flannery, who though recovered from his injury, made the moast of a bit of time off. Their relationship wuz curious too, but no one asked about it. What was the fella? He seemed a kind of father-figure to she, but on the other hand, she sometimes acted as if she were a mother to him too. There was a story there but no one could chase it down. No one dared ask, not even this Justin. One day though, he'd get her on her own – and when enough drink had been downed by the pair ov them, then he'd ask. He'd find out the truth. Maybe Gourgy or Luk would have a hand in it. He didn' think she could see them two, but she gave away little, so Justin warned them both to be careful at what they revealed.

There wuz one more important thing that everyone noticed about this Maddy O'Donahue. Around her neck was a long necklace that when she wore it, rested four loops on the upper part of her chest; the lower loop the longest, and which fell on the curve of her breasts. She touched this necklace often – feeling it for comfort seemingly – and with it maybe conjuring up some memory of the past. The necklace wudn' nothing ordinary neither – for it was made of sea shells – each one in the run of them selected for its specific shape, and maybe its specific qualities. Justin imagined her picking them up on a lonely beach somewhere on the Beara. Sometimes they jangled as she padded towards people. Sometimes, the sounds of the ocean were heard by the ears in the forest and they delighted at its sound. It was something they'd not heard before now.

Some humans of the camp these forest dwellers did not bother to watch (because they were unimaginative or dull) but she was different. Whenever she moved, they kept their eyes on her. She was special, that one; a bit like the girl Mabel, who they also noticed. Maybe it wuz because both of them 'believed' still. Es. Perhaps that wuz it. So this Maddy: well, she had human followers, but she was tracked by the little people of the forest too. Two worlds were watching her then.

Another person watched Maddy O'Donahue almost as closely as those in the forest. This was that beauty named Rosie Koskinen. They wuz naw love lost between these two – aw naw. And the reason fur that wuz becoming obvious to those keeping an eye on things. Despite her trade, this Rosie felt some yearning still fur Justin Nankervis, and she cudn' quite let un go. Es, the man, to be honest, was proper useless: a waster of the first order, who could barely get out of bed in the morning; but still, she kept a flame burning fur'n. Somehow, maybe, one day, he would realise who she wuz and he'd be enlightened that there wuz something good in them being together. But in naw way had this Justin been close to she, not for a long while, and so she took in other trade. Well, 'twas necessary work wudn' ut? – and somethun' wuz needed to pay the bills up on the mountain.

Maybe in her mind, she wuz trying to make un jealous, to make him want her even more. She hated the bastard some days but when she saw un' come up from underground caked in dirt, or when she observed him out and about, she cudn' help but crave after un. Either way though, her plan had failed, and now this Cussie spent more ov his time yipping up to that Maddy than she. Now jealousy's a bad thing as you know, but jealousy between two women is even worse. One of these days though, Rosie told herself; and then she'd peer into the mirror in her room, and wonder where it had all gone wrong. That Maddy knew ut too. She comed to see how this whore felt about Justin and she knew the power she gained from that knowledge. And Maddy

O'Donahue being Maddy O'Donahue, she lapped ut up – and gently touched her seashell necklace. Some days, although the men had seemingly stopped brawling, these pair might still set to.

None of this went un-nawticed by Trevorrow and Skews. These pair kept the mine pushing forward, knowing that (despite the on-coming season) the sap was rising in both this Francis and this Justin. Well, they were young men – and that is what young men did. Sap rises. They think of women and their bodies. They thought back and realised they had been there themselves, a long time ago. Of course, Trevorrow realised he was getting *that* bit older, and he was not much looking forward to the coming winter. He was glad the cage had gone in, because going down in the bucket or ladder wuz no longer pleasurable to him. The rheumatism in his knees (derived from years of constantly kneeling in the wet levels and checking over men's drilling) had started to become painful.

Trevorrow full well knew this wuz the last mine he would ever work. One time, he'd dreamed that he and Mrs Cap'n would take their savings and head back to Cornwall, and buy a small place (a rosebush-framed cottage) back in their home town of St Day, but of late, he'd realised that that wudn' ever goin' t'appen. He and she knew that there wudn' naw goin' back now. They'd be buried here. They'd become as much people of the Keweenaw now as those who'd been born here. Maybe this wuz why Mrs Cap'n didn' say a lot. She knew the failure. She was doomed t' pastry, turnip, yeast and saffron. Es, ee'd be ending his career with this place, which he knawed was bringing up goodly ore. That time wudn' yet, leastways he reckoned so.

Trevorrow and Skews had a notion of this O'Donahue maid too. They recognised her power; knew that she had some clout. Maybe she'd muscle in more than she wuz wanted. They cudn' make she out though. She wuz a sort ov woman they'd not encountered before – not back home or out here on the mining frontier. At least she'd been quieter about the uselessness of Cousin Jacks; now that her boys had got jobs within the mine. All that need watching too, for despite her silence, ut still seemed to lurk under the surface of her, and as everyone knawed, she was a dark pool, tha' one.

Now, Skewsy was profiteering from the mine's expansion in every way that he could. Anywhere there wuz money to be made, his thin face would be found. There was an old Cornish expression that went those who cen't schemey must *lowster*. *Lowster* meant hard work and Skews wudn' keen on that. Therefore with ee, ut wuz a case of those who cen't *lowster* must schemey – and to scheme wuz what Skews did best. His latest mad notion wuz to enquire about the possibilities of setting up a mineral tramway down to the harbour, so that even more tonnage could be shifted down there. The roadway wuz an inefficient way of getting ore down to the port, and he was thinking through various options of what might be done. It irked him that the mine was producing well but could not get enough ore down to the port to be processed.

There was clearly demand enough coming up from Detroit – and then there wuz all that new talk about the motor carriage industry down there. Copper wudn' be going out of a fashion when that stepped up. Brass an' electrics wuz all the rage. He'd managed to get the price back up now to where ut wuz, with New Diggings dominating the market on the tip of the Keweenaw. And sadly, in all of this, Skews almost forgot why he had first come out to the peninsula. He'd lost memory of what his wife and his family looked like. And that loss is a terrible fate for any man to endure. But as wuz his way, he did not speak about it to anyone, for he did not want them to know his weakness. He needed to keep that secret for now. He had other secrets too this boy – things you did not want to know. The thing though, is that secrets like that can't stay shut in, but more of that is to come, alongside the continual drilling and blasting of this mountain. Aw es. Only two levels have gone in so far. More will come, sure 'nuff.

In all of this, Doctor Jewell wrote up the extraordinary healing he had seen with this man they called Nimkii, and from the Nankervis brothers and Mr Trevorrow he learnt as much as he could about him. The procedure intrigued him for weeks, and between dealing with the minor ailments and injuries of the populace, he made it his business to try and learn about the herbal lore of these Indians. The task was not easy however, and even when he wrote to a bookshop in Detroit, asking for studies or anthropological accounts, he was told there wuz very little on it. It remained hidden; perhaps purposefully so, though he knew in his heart that conventional medicine could learn much from its approach. If only he could speak more with the individual concerned.

All went well for him – and he continued his services on Sunday at the preaching pit on the hillside. Realising that miners had no time for ranters he kept his services focused, and noted the approval given whenever he mentioned the protection of the good Lord underground. He'd tried to tap up Trevorrow and Skews for some money for the chapel building, but at this time, that was not forthcoming. Besides, he saw the benefit of what they had done so far, and indeed the schoolhouse was a major achievement, from which his own daughter had directly benefitted. He knew fully the problem: in order to build a chapel, substantial monies needed to be raised, and at the moment he was not sure where they would be coming from. Miners had other priorities. A lot of wages went on simply surviving and then sending back to starving families in the collapsed mines and communities of Cornwall.

Nonetheless, everything here was all about improvement and betterment: core values of the modern world. An ancillary issue was now that more Irish had moved in, they craved not Methodist services but something rather different. Indeed, he thought O'Donahue and her crew might begin some Catholic services but these did not pan out in the way that he thought. In fact, her crowd seemed decidedly sceptical of any form of organised religion. Whilst the Cornish seemed an improbable mixture of superstition and religion, these Irish carried the superstition, but seemed to say that although they had faith in God, God no longer had faith in them.

Yet things went well for this man, and so, surely and slowly his legacy and empire grew. All wuz as it should be. But that wuz just the surface. Underneath, lurked something else. That something else lay in his wife, who – to be frank – he had privately been concerned about for some time. Of late, she had seemed to be better. Certainly outwardly, she gave the impression of now accepting the world they were in and that she was coping well with it. But that kept altering and shifting – just like the landscape around them. One day, it shifted a lot. In fact, it was as if a fuse went off in her brain. See, this Clara had something in her mind and she would not let it go. So, whilst her husband was working, without knowing, without thinking of Wes-ley and morality, she left a newly-changed liddle James alone on the table, and opened the back door. She wrapped a bonnet around her head: a clean, white one that she had recently obtained from one of the bal-maidens, a woman named Sal Clemo. In this weather, this wuz just the item to wear: not too hot but enough to shield her hair from any light rain. She'd worn one a lot of late, almost in allegiance with the working women of the community.

Outside, a garden had been cleared for them, but no fencing had yet been erected. In seconds, she steadily walked to the end of it – almost as if she were floating on the heads of the grasses that had seeded there. Now she could pass into another world. She needed to. First of all, she put her hand into the forest, and noted the change of light on her forearm. A dappled energy fell onto it, and in the breeze, the shadows of branches and leaves danced on her skin. She liked the feel of it out there. There was a mystic smell to the forest which had taunted her for months on their arrival here. At first, she could not identify it, but daily living had made her both understand and crave it. At that moment, she was between worlds, but she did not like that, or want that any more. Something had to end here.

It gave her great satisfaction then to place one leg in front of the other and more fully move her body into the space between the trees. It was not like she could stop it. She looked ahead at the gaps between the trunks. At first, they were light and airy but as the forest became denser the gaps narrowed, until no light could be seen at all ahead of her. She liked that blackness – that unadulterated blackness. It was where she was heading. She could not stop herself, as seemingly, some force was yanking her in. Now she could learn about the forest. It had called her. The white pines beckoned her into them. She touched the sugar maples that bent down and caressed her. Prince Aspen and Princess Spruce all bowed to her. She reached down and smelt the flower heads of yellow violets, trout lillies, and trilliums. Her clothes accidentally spread the woolly hairs of pitcher's thistle and caught traces of red clover.

In this heady vegetation moved many creatures. She saw them all now. Whereas before, there had been glimpses – convivial sightings of this strange world – now, that altered. She became suddenly alert to a trail of porcupines and their younglings who walked down the hill-side. Some distance in, and beside an upland river, she saw beavers at work. On a lake, there wuz the sight of a trio of trumpeter swans. She followed the occasional butterfly. Then, she observed the croaking frogs in the river system and saw small, nimble, climbing toads on trees. High in the canopy called and cackled hundreds of birds, and in the night-time – which seemed to her, to come and go in mere seconds – flittered bats and owls. Grouse were disturbed as she walked through, but from their guttural cries she recognised they were not scared of her. Rabbits, pine martins, foxes and squirrels all noticed her, pricking up at her presence.

"Who was she?" they asked.

She wuz not ov they.

She had visions as she walked. In her mind, her almost Puritanical black dress no longer caught on the thorns or brambles of the forest floor and, as if on the cover of some flouncy New York fashion magazine, she was pulling a herd of animals; only they weren't a herd. Instead, they were birds: iridescent blue jays, each on leads with collars, and each obeying her command. She strutted as they strutted. She sang the same way they did, and when she echoed them, she felt whole again. She made her way as a dart of blue between dark bark and black bush. The blue jays were not flighty and obeyed her. They cooed at every word, and in turn, their colour soothed her. Cerulean feathers were everywhere now: a colour she had forgotten. And when she walked with them, her hands turned azure; her eyes transformed into sapphires (all her prior dullness now gone). This was perhaps the way all this talk of copper came out in her.

Es. The forest made her feel this way. There was not isolation here but in fact, glorious company: a brand new world. Wouldn't the girls love this? She knew that Rebecca would be intrigued, but Mabel would be the more delighted of the two: her dear, dear girls. She felt that James too, would be carried along by it in a basket woven from sticks, moss and lichens. She longed for them to see, like she had for a while now. But perhaps it was best now, that they were left behind: just like how it had been when she left. Es. That wuz best. And George too: she didn' need him now.

And then, when that dream dissipated, ahead of her there stood a tall stag. He was a magnificent creature; with a golden coat that was partially lit by the sun appearing in a clearing in the forest. Its antlers stretched skywards like huge branches on a tree, all out of proportion with the animal's body. Yet it maintained its glory; its intensity and grandeur and it looked at her unblinking, an utterly magnificent exemplar of nature. And on the twin sweeping curves of this creature's antlers sat a murder of crows, but they were not cawing or croaking. Instead, they were as serene at the stag itself. The tops of the antlers curved in, making a complete circle. The beast and the birds seemed to have been waiting for her for a long time: and when it turned and stepped away into the mist, she knew she must follow it. There, she came to a space where she knew she had to be – and then the forest enveloped her. All the while, she had been followed by those of the forest who, intrigued at what they saw, gossiped and yipped on about her.

And when later on that day, Doctor Jewell finally found his shaking son abandoned in the kitchen of their dwelling, he instantly knew what had happened. He searched for her high and low in the house. He stumbled around the township shouting out her name. And then, when people saw his distress they asked him what wuz wrong. And he tried to answer them, but he could barely say what he needed to, because he knew the dull awfulness of it; he knew that inside his wife lurked an unbearable instability which had been accentuated by their time here – and that she was enduring what psychiatrists in New York and Chicago would label a psychosis. He didn' want to label it in that way though because he knew precisely what that meant. He knew what would become of her, but also himself – and their children. In the end, when the Knockies Gourgy and Luk saw him failing in this way, they ran over to tell Francis and Justin.

When they stopped him from shaking and tried to get him to speak, all he could say was this, "It's Clara. She's gone into the forest... and she hasn't come back... I don't think she ever wants to come back. I knew it..."

His words put a new spin on everything. Clearly everyone needed to take a long walk in the woods to try and find her. With his trembling voice, the impression the Doctor gave though, was that she never wanted to be found again.

16

Knaw her did ee? What do ee do when someone disappears inta' thousands of acres ov woods? You morbidly search – but from the outset you knaw the invalidity of doing so, because in your mind you have already calculated the trajectories. You have mentally placed down trigonometry on the gloomy landscape and have noted all of the possible angles, and parabolas that Mrs Jewell could take. See, this was an unmapped world: one where the forest had seen only a little of the presence of humanity. It was raw, wild and impenetrable. From the forest sprouted the fantastic and the macabre. Anyone who walked its thousands of avenues realised it took them beyond their normal selves.

For those at New Diggings, the forest was also representative of all that was unknown: in it, there might be dragons, or other creatures (wolves, bears and the still undiscovered) that could rip the frail figure of Clara apart. No one wuz about to say that, but they certainly thought it. How could they not though? The Cornish, the Irish, the Finns, the Swedes, the Germans – were all deeply superstitious peoples – who responded to signs and signals. They saw tokens everywhere. They could observe layers in the landscape that others might miss. But were the clues comin'? Naw, they wudn'. The terror remained then.

Those who had Knockies or their magical equivalents sent them out to seek her. This was a quest that was not necessarily a happy one for them because such creatures preferred the confines of underground. Indeed, all of the Cornish Knockies went into the mine and consulted the ground itself; for, as was common knowledge, it could speak to them. Maybe it would sense the movement of this Clara above, and send it back down into the rock: a kind of reverse dowsing, where the tremors above would talk to the earth below. But although the Knockies listened hard, nothing came forth. All they noted was silence.

The truth, though hard to swallow, is that if someone does not want to be found, then they can disappear. It is the journey both to and from those points that is hard to bear. Doctor Jewell was beside himself, and although he did not say it, inside hisself, he contemplated how he had known for a while that his wife had stepped away from reality. She had cooked and cleaned and been the other half of his marital world, but at the same time, he knew of the distance between them. He concluded that, for a long while now, she had not been real. She had been almost a photograph of herself that was no longer three-dimensional. She'd already become a ghost – a resident of the spirit world. For him, she had born his children but now she represented decay and madness.

What had brought about this occurrence, in truth, he did not understand. But in part, he blamed his own ambition, his dismissal of her fears, his knowledge that she missed the social world of their previous life. He knew too, that she feared for their daughters and their son. What kind of life were they to have up here on the Keweenaw? was a core question for her. He realised he'd not given her attention enough. He'd become arrogant and now was paying the price. Sat on a chair in his home, he cradled his son; the being, the creature, the wonder that she had left behind, and that – through God's will – they'd made. He had read about such abandonment before in his medical studies, but this did not alter the fact that a woman's leaving of her own baby seemed outlandish and desperate. He even feared some kind of curse.

Briefly, as he had shouted for help in the settlement, he had even considered whether his Clara had left with someone else. Had she taken a shine to some Finnish miner and run off with him? But he dismissed that. He knew her loyalty: he thought he knew her Christian belief. She had been a stalwart of their square-set Wesleyan chapel back home, and indeed here, in their forest-formed preaching pit. How did her disappearance and her abandonment of her family connect with those principles of faith? Of course, on top of this, he stepped outside of himself to observe how the community would judge him. The man was supposedly a Doctor. What macabre act had he done to her to make her leave? Not only that, but a lay preacher too. He knew their doubts, and knew what dark discussions would be had over coffee pots on stoves.

"Where's Mam?" Mabel had asked, trembling slightly. He knew that question had been coming. Rebecca had brought her back home from the schoolhouse.

He did not know how to answer her. He knew not what to say. It wuz Rebecca who had to take over, and give her sibling a response.

"She's gone for a bit. For a walk in the forest."

"She didn' say she was going though."

"Didn't she? Sometimes adults are like that," but when she made this excuse for her mother, it felt like an abominable lie on Rebecca's part.

She quickly absorbed the situation and made a cup of hot tea for her father but in her heart, she knew that their mother had not been well for a while. It was she who had taken over much of the duty of care of her sister, and also assisted her mother with James. But her wandering off: it somehow was not so unexpected to the older daughter. In her mind, she had wondered intensely about her mother's relationship to the settlement and how it was growing and developing.

Maybe she was conflicted and could not take the imposition of grotesque industry on this place. Maybe the forest was luring her away from it, and she simply complied. The whole emotional upheaval of their long migration had also unnerved her. You had to be strong to survive (like that annoying Maddy woman) and maybe her mother did not have the strength for the new world. It was a sad realisation, but she had to contemplate it. She had all of these thoughts whilst she dealt with her father and her sister.

"I should get out there really," said Doctor Jewell. "I need to be seen to make an effort to find her. I can't just rely on other people."

"No," insisted Rebecca. "You are best off here. I don't need *another* parent heading out there too. Think about that please. Besides that, the whole of the camp are looking for her. They've fanned out all around, to see if she can be found. Even the mine's stopped working."

In the recess of a cupboard in the kitchen, Rebecca tried to find some food for her father and sister. All she could initially find, however, was a rusting tin box, containing some saffron buns that were by now, a few days old. She considered them for a moment, thinking that the food might offer them comfort, but in the end, their placing before her father and sister might only offer them more heartache. Instead, she opened the back door (the one that had been shut by her father when he'd found his wife gone), gathered up the buns, and broke them into pieces.

She threw this cakey-trade onto the earth. Her mother had a habit of doing this, and the local birds would soon flock to the crumbs and be off with them in their beaks. Crows and blue jays came most often. Instead of the buns, she brought in some ginger biscuits which had less of a physical connection to her mother, and although hard to the bite, seemed a more sensitive option. She brought the biscuits back into the main room of the house; her father sitting on the chair where she had previously dressed and stitched the wound on Francis Nankervis' forehead.

She made polite and positive conversation with her father, even though her mind was filled with a memory of her mother at a tea-treat when she was Mabel's age. There being no physical table, her mother had adapted what they had to suit the need of the anniversary gathering at their local chapel. She had taken an old bed-sheet and placed that on the ground. Upon it, she laid down the fresh tea-treat buns, and the children formed a queue to be given their treat. Rebecca had to dismiss that now though because if that memory continued, she knew that she would cry.

Mabel had picked up on the solemn atmosphere.

"Will Mammy be back soon?" she asked, a question that was both natural and grotesque.

"Yes," said Rebecca. "Very soon, I'm sure."

But when she said that, this older daughter thought she should better qualify what she had said.

"And if she doesn't come back today, she'll be thinking of you Mabel... of me... and Daddy... and James. You can be sure of that."

When the words came out though, they did not sound very secure. Mabel could tell that from her sister's tone.

"Why didn't Mammy say goodbye?"

"I don't know... Daddy and I think she was in a bit of a hurry..."

That too, did not sound very convincing but Mabel continued to sit on the floor next to them. Her father at least, seemed to be taking some comfort from rocking his young son to sleep. Babies were untouchable in such circumstances.

"What's that you're playing with?" asked Rebecca intrigued at her sister's creativity. "I've not seen that little poppet before."

Her sister was moving a doll towards a set of wooden animals in some quasi-fantasy world.

"Is it new? It looks new..."

"Yes," she said.

"Where did you get that then?"

Rebecca knew that such dolls were hard to obtain; especially one so well made as the one she was playing with.

"She's a piskie," announced Mabel proudly, "and this is her farm..."

Dolls were made for children in the camp. She'd seen them in the schoolhouse but usually they were just standard joanies: off-cuts of wood that carpenters shaped into the form of people and painted in bright colours. This was no joanie though.

"Did Daddy get it for you?" Rebecca asked. "It's nice. I bet there's no other girl in the camp here who has a doll like that."

"No," said Mabel. "There isn't."

Her definite knowledge of this slightly alarmed Rebecca though. There was something odd about the way she said it. Temporarily, she forgot about her mother's wandering off into the forest, and instead, focused in on her sister.

"How do you know?"

"I was told so."

"By whom?"

"Mr Skews said..."

"Mr Skews?! How does he know?"

At first, her sister seemed reluctant to answer the question. She carried on bobbing the piskie towards a wooden cow and horse.

"He told me."

"Did he? What did he say?"

"He told me that this doll was expensive and that no other girl here would have one. And that I'd have to look after it..."

This was news indeed.

"Did he give it to you then?"

"Yes," Mabel replied, still distracted by her imaginary play. "It was a present."

"What did he say?"

Mabel did not answer at first, and this annoyed Rebecca. In the end, she reached down and used her hand to turn her young sister's body towards her. Now she could see Mabel's face. She asked the question again. This time, there was an answer.

"He said that I was special and that this doll was for me because I was special."

"When did he say this to you?"

Mabel shook her head.

"I dunno," she responded in the way that children do, when they have such little sense of time.

Rebecca sat back. She was not aware that this Mr Skews and her sister had become so close. What was their connection? Why had he gone over and above, to supply this poppet to her? Something was not right here, and she needed to investigate.

"I's nice, isn't it?" said Mabel holding the doll up. "I love it. It means I can make up loads of stories..."

"Yes," responded her older sister. "But you're too old for dolls now."

She could not help but ruminate on what Mabel and said, and in her mind, there was an inescapable thought that her mother's disappearance might even have had something to do with the new information that Mabel had released. For a few moments she contemplated it, smiling at the imaginary world on the floor that her sister was creating. She also watched her father, now absorbed with his son, but still she decided to say something. She turned to him.

"Did you know that...?" but before she could continue her comment, there was a solid knock at the door of their property.

The shock that it gave brought her father back into a world of terrified insecurity and pain. She left her sister and went across the room to open the front door.

Standing there wuz a somewhat breathless Francis Nankervis.

"Thought I'd come over and give you a report," he said.

"Of course," said Rebecca, gesturing for him to enter the house.

Francis stamped his feet to make sure that any hardened mud from the mine fell off his boots.

"Doctor Jewell," he said, nodding a greeting to her father.

"What have you found?" he asked tentatively. "Any clues?"

"Well, we've scanned two miles outwards from the camp. We've gone up the mountain almost to the top of it... The higher-most fells. Nothing there. We've gone southwards, mainly because that looked like the direction she went in... but we've discovered nothing so far. The Irish have moved further to the west now, while the Cornish and the Finns have taken a more easterly route. We went below too – just in case – but no one's seen her. I'm sorry..."

"Thank you Mr Nankervis," said her father. "Your efforts are greatly appreciated. Indeed, I am so very thankful to everyone..."

"Justin and the O'Donahue woman have gone on a straight line from here. I've not heard back from them yet."

"I see."

"The problem is that there is no trail..."

"Perhaps our friend Mr Nimkii?"

"Cap'n Trevorrow said the same thing, but no one's seen him since all of that business with Flannery – and you know better than anyone else what he's like... Aw... only thing wuz that the Swedes spotted a lot of deer on the move... but I don't know if that's significant or no. A geht stag with them..."

"Just the normal migratory course of nature that... by the sound of it," said the Doctor, employing his usual logic.

"I wish we had some better news for you. I really do..."

"Thank you for everything you've done. We appreciate it, don't we father?"

She nudged him into a response.

"Of course, my dear. Yes."

"We're worried about night-fall," said Francis. "It gets cold out there at this time of year... Not sure what your mother had on."

"We know," said Rebecca, as if the obvious did not need to be stated. "Not much I think. Her coat's still here."

Desperate for something more positive, Francis quipped, "Rosie's got the saloon open... for the men coming back... a hot tod for anybody who needs it."

"That's appreciated..."

"I know people are praying for her," Francis said.

This comforted Doctor Jewell, and he sat down once more.

Rebecca moved closer to Francis. She noted his sweat.

"Is there really nothing more? Not even a trace," she whispered.

"No. Nothing, I wish there was, but really, we've so little to go on."

"How is he really?"

"Resigned to it..."

Francis wusn't sure whether he should ask her a burning question he had, but for the sake of the camp, he knew he needed to.

"Really Rebecca, I don't like to ask this... but wuz there anything wrong with her?" he questioned.

Rebecca encouraged him outside onto the porch.

"I don't think my mother was herself. I mean, if I am honest, I don't think she'd been herself for a while."

"I see. I mean, I understand..."

"This place... The Keweenaw... it scared her... somehow."

There wuz much in Rebecca's words. From the rear of the dwelling came the noise of birds.

"Damned crows," went Francis.

"I know. They fight the blue jays sometimes. I put out some stale baked goods earlier... to feed them..."

The staccato of their conversation somehow seemed awkward: as if they were drilling unrelenting rock.

"I wish I could do more," he said. "Truth is, I don't know what to do."

"Me neither."

"You don't need to keep up a front with me," he said, trying to scrutinize her.

"How do you mean?"

"I can tell... You're being strong for everyone."

"I have to."

"I'm here," said Francis. "If you need to talk..."

"I know..."

She was peeling herself away from him, back into the house.

"I do need to ask you something... But not here... Not now."

Both of them caught a connection in that. A trust... if you will: a new acknowledgment. He'd wait for her to come to him with this request.

"You know where I am Miss Jewell."

"Of course."

"Good."

"I know."

"I'll be off then..."

"Yes."

Francis turned to go.

"You are a good man," said Rebecca. "I want you to know that."

In other circumstances, he'd ask her to walk with him: for them to continue the search, but he knew the lateness of the hour. He knew what immediate responsibilities she faced.

"Be seeing you then."

"Yes."

And in this new world then, this was still how convention, es, convention, and Methodism, dictated the run of things. She went back into the still of the house and Francis made his way down to the saloon. There, he was bound to find Gourgy and Luk.

As well as these pairings back in the camp, Maddy and Justin found themselves searching together: following a straight ley-line from the Jewell's backdoor. Es. Although the pair had initially flirted and made suggestive and playful comments, there still seemed a jostling for control between them, even though it never needed to be that way. But such are the ways of people, and so too, the wiles of women and men up on the Keweenaw. As they made their way through the imagined space that this Clara Jewell had formerly walked through, the pair kept the barbs and humour coming, but gradually, this Maddy revealed a little more of herself to him.

"Ha. You Cornish, you're just a bunch of lazy bastards really, aren't ye though? I mean, you employ my people to do all the graft don't cha – while you all stand around talking about the best way t'tackle a job, stuffing yer fat mouths full of saffron and hog's pudding. It was the same on the Beara... I remember it well..."

"What do you remember? Tell me. I'm interested... genuinely. "

"Really? Well. Swarms of yous coming in, and swamping the place... Full it wuz – all the way along the cliffs at Allihies with you lot in tents and shacks. My family used to speak about the first mine at Dooneen: that's where your crew first came in. And then well, you was multiplying like fookin' rabbits all over Knockgour. Then up the Mountain Mine, you took over that place. No room fur they (like me) that had grown up there and knew the land... a right battering we had, all told."

"But we made it what it was, surely?" prompted Justin. "If us Cussies hadn' gone in, then you'd have had nawthun'..."

"We knew enough by then. How do you think I learnt? We could have done ut ourselves... nei problem."

"With you as Cap'n?"

"'Course," she smiled. "I was better than all the boys out there. Thaas partly why I'm here now. I've done my time in the earth."

"How come?"

"Got the magic touch," she said.

"You allays play your cards close to your chest..." stated Justin, eyeing up her form. "'Tis hard to tell what you'm thinking."

"Maybe I like it that way," she said seductively. "And maybe you like it better that way too... If there was no mystery about me, sure enough you'd be gone into the hills like the Doctor's wife... or you Cornish when your luck runs out."

"Maybe not," comment Justin. "Maybe I'd like to know the truth..."

"How do you mean?"

"Well, there's your bloak Flannery fur a start. What's the deal between you and him then? You like an older man, do ee?"

"Ha!" she laughed. "To be sure, Flannery's not my lover. He's not my type. Ha. Besides..."

"Besides what?"

She paused for a while, thinking carefully about what she was about to tell him. How much did she really to reveal to this man who a few weeks ago had lamped her one in the jaw.

"My ma's dead now. She worked the Beara mines all her life. A-cobbing. What do you call it again? A bal-maid. Aye, that she was. Well, my mother had me – and then, when I wuz on the way, this Flannery and she shacked up together now."

"So, he's your step-feyther then? That the deal, es ut?"

"Kind've I suppose... A kind of protector like... and he protected my mother too, after..."

She stopped her tale once more. After what? This was obviously an area she didn' much want to talk about. Justin felt it best to stay silent. He gazed out over the open stillness of the forest, admiring the collective radiance of the deciduous leaves: their golds, reds and oranges. Copper, it seemed, was above them as they walked onwards; and also below: for the floor of the forest was strewn with leaves carrying the same tones.

"And your feyther?"

"Gone... Buggered off."

"Before you were born?"

"Aye. Long before that... It was Flannery who saw my mother through my birth and so on... A wise woman, she wuz. Knew how to pick a good man... I know your brother hit un hard – but he's alright."

"I see."

Then, she blurted out her darkness.

"My father was Cornish..."

This came as a surprise. But there: she'd released it. She'd given ut breath.

"But your surname? O'Donahue? That's not Cornish..."

"No. See, well now, I took my mother's name. The O'Donahues are a big family on the Beara... it seemed the right thing to do."

Justin let her carry on. Despite the distraction of the conversation, they'd managed to go into the heart of the forest, but there wuz still no sight of Clara Jewell. It was as if she had been simply swept up into the misty air.

"Almost the first thing I remember," Maddy said, "were the engine houses... their stacks spouting smoke into the sky. The continual jarring and rattling – all the while like the earth was being shaken and hollowed to death..."

"It'll be like that here soon." offered Justin, "if Skews has his way."

"Comforting though, I suppose," said Maddy. "Maybe that's why I was drawn here."

"So you grew up with it?"

"Aye. Sort of. The mines weren't the only thing y'understand. I did my bit as a girl... and then, a bit of farming. Later, I took to the sea, fishing for crabs and lobsters... I remember the songs we used to sing back there... I can hear my mother's voice..."

Justin gestured for her to sing.

"Go on..."

Maddy responded by singing.

"'Twas opened by four Cornish men," she began, and then more confidently, "Again you'll find I am true.

But then the old Berehaven boys

Of mining little knew.

And when it progressed rapidly

With prospects fair indeed,

It was opened by the Pengellys

and managed by John Reed."

With her light voice, the ballad spread out across the forest and fell onto its damp leaves. In gulleys and hillocks, the forest people listened to her. She was special, this one. Her voice made her sound angelic, or perhaps angelic was wrong. It was less heavenly and more to do with the soul of the earth.

"Do you know any more?"

"I did, but I'd have to think about it. Write it down perhaps... I remember it because my ma used to sing it to me to go to sleep... It was a drinking song really but she altered it to a lullaby. That's just the way she was."

"Beautiful," said Justin.

"Aye, if you're tone deaf," argued Maddy laughing "Come on... let's push on... Maybe she'll be on the other side of this ridge..."

Maddy began striding away from him, and made good progress up the rocky incline.

"You didn' say who your father was..." observed Justin.

"Didn' I? Oh well, that's because I never met him..."

"Oh."

"You said he was Cornish though..."

"Aye. One of the Pengelly's... the 'heir' to the empire..."

Justin digested this information.

"What become of him then?" he had to ask.

"Dun't knaw. Won't ever knaw I reckon."

Her voice began to falter slightly. Up until now, it had been strong and cohesive. But then, in those words, she crumpled and, momentarily, let down her guard. It would be a fleeting moment and Justin knew he would need to grab the opportunity. In an instant, he imagined her thoughts: he could picture this world she grew up in; the mines trailing down to the Atlantic from the moorland, on the very edge of cliffs, just the same as his experience back home. He made a gentle reach to hold her waist. It was a move that he did not anticipate doing; neither was it a romantic move he had made intentionally. It was an act of care and it emanated from him as naturally as the growth of the forest around them. She did not push him away and neither did his movement shock her.

"He didn' treat my mother well..." she gabbled, her tone more serious.

Perhaps at this point, Justin now understood her reaction to the Cornish. All of them had been tarred with the same brush.

"We're not all bad," he offered in defence.

"No," she said. "I know... I shouldn't judge... shouldn't make judgements. I hate it when people do it about the Irish, so how have I the right to do it about your people? I mustn't."

She looked at the muscular arm that now held her. She gave a weak smile to him that conveyed only a sense that she was glad he was there next to her, but nothing more. As they walked into the damper, evening air now, she raised her hood, and the newly open Maddy then seemingly disappeared. She was coated in mystery once more, just like the leaf-littered floor of the forest.

Justin now struggled to determine her mood. He had tried to listen but felt that any further penetrating questions might evoke a more emotional and perhaps violent response. He'd gained some background though: about perhaps a rich, young Cornishman who'd fallen for one of the mine's bal-maidens, got her pregnant and then left; so too, had he learnt about her mother, and that this hardy Flannery had stepped in to care for them boath. In this, Justin felt he knew much more about this maid O'Donahue and that he had scraped away some of her hardened outer layer. He'd begun the smelting ov her. She seemed in no mood to talk further though, and did not want to ask him of his own background and childhood. Perhaps there wuz no need. Perhaps present acceptance wuz all she needed. He could not yet tell.

They had, by now, gone so deep into the forest, that they had lost all contact with the other Irish who were searching. Whereas before, they had heard calls for Clara, in order to try and locate her, now there wuz nothing but silence. Justin considered the fact that it was in such haunting space that the Doctor's wife had originally disappeared. The forest like this, went on for miles ahead of them. Fortunately, Justin and Maddy collectively had a good sense of direction and kept the lake below on their right-hand side. They could judge by their latitude the precise distance they were away from the settlement.

Maddy kept her silence. Perhaps she was now regretting revealing too much about herself to this Cornishman. She had shown him where some of her hatred had come from, and in so doing, she'd opened up a wound that would never quite be mended. By now, their actions had been watched by numerous sprites in this quarter of the forest.

They had found these two humans' interactions strange, to say the least. They sensed a possible connection between them, but then again, a residual distance; as if a repair could never quite happen.

Maddy knew the noise of this forest world. She knew it from home; and from her mother had learnt the wise ways of such people and how important they were. She couldn't see them yet, even though she tried hard to spot them in the undergrowth. She knew they were watching. She felt their gaze.

"You know where she is, don't you now?" she shouted out.

Her voice echoed long and hard in the vastness.

"Who are you talking to?" asked Justin.

"Nobody..." was her response. "Nobody. Not really. Just asking the world – that's all... I think... Yes, the forest knows..."

"But it's not saying," Justin continued, playing along with her metaphor.

But in reality it was not a metaphor. In fact, it was the full truth and Maddy could sense it and, so too, could the decaying forest. Intuitively, she fiddled with one or two of the shells of her necklace. He'd soon come to know very well that habit of hers.

"It's not speaking," Maddy said. "It doesn't want to."

Justin wuz puzzled as to how to react. She seemed to have a similar relationship to the green world around them as he and his brother had to the mining spirits beneath the ground.

"It's not good," she said – and at this – Justin felt a chill in the air.

But maybe in fact, she was thinking of their earlier conversation about her father. Again, the silence of the forest consumed them.

"I didn' tell you all the truth," she said. "I should have. You should know..."

Justin tried to respond but this time she put her forefinger to his mouth in order to hush him..

"You might think a little differently of me if I tell you this," she continued.

He could not respond though. Not even the forest seemed to be speaking to her now.

"There was just the one time you see. She had no interest in him. But he wanted her for himself. She told me that he grabbed her by the wrists... my mother... and him... next to the whim apparently. Had her up against it. She'd never go back in there. But yes, that's how I got scooped out of the earth Mr Nankervis... in an unloving act. And when you know that about yerself, you're never quite the same again... Part of yer's flawed then see."

For an hour or more, they sat amongst the trees and contemplated this, neither holding the other; neither really speaking much. Maybe they were listening though, still communing. We'll see. But now that this secret had been passed across, it felt like many more would follow. Es, there was an understanding between them now. The way that the sun was setting, up through the line of trees on the hillside, underlit the tree canopies and darkened their covenant. The evening light made the tall trunks cast long shadows: a sign which they both interpreted as natural communion between them and the earth. Were they now sparking? He hoped so. For the first time in a long time, Justin Nankervis felt like he was no longer in the confines of a shaft, and could now breathe.

17

Mazed days. Es. When Clara Jewell could not be found, a lingering unease came over the camp on the now very broken hill. It was certainly sinister that she had completely disappeared off the earth, but what worried everyone more, wuz the fact that seemingly, she did not want to return any time soon. No message came. No letter arrived. Whatever emotional distress had caused her to leave in the first place had not yet been understood, and it wuz that stabbing unknowing that was the most difficult aspect of her fading for her husband and family. There fell over the camp a view that maybe she wuz flawed inside in some way ('weak-minded' wuz what people really wanted t'say), but perhaps more immediately worrying, wuz the fear that she'd been carried off: that someone – or possibly something – had picked her up and carried her away under a tightly-clenched arm. This was an unknown world; all sorts lurked out there. Was this a one-off, or a portent of something else? One had to hope that it was the former and not the latter. Her disappearance laid a curtain of sorrow over the diggings high on the mountain, and it made the community's residents irritable and apprehensive.

Yew. Now in such situations, the previously hidden flaws of individuals come to the surface. Whatever they have managed to keep under and repress in daily life, bubbles upwards, and comes out in strange and alien ways. Es. That will zertainly show soon in this tale. An ominous realisation came over everyone that no matter how high or low they searched for Clara, she would not be found. It was as if she had become the forest's very moss and lichen; that her form had been consumed by the sugar maples and spruces. They'd made her their own. This realisation brought about the outward expression of their own fears; specifically that all-consuming one that they were going to die alone, distant from home. In order to offset this horizontal despair, the management of the mine pressed forward by going another fathom down. Maybe this wuz residual Cornish ideology at both its best and worst: if you don't like something, you drive away from it. The earth was the place where they took comfort. It would cradle and nurture them, despite what the surface was doing; despite the tricks it was playing. The earth shielded them from the grass-side of the world: it had always been that way. There was almost a grotesque drive into the underworld, to cavort in the canopies and the gunnies.

Nimkii never came – and when he didn' arrive, Doctor Jewell's body and soul collapsed. He stopped eating, and slept much. In trauma of this kind, sleep was his one comfort. Whilst awake, the thought of events was a constant, but in sleep, the situation could be forgotten. However, in the interminable waking comes that terrible transition from the fantasy and warm world of dream into the cold and bitter reality of the present. Everyone knawed he'd be going through this agony. To begin with, people called on him regularly, but in the end, they stopped doing that for there was only so much that could be said – and when all hope faded, they kept themselves in their own shacks and dwellings, contemplating in low whispers about what had happened. They avoided seeing the surgeon if they could. A quick bandage or plaster would do.

But still, happenstance, the Doctor had to carry on; he had family responsibilities. There had also been that awful moment when he had to explain to young Mabel that her mammy was not about to return any time soon. To his surprise, she did not collapse into tears. She had, by now, already sensed the atmosphere around her, and realised that something was wrong. Right now, it barely altered her countenance when she was given the news. She carried on half-playing with her piskie poppet in her own little imaginary world. But then, even the Doctor knew that this matter was not finished with yet, and neither was Mabel's lasting response. He predicted her rejoinder further down the track.

There had been a revelation though, and it came on one of the tighter, less accessible stopes on the third level. It was a new stope that promised a good yield, and after – damme – a morning of hard drilling, Francis, Justin, Luk and Gourgy sat down for their crowst. As in most mines, a small, improvised table had been constructed underground, so that at least for a while, workers could sit comfortably to eat. Old fuse boxes made good benches. Luk and Gourgy licked their lips at what morsels might pass their way. In their boxes and pails, the men had pasties and saffron buns, and after the physical labour of drilling, this sustenance was most apt.

"Some wisht, edn ut?" offered Justin, whilst turning a geht nub of pasty in his mouth. "Her feyther ent takin' it well, I knaw. Whaas tha' Rebecca say then?"

"She says ee's broken, but then, anyone would be, wudn' um?"

"Es Sos. Not sure how I'd react..."

"What? If your girl Maddy O'Donahue walked out the same way?"

"Get on with ee," said Justin. "She ent mine. Her got too much will in she t'ever be mine. Mark my words."

"That edn' what we'm all seeing. You'm sum sweet on she – an' naw mistake. Anyone can see ut a mile off. We all knaw the pair of ee are sparking. The Irish boys have nawticed ut. Flannery told me hisself."

"Tidn' like that..." came the protest.

"I reckon 'tis," chipped in Luk. "From what me and Gourgy have seen, you pair are well-suited..."

"You keep your nawse out boy Luk," retorted Justin.

"We'll see," said Luk. "When the weather gets a drop colder, you'll be wanting her warmth in your hut. Rosie wun't be happy. "

"'Ere, eat this," said Justin, tossing a piece of bun to Luk, "and be away with your views on my love life."

Luk accepted the end and ran away into the shadows to consume it. Knockies always did that for fear that any others of their species should steal ut.

"Whaas she like then, this O'Donahue maid?" questioned Francis. "I mean, you were out searching with her... Did ee have a yap with she or naw? Whaas er tale – the truth ov ut, I mean?"

"Oh, we talked," replied Justin.

"A'right... What about though?"

"Everything... Well, a lot anyway..."

"And?"

"Well, dun't judge she too harsh... She edn' had ut easy."

"Es. Fair 'nuff. But what else did ee learn 'bout she? I mean, some people wun't go near her for fear of her."

"What ee mean Sos?"

"Well, you knaw..."

Justin turned to Francis. He stopped eating.

"No brother. Go on. Say what you mean."

He took a hand to his chin in order to brush away a crumb of pastry.

"Well, people d'say she's different. You knaw: her clawthes an' tha'. I mean, I knaw she ent naw crone but she got certain ways... 'unchristian' ways if you knaw what I mean. Cen't say ut any better than tha'."

"What? Cuz she dun't gaw chapel? Cuz she ent a ranter?"

Francis didn' answer his brother. Instead, he tossed a pleading Gourgy the hard end crimp of his pasty.

"I dunno what she es. She's same as some of the cunning women back home... That's wha' people d'say..."

"She got skills," said Justin proudly. "She told me. Passed on from her mawthur..."

"Irish twaddle then? Superstition?"

That angered Justin. He had to respond fiercer now.

"She ent Irish. Not one hundred percent. She's half-Cornish. Her father wuz a Cussie..."

He said this proudly, but inside he knew there was no pride to ut. There cudn' be, knawing what one of they had done a few decades ago.

"Really?"

"Es. Really. Awnly she didn' take her father's name. He was a Pengelly apparently. She took her mother's instead."

Francis was now putting together some further pieces of the jigsaw,

"So thaas how she d'knaw copper then, idn' ut? In her blood."

Justin wuz so annoyed at what was being implied here that he would now let his brother think what he wanted. He knew of the Beara connection too. Obviously though, there was some information that wuz best kept secret, and stowed in a locked box. Ee didn' have t'knaw the full story. What Maddy had told him meant she had confided in him and there wuz no way now that Justin was going to break that trust. He knawed zactly what his brother was implying and ee didn' care fur ut t'all. Cunning woman? That is wha' he had said, wudn' ut? That was laughable, and s'wrong. Cunning woman wuz what they'd back home some days call a witch, and she zertainly wudn' nothing like that. How could they see her so wrong? Bleddy tusses.

Francis felt it best that he didn' say no more. He knew he'd been given the cold shoulder. He watched Justin sweep the crumbs of his crowst onto the floor, which Gourgy and Luk ran for. Then he shut down hard the lid of his pasty pail. It grated as it went down.

"If you'm the big 'I am'," said this Justin, "then how come you ent tracking towards that Rebecca a bit more? She's sweet on you. Anyone d'knaw that. If you didn' have claim on she, the other boys'ud be on her like a bear 'round honey. You want to make a move there boy, or otherwise she'll be snapped up. In this camp now, you ent the awnly man made of money."

His brother's words certainly made Francis think. He wuz fully aware of the attractiveness of Rebecca; he'd knawn ov ut since he first saw her in the Cliff Hotel. He knew enough too, from the stopes and galleries that there were other cunning boys in the mine who'd give anything to have a go on she. But right now, nawbody would be doing anything, because clearly, she was Cap'n Frank's. That made she untouchable.

Ut wuz the code.

Francis could have said a lot back but he chose not to, this brother. That wuz the way he wuz – more quiet and controlled. He didn' want to speak any further about Rebecca though, because every time he thought about her, it brought home his own inadequacies. She was properly educated. She wuz a lady (naw mine maid t'all), and she might expect something better than just a regular mine mucker. There wudn' even a chapel reading room or a Miners and Mechanics' Institute out here to educate himself further.

"She's keen, ent she boys?" Justin shouted to their Knockie companions.

"As mustard," observed Luk now back at the table, his eyes wide and pleading for more grub.

"She wants t'chow down on his..." but before he had chance to finish his sentence, Gourgy got cut off by Francis. He clasped his hand tight round his neck and only when he stopped, did he let un go.

"Enough," he said firmly. "I dun' need you buggers tellin' me what t'do."

"Well," said Gourgy innocently. "You need to get in there. You'm too slaw t'catch cold at the moment – not like your brother here. He's well in with the witch. Spellbound I reckon. Fanny-struck ee is!"

"What did you just say?" commanded Justin.

Gourgy checked himself and came to a realisation as to what he said.

"Mr Justin," he stated. "We Knockies view witches in positive ways. They ent all out of fairy stories. Y'should knaw tha' by now. We got enough ov um back home. One more here idn' goin' to hurt now, es ut?"

Although Gourgy had deftly turned his response around, in yet another way that saved his life, Justin still didn' look too impressed.

"Comus you on. We all need a cunning-woman every so often," said Luk. "I've been hundreds of times, me. Cure all sorts, they can. I allays swear by them, I do. You'n have your docs and surgeons and so on, but a proper hedgewitch, well, they'n sort ee out good and proper Sos. Charms and chants and whatnot... Nawthun' wrong with ut, is there boy?"

"No," said Gourgy in response.

An awkward pause ensued. A least ut had now been voiced. In the level, they'd only said what everyone else wuz thinking.

"I dun't reckon she had anything to do with the disappearance of Mrs Jewell though... I mean... do you?" stated Luk, realising he had overstepped the mark.

"No. Nawthun' to do with that... obviously," said Gourgy.

Justin turned.

"I'm watchin' you pair," he said, glaring at the Knockies. "An' as fur you dear brother, I think you should listen less to gossip, and a bit more to your family... Aw... try makin' your way a bit with Rebecca. She's like a good run of copper. She idn' goin' to be there forever."

The two Knockies cowered. Boy Justin wudn' takin' naw prisoners this morning. Francis nodded at what he said.

"Better get back," said Justin. "Get they fuses in... Best we blast a-fore the next core comes in..."

He was right. This was a male world in the mine, and all social niceties were not required. As he left, the three of them noted Justin scratch his crotch.

"Whaas' up with you?" asked Francis.

"Itchy ball-sack," he replied, smiling t'hisself in the way that only men can do.

"Nice," went Luk.

"'Andsome," said Gourgy.

They watched him go back into the limits of the stope.

"I tell ee. You pair best think about what you say to ee," warned Francis.

"We will, o great Master," said Gourgy, in his usual sarcastic manner.

"A bit less of yer cheek too," went Francis. "Be grateful for who's filling your bellies..."

"Es," said Luk, "and you pair be grateful who's watching the roots and ground overhead."

This was their usual symbiotic arrangement, but there was something that Luk said in that moment, that was utterly different.

"What ee mean?" asked Francis, his curiosity ignited.

"Wha'?"

"What you said about roots... You dun't normally say nawthun' about naw roots."

"Didn' us?"

"Naw... Whaas' on then?"

Luk gestured fur Gourgy to speak.

"We forgot to tell ee t' be honest, Master Nankervis..."

He paused for a while to recollect.

"All us Knockies – we've nawticed ut. We nawticed ut when we went underground to see if we could trace anything of Mrs Jewell... Thaas when we sensed ut..."

"What ee mean?" drove Francis. "Tell me."

"Tell un," said Luk. "Ee needs t'knaw..."

"Well, back home, the trees dun't seem t'say tha' much... But here, it's different. Their roots a-talk to each other... They communicate."

"Go on..." encouraged the brother.

"We heard them in the earth. Not just murmurings... but full conversations. Dialogues about what wuz going on... A lot of ut about the mine... At first, they were all scared, because there'd been a lot of lumbering, and then with the levels opening up, they wuz worried see – worried that you'd hack their roots off. Axes and dabbers."

Francis had heard a lot from these two over the years but this wuz on a new level.

"He's right," continued Luk. "They all talk to each other. They can tell what plants need water and who's short on sugar... They can redistribute resources. They take care of each other...It's like a grid... a network of them."

"You're having me on..." said Francis.

"No. We're not," pleaded Gourgy. "I's like what we've said. We can't hear it all but the forest is worried... concerned... That it's been let down..."

"By who?"

"Humans..."

"Human beings?"

"Yes... but at the moment, they ent keen on that Nimkii bloak either. They reckon he sold um up the river. Thaas what they said, wudn' ut boy?"

"That's right pard," noted Luk.

Francis thought back to the original deal that had been made, when he'd signed documents at the table in the hotel. It was a fair comment. In truth, the mine had exceeded the agreements made on its limits. Of late, ut had become a free-fur-all, especially since the arrival of the Irish, but not only they; several laker boats filled with Cussies had meant that expansion wuz inevitable. Christ knew what they wuz sayin' 'bout ut back Camborne or Redruth. Francis realised that they'd let ut tumble out ov control. In ut now, lurked the dispossessed. And when he considered tha' he realised too, that it wuz no accident. He, his brother, boy Skews and Trevorrow; they'd let ut happen purposefully. These pair needed further interrogation.

"But you said there were other creatures out there," Francis directly asked Gourgy.

"Aw... there are... definitely. I've seen um. Nice they were. To me, at least."

"Well, do they and the roots talk then?"

"Dun't knaw..." said Luk. "Maybe 'tidn' like they talk. 'Tis more like they both just knaw."

"Maybe," said Gourgy. "I mean, probably... You'd think so, wudn' ee?"

"But they cudn' tell you nawthun' about this Mrs Jewell and her whereabouts..."

"Naw. Not so we've heard," attested Gourgy.

"I wish you'd told me this before," said Francis. "This changes things..."

"How do ut?" asked Luk. "Ut dun't change anything. 'Twas zactly the same back home... y'knaw, with us lot and the landscape around us. Jabbering on all the time 'tis... from the roots right up to the tallest trees... and what we d'say t'the animals and what they tell we back... You've heard tell ov the piskie thresher an' the fairy ointment... I mean 'tidn' there all the time like. But ut's there if you need ut – kind-of- thing..."

Maybe Francis did knaw this and maybe he didn'. He'd not perhaps thought any wider than the relationship he had with the small people of the mines. Now here, he wuz being told that there was a whole interconnected world besides his feet, under his feet and over his head. Mad ut wuz. Es. Prop'ly mazed.

"Tell me again. How exactly do the roots talk?"

Gourgy looked non-plussed at having to explain ut again. He wuz like that. He gave a sigh as he spoke, and shook his head from side to side, so that traces of spittle fell onto the floor of the level.

"We looked at ut, didn' we Luk? And we d'reckon it's small things in the earth... they conduct the messages along, jus' like copper..."

"What kind of things?"

"Things smaller than we can see..."

"What – microbes?"

"Es. I believe thaas what I've heard them called. Seen ut in the papers I have... That yeah, but fungi too."

When Gourgy said that, it made complete sense. Now he understood the dominance of the damp smell of the woods; always that rotten, decaying odour of something oozing and percolating. Tiny life was reaching for hope.

"What else did you learn?"

"Gourgy don't believe me, do ee boy?" Luk responded, "But when I was listening I d'reckon they understand when there's a threat to um. They can sense ut..."

"What like?"

Luk thought hard.

"A'right then. Like they mad beavers... you knaw when they chop down trees... or when different insects attack (like they midges)... they're aware ov ut. I mean, I thought 'twas silent all the time, but Master, when we listened, we heard quite a bit, didn' us?"

From the stope, came a shout. It was Justin.

"You buggers coming or naw?"

"Coming," shouted Luk.

Francis warned them.

"Dun't say anything t'ee. Ee got enough goin' on already in his world without this coming up..."

"My lips are sealed," went Gourgy, but as always, that wudn' much of a promise. They could always be unsealed by the prospect of cake and ale.

"Best get we back into the stope."

Francis ushered them forwards and their gangly arms and legs moved into a crouching position at the end of the stope. Justin had already stuffed a couple of fuses into the tight drill holes. Soon, they'd be charging them to blaw the next section of rock away. He'd just had his world turned upside-down: ut wuz like a kibble had been emptied and shook his brains out. Now, they knew fur sure that this mine wudn' naw ordinary h'enterprise. There were forces here that were uncontrollable. The Cornish arrogantly thought they had roped the earth to their belt and braces, but at this moment, he could see that that wuz no longer the case. Ut put a geht shiver in un, that he'd cudn' shake off that day, not even when he hung his wet underground clawthes in the drying room. Es. Before that, he'd given a shout t'warn that they wuz about t'blaw. The ignition of the fuses just before noon made an explosion that rattled in all of the levels. But he knawed something had imploded in him too.

18

Well an' good then, all this Tom holla! Stories rely on a belief in the truth, dun't um? But half of all stories are lies: you d'knaw that. They are made-up, farcical exaggerations of the way things really happened. But were they not that way, then would you ever bother listening at all? Naw. You zertainly wudn'. You may as well live out your poor days never listening to romance, never hearing of fantasy, never encountering magic and never knowing what lies beyond the normal or over the horizon. Es. There idn' much left – when you take that away. All you have is the daily grind of things, the unending reach of betterment and survival, and that sounds like no life at all. Without story, where would us be? Here, maybe you are coming to see two sides of these long, storied days on the Keweenaw. But if half of all stories told are lies, then who do you believe? Where does your sympathy lie? Is it with the drive downwards of the mine – or is your heart with the forest? Now, you don't have to decide yet though, for there is more to tell. Es, this tale is still only a partially-worked stope, or the small, unravelling fiddle-neck of a fern in the dark, swirling forest.

Clara Jewell's disappearance got mentioned less and less. In fact, it wudn' discussed t'all fur fear of upsetting anyone. The Doctor took in a house-keeper, a nice maid in her early thirties by the name of Jenny Spargo. Now Jenny had worked the cobbing tables for much of her adult life, but when this opportunity came up for betterment, she leaped at the chance to help out with Mabel and James. She kept a clean house for the surgeon, though she never moved in proper like: that would never do for a lay minister. She stayed living with her parents. Jen wouldn' nawthun' much t'look at (she was too broad in the waist, and her face was scrunched up into a pine cone) but she did have a heart of gold. Already, she had nawticed that her hands had become softer, from not having to daily break ore, and hammer her days away on the side of this stupid mountain. The Doctor just stanked on. An' if his services in the preaching pit were slightly less confident, well, who could blame un? Ut would shake anyone's feyth – God or naw God – what happened to the bugger.

The weather got colder. Some blaw comed in moast days now. It seemed to transition overnight from warm days which carried the very last remnants of summer, into something wintrier. The sun was lower in the sky, and so the camp rarely received as much light. Indeed, the darker mornings felt like you were rising for forenoon core in the middle of the night, and before heading down to the shaft, there wuz a need to wrap up warm. The drying shack was a welcome place to be, and more often than not, the men congregated there. It wuz Justin and Francis – es, as Cap'ns now – who had to motivate them daily to go under; otherwise they'd spend the entire morning in there. The cool weather above ground was replicated by a dampness under it. It is hard for anyone who has never been in a mine to understand that wetness. It fell out of the walls and coated the timbering. The only way to offset it is a good session of shovelling or tramming, or an hour or two on the drill. That's when you worked up a sweat, and then wished to be up t'grass once more. Aw, the taste of the breeze when you comed up wuz 'andsome you.

Mining is slaw work. Some days it feels as if you are not making any headway but then, when you return to a stope and review it after another core has been in, gradually, you realise you are making ground, and that the level is opening up. So slowly the levels reached out from those first shafts sunk like a pair of lungs in the rock. Those who relied on the mine, but who never went down, only really had an image in their heads of what it was like underground. Those who ventured belaw knew it intimately. In essence, talking about ut was an abstraction: a theory of movement in rock, but every miner knows of it. A sense of ut becomes embedded, and when that is installed, an individual knows the entire landscape underground. Sometimes, they knaw it better than what lay just beyond the surrounds of the camp itself. Lengthy meetings were not required to discuss developments on the whole because steady courses had already been set. All knew what they needed to do: each had a specific function. You knawed each part ov the mine like the lines on the back of yer hand.

Word wuz that getting a serious steam engine or two was now on the cards, and that a brae crew of men would be needed to build two engine houses over the two shafts. Two pairs of shears would be needed as well, to connect to the bob. The difficulty with the two engine houses was their construction. See, nawbody much fancied any ov the stone from the mountain. It didn' have the density or abject hardness of granite, and that wuz what wuz needed: something lasting. Sometimes though, if the rock wudn' right, then the headgear would have to be a wooden structure, and here, that seemed the likely way of going. A lot of mines in 'Merky' were built that way, from freshly-cut lumber. The engines themselves could be shipped in below. From what the crew could gather from Mr Skews, they were already being transported across the Atlantic, and very soon they'd be taken up through the Great Lakes. What a day that would be, when they finally arrived. Apparently Skews was already working out the h'engineering ov ut – how they'd manoeuvre the geht pieces up from the harbour. 'Twudn' be naw easy job fur sure.

But this wuz fur the future. Nawbody expected that lot t'arrive until the New Year, an' when they realised tha', it wuz likely the gear might have t'stay down at the harbour fur a while before any attempt wuz made to cart ut up the mountain. They'd be in the full clutches of winter by then, and snaw and ice wudn' zactly worthy bedfellows t'be moving engines across the landscape they were working in. 'Twudn' like back home where an engine could be ordered one day and fitted inta' place the next week. The proposal wuz fur the mine t'get ahead of itself in terms of production. If there wuz enough ov a stockpile of ore already piled high, then that would allow the works a three-week shut down where all hands would need to be employed to fit the engines, and construct the houses around them.

After forenoon shift, Gourgy and Luk went missing – and only Francis had a notion of where they'd be. The two of them had comically taken to heading up to the schoolhouse after a core, sittin' in on Miss Jewell's lessons. Apparently, it wuz all about gaining the education they'd never had underground (es, rite on). Of course, fur Rebecca, the annoying thing wuz that she cudn' see um both, and despite promises, the strong likelihood was that the pair would sometimes mess around and disrupt others. Boath Francis and his brother had warned them 'bout ut, but ut was hard to keep control of them at times. The buggers did what they wanted.

In the school, the awnly pupil who could see them wuz Mabel. That wuz weird because none ov the other children were able to note individuals like Gourgy and Luk. They'd always aim to sit next to her – perhaps because she would help them with their learning. It was an arrangement that Francis, in particular, was not entirely happy with, but also it seemed like something he could not stop. If such individuals were being seen by Mabel, how could he put an end to ut? 'Twas near impossible to do anything 'bout ut.

She had some gift that maid Mabel, and the Knockies knew of ut. He'd nawticed that this pair were not the only ones she could see. He could tell from the way she looked, that she also noticed the Knockies of other miners too. The landscape must have been populated by both humans and other beings, so she wuz seeing a different world. It was no wonder that Mabel sometimes asked challenging questions to her sister, the school-ma'am. Francis had considered telling her more about the Knockies (it was clear she knew of the folklore, but not the reality of ut), but considering her circumstances, maybe it wasn't the brightest thing to do right now. There wuz already enough magic goin' on in the forest. Besides tha', the presence of Knockies wuz actually a closely-guarded secret, and although the miners lived up to the folklore, and put it on a plate for those who would listen, they were always careful to protect their companions true status. Giving them away too openly would be tantamount to issuing forth a roof collapse in the next fortnight.

Francis slipped into the back of the classroom. Despite its newness, the building already had that smell of chalk and books that he had long forgotten. He nodded to Rebecca. She was in the middle of reprimanding Mabel for fidgeting. Only Francis could see why. Luk was stood on the desk next to her, cavorting around like a court jester, occasionally hitting Mabel and, as a joke, putting her off her reading ov some storybook. Francis knew he needed a word. He moved to the rear seat where Mabel wuz sat and peered straight into the screwed-up face of Luk.

"Calm down my friend, and sit down," he said to Luk, "or I will dunk you in the slimes in the sump."

Luk had been unaware of the presence of one of their masters and the sight of Francis came as quite a shock to him. On another occasion, Luk might have come back to him with some wisecrack, but in the schoolhouse, it wuz a different matter. He sat down and picked up the book he was meant to be reading. Things became more orderly then. Rebecca had thought that Francis wuz talking to Mabel: asking her about what she was reading.

The calm air continued for a while, but Francis then nawticed the very odd learning behaviour of Gourgy. At first, the miner thought that the Knockie was attentive to his reading, but then he realised that Gourgy was, in fact, doing something quite different. Although the book was placed on his desk, Gourgy was not actually reading it. Instead, he sat fanning up the words from the pages of the book into his head, as if absorption alone would provide him with knowledge.

"What are you doing pard?" whispered Francis.

"Learning," replied Gourgy.

"Is it going in or naw?"

"Not really," said Gourgy. "None of it's goin' in..."

"'Tidn' goin' to is ut, you bleddy idiot... You can't learn like that..."

"Aw," went Gourgy, "I thought that's what you did when you do this thing they d'call learnun."

"Naw," said Francis. "You've actually got to read ut proper."

"Didn' knaw tha'" offered Gorgy. "I thought you just soaked ut in..."

"Pard. You got a long way to go... Me and you – we need t'talk about this back home."

Francis said nawthun' more. He knawed that they were trying but when the fundamentals weren't understood, then how wuz a t'progress? Knockies weren't stupid. They knawed the world. They could read and write. They could do sums. In fact, they were skilled mineralogists and mining h'engineers. They'd had a thousand years or more to practise. Francis knawed what this wuz – this wuz they pair poking fun. That was ut with them all the time: anything fur a laugh – anything to disrupt. The same pattern continued when Luk started to play with Mabel's doll that she was clutching.

"Whaas this?" Francis overheard Luk saying.

"A piskie," he heard Mabel say.

"That idn' naw piskie..." went Luk. "Dun't look like the ones I d'knaw. They'm oogly. This one idn'."

"'Tis," went Mabel.

"'Tidn', went the Knockie.

Francis thought he'd need to intervene again, but by now, Miss Jewell was at the front of the room, ringing the hand-bell she had, in order to signify that it was now mid-afternoon play-time. She had her class well-trained. They left in an orderly manner, each pupil placing their reading books into the wells of their desks, then closing the lids of them. Mabel, Gourgy and Luk followed her instructions, and they began to leave. However, before they could slip outside to cause more mayhem, Francis grabbed both of them.

"Eh. That's it now. Neither of you need to be here, and you'm causing all manner of mayhem and disruption. You'm really disturbing Mabel."

"We can't help it if she can see we," said Luk, defending his position. "She likes we there with her. She told us so."

"She starts ut, all the time," stated Gourgy.

"I dun't think so. Now, if you want any saffron later, get yourselves back home right now... and leave Miss Jewell alone so she's able to teach... Dun't disturb Mabel any more."

"Really?" Luk moaned. "But we like ut here. 'Tis better than in the mine. Warmer too."

"Yeah. Really," said Francis.

He could see the problem. These pair had got beyond their station in life. They'd got too comfortable living next to humans and wanted all the niceties and pleasures they had.

"You pair need t'get back down the mine or I will definitely have your guts for garters."

That wuz a meaningless threat fur ut had no currency. More likely they'd respond to the fact that they wudn' be getting no saffron bun any time soon. When that sank in, there wuz a change of mood, and some compliance.

"A'right... a'right," they went, "s'long as you ask Miss Jewell out. You knaw what we said the other day."

"Away with ee both," pronounced Francis. "Gesson with ee..."

Each Knockie laughed one of their mad laughs, and then left the schoolhouse.

"Everything alright?" Rebecca asked.

"Yes... Fine," responded Francis, lying somewhat. "How's your Mabel getting on then?"

"Aw, I've told you about her. She won't concentrate on anything. Says she knows it all already. Very wilful she is. An odd child..."

"I'm sure things will improve in time..." offered Francis. He knew they would now if the pair of Knockies were not with her.

From outside, there came the shouts and shrieking of the children who were at play. Despite the cold air, they loved the release from the oppression of the classroom.

"You alright?" Francis asked. "I wondered how you were getting on..."

"I'm fine, well, as fine as I can be. This place helps me to forget. You know, you can go a long time without thinking about her – and then suddenly it comes back and hits you. I keep asking myself why she did what she did. I find the abandonment hard to deal with..."

"Of course," said Francis. "I know... and your father?"

"Slow progress... but better now that Jenny is helping..."

"Jen's a good maid," noted Francis. He'd got to knaw her family.

There was a slight pause. Rebecca picked up the piskie poppet belonging to Mabel and transferred it from hand to hand.

"The mine's doing well, isn't it? I hear steam is on the way now..."

"Seems to be... Es. Steam will really help us shape things..."

"Bodes well for the future. Some people are saying that the place should change its name. Have you heard that?"

"Aw es. I knawed of ut... what um say? They want it called Mountainside, dun't um?"

"One idea, I believe," noted Rebecca. "Others want it to stay as it is."

"Not a bad one. New Diggings wuz a'right for a bit," said Francis thoughtfully, "but it's not very lasting, es ut? Hardly makes you want to come and visit, does it?"

"*If* people *ever* wanted to visit..." commented Rebecca.

"True 'nuff," Francis laughed, "but 'tis developing well enough by my reckoning... Maybe Mountainside would set it off... proper like."

The conversation stuttered once more. Francis thought back to the conversation he'd had with his brother and the Knockies the other day. He'd been right. There was this disconnection; this class issue between them that sometimes placed them into awkward territory that broke their attraction. Why were some women like this? He felt like he would never understand them, despite her knowing of his interest in her. She seemed to want to say more, but nothing came forth. Only eventually – after what seemed like an eternity – did she speak to un again; this time more covertly.

"I wanted to speak to you the other day. I've not seen you since..." she said softly.

Francis gestured for her to speak, nodding a 'go on'.

"It's a delicate matter. Something tricky... Difficult to say even..."

Was this the moment where she was going to tell him how she felt about him? Francis was aware that there wuz only a few minutes before she'd ring the bell again, and that the afternoon lessons would begin once more after the recess. But it was not as he wanted nor expected.

"It's about Mabel..."

He wondered if maybe Rebecca had the ability to see the Knockies too, but then he understood more clearly the direction of her conversation with him.

"You see that poppet? It's expensive. None of the other girls have one like that... She told me about it... and who bought it for her."

"Your father presumably? It looks well made. No plain joanie."

"I know... It is. It's from Detroit. From an expensive toymaker there."

"So who's it from then?"

"You'd never believe it," whispered Rebecca. "Promise you won't say anything..."

"Promise."

She mouthed a name: "Mr Skews."

"Skewsy?"

In an instant Francis was forced to think back to some of the earlier conversations he'd had with his brother and their Knockies. What did the forest say? Apparently, it (if he could believe in 'it') didn' like Skews either. The Knockies had discerned that Mr Skews wuz not to be trusted, though quite why and just how, had not yet been revealed.

"Yes. He bought it for her. She told me."

"Why?"

"I don't know. I can't work it out. They go for walks sometimes. He's sweet on her in some way... I can't tell... All I know is that it's weird..."

Maybe this is what the forest saw.

"You told your father?"

"Yes, but he's not listening... He doesn't see it as a problem... but I do... I don't like it Francis...There's something odd about it."

The more he thought about ut, he realised that he had noted how Skews behaved around the Doctor and his family. Maybe it was a front somehow: a deception.

"I mean, Skewsy's odd anyway," said Francis. "He's always been odd."

He said this but he did not want to reveal too much. How could he even begin to articulate what he'd been told and what he knew? It would zertainly be a way of pushing her away from him. For now, it was best not to reveal all his cards.

"Yes. I mean, everyone knows. He lives for the dollar, for greenbacks – but this, I can't work it out... Does he have any family?"

"He does, but they're at home... and he's not seen them for a while... Years maybe."

Francis knew this with more accuracy than what he said. It is the way of all of us sometimes.

"I know, but Mabel's got enough. She doesn't need his wealth."

"Perhaps he's just being kind? I mean, the man is an idiot but he has his moments..."

Francis could hardly believe himself. How could he ever call Skewsy kind? He was only trying to soften the blow; to not put everything he knew on the table. The forest? Sprites? Roots? It was all intermingling, and in the centre of the storm was Skews' keen face.

"It doesn't feel right."

Francis considered what she said. He knew her fears. She was sensing something reckless; something perverted, something unwatched, that had transpired here.

"What's she say about him?"

"Nothing. I can't get anything out of her..."

"But you said... Mabel's special... You told me..."

"What? – and he senses that..."

"Maybe..."

"Alright, but what is his interest Frank? I'm trying to understand it."

Francis tried to understand her fears. What he, as yet, did not tell her, was that clearly Mabel could see the *poble vean*. Gourgy and Luk suggested that she could see other creatures in the forest too. Was that, in some way, helpful to Skews? Maybe. Maybe it wuz another mechanism of aggrandisement. If this girl could communicate with the forest, then perhaps that would be useful. On the other hand, if his interest felt unnatural then that really wuz an unwanted entanglement.

"I'll make some enquiries," stated Francis. "If need be, I'll ask him direct."

He did not say so, but enquiries had already been made.

"No," said Rebecca. "Don't do that yet. I may be completely wrong. He may just have done a nice thing... a Christian thing... I mean, I see Mr Skews at the services and he seems such a good man... a noble man."

"Maybe," confirmed Francis, "but whatever we discover, I am glad you were able to confide in me."

"You understand my fears?" requested Rebecca. "I cen't have her consumed by the forest too. It would kill me – and my father. I can't have Skews change her forever either. Her innocence is at stake."

Francis knew what was implied by that. If he could, he'd not see it happen. What was the matter with this man Skews? What were his intentions? What had he seen about Mabel that no one else had? Es. 'Twas a keen problem but Francis would do his best to understand it.

"I wun't be naw bull in a china shop," he offered. "I'll try to get to the bottom ov ut though."

The reality was that Skews had long been of interest to Francis. Skews' oddities had already forced that on him.

"Thank... you," Rebecca stuttered. "I hate to ask, but you are the one person... that I can trust. Sometimes, it is very lonely here. I mean, do you feel that? This far up, this far away from civilization."

He knew what she meant. He understood it further because of the action ov her mother.

"Yes," said Francis. "I understand..."

The awful sub-text of these words were that both of them worried about the law in this place: that it remained almost ungoverned and unregulated. Some men could do what they wanted. The dismal forest too, was a threat.

"Look, I'd best get on," offered the miner.

"Of course. It's time for me to call them back in anyway."

Rebecca raced back to her front desk, in order to ring the bell.

"Thank you for listening to me. I appreciate it, Mr Nankervis... I really do."

She started to ring the bell, and it echoed out into the playground.

"You're a good man," she said in between the clapper hitting the rim of the hand-bell.

"And you are a good woman, Miss Jewell," stated Francis, for the first time releasing his true feelings for her. She stared at him, still a little unnerved by what he had said, but perhaps pleasantly so.

Francis tried to make his exit. As the children re-entered the schoolhouse he thought he observed that he had made the teacher blush. All that would have to wait now. There wuz one more final conversation between them though, before he left.

"One more thing. Can I ask? What do you make of that O'Donahue woman?"

"Oh, well, brother's keen on she. I dun't have a lot to do with her t'be honest... I steer clear if I can. Not sure I like her much. Another one I cen't quite make out."

"She was in here yesterday..."

"Really? What, about schooling?"

"No... Not really... She just asked to borrow a piece of chalk. Seemed nice enough though."

"Chalk?"

"Yes..."

"To mark somethun'?"

"I suppose so. She didn' say what."

Francis contemplated what on earth that could be about. He tried to understand this Maddy's motivation. What would she need to mark? Something underground? If ut wuz that, what business did she have to mark anything in the mine? He dismissed these thoughts. Maybe ut wuz something else; something domestic. What with Skews and this, there were mysteries developing all over the place right now: runs which had no ends to them.

As he entered the outside world, grim clouds gathered over the township. The children had gone back inside, just in time. A cold rain began to fall, which ensured Francis pulled up his collar, and then had to quickly dodge the growing puddles going back to his shack. He knew his brother wudn' be there. He'd be down underground, managing the afternoon shift. The time he had alone would allow him to think over how best to proceed with Skews, but also his attachment to Miss Jewell. This Mabel would need watching too. How could she be the daughter of a lay minister, but be so wayward? Honestly, 'twas like she wuz piskie-led, with Skews her controller and piper. And then, the pain-in-the-ass Irish woman too.

In his shack, he put a few sticks on the fire in the stove to get it going. A glow emerged from its door, which then he developed by placing in some logs. The fire burnt bright and helped to dry him out. Was this another implosion? He feared it wuz. In the last twenty-four hours he had learnt of the ability of the trees around him to communicate, of the seedy and mysterious side of Skews, and also his own instinctual desire to be with Rebecca Jewell. Suspicion and sexuality became forged inside him that night. All of it seemed to go against every bit of his Chapel upbringing: that core of morality at the centre of his soul. He wanted t'dismiss it and let it all go. But every time the fire blazed, it shone a new light on old truths – truths that were rapidly becoming outmoded.

After his core, in the early evening Justin did not go home. Instead, he walked up the mountainside past Rosie's saloon. He swore secretly at her as he passed. He spat curses. Es. He had good reason to. It wudn' like he had physical contact with her any more, not of late at least. He could not wait any longer. It was raining hard by now, and when the boy Justin walked into the Doctor's surgery, he looked like he'd come in with the tide.

"A'right Doc?" he went. "Need to see you 'bout somethun'."

"You're soaked," said a concerned Jewell. "Come in and sit down by the stove. Warm yourself up man... A cold rain like this is a recipe for a winter cold. I can't have you catching pneumonia... not out here."

"Thank you. I hope things... is, well, improving fur you..."

"Yes. Well, one still lives in hope...not that... er... Now, how can I help? What seems to be the trouble?"

"I's this," said Justin gettin' undressed in one movement – an' Jewell knew zactly what he meant.

"Oh," said Jewell.

"Do anything, can ee?"

"We'll certainly try."

Es. The conversation didn' go much further than that. 'Twas a condition the Doc had seen a thousand times before. Ee knawed ut wuz common in mining camps on the frontier and wuz a pain for those who suffered ut, but hopefully, 'twas caught early enough t'be treatable. And when the Doc had done, Justin left with a bottle of pills (he needed to take two ov they a day) and a quantity of regulation ointment. He paid the man with cash and walked out inta' the world like nothing had happened. This wudn' somethun' covered by Jewell's role as the mine's surgeon. Aw naw. This wuz something very different – but perhaps the less said of ut, then the better. As you knaw though, nawthun' stays a secret fur long, and so it wuz, with this Justin. To be frank now, he might even have been better off shouting ut from the roof-tops, considering what mischief comed ov ut. But that's the way ov ut always: one piece of past mischief leads to another in the present, and so too, wuz that the case here. But enough of that kind ov speculation fur now. All you need to knaw wuz that Justin had a condition and that ut wuz being treated with due care by Doctor Jewell.

Because ov the weather, moast of the town was now inside their dwellings, with their stoves lit. Those who'd come up from the afternoon shift were glad of the warmth of the drying room, after which they plodded across the camp to their own shacks and bunkhouses. Only in there, could be guaranteed dryness, and a decent meal. Late into the night, there'd be the usual passel of tall tales to make such evenings pass quicker and to negate the downpour. Some nights Justin would join in with them for such stories, as did his brother, but not this night. Naw. Something in Justin's bones made him think differently. He had in his mind the words of his brother and their pair ov Knockies, and their observations about him and the O'Donahue woman turned over tempestuously in his head. A shiver came over him but he was in no mood for more of their teasing, nor for a night of comedy. He'd cope with shivers that night if he needed to.

He looked around him: what would become of this place, this place in the middle of the forest that was still so distant from everything? What did they want to re-name it now? Mountainside. Skews would have had a hand in that, he deduced. Mountainside. That rang fine when he said it. The change in name reflected the change in the whole outlook of the camp. In a short while it had become a community: one which was now much bigger than the early diggings alone. They were hardly 'new' now anyway. They'd been at the strike for nearly six months now, and see how the place had blossomed. See what people it had brought to ut? He knew that the arrival of steam would bring many more in, and that inevitably it meant further expansion. Skews was talking about driving in another level, from lower down the mountain. Then there was still his talk of a tramway down to the harbour. What fancy, eh? How had ut come t'this, so soon, an' so quickly? What had once been timber and moss, was now a town with an industry as important as any other on the Upper Peninsula.

People were weird, Justin concluded. Sometimes, there wuz nothing you could do about that. Other folks did what they needed to do, and none of that wuz your fault. There was no point in even trying to understand them. He barely understood his own motivations sometimes, this boy, and so it seemed inconceivable to try and translate the desires and demands of others. That Clara Jewell: she was half-baked anyway he reckoned. Regardless of whether she was up a mountain in Michigan, she'd have lost the plot. Ut didn' matter if she was at home or away. 'Twuz best not t'tell the Doc his reasoning though. Justin knawed when to stay silent these days. Brave an' sorted he'd been ov late. Es. Brave an' sorted.

Should a go over now t'find she? That Maddy he meant. He wudn' sure. The last time they'd had substantial company together had been when they'd been out searching for Clara, and on that occasion, Maddy had revealed a lot to un. He felt he understood her more now. Before, she'd been a puzzle (she still wuz to moast other people) but at least he'd made some in-roads. Es. He'd had fantasies about her alright. In his dirtiest of dreams he wuz with her, and they were making love. But when that subsided, he dismissed any partnership with her. Ut wuz nawthun' like what his brother wuz workin' on with tha' Rebecca. Now that wuz a good woman. This, wuz somethun' different. How do ee work with ut when 'twas like nawthun' you'd comed across before? In the end, he decided to go over to the Irish house and see if she wuz in. He wudn' want to spend the night with the rest ov um, but when he'd sometimes sat on the porch with she – that wuz different. He knocked fur she, and big Flannery opened the front door. Although Flannery and he were on good terms, still from the Irishman (her protector), came an air of suspicion.

"So ut's you again, eh? If ut's Maddy you'm a-wantin', she's not here," he said.

"Where's she to?"

"Went out earlier..."

"Went out?"

"Aye."

"In this weather?"

"Rain won't stop her now. Don't ya knaw that Cap'n Cussie?"

Cap' Cussie. This boy was taking the piss, good and proper.

"She'll be soaked."

"Aye. Well, you'n tell her. Just like I've tried to do over many a year. You should try advising her. But I tell ya, my Cornish friend, the more you tell her not t'be doing of something, then the more she's likely to do it... and that's the truth of it now."

"No idea where?"

Flannery shook his great head, and shoulders. Justin nawticed him twist his lower stomach slightly. Despite Nimkii's healing ov ut, the wound there was obviously still smarting some.

"Your guess is as good as mine," the man said, looking over the soaked Justin in front of him. "Come in for a wet one if you like... Or maybe – by the state of you – you've had enough already!"

"No, thanks for the offer, but I'll look fur she..."

"Your loss," said Flannery beginning to shut the door on him. "You'll take my warning on she now, won't you? You try and change her, and she'll cast you away as if you're fool's gold. Remember that my Cussie..."

His Cussie? He wudn' no one's Cussie! He wuz perhaps trying to be friendly but his banter wuz off the mark. From Flannery however, Justin received the impression that Maddy was someone who did this kind of disappearing act quite often. Where the hell did she go to though? It wudn' like there wuz anywhere else in the camp for her to go. Ut wudn' like she'd be downing ale in Rosie's saloon. But also from this Flannery, he got the view that he had already sorted him out as a possible suitor, and that he wuz continually on her mind despite her denial. He noted his warning though: the man knew her better than he did. It was not like she was about to change overnight. There was a degree of merit in his advice. He cudn' let his lust fur she rule him.

Justin thought through the possibilities. Ut had to be that she had ventured away from the camp. His only opportunity for finding her would be to walk the circumference of the clearing and to scan the woods to see if she were, for some reason, out there. A little more rain would not affect him. His clothing was soaked already, but if she were out there, why now? What wuz she doing at this moment, when the rest of the camp were holed up away from the downpour? He trod the periphery and then went some way down the road coming up the mountain from the Cliff Mine below. He peered into the blackness; now a disturbing kind of blackness that was unlike that found underground. Aw, he'd been down belaw when he'd lost light: when the candle-wax had fizzled out, and he'd not a lucifer match to strike, but the gloom down there was nothing compared to what was in front of him. The Knockies said the forest was alive with creatures, with similar characteristics to them, but at this moment, it appeared dead and lifeless; in fact, so still, that it surprised him that anything could survive out here. How could something be both beautiful and disturbing at the same time? But then, he considered: he awnly had to look at she fur an answer.

A few hundred yards along the incoming path was enough. Wherever she'd gone, she was out of view. If she wanted to be concealed, then she'd achieved her aim. Yet she couldn't be too distant, not considering the conditions. Fur zertain, he'd have to ask her about it though: the same drilling into her mind and motivation that he'd had before. But in between the threads of rain, and the clouds in the night-sky, did come through some patches of light, where the moon poked its beams to the ground. And then, in the forest's blackened obscurity, he saw a flicker. It was a flame, he was sure, but nothing large; not anything from a fire, but instead, perhaps just a single candle. And when he listened further – more intensely – he could hear a voice, repetitive and monotonous. The language was clearly not English though, and when he first saw the candle, he instantly thought not of this O'Donahue woman, but in fact, of Nimkii. Es. That wuz who it wuz. Bound to be. This wuz somethun' he'd do he reckoned, and 'twas about time fur the mysterious bugger to shaw his face again. Not even she would be mad enough to be out here on her own; not in this weather – this distant from the camp.

As he eased closer though, and strode through the low ferns and bracken, he noted that his first guess was wrong. This ritual was not being conducted by Nimkii. In fact, he realised that ut was a woman, and from the precise way that she wore her shawl and cloak, that it was definitely Maddy O'Donahue. So this is where she'd come, eh? The stupid bitch. And he became exasperated at her position... Gah! She was sat off the ground, in a comfortable crook in one of the trees, and the upwards-turning branches matched the angle at which she was sat, so that her form wholly blended with the natural world around her. In the darkness, it was difficult to see the difference between her arms and legs, and the branches that threaded off from her position.

The candle was high off the ground too, and close to her; rested on a flat piece of branch. Incredulously, around her she had marked the trees in chalk, with spirals and circles: as a kind of portal that she'd entered. Although somewhat washed by the rain, these forms remained and could still be noted. Above her head dangled the long stems and berries of some fruit (probably poisonous) that was clearly parasitical, and had established itself on the host tree she was sat on. These falling stems and berries almost made a garland around her head: a kind of halo of autumnal colours, which she had not even noticed. With the candle, the moon and these berries she seemed to be caught in an ecstasy of light.

Listening further, he could not make head nor tail of the language being used, but then he recognised that what she spoke must be the Erse of her youth: the language of her foremothers and forefathers – and here it was being spouted in the middle of this remote forest, a long way away from where it had first risen from native mouths. What wuz she saying though – and what wuz she doing with her hands? It was a fairy tale he was witnessing. She was casting a spell certainly, for the force of her voice, made it clear that her words weren't without wider meaning or impact. In fact, it was language ready to conjoin two things together, to make something else – to create. It was weaving and binding.

As he looked up, he noticed her pull energy from the flame towards her stomach. He first watched in seedy fascination as she lifted her dress, to expose her belly (he could also just make out, next to the bark, the dark triangle of hair of her pubis), but then he realised that this energy was not being directed at her stomach, but instead, wholly towards the position of her womb. This was old magic indeed – of the kind used by no cunning-woman he had ever seen. This was no modern magic, of the mathematical, theoretical kind that allowed the earth to be mined and h'engineered: this was something darkly ancient, beyond all the knowledge that he had. On the one hand he wished not to break what she wuz doing, but on the other, so perversely intrigued and disturbed was he by her location and actions that he simply had to ask her what wuz on. He crept closer. Now he could see her face more clearly: whatever ritual wuz being completed, it was being completed in conjunction with the moon, for every so often, as branches, she would cast her hands up to it and say something.

Involuntarily, he gave a small cough and stepped forward, so that she would see his form below her.

"Wozzon?" asked Justin, gazing up at her. "Flannery said you'd be here in the forest. I came to look for you."

"Did a now?" she said in response, quickly lowering down her dress to cover her exposed stomach and vagina. She shifted her position in the crook of the tree to regain her modesty.

"I wuz worried. What the hell are you doing up there Maddy?"

She looked exasperated and embarrassed that he'd discovered her secret. Nervously, she touched one or two of the shells in her necklace. But did it in fact, seem like a surprise that he'd come? Perhaps not. She was contemplating this and, for a while, nothing came from her lips; then suddenly, something.

"Look, I think it be best if you say nothing to anybody about what you've seen here. You know I'm a witch. Don't think otherwise. In fact, you've always known," she said openly and directly.

"Have I?"

"I believe so..."

"You know me that well, do you?"

"We're similar, you and I," she said confidently.

"I dun't think so. It's not like I'm in the forest up a tree in the middle of the night..."

"I'm just working my magic…"

"On what? It looks scary…unchristian…"

"Aye. Well, I suppose it is unchristian," she said matter-of-factly. "All this was ours before any daft saint stepped onto our island and spoke their drivel. And I'm carrying it forward to this new land… I'm just doing what I need to do."

"What for though?" Justin asked plaintively.

"For Clara. For Clara Jewell," Maddy said confidently. "I'm trying to bring her back… why do you think I'm up here?"

"No. I dun't think so," said Justin incredulous at her attempted deception, and showed it by shaking his head from side to side. "You're lying."

"I was speaking to the forest. And you rudely interrupted me."

There it was again: that forest.

"Like hell…"

Maddy blew out the candle in front of her. Justin could smell the burnt wick. She gathered it in her hand, and in one fluid motion, turned to the side, and dismounted the tree as if she were stepping off some exotic creature that she had been riding.

"Oh, so you're an expert now, are you?" she asked.

"No," said Justin, "You must think me stupid. I know a fertility ritual when I see one… I saw enough ov they on farms back home. Old women working their cunning on cows and sheep. That's what you were doing, wasn't it? On yourself though… To make you fertile. What? To give you a chield."

At this, Maddy spoke something else fiercely in Irish, which seem to make the entire forest jump and contract. The leap was audible, the sensation real. Mosses moved, trees shuddered and lichens danced.

"Bejesus. I can see there's no dust on your senses Justin Nankervis. Maybe I need to explain… Indeed, up there, I invoked you – and you came… right on cue, just as I expected. So maybe you are not the problem. Maybe instead, you are my answer – right here on the mountain. Perhaps I just didn' see it before. Now I do."

Es. Fancying her wuz one thing, and so wuz getting his way beneath her dress, but this sorcery now wuz something else. If 'twas a fertility ritual, who exactly wuz she lining up to impregnate her? And then he came to fully realise what would transpire. Maybe his lust for her had not solely come from him alone, but somehow, had been implanted in him by this sylph. Now he was embroiled. At what she said, Justin was near ready to leave on the next available laker back down to Detroit, away from this mazed conjurer. Ut felt like he cudn' cross the Atlantic soon enough to get back to Cornwall. Some piece she wuz, this Maddy O'Donahue.

19

You party knaw how 'tis. Sometimes, things happen. In the drang of days, things... slip.

"Aw... no... not *him*," said a world-weary Trevorrow, clenching his fists. "Whaasmarrwiddee Samuel?"

"What's wrong with *him*?" asked a puzzled Mr Skews.

"You knaw what ee's like... naw use t'man nor beast, that boy..."

"Sorry," asked a confused Francis, "but who zactly are we talking about here?"

"Yeah, I mean, if you want my boys t'help build it, then I'd better know who you are meaning," stated a brusque Maddy O'Donahue. "Are y'tellin' of me that the man's an eejit?"

"Well, fur a start," articulated Skews, "he's the only h'engineer capable of this kind of work around the Great Lake basin, "and fur another, his expertise is what Harvey's recommend. He's their man over here."

"We'n do ut ourselves," went Justin in an attempt to be decisive. "Collectively, we've got the ability here. I mean, it's just a big kit that has to be assembled, ent ut?"

"You gotta' point boy," offered Trevorrow, "but the intricacies of ut see. Thaas the difficulty. 'Ave us got tha' or naw? The basics of ut, I agree but the finicky bolts and washers you."

"How do you knaw un then?" requested Justin, driving to find out more about Skews' selection for the h'engineering contract.

"Aw. I've knawn un a goodly while now. I've dealt with un in various mines all over northern Minnesota and Michigan."

"Sorry boys, but can y'tell us who you be discussing here? I'm not bleddy psychic now. I think y'all know tha'."

Justin was at a distance from this Maddy, sat with some sprawl on a chair on the opposite side of the room, but he still viewed her words with a good deal of suspicion. In point of fact, he considered her to be psychic, not that he'd said much to her since their strange night-time meeting under the moonlight, alone in the forest. Although she might not consider herself psychic in front of this lot, she bleddy well wuz. Perhaps that wuz why she flicked him a smile.

Skews meanwhile, looked sheepish. He knew precisely the look he'd get off Trevorrow the moment he dropped the name.

"A man by the name of Dicky Mint."

Trevorrow gave him that look.

"I think I've heard of un," said Francis. "On the grapevine like..."

"Oh, well, you would do," confirmed Trevorrow. "He's legendary... A lotta' Jackers will tell ee some tale about un."

"How come?"

"Well, the man's suppaused to be some kind of h'engineer, and to 'ave School of Mines qualifications an' tha' – but the truth is, ee's a liability... when ut comes to setting things up. Ee dun't knaw his h'ass from his h'elbow..."

"Cornish obviously?"

"Es. Been over here a few years now mind... Ee used to work the mines up Caradon way, when ee wuz younger. The Phoenix United so as I'n recall."

"Can a really be that bad? I mean, if Harvey's are suggesting him," wondered Justin. "They'd knaw, wudn' um?"

"I suppause they ebm got much ov a clue back home in Hayle. I mean, the boy Dicky is a continent away, edn a? Ee may have been alright once, but what they dun't knaw is that ee've lost it a bit over the years... Become complacent."

"What – because of old age, or infirmity?" Maddy demanded.

"Naw... he idn' that old t'be honest. He's just forgetful. Then he dun't follow instructions. And he wan't take telling – thaas the biggest problem with un," observed Trevorrow.

"Yes, well, they say some of that wuz because of that accident he had..." Skews tried to suggest tactfully.

All of them attending this planning meeting wondered what on earth had happened to him. What accident – and how had it impacted on him? Having a 'damage-magnet' mining h'engineer wudn' exactly the best ticket to be on. They wuz trying to avoid calling Doctor Jewell, not 'ave ee there watchin' this h'engineer's every move, or clearin' up the mess after un.

Skews continued: "I dun't knaw the full ins and outs of ut but I gather a few years ago now there was a bad collapse in some iron mine down in Wisconsin. Dodgeville, I think?"

"What, caused by him?" Justin worried.

"No. No. Just one of those things... Gived un a bit of a limp, so I gather... a gammy leg."

"Sounds like it affected his brain too maybe?" noted Maddy.

"Look, we don't have a choice. He's coming up from Detroit this next week, so that lot out there will soon get set up. As discussed, we've enough ore gathered to see us through the next few weeks. Plenty to go back down on the lakers, so this will give us time to set up the engine houses. The boys are up fur ut. And Maddy, I knaw your crowd are ready too... so once he's here, we can crack on."

Skews allays had a convincing logicality to him, which wuz one of his better points. That air of enthusiasm was matched however, by his keen ability to run away or hide somewhere convenient if somethun' went wrong. And now with this Dicky Mint's arrival ut sounded like things could easily head in a pear-shaped direction. Two problems faced the fledgling Keweenaw Copper Company: one wuz the fact that the days were not long this time of the year (meaning construction could take longer); another wuz that any work at grass level or above had to be completed in colder conditions. The air from the Arctic seemed to be tracking down over Canada and the whole location could feel its chilling gusts.

Stored on pallets just down from Skews' office, were all the parts of the structure that were needed. It had been one almighty task to get them up to the newly-named Mountainside community from the harbour. The biggest problem had been the two iron-forged beams themselves; these were great metallic and curving rockers, which could be attached at both ends and would have either pumped up water or the cage of men entering or leaving the mine. Beasts of h'engineering they were, like the exoskeleton of some busying industrial insects. Off them, comed the pump rods and the spring beams. These vast edifices had to be carted up the mountainside in some specially built long wagons which required the strength of six osses per go, to get them moving. Even then, they struggled to wedge the both of them along the track, and at one point, the lumberers had to go in again to help cut back the forest (a place near where Justin had encountered Maddy).

This amalgam of metal was not the only thing required though. Further wagon-loads brought up cylinders and valve boxes. Then there were the equilibrium valves, the exhaust boxes, and the condensers. After them, followed the valves (the geat and injection kinds) of varying sizes that seemed enough to provide for all of the rest of the copper mines on the continent. Spring beams were already being manufactured by the chippies and the blacksmiths were looking through the remainder of the supplies to see what else might need to be manufactured. Perhaps Harvey's gave such mines everything they could possibly require, for it was a long round trip to go back to Hayle Foundry and ask for another piece of equilibrium pipe; so too, would there be enough supplies for the future if anything became worn out or broken.

The arrival of all this kit would transform the town of Mountainside into something very different than it was before. Almost overnight, the town was now to become host to a fully mechanised industry. There would now be metal and steam in place over the last remnants of moss and lichen. Had they been able to listen – to quiet their minds enough – then all of those gathered might have learnt what the forest thought ov ut, what the sprites observed, and what the roots communicated to each other. But naw, they didn' bother. Who would? Dicky Mint, despite his various infirmities and apparent incompetence, wuz going to work as a magician in this place, and transform these backwoods inta' the industrial hub of the Keweenaw. The prospect of that both excited and terrified these two brothers, Francis and Justin. Slowly but surely, they were gaining a sense of the high stakes here. Steam meant more timber being chopped down. It meant more of the forest being decimated. They'd need to send out trusty Gourgy and virtuous Luk to find out what the natural world thought. Where wuz Nimkii when you needed un? That bugger seemed to have disappeared, though from what Trevorrow had said, tha' was nothing unusual.

Ut wuz incredible how these meetings with Skews and Trevorrow now started to be run. Each was accompanied by a reading through of the minutes from last time, and the required actions of those attending. Justin supposed that this must be what it was like running a mine properly. Francis wuz less certain of this being well-intentioned. Although all seemed professional, he could not help but think this was just a controlling mechanism put in place by Skews, to cynically keep everyone in line: to give them responsibility and then to question it if it was not delivered. Even Cap'n Trevorrow contested this regime; it clearly had not been the way the old Cliff Mine had operated. Maddy too, noted that this was not the way things had been conducted by the Cornish years ago on the Beara.

Perhaps all three cared more for a natural evolution of the mine, rather than Skews' minute detail. At this planning session, they'd noted that on a desk, Skews had now constructed (using *papier mâché*) a model of the landscape around the mine, detailing its layout and activities and showing his suggestions for the future. Indeed, his great future project was the mineral tramway down to the shore: something he clearly hoped to pull off once the engine houses had gone in. Another pertinent issue was the development of a telegraphy line to the site. This was a costly undertaking though, for it would need to be brought up all the way from Calumet, through several miles of bleak forest. As yet, the task seemed impossible, not least because of the expense of such an installation: but until they had telegraphy, the mine and the community would remain in isolation. Without it, somehow they would stay in the nineteenth century.

Ironically, at the same time as the parts for the engine house arrived at Eagle Harbour, so too did a further quota of glamorous ladies come in from below, who been specifically asked to move to this new town by Rosie. Of late, she had expanded the capacity of the saloon (she opened up further rooms and a dining facility) and in no small measure was it paradoxically starting to resemble the Cliff Hotel despite her earlier intentions. The arrival of more ladies into the camp was especially significant for it seemed to soften the world that was being built. It filled it with much-needed perfume and blusher, lace and silk. Rosie had contacts in Port Huron see, and they'd all come up from there. It was part of the deal: they had to be mobile – and go where the work was. Right now, it was here on the Keweenaw. This momentarily (whether anyone else knew), was the centre of the world, with all these Jackers. An' copper, well, tha' wuz the metal of the future.

Although many of the miners frequented 'Rosie's' as it came to be called, Justin visited less often. Maddy had scared him. He had worked out that her need (considering she was perhaps in her early thirties) was to have a child as soon as possible, and that she seemed to be suggesting, with her incantations, that he might just be the ideal father. This worried him for many reasons, but perhaps what puzzled him the moast wuz tha' Maddy herself had been created out of a rape committed by a bad egg of a Jacker: a Cornishman named Pengelly. It seemed twisted for her to even want company with him, let alone get down to procreation. He was still trying to decide what made him eligible. There were many other questions too: would they be married? Would they set up house together here in the camp? What were the implications of this? She seemed less bothered by those issues however than the conception itself. Indeed, there was the surface level talk of her gang and the mine, but underneath, et wuz this which dominated her thoughts and actions.

Somehow, almost by default, and because of the quantity of Irish labour present, Maddy had snuck onto the management committee of the mine. Maybe it irked her that she was not a shareholder like he wuz; and he needed to discover in some way if that was motivating her. Did she want to buy in somehow and have her own sixth of the deal? Jeez. She couldn't do that, not now. He fancied her – but all the witchery...? It was an aspect of her character that on some level, he did not care for very much. But then again, he knew of their mental and physical union – and what it could be like. He knew of their lust for life and what drew them together. He knawed their magnetism, and maybe tha' dark side of her wuz reflected in him. He knawed ee wudn' naw angel. Out here, he'd just struck lucky. Es. Chance had made ut so: a Jack O'Lantern was shining on his life. She wuz a strike indeed.

That night, when he'd found her alone in the forest, it worried him because she'd first lied to him about trying to find poor Clara Jewell, and then there was that sense that somehow (with all her clandestine powers) she had manipulated time and space to make him come there. He didn' like to be controlled like that, and wuz thus now worried about his own attraction to her. Every time he felt it, he wondered if somewhere, she was manipulating him: a-playing with her necklace of shells. Of course, in Skews' office, she was doing nawthun' but listening and offering her own insights, but he still hardened in his groin at the thought of physically being with her. She was dangerous but he wanted to taste her. He realised that as much as his brain was telling him to catch the next laker back down to Detroit that, in truth, in his heart he really wanted to be with her. Ee wanted to ingest some of tha' magic.

The meeting ended: all those present now concerned about the imminent arrival on the mountain of the irascible and infamous Dicky Mint. Trevorrow, Skewsy and his brother continued to chat about the construction of the engine houses, but Justin saw here an opportunity to talk further with Maddy. He needed to question her.

"'Ere maid. Can us two have a yap?"

"'Course we can," replied Maddy.

"Walk with me a while then – if you mind to..."

"Aren't you worried about being seen around town with me?"

"No. Why should I be?"

"A little bird tells me that that Rosie's sweet on you. Aye. The fierce looks that woman do give me."

"Don't worry about she," said Justin.

"Should I though?" Maddy asked, this time her questioning more serious.

"No... She's nothing to me. Never has been," he lied.

"Alright, I believe you. Well, since I saw you in the forest, you've kept your distance. Scare you then, did I?"

"A bit. It wudn' like I expected you to be doing any ov that..."

"Why not? It's perfectly natural. Perfectly human. I mean, I know well, it ain't like a Christian thing...a Methodist thing... but that's it with me Justin Nankervis, I'm a bit unconventional... Come on now, walk on with me here into the woods."

He had to trust her. He had to walk alongside her: his Jack to her Jill.

Saying little now, they made their way to the eastern side of the camp and climbed up the mountain, as ever negotiating the tall-trunked conifers. The going wuz hard, and so both of them became breathless. There'd be no conversation whilst they walked. Eventually, they came to a grove that let in some of the late fall sunshine. Maddy sat and rested. She never sat like other women, demurely with her legs closed. Instead, she sat like a man. There wuz tha' way about her.

"Come on then y'Cussie. So, you in or are you out?"

"How do you mean?"

"With me? I fancy you... and I think you like me. That's as good a reason as any in my book."

"For what?"

"To make a baby."

Justin laughed nervously. The openness of she!

"I'm being serious. I'm the wrong side of thirty. I'm old. My mother had me when she was seventeen. I don't want my tubes getting tight. All women have a clock and mine's ticking loudly."

"What – and get married?"

"This isn't Cornwall and it isn't Ireland. We don't need no certificate. We can do what we like..."

"Can we?"

"Yeah. I think so. We're adults. Who's stopping us? Plenty out here live together without bans and a license."

Justin did not want to answer but he did.

"I fear you Madelaine O'Donahue. Much as I like ee, you have the cunning about ee... an' well, I'm not sure what I make ov ut."

"That's yer Christian man Jewell speaking. You sound like a minister, not a red-blooded man."

"I have to think it through."

"Well, chapel this ain't, and I reckon you and chapel fell out a long time ago, just like me and my family did with the church."

Justin peered out over Lake Superior. He observed the golden leaf litter: the roots of trees poking into the ground, struggling for survival.

"And if we make a baby, who cares for it, eh?"

"I will."

"Not me too then?"

"Yes. Of course you too... if you want to, that is."

"But the responsibility ov ut? I mean, if we don't stay together."

"Well, I wudn' hold it against you. Some men can be bastards that way, but I know you're not. I've enough about me to raise a child... and I'd welcome your... contribution... but if you want to walk, then I'll understand. I get it."

"I don't want to walk... I mean, yes, I need a legacy too. No point in working in the mine all day, unless there's something to come home to... to work for..."

Justin turned to her once more. At least, she was being honest with him now – even if he wasn't being with her.

"Why me though? That's what I keep coming back to."

Maddy stood up and reached to hold his left hand. She held it tight.

"I see somethun' in you. I told you that. I dun't know quite what it is. But I see something in you..." she laughed. "You can give me what I need. Sometimes you just know. No magic in that."

The way that this Maddy said that, made his body ease into her. In the silence of the forest, he turned towards her and for the first time, they kissed, at first gently and then more intensively. Tomorrow, they'd feel the bruising. He felt himself being consumed, but ut was an absorption ee truly wanted. They were hurtling into each other. Her hands had soon reached inside of his shirt and jacket to feel his chest and she had hoiked up her dress high to allow him access to what until now, he had only briefly seen. She kicked off her decorated boots. Now she was encouraging him to touch her intimately. Suddenly, he forgot about the blackness of her, and instead, completely nuzzled into her form.

She did the same, making him feel strong and virile: a god in this new land. In a few further moves they were undressing each other and craving flesh and skin. Then, Maddy broke from him and lay down onto the floor of the forest. She found a bed of moss, and as Titania, encouraged her admirer to come close. He duly did so, and they became interwoven into leaf, fern and frond. The only noise came from their gasps of satisfaction; their realisation that they both needed this kind of passion in this harsh country. This far from the mine, this far into the forest, they thought no one wuz observing, but unbeknown to them a horde of voyeuring, wide-eyed creatures spied their every move, watching how this odd thing called humanity, expressed its love. Those gaking at the fumbling hands and bending limbs did not curse them though. In fact, all of them gave blessings which might have been uttered from Pan himself.

So there wuz this going on in the forest, and elsewhere too, was there activity. Boy Skews, somewhat annoyed that the rest of them had harshly criticised his appointment of Dicky Mint as the h'engineer to enable the construction of the pump house and winding house, decided that he needed some time alone. This was nothing new. He'd often take time out to walk in the woods and forget the fact that he was stuck here on this desolate peninsula. In his life, he had only two compensations for this: the first was money, which wuz coming-in in spades now and facilitated him quite a sophisticated lifestyle on the mining frontier (cash which also was being transferred to Trevorrow, Nimkii and the two brothers), and the second, was his sheer, irrepressible delight in seeing the doctor's daughter Mabel grow and develop.

He'd early on decided she was a sweet thing: a legitimate and different focus for him – away from assaying and mining. In reality, she was much too old for the poppet he'd bought her backalong (especially ordered up from a posh store in Detroit) but he knew she would love it (he knew she'd transformed it in her own mind into a piskie), and maybe come to love him, to see him as the voice of reason and guidance in her life. She'd always delighted in story and song, and seemed to commune with the forest. This all fascinated a man whose days were only used to touching minerals and ores. He noticed too, that of late, her father had neglected her. Doctor Jewell had become melancholic and full of remorse recently. Skews had visited and tried conversation but found the Doctor distant and uninterested. The Doctor had grown impatient with Mabel. With this, he gained another string to his bow in terms of making Mabel like him. He was becoming her father figure. Her real father had lost interest and was too consumed with himself. Mabel's flutterings were of no concern to him, but to Skews, they were enchanting.

So distant was Skewsy from home and so lonely was he that he had forgotten most of his own childhood and what had shaped him. In this way, Skews had become a mere shell of what he used to be, but when he thought over such matters, he knew that there was nothing he could do. His profession had made him so. The distant imagining of his wife and daughters did not help. He had been away so long that his daughters would have forgotten him, and his wife may well have run off with someone else. There was logic and good reason for it. Were things different here, he might do that himself, but no opportunity had come his way. Yet there was this Mabel and in his mind, she understood him. She wuz certainly the only one who cared for him. She had told him so, hadn't she? They'd played together.

In his walking, he considered the rest of the community. Trevorrow went back each night to Mrs Cap'n and although there wuz no love between them, there wuz at least mutual care. Jewell had had Clara. If only he had treated her better, and shown her the true wonder of the landscape, then maybe she'd still be with him. Now, he was in his house putting up with the sniffles, grunts and farts of Jenny Spargo. Likewise, he was observant enough to know that there was a growing relationship between Rebecca Jewell and Francis Nankervis. He knew from their looks, nods and glances that soon a wedding might come. That fool Justin too had probably got it on with most of the girls in the camp, and now seemed to be busying himself with the Irish slut: the one who never seemed to shut up. Es, they all had someone except him. That kind of knowledge has an effect on a man, chapel or naw chapel.

He knew where he would find Mabel. She would have gone up to the natural preaching pit and be there right now, cavorting about, singing to herself, and telling her stories aloud to anyone who'd listen. What, of course, he did not realise, is that this Mabel had an on-going conversation with the sprites of the forest. The way she spoke to them sounded like gibberish but it communicated to those who hid in the recesses of the forest and, in turn, they would watch her twist and dance. Maybe Mabel liked to come to this place on her own for it was usually where she had to conform and sit with her older sister. When her father wasn't there, she could do what she wanted: for Mabel was just about the only person in Mountainside for whom the forest was not dark or terrifying at times. For her, it was somewhere of supreme and joyful fantasy.

This man Skews often came to watch her from here in the shadows of the trees. She gave him a new sense of the world and he relished it. It made him feel alive again. It could not be helped. He guiltily wondered if she was pre-pubescent or pubescent now. He knew it was dark; he knew that it was twisted to think in such ways but it was not something he could stop. As she cavorted, he viewed the blonde curls on her head, the way her ribbons twisted around the strands of hair. He viewed her legs and imagined her soft skin against him. Es. Not good.

Skews did not know why he did what he did. At least in the forest no one could see him. At least, it was his secret. He undid the buttons on his trousers and pulled out his penis whilst watching Mabel. He needed to be careful not to moan with gratification for that would startle her. From this, he went into a kind of comforting dreamland as he touched himself and stroked himself hard. In this, he told himself that it wasn't him: it wasn't anything dark and depraved in him; rather it was something in her, or maybe even the forest itself. Yes, that wuz what was making him do this. Nothing else. So there stood Skews, a man who should have known better, but could not make himself better. He was watching this girl, and watching him was the forest. In the end, he had to place his hand over his mouth to stifle the relief of ejaculating. She did not see him this time. He had got away with it once more and his body buzzed at the relief. Mabel was clueless to his actions, though had they been crueller, then the sprites of the forest might have told her what he was doing, to warn her of him.

The white ore that had emerged now lay in spurts on a fern beside him and he quickly did up his trousers. He knew the danger of himself. He knew that he would sometime soon, impress his will on Mabel. He was sure she was sexualised that child. So he stood in the forest, breathing heavily but trying to cover up his orgasm. Yes, he told himself once more, this forest was dark. It forced him to do such things... it had a will of its own, and it had control of him. In the preaching pit, Mabel was now lying on the ground with her back to him, crouched in a foetal position, and playing with three or four flowers that she had picked. It seemed fitting for her to look this way, now that an act of love had been completed.

Mabel looked sleepy now, and this meant he could push back through the forest. Did he hear voices criticising him? He thought so. Maybe they disapproved. He would do if he could step outside of himself. When this occurred, great, breaking Atlantic waves of guilt and self-hatred raged through him, but this feeling had not stopped him yet. He knew what he must do: he'd go back to the assay office, and try to work out a way for Dicky Mint to get started. Es. That's what he would do. Beams and rods would take his mind off this girl's skin and lips. Cocky then, he wuz, this assayer: too cocky for his own good – blaming the forest for his own perversion; his own gratification. Ee wudn' about to tell anyone that though: of course not.

Now however, he was not the only one to know of it, or conceive of it. His traipse up to see Mabel and his subsequent arousal had been carefully noted by someone who had been keeping tabs on Skews for a while now. The shock of witnessing all of this did not leave Francis Nankervis for a long while, and as he followed the assayer back down the mountain, he felt like strangling ov un or picking up some heavy cobbing hammer and involuntarily bashing the man's head in. Despite the temptation he had, and the hammer he took from the dressing tables, and carried up widn', he realised that he could not yet enact his wish. At least he had the satisfaction of knowing that he had been right about the man from the start. The fact that he had signed a long-term contract with him, now made him convulse and retch.

20

Roarin' days, eh? Enough t'make ee balk up thaa wind.

The mine though, had a little pause. For a while, the ground did not shake to the rumble of drills and the resultant blasting ceased. Ut allowed a certain dignity to return. The forest hardly knew what hit ut. Conversing, reaching roots could hear each other again; and because the ground stopped rumbling, tiny, unclassified, unnamed creatures nosed themselves slowly upwards and emerged inta' the fresh air once more. They came out at twilight, and that remained the best time to see them – if you had those kinds of powers. They gaked at what wuz on and wondered why all the work had stopped.

Perhaps however, in such moments they already sensed that something bigger was coming: that this stasis wuz the calm before the storm. Certainly, although Luk and Gourgy saw them enough fur a quick yap, those sprites did not wait around very long to have much conversation with the Knockies, fur they were nearnly allays a-feared. However, from what the Knockies noted, the whole forest was glad of the rest; but anticipating only more destruction, more human reliance on its resources. Homes would surely need to be abandoned again. The forest-dwellers would also inform the multitudes of animals, birds, butterflies and other insects that they'd need to shift once more, to make way for the increasing want of humanity.

Somehow, they had picked up on the fact that although this was happening on their patch of the earth, in fact, it wuz happening all over America: not just down the bottom of the peninsula at Calumet, not just in Michigan, not only on the Iron Mountains of Minnesota, but everywhere. Soon the colonisation process would strip everything back. The world would become only further overrun with humanity and its waste. The future looked like snapped forests and piles of mining waste. Seemingly, they tried telling Luk and Gourgy of all of that, but their reaction was what you might expect: that was the way of mining, wasn't ut? Ut wudn' like humanity had been any different since the start of time. A Paradise had been created, and humanity had stanked on in there and made a mess: all fur lust and all for its habitual quest of metals, gems and minerals. And when one part had been used and abused (when the earth, had, point of fact, been bluntly and brutally gang-raped), they simply abandoned it and moved onto the next; the next patch of the earth ready for exploitation. They were smart these forest creatures though, and clearly some of them crossed many miles of terrain. Information passed between them. They knawed what wuz goin' on: knawed the true price paid fur the seductive red-brown glow of copper.

They knew, fur example, how all actions were interlinked. They knew what felling trees meant. It wasn't just the tree that went – but an entire community would tumble. They knew that digging into the earth upset the layers of soil and peat that had built up in particular places over millennia. They'd picked up on the fact that these proposed mine engines meant the use of water and steam. That meant the further diversion of streams in launders and shutes, and it meant dallying with fire (always a danger in a forest as dry as this one in summer). It meant billowing smoke, smeeching into the air, polluting an atmosphere that wuz once pristine. And then there wuz the effluent: all the by-products of these processes of mining: the arsenic and the rank tailings.

Nawbody seemed to give a damn about them, and gradually, from storage ponds and stagnant dams, the waste would one day leak into the Lake and turn its world upside-down just as here, high on the mountain. 'Twas always the way ov ut.

In picking up on these fears, Luk and Gourgy had sat down and touched pipe with both Justin and Francis, and expressed to them – somewhat bizarrely, ut had to be said – what they thought the forest wuz feeling. They tried to be diplomatic, because being Knockies, they could certainly see both points of view. On the one hand, they favoured the small creatures of the forest (there wuz clear fealty in both size and folklore) but on the other hand, they had sympathies with the humans. After all, the lifestyles of Knockies had evolved over time to be in allegiance with the humans. They could hardly say that they were impartial – and Luk and Gourgy guiltily knew ut.

For Justin and Francis, these concerns were valid enough (they'd learnt the hard way, like moast of us, in disbelieving the folklore) but they were less sure of how the destiny of all of this could be altered. There wuz a guilt about what they'd done to the forest, and what they would do perhaps to the air and the Lake, but that said, back home, ut wuz deemed fine. Why should ut be any different here? Besides, they argued, 'Merky' was a big ol' place. One little dent in it would make little difference – ut wuz vast you. Es, the two things that the continent had wuz land and resources in plenty; both seemed endless and looked like they would last until Doomsday.

Apparently, Luk and Gourgy had already put that argument across, and it wuz rejected by the forest folk because around the Great Lakes basin, there'd already been enough damage by people just digging a hole here, or a hole there, to see if they could locate some gem or metal in order to make them richer – or fatter. Their point wuz that the landscape was changing far too fast. Perhaps Luk and Gourgy could sympathise with that a bit: in their experience, back home, the quantity of magical creatures had declined greatly over the past century. Fur zertain, ut wudn' like ut wuz years ago, so es, they got ut – and tried to explain to them that they got ut. There wuz definitely confederacies see: between these Knockies and these other small people of the forest. But the Knockies knew they were more skittish and more nervous than Knockies ever were. You had to be quick in pinning them down to an answer.

Maybe this Justin (who, right then, wuz feeling satisfied that he had at last found a woman who 'got' him – understood him) and this Francis (who wuz still frustrated at his inability to properly pursue the affections of Miss Jewell) understood all of this, but felt helpless themselves. Somehow, the mine that sprawled out before them had spiralled beyond their control. It had become a raging, black beast of a thing that ate up the mountain. Ut had – almost overnight – transformed into a destructive giant (like ones in the old tales from West Cornwall). Where had they lost control of ut? How had it mutated and developed beyond what they'd imagined it would be? Neither of them wanted to say it, and neither of them wanted to admit it, but clearly there would be some kind of reckoning (there had to be) and once that wuz done, only then might they find some kind of redemption. But all that seemed a long way ahead, too far off, to be dealt with now. Besides, Justin, although delighted by what had transpired between he and Maddy, feared becoming a father, and next to him, his older brother wuz having nightmarish fears about the disgusting actions of one man. On that matter at the moment, he'd been too stunned to say anything.

"Dun't say we didn' tell ee," warned Gourgy.

"You'm right there boy. We've told um all the way along," stated Luk.

But maybe that day, Justin and Francis were preoccupied with other matters. Maybe here wuz the one chance to alter destiny and to make a corrective tweak. Here wuz the opportunity to change course and nudge things along a bit more carefully. Es. But ent that the way ov us all? We'm all sometimes too busy in the chaos of existence just trying to stand still, to even catch the true sight of things. 'Tis awnly later, when we have some introspection and self-reflection that we see a certain path wudn' the right choice t'all. An' knawing which path to take and which to reject awnly comes with wisdom, and in this pair of mucker-outters, these two Cussies, that wudn' installed yet, not by a long shot. But maybe by the tone of these Knockies, and from what else wuz happening, you can tell 'twuz comin', 'twuz goin' to embed itself in their thoughts and prayers for a goodly while. Somehow, eventually, 'twuz goin' to bring about a chapel ov renown.

"We appreciate you tellin' we though," said Francis, taking out his hands from his pockets. "Thaas one of the long-term benefits of working with you buggers."

Gourgy and Luk beamed a generous smile at their human masters. They tipped back their hard, felt miner's 'tull' hats on their heads.

"Have a bun or two," said Justin, and from his rusting crowst-box he 'eaved into the two Knockies' hands a pair of freshly-baked saffron buns.

A pleasure went through the pair, as their skin colour changed from the grey-brown of their usual tones, to something resembling a joyous admixture of pink and blue: a colour that always gave a visual indication of their internal pleasure.

If awnly these miners had seen and noted the warning from these two, in the same way they would note it if they heard a-knocking in the shaft belaw. In reality, ut wuz the same knocking here, the same tip-tapping, but you knaw how 'tis by now: neither of these two brothers would hear the sound ov ut. Never mind, eh? At least this pair would have full bellies fur a while and tha' wuz something not to be sneezed at. Once fed, they'd be quiet, a-snoring away down in the levels, and above grass. Knockies took pleasure in the simplest things really. A bit of food and pipe full of baccy – and they were made up.

While the camp wuz waiting for the arrival of the boy Dicky Mint (word wuz his laker had put in down harbour: Trevorrow had seen ut with a pair of ocular glasses), mining had temporarily ceased. In general, anyone who worked there had got as much of the groundwork done for the construction of the engine houses as they possibly could. Even deep foundations had been dug around the collars of the shafts; but no more could be achieved because they were waiting for the approval of this 'ere famed h'engineer. Ut wudn' be long before he wuz up on the mountain, overseeing construction – at least, tha' wuz wha' they 'oped. Word had comed direct from Cap'n: that ee wuz a cacky-handed bugger, so everyone had best watch un.

In order to alleviate boredom then, Trevorrow had suggested that age-old method of h'entertaining a mining community by having a rock-drilling competition. This had gone down well with all the differing nationalities in the camp, for there was always that draw of some bugger beating a Cussie's depth fur the first time. All hoped that ut would proceed in a good-natured way, especially between the pugilistic Irish and the feisty Cornish, because nawbody wanted a return to their erstwhile brawling in the streets. That said, a whole series of bets and side-bets had been made about particularly skilled drillers, but also entire countries and their successes. Money wuz dug from deep pockets and notes found in hat-bands.

The Finns and the Swedes were no drillers: they were woodsmen and their skill wuz in timbering, but working with creaking planks and gnarled logs had made them strong, so therefore perhaps despite their daily inexperience of the task, they'd always put in a good competitor. The Irish too, normally had a champion, and the Germans were not averse to having a go either. 'Course, the beauty ov ut wuz that every over-confident Jacker considered hisself to be an expert, bar none (best in the parish at least), and even though a man's daily task might not have been on the drill, they'd still have a go (and in tha', wuz much ov the fun ov ut). Ut was as much a Cornish pastime as say, a wrasslin' match, listenin' to a preacher on a Sunday, or an anniversary tea-treat.

The contest began at noon outside Rosie's and several squared blocks of rock had been carted up from the mine on a mule-drawn dray, and placed there. All the necessary equipment needed for the tests of strength had also been supplied, and the man who had been the stickler for any wrasslin' tournaments was appointed at the referee here too. This boy, who walked round continually with his hands in his suspenders, sizing stuff up, went by the name of Malcolm Edyvean, and he wuz straight s'die, so ee wuz a good choice fur the task.

Usually, there were two types of competition: single-jacking (which was one man on the end of a drill) and double-jacking (where two men assumed the same role). Double-jacking wuz often the actual way ov working belaw ground, because whilst one man laboured, the other got a breather in. Years of working the ground this way, had made the sweaty Cornish uniquely placed to do well in the competition. It wuz as if their whole bodies had evolved for this process: but then, other nationalities had their own skills, and many could equal the Cornish. The rules were that each driller – or each pair of drillers – would have five minutes in total. After tha', a measure wuz put in the hole to see what depth the drilling had gone to: the greatest depth wuz the winner.

A lot of brae an' strong men lined up fur the double-jacker. They felt this wuz where the real test wuz. The Germans had in Stefan Gries (a geht moustachioed bugger from Rammelsburg), and the boy Klaus Knickmeier (who allays preferred his own Harz mountain hammer); both wudn' bad drillers. They pair had shoulders like mine stamps. They wuz in with a chance, but so too were the Finns. They entered the blond Faas Jokinen and the even blonder Roope Toivonen (boath of whom contested they wudn' Finns anyway but Lapps instead): good, muscular drillers they were. There were countless more, and neither Justin nor Francis knew the full names ov they. The Irish had a few in too, in the form of big Flannery and his boy: a sinewy Kerry lad who went by the name ov Cillian. They looked a bit tasty.

Then, 'course, there wuz a run ov Cornish who signed up; among them, some of the decent drillers, like the bearded Walt Chegwidden an' his dark-skinned Spanish-lookin' pard, Howey Knucky. Now, boath ov they fancied their chances. Then wuz one of the old hands: a bloak originally from back Trewavas, named Bobby Moyle, with his partner Jack Hocking. Now, Moyle had arms like menhirs you and mehty with un, Hocking, had some forearms you. The suggestion around an' about in those about to watch this contest wuz tha' Justin and Francis should sign up too, but neither ov them were committed enough that day. Besides, wud it ever do fur the younger Cap'ns of the mine t'be knocked out ov a drillin' competition? Perhaps 'twas best they didn' take part – and instead, just watched from the sidelines.

One clang followed another almighty bash, as these pairs went through the rock together. 'Twas hard to even contemplate the speed ov they sometimes, so attuned wuz they in working together: every scat precision timed, with not a moment of energy wasted. The crowd liked to watch the rhythm ov ut. Even though, moast saw ut every day in the levels, putting ut in the daylight shone up how hard such pards worked belaw ground. Some of the wives and childurn observing could not quite believe the level of manual strength required: they'd heard it talked about at home during supper but never seen ut before. From the core holes, which on a normal occasion would allow the insertion of a fuse for the purposes of blasting the end of a stope, chipped up bits of stone.

Awnly when the men wanted to stop for a breather and to try and gauge the depth of the hole they were making, did they ever halt their unified attack on the rock. Usually, the men carefully sized up where they'd scat at ut, for the type of rock could make a difference – and in a cube as big as they were working with here, there were plenty of variations in terms of texture and type of stone being drilled through. Ut wuz best t'select well from the outset; otherwise, if you hit a particularly hard-veined piece, or some kind of crystal, you'd be buggered.

The double-jacker went to a series of rounds, where face-offs were deeply fought for. After each round, Rosie supplied a tray full of ale in order to help the competitors recoup from their exertions and satiate their thirsts. Those contesting the drilling had to be careful though: too much beer could see ee wobble, lose focus and mismanage the rhythm. That happened to the German pair: Stefan and Klaus, with the latter mistiming a hit and nearly scatting his pard off task fur a bit. By the time they'd recuperated, they'd crucially lost a minute ov jacking. Hauling a hammer overhead again wudn' naw easy business, and if you lost rhythm, well, you probably wudn' reach the right depth to proceed forward in the competition. In the end, ut comed down to a drill-off between Faas and Roope, and the be-capped Cornish boys Chegwidden and Knucky. They were experienced hands these four; and at the moment, they were working in the stopes beside each other on the third level. Here though, there wudn' none of that camaraderie. Here 'twas all out war you. Es. Some contest come to end up, but you had a mind as to who wuz going' t'win ut, and Chegwidden and Knucky worked hard together to gain their first win on Mountainside.

A surprise came toward the end of the double-jacker when the boy Edyvean began t'take down names for the single-jacking. Moast ov they watching reckoned a boy called Diddy Pasca t'win, because he'd won ut down the old mine for several years in succession. But then a new voice emerged. Justin tried to stop her – he really did, but she wudn' having none ov tha'.

"Now, let me 'ave a crack at it!" piped up Maddy O'Donahue who, up until this point was sittin' demure as y'like, beside all they who'd had a go at the single-jacking part of the competition.

"'Tidn' fur maids," a few Cussies shouted as a joke.

"Idn' it?" asserted Maddy, spinning in a circle to look at their jeering faces. "You haven't got any competition fer women have ya now? I reckon that I'n take the lot of ya on."

At that, the audience cudn' help but jeer she, but Maddy wuz havin' none ov ut. She wuz touching her shell necklace: what they all watching deduced as a sign of nervousness and of insecurity. At her mouthing off like that, a few bets got shifted and a few more were made. A collective grumble ov surprise went across the camp: this maid, she continued to be one who would not be shut up. So, the truth ov the matter wuz that in minutes, she an' the boy Pasca set to on the rocks, drilling as hard as y'like, like they wuz a-drilling fur their lives. A shake on ut, and off they went. Those in the audience could feel every strike, and every twist of the drill bit inta' the rock. Their efforts were accompanied by fierce moans and groans that sounded like the pair had been set some superhuman task by an ancient god. Heaving away they were, like there wudn' naw t'morra'.

Now, fust the boy Pasca wuz doin' a good job, whilst Maddy seemed to be struggling. Half-way through, she 'eaved off her shawl an' tucked her dress inta' her bloomers to free up her arms and hands a bit more. Tha' gained a goodly cheer from these Methodists. Pasca had removed his shirt, and despite the cold weather, wuz already glistening with sweat. And fur all they watching, ut looked like ut wuz goin' his way. He wuz makin' good progress, an' slinging hard, but then there wuz a clang that sounded wrong – ut had the wrong inflection to ut.

"Uh," he went. "The bleddy thing's filchered. Got a gad there, 'ave ee?"

He wuz shoutin' over t' a boy ov his to offer up the wedge ov a gad so he could lever the drill bit out and start again.

Maddy wuz slower in her actions, but she seemed t'be making depth in the hole. She'd chosen a good spot on the rock too. Because she'd stripped off, men were looking at her curvature, noting the fineness of her body. But so too, did they note the great muscles on her arms: tighter and stronger than many of they. They knew that they wudn' muscles born of simply collecting money or managing her boys. Na, ut wuz clear t'everyone watchin' that she'd had her time underground just as much as some of they had. Watchin' her moast intently ov all, of course, wuz the boy Justin Nankervis, who had alone traced the form of her body and felt the tight, erotic grip of her musculature. As the contest continued, Francis sidled up t'Rebecca. Amongst they watchin, 'twas expected. Many there knawed the score between they pair.

"This is great," Rebecca enthused.

"You not seen this kind of thing before?"

"No. Not back Bodmin..."

"Ah well, maybe not Bodmin..." Francis laughed, "but try down Camborne or up Minions... or perhaps right here on the Keweenaw..."

"The children love it... We'll talk about this in school next week. I'll try to get them to write about it."

"They'll graw up with it in their blood. They're idn' many mining communities where this kind of thing dun't happen... You wun't ever need t'puzzle now why there's allays a load of stones outside public houses with holes in them."

Standing by her, his hand was close to hers now. He wanted to squeeze it.

"Good to see Maddy having a go!"

"Yes... Justin said she was up fur ut, but I dunnaw ef he wanted she to go fur ut or naw. I wudn' like to take she on. She got more to her than moast of the bloaks competing. I bet she can single-jack a good length in. The stickler'll be there with his measuring rule soon enough. That'll tell the truth..."

And as Francis said that, Maddy gave another almighty heave on her drill bit and chipped out another inch or so of rock.

"Looks like she knows what she's doing," observed Rebecca. "I'd be useless. I've got no strength in my arms..."

"Ah, I don't think you need that." Francis said. "I think you should keep these hands soft, like they are right now."

He gently touched them and then withdrew again. This time, at his impress her fingers entwined with his, and they both smiled like a couple of kids, forced to dance together at a tea-treat; only with this pair, there wudn' now no force. It felt natural and they both knew it. It was funny how watching the violence of metal against rock had finally put them together.

"We should go to more drill contests together," teased Francis.

"Yes," said Rebecca emphatically. "Yes, we should."

"She'll do it, I reckon," said Francis. "God knows where she gets her strength from..."

"Women have got great strength when they really put their mind to something," suggested Rebecca.

"I can see. I can see that with her... and with you..."

As they watched, Rebecca pulled Francis more away from the body of the crowd. Seemingly, she didn' want anyone to hear what she was about to say to him.

"Listen," she said coyly. "I have to ask you something... Please don't be mad with me..."

"Ask away," Francis overlapped.

"It's just that... you know when you came up to the school... well, I asked around. I asked some of the mothers... some of the wives of the miners..."

"About what?"

Francis wondered what wuz coming.

"I asked them about your companions..."

"Companions? What companions?"

"You know... those things you're meant to have underground with you... All miners have them... you know, those 'knockers'..."

"Knockies, you mean?"

"Yes, that's them... Well, the women say that all their husbands have them... and that they look after them underground. I mean, is that right? I thought it was just a story... you know... a custom. A piece of make-believe?"

"That's it," asserted Francis. "A custom... a bit of folklore."

"Maybe," said Rebecca, "but that's not true, is it? I mean, it's not the reality is it?"

Francis noted the seriousness of her voice.

"Well, not really..." he said, not quite knowing the way this Rebecca wuz taking this conversation.

"Mabel, she tells me she's seen them. I didn' believe her first of all. I thought she was making it up... but now, I'm not so sure. And you, when you were in the classroom they were there, weren't they? I'm not stupid Frank. I know you've got some and they're no figment of the imagination, are they? They're real, aren't they?"

Francis wuz flabbergasted. How could he respond to this? This wuz the woman he wuz falling in love with, and he could not bear lying to her. On the other hand, by telling her the truth, he'd be breaking every miner's code and sworn oath to the Knockie species. He would not be compromised, though if there was ever one person to tell the truth to, then it wuz this Rebecca.

"Alright," he said. "You got me. And yes, they were there up the schoolhouse. They are real. I see them all the time. I can see some now... only you can't. I can't see mine... and I can't see Justin's either...ours are down mine, but there are others about. Just there, look, besides the steps up into the saloon... Do you see them?"

"No... I don't see anything."

"Well, I guarantee that they're there, watching the competition and drinking dregs of beer."

"You're kidding me?" she said, rather annoyed that Francis was still poking fun at her.

"No. Not now," he said. "They're there. I swear it. Either you're not looking close enough, or they're not allowing you to see them. They can change colour see. Sometimes, they blend into their surroundings. Their skins – they change colour according to their mood."

She noticed the more studied way this matter was discussed. Perhaps he was taking her seriously.

"You have to show me," Rebecca suggested. "You have to make them reveal themselves to me."

"A'right," said Francis. "I will... but only because it is you. But promise you won't tell another living soul that you can see them... not even Mabel... I'm already breaking a golden rule here by telling you."

"How many are there?"

"Where?"

"In this camp. On Mountainside..."

"Oh... about a hundred or so at any given time... Some are above ground, some are sleeping, and some will be in the mine bottoms... Some dun't come t'grass at all... unless they really have to."

"A hundred? Well, I don't need to see them all. How many have you got?"

"Two... between me and Justin. Each ov us has one."

"I see. And do you give them names?"

"We don't give them names. They have their own names. They've had them for centuries..."

Although Francis seemed to be honest with her, she was still not sure whether to take him on face value. Perhaps he was playing a game here – teasing her. The Cornish could be playful like that.

"Who are they then?"

"Well," said Francis, "mine's called Gourgy, and Justin has one called Luk."

But the way Francis said that made her change her mind in an instant. The way he wuz so assured about their names was convincing, so utterly confident that this pair were sentient beings who might just ride up in a kibble from the mine bottoms.

"I must meet them," she said.

"You will," confirmed Francis. "If me and you... I mean, if we're together... then you'll know. Maybe you'll know so much... tha' you wish you didn'."

He said this because he knew how hellishly annoying they could be some days. Suddenly though, it seemed settled. She was now being honest about her feelings to him by clutching his hand, and he too, had been honest with her by telling her that they lived with a couple of magical two-foot high mine spirits.

"Got any saffron buns?" he asked.

"I expect so," Rebecca said.

"Well, when you meet them, bring some of they, and they'll love you forever... They're easily pleased."

He nawticed her smile and she clutched his hand a little tighter.

By now, Edyvean, the stickler of the single-jack competition, was in there with his 'rule' ready to determine the winner. Up until this moment, the boy Diddy Pasca, had done pretty well with a fuse hole impressively drilled some twelve inches long. Now, under normal circumstances, a twelve-incher such as that would easily have won the competition: all the more so back home – since that likely meant drilling inta' hard granite. Here though, the rock wuz a mite softer, but he'd been up against this Maddy O'Donahue. Now moast of the boys watchin' knew this Maddy wuz keen as y'like, especially fur a maid, but she wudn't be naw match t' Diddy. 'Mean, Diddy had won every competition, hadn' a? Surely his reign would continue – up here on the mountain.

Well now, that afternoon, a lot of betting money changed hands, and tell ee the truth, a lot wuz lost from the Jackers, because come to end up, Maddy's drill-hole was precisely one inch longer than Pasca's. Es. She'd gone a full inch further in the time given, and that boy looked like a winnard when the results wuz announced. And the Irish – well, due to Maddy's magic and knack with a length of drill, they cleaned up, didn' um? At least 'twas one all: the Cussies winning the double-jacking competition and the Irish winning the single-jack. They seemed t'have the greater sway ov course, what with they winning with a woman and making the boy Pasca (the Cussie's drilling superstar) look somewhat pathetic. But there 'twas. He cudn' odds ut and shook her hand, well, like the good tributer ee wuz.

And the women of the camp, in that moment, had a new-found respect for this Maddy. Foul-mouthed she might be, and generally not their cup of tea, but when ut comed down to ut, there wuz nawthin in the world they liked better t'see than a maid putting a bunch of men right. And so it wuz with this Maddy. So maybe in that moment, in that final bell-tink of her hammer and drill, maybe thaas when the balance ov ut altered. Es, rite-on she wuz with ut all, blawin' over a kiss t'Justin that no bugger else even nawticed (well, maybe that Rosie saw ut) – but which only he caught and embraced. An' all the while he wandered what – ef anything – was transpiring in her womb.

All this yielded great fun, but Rebecca wuz still keen to talk to Francis about other matters concerning the camp. She'd not slept much, wondering about the presence of Knockies and now that something of that had been discussed, there wuz still the other matter: that ov Mr Skews. She wondered whether Francis had found anything out. She'd asked him directly: only in response, considering what he had recently discovered, he didn' knaw if this wuz the right moment to tell her of such happenings. Could he present the unmentionable to her? He knawed what he'd seen un doin' – and such information needed to be used wisely.

He wudn' sure telling her about Skews' activities wuz something she really needed t'knaw right now. He wuz resolved to tell her at some point, but awnly after he'd confronted Skews hisself and had it out with him. Skews wudn' there that afternoon: he wuz up his assaying office, looking over the plans ready to collude with Dicky Mint.

Otherwise, perhaps Francis might have confronted un in the here and now. Fur now though, the best thing Rebecca could do, wuz to accompany Mabel everywhere she went.

"Dun't let she go alone in the forest," Francis advised, and then a few seconds later he ruled, "Dun't take your eyes off her if you can."

"Why? Have you found out something? She's home right now with father."

"'Tis prob'ly just best fur now," suggested Francis; the rest of what he said was lost in the uproar of the crowd as smithied medals were presented by Trevorrow, first to the winning double-jack pair, and then the female single-jacking champion.

Now, whilst all these larks were occurring, elsewhere in Mountainside, something happened. You might have thought that such an activity might have drawn everyone together, but not that Skewsy – and not that Doctor Jewell. Jewell wudn' much for the drilling contests. He knew that come tea-time, a spate of minor injuries would be presented to him by inexperienced drillers, who wished fur the life of them, that they hadn' bothered to compete. He'd seen it a-fore back home.

Earlier, he had prepared the surgery to deal with a number of bruises, blisters and skin lacerations for those competing just a little too hard for glory. Such events wudn' very Methodist either. They were fair enough on their own: he had no problem with such a contest, but the fact wuz that every mining community in the world saw it as an opportunity to drink, smoak and cuss as much as they wanted. Therefore, any desire on his behalf for ut to be a Temperance event would fall on deaf ears. Indeed, so he had been told, the event was to take place practically outside Rosie's, which in his view would only exacerbate the issues of injury, violence and poor behaviour. He could already see the line-up ov broken fingers, blackened nails and sprained muscles.

He disapproved that Rebecca had gone along. He regarded it as an unseemly activity for a school-ma'am of her persuasion to watch, but, of course, she had contested that, saying that it was an important part of the community. That is what you got, he told himself, for bringing up a strong-willed, older daughter. He had contemplated her much of late, because he had become aware of her ever-greater closeness to the Nankervis boy. He feared this because of the actions of his younger brother. He had seen first-hand what his lifestyle had done to him. Yet, at the same time, he knew by now, that both brothers were individual entities. The behaviour of one should not precondition his response to the other. He kept telling himself precisely that.

Jewell had, however, insisted that Mabel should not go. He had no desire for her to see drunken men try and out-better themselves like primitive apes competing for leadership of their troup. He had her safely installed in their home by the fire, and as usual, she was happy to be in that fairy and piskie-led pretend world of hers. In fact, on that day, he delighted in it, for it seemed suddenly that all wuz back to normal once again, and that the imagined domestic world of the past had reappeared. Paradise had been regained.

In fact, a strange thing happened when he came in from the surgery. It was not only a strange thing; it was also a deeply embarrassing thing. For a while, when he entered the front room of his house, to his surprise, he genuinely thought that his wife Clara had returned, and that she was standing, warming herself, in front of the fire. Occasionally, she was responding to Mabel's narrative and the fantasy that she lived in, just like she used to. The scene was an appealing one to him: all seemed well again, like the woods had released her, and catapulted her back. The doctor could not help himself; seeing all of this – it put him in mind of earlier times – and so quietly, without her noticing, he crept up on her, observing the form of her body, and readying his hands to hold her hips. She wore that dress he liked of hers: the green one, with the pinafore now on the outside of it. The collar of her blouse was high, but there was still enough of the nape of her neck to kiss: just like he used to do to her in the old country before... before all of this happened here.

"You're back Clara," he said, laying both of his hands on her waist.

He could feel her jump at the attention: she had not been expecting it. At the same time, he placed his hot breath to her neck. He felt her fine hairline, and thought he could sense her perfume. Despite her slight jump back from him, he dared to kiss the soft skin at the back of her neck. It had been so long, and the touch and taste of it felt glorious. But at this, not only did this Clara leap away from him, but so too did she turn her surprised face to him. Only then did he fully realise the mistake he had made: the woman who turned angrily towards him was not Clara at all, but in fact, his domestic assistant, Jenny Spargo.

"Doctor Jewell, what do ee think you'm doin' ov?" she said, her voice trembling with fear. "I ent that sort ov maid. Whatever you got in mind, you'd best go down Rosie's and get out such urges there, rather than inflict they on me."

He stared at her, barely conceiving of what he had done. He saw her fir-coned, somewhat ugly twist of a face, noticed that his hands had been grasping at what actually wuz her generous ass. This was not the normal kind of woman he'd find attractive. Indeed, this was not the normal kind of thing he would do. What on earth had he done? How was Jenny to accept him in the future as her employer, when he had assaulted her senses and body in this way?

"My sincere apologies Miss Spargo," he blurted out. "I did not mean for it to be you. I mean, for some confounded reason, I thought you were my Clara... that you... I mean she... had come back."

"No," said Jenny instinctively. "I'm not your Clara. I be Jenny – here a-helping you and your family..."

"I know," said the doctor. "Really, I didn' mean to scare you... to do that to you... But for a moment... a single moment there... I suddenly thought you were her. You know that I would never do such a thing, if..."

George Jewell realised the futility of what he wuz saying. Whatever way he seemed to dress up his excuse, it seemed to make matters worse. What had become of him? Had loneliness brought him to this?

"The dress you're wearing. It resembled one of hers... the petticoat... She wore it just like that."

But then he realised: the more he continued that line, then the more perverted it sounded, as if she were acting as some erotic substitute for what had gone missing. Whatever he might say now would sound wrong. Had it come to his? Was he substituting Jenny in place of her – or had some kind of latent desire crept up on him, and overtaken him without him even noticing? If it were the latter, then he truly needed help. He suddenly realised that perhaps he had been repressing his desires: that his own inability to talk about how he felt had brought about this awful set of circumstances, where she would fear him forever.

Jenny, who was not a woman without sympathy, began to understand events a little more clearly now in her own mind. She could see how she had inadvertently deceived him and accidentally created an illusion. This realisation however, did not compensate for the shock of what he had done however, or the sexualised nature of his intentions. She had felt him upon her bottom: the kiss had been no brief peck of affection, but something more. The way he had held her waist was something she had not felt from a man before. But she saw the tears in his eyes, the especial pleading he was making. Clearly, the man had momentarily lost his senses; and perhaps that was to be expected. He had suffered greatly and although she knew he had tried to remain composed and dignified in his outward mannerisms, it was bound to come out.

"I'd best go," she said, now assured. "Best for you – and Mabel and James if I leave..."

"No. Please don't..." adduced Jewell. "I know I offended you. But let me make repair..."

"I think..." Jenny tried to say, "if..."

"Yes... I mean, I am sure you want to leave right now... but don't stay away permanently. I need you. Mabel, James and I need you... Don't make a decision now... Come back tomorrow... once you have thought things through. Be assured Miss Spargo... I am the gentleman you thought I was when you began service here..."

By now, Jewell had toned down his voice, for he did not want to be speaking in such a way before his daughter.

"I'll go now," Jenny said, "and yes, I'll think about what you said. I do understand Doctor Jewell. I do understand the pressure you've been under. I hope that I can return. I really do."

"Please do," he whispered. "I really don't know what I would do without you at this point in time... and I know... what I need to do... Perhaps I need to issue myself some of my own medicine, if you will... The mind... you know. It can play tricks..."

"Indeed," said Jenny, reaching down to put a fireguard up to the grate, and then straightening her pinafore. "Right now though, I think you need some time to yourself... Good afternoon Doctor Jewell."

She made her way in front of the crumpled form of the Doctor, heading towards the front door.

"Bye Mabel," she said softly. "See you tomorrow..."

"Bye Jenny," responded Mabel absent-mindedly, her mind as ever, on other matters of importance. Unknown to her father or Jenny a sudden thought had come over her.

The front door shut softly and Jewell collapsed into his chair, trying still to make sense of what had just happened.

"You alright Dad?" asked Mabel, now standing and seeing his indignity.

"Yes, Daddy's fine," replied Jewell, but in reality what he wanted to say was, "No. Daddy's very, very unwell."

Es. Such is the pretend world of being a parent at times. Who dun't knaw tha'?

Back down outside Rosie's, the cries of men and one woman at work on the drills suddenly stopped. Initially, as Justin and Francis turned their views up the street, to see why the now friendly competitions had abated, they thought the silence might have been to welcome this Dicky Mint. Perhaps he was making some kind of theatrical entrance to declaim his powers and ingenuity in the construction of Cornish beam engines. But when they turned, they saw that it was not his presence that had silenced all those competing and watching.

Walking down the street in his angular, padding way, wuz someone that they had not seen in a long time. It wuz Nimkii. Moast of the community had heard his name by now, and knew that an Indian was involved somehow in the operation; but they did not expect him to enter the camp in the here and now. Such wuz his stature and presence that no one noticed the small scurrying form of Jenny Spargo assert her way, crossing the road towards North Street. All eyes remained on the native; his jet-black, locked hair, this time, tied back around his head.

He liked a good entrance this boy: Francis and Justin knew that. Perhaps he'd come fur his money: there was plenty of that fur'n in the safe, and he could have his due reward. But there wuz a kind of solemnity to the way he walked that neither of the brothers had seen in him before. Those that knew ov un, also noted his stance. Almost opposite Rosie's saloon he came to a stop and surveyed the drilling competition that wuz occurring. He grimly smiled at it, either indicating his disgust with it, or that he knew precisely what it was all about. He seemed to note all the more Maddy O'Donahue's work, for she was the one now standing in front of everyone with a huge drill bit on her shoulder. Justin eyed their link, pondering what both of them knew about each other, for he realised, both knew the woods. And then the great man turned to survey the rest of the camp. They wondered whether he had already noted the new equipment for the construction of the twin engine houses – and that he'd come to quickly realise that the operation he had left a few months ago, was growing and expanding rapidly – without his or the forest's permission.

In the end however, that was not the reason for his presence. In his time-worn satchel, the one that they had earlier seen used to carry the first ore down the mountain; he was clearly carrying something of significance. Everyone's eyes focused on his right hand as he reached to open it up, and then pull from it a small object. It was made of cloth, and at one time in the past, had been starched white. Now, however, it was stained and dirty. Gently with his forefingers, Nimkii pulled out the object's four corners such as they were, and bent down to place it on the ground, lowering his head as he did so.

Everyone present gazed at the object he had brought. At first, they thought it might have been some sacred object from his tribe, something of Shamanic or ritual significance, but it wuz not that. In fact, what he had placed before them wuz a torn woman's bonnet. Rebecca alone recognised its place and its value.

"I know it," she said. "It's my mother's! It's my mother's bonnet."

Es. 'Twas her discarded gook, sure 'nuff.

21

Now, as you might knaw, a lot ov individuals in the camp were in line fur some scolding tongue pie tha' week. Rebuke and reprehension. Es. Thaas the way. There wuz plenty too, who might be given what fer in their awn shacks and homes. You'n fully see how 'twas unfolding, inch-by-inch, day-by-day, on the geht mountain: how all these individual tales came t'thread and bind together. Es, true 'nuff. But fur love ner money, nawbody could tell ee how next ut would all pan out. You knaw enough now though (in all a person's striving and stroathing), t'understand that a warm saffron bun placed on your kitchen table dun't come easy. An' chapels, well, they ent just about sin and transgression: they'm about love and salvation as well. You knaw too, that the world is crammed full ov magic and redeeming hidden moments that you had no idea about. Some people think thaas all gone – but ut ebm gone t'all. Aw naw, my 'andsome. 'Tis right here in front ov ee.

The blustering arrival of Mister Richard Mint, an h'expert mining h'engineer graduate from the esteemed an' world-renowned Camborne School ov Mines, wuz supposed t'be one of they great moments fur the mine. When ut wuz recognised on the Wednesday ov that week in mid-November that he wuz on his way, naw amount of preparation went amiss fur his arrival. Skewsy had organised a flash photograph of him to be taken with a special commemorative pick-axe breaking ground of the first of the engine houses to be built (in fact, the generous footings wuz already in, but tha' didn' matter), which he duly did; as well as a high tea of all manner of nicies and buns for the respected technician. Had there been a parping brass band available, then one might have been employed at this point. Skewsy had paid for a photographer to come up all the way from Calumet: money t'burn see.

This very de Vinci of 'Merky' wuz now walking in their camp: he wuz there to set they up good and proper. The great and the good of the town (or at least as many as Skews could dig up) had been invited to meet un' but within just a few moments of his arrival, it was quite clear that the articulate Mr Mint had only one word that he liked to use more than once, and that word wuz "Grand". When people fust asked ov un how his journey up from Detroit had been, the response wuz "'Twuz Grand." And when this Justin and Francis Nankervis asked him whether he wuz looking forward to getting started on the engine house's construction, the same response came from out of his geht shaft ov a mouth. Gradually, those there realised that for a man who dealt in tight angles and deft precision, he wuz initially at least, somewhat nervously monosyllabic. Perhaps thaas what happened when you gave too much time to calculus, the thicknesses of walls – and the safe insertion of pin-rods.

The awnly man ee talked to a bit more affably wuz John Trevorrow because as everyone knew, the pair had worked together before. Trevorrow (who, as we shall see, had been having his own issues of translation of late) greeted him like an old colleague long missed, but that wuz the way ov ut sometimes. Appearances like tha' can be deceptive. You do what's needed fur the greater good. 'Course, boy Skews wuz all over un like a rash, trying to grease the wheels, and oil the pump so t'speak. Skews wuz full ov ut too, coming out with every obscure mining-h'engineering term his seedy brain could lay its hands on. Anyone else knaw what a zyghyr wuz? Well, Skewsy did. Francis kept his eye on un, never relenting in his fixed gaze on him. His purpose wuz to try to make Skews feel uncomfortable and for him to knaw that he wuz under surveillance. Indeed, it wuz his long-term plan to induce Skews to ask him if anything wuz wrong. Then he'd have his moment. At that point, he'd reveal what delicacies he saw him doing in the forest.

This Dicky Mint turned out to be a proper short-ass. Aw, now. Ee wuz one of they boys who seemed t'be all head and torso but with two small, bandy stumps fur legs. In another world, through different spectacles (perhaps ones with a lot of dust, drill grease and grime on them), you might almost have mistaken un fur a Knockie. In all honesty, that wuz perhaps not a bad thing because he wuz directly concerned with the safe installation of important equipment in the mines of North America, and this job took un all over the plaace. Ee wuz suppaused t'knaw his onions – just like the Knockies, not that he believed in any of they – so ut wuz discovered. Several people had picked up on the fact that he didn' care much fur superstition or any of tha' nonsense. His jag wuz measured science alone. Maybe the Dodgeville collapse had taught un tha'.

He walked with a tin-tipped walking cane: t'compensate fur the fact that one of his legs got twisted in tha' accident down in Wisconsin (which nawbody dared t' question un about); an' therefore, in such grandeur he looked like he knawed what he wuz doin' ov with any piece of mining gear. That perhaps wuz the point though: he *looked like* he knawed what ee wuz doing. Whether he did knaw what he wuz doing wuz a different matter, as the community at Mountainside shortly came to discover.

Minter, as he swiftly became known (the Cornish were allays hellers fur giving people nicknames, especially they with a bit ov power and swagger) wuz certainly goin' to make his mark here. The man wudn' no more than say forty, but he was prematurely aged: a thin wisp of greying hair tried an' failed to cover the dome of his head in a piece of extreme h'engineering, whilst he used his cane in a remarkable range of creative ways to illustrate any crucial point about the construction of the engine houses tha' he wuz making.

Skews housed un in a newly-built cabin on North Street, not far from the Spargo property which he hoped would give un the space enough to contemplate the detail of the project being undertaken. Ee cudn' be found there very often though. Es. This Minter wuz minted enough to soon gain the attention of a fair few girls down in Rosie's place. In fact, it felt like he'd awnly been at Mountainside for five minutes a-fore he wuz down there in the evening, enjoying a brae ol' bit of convocation and cavorting with the maids. Limp maybe, but he knawed where t'put his hands an' cop a feel.

He'd strammelled inta' the camp a couple of days after the drilling contest. People soon began to knaw who ee wuz. Not awnly did a have the appearance of being the mutant offspring of some Knockie and human interaction, but he was also boss-eyed so when you looked at un' straight, his vision gave the appearance of not looking at you directly but almost through you, several yards down the road. T'compensate fur that, he wore thick, bottle-lensed spectacles which rather exaggerated the proportions of his eyes compared to the rest of his head. The Minter was well-dressed though: clearly, he'd made a bit working for Harvey's operation in 'Merky', and he'd spent his money on fine fashion from some of the bespoke downtown tailors in Detroit. Aw es. In that sense, he even took it up a notch from the kinds of outfits Doctor Jewell had become well-known fur wearing. Like a relic from the previous age, somehow washed up on the shore here at the northern end of the Lakes, he also wore a stove-shaped black hat; perhaps with some nod to the fact that he wuz an h'engineer, thus evoking the inventive spirit of Brunel.

But he wudn' zactly naw Isambard Kingdom. The reason fur tha' wuz that much as he had knowledge of wha' needed to be done, the man wuz a tad complacent in everything ee did. In point ov fact, despite his distance from Cornwall, he latently carried with him that most grotesque of Cornish sins: which wuz that he fully embraced the concept of dreckly. Now, dreckly is fine sometimes: when you've just comed home from a full eight hours of hard jacking in the third level of the mine, 'tis fine enough t'say that you'll put the rubbish from the spence out dreckly. All well an' good, an' so on; but ee? Well, ee wuz on a contract see, signed with Skewsy, an' you didn' need t'knaw much beyond that – other than that ee was being paid by the hour fur his time and input.

Ut wudn' like ee wuz on a 'go slaw' button all the time, but whenever there comed a difficult piece of the h'engineerin' puzzle to solve, he'd state that that particular problem would be dealt with dreckly. An' so, in this way, maybe that wuz what these h'engineers did, but maybe too, he was conforming to ethnic type. In his mind, dreckly was a kind of moment to think over something, give ut due thought and consideration in the mind, which wuz one positive way of looking at ut, but on the other hand, time wuz money. When he got one of they dreckly moments, well, sometimes those around him made the decision fur'n – an' cracked on anyway. This wuz the response of Justin and Francis who wudn' well known fur their drecklyism. They wudn' have got this far now, would um, if they had a dreckly mindset?

"So, when shallus begin then Mr Mint?" asked Justin, trying to inject some enthusiasm into proceedings.

"Well, I shall settle in t'day Cap'n Nankervis, and I reckon early tomorrow morning, at eight o'clock precisely, we'll start setting things in place. Ut won't take we long once we get going. And you've made a heap of progress already by gettin' the footings in. 'Tis all upwards from there I'd'reckon," the h'engineer said with some measure of confidence.

This Minter had an accent which wuz an absurd-sounding combination of Cornish and American English. He'd kept the old words and phrases in place, but they had a new spin to them. At first, Francis found that dislocating but then he realised that he, his brother and a lot of the rest of those who laboured at the mine, were just a few stages before him in terms of becoming Americanised. Ut wuz the way of things: you cudn' help but soak ut up, and then it comed out when you weren't looking. He'd nawticed ut with everyone: Rebecca, Doctor Jewell, and even a shift in the voice of Maddy.

"How long do you think ut will take?" he questioned.

"Aw, well, hard to say. But things are looking grand now, so if the weather holds, we might get one of the houses built by Christmas. Best to get the pump active fust I d'reckon, then whilst the mine's being cleared of any water we can start on he second..."

That made sense to Francis. Maybe this boy wudn' the daft bugger Trevorrow made un out t'be.

"Everyone's ready to go..." offered Justin, then tried to make a joke by continuing with, "All hands to the pump then..."

"Yes, Mr Skews informed me of the quality of the ores coming up, and that you've enough to keep supplying Detroit, while our h'operations continue."

He paused for a while, and then reflected, "You really are in a marvellous position here you know. All sorts of discussions down below about opening up the motor-carriage industry. Yes. Grand plans, Mr Nankervis... and I hope Harvey's will be able to do you good service. I've had no complaints over my years of work for them and pray that can continue here."

His enthusiasm though, impressed Justin. He liked the way he brought a technocratic drive to the place. Sometimes, he didn' sleep thinking about all this mumbo-jumbo up on the mountain: the Knockies going crazy about the forest speaking to them, roots conversing, and the story of Clara Jewell's disappearance and its consequences from yesterday. Es. Mehty here in front of them looked like just what they needed at this point in time.

"Whaas fust then?" enquired Francis.

"We'll get the weight-bearing wall in t'start with, then best build around ut. Fur the beam see. I d'reckon thaas best fur what we've got here. I'll devise a set of pulleys and so on to lift the beam inta' place. Got enough mules and osses here, 'ave ee? Because it'll need some strength t'raise ut."

"Reckon so," Francis said. "A lot of the wagon osses can be put to use elsewhere during this phase..."

"Grand... grand..." the h'engineer offered in response. "Once thaas done, I'll then commission work on the chimley stack... The scaffolding there will be the main thing. Your Finnish boys up to the job? Swedes too, I hear..."

"They'm ready. They'm good at what they do. Tell us whaas needed and we'll convey it to our crew here."

The Minter nodded in appreciation.

Observing this conversation was Maddy O'Donahue. She moved closer to Justin, maybe to overhear better, but also maybe to overtly state that she and Justin were together. He'd already met the Irish woman and wuz intrigued to know more. He'd awnly been in the camp five minutes and already he'd heard stories about her activities of late.

"I'm sorry," Minter went, "I know you were introduced to me earlier on but I've forgotten your name my dear."

He said "my dear" like Maddy wuz some grand dame. She gave it to him again. He did remember something about her though.

"And you say you're from the Beara... Now, that wuz a plaace! I never got out there myself, but I gather some good ores were found... Harvey's have sent several beams out there over the years... See from Hayle to south-west Ireland... not so far, is ut? Not compared with taking something across the wide Atlantic. Delighted to meet you..."

"Maddy's just won our single-jacking contest..." offered Justin. "She's a bit special, this one..."

Maybe in saying this, he wuz trying to offset what else he'd heard about her.

"Really?" Minter squealed in delight. "Goodness gracious, my dear! Wish I had that kind of strength."

In these few seconds of discussion, Dicky Mint had already picked up on the fact that one of the Nankervis brothers wuz obviously either married to or courting this Irishwoman. The politics of mining communities, as he had come to know, were just as important as the precise diameter of a cylinder.

"So, that matter's settled then... And do you have a good lady Mr Nankervis?" questioned the h'engineer, now turning his attention to Francis.

Francis blushed slightly and seemed unready to give an answer. He mumbled something, which was unintelligible to those around him.

Justin answered for him.

"Early days, Mr Mint, with my brother here – and a lady in the town... but yes, they'm sparking a brae bit..."

Francis gave his brother a look. Temporarily, his gaze turned from Skews to reprimand his sibling. As yet, this was not the kind of information he wanted bandied about. Rebecca and he had not even told her father that they were a-courting proper. Hell, he wudn' sure even if they wuz as yet. There wuz much still to be discussed.

"Grand. Grand. Glad to hear it, glad to hear it. I hope I may meet her soon."

At that moment, comed a pause in the conversation, and twice, Dicky Mint tried to open his mouth to seemingly address Maddy, but twice, he relented, and what he appeared to want to mouth wuz never said. Perhaps at that moment, he deemed his inner voice inappropriate. There wuz perhaps something this skilled man wudn' givin' away, or even that despite his wish to be convivial, he realised he needed to be circumspect. They'd all seen ut though; all noted his cessation of dialogue. This wuz all well enough because the oily force of Skewsy wuz back with the group now.

"Another saffron bun Mr Mint?" offered the obsequious Skews. "They are straight from the oven of Mrs Cap'n... Mrs Trevorrow... and she is, I gather, a splendid cook... Fresh saffron grown right here."

"No. No," said Dicky Mint. "I'm full enough. I've already had three – an' mighty 'andsome they were Mr Skews, but I could not eat another..."

In this discussion, Skews wuz clearly trying to pull Dicky Mint away from them. But even they nawticed that the Minter seemed to prefer their company to Mr Skews. Maybe this man had already h'engineered a way through the politics of the camp, with him coming to know precisely what kind of man he wuz dealing with in the form of this Mr Skews. Perceptive as he wuz, and despite his drecklyism, Mint wuz able to see the overt tension between this one brother Francis, and his co-adventurer at the mine here. Skews himself was also very aware of the way in which Francis Nankervis wuz looking at him. The pair pulled slightly away from the Minter, Maddy and Justin. They spoke in hushed tones.

"Do you suddenly have a problem with me Mr Nankervis?" Skews asked Francis directly. "It looks like something is troubling you."

"Something is troubling me," said Francis in a low voice. "But I'll air it another time... You'll find out soon enough."

Skews nodded and stepped back, nudging Mr Mint once more to join another conversation. Mint had not heard what wuz said but knew by now, that he'd need to step carefully between those two. Maybe the best policy was to work with Trevorrow and this other brother Justin in matters ov h'engineering. But then, what mining camp in the world wuz there without such tensions? Ee'd seen ut a thousand times.

What wuz ut about here though, that wuz different?

Fur the moment, he cudn' put his finger on ut, but there wuz something different goin' on. Ee cud feel ut in his bones. For the rest of the afternoon, he indulged Mr Skews, and several important matters were discussed regarding the construction process; but at the same time, he craved a simple beer and different company. That is why he went down to Rosie's and there, propping hisself up at her bar, he contemplated this strange, new world he'd stepped into.

Skews wobbled mentally as he walked away from this group. Mr Mint was conversing with him about some matters, but he could not fully ingest what wuz being said. Skews' mind only ran to one thing, and that wuz the way in which Francis had changed his response to him. What did he knaw about him now? What new information had he somehow gleaned? 'Mean, the brother spent moast of his time down the mine, so what could he have seen him doing? Frantically, Skews contemplated all of this over and over in his mind. He ran through some of the dodgier aspects of his own financial practice with the mine, the cuts he made here and there, and the way he brought in extra coins to his own purse, but it was not that, surely? Francis, Justin and Trevorrow joked with him all the time about that. So what wuz ut? And then, as he put the empty plate of saffron bun crumbs down on a table in his assay office, he began to reflect on other actions of his, and wondered if those were the reason for the brother's now overt dislike of un. In this, he wuz forced to reflect on his own misdemeanours. Some tongue pie – or worse – wuz clearly going to come his way and he'd need to be ready to catch ut.

Ut didn' take much imagination t'realise that this Maddy and Justin later went back to his room, and continued to express their attraction to each other in various amorous ways. Aw, she wuz keen this Maddy. She knew when it wuz a good time: she'd learnt from generations of women before her. Ut wuz all about improving her chances ov conceiving. Justin wuz rather more like men can sometimes be – interested awnly in getting his end away. Shame t'say ut but thaas men sometimes fur ee. Still, tha' seemed t'be the way tha' boath of they liked ut. Naw preacher wuz breathin' down their necks, wuz a?

Francis stayed silent though, and went for a long stroll in the woods. He retraced his steps up to the preaching pit, and contemplated all that had transpired. His mind was set on two things: the matter of Mabel, and of course, the will of her older sister. Rebecca had spoken to him about some incident regarding her father's help, the maid Spargo, who apparently, had been a bit difficult of late, and then, of course, there wuz the on-going mysterious matter of the bonnet. He parked both of those matters for the moment though, and made sure he did not stray too close to where Skews had been,

The day before, the bonnet had signified the cessation of the drilling contest and caused much upset to Rebecca Jewell. All understood what Nimkii had done however. He had found an item of clothing that belonged to her mother, and he had brought it back. He was being honest (a rare thing in this place at times!) and whilst the crowds for the contest abated, it wuz Trevorrow who stepped in to try and communicate with him as to what the Indian had found. Of prime concern wuz the whereabouts of the bonnet when it had been found: both its wider location in the vast forest around them, but also its more intimate status in that area. Had it, for example, been found by a shallow stream – or caught on the spiky lower branches of a tree? The question as to whether anything else had been found was a mute one, for surely if Nimkii had found any other clues as to her whereabouts or state, then he would have brought them back as well. This thought reinforced the notion that the bonnet wuz all that had been found.

It wuz such a bizarre object as well – and back home, wuz not normally something her mother would wear. In fact, she had borrowed one of the white gooks from a balmaiden by the name of Sal Clemo, in order to wear whilst cleaning the Jewell household: maybe to show she could be working-class too. And then there wuz the way it looked right now: covered in grime and mud. That colourisation seemed to suggest that it had been flailing around the forest floor for a while, and obviously that it had become detached from her mother. This brought two further notions into play: if the bonnet was discarded, then had she somehow carried on and, in some capacity, was still living in the forest, but also, there wuz the more worrying prospect that this was all that wuz left of her mother: one notation suggesting complete disappearance, or even a kind of alarming absorption into the forest. Whatever was being contemplated, Trevorrow had been at pains to try and make sense of it for her. He and Nimkii were crouched together, with Nimkii drawing fiercely and intensely into the sandy layer on the main drag through the town.

For Rebecca, it had felt like the fate of her family wuz now in this Indian's hands. Whatever he said, would be gospel. Several people hung around to see what he was saying (or rather what Trevorrow wuz translating). As this process took place, the awnly thing Rebecca could really contemplate, wuz how she would deal with this matter with her disturbed father and her awkward sister. By now, she herself had moved to the bonnet, and picked it up to examine it. Involuntarily, she smelt it. She knew the lack of purpose in doing this, but something in her made her want to seek out her mother's smell. Of course, the bonnet smelt only of the dank earth and nothing more. But at least this Indian had been right. Somehow he had known it was her mother's and so brought it back. Perhaps there wuz some comfort in that and the kindness of this act.

'When Nimkii and Trevorrow had finished their long discussions, the Cap'n eased his rheumatic frame upwards, and began to orate what he had found out.

"He found Mrs Jewell's bonnet about five miles due south of here. Nothing else. Only that. There was no trace of her, just this... He's been aware of her having gone missing for some time but he hasn't been able to find her. There has been no trail. No scent. No nothing."

A collective gasp had gone around those gathered, and Miss Jewell needed to lean on Francis, in order to steady herself. Nimkii seemed to here be confirming her worst fear: that somehow her mother had stepped clean off the earth, or had even fallen into some unprecedented theoretical void. After Trevorrow first spoke, Nimkii spoke once more, and made his translator notice something else in the picture. The Cap'n nodded and continued – even though it seemed he did not want to speak much more.

"Nimkii here found the bonnet... in a glade... on the floor... es... in a circle of toadstools..."

Nimkii had pointed again at the diagram he had etched on the ground, and with his eye and finger, commanded the frankly by-now, nervous Trevorrow to continue.

"Toadstools and mushrooms," he said hesitantly, "all brightly coloured... reds, and oranges and yellows... that's what this Nimkii says."

The decay described seemed to link with death. There wuz not a person in the camp listening who did not think of the fungi named dead man's fingers pushing out of old, fallen bark and the carpet of moss and lichen. With Trevorrow's words, those attending could almost smell the rancid putrification. They were imagining her dead body below and those toadstools pushing up from her buried form.

How long had she been gone now?

Long enough maybe. Sometimes, you try not to think that way but you knaw nothing can alter the way you imagine it. After what Trevorrow said, the street went quiet. In the distance the awnly thing that could be heard were the crows gathering in the west. Wuz this some kind ov closure? Ut didn' feel like ut because Nimkii's knowledge only – in fact – caused more questions to be asked. It sometimes felt like her disappearance would never be solved: that it might never go away. It would stay with everyone until the end of their lives. Death could do tha' sometimes. Linger.

The silence persisted for some time, until further up the street came the sound of a door slamming shut. It startled everyone present, and once that noise echoed through the camp, the sound of running footsteps could be heard on the sandy covering of the route-way. Coming towards them wuz the hurried form of Mabel Jewell. Breathless in the way that all young people are when they run at speed, she entered the circle of by-standers, not even giving a look to her sister who held the gook in her hands.

"It was in the fairy ring, wasn't it? I know. I'm right, aren't I?"

Precisely what devilment this wuz nawbody knew, but the child had zertainly sensed ut. She could never have heard what Trevorrow had already said to those gathered there. Something else had driven her here to come and stand amongst them. Maybe she'd realised what her father had done with Jenny Spargo.

"What?" asked Nimkii, for the first time speaking in English.

"Mam's hat..." answered Mabel. "Her bonnet,"

There were gasps of surprise at what she said – but Rebecca and Francis did not recoil. To them, Mabel's prediction – her foresight – her way of understanding the world wuz nothing new. They had known of it for a long time. For the rest though, well, it singled out the middle daughter as having powers that could barely be contemplated. But it did not stop there.

"You knew, didn't you Miss Donahue? You knew it was there too."

Maddy stepped forward.

"Who told you that?" asked Maddy, now placing down the drill bit she wuz still carrying, and moving in sympathy – but also surprise – towards the girl.

Mabel didn' want to speak. The fact that this Irish woman responded to Mabel wuz enough to scare her, but now that she had spied the actual bonnet in Rebecca's hands, the enormity of events started to take hold in her, and she began to tremble and shake.

"Don't be scared," articulated Maddy. "Please... You hear it now, don't you?"

Mabel wuz still trembling, but she managed to nod a "Yes."

"Does it speak to you Mabel?"

"Yes..." she shivered out.

"You and me both then..."

Maddy had reached Mabel by now, and was reaching out to hold her hand, aiming to comfort her. Mabel no longer saw Maddy: intrigued, she was reaching out for the runs of sea-shells around her neck.

"Who?" loudly demanded Rebecca, trying to make sense of what she was seeing. "Who has been speaking to you?"

But the answer she was looking for did not come from either Mabel or Maddy.

Before they could reply, ut wuz Francis who quietly responded with the words, "The forest."

At this, Maddy and Mabel nodded, and Rebecca violently broke from him, to push her way through the crowd and go back inside to tell her father precisely what had been discovered. She had no idea, of course, of what else had transpired earlier that day, and did not fully understand the reluctance of her father to even process the information that his oldest daughter wuz telling him.

A long way back up the camp, on the very edge of the woods, a lone figure had looked down upon this scene, and saw the way this woman Maddy O'Donahue was comforting his Mabel. He knew something incredible had just happened, but not one bit did he care for the association of his curly-haired star-girl with that damned Irish witch. He could awnly think of Mabel one way – and didn' want her corrupted by the likes of she.

Another figure watched closely too. It was Justin Nankervis. He was starting to see an unholy trinity open up before him: there was Mabel, there was Maddy, but then, so too, there wuz Nimkii. All ov them were connected in some way to what wuz going on here, but for the life of un, he could not put his finger on precisely why they were linked. This portal that they had formed together merited more inquiry. Fur zertain now, Maddy would entertain this Mabel, and in a short while, with his foot, Nimkii had scrubbed out the image he had drawn and the crowd started to disperse. Trevorrow looked unsure of himself, as unsure of himself as he'd ever been, and Justin and Francis knew that the same look had crossed their faces. This little maid Mabel – the Doctor's daughter – what wuz she like? Where did tha' come from? The child had some kind of foresight fur zertain, and ut wuz not just the Cornish who went home that night with a sense of renewed superstition: they all did – the Irish, the Finns, the Swedes and the Germans. Hell, some went home swearing 'twas time they went a bit more sprightly t'chapel ov a Sunday morning – an' tha' wudn' just the Cornish. And somehow, there and then, ut seemed like tha' might well come. The h'unexplained can h'always make a man more religious.

There wuz a good deal too, to be discussed with Nimkii who, on this occasion, understood a need for him to remain at Mountainside. The two brothers hoped that this time, he would stay for a while. and that working with Trevorrow as translator, they might be able to ask him some more thorough questions about the forest around them, and to then see if they could confirm what their pair of Knockies – honest Gourgy and reliable Luk – had said about ut: that ut wuz unhappy at the way it had been treated, how the mine had encroached on land and churned up more of the woodland than anyone ever expected. Maybe there wuz still time to put ut right. Earlier, in seeing the abandoned limp rag of her mother's bonnet in Rebecca's hands, lots of things suddenly seemed to connect. At precisely the same time, they wondered if Clara Jewell's strange disappearance wuz somehow related to their actions: their wanton and ill-judged destruction of habitat. Trouble then – and then t'morra', anticipation ov the glorious arrival of this boy, Dicky Mint.

22

My Gar, Rebecca tried. My dear life and days, she really tried. She attempted to get her father George Jewell to engage with the relic of the bonnet brought back to the camp by Nimkii. When she showed him it, initially he dismissed it by saying that it was not his wife's, and that it was a bal-maiden's. That was convenient for him, for that way he did not have to deal with the present (he was still reeling from that awkward, fumbling encounter with Jenny Spargo). But, he was forced to acknowledge that it was his wife's when Rebecca showed him similar bonnets offered to her by Sal Clemo, still remaining in her mother's wardrobe. The odd thing was that even though he listened to Rebecca giving him her version of Nimkii's story about what he had found, he neither commented upon it nor discussed it with his daughter. He had no need to. It seemed now that his ghost-wife was off-limits, and to no longer be openly discussed. Jewell had located it in the deepest, darkest level of his mind, and stowed there, never to be opened again. It was his way of dealing with it.

Rebecca understood this process but nonetheless found it frustrating to cope with her father. It felt like she alone had to bear the burden of the discovery made in the fabled forest. Her father busied himself with matters to do with the mine, working in conjunction with Mr Skews and Mr Mint on the engine house's construction, and contributing to the detailed discussions about safety aspects (he had, by now, picked up on the fact that apparently Mr Mint did not have the greatest safety record going). The three of them, to an extent, became thick as thieves, with them presenting outwardly the face of an educated autocracy in the community; at times, a little in opposition to that of the official mining Cap'ns: Trevorrow, Justin and Francis. Rebecca knew of his need for diversion, to pour his energies into the community instead of facing what was inside himself, but likewise, she did not like the way that her sweetheart was now being sidelined in the construction process. She put her mother's bonnet in the drawer of his bedside table, and hoped at some point, he would find it and reconnect with it. That bluster and pretence of his could not last.

"I haven't washed it," she asserted. "I've left it just as Nimkii found it."

"What are we to have for tea tonight?" was her father's response. "I'm in the mood for some urt pie and clotted cream."

Because of this, Rebecca spent more time with Francis. She was starting to feel comfortable in his company now, and perhaps he too, in hers. Gradually, they opened up their relationship to others in the camp, and the general view was that their coming together was a natural pairing: an evolution of like-mindedness. If two people were more suited to each other, then the community of Mountainside did not know it. By this time – it was early December – and Francis was thinking of having that difficult conversation with her father about his intentions towards his daughter. Already though, George Jewell had known what was in the offing, and had come to understand that this Francis was a very different kettle of fish to his brother Justin (who wuz still requiring treatment at the surgery – his complaint had not gone away).

In different circumstances maybe, her father might have protested a bit more (a mining Cap'n out here in the wilds wuz not exactly his first choice) but then again, he saw no other better offers. A more pertinent issue, of course, was the fact that Francis

Nankervis and the Keweenaw Copper Company were supplying the doctor's wages, so in this way he had no choice but to approve the match. He'd been pleasantly surprised by Francis though and the way he conducted himself. He could see why Rebecca liked and admired him. He saw the potential they had in this community, and knew that any thoughts from the past had to be dropped. This place was now the focus of everything. Cornwall was a world away – almost on another planet – and maybe his silence about his wife was helping him to confront that reality. If they did marry, then children might come, and that would take his mind off things. Yes, Francis Nankervis was a good man, a kind man.

Jewell guessed that it would not be long before Francis asked him for his daughter's hand. This was fine, but a realisation did come upon him, that then he would be left in the house alone with James and Mabel. Thankfully, Jenny had come back but was now more guarded about being in his presence. He'd again apologised. He said he'd taken medicine (he hadn't). At least she could care for James (that was one matter off his mind). As for Mabel, he did not know what to think. He'd been told by Rebecca about this girl's obsession with the forest talking to her, as well as the dreamy fantasy world that she continued to live in – almost as if she wudn' grow up.

The problem seemed that she was growing physically, but was almost staying young in her mind: to him it was still full of fairies and pixies, and he felt she needed a substantial dose of reality. He sometimes could not sleep because he worried that there was something mentally unhinged about her (that her mind was not developing as it should) – and maybe in his darkest thoughts, this was a direct legacy of how his wife had acted. It was hard to hold a conversation with her: to obtain her true thoughts on the world. She gave nothing away. He had put this down to adolescent moodiness, but in his heart, he knew it was something more. She was menstruating now: was it a woman's monthly ailments that consumed her? He did wonder.

What too, was her connection with Maddy O'Donahue? He knew, by now, of their link, and he did not like it one bit. Although he had not commented much at the time, Rebecca had one morning informed him of the relationship that Maddy, Mabel and this Nimkii seemed to have with the environment beyond the camp. At least maybe her link to Nimkii might be productive: he still had hopes of connecting to the Native American's brain in order to learn some of his shamanistic medicine. That *would* be something: perhaps one day, Mabel might be able to offer him that link and that access. That Maddy wuz something else though. Perhaps he needed to talk to her. In all fairness to her, they'd not directly spoken. Besides, there were other important matters which dominated above and beyond the gossip of the Mountainside community.

Over an intense three-week-long period, the first of the engine houses got built. You know all those engine houses back home in Cornwall, that are pistols shooting the ore skywards from out of the ground? Well, in all honesty, what was constructed at Mountainside looked like some kind of mutated offspring of that, because the normal building resources were not available. Any notion of chunky granite for the exterior walls of the engine house had already been dismissed. There were simply not the quantities of stone available, and any good stone excavated from the mine was to be used solely for the end wall, on which the beam would be positioned. Outside would be the usual geht pair of shears and inside, all of the equipment brought up the mountainside (and lying on pallets) would be connected up. To give the Minter his due, initially, he did have a plan, and having supervised the building of other such mines across the frontier, he was able to freely adapt his ideas to the situation here on the Keweenaw with remarkable ease.

"We'll cut in there on the left. Thaas solid enough, I d'reckon," noted Mr Minter, pulling on one of the struts that had been concreted in.

"Now, upon my life, I don't think anything will be moving that anywhere soon," confirmed Flannery. "A tornado could go through here and that would not be moving an inch."

The main frame of the house needed to be constructed with substantial pitch-coated timbering, and around this timbering was placed a galvanised steel wrapping. Thus, as the frame grew ever higher, around it grew the scaffolding too, and an army of individuals was concerned with positioning and fastening the steel sheets to the timber. Despite the galvanisation, they would still rust, so eventually, the whole of the metal casing would turn a red-brown as a result of oxidisation. There'd be the furrows of the steel all turning as rusty as the earth, just like the roofs of the thousands of sheds and huts all over Cornwall.

"Bang un in right," shouted up Walt Chegwidden.

"Dun't ee worry y'bugger." said Knucky at the top of the scaffold. "I got un."

The temperature dipped during the month of December but still miners pursued this growth upwards. With mittens and gloves, they positioned the sheets of metal around the gargantuan wooden house, which, as it was being built, emerged upwards like a fairy-tale castle, unfolding almost in one go as if a pop-up book was being opened. There were drangs, entranceways and openings to allow people and equipment entry into the frame. Space was made for windas and connecting rods and cylinders. Es. Just as it should be. And looking fine and proper ut wuz. Once the main structure around the pump engine was built, and the massive beam had been placed in, then the rods and mechanisms could all be added. Manoeuvring the huge beam into position had been tricky but via a clever system of pulleys and leverage (devised and supervised by Mr Mint and his h'expertise) – and by making good use of every horse and mule available – the beam had been raised to its necessary height. In the end, 'twas rocking lovely with a smooth action.

"Grand," went the Minter. "Not bad t'all."

"Near 'nuff perfect," said Trevorrow. "I got t'hand ut to ee meht. You've done a bewdie job here with ut."

Trevorrow didn' really want t'say that but felt like ee had to. At this point, there wuz no drecklyism about the boy at all. Perhaps he'd changed.

Thereafter, now could be built the boiler house and the chimley. The latter was perhaps a bit more iconic, and resembled far more the mine engines of back home and on the Beara than the rest of the structure here. The Cornish were skilled masons and the tight brickwork rose fast, so that now, over the forest, an artificial tree grew skywards. For its bark, it had brickwork, and for its canopy, soon enough it would spurt smoke from the fire that lit the boiler. So far, so good then – and daily, Mr Mint could be seen in the morning down by the structure, standing next to Skews and Trevorrow, sizing up the progress and deciding what the next priority should be.

They were joined too by Doctor Jewell, keen to make appropriate comments on the safety of those working at height. Generally, the Jackers were happy to walk along the great beams of the structure like balancing birds resting on perches, but Jewell insisted that for safety purposes a line should be strapped to them to help break any fall. The mechanics of the pump belaw ground were taken care of by Francis and Justin, and a host of other miners and Knockies under the surface. It was crucial that the pump's depth could be added to, as in the future, the mine would potentially sink further levels into the mountain. The pump would counter the continual need to bore in new adits.

From a distance, this grey castle became the defining feature of the community. Its huge shadow now dominated everything, and its skyline could be seen from miles away in the deep forest, even so far down on the lake shore that it sometimes shone in the easterly morning light, and could be seen down at Eagle Harbour, poking upwards above the trees. Everyone working on the structure realised now that this building (and what it contained) was going to massively change this community once more. Gallons of water could now be pumped from the lower levels if needed. Before now, it felt like they had only been playing at mining. This structure gave them a new purpose, with everyone knowing that what was about to be released from the ground would be coming up on an industrial scale. Skews was already readying his mind about the proposed mineral tramway – he wudn' let that go. Aw naw. Plans see, clearly above and beyond the reproach and look of this older Nankervis boy.

For those sentient beings watching in the forest, it was hard enough to see former friends hacked and sawn into lengths of planks and timber, let alone see them jointed and hammered into position. But that was less of a shock than seeing the quantity of galvanised steel go onto the frame and make the shell around the building. This unnerved them because they'd not ever seen steel in such quantities before (all shipped up from Detroit see); they never knew there could be so much of it, and that the mine would come to dominate so much. The sounds it made scared them: the ground shook more and, in their chest cavities, a continual rhythm could be felt. It was as if the very air itself had changed. They all viewed Nimkii with suspicion. He had told them different. He said it would be fine. And even when Yolkai, the great Moon Goddess passed over the structure, it seemed to make no difference. In fact, all her light did was to highlight and throw illumination on the steel structure as if she was celebrating its achievement. That wudn' good at all fur they.

Some felt angry. Some felt let down. All knew that their way of life (established for millennia) was about to change very quickly. The mine caused old routes and runs across the forest to cease. It changed age-old pathways that had been determined by those long before their great-grandparents. It broke every rule about how one should move around the woods. Some cried tears and did not leave their hollows. The dystopia outside was too much to bear. That wuz the way ut wuz for these forest-dwellers – the small people who lived between the roots, the rocks and the moss. Dear obm. You could understand how they felt, even if you cudn' hear what they said.

Gourgy and Luk sensed it, but so too, did other Knockies (at least the ones who sometimes comed to grass). They not only felt it mentally, but could physically feel the hurt and hate emanating from the forest. It was maybe a place they no longer liked to go. Gourgy and Luk were all part of the folklore, but when it comed to dialogue now with those in the forest, they out there did not want to know. The Knockies were part of the same machine that was uprooting everything else: these pair who once perhaps they found confederacy with, were now just minions of the men who scorched the ground. The forest-dwellers knew who wuz conducting operations: they recognised that direction was coming from Mr Dicky Mint. What scared Gourgy and Luk though was that, in fact, they knew the truth: that it was their humans who had started this whole thing – their great quest fur a decent strike. Minter was just a vessel: a conduit, a launder through which the activity flowed. But the forest wudn' have ut. The roots and fungi raged.

They actually all steered clear of Minter. It had soon gone about the camp that the h'engineer had little time for folklore or superstition, and that his marvels were built solidly on mathematics and physics alone. Now, knowing what the forest felt about him and also what was being said by Minter about mining spirits as a whole, it didn' make for an especially good combination. Doctor Jewell could do what he liked about trying to offset accidents. If the forest wanted something to happen, it would enact it. It did what it liked. Gourgy and Luk worried that if it came to that, then they hoped they were in the right place at the right time to save not only their humans, but others too. Word went out around the levels to warn others.

The Knockies then, were on high alert. Ut went like that sometimes. They listened carefully to every creak, every fall; each clamour and each squeeze of timber. They did this underground, but also under the very frame upon which the beam wuz placed. Ut looked precarious enough up there, and with levers and rods moving in every direction, ut wuz easy to see how something could disconnect and fall. Listening, they dodged the cynical, bandy legs of Dicky Mint, avoiding the thrusts and parings of his tin-tipped cane. If Minter thought everything was based on the security of science and mechanics, he'd best think again – or he might wish his crowst-time saffron cake dough.

This went on for a while then, in the run up to Christmas. No one knew what that would bring, nor did they knaw ef the great structure would be fully functional by that festive marker. The days did become much colder, and this far north, on the geht continent of 'Merky', the days got very short. Dawn broke late, and first light only came at eight in the morning. It started to become dark once more by the middle of the afternoon, and this slowed things down, as you might expect. Es. There wudn' the speed there like in the summer months. 'Course, boy Skews wuz adamant that the first house would be complete by Christmas, and so he tried to manipulate their employees so that work carried on into the evening, and miners and surface workers conducted their tasks in the semi-darkness. This was always a bad recipe, and Justin and Francis knawed ut. Even Trevorrow, and the Minter himself, took in sharp intakes of breath, when Skews first suggested it. But even though there wudn' agreement, Skews seemingly still had his way. Only the Doctor complained – especially when ut came to men working at height into the black of the evening. 'Twudn' the best combination now, wuz ut?

All this time, Skews had been aware of the gaze that Francis had been giving him and because of intrigue, or guilt (or perhaps both), Skews made every excuse possible not to be left alone with Francis. The pair didn' say much to each other through the whole construction process, and only conversed when it was absolutely necessary and only when others were present. Francis would often look for Skews but too often, he made sure he had the defence of Doctor Jewell and Mr Mint around him. At that time, Francis did not necessarily enjoy the cruel power he had over Skews; he simply wanted, at some stage, for him to be brought to book. The problem wuz that the mine needed to be the priority. At least, Skews now had very little access to Mabel. This separation from her must have caused him some degree of anxiety though. He'd nawticed of late that

Skews had gained a nervous tick with his left eye, and constantly patted his forehead with his handkerchief to remove globules of sweat. It was winter, and the man looked feverish and distracted. He still managed to keep up his hypocritical pretence of respectability: at one point even denouncing some of the workers by saying they were spending too much time in the warm boudoirs of Rosie's girls. What a tusser!

Francis spent a good deal of time with the doctor too, both of them examining the structure to ensure it was as safe as possible. Once he had admitted to him his affection for his daughter, then, he felt, that they'd got on better. However, one thing concerned him: if Jewell found out about Skews then there'd be hell-to-pay. It would be a hell-to-pay that probably would break the doctor, and his fear was, that after gaining knowledge about Skews' interest in Mabel, Francis would see the Doctor throw himself off some ravine, or even worse, off the collar of the shaft. The Doctor would have an epiphany and see his own neglect in action – just like ut wuz with his wife. Maybe even that bastard Skews realised this. Francis wudn' put ut past un.

Whilst all of this construction had been taking place, and the steel castle rose from the floor of the Keweenaw, Justin and Francis had tried to nail down Trevorrow to gain a meeting with Nimkii. Ut wuz perhaps a meeting that in their hearts, they did not really want to have, for in truth, what they had done to the forest, and the liberties that they had taken with the original agreement, seemed to them to be a problem. In order to progress, they needed their fifth shareholder's response. Before now, Nimkii had been an enigma, ever since their first phosphorescent meeting at this spot in the then untouched forest; but there were clearly more things going on that Nimkii wasn't speaking about. It puzzled them more and more as to why he went off on walkabout for such periods of time, almost as if he no longer cared about the situation here. And when they asked Trevorrow, what came back completely amazed them.

Nimkii ranged much more widely than they'd ever fully considered. He'd probably walk right around Superior, he'd enter Canada – for him, this whole area was the same land. The delineation they conceived of wuz an artificial one. He'd go down as far as Minnesota and back again. He'd walk through the forest; but apparently, lower down the peninsula, his people had horses, so that greater distances could be covered. But crucially: what about the bounds that they'd broken? Was he still tolerating their presence? The answer came back that he was. Apparently, he was untroubled by it, and as long as money and copper kept coming his way – then he was happy.

But the forest? Surely in some way, it communicated with him. And Trevorrow said the forest and Nimkii had had dialogue. He'd talk to it often. What wuz clear wuz that Nimkii had been very angry when the forest called for Clara Jewell and did not return her. That sharply divided them, and since then, apparently he'd had less respect for the creatures here. There'd been a schism: a schism that was not repairable until that woman was released and returned. Trevorrow indicated there was no movement in that. Ut wuz where the line had been drawn – and wuz where ut stayed.

And what about the Irish? What about all the new people who'd entered the camp since they'd signed the agreement? What did he feel about them? Trevorrow said that he seemed to feel nothing. The response was something like the idea that people should wander where they want. The world above ground (and belaw ground) wuz to be explored. Ownership ov land wuz an illusion anyway. And the metal structure? Nimkii did not like it, but knew it was necessary. He'd seen European people use them before down in Calumet and Houghton. They seemed a necessary evil. And for both Justin and Francis that seemed apt for everything their people did across the globe. The Cussies were a necessary evil. Frightening.

But what wuz he needing now? He had offered them so much, given them so much. He had been so forgiving. What more could they do for him? The answer that came back wuz that he needed nothing.

Was he angry though? The answer wuz no; he wuz not angry.

It being winter, the solstice coming, it seemed that this Nimkii would stay at the camp for a while. He had no thoughts of leaving now, because soon the deep snows would come and he was better off here in this part of the Keweenaw, which although north was warmed by the waters of Lake Superior. But perhaps even then, this Francis and this Justin still had a feeling of concern (some latent doom in their hearts) that what he wuz telling Trevorrow wudn' the full truth.

"Naw," said Trevorrow, "I dun't think so."

And they got to thinking too about how true Trevorrow was to them. They cudn' help but feel that way.

Francis wanted to ask Nimkii about Mr Skews and what he thought of un and Justin wanted to ask the Indian about Maddy, and what he thought of her; but that would have to wait another time. Nimkii had, over time, picked up a few words of English but the communication still had to be completed mainly through symbols and signs. Zertainly, fluency wuz a long way off. Right now, the brothers had to be happy enough with the responses that came back.

Bizarrely, Nimkii would still not accept accommodation within the community. He'd been offered his own shack – or if he wanted, his own house – or perhaps even a room at Rosie's, but in reality, he declined all. It was cold weather, Trevorrow had apparently argued, but still no internal room was needed. And then they all nawticed where he decided to make camp: right beside the collar of the mine; in actual fact, not too far away from the place where all those months ago in the height of summer, Justin and Francis had first encountered him. Seemingly, he was finding a comfort there, a recognition that this wuz not only part of their doing, but his too. And for that reason, those in the forest viewed him dismissively. How could one of their own act in this way? The Knockies saw un there on the collar, with a fire and his sleeping mat, and somehow they could sense what wuz coming. They could feel it in the air. It wuz the way the air smelt underground; the way that candles blew out all too quickly on the top of felt 'tull' hats. Forces were at work, as large as those which millions of years ago, had stained the landscape and formed the bright blue copper beds here.

It wuz on his way home from this meeting with Nimkii that Francis finally ran into Mr Skews. Their collision arose from the fact that Justin went back to Maddy's accommodation and Doctor Jewell had, earlier that day, returned home for urt pie and clotted cream. Toasting his own success so far, the chaos that wuz Dicky Mint had, by now, found his usual position in Rosie's and wuz already buying a drink for a maid he wuz sweet on. She had a dubious reputation but what did tha' matter to ee now?

Skews didn' want this meeting, but as he hurriedly left his office, he turned straight into Francis. It took boath men some seconds to adjust to the fact that this had occurred and that they were now alone.

"Come on then," said an instantly angered Skews. "Finally! Now, what do you want to say to me? Let's have it."

"I dun't need t'say very much to you," retorted Francis, trying, by now, to control his breathing. "You know your wrongs."

"What wrongs?"

"You go each week to lower your head before the preacher, and you say the right things... but really, God knows the full truth about you."

"Does he now?"

"He does... and I do."

"What do you know?"

Francis reached in, grabbing Skews' string tie – and pulled him towards him. The man wuz not as heavy as he imagined, and so he fell closely into him, with Francis recoiling at his yellowing teeth and ripe breath.

"I know that I saw you in the forest..."

"Am I not allowed to walk in the forest now then? Not like your brother and his little Irish bitch?" he interrupted.

"I saw you in the forest, and you were watching Mabel in the preaching pit. Don't deny it. I saw how you were touching yourself. What you did."

Now Francis wuz getting somewhere. The moment he said 'What you did' Skews became sand falling through a hour-glass. His body lost its bone and muscle, and he weakened in an instant. The arrogance that had been there seconds before dissipated in an instant.

"There too, up in the preaching pit... where you sit and pray with the Doctor's daughter... and there you are... having your own perversions... What is it, eh Skews? Can't get any adult action yourself, so you choose a maid..."

Francis needed to steady himself as he spoke these words. He used Skews as a frame, for that wuz all he wuz by now.

"I... ah..." Skews tried saying, but nothing more could come from his mouth.

"You know what you are," Francis said, "and I hope that disgusts you..."

"She... ah... tempts me... something about her..."

"You are an adult. She's still a child. There are no excuses. You ought to know better. Whatever devilish urges you have here, control them... You take one step closer to her... You buy her any more presents... and I promise: I will single-handedly kill you."

Francis cudn' believe he wuz saying what he wuz. This wudn' him, wuz ut? He wuz the good brother after all: the sensible one, and here he wuz, threatening death and bloody murder. Wuz there somethin' evil running in the Nankervis blood?

"Do you understand me?" he drilled.

"Yes. I understand," replied Skews, seeing his life pass in front of his eyes.

He let Skews drop. There wuz now nawthun' to un. He became a greasy rag on the floor of the pump house. But in fact, that wuz all he had ever been.

"Do you get my meaning Mr Skews?" Francis reiterated.

"I do, Mr Nankervis. I get exactly wha' you mean."

"Good. One sight of you near her, one sight of you even looking at her," Francis threatened, "and I'll make sure you come to a grim end."

Skews wuz now quivering.

"Who else knows?"

"Awnly me, but Rebecca's not keen on ee anymore than I am... She's been worried about you and Mabel for some time."

"The girl..." he panted.

"What about her?"

"She sings to me... I don't know what it is. I really don't. She has this quality... I like to hear her talk about the forest..."

"Not anymore."

"But Mr Nankervis, you must understand. It's involuntary... I am pulled to do it..."

This Francis did not really want to be having such a dialogue with Skews. He'd wanted the conversation to be short and sharp: like Skews would walk away knowing zactly how 'twas. But here again now, he was wheedling, pleading, excusing: just like the practised Skews of old.

"Pulled by what?" he had to ask though.

"The trees... the forest..."

So here it wuz again: that same excuse as everything else. Francis did not want to know.

"I'm tired of hearing about the forest. Ut seems the forest is now the excuse for anything..."

In his mind, Francis felt Skews wuz still not taking responsibility for his own actions, and that the wider fear of the forest (which had descended on the camp) was now a convenient excuse for this pathetic pervert of a man.

"Mabel – she feeds me," Skews pleaded, now sounding fully mazed. "Her energy, it comes straight to me from the forest. It's why it makes me do that."

"What – toss yourself off in the forest?"

"Yes," Skews said, dejectedly.

"I've seen what you do," shouted Francis, "and I was disgusted by it. Now, so too wuz the forest. It's watching, I reckon. You left your seed abandoned there. How is that respecting the forest? It's as big a piece of pollution as an arsenic lagoon."

"I don't know," replied Skews, not now believing even his own argument.

"Take this as your last warning. Anything else, and I'll nail you and your bollocks to the top of the engine house shears and leave you there for the crows to feed on... Got ut?" he bawled.

"Yes. Will you tell anyone else?"

"No. Not yet..."

"You promise? Please?"

"I'm not negotiating with you, Mr Skews. Not these days."

"I'll aim to keep my bargain. Thank you for the correction. You're a good man Francis Nankervis."

"Don't bullshit me Skews. Don't even try your usual ways ov workin'. I mean what I say."

"Alright," responded Skews nervously, his tick now worse than ever.

"I'll see you for our outside chapel service on Sunday," observed Francis, "and when I see you I want to be sure that you are praying for forgiveness for your sins. You make sure of that when Doctor Jewell is a-preaching... Mind you do now, won't you?"

These were commanding words from the older Nankervis brother. Skews wuz fully aware of their consequences. He would never be able to look at the engine house shears in the same way ever again.

Francis started to leave. The frail body of Skews was coming around on the sand of the road. He wuz no longer the man they'd first taken the copper ore to, to test its quality. The mine or the forest or something had broken him. It had sucked all vitality from him. But he still shouted after Francis.

'"Is there any way of redemption for me?" he bawled.

"Not so as I can see it right now," came the response back.

Francis Nankervis wuz gone now and Skews stood up in the middle of the road. He thought over all the times he had been with Mabel and still treasured those moments. He weighed up death at this man's hands over reform and knew which one he had to take. He knew his sin more than ever. He had known it long before, but now that it was exposed – and given air, true air and voice – then it was even worse. Was this the moment that he changed for good? He could not tell as yet. All he knew wuz that there needed to be a new way now. Es. That wuz ut: how could he even grasp at redemption without understanding tha'?

Es – that all happened. Sometimes painful things have to happen, so that good things can come from them. You knaw tha'. Gar – what would ut be like ef 'twas all plain sailing? 'Twud be the same ef you had saffron bun every day fur eternity. You'n always have too much of a good thing.

Elsewhere in the camp, other deeds were being done. Ut had been a while, and this Justin and this Maddy O'Donahue had still been goin' fur'n like the clappers at every intimate moment they could grab together. Justin had tried asking ov her about the forest, but she just said she liked to be in the natural world and drew strength from ut, though she'd had an idea fur a while that Mabel was special, and could see things. Had she seen creatures in the forest? He'd asked her tha'. He'd tried to pin her down on it, and she'd answered openly enough. No, she'd not seen anything unusual. She did however, say that there wuz a twilight world out there, made of small creatures and beings, and in that, Justin had some sympathy for he had already heard Luk and Gourgy saying the same thing and thus he knew some of its ways.

Maybe they needed to be more honest with each other though: more truthful about each of their connections to the liminal world. But you knaw how 'tis with humans – and you knaw how 'tis with lovers too? Maddy's concern wuz for they to make 'iss on their love-making for they urgently had a baby to create. Hell though, they wuz two months inta' this thing and still, she wuz sensing naw planted seed. Nawthun' as yet, wuz grawin' in her womb – and it wuz with disappointment, that she again had her period. 'Mean, there wuz passion enough between they two. Questions need t'be asked though: was ut his seed that weren't good enough – or wuz ut she who cudn' conceive?

Maybe, fur the fust time, she have to go to see Doctor Jewell and lay ut on the line. He might be able to tell she what wuz wrong. She feared that conversation though: that she'd be childless for eternity. An' if tha' didn' work, maybe he'd arrange for her to go for some tests – what, back down in Detroit, or maybe Calumet? – t'see if she could conceive. An' if tha' wudn' naw good, well, her Justin too. Maybe something wudn' right with 'ee. 'Mean, the boy spurted enough, didn' a?

But she knew too, she had other ways. She'd performed the ritual before to set her on this path: maybe ultimately, something stronger wuz needed.

23

"**U**nderstand, do ee?" warned Francis, pointing a warning finger at they. "Naw acting up!"

That Saturday morning, Justin wuz on core, assisting the Minter with the pump's installation underground, and so Francis invited Rebecca around to finally meet Luk and Gourgy. The somewhat humble dwelling-house that the two brothers lived in thus far had been expanded by the carpenters over the course of the autumn – with extra space and rooms being added. Their monies from the mine had made them wealthy. Detroit kept paying out. Of course, you might be able to guess that the boy Francis saved moast of his money for the future. He was one of those people who knew that the good times of the present might not last forever, and so he put some money by. Nawbody knawed when rainy days might come; 'twas best to be prepared fur um.

That Justin lived more for the moment (ee always had) so ee spent his more or less as soon as he had earned it. There'd be more in the pot soon he allays reckoned. His big plan wuz to build Maddy and he a place to live together (land had been sized up in the south of the community). In the meantime though, in contravention of wha' he'd promised his brother and his supposed commitment to Temperance, a goodly proportion of his wages were still spent on liquor and poker, on dicing an' rounds ov ale, and making himself a Cap'n of the people. 'Mean, he had a 'girl' on his arm now, so that wuz one expense down, and Maddy, well, she wudn' too demanding of finery. She still liked his abandon though, and saw something of herself in un. Despite their difficulties in conceiving, ut wudn' ever like they stopped the impulsive fancying ov each other. Besides, she had a good income too from her collective of Irish boys. Things were set though for perhaps both brothers to move out of this place where they'd first stayed, in order, in the long-term, to be with their respective sweethearts. Now, 'sweetheart' wudn' quite the right word t'describe Maddy O'Donahue, but 'twill do fur now.

Before Rebecca arrived, Francis had the knockies sat down, regimented in the recently extended kitchen. They looked some wisht since their master wuz going through all the rules of the encounter with his lady-friend, the school-ma'am. There wuz a whole manner of things that they needed to be aware of: chiefly, no touching ov her, no swearing, no begging for food (she was sure to have some anyway), no burping and most importantly, no farting. They were also to mind their p's and q's – whatever they were. Francis was a little paranoid about their display.

"Try to stay the same colour if you can," he stated. "It's really off-putting for anyone if you change colour before them..."

"Rite on," went Luk, patting his skin to check it.

"We'll do us best," said Gourgy.

"Oh... and no merging into the background. Not today, alright?"

"Whaas' in ut fur we though?" asked Gourgy.

"It's about the future," said Francis. "You're going to be seeing a lot more of Rebecca, and 'tis best if she knaws the truth about you pair. No point in hiding ut, and revealing it half-way through the m..."

Francis stopped himself but Luk was intelligent enough to pick up on what he wuz saying. He leaned towards his compatriot.

"He's talking marriage boy. He's talking about getting wed..."

"I knaw," said Gourgy, "but what about we?"

Francis realised that he and his brother had allowed them to get away with too much. They had become used to the fineries of life, instead of sleeping in the levels like the rest of their species. He knew the warning Justin had once given him about the pair: give um an inch and they'll take a mile. And to an extent, that is zactly what had happened. They'd got used to home comforts. In order to offset their complaint, Francis offered them something.

"Look, when I move out of here, you pair can stay on here permanently in this place. How about that? Lords of your own manor, eh?"

Both of the Knockies considered it. They nodded. It didn' seem like a bad offer. There'd be room for all-night parties and inviting tasty girls back from Rosie's.

"A'right," said Luk. "My companion and I accept your kind offer."

"She'll be here soon," panicked Francis. "Now remember what I said. Aw – make sure you put your pick-axes somewhere, will ee? She dun't need to see those, do she? Oh, and be sure your loincloths are in place. She dun't want t'see anything else."

The boy Francis was thinking of Skews here and, of course, he still wondered about the ramifications of his recent words with the assayer.

"I'm nervous," confessed Gourgy. "I mean, it's been a while since we've been properly introduced to a non-miner, idn' ut? "

"Reckon so boy," noted Luk. "Couple of hundred years, at least... maybe more."

Aw, they did go on sometimes this pair.

Justin looked at his watch. The large hand wuz going around to ten o'clock. Rebecca would not be late. Being a school-ma'am time wuz everything to her: her whole day was organised around time. At least today was a Saturday and she had no other direct responsibilities that day (aside, of course, from tip-toeing her way through the lives of both her father and Mabel, not to mention young James too).

When the knock came, the two Knockies sat bolt upright on their little chairs and adjusted themselves one final time to ensure they gave across the most respectable look they could possibly give. They recognised the importance of such a moment. With a young miner such as Francis, it wuz to be expected that, at some point, he would take a wife. Here, it wuz slightly different though because everything about the mine wuz in such close proximity. Back home, ut might actually have been easier to have kept them a secret, because the mine and the domestic environment were too very different things and kept far apart. The mine wuz down on the cliffs and the homestead was up near the carn.

Francis opened the door and, out in the hallway, they could hear the usual polite greetings.

"I've brought them some fresh saffron buns, as you suggested," this Rebecca wuz saying. "I hope they're good enough..."

All of them could hear the nervousness in her voice. She wuz a school-ma'am but the way she spoke sounded like she wuz nothin' more than a mouse.

"They'll be fine I'm sure," Francis wuz saying. "You'll easily win them over with those."

"Hear of un..." went Gourgy. "Ee d'think we'm some kind of pushover..."

"I knaw," replied Luk. "Laughable, idn' ut?"

Finally, Rebecca entered the room. Francis worried that he was going to have to tell them to "Shaw themselves," but in the event, they were both sat there together, each twiddling their thumbs and looking contented, like butter wudn' melt in their mouths.

"Boys, this is my sweetheart, Miss Rebecca Jewell. So... that one on the right there is Gourgy, and on the left, that's Luk."

"Delighted to meet you," said Luk holding out his cakey-looking hand.

Rebecca reached out and shook it. This thing's hand felt cold and damp like nothing she had felt before. It made her think of what touching the skin of a toad must feel like.

"A pleasure," said Gourgy, standing and bowing before her, then offering his hand in the same way.

Rebecca couldn't help but giggle at their funny little voices. She'd not heard anything like it before. Clearly however, she wuz fascinated with their form: the fact that they even existed. Here was a piece of living folklore. 'Course, she'd heard about these Knockies – if you grew up in Cornwall, everyone had heard of them, but to see them in the flesh – their toady flesh – was indeed, quite a marvel.

"I'm so pleased to meet you both," said Rebecca. "Francis has told me a lot about you. I suppose we have a mutual interest in preserving the lives of Francis and Justin."

"True enough," replied the pair in unison.

"Welcome to the club," added Luk.

"Justin and I have been working with this pair all our lives. They've saved us from being hurted many a time..." stated Francis. "but they've had other owners over time – all the way back to when the Phoenicians came. Tin and copper – they've done the lot. Ent tha' right?"

"Es," said Gourgy. "When we first see'd Francis and Justin we knawed they'd be a good pair. And ut have worked out well s'far... Better than a lot of our Masters over the years."

"That's right Gourgy," added Luk. "We've had some ripe ones sure 'nuff. But then, I dun't 'spect either of us thought we'd been journeying out to 'Merky'... Then again, Miss Jewell I dun't 'spect you did either."

"No, I had no idea we'd all be here like this..."

This comment seemed to underline just how magical this experience wuz for Rebecca. Francis still thought she would run a mile at the oogly sight of them.

So far, so good, thought Francis. So far, the pair were behaving very well.

"So does this mean I can now see you all the time?" asked Rebecca "Now that you've..."

"Shown themselves," added Francis. "We call it that: 'show yourself' – dun't us boys?"

"Thaas it," said Gourgy.

"Yep," went Luk.

"But best if you keep ut secret," offered Gourgy. "Like you know and I know, but we keep it to ourselves like..."

"Yeah, because we'm breaking the official code here really," said Luk. "We dun't mind – us pair – but some of the old-timers can get a bit feisty and moan on about ut."

"I will be circumspect," Rebecca said. "I promise. But if you see my eyebrows raised... it's just because it's so wonderful to know you exist. My sister..."

"What, Mabel?"

"Yes. Mabel... She says she can see you though. Why's that?"

"Dunnaw. Sometimes, some humans who are not miners can – fur whatever reason. It's like a kind of gift... You got to be tuned in to we though. Gotta' knaw where to look so t'speak..."

"I see."

"She's a good maid that Mabel," observed Luk.

"And has she been seeing you since we, as a family, first arrived?"

"Reckon so – dun't you Gourgy?"

"Es. She seen we the moment she fust arrived. You cen't say nothin' mind. Say anything to she and that'll break the code. Ruin the magic, like. So dun't do anything like tha' if you can," advised Gourgy.

"I won't. I promise."

"You alright still?" checked Francis.

These funny-speaking, two-foot high mine sprites were enough to scare anyone, but his sweetheart seemed to be taking it well. There wuz however, anticipation on each of the Knockies' faces, and the smell of fresh home-baking was already in the air.

"Eh, Miss Rebecca" asked Luk, as if he had known her for a millennia, "You got any buns with you? Francis here said you had buns, and me and my meht here, we'm mighty fond of a bit of bun."

"Oh yes. Of course," said Rebecca, slightly panicked at the request, and realising she was carrying a basket full of saffron buns. The basket had been her mother's and on top was placed a white tea-towel to keep the basket's contents warm and moist.

"Straight out of the oven, are they?" enquired Gourgy. "Be lovely to taste a bit..."

"Certainly," said Rebecca. "Here, have the lot..."

Luk and Gourgy raised their eyebrows to an extreme height. No one in the world had given them that much bun before.

Francis made an intervention.

"Boys, I d'reckon one is enough fur now. I'll keep them locked in the spence and we'm have some more later on – but fur now, one's plenty, idn' ut?"

"Sorry," Rebecca whispered, handing each one of them one of the large-sized saffron buns. This is where it potentially could get messy. Francis hoped they'd follow his advice and take small, gentle bites and not wolf down the bun in one go. At least Gourgy and Luk tried to dine politely. There wudn' quite s'much chomping and gulping as usual, and crumbs didn' fly off in different directions – like ut usually did. Having said that, the buns were demolished and fully into their bellies in under a minute.

"Lovely," said Luk. "Thaas the best bun I've had out here... well, since leaving Cornwall."

"You're not far wrong there," commented Gourgy. "Better than the ones Mrs Cap'n d'make. She d'put too much orange peel in. You awnly need a bit. Just like the one I just had."

Francis smiled a thank you to Rebecca.

"They'll probably change colour now," he said.

"How?"

"Well, when they're happy, they do it. Involuntarily. They can't help ut, see..."

Gourgy and Luk were turning a bit bluey-pink.

"I see..."

"Sometimes we do ut to wind him and his brother up," smiled Luk. "Just so they dun't knaw what mood we'm in."

Now the pair looked a little less like toads and more like little men who worked the mines. Their faces beamed out smiles that were cuter than even her baby brother.

"Glad you liked them," said Rebecca. "I'n always make you some more."

"Would you?! That'd be proper."

"I'd love more of your buns."

Here, this wuz getting a bit out of hand now. Prior to now, Francis had agreed with the Knockie duo that once they'd been fed, then they'd go off down mine to help with whatever Justin wuz doing.

"Time you pair got t'work I reckon," suggested Francis. "They're goin' t'start up the pump today, so brother said."

Realising that they were not meant to outstay their welcome, the Knockies stepped down off their chairs, like refined gentlemen of a previous age, and picked up their pick-axes and strapped them to their backs. They looked slightly downhearted at the fact they had to leave. This Rebecca wuz alright, wudn' she? She wudn' just a school-ma'am with a shouty voice. Francis had done well there; good decision all round.

"Bye then," said Luk.

"Nice to meet you," said Gourgy with a twinkle in his eye. "Nice buns."

"Yes... the same with the two of you. Lovely to meet you both."

"Keep an eye on the Minter for me, won't you?" Francis shouted after them.

"'Course," they returned. "Dun't ee worry none."

Francis sat down at the kitchen table. He looked over at the now vacant little chairs that they had been sitting on.

"Well, that cudn' have gone too much better now, could it?" he asked Rebecca. "Some people might find them scary. I mean, they ent purty, are um?"

"No. They were lovely. Really! I mean, I never knew... never knew it wuz even possible... but there they were, just like the stories say."

"You got friends fur life there," noted Francis, "if they like your buns that much, they'll do anything for you."

Rebecca laughed.

"I'm glad. Glad I made them to their taste..."

"Connoisseurs see," stated Francis. "Dun't your feyther appreciate your cooking then?"

"Aw he? Well, he used to. Likes pies and clotted cream but anything else... well, it's as if he doesn't nawtice. With him at the moment, it's the mine *this* and the mine *that*..."

"I know. A distraction for him then, I believe?"

"You're right. I'm not sure he'll ever get over ut."

Francis wondered if this was the moment to tell Rebecca what he had discerned from their discussions with Nimkii – that he and the forest were at loggerheads over the disappearance of her mother. He went through the narrative in his own head, but when he actually had the moment to tell ut, to explain things the way that they truly were, he stepped back from it. Ut sounded too bizarre, too strange for him to even give ut voice. He needed to work more on Nimkii with a hope that one day, Clara might come back, and tha' she'd be released. What worried him more now though, were the changes that would have occurred in her if she wuz out there surviving somehow? She'd not be the same. So, for the moment, best not to say anything. He could, however, tell her about Mr Skews.

"I... ah... finally saw Skews," Francis said, a more serious tone shaping his voice.

"When?" she asked.

"A couple of days ago... after brother, Trevorrow and I met with Nimkii..."

"I thought you said he wuz working hard to avoid you."

"He wuz, but he didn' see me coming. He more or less walked straight into me. I couldn't help but have that conversation widn' after that."

"What did you say then?"

"I put un straight."

Should he tell her now what he'd caught Skews doing? No. It would destroy his sweetheart. Best that she knew nothing, but that he'd made Skews aware of his obsession and that people nawticed it.

"And he? What did he have to say?"

"Well, he admitted it." "Said he was a bit obsessed with her. He knew ut wuz wrong and that ut would certainly be misinterpreted. I put him right on all ov ut."

"But what was ut specifically about Mabel? I mean, there are other girls in the camp. Why her?"

He understood what she wuz driving at. Francis knew the answer to this, but he did not want to say it. He considered saying the truth but carrying on the lie seemed the best course of action fur now. If she knew that Mabel also had some odd and intimate connection to the forest beyond what wuz already known, then Rebecca's world would collapse and implode.

Perhaps he should have been brave enough to tell ut like ut wuz, but who would do that? Not many. There wuz too much at stake.

"Dun't knaw," he said, which wuz a lie.

Fur now, as long as his sweetheart knew that Skews would not trouble Mabel again, that wuz good enough. With that, he knew the forest would have to do its worst, but even though he believed in magic (he'd just presented two folkloric creatures to Rebecca) he still had a hope that this forest thing could somehow be denied or subverted. Underneath all of these thoughts, of course, he felt guilty, for he knew it wuz he and his brother who had altered the balance to begin with. Es. Putting off Skews wuz enough. Shawin' Rebecca the Knockies wuz enough fur now.

Rightly, Rebecca's questioning ov un wuz relentless though.

"What did Skews admit to then?"

"I think it's like we said. He's lonely out here. He perhaps needs more company. He lets work dominate his life too much. He becomes obsessive."

No, he most certainly could not tell her how obscene things really were. There wuz corruption and then there wuz *that*.

"Will he make repair then?"

"I hope so..."

See, there wuz long-implanted Methodism in they. And when Rebecca asked this, his mind went to what the assayer had said about redemption.

"He's trying to find a way forward I think..."

"At chapel? In hearing my father preach?"

"Yes. Definitely. I mean, he's usually at the preaching pit, isn't he? But I think maybe he's become a bit corrupted..."

"Mmmm... how do you mean?"

"Morally corrupted..."

And when Francis said that, it seemed right. It seemed like that could happen to anyone at anytime from any place in the world. Such moral corruption could creep up on everyone, so it felt like a truth wuz being spoken. But even as he said all of this and had this important dialogue with his sweetheart, ironically, he himself, wuz the one who felt morally corrupted. Now, how mazed wuz tha'? 'Twuz proper silly.

Francis became silent for a few moments as he stowed the remainder of the saffron buns in the spence. There wuz now a lot to think through. Six months earlier, and life had been simple. All he and his brother wanted wuz to make a bit; not t'live hand t'mouth like ut wuz back home and to turn their lives around on this new continent, in this new country. The complications that had resulted from that now seemed huge though.

Momentarily, he even wished he wuz back in the bunkhouse of the old Cliff Mine, and he and a group of Cussies were sat around, touching pipe and telling ov' a few good yarns. All of that seemed a long way away now, and although he had this thought, he knew it was not a world he could go back to. His life was bound here to Mountainside, and in so many respects, he wanted further permanence. That is why, when he came back into the kitchen, he asked a question that had been burning in his mind for some time. He had no ring to offer, but what did that matter? The important thing was his asking: what he said to Rebecca – and therefore, he said it.

"Marry me?" he went, saying it almost too quickly, so that Rebecca wuz unsure what he'd spoken.

"Pardon?"

This time, he went down onto one knee and held her hand.

"Marry me," he repeated: now making it a statement, as if there wuz no doubt in his mind. But then, whilst on his knees, he thought he'd better sweeten what he was saying.

"Rebecca Jewell, would you do me the great honour of becoming my wife?"

He had not checked with Doctor Jewell that such a request wuz possible, but even so, the surgeon knew that such a question would be asked at some time soon. He felt there wuz tacit, if not official approval. He did not give Rebecca time to answer. So ensconced wuz he in his own thought patterns, and such guilt did he feel about not telling the truth about Mabel, Skews and the forest, that he found himself blithering on.

"I've thought about it a lot of late. Have you sensed that? I mean, there is really nawbody I would rather be with for the rest of my days than you, my dearest Rebecca."

Rebecca noted the shift in his voice. He'd become more formal: perhaps that wuz what he thought such a proposal required; but there wuz no doubt of the honesty in his request. She knew that he genuinely loved her. She knew too, that she had similar dreams and wishes for the future. He wuz, despite what her father might think, just the kind of adventurer in life that she wanted to be next to. It was therefore easy for her to answer him. She paused though, just enough to see if his countenance would shift or alter. She wanted to make him laugh; perhaps even to give the impression that she needed a few moments to think it over. But such wuz her sweetheart's energy and passion, such wuz his courage in even asking her, that the answer came easy.

"Yes," said she. "I'd love to marry you Francis Nankervis. If there is one thing I am absolutely certain of is that I want to spend the rest of my life with you."

Francis beamed a smile back to her but now on his knee, he could barely move. Suddenly, the weight of what he had just asked her came over him. Because of who she wuz, and her sensitivity in such matters, she understood the moment. Instead of pulling him up, she knelt down as well. How gorgeous and wonderful she looked to him! In her beauty, all that original hope of this place came back to Francis again, and he began to relax.

"I was worried that you'd say no... especially after meeting those pair this morning..."

"No. Not at all," said Rebecca. "You, Francis Nankervis, have a way of opening up my world, and I will be with you every step of the way."

Es. Well, ut all sounded good there, didn' ut? But naw married couple ever knaw what troubles will come their way – and what strife will walk inta' their lives, and so ut wuz with this pair. They didn' cause ut. Indeed, unlike the mine and its surrounds, they cudn' even conceive of ut, but happen ut did. Es, happen ut did. And although ut looked all rosy and romantic at this moment, the fust ov ut, tell the truth, wudn' far off. Ef they boath knawed what wuz t'transpire then maybe they'd have paused and reconsidered, but no bugger does that, do um? Things wuz set and they had a ready-made family in the form of Gourgy and Luk, and just across the camp George Jewell, Mabel and James; and at some other juncture, the support of Justin and Maddy O'Donahue. Rite on then. Es. Rite on.

Down mine, 'twas all goin' on well enough – sort ov. Bellies full, Gourgy and Luk went down the main shaft in the kibble, and joined the several men and their Knockies working down on the third level. More ore had been discovered there and so the second level had been somewhat abandoned of late. They were digging away on the northern end of the mine, directly belaw where the pumping rod and cylinder wuz being lowered down. Trevorrow and Justin were belaw, and up top wuz the affected Dicky Mint, accompanied by a quieter Mr Skews and another set of labourers. What they were trying t'do wuz make the shaft coming down accept the pump without any hitch, yet because of the hard run of the rock on the furthest side, the cylinder of the pump kept catchin'. There wuz only two options: either t'blast ut out, or t' dig ut out carefully. The former is what would normally happen, but now that the pump wuz in place, well, you hardly wanted tha' to be scat to smithereens, did ee?

Na, Justin made the right call on ut. Ee wuz down there, supervising the careful digging out of the shaft on the far side to facilitate the access. Trevorrow agreed with un. It was the safest way t'do it and the best way to do ut. But then, up top see, you had Skews and Mint trying to edge um on a bit. Minter ought to have knawn really, but the bottom ov the shaft wuz left t'be sorted dreckly. The reason wuz that this needed to be sorted before Christmas so the mine could re-start again. Skews knawed they wuz running out of processed ore to send down to Detroit. Ut wudn' like you wanted to stop they receiving: if that were the case, then they might take up with someone else. Thus, fur Skews, it wuz critical the mine re-started on Monday.

Now, say what y'like but tidn' naw good having hurriedness when it comes to mining. 'Twill go the way the earth d'want ut t'go and the earth idn' goin' to be hurried along by naw bugger, not even a man with the sophisticated h'engineering skills of someone like Mr Mint. So they wuz definitely annoyed up t'grass that things wudn' moving along a bit quicker. But as Justin protested, shouting up the shaft back to um all in the engine house, ut cudn' be hurried. The expedient Maddy wuz in there too. She wuz agile that one, and could swing upwards easy-like. Ut didn' take her long to climb up beside the pumping mechanism, and in a few minutes, she'd be up t'grass. She wuz a marvel in tha' way, and although Skews didn' like her, even he knew that right now, she was useful in offering more accurate communication between top and bottom. She wuz skilled too, in moving up and down ladders: caked with slimes and dirt, that any normal man would slip on. What wuz ut about she? She moved with an agility that others found amazing. 'Twuz magical t'see. Honest. Naw wander Justin had eyes fur she. There wudn' a man in Mountainside who hadn't considered what *it* would be like with she.

"I rode the man-engines many a time on the Beara," she told Dicky Mint. "You get a feel fur it. You knaw where to step. When t'step. Where not to as well."

But 'course, there wudn' naw man-engine here. The system of reciprocating ladders had already been viewed as a death trap by moast mining h'engineers and surgeons, and so had long since been retired. But her, she looked like she could step down to the depths on one ov they at any given moment.

Up top, there wuz some discussion on extending and moving the rods and levers across a bit, so top-side this would bring the pumping system back this way a little. But considering the wood and timbering that would be required in the engine house, nawbody seemed much up fur ut. As Doctor Jewell noted too, such insertions high over the shaft would also be incredibly dangerous. Maddy looked at un whilst he wuz chitterin' on because she knew he was the man she needed to go and speak to. Maybe he could do a test on her or somethun' – an' see what wuz wrong: why her womb wudn' workin'.

Once she'd finished here, she swore she'd arrange ut with un. Her infertility or Justin's infertility wuz beginning to dominate her every waking moment. She needed to be careful concentrating here. Ut would be all too easy just t'daydream ov holding an infant in her arms. She wanted to feel the chield nuzzling at her breast, suckling her teat and accepting her milk. She craved ut in ways that were dangerous you. She needed that warm glow of infancy to make her feel whole somehow. An' what wuz she doing now? Telling a bunch of bloaks what t'do down a mine: the outward career that had for too long been set fur she. But as y'knaw, that wudn' the awnly thing she could do. She had many arrows to her bow did this O'Donahue woman.

"Any good?" she shouted down. "Mr Mint's a-wondering how it's going."

"We're goin' as fast as we can," came back up Justin's echoing voice. "'Tis tricky though. Some awkward bit of rock you."

Everyone knew the immensity of what wuz happening belaw. Up t'grass there wuz all this brand-new, shiny kit ready to be operated. The furnace and boiler had been tested and the beam was rocking lovely, but hell, none of that made a blind bit ov difference, if they couldn' get to bottom belaw. T'Maddy, ut seemed simple enough, and that maybe in his work, Mr Mint could have sized up the shaft belaw and made allowances in his design, but that didn' seem to be the case.

Trevorrow had looked at her a bit sneaky like. Although he had his reservations, as time went on he wuz beginning to like this Irish woman. She had some fire to her, and boath of they knew the problem. This should have been thought through in the initial design, not at this late stage ov proceedings. But you cudn' say anything. If you did, then Mr Mint might walk – or rather catch a laker back to Detroit – and there wuz still the second engine house to put in yet: over the main shaft to power the cages. This wuz just the air-shaft and the water pump, not even half of what was fully needed. Considering the schedule, ut didn' look like that would be done any time before the spring.

Now, as Justin and his crew wuz working on removing that fair weight of rock, ut becomed clear to they what wuz actually the problem. Before the mine went in, then one of the great sugar maples that had been located here, had a set of long roots, that did not just go down under the earth of the forest, but went down much further, into the bedrock itself. That was what they were encountering because try as they may with gads, axes and spars, they could not get the rock to shift. It wuz enchanted somehow. The reason for it became clear to the boy Diddy Pasca, who was small enough to crawl up in between to see what wuz preventing the rock from being moved out of the way of the pump cylinder. What ee found was that a fist of tree roots were tightly wrapped around the back of the rock. Awnly if they were removed would this rock in the shaft be extracted. Ut didn' look like they wanted t'let go though.

"Bleddy geht roots in there," shouted out Pasca, from up and within. "Goin' t'need a sharp axe t' cut through them."

An axe was passed up to un, and Pasca wuz wedged in there by Justin and Chegwidden. The German pair, Stefan and Klaus, were holding they in there too. 'Twas some job you, and the pyramidal form of the five ov um looked more like a circus act of gymnasts and tumblers than a team of miners. There wudn' naw choice though. 'Twuz the awnly way the rock wuz goin' to move. Nature wuz clutching onta' ut at the moment, like ut didn' want t'release ut. The message went up top and Maddy relayed ut grass-side. Well, Doctor Jewell wudn' too happy with what wuz goin' on below. Ut sounded like a disaster before they'd even started. He'd have preferred they to cut their losses and come back at ut at another angle, rather than go mazed on ut like they wuz now. Miners never learnt.

"Mining is 99% perspiration and 1% inspiration Doctor Jewell," offered the Minter, looking supremely confident that what the boys belaw were doing would bring about the right end. In his impatient mind, ee wuz looking forward to this agony ending soon, so that he could head down to Rosie's and then rest up a bit over Christmas.

For a while, ut went silent. Belaw, above, all that could be heard wuz the gentle chink-chink of Diddy Pasca cutting his way through the roots. But well, you knaw this place by now. You knaw the way things can go. It wuz Luk who heard it first. He wuz always attuned see. And he wuz Justin's Knockie, and right now, 'twas his boy who wuz in there. He checked with the other miner's creatures too, to see what they could hear.

"Hark!" shouted Luk. "No noise t'all from anyone..."

Justin repeated his call, and the level went deadly quiet. Pasca stopped hacking at the root. But there wuz a sound that could be heard; scarily, it was precisely what Luk thought it wuz.

"Can ee hear ut boy?" he asked Gourgy, who wuz there too in the shaft.

Above, they heard ut go quiet belaw.

"Wozzon?" asked Skews.

"Don't say a word," Maddy told him. "They'm a-checking..."

Even Skews knew not to say any more.

"Es," said Gourgy. "You'm right boy. There's a distant knocking but 'tis getting ever closer."

Gourgy produced out of his pocket a small and ancient ear trumpet and placed the widest end of ut upon the rock closest to him. He raised his hand to indicate that he still required silence.

"Es... I's coming," he said.

"What?" asked Justin.

Instantly, his tone changed.

"Get out of here now... Collapse coming..."

When Knockies spoke like this, everyone knew what to do. The circus pyramid collapsed and like fluid, those who'd be in ut, squeezed past the pumping cylinder. Anyone else in the shaft at this level moved back along it as far as they could, at least to other safer stopes and places where the timbering above and at the sides looked solid. They knew how to take cover and grasped hold of their hardened-felt 'tull' hats to ensure that at least their heads would not be hit by falling debris. Above, Maddy could sense the change. She instantly understood what wuz coming.

"Move away from the collar," she said urgently to all those looking into it.

"Why?" asked Jewell.

"They know a collapse is imminent. That rock's going to fall, and when it does, all sorts of crap is going to fly out of the shaft... Move!"

"How do they know?"

"Knockies," said Maddy. "I can tell."

She urged them away now with pace, and they stood outside of the engine house and on what she felt wuz safer land. At this point, she worried that the whole of the house might go down as well.

"You believe that claptrap?" asked Mr Mint, smirking.

"I do now, if it saves lives," said Maddy. "I doan' go down far, unless I've got some Knockies around me. And them buggers, Justin's one, Francis's one, they can hear a pin drop beneath the earth..."

Minter said something like humbug, which wuz enough fur Maddy t'mark his card. All they could do now wuz to listen.

Ut wuz the same belaw ground but the collapse maybe wuz not so imminent as the Knockies had predicted.

"Where's ut to?" demanded Justin; his voice frantic. "You said ut wuz coming..."

Luk was sat upright now, contemplative and calm, but definitely sure of his prediction. He'd crossed his legs and shut his eyes in a meditative state.

"Sometimes, a fall has to work its way through. Luk, he's good. You just got to trust him. You should knaw that by now."

"Is ut still knocking?"

"Es... more taps now. Big knocks..."

In a sense, their dialogue made ut worse. Ef the place wuz goin' t'collapse, ut should just get on with ut, rather than hang around, having everyone waiting.

"I's the roots, idn' ut?" asked Gourgy.

"Yep," said Luk, breaking his focus. "They didn' like ut."

Along the level, in the shaft, those roots were talking to other roots: the remnant of the forest that wuz once here. The feeling wuz that ut wuz enjoying this moment, toying with the miners, and that the delay wuz its tease: like the stockings and suspenders of one of Rosie's girls. But ut wudn't the stockings themselves. Ut wuz the bare leg above.

"Keep still," said Luk. "Almost here now."

And up t'grass, they did the same thing.

"I can hear ut still..."

Everyone else tried, but only the Knockies had the sensitivity. This now, wuz why you had them, and yet again, it seemed they were about to prove their worth.

"Nice buns, weren't they?" asked Luk to comrade Gourgy.

But Gourgy didn' have time to answer because the earth groaned like a ghoul and several tons of rock suddenly fell down into the shaft, right from where Diddy Pasca had been working, sending a spume of smoke and dust up to the collar and out of it, and scattering the same along the level. For around five minutes nawbody could see anything, but when the dust settled, the chaos revealed that the rock fall had bent to buggery the pump cylinder on this level, and that all that wuz left wuz a mangle of metal. The blocking rock had been removed, but now the whole of that side of the shaft would need working out. There were hundreds ov barrow-loads of rock to get out before any work could recommence on the pump. At least nawbody had been hurted. Luk and Gourgy got congratulated by all. They felt pride in the fact that they were able to demonstrate their age-old way of doing things. Ah – another generation ov miners saved.

"See," said Luk, to anyone who doubted him.

"I see," said Justin, "and I'm indebted to you my Knockie friend."

"Told ee we'd get all they saffron buns," Luk whispered to Gourgy. "We're the best..."

High above, Skews got the message that everyone wuz more or less fine but that the rock fall had caused major damage to the pump.

"Ah well," Mr Mint observed. "'Tidn' nawthun' tha' can't be fixed. I mean, dreckly, they'n dig out the fall, and we'll get some more cylinder lengths down there. Dun't ee worry Mr Skews. 'Twill work itself out."

Maddy cudn' believe the arrogance of the man, and with distaste, she watched him walk away from the scene, as if the chaos of it did not matter to him. Trevorrow had been right about this man.

"He wudn' be saying that, if ut wudn' for the Knockies," she said to Skews.

And Skews nodded, because he knew she wuz right, and well, he knew he needed to be putting a few things right.

"Redemption for those below," said Maddy. "Could have been a lot worse. A helleva' lot worse."

Skews turned away from her to survey the scene. He knew the paperwork that would now need filling in to the American Mine's Safety Committee. Beside him, George Jewell wuz getting ready to deal with those coming up from below. Skews hoped t'God that there were few injuries. This mess wuz something he didn' need. Maddy stayed to help Doctor Jewell, who wuz now joined by other workers and wives in the community. The service at the preaching pit on Sunday wuz bound to mention this lot, and God's way ov somehow protecting all they belaw. 'Twud be all about feyth in the Lord Above naw doubt. Feyth wuz wha' got miners through. Everyone might say that on the outside, but inside they knawed they'd been saved once again, by a magical creature who wudn' even s'paused t'exist.

"Over to you now then Doc," Maddy said.

It would take a while for the patients to emerge up in the cage and kibbles. Fortunately, they'd be walking wounded.

"I need to come and see you," she stated. "I want some fairly urgent medical advice."

"Of course, Miss O'Donahue. Come up to the surgery, any time this next week."

"I will," said Maddy.

Maybe she did need science: not just magic.

She prayed to God that Justin had survived intact. Tha' wuz something she had not done fur a long time, and wuz unlikely to do in the near future. By the time all of those on the third level of the mine had been brought to grass, the moon had ascended over the camp. Yolkai wuz watching once more – and out there, in the darkness, the malevolent forest laughed at men and women, and their stupidity.

24

Ut comed in proper dirty fur the rest of December. Michigan winters are cauld and ut wudn' long after the collapse in the shaft, that heavy snow started to press. Arctic weather systems pushed down across the northern half of the continent and coated Copper Mountain and the forest around ut in an oppressive layer of blinding-white drifts. When this occurred, absurdly, the forest and the mine merged. For a while, it became hard to tell one from the other. Great swathes of snow and ice covered the upper branches of the trees and continually sent groundwards sparkles of flakes, which made any light percolating through the forest glow blue.

The line between the forest and the camp blurred: no one could tell where the border wuz anymore. Churned-up earth wuz assimilated into the white carpet, just the same way as the covering of forest-floor detritus. Maybe the awnly differences between the two zones were the regular and patterned bootprints of the camp, compared (bar a few small bird's feet and animal prints) to the untouched snow of the forest. It got cold. Between shifts in the mine belaw ground, men huddled around stoves and braziers and did their best to keep warm. Skews had a new load of insulated clothing brought up from Detroit down below. The moment the cargo arrived, ut wuz seized upon by the workforce. They needed this kind of gear now, just to keep mind and soul together. And in winter, mind and soul are essential. Es. Letting one slip can unsettle the other.

While the snow settled, the priority job was to clear the shaft of the several tons of rock that had fallen in onto the bottom of the pumping mechanism. Above, Skews' dream of operating the pumping house before Christmas wuz not about to happen. This wuz because all endeavour wuz spent on cleaning out the rubble and twisted metal away from the location of the accident. The carpenters and blacksmiths devoted their time to constructing new wheelbarrows to help with this process. Because other work top-side had more or less ceased of late, any man who could labour was either in that level or operating the cage and kibbles to bring that material t'grass.

It wudn' naw simple job. Whatever the forest wuz saying from its roots wudn' no little signal. In fact, the whole of the spreading rootage under the pump house seemed to be having fun with the men working belaw. Toying and tickling ut wuz. There were a few further fall-ins where lightweight rock decided to descend too. The work wudn' easy; tributers carefully inched their way through and made damn sure the Finns and Swedes got in there quick with hefty timbering. At least the sides of the pump and ventilation shaft got reinforced. Maybe ut wuz truly work that wuz needed. Maybe ut should have been spotted before, awnly the Minter – as you knaw by now – wudn' quite on ut the way ee should have been: too much ov a dreckly-headed boy see.

Whilst all of this wuz carrying on – mainly supervised by Justin and Francis – Mr Mint kept his distance. Apparently, he wuz working on designs for the winding house which wuz the next thing to be built. It wuz suspected, however, that half the time he stayed in bed, or toasted his unstockinged feet by his stove. There wudn' a great deal of debate and discussion goin' on fur sure. Trevorrow had, however, conveyed to un the company's disappointment about the cave in, and at least given un an indication that the planning should have been better.

Justin hadn't said much. T'be honest, he wuz more concerned with getting the mine back on track, but when Francis discovered the disaster (remember he wuz at the time busy congratulating himself on a successful marriage proposal to Miss Jewell), he wuz keen to have a word with Mr Mint. An' on such issues, just like with Mr Skews, the boy Francis told un like ut wuz. So his words went along the lines of what the hell wuz he thinking ov when he wuz considering the pumping system at the bottom of the shaft, and how come he hadn't properly surveyed the situation? Es. Tha' wuz ut. Boy Mint had not tasted tongue pie like that fur a long time.

Francis didn' get much ov a response, though in explanation, ut could really be worked out that the Minter didn' much like getting his fine clawthes dirty, and so he hadn't taken ut upon hisself to check the third level. His view appeared to be: first level fine, where a well-dressed man didn't even have to get grease on his hands that far down, but third level? Now, that wuz something else. Why should Mr Mint be down there crawling around when there were other baissly-looking buggers who could just as easily do that? Come to end up, Francis told un 'twudn' good enough. Na. 'Twudn' good enough. And the Minter, well, ee didn' like that much, but ee had to suck ut up. T'assuage his guilt, or even forget what had happened, he spent the whole of the run-in t'Christmas, eating well and spending his money on good brandy. As Maddy said, the man wuz a complete eejit.

Trevorrow and Skews did employ enough men in the other stopes to bring up some ore, because obviously, during the construction of the pumping house, stock had become depleted. So more ore wuz piled up on the surface, but because of the weather, ut wuz harder to cart it down off the mountain, and also fur the lakers to head to and from Detroit. When the snows came in, they were always worried about the lakes icing up and getting trapped up in the inhospitable north fur weeks on end. Therefore, despite Skews' objectives to 'up' production and keep Detroit supplied, ut didn't quite work out in the way he wanted. Still, with the snow in, ut probably meant that the stocks down there were not being processed as quickly as normal anyway. Skews therefore transferred his ambitious plans about the telegraph and the tramway into the coming New Year. He tried not to think about the delight that wuz Mabel Jewell. He needed distractions.

The awnly day before Christmas that mining ceased was on so-called Chiwidden Day. For some reason, this miner's festival had been cleverly transferred across the ocean, and basically, in the midst of mid-winter, ut allowed miners a bit of a holiday, accompanied by the usual telling of comic Jacky tales, wrasslin' matches (inside, this time) and a fair bit of fine food. Ut was allays celebrated on the last clear Thursday before Christmas. All the other nationalities joined in. Some of the Cussies still called ut White Thursday, and that wuz because apparently, the holiday originally commemorated the first time black tin was smelted to prop'ly produce white tin. Hellers fur superstition see, these Cornish buggers.

Whether tha' wuz true or not naw human knew, but having been there all them years ago, Luk and Gourgy reckoned 'twas true. Ironically, of course, the holiday concerned itself with tin and they out here, solely dealt with copper, but naw matter: ef 'twas a miners' holiday, 'twas best to leave ut be. Like ee would, Skews complained of a loss of productivity, but Trevorrow, Francis and Justin all knew its importance. When they were in the same shoes as the tributers and tutworkers, ut wuz a welcome break in the routine of industrial life, and wuz looked forward to, for weeks on end. 'Twud be a very unwise man to ever say that ut should be cancelled or toned down a bit. Now that the shaft wuz clearing, and the debris from the crushed cylinder was taken top-side 'twas time fur some rest an' recuperation. So the miners did what they did and took advantage of their traditional holiday. Fair 'nuff you. The Keweenaw Copper Company awed um tha'.

Maddy had not used the time fur magic (tha' wuz still to come) but fur the here and now, for science. Moast women enduring a gynaecological assessment would be utterly embarrassed at what Doctor Jewell wuz asking her to do, but not she. Not a blush or a moment of doubt crossed her face, and she lay down on his examining couch, hitched up her skirt and spread her legs before he'd even asked her to do so. They had already been through a consultation process. She'd already confessed that they were trying fur a baby, and despite their efforts, nothing wuz taking root. George Jewell said that he understood and wuz sympathetic, but he realised as soon as Maddy said what the problem wuz that he would need to tread very carefully. His mind instantly ran to the treatment he'd already offered her partner – the other Mr Nankervis – in these events here, and that, to be honest, gave him palpitations. He knew that he wuz about to have a very frank and deeply personal conversation with this woman: that potentially wuz goin' to shock the life out of she.

'Mean, they'd been through all the usual checks: talked about her ovulation and cycle, he'd shown her a detailed diagram in one of his heavy medical books as to a map of a woman's cycle and when conception could be best guaranteed. It appeared all wuz well with such matters. She already knew a great deal. The woman wuz a kind of hedge-witch, after all. However, she wuz questioning where they were goin' wrong. Nothing wuz happening! Now, Doctor Jewell didn' want to pry too far. In fact, he wished he didn't know what he knew (but that wuz sometimes the way of doctoring you). He was certain there would be ramifications, and very serious repercussions. But then again, he'd made an oath: he had to tell ut like ut wuz. Ut wudn' somethun' you cudn' disguise or brush over. Hell, ut could kill ee. That should be enough for she t'understand why he had naw choice. But he wuz still imagining the conversation that at some point, the pair of them would need to have.

Perhaps up until this moment, he hadn't necessarily thought about them making a child. He hadn't pictured them making love. She'd openly told him about ut all though, that they went into the forest and did *it* there. Neither of them had the Christian respectability of marriage to their names either: living in sin wuz fine enough fur um. But even as he thought ut, perhaps now they might understand better the consequences. The preacher in him wanted to say more but he resisted. That wuz a different role; he'd save that for another day.

He gave Maddy a cursory look. He didn't want to look too much. Ut wasn't like he was extracting a precious gem; neither wuz ut ore that he'd never seen before. But his examination glass gave him enough of a view, and ut was clear enough to see what wuz there on her skin. He could view the ulcers. Likewise, he noted the growths around her vulva: they were unsightly and wart-like – but maybe, as wuz so often the case on the primitive frontier – she had not noticed them.

"You can sit up now again," he said to her. "Hold out your hands for me please..."

She did as she wuz instructed. He wuz recalling a similar diagnosis that he had made with Justin some months earlier. Yes, they were not big yet, but there were some patches of red rash on her hands. Because of this, he moved along the couch towards her feet. Now, Maddy liked walking barefoot around the camp – even in the snow – but, under the dirt and patches of hard skin, he could observe the beginnings of a rash there too. Bad news.

"Say ah!" he asked.

He moved to look closely in her mouth. Her teeth, overall, were in good shape (if slightly sharp and pointed), but there were definitely some white patches inside of her gums. He looked above and below. Yes, definitely there.

He then felt for any swollen glands in her neck and moved his hands gently up from her shoulders to her jaw-line. No, nothing there, as yet.

"Have you been feeling tired of late?"

He barely gave her time to answer. Another question came quickly.

"Any headaches?"

"Maybe a bit. Some headaches now and again. I had some after the shaft fell in. Tired? Perhaps so, but I thought it must just be the time of year... December makes you feel jagged doesn't it?"

"Mmm."

Doctor Jewell gave her a good look up and down. What could he tell her? How could he relay this news to her? She wuz angry and confrontational at the best of times, this woman. How would she be with this grim news?

"Give it to me then," she said. "Tell it to me like it is."

How like her those demands were!

"Alright, well, I won't beat around the bush Miss O'Donaghue. Unfortunately, you've picked up a venereal infection."

Her response was instantaneous and full of venom.

"The bastard," she said, referring to Justin. "Him. I must have caught it off him. And the cunt never told me. I mean, I can't just get ut, can I? I haven't been with anyone else."

"No. You can't just get it. It's syphilis I am afraid, and yes, you've probably contracted it from your partner."

"And that's why I'm not getting pregnant?"

"Well, the disease can definitely affect fertility in both men and women... so yes, probably so. As you say, it's a likely side effect."

"The bastard," she repeated again. "He'd know now, wouldn't he?"

That wuz the question Doctor Jewell did not want to answer. Besides, he needed to follow patient confidentially. In reality though, his mind wuz working just as quickly as Maddy's. Maybe Justin hadn' informed her of his condition. Maybe their tumbles and fumbles in the forest had made them both neglect to look in detail at the intimate health of their bodies. 'Mean, that wuz possible, wasn't ut? The Doc said he'd certainly seen that before.

"Has he come to you about ut? I mean, if he's come to you about ut, he could at least have told me about it now, couldn't he? Me there, hoping fur the world with a new baby, and him fooking it right up... with a scabby cock."

Now, she wuz getting down to the detail.

"Will ut kill me? I mean, I hope ut kills him like."

"It will, if it isn't treated," said the Doctor.

"What do I need then?"

"A course of antibiotics. They're new but I have them here in the surgery."

"Tablets, are they?"

"No. It's an injection. To be given in the buttocks."

"In my arse?"

"That's right. Yes. We do one first of all and then maybe some further injections to help things along."

"Go ahead then," Maddy said. "As soon as you like. Tell me when you want me t'show you me jacksee and let's crack on and get it done."

Doctor Jewell made the necessary preparations. He opened his normally-locked medical cabinet and pulled out a canister of cloudy fluid alongside a hypodermic needle. As he did, this Maddy continued to comment.

"It's a risk then, I know. I mean, it'll have been stopping me from getting pregnant, and if I don't get it treated I'll be infertile... That right, is it now Doctor Jewell?"

"Yes. That's right," the Doctor replied, pulling up the solution into the syringe.

"And that bastard Jacker I'm a-cavorting with – he'll need ut too, won't ee?"

"He will," said Jewell, but in saying this, he was lying because Justin had already had a quantity of the antibiotic, both in tablet and solution form. The last time he'd examined him Jewell thought it wuz going away, and reducing in proliferation, but maybe not though, considering what Maddy had now caught as well. There wuz no way that Jewell could even have given Justin Nankervis warning as to what she had discovered. Most likely, she'd be right around to his place the moment he'd finished with her, an' likely to knock seven bells of shit out of un. The Cussie ought to have knawn better. Couldn' a keep ut in his pants 'til he wuz cured? Obviously not.

"If you would like to lie on your front now..."

Maddy manoeuvred herself this way around.

"At least I shouldn't feel the prick of the needle," she said, trying to offer some comedy to the situation. "My arse is fat enough already. Plenty of cushion there, eh Doc?"

Doctor Jewell did not comment. He kept professionally quiet and did what was needed. His thumb pushed the cylinder down and the fluid gushed into her blood and muscle.

"Thank you," he said. "Keep an eye on it, and come back to me if it gets any worse. But really I'd like to see you in a week. We'll check to see how things are going."

"Alright," said Maddy. "I mean, thanks fur taking a look and talking it through with me... I just want... you know..."

Jewell knew. He knew how much she wanted a baby.

"Look, Maddy," he said, with a serious expression on his face. "I have to tell you: catching syphilis can compromise things..."

"How do you mean?"

"Having children... Your fertility might recover but sometimes, there's a longer term effect on the embryo. It can be congenital. It can lead to problems... I need you to know that."

But Maddy did not want to hear this science. Right now, she urgently again needed some magic. Ut wuz almost as if she had partially put a pair of ear protectors around her mining helmet. What he wuz saying made naw sense. She did not want ut to make sense. Aw, now, she should ov listened – and have been warned – but who reads signs like that, eh? Blasting. Fuses Dynamite. Babies. They're all the same. They all generate signs saying "Danger".

"I'll make sure I come back."

"Please," said Doctor Jewell. "If you could. It's essential if in the long term you want to become pregnant. And that man of yours... tell him to come and see me too."

He'd lied a second time and it did not sit well with him. Perhaps the reason why he no longer had Clara in his life wuz because of such lies. He disturbed himself with his pretence. He realised he'd done it many times before now. Perhaps, he reflected, his dishonesty about everything had made Clara go into the woods.

"Take care of yourself," the Doctor said. "Rest up."

But you know this Maddy. You knaw she wudn' about to do tha'. Aw naw. She wuz goin' t'drag that fooker Justin Nankervis out of a hole in the earth ef ut wuz the last thing she did in the world, and she wuz goin' t'lay into un like there wudn' na tomorra'. To top it all, when Maddy left the doctor's surgery her arse ached. She could feel the precise place where the large needle entered her posterior. She had questions now. How come they hadn't nawticed anything? Were they that stupid? Wuz she that stupid? – or had ut just been him?

Her mind wuz so focused on this that she failed to acknowledge Mabel playing with Jenny Spargo in the garden. Mabel had waved a hello, but Maddy wuz in no mood to talk. See, all of this took her back. Ut took her back to the Beara and the kind ov sufferin' her mother had endured with the man Pengelly. Maddy had sworn that nothing like that would ever come her way – and here she wuz at the end of the year nineteen hundred (supposedly the start of a brand new century), feeling something familiar.

This wuz vile enough, but as she processed her condition and what she suspected wuz her lover's condition, she realised that he must have caught ut off someone at some time. She knew he wudn' naw angel, and that he'd a past. But she wuz different. She'd not ever come across the right bloak before and so she'd been still a virgin. There'd been dallying – es – dallying, but nawthun' more. Justin however, had been with someone and she knew in her heart precisely who that wuz: ut wuz that bitch Rosie Koskinen. Considering her professional duties, ut wuz odds-on that she'd given ut to un, and although she'd considered that at one point their prior relationship must have been intimate, she didn't really want to address that issue. Ef the bitch died ov ut, then so be it. That wudn' make naw difference to she. But Justin? Tha' wuz different. He'd infected her, but the problem wuz that magic had made her love the tuss, and in the deepest part of her soul, she still wanted un to be the father of their child. They needed this to be sorted though, if their dream of a family wudn' goin' to just collapse around her ears overnight. There wudn' naw Knockie goin' to call out an' save them – or wuz there?

One final concern raged through her. The news goin' around the camp wuz that Francis and Rebecca Jewell were getting married. Now, what would tha' be like if that pair had a chield before they did? She could see the map ahead, and she could see that coming. Even over the Christmassing, they could marry and then, soon enough, Rebecca might announce the news. She could foresee it, using that ancient cunning inside of her. Rebecca had told Maddy she wanted children, though Maddy had kept counsel on her own true wishes. She desperately needed the disease to go and let her ovaries and womb to be ready. Es. She truly wanted to mine children, did this maid.

Ut wuz coming up to Christmas. News of her being clear and healthy would be the best thing that could happen. This Cornish asshole though, he still needed confronting. He still needed placing under the wringer, or even better under several hundredweight of iron stamps. Some honest talking with ee, and maybe the slag in the saloon would be needed. As she walked down the street away from the Jewell place, she didn't want to scratch herself but found ut impossible not to. Es, not very ladylike she wuz that day. Who could blame she though?

Before she minded to do that she went out to a place that the people of New Diggings, and then Mountainside, had started to call the Deads. She didn' knaw quite the reason fur its nomenclature but that area of the camp wuz where nawthun' else stood or grawed. Fur them ut wuz a wasteland, and hence its name, she s'paused. Ut wuz where none of the mine had come to be built on, and wuz just a place where people thrawed their groushans or old rags an' clawthes. Indeed, the ground there wuz still stained by some of the early processes of refining before the more lasting sheds and buddles had been constructed. Launders ran used and dirty water there and let ut drain. This gave the ground there a somewhat boggy consistency, and this wuz increased by the forgotten pools of chemicals and nitrates that no bugger had ever bothered to clear up. The whole place stank for some reason, of sulphur (and perhaps even brimstone), like anyone going there might well have stumbled upon some outer layer of Hell.

Despite the snow elsewhere, the Deads kept its usual orange-brown, turdish colour. Maddy didn't tell Justin, or even Flannery that she liked to go out there, for in her view, her fascination with the Deads wuz beyond reason. Maybe ut wuz because it reminded her of home, and made her recall the kind of polluted landscape she wuz formed in. Also, gazing at ut, gave her the drive to escape it. In essence, the stench and look of the place drove her away from ut. She knew awnly too well the strength of that feeling, and she knew herself the danger of wanting something too much. That could sometimes take you to a dangerous place, and right now, as she trod along the boundary to the Deads, she knew she wuz close to ut. Trevorrow always complained to anyone working top-side that the Deads wuz not the place to just 'eave anything but still, they working up grass, did ut. The place, a year ago wuz fresh forest but now ut wuz this alone – and cudn' be changed. In seeing its limits, she knew she could not have it. No, she had come too far now, not to cross this slough. There were words needed, things spoken, treatment needed, but she told herself she would cross. By hook or by crook, she would transcend the real Deads and the imagined Deads of her life.

The Doctor meanwhile, wearily sat down in his chair in the surgery. He felt exhausted by this secret he would have to keep: all because that fool Justin had not even told Maddy about his condition, he'd had to pretend he had not seen the man nor dealt with him before. He knew, probably like Maddy, that there were suspicions about the whole of the populace of the community and their own reproductive health. If Justin had caught the disease off Rosie, then there were bound to be others suffering the same fate. That wuz all he needed. What purpose was there in all these lies? Lies only led to this. He sensed that the community wuz about to topple before him like a set of stacked dominoes played on a bar-room table.

He also had a choice to make: should he now tell Rosie? Indeed, he perhaps should have made an intervention before, but that would need to have been when Clara first disappeared. He'd gone against usual medical advice: that prevention wuz better than cure. Now, there might be an entire community to cure. The problem wuz these hardened men and women out here: there were dark days, dark nights, and not the best washing facilities in the world. No wonder there wuz spread. In his mind, he turned over the need for some kind of public health campaign, and he might well need to enlist the services of Trevorrow and Skews. He need not make it about individual people's reproductive health alone; he might suggest some kind of check for all on Mountainside.

Fortunately, other matters in the Doctor's life had moved on to a more even keel. Jenny Spargo was now ensconced back in the house, and seemed to be carrying on her household tasks without worry about him. They'd spoken no more about what happened. Maybe if he had been close to another colleague he might have asked for advice about his own mental well-being, but there, that was simply not possible. The nearest practice would be down at Calumet, and that was a couple of days journey away. No. He didn't need anything. He felt better now. His work on the mine had helped. He'd even considered the bonnet that had been placed in the drawer of his bedside table. At first it had appeared ghoulish and unpleasant, but maybe Rebecca was right. Now it offered him comfort: that a piece of her was with him. He was yet to pick it up though and inspect it closely.

Word, of course, had come to him that his daughter and Francis Nankervis intended to be wed. Francis had been to see him, to officially seek permission, though judging by Rebecca's countenance, it was clear that the man had already asked her. They intended no long engagement but to be married as soon as possible: perhaps even over the Christmas, or shortly after. He knew the implications of this. As a lay preacher, he could not perform the ceremony alone. Maybe a blessing could be held in the preaching pit, but if they wanted official marriage, someone from Calumet might have to officiate. Given the weather, that might be difficult, yet it was not impossible. He was keen for them to make their marriage official (just like his own marriage). But he knew how ut wuz for the rest of mining communities such as this. Common-law marriages were common, or indeed, people just lived with each other and said that they were married if ever there was official enquiry. Nothing was vowed before God, and that, Jewell felt, was this place's problem. No wonder venereal disease was rife, when such a lack of commitment generated an 'openness' in the population. These were matters that also would merit discussion with Cap'n Trevorrow and Mr Skews. It was his sincere hope that Rebecca and Francis would be married by the end of the year.

Mabel had grown of late. Rebecca said she was now concentrating better at school. Perhaps the colder weather meant she had more time inside, and given the fact that there was little else to do for children of her age, she seemed to be applying herself to her studies better. Maybe there were not the distractions of the summer. Had she finally finished with fairy stories and all that nonsense she seemed to spout at times? She seemed to be attracted to Nimkii though, and the gentle Indian had encouraged her presence. Jewell could not quite work out what they had in common, but Nimkii was still encamped near the mine's collar, and the rest of the community worked around him. To Jewell, he still seemed like some old memory of another age, now finding himself in the deplorable and industrial landscape of the mine, but seemingly, he liked it well enough. He'd adapted various items (including pieces of galvanised steel) to form accommodation and with the lengths of metal constructed a kind of tepee. In it, he kept a fire, and kept himself warm.

How he and Mabel communicated he did not know, but he certainly initially saw no danger in their friendship. Indeed, he hoped that Mabel might be able to draw Nimkii close to him. He had not dropped the fantasy that the name Jewell might be associated with him coming to write the leading sources on Shamanistic medicine of the Native Americans. Now wouldn't that be a thing! Maybe in the long term, he could pull that from the chaos. Of course, Mabel's liaison with Nimkii was carefully scrutinised by at least one other member of the camp, but at the sight of it, that individual could only return to his dwelling-house and cry, for he knew he had no way of gaining her back. And this Indian, what was he to her? Such envy, such jealousy – that could only be a bad thing, couldn't it? And what could he do now that he had been warned? The answer was nothing. He'd need a new outlet; a new obsession.

As Rebecca was soon about to leave his household and start one of her own, he knew that he ought to spend more time with Mabel and with little James. He was glad that the former was at home more often, so maybe he could intervene and talk to her about Nimkii. He was pleased that she did not wander in the woods as much as before. His sole joy perhaps came in his time with James, who wuz as yet, too innocent to know anything of the world and who might be shaped in a better way by this new century. In the growing darkness of the mid-afternoon, as he shut and locked the door to his surgery, out there across the camp, he could hear the carousing and laughter of the miners celebrating Chiwidden Day. A slow chill still ran down the back of his neck though.

25

'Twas comun'. Es.

Whatever you might say, 'twas comun'.

Maddy bided her time. She hadn' let un near her for a few days. She'd given ut due thought, and daily checked herself, to see if she felt different. Truth be told, she cudn' tell. Ee'd been next to her alright, but she'd kept her distance. Justin nawticed. After the passion of the last few months – doing *it* as often as they could, whenever *they* could – the atmosphere inside patterned that found outside on these frosty mid-December days. Justin thought he knew the score. He knew her frustration that she was not yet falling pregnant. He realised that it might have been him: but being a man (and as all men are fools) he did not go to the Doctor about ut. He wanted an easy life: naw critics and naw advice. Unfortunately, because of certain actions he had taken in the past, tha' wuz no longer possible.

Turned away from Justin, Maddy contemplated her time in the Deads and this memory reaffirmed what she needed to do. Whilst others had spent these wintry days holed up inside their cabins, shacks, bunkhouses and dwellings, she'd often gone for walks in the forest on her own. Justin had attempted, and asked to go with her, but ut wuz clear she had no want of company. She wanted to be on her own. But he gathered she would not be sat up a tree casting spells like before or communing with the universe. He knew that the isolation she craved wuz because of him. Any man and woman in a relationship know when things are wrong. There is distance, and struggle. There is love and concern; but brick walls were being built as quickly as those that went up on the pump-house chimley stack. Such walls can be broken down, but when thick snow settles on them, they are hard to see, to distinguish from the rest of life, and so battering them down becomes near impossible. Justin and she, they'd always communicated. It was that which had brought them so close, but now, nothing. The imminent Christmas ought to have been a time of togetherness, but it didn't look like ut wuz heading in that direction. 'Twudn' goin' t'be naw nativity fur zertain.

The last time Justin felt that they had been truly together wuz at the preaching pit a couple of Sundays ago, when Jewell wuz giving geht thanks to Lord God above for preserving the lives of those working belaw. He'd invoked several long passages from the Bible about triumphing over difficulties, and Maddy seemed genuinely grateful that Justin had made ut up to the surface. What wuz ut she had said? Something about her life not worth living without him. But that wuz two weeks ago. What had changed?

Maddy had tried to jackhammer and drill into the core of herself to get over the issue. At first, she had wanted to batter him. In her kitchen were various tin and pewter plates and bowls. There wuz a point where she'd wanted to throw the lot at him and snap every single bone in his body. She'd wanted to drag him out to the Deads and bury him there: let un sink down to Hell. How could love inflict such a feeling? How could love inflict such harm? It seemed unfair, in precisely the same way that Clara Jewell had gone missing. All of it was unfathomable. She could usually find answers. She could usually touch her shell necklace and know what to do. But in this time, in this moment, she couldn't. And still, there wuz the memory of her mother and the Beara. Still, there wuz in her mind, men and the mistreatment of women. Was this man she lay next to of the same stock? She didn't think so, but his inconsiderate actions here, they troubled her.

"Let me see," she suddenly said.

She reached over to Justin, who wuz dozing – and pulled down his saggy underwear. Ut wuz not fully light yet, but enough of the dawn shone through the shutters for her to see what she wuz doing.

"I wuz asleep," announced Justin. "You should've said... if..."

In one movement, as fluid, just like the way she manipulated herself up on the ladders of the shaft, Maddy pushed one leg upwards, turned almost on a penny and came to straddle him.

"Let me have a look..."

She did that. She peered close at him, and examined his body. Were there any traces? Justin wuz still coming around, but certainly his morning wood grew. Finally, ut seemed like there might be joy again. But ut wuz not that at all.

Maybe there were. Some of ut looked red and sore. But ut wuz not as bad as hers. She'd looked a thousand times in the mirror.

"You gave it to me," she said, her voice calm.

"What?" Justin mumbled.

"You know what," replied Maddy.

"You caught it off that Rosie, didn't you?"

At that, Justin jerked into action. The doze he had been in fell away from him and he opened his eyes wide.

"I saw Doctor Jewell. He examined me. No doubt about it. Syphilis, he said."

Maddy let that sink in.

"Did you know you had it? I mean, didn't you notice? Couldn't you even tell there wuz something wrong?"

Now fully awake, Justin began to process ut all. He knew his error. He knew he had to respond quickly but say the right thing. He'd have to lie. In the next room, slept Luk and he hoped that bugger wudn' hear ov un, for he knew the truth. Knockies have that way about um.

"I didn't nawtice. If I'd known, I'd never have..."

"Really?"

"Doc seems to think you never saw him... but maybe you did. And if you did, what the fook were you thinking – having it away with me?"

"I never knew," he lied.

"That better be true Justin Nankervis," she said venomously. She sat back and tried to control herself. All these days – that time in the Deads – she swore she wouldn't go at him this way, but there she wuz, breaking her code.

Justin had processed much in the last few seconds. No wonder she had been like she had been. He saw the damage, and realised his own stupidity. He thought that Jewell had said he was out of the woods. Obviously not. The infection remained. And shit, ut didn't bode well that Maddy knew of the interaction between he and Rosie. He knew the maelstrom that might result from that knowledge.

"I thought you were a different kind of Cussie," stated Maddy slowly and confidently, "But maybe yer just the same damned saffron-bun-headed scumbag that the rest of your race is. I mean, do you know what you've done now?

"No."

But he did.

"No? Well, obviously if we two have this, then it makes both of us temporarily infertile. No wonder I can't conceive."

"I see."

"But do you? If you don't get this treated, you're going to be infertile for life... and even if we do manage to make a baby, it might be still be damaged."

"Damaged?"

"Yes. Not born right."

Now Justin understood the implications.

"Get yourself up to the surgeon... You need to get this sorted. Today!"

Justin knew the irony in this.

"And you?"

"Y'twallop! I've already been. I got an injection. In my rear."

Justin had already been. He'd endured the same injection twice already, and had a brown-glassed bottle of pills that he'd told her nothing about.

She was shaking him now, beating him into action. Her assertions were almost as if she were trying to urge the disease to leave both his body and hers.

"We can't have this," she said, regaining more control of her emotions.

But then the memory of what occurred before arose. This wuz why relationships like those of Rebecca Jewell and Francis Nankervis were less complicated.

"That whore gave ut to you then? Long before I came by."

Justin didn't want to answer that question, but es, his mind wuz on Rosie. Ut wuz on that night in the Cliff Mine Hotel when the world wuz younger and a very different place. There wuz his success at the poker game and the raising of the money for that first, essential assay and all that initial gear.

"I'll sort ut," said Justin.

"What? With her?"

"No. Bugger her," he lied. "I don't care about her. I'll go straight up the Doctors."

But the fact wuz he did care about Rosie. He'd found a better option with Maddy, but ut wudn' like he hated Rosie. She'd need to be told. A double-guilt raged in him, because the reality of it fell in on him: he should have told her before now as well. He'd let ut continue in she, and maybe she'd spread ut further. There wuz probably other men in the camp now too, suffering from the same disease, but 'course, nawbody had said. Somehow, in all of this, he'd need words with she. And she too, would need to be seeing Doctor Jewell. Es, ut wuz a pyramid ov cards that wuz collapsing around un. He pushed Maddy off him and pulled up his underpants.

"You going now?" she asked.

"What do you think?"

Justin was now standing, and after trailing a shirt around his shoulders he pulled up the dungarees he'd left overnight on the floor. When he'd fixed the straps, he next sat on the side of his bed, putting on his boots, and scrabbling at their laces.

"It's freezing out," Maddy said. "Wrap up warm. Put a good coat on."

At least, so it seemed, there wuz still some care for him, despite the way he had acted. He felt the guilt pounding through him. He'd not felt this way, since he'd been at home. All had been set fair, and now this. He and Maddy they had something. He knew that

– and here he wuz, jeopardising it all.

Maddy was now hunched up on the bed, an awning of sheets around her, sat just the way that Nimkii did as he watched events in the camp unfold. Justin knawed what this had done to her. She wuz covering her body. She wuz afraid to show ut to the world. An' all tha' wuz his fault. He cussed himself on the inside.

"I'll see you down the mine later."

Justin tossed those words at her, as if she were his torturer, and not his lover.

"What for?" she asked.

"You know?" Justin said. "For the curls..."

By this, he meant the traditional carols that were always sung by Cornish miners on Christmas Eve wherever they were in the world.

"I'll be there," she said. "Good luck!"

Justin breathed a sigh of relief as he left the bedroom, but as he came out into the hallway of Maddy's place, he saw Luk looking at him. Luk had a face on un like thunder.

"I knawed ut," he said disparagingly. "I knawed you'd cock ut up..."

"What are you doing here anyway?"

"Maddy said I could finish off the last of her Chiwidden Ale... There wuz a fair bit to be got through."

"Did she now? You were listening in on us then?"

"Well, I could hardly avoid ut, could I?" stated the hungover Knockie. "You pair are noisy at the best of times, not least when you'm in the bedroom. But es, I overheard... Some wisht you."

"It's private business," protested Justin.

"So what?" said Luk. "It's good that I knaw. You need a proper kick up the ass, y'tuss... I thought you got that sorted. I said to you about ut long ago when you were scratching your bollocks down in the level, and now see where ut've got ee..."

"I went before," whispered Justin. "I've already been to see Doctor Jewell 'bout ut."

"What? But you didn' tell she 'bout ut."

Justin looked sheepish.

"Boy, you'm a bigger tuss than I thought. You with that maid in there? And you cudn' be bothered t'say nawthin. You ent right in the head. You'm beyond help, you are. Zactly like Penzance this is."

"I dun't need naw Knockie tellin' me how t'live my life."

"Dun' ee now? Seems t'me that you definitely do. Because you ebm got a clue yourself. And there I wuz under the illusion that you were a bit more sorted these days... Ah well..."

This wuz the last thing Justin wanted: a bleddy moralising Knockie. Wesley-like ee'd become.

"I'll get ut sorted, dun't ee worry," said Justin.

"You'd better. That maid in there d'want a baby with you, and you – with your sticky-out ears and skew-whiff teeth – wun't get no better offer."

Justin wrapped his wool coat around him and shoved a cap on his head.

"Make sure you tidy up when you've finished," Justin stated, addressing the Knockie and the empty bottles of ale that were stacked on the floor.

"I'll tidy my end meht," said Luk. "You just make sure you tidy yours."

What a cocky little bastard!

"Who are you to call me meht?" went Justin, and involuntarily he gave a hard kick to the Knockie that caught him in his belly and scat un over, good and proper. In Cornwall *meht* wuz a word reserved for only those closest to you. Say ut the wrong way: sarcastic-like, and there is nothing more that winds up a Cornishman.

"You ent no *meht* ov mine," stated Justin.

"We'll see," said Luk, recovering from his master's anger. "We'll see."

But the way this Luk said ut, wuz full ov pain and anger, and well, ut never did a miner any good to mess with his Knockie.

Awnly when Justin got outside, did he realise the numerous errors that were building up in his life. Luk caught un at the wrong time. Hell, but what a thing to have done to the little bugger on Christmas Eve? Unless he made quick reparation, that would drive a geht gad between um and that wudn' naw good at all. Shit, chaos seemed to be engulfing this brother right now.

He carried on striding across the white-coated landscape. He strode on by the Deads, and acknowledged with his hand, the form of Nimkii still sat in his steel tepee, watching over all that wuz happening. Aside from the sound of his own footprints in the morning's fresh snow, there wuz no other sound. Even the murder of crows that seemed to watch the camp had gone. Their companions, the blue jays, had gone south much earlier in the season: heading to warmer climes before the snows came. So this wuz Christmas, wuz ut? – he walking through his life's work to have some tuss of a Doctor shout at him. He'd already had his missus and a Knockie gibm' fair jip.

He knocked on the door of the Doctor's house. Inside, a grate glowed and he noted the morning forms of Jenny Spargo and Mabel. Ut looked like they were playing a Christmassing game, and on the table were swathes of paper chain decorations that they had been making the night before. In seconds, they'd be pinning them to the durns of the doors and running them from the lampshade into the corners.

Doctor Jewell answered the door and peered at the form in front ov un.

"Oh, I wondered when I might see you," he said. "She's told you then, obviously. Had it out with you."

"Es."

"And?"

"Wants me to get it sorted."

"Well, you've tried that... and it almost *was*... Didn't you think to tell her? I mean, I never thought you would... the two of you would..."

"I know," said Justin. "Hands up Doc. You caught me. I admit everything."

"I didn't say what I knew. I had to lie to her."

"Sorry."

"You're a fool Justin Nankervis... and no doubt, there'll be a price to pay."

He expected that, but not quite the tone in which the Doctor said ut. Ut was almost the way the forest spoke: the way that he had heard Luk and Gourgy talk about its need to get its awn back: to enact revenge.

"Can you cure it? I mean, properly cure ut."

"Of course. But you jumped the gun. If you held fire, you would have been alright. If only you'd let the infection ease. You'll need a final dose I reckon. Best that you come up surgery with me right now."

"And Maddy? How bad is it with she?"

"She knows what she must do. Luckily, it wasn't too bad. Not much advanced. She might be alright... But with women... sometimes, it can be harder..."

All these things were not really the kind of things that Justin wanted to hear, but the thing wuz – as his Knockie, good Luk had suggested – ee needed to hear them.

When they got inside the surgery, Justin leant back on the examining couch and for the second time that morning, pulled down his underpants.

"Not too bad by the look of it," observed Jewell. "One more shot I think... If you could just turn over."

Jewell did what he needed to; then, came something unexpected from him.

"You'll have caught it off Rosie then, I suspect?"

"Yes."

"You ought to tell her..."

"Yes. I should..."

The Doctor said nothing more until they were back in the street again. He had finally released Justin back into the cool air of the Keweenaw Christmas Eve.

"Listen," the Doctor said. "I misled you just then. You've no need to speak to Rosie..."

"How come?"

"I used my initiative."

"Eh?"

"I went to see her. I gave her my advice. She came in here a few days ago. Had the same treatment as you and Maddy. Told her no more clients: not for a while at least. I'm to check the rest of her girls too. Best fur the whole camp, eh?"

"Thank you," Justin said. "I appreciate that."

He was a good man this doctor: a skilled man, a subtle man. He never deserved the loss of his wife. Maybe he wanted to say that to Jewell, but in the end, Justin didn't. Sometimes silence wuz still best. So fur now, Justin trudged back to the mine. But from beneath ut, he could clearly hear the sounds of men singing in the levels belaw. Nimkii had caught the sound of ut too, and wuz clearly intrigued. Who on earth were these people who felt it fine to sing forth in the hollows of the ground?

That time of the morning, the miners beneath ground were awnly practising, but this wuz always the way ov ut come this time of the year. See the Cussies had a whole barrowful ov curls t'sing and praise the Lord, and even though not many ov um wuz truly Christian, ut seemed the right thing t'do each Christmas Eve. The tradition went back centuries, for the Cornish were always famed for their singing of carols. Now you may ask: how cud they be truly Christian when they had such faith in Knockies? All that the preacher had said about faith and praise for protection, well, that wudn' nawthun' to do with the Lord God above: that wuz solely to do with the Knockie Luk, who had very fine hearing, and sensed the knocking in the ground. Ee wuz the true one to be thanked; so even though these Cussies perhaps had a pretence of Christianity about um (as seen every week at the preaching pit), something residual – darker and older – lurked inside of um. An' tell ee wha' you, Wesley could spout his sermons every day ov the year and ut wudn' take that pagan and darker past away from these Cornish. Yet Methodists they were on the surface and so that wuz a good enough reason t'sing.

So too, wuz there history though. There'd allays been a connection with the miners and Joseph of Arimathea. The Knockies all confirmed that ee brought the child Jesus to Cornwall when he wuz still a boy, and he wuz the same man who took Cornish tin and 'eaved ut atop of Solomon's temple, so there wuz perhaps some mythic reason why these Cussies continued to celebrate the birth of Christ. No matter where they wuz to in the world, you saw the Jackers go down to the bottommost level and sing their hearts out. And even though many of they wudn' naw chapel singers, ut sounded lovely because it resonated around the caverns and gunnies, and made ut sound like angels a-singing. Es. Tha' wuz what ut wuz like when you heard a full voice ov men singin' tha' way. Like angels 'twas. The current tune was 'Joseph was an old man' which wuz being led by Walt Chegwidden:

"Joseph and Mary walked
Through an orchard green,
Where was berries and cherries
As thick as might be seen.
O then bespoke Mary
So meek and so mild,
Pluck me one cherry Joseph
For I am with child."

Es, the Irish, and the Swedes, and the Finns and the Germans were puzzled by ut all, but they were also intrigued by the madness of their workmates. They'd never seen the hollowed earth used as a cathedral before, nor felt the resonance ov ut in their chests when ut wuz used as a soundboard to amplify the Cussie's voices. And so they sung loud and hard belaw, and even the earth responded. The fungi and the roots and the microbes ov the earth all listened, and temporarily, for those few hours, maybe thought the Garden of Eden had somehow returned.

In the hidey-holes, the sounds even seem to wake those sprites and creatures of the forest who had decided upon hibernation. Some woke from their dreams to hear these angels, and would later ask Yolkai what those delicious sounds were. Others did not wake but incorporated the symphonic voices into their dreams where they swirled melodiously. They knew not this God or this Jesus being prayed for and celebrated, but they still sounded like songs of the earth: songs that could arrest destruction, and which, like those humans watching and listening up high t'grass, or belaw in the mine itself, gave them comfort and relief. So at this moment, perhaps there wuz harmony. There had been many changes of late: Skews wuz adapting to his new world of distanced celibacy; whilst very soon, this Francis and Rebecca would only be getting closer. Justin and Maddy hoped that the Doctor might be able to offer a cure for their ailments and that very soon, they could begin once more the processes of procreation.

At grass, George Jewell sat on a wooden pallet and watched the singers and wished for more. He could only hope that somewhere, the music might fall on the ears of his missing wife. Mabel made communion with Nimkii, for in all of this, maybe awnly that pair knew the truth about the way this wuz goin' to go. But Mabel said nothing because she wuz too young, and Nimkii said not a word, not least, in English, because he cudn'.

In the depths they listened and celebrated, and drank tay and ate fresh saffron buns made by Rebecca Jewell. The Minter had even 'eaved a pair of boots on his feet, and had rode the cage down to the third level and he now stood there watchin' ov the choir singing away. Ut took un back, tha' did, to the auld country, and even though the man wuz now more about brandy and girls, those watchin' seen un wipe a few tears from his eyes. An' proud Trevorrow stood there, snugly next to Mrs Cap'n, knawing how such songs could break a man's heart. An' knawing what he did about hisself, he knawed some big changes might have t'come after the Christmassing.

And in the levels too, were sat all of the Knockies listening intently as ever. And when they recognised the words, they joined in too.

That Gourgy and Luk stood away from their masters though, for they could feel somethun' in their bones. Luk especially, shied away from his miner. Who the hell did Justin Nankervis think he wuz? Gourgy knew that the marriage of his miner might result in the realisation that they were soon goin' to have to compete for attention in a another strange, new world of babies and children. And wha' a bugger tha' might be.

These were not the only changes. As the curls were sung, in the dark recesses of the drawer in the bedside table next to the bed of Doctor Jewell and his former wife Clara, something sprung into life. From the fabric making up the bonnet that Clara had worn into the forest and had been found by Nimkii, a culture of fingers reached out and pushed for space. From the hat spread hyphae and mycelium strands all questing for space and affirmation. The fungal development responded to both the wood of the drawer, and the damp atmosphere of winter: the grate in that room never produced much heat. The mass expanded and turned in and spun the space, and soon became a colony. Fruiting bodies of red and white caps were ready to unfurl as soon as the drawer was opened. Beneath them lurked the gills of hymenium ready to cast out its spores far and wide, those dispersed cells ready to colonise new landscapes, new continents. It all crept so silently that the doctor heard nothing when he wuz asleep, and gradually, the muddied gook became consumed by the emerging stems of toadstools.

In the caverns and levels belaw, the miners still belted out their curls:

"Hark, what music fills creation,
    Circling thro' the boundless sky,
Shepherds, fill'd with consternation,
    Hear seraphic harmony.
See them, from the Realms of Glory,
    Shedding lustre o'er the morn;
While they chant the wondrous story
    Of the great Messiah born!"

Crowst-time

They always had saffron buns fur crowst, or as her grandfer used to say in that distinctive American-infused way of his, *Sef-fren*. Hard to think how something so delicious could be made from something so small. If you see it still for sale now, it's in tiny plastic bags. She remembered them hung up beside the refrigerated cheese counter in the village shop, close enough though to other items of baking: the bicarbonate of soda and the self-raising flour, the sugar, bags of currants, tubs of glacé lemon peel and other candied fruit.

Those fine dried threads could be seen inside those packages; the package itself being no more than a couple of inches square: a tiny parcel of golden stamens. She couldn't remember the company who manufactured and distributed them, but this was in the days when everything was home-made, when 'boughten' standardised products were considered inferior, and not a patch on what could be delivered in one's own kitchen: in one's own range or oven. 'Boughten' meant skimping on the ingredients and a lesser taste: an inferior substitution, which one only purchased if desperate. Her grandmother always avoided it. There were about twenty packages on each card: some money you, for what it looked like. But they went. When you paid, you popped the package not in your basket, but in your purse. It was to be kept safe – like a ten-pound note. Every baker in the area needed them. Imports those were, all from northern Spain or Italy probably. And now they come from even further away. Nothing is grown local like it used to be.

See, they've gone now. There are only trace elements left, but in the past – in the last century and the one before that – there were plenty of fields in Cornwall where saffron was still grown. Every village once had a saffron meadow where the fields turned blue-purple or pristine white with the emergence of crocus plants. Specific south-facing meadows were given over to them. They were so endemic that nobody bothered to write them down. It was never like they would fall out of fashion or be forgotten, was it? So their remnants are still there apparently: in Stratton and Launcells, in Fowey and Feock, in Mylor and Penryn. One time, they could be located in every parish. They small fields sustained a people – and fed a nation.

They grew it in private gardens sometimes as well: it always did well between the angelica and caraway plants. Some of it was for food; some of it was medicinal, and those same meadows got passed on in wills because they were valued and important, just like the deeds and bounds of mines and river courses, the foreshore and age-old adits and access caves. Those old owners knew the value... but now, well, those expanses are of late covered in either new housing or industrial estates, with perhaps just the memory indicated on a signpost or an ancient street name. But somewhere in the mind, it still lurks, that memory – maybe just two or three generations ago: the spice from the stigmas of *Crocus sativus*, a species that blooms in the autumn in Cornwall. Your grandmother's hand is pinching the cup-shaped salverform flower, which runs down organically into a narrow tube. The flowers can vary a lot in colour you. There are mauves and lilacs but also the dark yellow is sometimes strewn with white flashes.

Their leaves aren't that special though: just grass-like with a white central stripe along the leaf's axis: not much maybe – for something talked of in the same breath as frankincense, myrrh and cinnamon. Inside the flower, the three stigma; each bursting with filaments of 'red gold'. Half-remembered delicate fingers reach in and gently pick them, sensing the anatomy and then moving on surely to the next. These were the female parts of the flower and they were not made for men to pick – they who drove charges into hard rock here and back home, to mine a living. Instead, its form became the work of girls and women.

So there is a need to ask: when did all that pass then, and when did it move into legend and story, and how come the stupid Cornish have to import saffron from hotter climes just to make cake and revel buns for chapel anniversaries? Perhaps when Methodism declined, and seemingly overnight the territory became secular, that is when the forgetting occurred and the replanting ceased. And that was the moment when the young forgot the skill, or lost the patience to pick the hard-won stamens, knowing that even after a whole day of picking, you'd only gain a small handful. Our world is too daunted by that. It needs instant gratification, not sorry threads of yellow.

And so sadly, the young let it go – and why bother anyway when every high-street baker sells buns and cakes, and when the very same can be ordered on-line and next-day delivery can be offered anywhere in Britain? Time had sped up – and somehow the crocus and its stamens got left behind. That's for others to pick now, others to grow, for girls and boys who have patience, who still don't mind the stain of yellow between forefinger and thumb, and do not worry if a white blouse or shirt becomes dusted with golden particles.

Somewhere now, it is cheap labour. It is a group of low-paid individuals (children maybe) who are tasked with the extraction, who pull the spice out and deposit it by weight into shipping sacks. They are at it now, in the Middle East, in Africa, and in Afghanistan, making sure our appetites are supplied with enough of it; so that what was once local is now global. All of that slow picking and making has long since disappeared into the atmosphere, and reminds us of that time when tea-treats issued forth that revel bun – and the world felt a better place.

So that day, when the revel buns at 'Saffron-Bun Chapel' are brought in by adoring and smiling women, it is both an annunciation like it is used to be, and a confirmation: a noting that whatever transitions and technology have come and gone that this remains – and stays the same. Buns here connect with God – and God connects back – for He knows it is the chosen food of this nation and its people. He knew what happened here. He still knows. And when on that day each member of the congregation is offered such a revel bun for this re-opening ceremony, then time stops and all are back here at the chapel's foundation, which as you can guess well enough by now, was not quite the thing it was elsewhere. For as we know, some pollen drifted here once, pushed upon a wave and a wind, and what it found was a new land where old ways got transmogrified and mutated. In so doing, not only did they seek a Christian God's approval, but also other gods, other spirits and sprites, who came, in that time, to add a little spice to humanity's waywardness.

There are names of those first founders, those first congregations, piled up in ledgers and listed on the walls inside. Such names mean very little to most of those of the present but maybe a little more to her. For her, they held deep meaning. For others present, they are dust though: bygone individuals who were simply doing their best in difficult circumstances. We note that and we sing hymns. We talk about remembrance. We talk about anniversaries and connections from the past to the present. But under the planchen floorboards, mythology stays: still lucid, still liminal. There may be breaks and pauses, but that remains.

26

Some time had passed you. Christmas and New Year were distant memories, but the year had been good so far. 'Twas givish fur zertain – in all kinds of ways. The days skittered on. The loud singing of heady curls in the deep levels felt a long way off in the run of the year around to October. Almost ten months had passed by at Mountainside. Not much work wuz completed at the mine's surface during January and February 1901, but a new, fourth level was sunk belaw the snow and ice that offered swathes ov fine copper.

Here, the miners broke into a new corridor of phosphorescent and startling blue, where the copper had already oxidised, and which, when they walked along it, felt like they were in an all-consuming tunnel of water, deep beneath the ocean. It wuz the same colour as the sea down Nanjizal or Porthcurno, and mesmerized anyone who entered the lode there. The colour stayed on your eyelids and made them glow in the darkness of the crowst-hole. When spring came, work above resumed on the winding house, and because a good amount of this copper had been brought to grass in the previous months, this again allowed mining itself to pause, and time could be given over to the construction of this new building.

Es, the boy Dicky Dreckly had not been so tardy this time, and accompanied by Skews, Trevorrow, and the Nankervis brothers he had designed a counterweight winding system with, what effectively were, two cages. Thus, as one cage delivered workers to the levels, the other – intentionally built larger and wider – hosted wheel-barrowfuls of ore which could quickly be dispatched to the surface. During the cores themselves, ut wuz then possible to have the north and south sides of the mine feeding-in laden barrows into the cages. Production increased. Skews determined that underground, he planned on getting in trams on tracks (with loaders) to help move the ore more efficiently from the stopes to the cages. He had discovered that an iron mine down in Minnesota was closing and the gentlemanly prospectors there offered the Keweenaw Copper Company all of their old gear cheaply before they flooded the levels and abandoned it. Gradually, over the early summer, this equipment was brought up from the bottom of the peninsula to the very top. The transferral of the trams (one at a time on a horse-pulled wagon) seemed a momentous task but once they were in, conditions belaw ground would be improved immeasurably. A new job evolved, with the laying of tracks in the levels.

Overseeing the arrival of the trams and their integration into the levels wuz one of the last things that Cap'n Trevorrow had a steady hand in doin'. Trevorrow see'd ut like this: in approaching the end of his sixtieth decade, he'd had a good run in mining in 'Merky' and, considering his painful arthritis and rheumatism he rightly felt that this wuz the right moment to hang up his bowler hat. He'd still have an interest in the mine (he remained a shareholder), and despite his retirement everyone somehow knawed that he wudn' be able to keep his nawse out, but as fur the big decisions now, well, he reckoned on the boys Justin and Francis being about ready to take over. They knawed that he wuz there if ever they needed his advice, or wanted to pick his brains over any matter.

Trevorrow would lose his wages but keep his shares, so there should be a goodly amount for his and Mrs Cap'n's retirement. They had a notion of building a new property somewhere to the north of the mine, with views out over the Lake. Ending their years there would be fine in his view. Trevorrow felt satisfied with what he'd achieved. This wuz a better mine, a well-planned one, compared to the ragged chaos that had been the Cliff Mine. 'Course, he thought back to his earliest experiences in the mines back home, and, in this time, accepted the fact that he wudn' ever be goin' there again. Instead, es, maybe he'd do his bit to help the Doctor with his aim to establish a proper chapel fur worship and so on. Now, given his retirement, you might think tha' wuz the end of ee and she in this tale, but naw, that idn' the case, as you'll soon discover. Nawbody's ever forgotten in a place like this. 'Twas allays the same back home too. You live on in the tales and stories.

Moast of the construction of the geht winding house took place in March and April when the ice and snow ceased and the peninsula started to feel the fresher, southern breath of spring. Its structure wuz slightly more compact than the pump house, but like the older structure, it had been built mainly of timbered struts with galvanised steel cladding. At the top of the house sat the two massive wheels of the winding gear that held the steel ropes on which were attached the cages belaw. By the end of April, these wheels could be heard humming and whining all day long, and along with the continual shudder of the pumping mechanism, the mine now curiously felt as if it had joined the twentieth century. The ground rumbled continuously like some earth demon would burst forth.

The erection of the winding house, of course, wuz fully noticed by those in the forest, who flinched and gasped at its noise, and in leaving their age-old places of hibernation, many gave up on these surrounds, and headed southward, away from the clamour. It upset them too much to see what had been done. The winding house was constructed not far from the Deads, and there, further waste was added, which seemed by now to be seeping into the river systems, confusing the water nymphs and forcing them to move to cleaner, crystal waters higher up the mountain.

Some stayed and watched, and wondered, but now they avoided the Knockies. Once, that species had seemed friendly, but now the sprites regarded them as traitors. Every night, in consolation, they called forth Yolkai who illuminated all, but seemingly could offer little comfort. All she said wuz that one day the land would get its own back, which none of the sprites really understood. In the here and now, their homes and hollows were at risk: for they knew that the kind of mechanisation recently installed would bring further miners in on the lakers, and that the community would expand further. Anger which once had just been discussed (these sprites were not normally a vengeful people), now turned nasty. They thought of ways in which they might have an impact. Their attempts before at instigating a collapse had failed. A more coherent strategy wuz needed – maybe one that would affect those who had brought all of this agony to their door. They'd need to converse with the roots, the fungi and the lichens once again.

The rest over Christmas had clearly done Dicky Mint some good. There were no difficulties in him finishing the winding house, and the Keweenaw Copper Company was keen to now let Mr Mint go. When summer wuz approaching, maybe ut wuz time that his formal contract ended, and all assumed that he would head back down through the Lakes to Detroit. He seemed in no hurry to leave though; perhaps he wuz actually enjoying his life in the community of Mountainside. One might ov felt that more work might come in for him from Harvey's but perhaps he'd had enough of being a travelling representative for them on the mining frontier.

Perhaps here, in the vastness of 'Merky', he had found something that he longed for. What once had been lost had now been found again. The management of the mine had to make a decision about his future. Two things persuaded them to keep him in place: the first, wuz that during the early summer, Skews had enacted his plan to bring telegraphy up from Calumet; the second wuz the mineral tramway down the mountain to the harbour. The fust job wuz a major piece of h'engineering which would hopefully keep the Minter occupied. Ut wuz certainly the right time of year to complete the work: for ut necessitated surveying the forest all the way down to Calumet, and finding the best route to run cabling through the trees, without encountering lakes or ravines.

The most difficult bit of the task wuz running the cables over some of the tops of the mountain passes, for that would be the most efficient route. However, sometimes (as Mr Mint well knew), it may well have been worth curving around the side of the mountain, in order to not let such extreme weather affect communications in the future. He seemed to know precisely what wuz needed and ordered both pitch-preserved telegraph poles and cables brought up from Detroit. The process kept Mr Mint occupied from May until September. A gang of men were selected to complete the work: mainly composed of Finns and Swedes who knew well how to work with wood. Holes would need digging, and then the poles concreted in. Having begun from Calumet, there was suspicion that from there he had sent a telegram back to Detroit, telling Harveys in America that he no longer wished to represent them. He told no one about such matters though: for very secretive sometimes, that boy Minter could be.

Contact with Calumet meant contact with the wider world. Once the system had been installed, then no longer would the mine have to complete slow, written correspondence with Detroit. Telegraphy meant swifter messages could be sent and received. Indeed, the mine could then be seen to be operating globally. A great deal of equipment could be ordered by mail now, and when the telegraph wires were in place, no doubt Calumet and Houghton would have much more to do with Mountainside. Births and deaths could all be registered if need be. It seemed the kind of progression that wuz needed. But Skews and Mint did not end things there: if the telegraphy wuz installed to the mine's satisfaction, then it wuz clearly Mint who would have the first shot at trying to design the mineral tramway down through the forest to the port at Eagle Harbour. That wuz the boy Minter sorted then. He'd had a goodly run here up on the Keweenaw – and 'twas looking like he'd never want to leave. Some mines, you cudn' wait to get out ov, but this one here wuz different.

Skews not only expanded the mine, but also expanded his mercurial empire. To give un credit, ut wuz somethun' that wuz sorely needed, and his efforts made many happy in the wider community. He organised some more shops for the town (a baker's, an ironmonger's and a tailor's), and expanded the produce available to those on Mountainside. Rosie had almost paid un back her loan. The Cliff Mine Hotel closed and the settlement down there became a ghost town. Everything moved to Mountainside. Direct contact with Eagle Harbour wuz now all through Skews, and he saw to it that many new items became available: home comforts, better furniture, new and fashionable clothes, not to mention wallpaper, better food (including fresh fruit and vegetables), and even bottles of soda.

He also invested, under advice from Cap'n Trevorrow, in a set of benches that would be placed in rows before the pulpit rock, making the services there more comfortable. Jewell and Trevorrow kept pressure upon Mr Skews though for a Wesleyan chapel proper to be built, but that, for the assayer, wuz not a priority. Jewell considered subscriptions instead, hoping that the community would realise the need for such a building, and contribute some money each week. Trevorrow wuz a great promoter of this idea: for in retirement, he fancied himself as one of the founders of a chapel. For the winter period, Jewell had had to move services inside of the schoolhouse. Spring enabled them to return to the routine at the amphitheatre on the edge of the forest. Skews kept hisself occupied. When he was engaged upon something like the expansion of services, or indeed the telegraph, then he appeared to be fine. But there wuz always that inherent danger in him, so Francis still kept a close eye on him. The problem wuz that with Skews there wuz always more than met the eye: that wuz the manner of the man.

Aside from his chapel project, George Jewell immersed himself in the life of the community. No longer were there just the cuts and bruises of miners to be dealt with. People became infirm, they caught colds, they became rheumatic like Trevorrow, they fell down staircases, and they broke bones. Women became pregnant; they had babies. Old miners coughed up dark phlegm. There were children's winter ailments to be engaged with. He suggested programmes of vaccination and inoculation. When Mr Mint first travelled down to Calumet, George Jewell accompanied him, so that he might investigate the latest medical practices that had got as far as that town (coming up from the schools in Minneapolis and Chicago) but which were possibly still unknown to him: the Keweenaw hardly being a laboratory of innovation. There wuz a lot to take in, and bring back to the community. Practice had altered a lot, and he at least wanted to feel like he still kept his ear to the ground and could refresh his surgical skills.

Clara Jewell disappeared in people's memory. Her wandering had been an event early in the formation of the town, and it had become myth: something that almost hadn't happened. For those who'd been there, it wuz still in the front of their minds, but for the rest, it was folklore. No one could do or say anything so they stopped talking about it. This paradoxically, wuz something that pleased George Jewell, for her memory was best sunken into the Deads of time, just like everything else. Jewell, however, felt he should perhaps take a new wife, and this was an ancillary reason for his visitation to Calumet. There, could be found culture. The town had a theatre, an opera house, libraries and parks. Maybe he could meet someone, a sophisticated and cultured lady. The boy James wuz no longer a piskie-like baby, but a rampaging toddler and Jenny Spargo had her hands full containing him – preventing him, for example, from climbing his way out of his cot, or hindering the studies of his sister Mabel.

Es, there were other curiosities too. Sometime early on in the New Year, Jewell had smelt something disturbing in his bedroom, and he searched high and low as to where it was coming from. In the end, of course, he opened that drawer and found a colony of now bright bluish fungi. Their closeness to his head whilst sleeping at night, wuz what disturbed him the most. It wuz almost as if they were reaching for his mind, to assault and enter him. At first, he could not understand the find, but then he realised that some spores had somehow remained in the gook belonging to his wife. When he came across the pungent mass, he used a fire shovel to scoop the whole into the grate, and there, the caps and stems burned, alongside the metamorphosised bonnet. Ut felt like an offering to the gods. Maybe ut wuz.

He realised he should have looked before, and taken more care. Had he really valued the object, he might have washed it, and kept it safe, but this wuz the way of this boy Jewell. Es. The drawer could not be saved – for it was too heavily impregnated with the fungi, and could not be bleached clean. When he realised that, he took to breaking apart the wood. It fell into pieces easily, and he burned them too, on the fire. He'd have a replacement made. These were all matters he did not discuss with anyone else at Mountainside, nor wuz he likely to say anything to anyone in the cultured buildings of Calumet. The incident disturbed him deeply though, and in the carriage ride, running down to Calumet, although Dicky Mint tried to engage him in high-level conversation over opera, lady's fashions and baseball, Jewell could not respond. It wuz as if his mouth were full of hot button mushrooms on toast, and so he did not speak. He did not like the taste of them, and they clogged his tongue.

In nine months, this Mabel Jewell had transformed, and grown from a girl into a woman. The curls on her head remained, but they grew longer down her back, and Jenny Spargo tied them in new ways with fashionable, patterned ribbons. Mabel started to ditch her skirts and dresses for trousers, which she preferred to wear when she sat with Nimkii: still enthroned in his steel tepee at the mine's collar; now disguised by the winding house. Although often separate from the rest of the camp, the Indian and she had a rapport. Nimkii had taken to teaching her about the fauna and flora of the forest, and shown her how to make tools and objects from the natural world. Such activities pleased her very much for she had an engaging and interested mind. It wuz thought that her time with him allowed him to learn English and she learnt some native words. Skews tried hard not to look when (unusually for him) Nimkii set up some targets on the edge of the forest, and sportily showed Mabel how to throw a tomahawk. This aggressive activity was so very different from the path he normally chose. She got good in the early summer, and wuz able to throw a tomahawk a fair distance, with considerable accuracy. Boys could only stand and watch, with her liking the fact that she wuz gaining new skills, and completing tasks that they could never do, not even in a hundred years.

Mabel could clearly still see the Knockies. Her growth and maturity had not taken away that from her. So the Knockies had learnt: with some human beings, when they were young, they were somehow attuned to the small people, but when they grew, and left childhood behind (forgetting stories and imagination), sometimes their capacity to see their species fell away. But not with she. She'd often catch Knockies trekking up to the shops (they'd often gain fresh saffron buns by devious means) or heading for Rosie's saloon. She'd see them come up to grass, and she'd scrutinise them going about their business. She'd say nothing though, as if speaking to them would make them disappear from view. She wuz no longer a kid, this Mabel. Aw naw. She wuz a young woman, and the early half of this year, wuz the time in which she blossomed. She knew what the forest wuz thinking did this peach of a young woman, but she said nothing (awnly except to this Nimkii, seemingly now her confidant).

Further lurid medication and checks were given to Maddy O'Donahue and Justin Nankervis over the Christmas period, and when he saw them around New Year's Eve, Jewell gave them both a thorough examination, concluding fortunately, that the dose had cleared up. They were now free to engage once more in sexual relations, and realising that her time would not be there forever, Maddy indulged. And when they did this time, ut became clear that she wuz now pregnant. Oh, the celebration that that news brought! You will know it. You will know how she thanked Doctor Jewell, and this Justin (who'd mindlessly completed the deed of insemination), and how she joyously went into the wilds to thank nature and all of the gods and goddesses who would listen.

Maddy had mapped her cycle meticulously and she thought there might be good news (for she held her shell necklace all night), but it took a further visit to Doctor Jewell before the pregnancy was confirmed. A simple urine test made ut so. But Maddy kept ut quiet. She carried on like nothing had happened, until she could no longer disguise the rounded bump in her belly: a kind of Irish fairy mound. Partially, this wuz because she did not want to jinx this wonderful thing growing inside of her. Maddy did not spend her days adroitly levering herself through the ladders and platforms in the shaft. Instead, she took it easy, and when the spring came, she supervised (alongside Justin) the building of their new home together.

She spent a goodly amount of time making sure that nursery items were purchased and that she had everything she needed. In this sense, Mr Skews became helpful in procuring all that she wanted for the arrival of her baby. What joy indeed, this brought to her! Justin celebrated too, but perhaps he had not truly considered the consequences and responsibilities of parenthood. Remember this wuz a young man who barely could take care of hisself some days, let alone another tiny human. Still, so ut seemed to her that, just like in mining, science and magic had worked in union; and that pleased her greatly. She told her boys, and her man Flannery, and they and he were pleased for her. George Jewell kept his eye on her condition, examining her weekly, to make sure that her blood pressure was stable and that he could hear the faint sound of the beating heart of the baby forming in the gunnies of her womb. Maddy O'Donahue, as a mother! Now who'd have believed that? But es, 'twas happening, and the baby wuz due at the end of September – more or less, a year on, since she'd first become enamoured of this Cornishman. There's uplifting fur ee, eh?

Now, not everyone in the camp wuz happy to hear this news of theirs. Dear Rosie, for one, wuz not glad, fur despite everything, despite other lovers and the passing of time, she still had a deep hankering fur this Justin. There wuz definitely somethun' about that bugger. She cudn' quite put her finger on ut, but all the while she'd a-hoped that the boy Justin might come to see the light with this Maddy, that she wuz a proper witch (one destined for evil), and that he might come back to she. Like many others in her profession, she'd had enough ov ut, and would do anything almost to make ut stop. Es, the saloon wuz sustaining her living and the now clean girls were doing well, but something else drove her now. What she wudn' give for a chield too, and maybe she considered her time wuz past all of that, and she'd go inta' old age just a lonely ma'am with not much more than good rouge and perfume to her name.

She could see the reality of ut though. She knawed talk of them pair having a baby wuz part of the world ov the saloon, and many had naw idea of her and Justin's past, of course. Like us all, she tried not to be hateful and to not have that pain arching through her body, but late at night, when the saloon wuz closed and the camp wuz quiet, ut was still there, pumping away at her. The awnly light had perhaps been the course of antibiotics she'd endured, and the offering by Doctor Jewell for her and her girls to attend regular check-ups. How long she could go on like this she didn't knaw.

She looked at her face in the mirror of her room, and she could see lines forming by her eyes. She could feel her skin tightening and stretching like time wuz beating ov her down each day. So an anger raged in she, although she never told no one. And that Justin – coward sometimes as he wuz – ee cudn' even be bothered to tell she wha' wuz on. She never felt that way about any other Cussies: they wuz just clients, happy one minute t'have she against the wall, and next minute t'be up sitting pretty on the benches in the preaching pit swearing against sin. Es. 'Twas a rare old world fur she, and ut seemed to be getting more and more unfair. Selling up would be the best thing she could do, but why waste an opportunity? The mine wuz still grawin' every day. Boat-loads of Jackies would be coming in over the summer to work the levels. She wudn' about to thraw ut away, not yet, at least. She'd have to bide her time.

So some wuz blessed that summer, and some wudn'. But that is the way ut always have been. Such is the way life throws its dice. Another pair had rolled a six though – or, so it seemed. And you knaw this pair too: Justin and that Rebecca, who on New Year's Day, had tied the knot. Oh es, they'd made themselves respectable in ways that some men and women wudn' normally dream of out here on the Keweenaw. A minister had been brought in and done the deed for they, and this wuz followed by a celebratory tea-treat in the schoolhouse.

Luk and Gourgy knawed 'twas coming, and when the knot wuz tied, they became mightily reflective on their own experiences, and wished they had not given all their born days to humans, and looked more for female company of their kind, deep in the earth. But that is the way sometimes things go, and they knawed all of that. So they took joy instead in seeing their one boy shack up with Maddy, and the other, get hitched to this maid. 'Course, they already knawed what would follow. Before long, Rebecca and he wuz trouncing up to her feythur's too, to see if she wuz pregnant. Ut didn't take the boy Francis long, did ut (up there like a spriggan ee must've been)? Suddenly then they wuz set too, fur family life, awnly she wuz much more open as t'what wuz happening. So this maid, she told everyone, and everyone partook of their joy. Luk and Gourgy cared maybe a little less about that but instead, looked forward to the fact that they were about to take over their own residence.

So there were these Cornish pair now, these tusses from nowhere, on the other side of the Atlantic, turning up here and makin' something of themselves with all these other people. An' fur a moment that felt good. 'Course, the forest comed t'knaw, just like ut did with Maddy and Justin's baby; yet it wuz awnly half-way through the pregnancy, that this Justin and this Maddy decided to reveal their news to what, effectively, wuz their brother and sister-in-law. Rite on then. Es. Not bad fur a couple of useless buggers from Cornwall. Both pards were now paired up with women, and both women had buns in the oven. Es, well, ut do go like that sometimes, dun't ut?

The mine now had a pumping engine, a winding engine, trams, a telegraphy system and a ready stock of ore. Meanwhile, in the wombs of these two women, another extraction would soon need to take place. The mineralized gems sought after in there were far more precious though, far more important. Come end of September, these two pards wuz expectant fathers, hoping fur some good news. How that wud go, wuz like the rest of hard-rock mining. 'Twas proper guesswork you, and nawbody in the world could tell ee what the lode would reveal.

27

"A'right?" came an enthusiastic greeting from Walt Chegwidden across to Nimkii.

Nimkii knew how to respond to this in the Cussie-style.

"A'right," he shouted back, affirming that he was fine and well.

One morning – ut may have been late September or perhaps early October – ut wuz certainly when the deciduous leaves of the forest had already started to turn golden yellow, red and orange – this boy Nimkii woke up inside of his steel tepee and heard Chegwidden's salutation, and knew what he needed to do. He had contemplated ut many times before, but he did not know anymore even how to confront the issue. A lot of water had passed under that bridge. Around him and above him sat the leering menace of two massive steel-clad structures, which a year ago, were not here. All that had once been here wuz a small hole in the ground, where he had dug out rock with these two brothers: Justin and Francis Nankervis. Before that, there had been nothing but forest.

He was reconciling all of this, trying with meditation and reflection, to understand the changes that were happening to the world. Yes, those changes were here on the Keweenaw, but they were everywhere from what he had gathered. They were lower down the Peninsula, they were in Minnesota and Wisconsin; they were also down on the lower peninsula of Michigan. All those places and names anyway, they were false appropriations of what wuz there before, symbolic of how the Europeans had altered and divided up the landscape. Yes, his people had got richer. They'd more money than many of his kind, but what did that mean in reality? What had been lost? And maybe he realised that he had been far too innocent in this process. It was not like he had been deceived, for he knew what would happen: but it was more him coming to a new understanding of the way in which a small area of the world can be ruined, and seemingly that did not matter, because there are many more like it elsewhere. But when the 'many more elsewheres' are enduring the same process, then there really is a problem: a repetition all over the Earth.

He'd tried with the forest before. Es. He had tried with it when Clara Jewell went missing first of all (all those events he observed from close by); he had tried again when he had found her bonnet in the fairy ring of toadstools and mushrooms, deep into the southern forest. He had shouted at the trees, the animals, the birds, the insects, the butterflies, those usually hidden sprites of the forest and told them how disappointed he was: how the forest's ensnaring of this women was no act of kindness. The forest had sacrificed much and seemingly, Clara Jewell was the human's sacrifice back.

But the forest – the great and wide forest – so disappointed and full of such bitter mistrust as it was, did not want to engage in dialogue. It did not want to listen, and he (he, for what he did, for what he had sold), he was the most evil man on the planet. That had never been his intention, he had pleaded. So all this while, he had sustained and nourished his guilt. He had witnessed construction of the pump house and the winding house; he had seen how the Deads had spread, and how pollution had seeped into the land's rivers. He knew that bit-by-bit, the edge of the forest wuz receding. He had felt stasis and a sense of embattlement: that unless the forest put an end to its siege then things might escalate still further. No one needed that: not the fairy and fay creatures of the forest, nor the humans.

Intervention would be needed or the wickedness might continue. He'd become close to this Jewell woman: she was a young woman now – and no longer a girl. She liked him, and at first, he did not understand why she wanted knowledge of him, but as the year unfurled, he realised that she was completing this action for good reason. She saw him as an ally in her growing communication with the forest. No one else understood. She saw the debate in his mind, and as all of this tumbled into close perspective, he began to realise that the two of them might be able to work some magic together.

The other miners and surface men were surprised to see tha' Sos Nimkii wander through the camp that morning. He generally kept himself to himself, but now, for a change, he was out and about: and his awkward, angular presence was noted. She was waiting for him outside of her house. They did not need to speak, for they knew what they needed to do. In silence, therefore, she joined him. Mabel had lied to Jenny Spargo about where she was going. Her father would certainly not have wanted her to wander into the forest, but he was too occupied with new medical books he'd purchased in Calumet, as well as a bevy of letters to potential replacement wives he had encountered there. She knew all of that but this time, it was necessary to break that rule. She knew when Nimkii would pass by, and so she had made excuses about needing to fetch something trivial for her pregnant sister. She was clever this Mabel, but then, you knaw tha'. So no one nawticed them quietly slip into the woods together, not even that Skews, who normally kept a distant, if jealous eye on things, but who that morning wuz too busy talking to Dicky Mint about the mineral tramway's possible funicular design.

The pair of them headed south, into the deepest, darkest part of the forest, when the light soon faded; and where the trees assumed an austere blackness. Even the mosses and lichens were dusky here. Further to the west was where the great run of telegraph poles ran through the forest, a job recently completed by Mint and his Scandinavian team. Here though, the forest was primitive.

"We must wake it up!" said Nimkii.

He could not – even now – speak in long sentences of English, but Mabel had managed to go beyond the level of broken conversation with him that Trevorrow had begun some years before. Even if he could not deliver long pieces of language, he understood a little more now. Mabel had been teaching him, and with the time he had spent with her, he'd gained confidence. She was a good conversationalist; non-judgmental and tolerant of him. On the other hand, Mabel had picked up some words and phrases from him: the native names for certain things, but she could not communicate in his language beyond that. She did not even know fully what tongue he spoke. To her, it sometimes sounded like the words of the trees and the earth.

To wake up the forest from its slumber that morning, they took sticks, and banged them hard against trees. The first thing this did was to wake up the birds, and it sent the crows and the blue jays tumbling out of the branches and into the sky. With the echo of their work, they realised the vastness of the terrain. Much was still untouched, but both of them knew that was hardly the point. The nearby telegraphy proved that nothing was off-limits as far as the humans were concerned. It was their world and no one else's. Anyone who tried to contest it would be bull-dozed away or consigned to the pollution oozing from the Deads. Even this far into the forest, still could be heard just below their noisy beating, the low hum of the winding gear; the greasy bob of the pumping engine.

"We need to speak to you," shouted Mabel. "Me and Nimkii here. We want to talk with you. Please come out."

For a long while – indeed, for the whole of the morning – these words had no effect. She kept shouting them, or similar phrases of encouragement. But the forest was always careful not to respond too quickly. It had learnt patience, and in order to converse with it, it was best to be persistent. Gradually though, the sprites of the forest emerged. They poked their long noses and sticky-out ears forth from hidey holes and uncovered themselves from moss and lichen. They came to trail behind Nimkii and Mabel in a kind of wild procession of forest-folk. There were all kinds: fairies and nymphs, and piskie-like beings, as well as others that she had no clue of the names of: little people covered in maple leaves for clawthes, and bizarrely, others encased in fungi. It was a strange carnival indeed, and they had only responded because it was these two humans who were trying to engage with them, and they had seen them before: recognised their intent. When the imperialist and destructive Minter and his men had walked close by, they squatted below, not making any movements, not even making a sound, but this was different.

When enough of them had gathered, Nimkii addressed them.

"We seek peace," he said. "We do not want war."

Those present gave him their ear.

"There have been mistakes," Mabel said. "Misunderstandings, but we want to change those. That's why we're here."

None of the forest sprites answered. Individually, this was not the way they did things. But they could talk in union: a kind of collective consciousness. Mabel picked up on it.

"They won't speak now," she said. "They want to wait for Yolkai – when it's dark."

"We wait until the moon then," offered Nimkii, sitting upon a fallen tree, and preparing himself for a long delay all afternoon. And so, for some time, Mabel and Nimkii sat there, with the eyes of the forest on them. Out there, they saw a landscape of small beings, and of individuals who had no human name, just sat there watching them intently.

"They say there is another human in the forest today... a woman..." said Mabel realising what was being whispered.

And then Mabel listened some more.

"It's Maddy. They say she is out here with them. With us."

Mabel heard what they were saying and in knowing what was happening to Maddy, she realised that she and Nimkii had to try to get this right. There might otherwise be consequences.

Eventually, night came down. All that could be seen now were the whites of a thousand eyes peering at them from every corner of the forest, and in scanning these and their intensity, both Nimkii and Mabel forgot to look skywards. Soon, the moon goddess was with them. She was in the sky, but also too, in this part of the forest where they had come to a halt. Mabel had not seen Yolkai before, and she was the purest and most beautiful thing that she had ever seen. With her arrival, the veil that had seemingly clouded Mabel's mind for the whole of her childhood was now brushed aside. This was what her reading of fairy stories and her role-plays had prepared her for. There was not doubt that she was attuned to the world of the fae.

"What brings you back to us Warrior Nimkii?" asked Yolkai. "Your betrayal is everywhere."

Obviously, Nimkii could hear Yolkai in another tongue, but to Mabel, the forest offered translation.

Nimkii denied all.

"You have taken profit from our pain."

He protested again.

"Suffering is the only way now."

Nimkii shook his head, and knelt before her.

"Who comes with you here to the forest?" Yolkai asked, at last acknowledging Mabel's presence.

"Mabel Jewell... She is the daughter of Clara Jewell, the one you took away."

"And what of that?"

"Return her mother please, and all will be well again..."

"But Clara Jewell made a choice to be at one with us. There is no return..."

"There must be," Nimkii pleaded. "Think of her baby boy... her children... You know you are lying. You took her as a sacrifice. You tempted her to you."

"We care not for babes or children, just as you have not cared for our young... There is a price to be paid. Humanity must learn this."

"We know it."

"Tell that to those that work the mine..."

"We shall," interjected Mabel.

"Tell that to all those who cross this land to plunge into its depths... and steal what is not theirs."

But Mabel could not respond to that. It was too big an ask, but still, she understood the point. Even she could see the way the world would go in this new century.

"It will be a long time before we reclaim the mine," stated the Moon Goddess.

"But one day it will come," offered Nimkii.

"But by then, will all those around you here have been decimated? What new world must theirs be now? I know those men of the mine. I know what they did to their own land. I pass over it every night. I see their destruction. And now, they inflict their evil on us here."

Now Mabel understood. Now she could see what these Cussies had done, and how it had upset the balance. She wanted to run and tell the Cap'ns of the mine, to tell her father, to let the whole world know. But all of this was bigger than her. It felt overwhelming.

"We have some knowledge for you as well Mabel Jewell."

Mabel was uncertain where this was going.

"Beware of the man named Skews. We have seen him and his actions. He has bad intentions... Trust us. We know..."

Mabel thought back to her earlier encounters with him. She had found him kindly when she was younger, though it was true of late, that he had kept his distance from her.

"Why?"

"Harm is in him. That is all you should know. We are glad to have met you Mabel Jewell. We have now put right a wrong done to us."

For the first time, the forest now scared Mabel. Before, it had always intrigued her, but this now, was something different. She saw its malevolency. She understood why it had embraced and enveloped her mother: and now she had learnt why she would never be released. Skews was another troubling matter.

"We came to you with compassion," stated Nimkii, but you appear to not want to listen."

"We are listening," responded Yolkai. "We have been listening long and hard, and we have become wise with it. There is still much to be decided. So much is unwritten. There is new growth under the carpet of leaves, but neither you nor I can see it. But I've said enough. You know what you must do. We know what we must do. Have faith in us and we will in you."

The encounter with Yolkai then ended as suddenly as it had begun. Dawn was breaking across the landscape, and the sun rose in the east, trailing its beams across the Lake to the north of this location in the forest. Early morning shadows of the tall tree trunks provided enough cover to allow those watching to slink back to their burrows and hollows. It was only at this moment that Mabel and Nimkii came to realise that they had been in the forest for almost twenty-four hours. Their conversation with Yolkai which seemed like it had lasted for only a few minutes had, in fact, continued for much longer. Dialogue with the forest creatures it seemed, was always slow and dream-like, and so too, was discussion with the Moon Goddess.

"We tried," said Nimkii. "Now you see what I battle. It is hard to shift them... hard to get back your mother. They were the ones who entranced her. It was not your father's fault."

"There seemed some hope though," observed Mabel. "I have to believe that."

"What about Mr Skews? Did you know that?"

"No. He's been kind to me. I mean, really kind, especially when my mother went missing... so no, I don't know what it's saying."

"The forest sees all," said Nimkii, "I don't agree with it always but respect what it says. It has seen something it does not like. Be wary of him. Tell your sister. I make a promise to you. I will keep an eye on him."

So in that, Mr Skews became watched by not just one protector, but two.

They realised the need to return to Mountainside. She had been out for almost twenty-four hours with Nimkii, and her going missing would perhaps already have prompted worry and a search. She doubted her father would have noticed but her sister and Miss Spargo would be concerned. She'd spent nights out before of course, but that had been in the summer. It was now early October. Perhaps it would be best if they came back into the camp separately. Nimkii could see the sense in that. Who would have believed them anyway if they had said that they'd been out talking to the forest? Not many, though maybe they could tell Luk and Gourgy. They'd know. They'd understand. They'd already worked it all out.

On the same day, a heavy Maddy waddled into the forest. She'd been working on a place in which to give birth. Her chosen destination wuz formed from a bowl-shaped dip in the rock underlying the soil, and it was surrounded by low trees and ferns, so felt private and safe. For a few weeks, she had taken provisions there, and stowed under a tarpaulin everything that she felt she would need. In a wicker basket she'd brought a bowl, some soap, water, whiskey, blankets and a change of clothes which were all positioned under the grey material, and kept in place by heavy stones. She brought things for the baby too: some swaddling, and a blanket. She'd at least been witness to a number of births back home. She knew what to do, and what ut would be like. Her mother and her grandmother before her had given her that knowledge.

In her mind, there wuz naw necessity to have Justin there (the sight of her in labour might put him off her for life) and neither wuz there any need for Doctor Jewell to be present. This moment wuz a womanly thing in her view – and she wanted to do it her way. Since its conception, she knew she wanted to give birth to her child in as natural a set of surroundings as possible, so the forest seemed the place to do it. She didn't care what small ethereal beings watched her, or came to be intrigued by her groans or moans. Ut wuz better here than being in the middle of the camp where everyone human going about their daily tasks would be able to hear her.

Es. She had tunnel-vision in her objective, did this Maddy. She had not really contemplated the consequences of anything going wrong, or the fact that having the Doctor present might actually have offered her greater physical comfort during the process. He could give her air; perhaps help with pain relief, but none of that wuz fur Maddy O'Donahue. Women preceding her – all over the world – had done this before without the interference of modern medicine. She'd be the same. Besides, she wuz confident about how things would go: for a long time now, she had made rituals to ease her child's birthing.

There were traditions she remembered from home: candles lit all night in bedrooms, avoiding graveyards (she kept away from the Deads of late), not seeing rabbits, and washing windas in a clockwise direction. When her time came, she'd carry an image of St Brigid (an old goddess, she had inscribed into a ring; kept on her fourth finger on her right hand) and it wuz good, so it wuz said, to pierce one's clothing with pins several times. All this, she duly did. She had meditated on what her body would endure. She had asked the universe to assist her: to make the birth easy and to give her a healthy child. She had placed her shell necklace on the mossy bed she had made and given it blessing. She spoke not Christian words but something older: something more important, more instinctual.

In all of this, she said little to Justin Nankervis. There were things about birthing that he did not need to know, but there wuz an additional layer of mystery put on the task by women. It was her most sacred moment: and ut needed to be her, the child and the world. No other soul need intrude. In fact, Justin had matured greatly during her pregnancy. He truly began to understand the significance of their union, and what bringing another soul into the world really meant. He too had been keen to assist her, but she had lied to him, and told him that other women of the camp were ready to assist when her time came. Now, in such circumstances, men have little sway, for the extraction of babies generally, in this time, wuz women's work; and so he assumed – as any man would – that she would be cared for and assisted.

Of late, she had become less mobile. Her awnly real exercise wuz to go up to the Doctor and check that she and her baby were still healthy; and this, she did regularly. Jewell had wanted her to work with him on a birthing plan, but she purposefully muddled him with her intentions, and kept to her own secret agenda. He chided her and raised his eyebrows at her lack of concern, considering he had nursed her all this way (and from such grim first circumstances), but this final stage, ut would be hers and no one else's. She wuz adamant in that. Her ultimate aim wuz to walk out of the woods clutching a new, umique piece of creation, and she knew deep in her heart that that moment would soon be there.

She'd recognised that the birth was imminent. In the same mirror where she had examined herself to see if the disease was still promulgating, she now examined herself to see if she was dilating. Yes, she marked a difference and could already feel the contractions. She needed to be wily about this. No one could know. The baby might not come for a while, but she'd need to be at her place in the forest. It was well and good that Justin wuz on forenoon shift. He'd had a kettle-boy stand outside the house to let him know if anything was happening, but Maddy had paid him off with money and some pointless errand. Everything she needed was out in the forest already. What she didn't need were prying eyes watching her cross the camp. Fortunately, that Nimkii was not in his temporal housing at the mine's collar, and given the time of the day, moast other people were at work. She wanted to shout out the pain, but knew she couldn't. She daren't look underneath her skirt for she could feel herself opening up to let the mite out. All she needed to do now was to get to her prepared place in the forest.

In the day-time the weather was not uncomfortable. She compared this with what she'd experienced in the prior winter, and right then, at this moment, the sun felt balmy. This act would be fine, she told herself. She could hear her mother's voice, advising her, telling her how to walk and stand. All would be well. She just needed to be careful not to trip over any brambles or tussocks. There, in the background, was the sound of the grind of the pumping mechanism and every so often the slam of doors on the cages of the winding gear. Her footsteps imitated the rhythm of their movements.

When she came upon the prepared place in the forest, she gave a final check to ensure no one saw her. And then, in the midst of the wood, she stepped out of her skirt and exposed her rounded stomach and dilated body to the morning sun. Her waters had already broken. She lay back onto the soft moss, and counted her breathing patterns. She readied a knife and scissors beside her and had swaddling in which to wrap her longed-for baby. Despite the pain, she dug deep, and in her mind, welcomed all the animals of the forest to witness what was about to happen. It took some generous pushing and gasping of air to reach the point at which she could deliver that oh-so-wanted ore. This was the point, she supposed, that under different circumstances, Justin would have held her hand, and wiped her brow. In the same moment, she considered the Doctor standing over her, offering her extra oxygen. But there was no need of either of them. She felt the infant's arrival below.

Out slid the form of a baby onto the moss, coupled with a sluice of afterbirth. She sat up and readied her knife. In the end though, the knife looked too angry, too aggressive. With her too, was a pair of scissors and she began cutting the cord close to the baby's stomach. In reaching for the cord, she saw that the mite was a boy. In these moments there was real joy, but that joy soon turned into something else. The birth had been relatively easy, so what was wrong with him? Why wasn't he crying? Why weren't his legs moving or jiggling in wonder at the new world he had just entered? And then she realised. He was still and silent; the only thing that moved on him was the still wet blood and embryonic fluid from inside of her.

For a moment, she pressed his heart and tried to urgently start him into life, but it soon became clear to her that all hope of life had been taken from him some time ago, most probably when he had still been in her womb. She dropped his still bloodied form onto the moss, and gathered her thoughts. Under the blood was the luminous blue of her dead baby's skin. It wasn't meant to be like this. She had done everything right, but her mind, of course, ran back to those conversations she had had with Doctor Jewell at the time of conception. There could be problems, he'd said. He had warned her: offered her the Danger Notice. The syphilis could have a lasting effect, and here it was. Was ut really that though, or wuz it what everyone else said about the forest? That thought did race through her mind but no, this was congenital. The forest had had no impact.

Her life had taught her to think on the spot. Within minutes, she had formulated a plan, and knew what she was going to do. Nothing was goin' to stop she becoming a mother, and she knew that very soon, another child would be born. A plan formed in her mind: one that she knew would work and one in which science would have no place. She'd have to go back to some powerful magic: magic that maybe she had not even admitted to herself, but which she knew was inside of her. Nobody would need to know that yet though. Timing would be all. So powerful some times is the desire for a child that women and men do great wrong, and make bad decisions. And so she made a decision – and wrapped the lifeless form of her boy into a roll of tarpaulin. She tied it at its ends with mining-company string so it instantly became an industrial winding sheet. She knew right then where to place it.

This act of cunning would need no small measure of disguise and distance to allow what needed to happen, to happen. She could barely stand. Who would be able to after giving birth, after suffering such trauma? But she was hard, this Maddy. Es. Nothing wuz goin' to stop she now. Venereal disease hadn't stopped her before, and now, even a still-birth wudn' about to ruin her dream. In order to help process what she was about to do, she uncorked the bottle of whiskey she'd stowed there and took a long swig from it. The sour liquid numbed her mouth but as it trickled down her gullet it gave her some resolve. With this inside, she turned over and scattered the mossy bed that she had made. No one would note it as a birthing chamber now. Then, she got some of the water (its coldness made her shriek a little) and a flannel she had brought with her, and using the bar of soap, she wiped herself down. Her legs and vulva had been bloody but soon, this stain was erased.

She took another swig of whiskey. The alcohol was just what she needed. She knew that she'd have to simulate the fact that the chield had not yet been born, and that she was still pregnant. In replacing her underwear therefore, she stuffed in them, the spare clothes that she had brought and refashioned the fairy mound of her belly. For a while, she shaped it like clay to make it as natural as it could be. There'd be no going to the Doctor now or lying next to Justin, for both of them liked to listen to her bump. This bump now was a fiction: a piece of unreality. But if she could maintain it, it would pay dividends. In so doing, she would enact a very old piece of magic.

She checked around the site. She moved the form of her dead child into the basket, and carried it away from the scene buried by other objects of importance: soap, flannel, a water jug and a half-drunk bottle of whiskey. Anyone else might have called her an eejit for what she wuz doing, but not she, not now. There was too much at stake. She could manipulate it, she knew, and make the world think otherwise. She had those skills inside of her. She would call back across the ocean and pull over every ounce of wonder; there was a very specific device she would conjure.

Checking over the woodland birthing chamber once more, she was able to consciously hold back any tears. She'd had to pretend things were right for years, so this was no great difficulty for her. No, nothing had been left. This was important because she didn't want anyone finding anything to do with what had just transpired. There'd be no finding of a Clara Jewell gook and bringing it back into the camp from out of nowhere. All she had to do now was hold fire, keep counsel and let no one examine her. Es. Just act normal and wait for the right moment.

"Fook," she said to herself under her breath.

There she was then, this Maddy O'Donahue, walking bold as brass, back into the camp, like nothing had happened.

28

Es. What a story, eh!? Who'd ever have thought she'd do such a thing? But her act wuz convincing enough to fool Mrs Cap'n as Maddy saw she on her way back into the camp.

"How's Cap'n? Enjoying retirement is a now?"

"I wish he'd bleddy well go back t'work," Mrs Cap'n replied. "Under my feet all day long ee es."

"A man's bound to miss something when he's had a lifetime at ut."

"True 'nuff. Eh, you'm looking some uncomfortable maid," Mrs Cap'n observed, "but 'spect ut wun't be long now."

"Hope not," said Maddy back to she. "My back's hurting somethun' terrible!"

"Es. Well, 'tis some geht load t'carry. You need a tram brawght up from down belaw. The baby'll come when he or she is good and ready."

The thing wuz, he had been ready, but whether he wuz good or not wuz another question. Maddy waved bye-bye to Mrs Cap'n. She realised that she'd lost all track of time. Clearly, she'd been out overnight though, for the morning shift wuz just getting ready to descend. Nimkii wudn' still where he wuz normally encamped and the rest ov the camp wuz waking up to another day of fall, and another day of toiling underground.

As she walked, she made sure that the pretend bump did not move, so she kept one hand right under it; the other she used to carry the heavy basket containing her dead son. Ef the core wuz about to go down belaw, then that would mean that Justin would already be in the levels – and this suited her purpose fine. Of course, she'd have some explaining to do, but hopefully, once he saw that she was still pregnant, he would ask no further probing questions. She knew how to cover it. She'd tell him she'd been in the forest completing birthing rituals and he would accept that. He knew her tendencies by now.

The important thing at that precise moment was to ensure that no one else touched her or got too close. She'd definitely wudn' be sleeping with him. She'd tell him she wuz restless and uncomfortable and instead, doze in one of the chairs in the parlour. Ut wudn' like this Maddy wuz hard-hearted (though it may well seem so) for she wuz still grieving mightily on the inside, but at the same time, she knew she would need to dispose of the body. She would need to place it somewhere where it would never be found, and already, she had an idea of tha' in her mind. She'd complete that a bit later. The dead body now she'd hide under the planchen in the kitchen: a couple were loose and they'd do just fine.

The time on her own would do her good. It would allow her to regroup and collect herself. She could bathe properly and do a better job with the deceptive bump. All that she had gathered erstwhile in the basket, she could put back. Now that she had this time on her own, she could also think about where she would have her second birth. Stowed away somewhere wuz a journal of hers, with the ghost of an idea about what once happened on Beara back home. An old woman had told her what to do, and how something could be made 'unnatural' like. She'd have to employ that now. Aye – and do the thing she never ever wanted to do in a million years: conjure a Pooka.

Had she perhaps stopped for just a moment, and reflected and reconsidered, she might well have done things very differently. Had she told Justin of the still birth, then he would have comforted her, but the drive in her towards motherhood was so overwhelming that she could not think of any other path. The *obvious* thing would have been to have paused, let her mind and soul recover, and then to try again. But you know this Maddy. You know how *obvious* wudn' a word in her vocabulary. She did things her way, and this desire was consuming her. Her breasts were already delivering milk fur Chrissakes. The wet blobs on her blouse would need dealing with. No one should see that; not yet. Weighing all ov ut up, a Pooka might suit after all.

Her isolation could not be complete however. She'd need to know what wuz happening with Rebecca's pregnancy. She realised, of course, that in fact, she had conceived earlier than her, so whilst being patient she would need news of how she wuz progressing. Ut could not be long now. Rebecca herself had told Maddy a few days ago that she knew she wuz near her time. News would come through the camp: she wuz sure of tha'. The alternative wuz that Justin would know because he and his brother were close: thick as thieves sometimes, she'd say. She needed to avoid Jewell too. She didn' want ee touching any part ov her because that would certainly give the game away. Hopefully, he would be too busy gearing up for the delivery with his daughter. Sensible as ever, she had informed Maddy that she definitely wanted her father close by, in case things did not go as planned.

Elsewhere in the camp that morning, Mabel Jewell returned home. Her father had not even noticed that she'd gone, so consumed with preparations was he, for the imminent birth of his first grandchild. But Jenny Spargo knew she'd been out all night, and had fretted hard as to whether she should have raised the alarm. Sensible though, wuz this Jenny Spargo, because she'd had the resolve to go down to the mine's collar and see if Nimkii wuz there. When she discovered that he wasn't, then she put two and two together and realised that the strange, but kindly, Indian must be with her. Mabel had in the past stayed out late to watch the night-time animals with him. She wudn' put ut past them that they'd done something like this again. She'd hadn't slept well because of ut, but over the past year had learnt that Mabel wuz not the kind of girl to respond well to rules.

When she arrived to complete her day's shift, she found Mabel back at home, calmly sat at the breakfasting table, with two slices of toast, spreading butter and marmalade upon them. Jenny's face must have given a broad look of surprise, but Mabel resumed her eating.

"You could have told me," Jenny said, leaning in, trying to show that she was being complicit. "Just t'stop me worrying."

"I will," Mabel offered, "next time."

"Went with Nimkii, did you?"

"Yes. Ee wanted to show me something..."

"What wuz that then?"

"A moose and her calf... about two miles away..." she lied.

"Really?"

"I'd never seen a moose before," Mabel articulated, though she might well have replaced the word moose with Moon Goddess.

"Good for you," went Jenny. "Now, tell me, where's James to?"

"I wuz back by the time Papa awoke. He left James with me. Down there look."

Jenny strained her neck around where Mabel was sitting and found the dribbling form of James, on the kitchen floor. He was bouncing as he sat, placing a teether into his mouth and half-playing with a wooden toy train.

"Has he been alright?"

"Yeah. Fine," answered Mabel.

"You off to school today then?"

"No. There's no school at the moment... you know... because of Rebecca's pregnancy."

Jenny considered this. She had realised the pause in the children of the camp's education and had asked the question more out of habit, than direct interest. So ut wuz said, Sal Clemo might cover the lessons for a while. Although a bal-maid, she did have a brain on she.

"You'll be replacing your sister soon, I reckon," offered Jenny. "With your imagination, I reckon you'd make a fine teacher. I mean, I doubt whether Rebecca will have much time once she has her baby. Babies take over like that."

Mabel weighed up this option.

"No," she said. "I'd never want to do that."

"What might you want to do then?" asked Jenny, curious about her charge's future plans.

"Dunno," Mabel responded. "I haven't got anything that I really want to do. I don't want to have children though..."

"Oh? You've decided that?"

"Yes. Definitely. Children are hard work. Besides, all they do is consume. All they want is more and more. Look at James there. He's just the same. People have enough children already."

In a way, Mabel's answer wuz what Jenny might expect ov her. She had knowledge beyond her years this one, and that wuz why she felt she might make a good teacher. Obviously however, she had seen the pressures on her sister and had come to recognise the stresses of that profession.

"Maybe you could be a doctor – like your father."

"Do ladies train as doctors? I thought ut was only fur men."

"Oh yes. They do now..."

Mabel considered this prospect, as she finished her toast.

"No," she eventually said. "I don't think so. Too much blood and gore."

Jenny realised again that she had a point.

"What else then?" asked the housekeeper. "What else would you like to do?"

"Go back," Mabel answered.

"Go back where?"

"Home." she replied.

"You are home."

"No I'm not," stated Mabel. "I mean home home."

"What – back across the ocean?"

"Yes, back to Cornwall..."

"Oh. Do you remember it?"

"No, said Mabel. "That's why I need to go back. But then, there's an awful lot of America to see. I saw it on the map."

By now, James was crying and needing comforting. As she had been talking to

Mabel, from the stove, Jenny had prepared him a small bowl of milky porridge oats which she wuz spooning into his mouth. Meanwhile, Mabel knew the real reason she wanted to go back. She wanted to understand better these people around her, whose transported culture had shaped her. She wanted to eat a pasty, and afterwards, taste clotted cream and saffron cake at a village tea-treat: just one of those things she'd observantly picked up from here. Then again, there wuz so much to see and experience here.

Foremost though, that morning she'd been thinking about what that Yolkai had said about the Cornish and the way they destroyed their land. She'd seen ut here, and she needed to see ut back in their homeland too as a kind of confirmation. These were thoughts she might try to tell Nimkii, but they could not be outlined to her father. He knew his line: Cornwall was a dying country. Here wuz where the future wuz. Maybe hers wuz too.

James had stopped crying now.

"What are you up to today then?" asked Jenny.

"Dunnaw yet," responded Mabel. "Go for a walk maybe."

But all of this wuz a lie. What she didn't tell Jenny Spargo wuz that, in fact, she wanted to investigate Mr Skews. She needed to discover why he wuz bad news. The prospect of this scared her somewhat, but in other ways, it wuz just like a *Girls' Own* mystery, and the prospect ov ut thrilled her no end. Maybe if her sister were present that morning, she might have asked her about Mr Skews and his intentions, but she obviously wasn't. She wuz too busy being pregnant. Mabel would have to use her initiative. She'd have to lure him out. If Nimkii knew this, he'd never have let her embark on such an exercise.

As the cages were going down with the forenoon core, Nimkii wuz back in his steel tepee. He sat facing the low, eastern sun, whose aura now reflected on the stagnant waters and wasteland of the Deads. He meditated, involuntarily scooping his dark, locked hair behind his head. He hoped that the angry forest was considering again the bargain he had offered it.

Maddy cudn' precisely recall the number of days after her own stint at giving birth before news came through that Rebecca Jewell had gone into labour. Was it four days? Yes. It must have been. But maybe it was five – or even six. It wasn't quite as long as a week though. After all, conception had obviously been at a very similar time. It had been that hard January. What else wuz there to do but cuddle up? What better way to spend one's time than under furs and blankets? There were always more births in the summer and early autumn.

The same slightly jug-eared kettle-boy who'd been employed by Justin to alert him of Maddy's imminent birth, had now been employed by Francis Nankervis and upon knowledge that the birth wuz imminent, he had dispatched the boy to the mine, to let his brother and others know. The boy had skedaddled down past Maddy's place, and on the way shouted across the news to her, before turning up at the mine near breathless and unable to speak. Within a few minutes, he'd step into the first cage that came back up and then plunge down into the mine's depths to find Justin. This wuz a completely different way of dealing with a birth than her awn. Here, ut seemed the entire community would instantly come to know what wuz going on, and would be wishing the mother well with every single push she was enduring.

Maddy reflected on further differences. She'd nawticed that Rebecca had blossomed during her pregnancy. Her mousey appearance changed. She wore her hair differently, as if there was now a new confidence in her power as a woman. She'd applied make-up and lipstick. Compared to Maddy, her bump sat higher on her frame. It was smaller and more compact and manageable, whereas Maddy's had felt wobbly and wuz low-slung. Her mound had caused her to walk bent over, and it had certainly hurt her spine, as she had expressed to Mrs Cap'n. Rebecca had seemingly not suffered the same fate, as if pregnancy was just a minor challenge to be got through, not the all-consuming event that Maddy's wuz. Then, a still-birth could do that.

Both women gave it different significance though. No doubt, Maddy imagined that as soon as Rebecca had finished pushing, she'd be upright and dressed in her best nursing frock. She certainly wouldn't be swigging on a bottle of whiskey fur comfort. A cup ov strong tay would do the job. Age wuz certainly a factor. Rebecca was but twenty-one almost, whereas Maddy wuz more than a decade older. Women back home used to say a young mother's birth was always easier. Perhaps this Rebecca had flexible hips and a fanny made of rubber. She wudn' like that at all.

There'd be a team around her, ready to assist with any matter, and the child would be delivered at home, most likely with her father next door, readied for any eventuality. He'd have sterilised a table and laid out all manner of forceps, hemostats, amniotic hooks and laparoscopic sponges. He'd even have sutures at the ready. Jewell would have read up on every possible eventuality, though Maddy sensed that her delivery would go smoothly. Her contractions would be gentle and her baby would step instantly into a world of love. The very thought of it made her shudder with jealousy, and also inside of her raged a charge of unfairness, as to why she was now childless and this women was up there now, bursting open her fecundity.

Maddy kept her eye on the cage in the winding room. It was now a device she knew well. Her expectation wuz to see Justin emerge, and she wondered whether he'd check on her first, or head up to his brother's dwelling to see how the birth wuz progressing. He must have been a long way into a level because it was well over quarter of an hour before he came t'grass. By now, she wuz outside their dwelling, sat on the porch, ready to greet him.

"You've heard, I take ut," stated Justin.

"Yes. You're going to be an uncle."

"I thought I was going to be a father first. Me and Francis: we both reckoned on your bursting before she..."

"You never can tell."

"Naw. S'pause not. Any news come down yet?"

"No. Not heard anything. Shall we boath go up then to see whaas' on?"

Maddy gestured to her belly.

"No. Look at me! I'm like a beached whale. You go on up. I'll be alright here."

"Shall I leave the boy with ee again?"

"No," said Maddy determinedly. "I'm a'right on my own. I haven't had any signs of anything yet..."

"Well, I won't be long," Justin said, reaching in to lovingly kiss Maddy. "'Spect Doctor Jewell is on ut anyway."

"No doubt," offered Maddy.

She ought really to have gone up, but considering her size (or even her pretend size), people would understand. She imagined Francis in there with his wife. He'd definitely be the kind of man who'd want to be there in the room: a modern kind of man, that she knew hers wuz not. One drop of blood and she imagined that Justin might faint. He'd certainly stay well away from the centre of things. He'd be outside touching pipe with Trevorrow she expected. Other fussing women of the camp would be gathered there: no doubt Jenny Spargo readying Rebecca's sister and brother to meet their new nephew or niece. Sal Clemo in there too. But she had to check herself at such thoughts. In reality, she had not really want any of that happening. The sooner a swap wuz made, then the better. Babies change a lot in the first twenty-four hours: that would be the best time, when even a mite's parents are still unsure what he or she looks like.

One thing more was needed. She could not act yet. She could not complete the calling and the conjuring she needed, until she knew the sex of their baby. Only then could she act. Everything else she needed wuz prepared. She knew the forest would love this: it was a game that the natural world loved to play, and she would fully partake of ut. She knew not where it would lead, but the compulsion to do it, consumed her very core. She waited for what felt like a very time. Time dragged far more slowly than when she herself had been in labour, and the nervousness at what she wuz about to enact started to snap at her as a swathe of midgees coming up from the Lake.

In all this time, she was not awnly contemplating the conjuring, but also how she would enact the exchange. Ut cudn' be done too quickly, for whilst the swap took place, she would need to still be pregnant. But then, once the transfer had happened, then she'd need to give birth once again, but this resolutely had to happen somewhere where no prying eyes would see. The birth would necessarily need to be quick: perhaps within minutes. She would not be able to announce her labour, for all that would do would be to draw others around her. It had to be enacted as if the delivery suddenly happened to her, almost by complete chance. Such things happened. Women had babies that way all the time, and sometimes, even without the trauma of labour and painful contractions.

For a while in the camp, there was a stillness. The noise of both of the engine houses continued, for most of the shift gang were still at labour belaw, but despite that rocking and rumble, all other dwellings were silent, sat in anticipation of new life. The day dragged though. Maddy thought the baby would have come before, but in fact, it was not until the afternoon shift had finished up that news filtered through that mother and baby were doing well, and that Rebecca Jewell had given birth to a fine boy. This time of the year, the evenings were drawing in early: and it was in the twilight that Maddy left to concoct her recipe, and pull from the universe, something startling and strange. Es. Right then: a Pooka. A boy. That is what she would need. She could predict that the men would go down to Rosie's to wet the baby's head. She could imagine the congratulatory comments, the slaps on Francis' back, and elsewhere, the cooing, congratulatory women and puzzled children (not quite knowing how babies could somehow be pulled from thin air – nor how they were actually made).

Aw. You knaw by now what this Maddy needed to do. You know the story. And strong she was and so determined that not even the most powerful deities in the universe would even try to stop her. So, on hearing the news, she picked herself up and, carrying a lock of hair she'd earlier cut from her dead son's head, she walked straight down to the Deads.

In this place she could now operate in the way that she wanted. Here were the compounds that she needed for her crafting. The place stank of sulphur and nitrates but that did not matter. Lots of good things are born in bad places. She'd need to select clay without arsenic staining though, for that would not assist. She'd need only a small amount. Now back home, on the rocky Beara, clay was hard to find. Ut would have to be nabbed from a potter or some such artisan, but in these soils of the Keweenaw, under the leaf litter, but before the copper-bearing ore, there wuz enough of it. The autumnal rains had made it malleable which wuz precisely what she needed.

She squatted down beside the run of this area of the camp. Oils and waste products were illuminated on the human-formed lagoon. This wuz perfect for the deed. She touched her shell necklace, and knew that the magic she wuz about to enact wuz very powerful. No one, in her family, not even her mother, had had to enact it in recent times. In the event, such an action wuz actually quite simple. What ut required was fur her to form a body out of clay first of all. So she found a good amount of clay, and shaped it with her fingers. She formed first the trunk of a body, and then from it pinched arms and legs. She then refined those limbs by squeezing out hands and feet, all perfectly proportioned in the best way that she could. Then carefully, from the torso, she formed a neck and a head. Peering closely at the head, she took from her cloak, a pin (the very same pin that folklore told her to weave through her clothes before giving birth) and in the clay of the head, she formed two eyes, a nose and a mouth. Turning the figure first to the right and then to the left, she added two rounded ears. Into his head, she pushed strands of hair cut from her still-born child. In all, ut wuz as if she had sculpted the air. It had been this being's womb. There. He wuz now complete.

What magic then issued forth from Maddy's mouth, who can say? But the words were familiar ones to her at least. They were in Irish, as old a language as that spoken by Nimkii, and she spoke it quietly but assuredly for she wished no one to hear her machinations. And if ever you doubted that this O'Donahue woman was a real witch, then maybe you would be surprised here, for her conjuring wuz very real and very bold: high magic indeed. She placed the clay figurine into the polluted lake and left it there a while. She knew very well what would form. Checking around to see that no one had noticed her activities, she readied her wicker basket. When he arrived, this would be where she'd place him. It would be his temporary cot.

In doing all of this, she stooped over the lagoon to see if anything wuz forming. She made a check that the string holding her pretend bump wuz still in place. She consoled herself with the fact that it would soon be gone. The dead landscape of the mine wuz not a place she had expected to find herself, but given her circumstances and her desperation, it now became a new cradle of life. Perhaps such places could still offer something despite their infringement on the natural world. She knew full well the irony of this: the unnatural making something natural, or wuz it truly the other way around? Minerals and nutrients were coalescing and coming together in the gloop.

What would Justin say if he knew? Actually, as a partner during her pregnancy, he had improved immeasurably. He was evolving into the nurturing father that she had always believed was there, a view she'd had of him, perhaps ever since she'd first seen him. He knew enough about her not to ask about certain things. Discovery of this though, would be too much. She believed it would damage him forever, and when she considered that, she instantly let the thought drop. There was also the devious act she was about to complete: how could she enact a piece of age-old folklore without any guilt or regret? The answer wuz to be found in the old stories: childlessness was a powerful motivator. She could not think any further ahead than that.

There would be consequences surely, but Francis and Rebecca would be able to cope better than Justin and her. She wuz a school-ma'am after all – and he was a far better manager than Justin. Waywardness could easily be corrected. Ut wudn't be the case with her and Justin. She knew that they'd awnly compound it, and make ut worse. This is the mazed way of us human beings. We still do things, even when we know they are wrong. That capacity has been drilled into us. It is part of our journey. Yes, that wuz why she wuz doing this now. She cudn' odds ut. It was almost instinctual.

What came next thrilled her. She did not know whether the spell would work, nor even whether the incantations made would help form the clay into what she needed. But soon the lagoon waters parted, and instead of the surface of it being oily and polluted as before, it turned crystal clear, and the darkness from above seemed to pool into it. As if in amniotic fluid, she first saw a baby's head, intricate and cute, and below that, the rest of his foetal-formed body, his arms facing upwards at the elbows, his knees bent; one leg higher than the other. There he wuz. Her Pooka. Now she had something to play with, something to substitute with, and something that could change her life forever. They were meant to be noisy, bad-tempered and aggressive, these beings, but she couldn't see that now. In the water he wuz placid and peaceful, as if absolutely, a chapel cherub. But in thinking that, she had to check herself: because for all intents and purposes, he wuz real. She had crafted him out of clay, air and water.

She reached both of her hands into the water, and in one motion yanked this creature out. Once in the air, he started to cough and breathe. His eyes opened, and when he realised he'd been torn from safety out into something else, he squalled loudly. Alive then. Very much alive.

"Shhh, my baby Pooka! Welcome little thing," said Maddy softly, trying to rock him into peace. "Dun' be deceiving me. You'n save all that. There'll be plenty of time for your antics!"

The little being stared love at her but she couldn't cope with that. Aw no. This wuz not the thing she wanted at all: she knew what they could be like. That wudn' the reason she'd made him though. Ut just came with the territory. Ut wuz embedded in them from the start. They could have this one and she could have theirs. Now that he'd arrived, a swop would be simple. See the cunning of this maid, eh? See what she wuz trying to achieve. She looked around once more, hoping that nobody saw she.

The land had given her this changeling and all she had to do now was place it in another's cradle. Hell-fire, you. Some job.

29

Some pair they wuz. Damme. There was the good one. And then, there was the other one. Two babies, es – if you could call one a baby. That one certainly looked like a baby but it wuz from a different realm. Ut wudn' quite human, so to speak. The Pooka wuz a monstrosity really but the problem wuz tha' ut didn' look like naw monstrosity. Ut wuz deceptive to the eye. That is the way of magic see. Ut's all to do with tha': deceit and deception. Whereas one had been a goodly ore extracted from the cavern that wuz Rebecca Nankervis' warm womb, the other had been misshapen but ut still coalesced and fused. Ut wuz as if ut wuz awnly half-baked, and comed out of the oven still a little cakey in the head. In Maddy O'Donahue's mind, she'd tried to make the one that she wuz carrying resemble what the universe told her about what Rebecca and Francis' baby looked like. He'd have their hair, he'd have Rebecca's intelligence and kindly face, and Francis' stamina and morals. Both of them had brown eyes, and so did this little bugger she wuz hastily carrying away from the Deads. At this stage, the creature knew he needed to be quiet. Ut wuz instinctual in they, fur they always knaw what wuz about to happen to them. They could read human beings like a book you. Es, like a book. He'd knaw how to wind up the key and set um off.

Awnly when they were ensconced in their final cradle could they let rip and show their true colours. Unfortunately, that wuz the way ut had to be. Maddy would have preferred it to be different. She wished that in another world – some distant, future world perhaps – an extract of the other one could be taken, and that it might be replicated in some astonishing way. One day, science might be able to do that, but not now, not in the age that she lived in. And so she had to make the moast of what they wuz – and she had done just that. Guilt consumed her as she trudged across the camp, but this never superseded her desire for a healthy child of her own. 'Twudn' ideal at all – none ov ut wuz – but sometimes, these were cards that life dealt you and you were forced to play them. She knew too, what kind of an imp she'd be handing over to Francis and Rebecca, and she did worry for them. She could predict what difficulties there might be: how wayward this little thing might grow, and how he'd push them to their limits. A right scamp he'd be – an' then some. Then came the guilt again, but she pushed it down into her core and left it to fester there, with other bile.

Aw, there he wuz in the basket. She'd told un to hunker down inside ov ut. Naw noise mind. The contents that she carried would now become a gift to the proud parents. To be honest, in a certain light, the creature could almost be a young Knockie, so unhuman wuz he; but he had not the age of them. He was still fresh to the earth. But he could shape-shift too. In that light, yes, ut wuz true, he could even be a Knockie, but when the moonlight caught his face, he was quickly back to being a cherub. Sometimes, both forms of him swapped over all too quickly like a flickering image – back and forth. When she got close to the Nankervis property though, she placed a red-and-white chequered tea-towel over the top of him, and as he nestled into the space, she made sure both of his tiny feet wuz tucked in. Aw, the dear of un. But t' be frank, 'dear' wudn' really the right word for a Pooka of any type.

She could tell by the light on in the house, that there were several people gathered inside. The main person to avoid would be Doctor Jewell. She hoped he'd be too full of his own self-importance to bother about she. The last thing she wanted wuz he giving her a look over. Everyone there would knaw that her time wuz close. She didn' need another examination. Knocking on their front door, she checked the basket once more, and made sure that the pretend fairy mound wuz tucked where ut needed to be. She could hear raised voices, convivial laughter and celebration. This wuz going to be hard work, but she'd committed to it now. Ut was like mining: once you targeted a lode of copper, you followed it all the way through. She knew that from the Beara. Come on now. Steel yourself. Ef anyone can do this, then you can. Remember when the Irish first arrived, and undercut those Cornish buggers. That's the spirit.

Ut was Trevorrow who opened the door. His response wuz seemingly not because of any particular purpose or that he'd been designated to deal with new well-wishers, but just because he wuz the closest individual to the door. He'd been drinking, like all of the men inside had been, and when he stood there, she sensed he wuz already half-cut.

"Maddy, me lover. Come to join the celebrations, have you?"

"Aye. Well, I hear it's good news.."

"Es. A baby boy. Wonderful news, eh?"

He gave her a look over.

"And yours'll be along soon no doubt. Justin's been keeping me posted... Come on in maid, out the cold."

He helped her up the step but clutching hold of her arm; actually, the one that she wuz carrying the basket with.

"Thaas ov ee," he went.

Maddy entered carefully, making sure she did not hit the basket on anything. She did not want to disturb the creature contained inside it any more than she needed to. The Nankervis' parlour wuz packed with people. They wuz all there, as you might expect: the boy Minter (fatter than ever now, on cake, cake and more cake) had nabbed Francis, and in overhearing their conversation they were clearly talking about how a potential water propulsion system of the mineral tramway would work; clearly, the father's baby didn't matter any more (that wuz fur dreckly), and the mine again took priority. Also in the room was Doctor Jewell, who wuz talking to an unnamed elegant lady she had not seen before, and who turned out to be from down Calumet. She wuz staying at Rosie's saloon at Jewell's expense. Present too, wuz the slag that owned the saloon and in Maddy's view, whose uncleanliness, had first stopped any conception (Rosie pretended not to nawtice Maddy, but her eye was pinned on her every move nonetheless). She s'paused the Doc wuz finally moving on with his life and this new women wuz a Clara replacement. She looked more cultured than anyone else in the room, as if she had mistakenly stepped into this story from another melodrama.

Maddy made small noises of greetings and brief hellos to the people she passed. They all made note of her form, knowing that soon her day would be coming; just like dear Rebecca and her little babe. Compared to the earlier blackness of the Deads, the parlour felt very brightly lit. She'd been to the dwelling of Francis and Rebecca before, but it had now been transformed into this celebratory venue of light and new beginnings. The oil lights were turned up high and hurt her eyes. On a long table was a set of pies and fancies: all kinds of nicies that had been baked earlier by Jenny Spargo, moast of which had already been wolfed down by those attending. Other miners were in there too: several she'd beaten at the drilling contest last year, and who she joked with about a return match.

"Not in this state," she'd said glibly to them as she passed through.

In all this though, she wuz seeking Justin. Maybe, at this precise moment, in order to complete her endeavour, she needed him close. At present though, frustratingly, she cudn' see him. Nimkii wuz there though, standing in the corner – tall and erect as a totem – somewhat puzzled as to how these Europeans celebrated the birth of a child. She nodded at him. Could he tell what she was up to? If anyone could guess at her intent, ut wuz he. But thankfully, he wuz not looking at the basket she wuz carrying. Instead, he kept a more serious eye upon Mabel Jewell. Wasn't that always the way though? Those two were close, she knew that. And she knew her own connection to them too: she could sense it.

She hoped too that Mabel wouldn't notice her. That child wuz awkward. She didn't fit in the way others did. Child? She wuz hardly that now. She wuz more a young woman. That much wuz very noticeable in the way she carried herself, and indeed, in the way in which she wuz dealing with her brother James. She looked after him attentively, knowing the score with her father and the woman from Calumet. Despite the dream-like state Maddy wuz in, she wuz able to give a little wave to James. She knew that had his timing and arrival been different, then he might well have been the one being swapped. Lucky fur him then, not to be involved. A near miss. He wuz too old now: too old for the process to work. You needed pure innocence and maybe his was already gone.

Her sole task wuz to locate Rebecca and her baby boy. She said 'her' but really Maddy meant the boy that would soon belong to her. Ut was both a terrifying but exhilarating thought. Still in her mind, she wondered where her Justin wuz?

Sat alone, and looking more downtrodden and down-at-heel than usual wuz Mr Skews. She sometimes liked to call him Samuel and addressed him as such. Using his first name reduced his status. She wuz clever like tha', this Maddy.

"Now Samuel, have you seen my man Justin about of late? I thought he'd be here, but I see nothing of him."

Skews looked up at her. She tried to be convivial with him, even though he knew in fact, that this woman despised him. He couldn't help but respond sneeringly.

"Next door I think... In there with Rebecca."

The way he said that wuz intentional. It was spoken bitterly, as if momentarily making Maddy assume that the pair were in the bedroom having an affair and passionately making love together.

"With the baby?"

"I believe so... They've been in there some time."

Again, she noted that bitter intention of his. What wuz wrong with the man? He took his own trauma out on anyone who'd listen, and now, even the likes of Jewell and Mint had realised what he wuz like, and so avoided un.

Maddy could not as yet force her way into the bedroom, because others were still helping themselves to food. She wuz temporarily forced to continue to speak with Skews.

"Do you know if they've named the bab yet?"

This wuz obviously something Samuel Skews had not really contemplated. Such a moment wuz below him, and that wuz just who he wuz. People never mattered: only profit and gain did.

"I don't know. No one's mentioned any name as yet..." he responded glumly.

There wuz not a long time now before those piling food upon their plates moved away from the table, and she had access to where her man and this new mother were. She gave Skews another look over. She noted his grey form; it wuz almost as if he wuz collapsing into hisself. His body seemed hollow, like all the goodness had been sucked from it. By the look obm, Maddy didn' think he'd survive the forthcoming winter – and maybe Samuel Skews knew that. His form unnerved her slightly. He'd made her re-evaluate what she wuz doing. Maybe evil meeting evil had somehow done that to her. But she gathered her senses once more, and when there was clear access to the bedroom, she knocked upon it.

"Come in," a voice said. It wasn't any voice though. It wuz Rebecca Nankervis'. How different it sounded when she wasn't just giving out instructions to school-children.

When she walked in, Rebecca wuz just finishing nursing her baby boy, and somewhat surprisingly, sat on a chair close by her wuz Justin. He had been entranced at the child, and had clearly been helping the new mother. Unlike Francis in the outer room, Justin wuz not drunk, and soberly seemed to be watching Rebecca for any tips on being a good parent. She'd suckled her child before un and tha' didn' feel right t'Maddy.

"I brought you some buns," she said. "They're fresh... Wanted to come up and see how you were."

"I'm fine. The birth went very well. Fortunately, despite his preparations, I had no need to call on father, and now, look... I've got this one to look after."

She lifted up the child so that Maddy could see him more clearly. She observed his tiny screwed-up face, his button nose and his twinkling eyes. Thank St Brigid they were brown.

"Bewdie, idn a?" said Justin. "I can't wait for ours to come out. Rebecca's been giving me some useful tips..."

"Well, my husband has had a mighty bit to drink today. I'm not sure he's capable of very much at the moment. Your fella here's been helping me greatly. Do you want to hold him for a bit Maddy?"

"Please," said Maddy.

She dropped her basket containing its special load onto the planchen of the bedroom, and nuzzled the warm child into her. Under any other circumstances, Maddy would have told Rebecca that he'd got her eyes, or that he had a mouth like Francis, but to say tha' on this occasion, would be utterly wrong. Regardless of morality though, she couldn' say it, for in her mind, already she had made a leap, that this little being wuz hers and that ut had been pushed out of her womb a few hours earlier.

"Aw... He's so lovely. I can hardly wait... We're both so excited, aren't we Jus?"

"If ours is as lovely as this mite, then we'll have done well," went Justin.

"You named him yet?"

"No... well, yes... Well, we've considered a few names. We had Jennifer in mind if ut wuz a girl, but ef ut wuz a boy then we wuz thinking Richard..."

That wuz ut then: that wuz what their changeling would be named: Richard Nankervis. Dicky Mint. Now Dicky Nankervis.

"We haven't decided yet. Of course, we'll have a baptism. Make it official... Put him on the Roll of Honour."

And then Rebecca realised.

"Oh, but we haven't got a Roll of Honour have we? Not yet at least."

She wuz referring to the supposed plan for building a Wesleyan Chapel that had been batted back and forth between her father and Trevorrow, and which had now seemingly been put on permanent hold by Skews.

What Maddy wuz meant to say what that the child looked like a Richard and that the name suited him, but much as her brain told her to say that, her heart solidly prevented her from doing so. She had other ideas in mind.

"I'd best burp him," said Rebecca, and she reached over for her child, but there wuz something in Maddy that wuzn't ready to give un back, and that delay – that ever so slight delay – momentarily troubled Rebecca a little. But then, when Maddy did give her boy up, she understood. She saw his cuteness, and she knew how wished-for their own child wuz.

"Can I do ut?" asked Justin. "I need to learn..."

Fook. What wuz up with her man now? What had this Cussie asshole turned into? He wuz behaving differently now. It wuz difficult fur Maddy to imagine him any other way than the liquor-drinking poker-player she'd fallen for, but here he wuz trying to be a responsible adult. Wonders would never cease. A minute ago he had been paying attention to his sister-in-law's breast.

"Alright," said Rebecca, who already seemed to knaw everything about babies. "You just need to get the angle right."

She carefully handed him over to Justin.

"Hold him on his bottom, and then rest him on your shoulder, facing you... here's a cloth. Catch any milk burps with that."

Justin did what she said.

"Shall I rock him a little bit?"

"Yes. That always helps."

As these classes in parenting took place, Maddy realised she still needed to enact the exchange. And bugger, if one of the creature's hands wudn' making its way out of the basket between its side and the red-and-white chequered covering. He wuz being noisy too: she thought she could detect a slight snuffle. With her foot she gently kicked the basket, so that its hand moved back below and so that it might cease its loud breathing. Never mind un, eh? So focused were Rebecca and Justin on her son's burping that they did not notice her covert actions.

"How are you feeling now?" asked Rebecca, with the apparent wisdom of someone who has given birth talking to someone who hadn't.

"Be glad when it's all over."

"Justin said you're not sleeping... I was the same. It was easier to sleep in the chair than on the bed... Much more comfortable."

"Be nice when things go back to being normal... well, as normal as they can be with a new baby on board. Yours is so quiet. Does he cry much?"

"Not so far, or not so I've noticed... I think it's something they learn. They get to know it will give them the attention they crave. Done?"

Rebecca said this final word to Justin, and he affirmed that he felt the infant had now been winded and wuz ready to sleep again. He handed the baby back to her and she gently put him back down into the cradle, tucking a white blanket over him. Annoyingly, boath did this with an air of being accomplished parents.

"Aw!" said Maddy, craving him. "They change a lot in first few hours of being born... Someone told me tha."

Maddy didn' reveal who. She didn' need to. She was preparing ground. There then came an awkward pause, like none of these new parents knew what to say to each other.

"I'd best leave you girls," Justin announced. "'Spect you got plenty to talk about."

He seemed to pick up on the fact that they needed to discuss women's issues, details of the pregnancy and what the birthing process wuz actually like.

"I reckon I've done my parenting bit for the day," he joked.

Both women responded with a dull laugh. Es. Tha' wuz the way of men sometimes.

Justin gingerly stepped out of the room. He did not want to wake the baby. It was almost a minute before either of the women spoke again.

"I see your father's got a new lady on his arm..." Maddy noted.

"Eleanor, she's called. Eleanor Prowse I believe. I think he's keen on she. Not sure she is on him though. I mean, Calumet and here. They're like chalk and cheese, aren't they?"

"Good that he's moving on though."

"Yes, it has put him in good spirits. And now this little one... Do you know Maddy, I thought you were bound to have yours before mine? You always looked like you were ahead of me, ever so slightly. Father said so too, but look how it's ended up... Who'd have known, eh?"

"Aye. Well, I thought mine would be here by now, but there you go..."

Maddy wuz struggling now. She hadn't expected her man to have been in there with Rebecca. That seemed an odd kind of distortion to events: him watching her breastfeed. And then Skews outside too. He'd managed to put her off her stride. She contemplated all of this and dug deep. The exchange would have to be made tonight. There would be no other opportunity. Ut wuz the way with all changelings. The opportunity did not last forever. All she needed wuz Rebecca momentarily out of the room.

"'Spect you're exhausted?" tried Maddy. "I mean, all those people out there as well. Bet you could have done without that, eh?"

"Definitely," attested Rebecca, "but Francis, you know, he wanted to invite everyone... it's a big thing, isn't it, I suppose? Your first child."

Maddy could not admit that wuz true, even though she resoundingly knew it.

"Will you keep school still then?"

"Partially I hope. Maybe find another teacher. Jenny's agreed to some child-minding... An' Sal will help cover my school-keeping too."

Shit. Maddy realised what might be coming the way of her prior housekeeper.

"And the birth?" Maddy asked. "How did that go? I mean, you hear so many terrible stories..."

"It was fine. I mean, it's just something you deal with. Oh, but when you first see him Maddy... there's nothing like ut. It's the best feeling ever."

Maddy knew. That wuz why she wuz here. She had returned to being collected and assured. Ut wuz better now that Justin had left.

"I'll just lower the lamps a bit, if you don't mind," Rebecca suggested. "Too bright in here, and I want him to sleep..."

She went about the room, adjusting the burn on the wicks. This wuz good. The half-darkness would muddy the act still further. Fortunately, the creature wuz still behaving himself.

"Would you mind staying here for a bit Maddy? I know I can trust you. Look, it's just that with so many people here, and them all wanting to chat to me, I haven't even had time to visit the water closet..."

Water closet? What did she mean?

"Oh, you mean the john?"

"Yes..."

Like most of the dwellings in the camp, their single toilet wuz still placed outside in a wooden hut. There wuz no one here yet with posh ceramic, like they had down in Calumet: the kind that this Eleanor would know. Rebecca would have to pop outside. Given the fact that she'd have to re-enter the parlour, and that a tide of people would want to know how she and the youngster were now doing, this would give Maddy plenty of time to make the switch. Her patience had been rewarded. What she hoped would not happen wuz that anyone else would come in to see how things were going, and that she be caught mid-substitution.

She derided herself again. She knew the evil she wuz about to complete, but ut wuz as unstoppable as the progress of the mine. No force of nature on earth could alter what she wuz about to do. However, as Rebecca shut the door of the bedroom and stepped into a guffaw of enthusiastic voices in her parlour, Maddy did have a final doubt. That evil in her: maybe it had been instigated long ago with her mother's encounter with that pig Pengelly. Underneath everything, wuz that what wuz driving her? Had ut been ingrained in her all this time? Wuz this action just an unchangeable part of her destiny? Maybe it had even been written before she'd been born. The ease at which the creature had been formed suggested that this might be so. She writhed and wrestled with these feelings which came over her like wintering Atlantic waves on the cliffs at Allihies.

But when it came, the swap wuz decisive. She lifted the lid of the tea-towel and lifted out the pungent form of the creature. She lifted him across the planchen and then carefully tucked him in next to the real baby. Both were sleeping, and in that moment, they resembled brothers – or twins even. Sweet were their expressions. Although Maddy wuz swift in these actions, there wuz still time to note a similarity between the creature and what it wuz now replacing. The universe had moulded this creation well. The pair were very similar physically, though clearly not in mind or spirit. Aw naw. Not t'all. She'd learn of exactly how different very soon. Seconds later, she found herself untucking the real baby's blanket and lifting him out of the cradle. She kept one foot rocking the device, so that the changeling would remain in the land of Morpheus. Now that this true baby wuz in her hands, there wuz just time enough to press him to her cheeks, and for her to smell his earthy newness. This is what she had craved. Thankfully, both these boys were of the same size: their eyes and hair colours identical.

She placed the baby boy into the basket and hoped – or rather prayed – that he would not wake up and begin to cry. If she'd been careful with the basket before, she'd need to be even more wary on the way out. Inside it too, were a stacked pile ov day-old saffron buns, and these would need to be placed on the table for guests at the Nankervis house. That too, meant she would need to be delicate in her actions, but there wuz no other way.

One other task needed to be completed in the time she had. There was a pile of clean towelling nappies sat on a dresser. Besides them was a jar containing large safety pins. Quickly, Maddy grabbed a nappy from the top of the pile and reached into the jar to take out a pin. She noted how Richard's nappy had been folded and set, and she tried to imitate it on the lower body of the Pooka, the new Richard. The one on the real Richard she would keep in place. Ut was extremely unlikely that Rebecca would note that one, from the total number of nappies, had gone astray. With that, all wuz complete. She took a deep breath.

Seemingly, a long time passed before Rebecca returned. Her actual time in the water closet had been small. Her perambulation back there had been delayed of course, by those outside, still wishing mother and baby well. Maddy had overheard a conversation she'd had with Skews as to the mite's well-being, and had witnessed the inane questions that others had asked her, as she made her way back.

"Any problems?" she asked. "Alright, is he?"

"No. No trouble at all. Sleeping soundly. Might need a change soon perhaps. I thought I smelt..."

"Don't worry. I'll deal with that. Little so-and-so. He'll be sure to wake in a while... I'll do ut after people have left..."

"You should get some sleep," Maddy advised the now surrogate mother.

"I think so. You should too. You never know when your time's going to come," advised back this other surrogate mother.

The fact wuz though, that Maddy did know. She stood up. She'd been sitting in the chair where Justin had been before. She had double-checked to make sure that no arm or leg appeared from the lip of the basket.

"I'll put the buns on table," Maddy said. "You're going to be wonderful parents – you and Francis. I know it."

A few tears fell from Rebecca's face, and sentimentally, she reached out to hug Maddy. This wuz the first time they'd physically been so close. Maddy did not get too close though, for she did not want Rebecca to feel too much of her substitute mound.

"If you see my 'worse-for-wear' husband out there, can you tell him to come and help me?"

"Of course I will. He'll be in soon," said Maddy.

"Thank you... It's really nice to share all this with you. Who'd have thought it, eh? Me and you, and those two..."

"I know. Looks like it's going to be a lovely time for us both," said Maddy, though she knew that wudn' quite true. Still, ut wuz what you said. Maddy did her duty. So then, this Maddy left her, and marched out into the parlour again. It had emptied a little. She quickly deposited her buns on the table, and made her way to the door leading to the street outside. She could not be too bothered with Justin. He wuz now though, in conversation with his brother and she'd need to interrupt.

"Francis, Rebecca's asking for you..." she said briefly.

"You going home?" asked Justin.

"Yes. My ankles are swollen. I need to rest... Don't fret though. You stay on here."

"You sure?"

"Absolutely."

She didn't need this. None of this. She needed the infant home and out of the way.

Her plan would fail if there wuz anymore of this, and now, in the corner of her eye, she could see Jewell convivially heading towards her. She turned away from Justin to the Doctor in order to make the first move.

"Congratulations Doctor Jewell! What a lovely baby boy! You will make a splendid grandfather."

"Thank you. Sweet, isn't he?" said the Doctor, clearly wanted to extend the conversation and introduce the lady he wuz with.

"He's a darling."

"All well with you? No problems? I mean, I thought you were bound to be the first to have a delivery. But such is nature, eh? She dictates all..."

"Fine. Just a little tired.. That's all."

"But no issues?"

She knew what he'd want to do. Doctors think they may touch a woman's body whenever they wish. He was reaching now to check one more time.

"No," replied Maddy, edging back from him. "All fine."

She nodded courteously to this new lady, and turned to the door, so he could no longer examine her.

"See you later then," said Justin. "I'll just stay a while longer, and then come home."

"Fine," said Maddy to him but he could sense her tenseness. He knew ut would be her wish to see the birth got through. Ut had dragged on long enough, and now Rebecca, in there with her son. Ut wuz enough to make any woman jealous. He understood.

Maddy left the Nankervis property and hurriedly stanked down the street.

She reckoned on ut being her time again.

Back home – as if by magic – she had another birthing and held up a new baby boy. She placed him temporarily in the cot they had already assembled for such a moment. Undoing the tightly-tied string, she 'eaved the fairy mound into the wardrobe's depths. She took some water and wetted a patch on the planchen in her parlour. She then took a pin and pricked her forefinger. In the pretend wetness of broken waters, she wove some of that blood. With that, she could create an illusion that would convince the Devil himself. Awnly God knew what Rebecca and Francis were now cradling, but when Justin came in to their bedroom, she wuz able to present to him an unquestionable picture of her having given birth on the floor in the other room, and their coveted baby boy now nuzzling at her milky breast.

30

Darny heck! Babies and Pookas – and now a crafty little changeling afoot. Who'd have thought ut? In this time and this place, in the opening decade of this brand new century, all of that should be out of mind, shouldn' ut? But naw, tha' wudn' so. Here 'twas right in the here and now, when men and women should knaw better. Here it was on Copper Mountain, high in the forest, high above the clear waters of Lake Superior. Here 'twas lurking in the middle of the township ov Mountainside. And right now, moast people knawed nawthun' 'bout ut. They'd been deceived. They were blind to the machinations of someone else. The deceit ov ut, you! Back 'ome, it wuz the piskies who stole childurn from their mawthurs. Here though 'twas a woman that some might call a witch, who'd decided to enact a plan, who'd caused a change in fate, who'd manipulated circumstances for her own end. But you, and awnly you, d'knaw why she made ut her purpose. But no one knawed, not fur now at least. And all of this you, would one day have an influence on a building that was yet to be constructed upon Mountainside, but that's not worth mentioning now. That's fur later, when things follow a new run ov ore, fur when in the parlance of this new America and its beautiful subtleties of language, the shit really hit the fan.

In boath of their houses these two brothers tried to sleep then, and next to them were two doting mothers. And, as is the way with all doting parents, when they fust saw their offspring, they could not sleep well, because at every gurgle and movement of their babies, they rushed to look at how they fared, and checked to see if they needed anything: to ensure they were not hungry, not suffocating and were safe. A few years down the line, and a fussy child's request would frustrate and annoy a parent, but right here, right now, along with the excitement that goes with a new birth, each parent would have done anything for the mite that peered over the blanket in their respective cradles. This wuz so fur this Maddy and this Justin. Although neither could see ut, at the same time, Rebecca and Maddy could not sleep, and got out of their bed to look once more at their offspring. It wuz hard to take in the enormity of things: how far they had come. And when at the same time, these two brothers, Justin and Francis got out of bed to relieve themselves in the piss-pot, they too, stole a fatherly look at the chield that they had made. Both of their bladders had been full of beer, Francis more so, because after all, it had been his and Rebecca's party to wet baby Richard's head, and he'd had his fair intake of ale.

In this moment, it seemed like these two brothers, these two mucker-outters of old, were destined to do everything the same, and here 'twas again. How different now were their lives? How wondrous 'twud be to go back 'ome and shaw they who always doubted them what they'd made of themselves in this new land. 'Twudn' somethun' that wuz goin' t'appen overnight, but one day they both swore they'd do ut. Put um right. And when they thought about tha', they called back into bed their respective women and nuzzled even more closely into them, and held them that little bit tighter, which likewise, made the women glow with pleasure, and believe that a projected future happiness could be considered. 'Twas a nice feeling; thaas fur sure. Babies sleep but Pookas, well, they like to play with humans and love to push them to their very limits. Es, thaas all to come see.

As Rebecca lay there and tried to sleep, she considered the immensity of what had happened, and thought of her own mother; her eldest daughter still wondering why she had gone off into the woods like that. Perhaps, she considered, her baby and her mother's transition into a grandmother, would have kept her here, a tie which would have stopped her ranging. But at the same time, she had to think of the future: her child and the one that Maddy had had (a breathless Justin had rushed back up late at night to tell them the good news) were the future of this township. Not only that though, they were the future of this country – a country that had enveloped them so much that the old land and its lore seemed ever distant. She hoped she could bring it up in the ways of her faith, and still connect back to the culture of home. Es. Saffron buns, pasties, sugarless tay, choirs, brass bands and chapel anniversaries: the markings of Cornishness.

Maddy too, wondered about the immensity of things, but not in the same way as this naïve Rebecca. Instead, she pushed down deep inside of her the cancerous lie that she had completed. She felt satisfied though that from clay and magic she had conjured the Pooka; the old ways were still there, still part of who she wuz. She repressed everything as much as she could. She buried it deep into her heart, so that no one would find it, not ever. Ut wud be somewhere where even Yolkai's moonlight would not be able to shine onto ut. In this way, she could ensure that the truth would never come out, not unless she blabbed it herself. The last few hours had all passed by like a dream, and in her mind, ut would now stay that way. There wuz just one more thing to be taken care of, and at present, ut lay cold under the planchen boards in the other room.

She realised that her life was about to change immeasurably. She would no longer be able to always be down the mine with the rest of her boys. Instead, she'd have to be at home, looking after this little one, making sure that his every need was taken care of. This Richard was hers now. She'd taken full possession of un. Guilt hadn't come into it. Maybe it would one day, but not for now. She placed their baby boy between them in the bed, and the small being unified them in a new way. Before now, it had all been about passion and sex with this pair. Now, something else bonded them. The bond may have been false – but matter do ut?

In the end though, Justin had to leave them, for he had work to attend to. Across the township, a weary Francis did the same, taking one final look at the being he thought he had made. How sad a day it would be if he discovered that the mite between Rebecca and he had no connection to them? But let us leave that for now. There was no way that would ever be discovered, and so this new Richard would be brought up and loved in just the same way as the old Richard. Aw, dear obm. But maybe ee wudn' naw dear. That we might well get to see. Changelings have a way about um.

"See ee later my bewdies," wuz the final thing he said to a sleepy Rebecca and that beautiful boy of his. He kissed them both goodbye. That wuz the kindness and the lovingness of that brother, but you d'knaw that by now.

Minter, Skews, Francis and Justin had a meeting at crowst-time the next day. They were joined by Cap'n Trevorrow, who although now retired, very much liked to keep his nawse stuck into things. When you had lived and breathed mining as long as ee had, ut was some hard to leave it go. The meeting to discuss construction of the inclined mineral tramway though began with a round of congratulations for both of the brothers and their offspring. Whilst Francis and Justin had been busying themselves with becoming parents, Skews and Dicky Mint had taken it upon themselves to survey possibilities: and then design a route, for the tramway down to flatter land nearer the shore of Lake Superior.

The idea wuz that although there would be a big outlay in constructing the mineral tramway from the mine down to the level land, and then the harbour, this would avoid the somewhat circuitous and time inefficient route down through the forest for the ore wagons. Skews had calculated that if the mineral could be transported down from the mountain more efficiently, then the whole operation could step things up a gear. At the moment a laker pulled in to Eagle Harbour every couple of days. But with the tramway, this might rise to two lakers per day coming in. The rise in production would be enormous and with the way things were going in Detroit (even more plants and factories; brass and electrics), yet more copper was needed. By this time, the endeavour had already been agreed upon.

"Lead we through ut then Dicky..." demanded Francis. "Tell us your thoughts..."

"Well, as you knaw, I've looked at boath, and I realise there are very respected dissenters here in the room, but I d'still reckon ventricular is the way to go. Moast of the h'engineering systems here on the Lakes are set in place by such mechanisms... Many of the locks. 'Twud be an easy thing to get a crew up here from down Detroit, and put in place the pipe work," stated the Minter, perhaps a little over-confidently.

"Remind me. And it works again by?"

"Water pressure. The down-going trucks force water uphill to drag the skips up with ut. Simple."

"What gauge again?"

"Standard five foot. Same as all skips in the US. Easy to repair. Easy to get hold of..."

"And then, as we agreed, a drop into the hold of each laker. Turntables each end?"

"Yes... so you'n have a swift turn around. The moment the skip comes up to Mountainside, then it's filled and sent down. Same down the bottom when they get emptied."

"I knaw," said Justin, "but how many boys on tha', and can they turn it around fast enough before the next skip arrives?"

"They should be able to," indicated Minter.

Nawbody wuz never sure with his estimates though. You had to check carefully with the bugger. Ef there wuz one thing they'd learnt working widn, 'twas tha'.

"Perhaps, ef I might suggest, we should try ut... before we commit," said Trevorrow.

"Right enough. We've got a couple of spare wagons. They carry about the same tonnage. We'll have to measure how long it takes. What time intervals are you proposing Mr Mint?"

"Well, I was reckoning on ten minutes say between each one... We can have more of a gap but I was thinking about profit. The more boys you have in there to fill it with ore, then the swifter it would be."

Mint was right about tha'. Ut wuz the same underground with the tramming.

There wuz a pause in the proceedings. Skews hadn' said much so far. Francis and Justin knawed why. He preferred the cable variant of the design.

"Lot of clearance to do," argued Trevorrow. "Down the slopes... and then, we all knaw, then there's the land issue."

Everyone knew what he meant by that. Things kept on growing. Maybe ut would be easier now that Nimkii wuz camped with them, and didn' keep going on walkabout around the peninsula. But still, ut needed considering. From the look ov un of late, Nimkii seemed to have given up the ghost on ownership of the area. Maybe it was just him, or maybe it was the fact that he knew he'd made a mistake a year or so ago in letting them mine here in the first place. The awnly thing that you could say is that mines allays eat up land. That is until they go bust. Awnly then, can nature an' the forest reclaim ut as their own. Awnly then might the refugee sprites make their slow way back.

"I reckon we'n strike a deal... I mean, 'tidn' that much land really, es ut?"

No one wanted to respond to Trevorrow. They'd heard this before. Sometimes ut didn' feel right or proper. Then again, it was a kind of necessary evil, happening all over America, and come to think of ut, all over the world. 'Mean, did um want to carry on living like they did or did the tribal nations wunt a few more luxuries and wealth for their childurn?

Justin and Francis knew a little more beyond this. They'd picked up on some underlying fears from their Knockies. As odd as ut wuz, they talked about the forest a lot. Nimkii and that sister of Rebecca's, Mabel, seemed to be aware of ut too. The proposed tramway would be a thin slice of land, Dicky Mint argued. In a way, ut would do about as much damage to the natural forest at the telegraph lines coming up from Calumet. But then again, over time, thin slices tend to became thick slices, and once a slice was made, it soon got added onto. Boundaries got removed. Limits shifted. The process was unstoppable, and all because of these two brothers sat there right now: that Francis and that Justin. Maybe at that moment, these too knew they were culpable.

Skews let ut all be talked through. Ee allays played his cards very close to his chest, and so while Minter elaborated on his 'grand' designs, Francis carefully watched his reactions. There'd bound to be some backhander in ut fur ee. Ef the ventricular mechanism wudn' to his liking, it didn't matter if the cable system was more efficient or cheaper to install: it would be because someone from the cable installation company would knaw un, and they'd come to a mutually beneficial agreement. Thaas why you had to watch Skews like a 'awk. Corruption runned through un like a stick of rock. Of late though, he'd distanced himself from Mabel. Francis knew why. He'd become aware that he'd been replaced in her life by Nimkii. Francis understood the pain that that would have brought him, but then again, perhaps this wuz a good thing. He deserved ut fur what he used t'do: Nimkii wudn' a bit like Skews.

"Well, my considered view," said Skews, "is that although Mr Mint's ventricular system is a sound one, his alternative cable design is the one we should select. My reasoning is that it can be installed more quickly, we can complete a good deal of the construction ourselves and most of the equipment is already available. Organising the other project will take longer because we will need contractors from down below."

By this, he meant the Lower Peninsula of Michigan. An' when tha' was mentioned everybody knawed ov the cost ov gettin' um up there.

"There is a further problem as far as I can see. We spend a considerable amount of the year in snow and ice. Introducing a ventricular system here might be tricky. One crack, one frozen pipe will render the system inoperable. At least with the cables they might break and fracture, but we can replace them in a day."

Francis had to hand it to him though. Skews had understood the problems. Did ut matter that he'd get a back hander out of ut? Maybe not. Maybe not anymore. It was just the way of things, and sometimes you have to accept that. You had to think ov the greater good.

"How do you feel then gentlemen" asked Cap'n Trevorrow. "Shallus vote on ut?"

Francis and Justin laughed to each other. This wuz Trevorrow being hands off, wuz ut?

"Those in favour of the cable system say aye."

Four ayes came back.

"Those against the cable system?"

No one responded. Minter said nothing except "I feel I shouldn't vote, not being on the Management Board of the mine."

He had a point. Was a suggesting he should be? Maybe thaas what he had in mind. Why did a worry anyway? He wuz on good money you.

There wuz naw point in asking about the ventricular system because ut was unanimous anyway.

"Agreed then. We'll start work on the cable system as soon as possible," said Skews.

"Grand," went the Minter knawing that with any luck he'd have another winter ov ut up here on the mountain. In point ov fact, ee'd made ut his home. Ee'd got to like his brandy every evening and some of the girls at Rosie's.

"Who's going to go an' see Nimkii?" asked Francis.

"We will," said Trevorrow. "Samuel and me."

Justin and Francis nodded in agreement. How time changes things? Once these pair were nawbodies. Now they were somebodies. Tha' wuz 'Merky' fur ee. Hell, they had two engine houses, a fleet of wagons and 'osses, several sets of stamps and now they wuz going to have a bleddy geht inclined mineral tramway. How had ut happened, and how come too, they both had childurn now? Those questions could be easily answered though. What could not be answered so easily was why still the forest was listening to this meeting. Oh, good they were, those sprites of the dells and groves, and the ponds and the clearings, of knawing when to listen and when not to. And today, they had listened. And after they listened, they went and told the tree roots and the fungi.

Had they anything about um, this pair, and the rest of this town, then they ought to have been fearful, fur like Clara Jewell, forests have a way ov creeping up on ee an' never lettin' ee go. But let's call a halt to ut there. We'm gettun' ahead ov ourselves.

On his way home, Justin saw Rosie Koskinen outside her saloon, sweeping the step and tidying the porch.

"Ah Jeez," Justin said to hisself.

He wanted to avoid her; they had not spoken for months. Ut wuz silly but ut wuz the way things were. Sometimes men and women who once had a connection choose not to speak about ut.

"Alright stranger?" asked Rosie. "I hear you've had some good news *pupu*... Congratulations."

She kept up a pretence this Rosie, fur still in her mind, in some projection ov fantasy, she an' Justin were still together, and they'd be celebrating the birth of their child, and not he with that Irish slag. But she was good at repressing all ov that, this Rosie, and she tried – although her heart hurt – to give him her good wishes.

"Thanks," said Justin, and as he said ut, he remembered their fumble of a time together in her room down in the old Cliff Hotel, now a ruin on the plain below. Happenstance, the new tramway would go right through ut, and necessitate its demolition.

Neither she nor ee really knawed ut, yet their actions had involuntarily contributed to the way things were panning out around them, thus also, of course, how it would go in the future. Ef Rosie had not given Justin syphilis, and if Justin had not passed ut on to Maddy, and if Maddy had not got syphilis, then maybe her first-born would have been healthy and not still-born, and if that was so, then maybe she'd have had no need to conjure up something nasty from the Deads. But neither ov these pair were going to speak about tha', wuz um? That wuz because neither ov them knew the chain of events: the knock-on of ut all.

"You alright?" asked Justin politely. He thought he'd better ask. "I mean, is business good?"

And then he regretted asking that. It sounded like he was asking her about her past, and Rosie had progressed. She'd moved on, just like he had.

"We're doing well enough," she replied. "One staying guest right now. The Doctor's lady-friend. Pleased to see things are opening up more and more... Is it right – the rumours I'm hearing about the tramway?"

"Es. Hopefully being put in soon."

Justin didn' say nawthun' about the proposed route ov ut.

"I'll have to expand," Rosie said buoyantly. "More labourers and navvies I reckon, don't you?"

"'Spect so," was Justin's response.

Ee really wanted to move on. Ut felt uncomfortable speaking to she again, especially when, in his mind, Maddy had just given birth to his son. There wuz an awkward pause in their conversation.

"Best get on then," stated Rosie, but then she stopped sweeping once more and asked him a further question.

"You got a name for your baby? A boy, wasn't it?"

"Well now, I want him named Jago, but Maddy ent so keen. Jago wuz my grandfer's name."

"What's she want then?"

"Oh, you know, something Irish..."

A battle over the name of a new baby seemed to be something Rosie wanted. It was a nice battle, something important. Ut wuz a battle that she wuz unlikely to have any time soon.

"You'll have a job there then *pupu*..." Rosie observed. "From what I've seen, she's a fierce one."

She wanted to say that Maddy wuz a tricky piece of work but she controlled her tongue.

"Tell me about ut," said Justin, a comment which at least made Rosie smile, and think that at least not everything was perfect in the Nankervis and O'Donahue household. A quick dose of hope came over her.

"And Rebecca and Francis, well are they... with their new one? Richard, isn't it?"

"Happy as Larry from what I gather," said Justin. "Who'd have thought ut, eh? Me and he as parents..."

"I knew you both had it in you. I always had faith in you Justin Nankervis."That seemed an odd thing to say, and Justin didn' knaw rightly how to respond to ut. Ut seemed Rosie still wanted un t'knaw that she still lit a candle fur'n in spite ov everything, despite all the secrets that awnly some even knawed about.

He tipped his cap and said, "Best let you get on. Look after yourself."

As he did this, maybe he thought now he should dispense with this cap, and get a Cap'n's bowler, just like Trevorrow.

"And you," she said, retaining her false smile still.

As he walked away, Justin knew inside that if there wuz one person he'd wish would move away from the camp, then ut was she. Her reminded him of everything that was broken in his past. That wuz why he now kept away from the saloon; it wuz why he let other buggers like Dicky Mint go there. Ut wuz a world away from where he wuz now. All ov this aligned with the new sense of himself as a responsible parent: whereas before he cudn' wait to finish a shift and hit the beer and the carding tables, now he desired to be home with Maddy and the boy, to see how he was daily changing and developing. Temperance es. Well, ut seemed 'twuz best followed.

Elsewhere, Francis went home from the meeting with the same sense of joy; but when he entered the dwelling he found an exhausted George Jewell sat in one their armchairs, looking dejecting as if he needed to solve all of the world's problems at once.

"Wozzon?" asked Francis. "You look wisht."

"It's Rebecca... well, she and the boy..."

"What specifically?"

"She can't feed him. The boy won't take no milk."

"Have you advised her? I mean, you must have seen this before."

"I have, but not quite like this... I mean, she've been trying all morning. But it's still no good. It's almost like the mite don't want it. And you know, babies need their mother's milk. It's crucial at this stage."

Francis knew the need. He was acutely aware of ut, but this didn' look good, not if her father, the doctor, was worried.

"She's in the bedroom. I let her go. She was getting taissy with me about everything I advised her to do. Maybe you'll do better? Perhaps I haven't got the patience anymore."

"I'll try," said Francis, slipping off his boots and jacket.

"Anyway, how did the big meeting go about the tramway?"

"Well, it's going ahead. Cables we reckon... Might be easier to build than a ventricular..."

"I said that all along," said Jewell. "Dicky's keen on the ventricular idn a? He's always telling me about ut..."

"Well," said Francis, "the main issue es the cost. Getting in an underground water system would cost the earth. But you knaw what Dicky's like with his grand designs – always wants the latest. Me and Justin, we were always keen on the cables... and Skewsy too. I think Dicky's coming around to the same view now. 'Tis voted on anyway."

"Proper... well, look, I'd best leave you to it," he sighed. "See if you can get the boy to latch on to her. She's in tears about in there. I'd best go down and see how 'tis with Maddy. I hear there's good news there too..."

"Es. Last night apparently," offered Francis. "By the time brother got in from being here, the baby had decided to enter the world."

"Good news though. I wuz worried fur Maddy," Jewell said, though he gave no reason as to why.

George Jewell stood up and moved to the door. How different the room looked now. Last night ut had been filled with everyone from Mountainside. Now the place looked sparse and bare.

"I'll... ah... leave you to ut. 'Tis awnly a little hiccup. But be gentle with her. She's been through the mill this morning..."

After this, the surgeon left, and gingerly Francis poked his head around the door of the bedroom. He found Rebecca face down on the bed, with the baby – or non-baby, as 'twas rightly the case – left in his cradle.

"A'right?" he asked in the way that all Cornish do. "Your feythur's said the boy ent takin' no milk. How can I help? What can us do?"

"Don't start," Rebecca replied curtly. "It's like he won't take it – whatever I do... Almost like he doesn't want to be next to me. I mean, yesterday, he was fine, but today, completely different..."

"How do you mean?"

"Like as if he isn't the same child."

"Dun't be silly... It can happen... I read about ut. You know, in one of them instructional books your feythur gave me. What to expect after the baby is born."

"Aw, I read all of that too... about what to do to encourage him to latch on to me... but honestly Frank, I've tried everything... I got sick to death with everything my stupid father was saying to me. How does he know? He isn't a woman."

"Maybe you've got tense... Maybe the boy can feel that... Try to relax a bit more."

"Don't you think I've tried that?" she replied, tenser than ever.

Such are the ways between men and women.

"I know... I know... But try to be calm. I'm sure we'll solve this."

"We need to," said Rebecca. "He cen't go on without milk for very long. He'll be malnourished. 'Tidn' good fur his body. Father was talking about his immunity. Milk is the best thing for un. I want to get this right."

Of course, what this pair didn' knaw was the truth of the matter; they thought ut was still the same Richard who'd nuzzled proper into she. But now 'twudn'. The truth ov ut was tha' Pooka babies dun't like milk one bit, and thaas why Rebecca was struggling t'offer un her breast. Ut d'take a while to even get them to take a mouthful ov milk, and this one, well, ut seemed ee wuz havin' none ov ut. See, what Pookas like ee really like is fresh, morning dew gathered in a bed of moss, or found in a still pool in the stump of a fallen tree, blown down by the wind. But he cudn' say ut and they didn' knaw ut, so that is why there was an impasse. And when Francis looked at the baby who they thought was Richard, and held him close, he screwed up his faace in anger and loudly squalled and squalled until ut seemed like he'd have naw energy left. But Rebecca cudn' stand ut. She had to go outside fur a while; her brain and heart full ov fear that she cudn' be the brilliant example of motherhood that she wanted to be. Looking back, maybe ut wuz that moment when things changed, when a realisation comed over of both ov they two parents that wha' they had embarked upon wudn' goin' t'be plain sailing.

Whilst Rebecca pondered her failure, Francis did his best with the boy. He wuz, as you know, not one to give up easily. Somehow, ee'd tame this little thing. Why wuz a so unhappy? He checked over him, though he was sure that Doctor Jewell would have done the same thing. Maybe he felt a little clammy, a little damp. But he knew not what to do about that, for he'd not much encountered babies before now. Maybe they were all like that.

With a great deal of effort, and with Francis' ears hurting at his continued crying and mewling, the boy finally calmed down a little. Francis found it best to take him over to the winda', upon which the boy's eyes could look out on the forest. His squalling had certainly woken up the forest: and ef Francis could see, he'd have observed a mass of tiny sprite faces gathering to look at one of their own, now being taken care of by a human. At least, this seemed to be calming him down a bit.

At that point, the bedroom door slammed open, and in walked Gourgy. Ee wuz back from forenoon shift.

"I just seened of Becca outside," he said. "She looked proper wisht... She told me the boy wudn' take naw milk..."

"Temporary problem," said Francis. "She's upset because she wants to be a good mother to the boy."

"Of course," said Gourgy. "Let me hold ov un fur a bit..."

"A'right, but be careful. I've just got un to calm down..."

Francis handed over the changeling to Gourgy. What a moment there: one magical creature being handed to another you!

"Grawn a bit ebn a?" noted Gourgy. "'Tidn' long since I last sawed un, and he've altered a brae bit."

"They say that," said Francis. "A book I read said they change a lot in the first few days. Somethun' about all the bones fusing and being activated."

"Well, ee d'look alright to me," said Gourgy. "Perhaps he might like a drop ov this..."

Gourgy produced from his waistcoat pockets some freshly-cut dandelion stalks.

"What you doing?" asked Francis worriedly.

He was moving the dandelion stalks to the baby's mouth and squeezing them between his green-brown toady fingers so that the white juice from inside them fell into his mouth.

"Doing what Knockie mawthurs do. Feeding un some milky daishals."

"You can't do that..."

"But see, he likes it look," said Gourgy, very confidently.

Francis peered into this face of his boy Richard. Clearly he was liking what Gourgy was feeding un, despite the oddness of the food stuff.

"Nutritious see. Just like breast-milk. Full of goodness... I reckon you'll be alright now."

Gourgy handed the baby back to Francis. The wisdom of Knockies never failed to impress the miner. Just when you thought you knew everything about them, they'd go and do something that surpasses everything else.

"I'll go and get Becca, shall I?" asked Gourgy.

"Please."

Francis looked at his boy again. He still had no idea that what he held was a troublesome Pooka that had been formed in the mine's Deads. Ut had been made not by a sperm and an egg but instead, by clay, sulphur, residue and magic. A clear thread of naughtiness runned right through un. Francis had no idea: but maybe the forest peering in, had a bit of a clue as to what wuz going on. He tried to sing and hum an improvised tune to the baby to try to keep him calm, but perhaps the liddle mite wudn' nawthun' fur songs or airs. Francis certainly did not want to hear any further crying. Perhaps Gourgy did have the trick. They'd soon see.

"Try now," said Gourgy as he led a somewhat-still-broken Becca back into the bedroom.

"What's changed?"

Francis explained.

"Daishals?! You can't feed a baby daishals..."

"Not daishals..." clarified Gourgy, "but the *milk* of daishals..."

Both Francis and Gourgy observed that Rebecca did not seem impressed by this delicacy at all. She looked at them both with derision.

"He will take your milk now," said Gourgy assuredly. "Mark my Knockie words."

"Try it," said Francis. "One more time..."

To allow for this, Francis and Gourgy handed the baby to her, who began to unbutton her blouse. They turned around to let her try to feed the baby. For a while, there was only a breathless silence, but then a russle and some adjustment of her form as Becca sat down onto the bed. She gave a small grunt of motherly satisfaction.

"Any good?" asked Francis.

"Yes, I think so," said his wife. "He's better now... more comfortable... Yes... he's taking it. You must have done something right."

Gourgy looked over and smiled at his master.

"See," he said confidently. "You owe me one... as well as all the thousands of other favours you owe me..."

"Thank you," said Rebecca. "Truly, we're so grateful."

"Right," said Gourgy, "I'm off down Rosie's... Aw, best not say anything to the Doc about all of this, eh? He might ask the wrong kind of questions."

"Don't worry."

Gourgy looked over to the mother and baby.

"See, he's a right guzzler. My advice is always keep some daishal milk. Get on tha' first of all every time. See ee later."

Gourgy tipped his hat and left. Then, as he made his way outside, he did wonder briefly – ever so briefly – why this chield liked daishal milk so much, but a moment later, ut left his Knockie mind.

"You alright?" asked Francis to his wife.

"Much better now," she replied.

So there 'twas. Something wuz solved. But come to think ov ut, that wudn' half ov what wuz t'come, and when that comed, nawbody – not even a wily Knockie – could solve ut.

31

As George Jewell left the Nankervis house earlier, he knew precisely what difficulties Francis was about to face when he talked to Rebecca. His daughter had come over earlier when he was about to go for a stroll with this ladyfriend he had grown fond of named Eleanor Prowse, so he had to send word to her at the saloon that he'd have to attend to some doctoring matters before he could meet with her. What he liked most about Eleanor was that she was a committed Wesleyan. She had lots of ideas as to how they could raise money to build a chapel. She'd already been involved in the erection of a couple of Methodist chapels down in Calumet and George figured that he could use her expertise here. She seemed a perfect fit, as long as he could tempt her away from the sophistication and glamour of Calumet. In all honesty, he'd not thought of Clara for months. He knew inside that the drawer of fungi had been the last straw for him in that matter.

Now to Maddy. He had wished that he had managed to get down there sooner to see her, since Maddy was certainly more at risk in matters of childbirth than his own daughter, but when the latter's baby would not suckle, then he knew he had to divert his attention away from the Irishwoman. As far as he could discern, there had been no problems with Maddy's birth nor the infant itself. This was very good news for deep in his heart he had worried about the condition of the mother and the resultant baby. This was all curious since there had been the very serious matter of the venereal disease – and that had not only unsettled them, but him as well. He'd have liked really to have been there at the birth, but of course, there was no way that Maddy would have that. She was too full of superstition and hard-nosed womanhood to allow a man like himself to be present. But it did puzzle him how swift the delivery had been. She had seemed perfectly fine at the party held by his daughter and Francis. To suddenly have given birth like that was a marvel indeed. Still, he knew it was not unknown. Births varied. Some women went to Hell and back with them. Others had babies who seemed to slide out on a whim, as if greased in pump oil.

On the way through the camp he noticed Nimkii in his now expanded set-up by the collar of the mine, right next to the rumbling and juddering engine house for the winding up and down of the cage. He was busying himself with something inside of his galvanised steel tepee though, and Jewell knew, of course, that where he was these days, Mabel seemed to follow. She wuz sure to be completing some task for him, or learning some of his language. Mabel, he knew, was not going to be like his elder daughter. She was never going to be compliant. She was never going to take over the running of the schoolhouse. She'd never be a stalwart of the chapel in the way that he was. He could only blame himself. Rebecca had emigrated at an age where she could process the changes and cope with them. Mabel's transition had come at a more difficult time in her development: knowing her, she was going to end up like one of those crazy theosophists he heard spoken over down in Calumet.

He could tell that she and Eleanor would never be friends. He had already realised that Eleanor wuz a realist and Mabel, well, she was still dreamy as ever, like adulthood would never ever come. He genuinely worried that very soon she might go feral. Perhaps there was a disproportionate number of her mother's genes inside of her. Still, the Doctor put these thoughts aside as he made his way to the other Nankervis brother's house.

Coming in a northerly direction from Rosie's saloon, in the corner of his eye, he spotted Justin Nankervis, mozeying along at a steady pace. The Doctor stopped to greet him, but as yet, Justin had not even noticed him standing before his property. The man seemed to carry the weight of the world on his shoulders and did not look a picture of paternal joy.

"Yo!" Jewell shouted, trying and failing to sound like a miner.

He caught Justin's attention and the man looked over to the Doctor.

"Some congratulations are in order I believe," shouted over Jewell. "A baby boy, isn't it?"

Everyone seemed to be congratulating him today. Justin picked up the pace to meet the surgeon. Jewell leaned in a hand for Justin to shake.

"Yes," he said. "Ut comed quick. Last night, while I was still at brother's."

"So I gather!"

"Wonderful news... considering..." offered Jewell.

"Considering?"

Jewell realised his error.

"Well, ahem... considering the difficulties of the boy's conception..."

"Ah. I see what you mean," said Justin, unbothered by the Doctor's assessment. "I think we'm over that now."

"Good. Good."

There next followed a slight pause as each realised the immensity of the achievement.

"She's inside if you want to see her," gestured Justin. "She's been here, sorting out, but I had that meeting with Skews and Dicky..."

"Yes, so I gather... The tramway sounds a wondrous project. Francis told me a little about it. I hear that the cable mechanism is the favourite device of propulsion."

"We'm settled on ut now I think, yes... Work should begin soon."

Jewell and Justin were about to climb up the three steps into the property but by now, the door had already been opened by a beaming Maddy, who was standing there holding their baby in her arms. She had heard them speaking outside. This would be the first of a lifetime ov performances.

"Look what I've got," Maggie squealed in delight at Doctor Jewell. Aw now. The front ov she. Sometime soon, someone wuz goin' to give she a big slice of tongue pie too. Not you or I though.

He took a closer look at the baby.

"I know," said Doctor Jewell enthusiastically, "Marvellous news... I'm so happy for the two of you."

'Course, what ee didn' have any notion ov wuz that when Maddy handed him the chield, what he was actually holding was his awn grandson. But that's the way of all of us sometimes, idn' ut? We can't see what's right in front of our faace.

"There's a family resemblance I see," said Doctor Jewell peering up at un. "He's just like Richard. Got the Nankervis eyes and brow... and, of course Maddy, your fine looks..."

Smooth, Jewell wuz. He knawed how to doctor; knawed how t'build trust and confidence.

Maddy thought back to what she had conjured and knew that somewhere, ut would make two other parents mazed. It was the way of such Pookas. Always.

"And a name for him?"

"Jago," said Justin, like it was written in stone. "My grandfer's name."

"Not on your life," said Maddy, half-joking, half not.

"What are you thinking of then?" asked Doctor Jewell.

"Ciaran was what I wanted."

"Alright then, Jago Ciaran Nankervis ut es," stated Justin.

"What are you saying there?" asked Maddy. "We ain't even married. Not even betrothed. Ain't that right Doctor Jewell? I think at the moment he's Jago Ciaran O'Donahue, least till you make an honest women of me y'Cussie shit."

Silence ensued.

Jewell tried not to intervene, but in the end, he felt forced to speak.

"Whatever he is, he's certainly full of beans... Would you mind if I checked him over?"

"Oh yes... Of course... Come inside now..."

"It ah... might be good if I can speak with you Maddy as well..."

Justin knew this was his cue to be elsewhere, He took off his boots and padded his way into the kitchen. Time t'boil the keddle ee reckoned. The Doctor went into the living room with Maddy. He noticed a table. This would do for an examination of the baby.

"May I?"

Maddy cleared a table of papers and carefully put down Jago or Ciaran onto the table. He may even have had another name this mite, but no one knew that.

"Can we just?"

Jewell indicated for Maddy to remove his swaddling and then the nappy he was wearing. She remembered the chaos of the swap: the nappy had been the trickiest bit ov all.

"Best get a good look to see if everything is in working order," noted Jewell.

Somewhat nervously, Maddy stepped away from where the Doctor was conducting his examination. He pulled out a stethoscope and other instruments from his bag, including a device that emitted a small light. He shone this into the baby's eyes to see if they would follow it. As he did this, he spoke to Maddy about the birth.

"Things came on quickly then?" he asked.

"Yes," lied Maggie. "I got back here after I saw you, and then whoosh... it all happened..."

"Where?"

"In the other room... the scullery..."

"Much fluid was there? I should like to have seen. He was laying low on you... often a sign..."

"Quite a bit... um yes," she lied, trying to recall what actually happened in the forest.

"Much blood?"

"A fair bit yes..."

"Mmmm..."

As they talked, the doctor examined the baby's limbs and bones.

"A lot to clean up I expect..."

"There was. There's still a stain... on the floorboards. Have a look if you like."

"No need. But ah... no problems then? No prolonged labour?"

That blood-letting had been pointless then.

"A few minutes or so, but then I could suddenly feel his head..."

"...and what, he just came out?"

"That's right. I pushed and there he was. That's the honest truth now. "

"Was he crying or did you need to slap him? Sometimes you do, you know, to make them realise where they are... helps them to take their first breaths, you see."

"No, crying right away," said Maddy. She hoped that her voice did not carry any trace of her deceit.

The stethoscope was next employed to check Jago Ciaran's heartbeat. No conversation occurred between them for a while. Maddy thought this was because he was listening hard to the sound of her son's heart but it was not so. Instead, Jewell had been thinking.

"You were lucky, you know. I read up on it. The chances of a healthy baby after syphilis... well, you know they're not good. I think I explained to both you and Justin. I did not mean to fuss over you but I mean, I expected..."

"What?"

"Well, maybe it could be deformed... blind... deaf. These things do happen. Sometimes, a still-birth. By good hap, not here though, eh? "

At this, Maddy crumpled a little. She'd have to maintain her cool.

"I was worried for you both... of course, I couldn't really say anything... but by the looks of it you've managed to swerve through the obstacles. This little fella is in fine form. He's in perfect health."

Maddy knew this already inside, but to have it confirmed again felt reassuring. She could not let talk of a still-birth upset her, not least in front of him.

"You did a fine job," the Doctor stated.

"How so?"

"Looks like you cut the placenta close to the stomach. The button is precisely the same as your ah... brother and sister-in-law's child. Must run in the family eh? Did you use a knife or scissors?"

"Knife.. No... scissors..."

Maddy could feel herself panicking. She knew she must not let any crack show.

"I mean, I had a knife but in the end I used scissors. New, sharp ones I bought for the purpose."

"Well, I must admit, I couldn't have done a better job myself. Looks very professional I must say. I always knew there was more to you than meets the eye Maddy O'Donahue..."

Maddy changed the subject.

"So Jago's alright then?"

The unnerving nature of this process had made her call him what Justin wished.

"He's fine. Is he taking suck?"

The interrogation seemed unending. She had to comply though. To usher him out would be an obvious give away.

"Yes, very well. Seems to latch on to me well enough..."

Maddy had sizeable breasts the Doctor had noticed.

"Good. Good. I shouldn't really say, but Rebecca's having a hell of a job with Richard.

I was there earlier. You might want to chat to her about it. Share experiences if you like... Not really something I can do."

"Of course," Maddy said. "Don't worry now. I won't be saying you told me so."

"Thank you for being discreet... And now, well, almost done..."

"What else is there?"

"Let's consider mother's health, eh?"

This was the part she didn't want to talk about. No woman does. Where was Justin? Couldn't he come in right now? Why did he have to be so polite in that Cornish way of his?

"How are things below? Alright are you?"

"I think things have returned to normal."

"Any blood? Mucus? Fluid? Perfectly natural, of course."

"Initially there was a bit," Maddy observed, "But only straight after... nothing else."

"Good. Good. Well, we won't do it today but in a week or so, it might be good to come up to the surgery just to give you an examination..."

"Oh yes. Absolutely," agreed Maddy.

"That seems to be it then... Any problems give me a shout. Anything, remember. I will be twiddling my thumbs before I commence health and safety work on that dashed mineral tramway."

"Thank you," said Maddy.

By the sound of their movements in the living room it appeared that the Doctor was about to leave, so Justin joined them. He tapped on the door before he entered.

"Everything alright?" he asked, supping from an enamel mug of hot tay.

"All tickety-boo as they say," said Jewell. "You've a great parcel in there. The stork's brought you a very fine little son."

"Thanks Doc," said Justin.

Jewell made his way to open the front door.

"I'm ah... still trying to work with Mr Trevorrow," he said, "on funding our chapel... eventually..."

The Doctor need not have said any more.

"I'll make sure some monies head your way Doctor Jewell," offered Justin. "Doan' worry. I want Jago to be one of the first on the Roll of Honour..."

"Marvellous..."

"You've decided he's a Methodist already then?" stated Maddy sarcastically.

Justin did not answer.

Ee perhaps knew deep in his heart that Maddy didn' just mean that their son should be a Catholic. He knew she was talking about an older way, an older path. Ee recalled her sat in the tree: what others said about she. There might be a bit of a battle ahead of him. Having sorted his own life out and got hisself on the straight and narrow, and on the Temperance road, he very much wanted his son to carry on in the same way. With Maddy though, tha' might not be possible. But there wuz nothing he could do 'bout ut, because ee knawed ee loved her. Ee loved too, what they had made together; well, what he thought they had made together. What wuz in the living room wuz actually his nephew.

Once the Doctor had left (his parting words were about going to see that woman Eleanor Prowse), Justin checked with Maddy that both she and the baby were well.

"We're both fine," she stated. "Don't you be worrying."

Ef Justin had known just one iota ov what had gone on then he very much would be worrying. But worrying only ruins tomorrow, and so that must rest for a while. Maybe it would come back to bite him in the ass, and maybe it wudn'. You could never tell.

As ee wuz thinking through the next few years of his life, in walked a flustered Luk. He was gibbering and gabbling on to himself about somethun' in the way that he did sometimes, and kept rapidly changing colour, which with Knockies was allays a bad sign. He was turning from pink to yellow and then black, finally ending up green and brown again. He sat on the floor close to where Maddy had pretended she had given birth. Below him were the tied-up remains of another chield. Ee wuz still jabberin' on though.

"What's wrong?" asked Justin. "Why are ee all s'flustered?"

"The forest," Luk stated solemnly.

Justin was aware of his annoyance with the forest.

"It's been bullying me..." he sobbed.

"Bullying you?"

This wuz a turn up fur the books.

"How come?"

"They ent happy out there. They say that we'm goin' to build a tramway right down to the harbour. Is tha' right?"

"Well, it's being planned for, yes."

"They think we and all the other Knockies have caused ut... they say 'twill be the ruination of their world."

Ee wudn' making much sense now. But this wuz the way of Luk sometimes. Sometimes, he took criticism very personally, not like Gourgy at all.

"They've told we t'stop ut or else..."

"Or else what?"

Ee gived a geht sob again, blawing his nawse on a hankey Justin had just given un.

"They said they'd feed me to the bears..."

"To the bears, eh?"

"Yes... and to the wolves..."

These were all creatures that for Luk, were straight out of books of tall tales. Back home, he'd dealt with scary seals in adits and biting badgers in old men's workings, but this wuz different. Despite Luk's usual exaggeration, this felt different somehow. He'd stepped outside the surrounds of the camp looking for daishals, and the forest had surrounded him apparently. All sorts comed to speak to un.

"Then they told me they'd bury me alive..."

And in this way, fur the fust time, even this Justin had some manner of belief in um. When Maddy walked in on them talking, she instantly recognised the seriousness of what was being discussed.

'I'll have a word,' she said. 'Don'tcha be worrying your heart out Luky boy.'

They talked a lot and then they had a high tea of boxty and saffron buns. Maddy said a lot to it. This forest thing wuz getting too much. But then, she realised too, that this mine thing was getting too much as well: a little too big for uts boots perhaps. As it wuz though, that wuz set t'be the way ov things in that daft and sprawling century. In the night Maddy woke and found little Luk sleeping right next to little Jago in his cradle.

She did not disturb them. What Maddy hadn't said to either Justin or Luk was that earlier on, she'd reached beneath the floorboard planchen and pulled out a canvas-encased tiny body. She'd had in mind somewhere she could hide it where it would never ever be found, and so she placed it there, almost without a second thought. She did the deed under Yolkai's moonlight.

32

Hell. Bit Rory-Tory idn' ut? All the ups and downs ov parentin' and ov running a copper mine. A bit unnerving too, knawing that the forest wuz out to get ee fur some ov your actions. 'Tidn' naw use beating around the bush with ut, because there wuz some stark facts t'face. All the way along up on Mountainside ut had seemed that something malevolent lurked in the background; and after what liddle Luk had said, Justin, and then Francis knawed that they'd need to be careful. If the dark woods weren't unnerving enough when the two brothers had first hiked up the mountain that day from the old Cliff Mine, then they were even scarier now: and when they'd had a few days t'contemplate everything, they wondered too ef what wuz goin' on wuz in some way connected to that earlier weird disappearance of that Mrs Jewell, the doctor's wife. Wha' wuz her name again? Aw es. Clara. That wuz she: Clara Jewell.

Still, despite thinkin' this, they boath decided not t'say anything to her husband, nor to individuals like Samuel Skews, Dicky Mint or Cap'n Trevorrow. Francis had considered tellin' ov Rebecca – and ee wuz about to, a couple of morning's ago – but t'be honest, she was still getting used to caring fur who she imagined to be Richard (and that was strain enough), so ee decided not t'say anything. 'Twas different with Maddy though. She knawed all about ut (well, she wuz like that: allays ahead of the game tha' one) and she swore t'they she'd do somethun' 'bout ut. Zactly wha' they were still unsure, but she reckoned on havin' a bit ov a plan up her sleeve – or her shell necklace at least. In all, ut seemed absurd to even think or talk about ut. They never heard the like ov ut back 'ome. Then again you, perhaps nawbody back in Cornwall was watchin' or listenin' hard enough. Maybe here, ut was easier to see, easier to listen.

Fur now, the timid Luk wudn' go very far without Gourgy by his side. They wuz always a pair you, a comic duo from music hall even, but now they were even closer. Luk wuz on edge all the time; Gourgy less so, but then, tha' had allays been the way ov they. Maybe though, Luk's fear had rubbed off a little on Gourgy. The buggers didn' spend much time exploring the forest naw more. They kept to their miner's homes, unless they wuz working underground. Maybe other Knockies too, an' the other migrant magical creatures working underground, were a little more careful: after what they heard about Luk's experiences. No one questioned un. There wuz naw need to. Knockies never lied. So underground, they were prepared to knock that little bit more, to double-check the timbering (that wuz in itself part of the problem, since it wuz, in effect, murdered forest) to ensure there were naw collapses. Somehow, they felt a presence down there at all times. When they felt that (they'd not had ut before backalong, back 'ome), they knew the need to be a tad more watchful. Still, the digging and devouring of the rock underground carried on nonetheless. Allays the way see. Nawbody dun't ever learn, do um?

These worries went with the brothers but there wuz some temporal release from all ov ut when after Justin's encouragement, the two of they ordered in from down a posh Calumet outfitters, a set of clawthes befitting their role as Mining Cap'ns. Maybe ef you don't knaw Cornwall and nawthun' 'bout mining, then you will not understand the status of Cap'ns in that community. Becoming one meant everything. Ut shawed your intellect and skill, but also how you managed a team of men and women.

Becoming one, elevated you in that society. Were they back home, then it would be an instant ticket to be invited to every social occasion goin', an' to be given time ov day and respect by everyone you encountered. See, Cap'ns were the life and soul of a mine, and ut was around them tha' everything else circled. Ut wuz they who did the hiring and firing, but ut wuz also they who offered reward and support to those striving fur betterment of the community (fur they institutions such as Miners and Mechanics' Institutes and chapels). Put simply, ut gived um a new status, and whilst everyone in Mountainside knawed they were the Cap'ns, this uniform they were now putting on sealed ut.

When the boxes of fine clawthes arrived, Justin hurried up to Francis' place and they opened them together, as ef 'twas Christmas Day. In a few moments they'd stripped off all their ragged normal gear, and put on what had been sent: one of the crisp new shirts (with a plentiful supply of collars to pin on), the comfy trousers (these were always made wide in the thigh for lots of bending over and gaking in gunnies underground), suspenders, and then a waistcoat, onto which they would attach a timepiece on a chain. These new pocket watches had arrived too, and they looked great, the chain linked with a long brass bar to the button hole. Good and proper ut looked. Next comed the tail-coat style jacket. The latter eschewed an earlier era, but ut wuz what they wanted. Ut wuz what people expected.

'Course, all this meant tha' neither ov um would be doing quite s'much drilling, blasting or digging in the way they had previously done. Also, there were brand new, leather hob-nail boots: ideal for when they needed to go belaw and walk the muck-filled levels. Their Knockies would probably not even recognise them and maybe even laugh at their pretence, but like Justin said, ut had to be done. Finally, of course, there were separate hat boxes, in which sat black-felted bowlers. Now this wuz the real marker of any Cap'n and when Justin put his one on his head, he felt like King Arthur drawing Excalibur from the stone. A similar aura passed over Francis, as he checked his profile in the awnly mirror they had in the house.

"Bewdie," said Francis. "We'm lookin' some sharp Sos."

"I knaw. That wun't stop folk from taking the piss..."

"Who do ee mean?"

"Ah, y'knaw... Minter and Skewsy I 'spect. I reckon Trevorrow'll have something t'say too."

"Naw. No they won't. They'll be glad to see ut."

"What about they others? Bloaks in the levels, up the stamps, working the timber yard..."

"Boy, they ent goin' to say nawthun'. In fact, all ut'll do is that they'll give we more respect than ever. This is a badge boy. Think ov ut as a talisman... people knaw already that we'm the Cap'ns."

Seemingly, all they had to do now was graw a bushy, handlebar moustache and beard, and they'd look like a younger version of Trevorrow. They laughed to themselves at this.

"My! Don't you pair look dandy?" wuz what Rebecca said when they waltzed in on her with their new gear on.

"What ee reckon?" asked Francis.

"Suits you. Looks fitty."

"And me too?" asked Justin, as if he was parading like a model on the front of one of they new magazines comin' over from New York.

"You look splendid," Rebecca said. "Maddy'll love ut..."

"You reckon?"

"Yes!"

"I dunnaw. I think she might take the piss..."

"I don't think so Justin. Maybe at first, but then she'll realise what a finely-dressed gentleman she has on her arm. She told me you were expecting the parcels to arrive today..."

"She's been here?" he asked with some degree of surprise.

"Oh yes. She and Jago came up this morning. We... ah... compared notes so to speak. Us women have to stick together."

"Of course... The boy alright, wuz a?"

"Aw, ee's lovely. A real smiler that one. Bit different to Richard. We were talking about getting them down each night. Richard's so fussy, idn' ee Francis? Sometimes you wonder what else he wants. Never settles, does ee? But Jago, oh, what a lovely little thing. Maddy said you've had naw trouble widn' at all..."

"Es," said Justin. "Ee d'sleep good through the night. All the way through..."

"Wish we could say the same," said Francis. "Our liddle bugger like t'fuss all the way through from dusk to dawn... Dun't think we've had a good night in days 'ave us Bec?"

"Least he's feedun' a bit better now," noted Becca, though perhaps in her heart she knawed she shudn' have to tempt un with the milk from a daishal. 'Course, she didn' knaw nawthun' 'bout her boy's primitive self and his baser needs. Pookas are very specific see. They like things just so. Just so you knaw.

"Maddy tell ee what she do, did her?"

"Oh yes, she was very helpful. She's way ahead of me on all of this mothering stuff. You got yourself a good one there. When are you goin' to make a good woman of she?"

Justin laughed embarrassedly.

"Aw... one day soon I spect... Maybe when the new chapel es built..."

Ee'd said this purposefully, knowing tha' in reality the geht project was securely placed in the dreckly category.

"Well, she'll be waiting a long time for tha', wun't she? They'm some slaw on tha' really. I mean, father and that Eleanor they were asking me if they could use the schoolhouse for services, during the winter, which of course, I agreed to. They're still up the preaching pit for now though."

"I made a donation to your father's fund," said Justin, "after what he did fur Maddy, me and the boy..."

"Oh, that's kind of you Jus. He'll appreciate tha'."

All this while, Francis had stayed quiet. This talk of chapels and Methodism was all well enough but ut didn' much interest un. He knew he needed to shaw willing. Ut wuz, after all, wha' Mining Cap'ns did but 'twas hard fur'n to rustle up any enthusiasm. Ee put ut down to tiredness. His wife wuz right. Their son had been trying and he knew himself, ut had tested his patience. But wha' could a do? If you'm old enough to have one, then you'd best care fur un no matter how hard or how mazed ut got. All this chatter made un realise that seemingly Maddy and his brother's son was of a very different nature. Tha' annoyed un.

A loud crying suddenly came from the Moses basket that had been placed on the kitchen table.

"Excuse me," said Rebecca. "Best see to this little gentleman's needs..."

A gentleman now then, this Pooka. Who'd have thought ut?

Francis gave his brother a look of embarrassment. Ut wuz a look that told his sibling that he wasn't quite sure what he had produced from his loins. Justin could tell that the stress of ut was gettin' to him. In the past they'd probably have had a beer or two and straightened ut all out. Not now though. That seemed impossible. So many hopes an' dreams are threaded into childurn, aren't they? Ut looked like Francis felt things weren't goin' in the way he wanted, bowler hat or naw bowler hat.

Rebecca wuz right. The boy wudn' settle. There wuz a restlessness in un. Perhaps that wuz some inherited aspect of his line. Both Justin and his brother allays had itchy feet, and hence why they were here now on the Keweenaw, so maybe that comed out in the next generation.

"I'll make ee some tay boy," said Justin. "Bec, you got any buns?"

Taa and buns see. The Cornish way t'set things straight.

His brother stood silent, seemingly unable to respond to the needs of his son. He'd need support. Who'd have thought ut? Ee'd allays reckoned on Francis being the one who wuz sorted, and who did things right. But then, none of us are perfect. Childurn are never perfect either.

Justin filled a keddle an' put it on the stove and with Becca pointing to a basket, he found some saffron niceies.

What wuz clear wuz that their boy had a lot more niggling energy to un than Jago. The little mite seemed never to be wanting to be wrapped in swaddling and in a nappy. Indeed, by the look ov ut, he seemed happier when he was naked and in his awn skin. Only then did a stop trying to escape and cease his crying. Now, that wuz the way of changelings though; only nawbody there knawed ut at the time. They dun't like to be indoors do their kind. They'd rather be outside (well, thaas where he'd been born, wudn' ut?), and Pookas like ee allays wanted to wander and explore. They liked to find mischief and put their nawses in places where they wudn' wanted. They could be proper wicked too (you'll see tha'!). And this wuz the way of this Richard here, allays trying to undo his nappy and put his legs out ov ut, and allays reaching beyond the confines of the basket.

Francis wuz still silent all this time, knawing in his heart what a struggle this all might be. Becca hadn't come to that point yet, but she soon might. Whilst the keddle boiled, Justin leaned in to have a look at the boy. Ee hadn't seen un fur a while, and when he looked at un, he first of all, grizzled up nice but then when Justin got too close, something altered. His face became wild in some way, and had the boy teeth he would definitely have bitten him. Even now, ee was gumming away in anger and distress.

Justin didn't say anything ov course, but the boy had changed a lot in the last few days. Froth on his mouth there wuz, and his eyes were piercing like a cat's. His skin tone too, seemed somewhat green and mottled in colour, not too dissimilar to the way Luk and Gourgy's octopus-like skin looked, and then his limbs, well, they weren't like Jago's. His were cute and clasping but Richard's were all gangly and bent, as if his bones were made of twigs. He wudn' naw oil painting thaas fur sure. And a geht nawse on un. Now, was ut pointed or naw? In point of fact, Justin didn' like t'look and 'course, ee didn' like t'say either. After the growlin' and the grizzlin' at un, Justin stepped back to the keddle which had boiled by now, and began to make the tay.

"Bit lively, idn a?" stated Justin.

Tha' wuz the understatement of the year.

"He is that," said Rebecca, doin' her utmost with un."

"What say you brother?"

But Francis didn' answer. Justin wudn' even sure if he'd heard his brother's question. Francis wuz in some distant place, maybe back across the ocean, maybe in their parish, when they wuz innocent youngsters and the world wuz young. The pouring of some tay was the awnly thing that seemed to jolt him back to reality. He also placed down a saffron bun on a plate in front of him. Maybe some crowst would help. He drank the tay and ate the bun, but the liddle bugger kept on and on. What could ee say? Nawthun' much. Justin had runned out ov advice, seemingly in the same way that Francis had almost stopped communicating with his wife. This clearly wudn' naw parlour game of 'Happy Families'.

"I reckon ee'll calm down soon," said Justin, and ee said ut in that way that all people do when there is something wrong and not a lot else to say. Ut had the same tone to ut when people spoke at funerals or when someone is leaving home and you might not see them again for a while.

"Wha' did Maddy say?"

"Aw. Well, when she held un he wuz alright with she... not a peep out of un..."

"Perhaps we should swap," suggested Justin, for a laugh, to try and lighten the mood. At least that made Francis smile a little, even if rather wryly.

Ef awnly boath ov they knawed the true facts.

"You two might do a better job than we're doing," came his brother's response.

"Let me try again," said Justin.

He leaned over the basket and took his shiny new pocket watch and waved ut back and forth in front of the baby. Something about this seemed to work, for Pookas, well, Pookas are like magpies. They allays like shiny objects, and that morning the sun came through the kitchen winda' of the Nankervis property and glistened on the back of the brass. This, the Pooka greatly liked for now he smiled and reached up at the swinging watch before un. Ef ee cud have stolen ut fur a nest, or even fur his crowst, ee would've done.

"You hypnotising un," asked Francis, "like the shaws they used t'have down 'Zance?"

"Dunnaw. Not intentionally," said Justin. "Ee seemed t'be calmed by ut."

Justin wuz right. Metal attracted Pookas. So did sunlight. Eventually, this awkward Richard became drowsy and started to doze. He seemed to be fighting against sleep, and at one moment he became wide-eyed again (there wuz some charming darkness in his eyes you) but then settled once more.

"You got the knack," said Rebecca joyfully. "You can come again! You're just like Maddy... you know how to soothe him."

Justin looked over at his brother whose stare at him did not deviate, and which was unrelenting. And in tha' look there was, fur the fust time, between these two brothers (who, after all, had been through so much), the inkling of jealousy, and a feeling of inferiority. This is sometimes the way with such small things. And such small things can be intensified in families. So maybe after that, things were never quite the same again, but such is life. We never knaw when the well of jealousy will spring out of us, and so ut wuz here, for in that moment Francis hated his brother. Maybe too, as hard as he was trying to repress it (knowing that he was feeling maybe just like Skewsy), he wanted that thing in the Moses basket out of their lives.

His jealousy was born of his brother's actions but also the fact that he could sense what wuz coming at them over the horizon. His brother wuz a fool and a layabout, a drinker, smoker and gambler and others things too, and there he wuz soothing his son, a job he should easily be able to do but cudn'. Neither did he like the look, that momentarily, Rebecca gave un. Francis chose not say much more but instead collected up the used cups and saucers, as well as the plates. The saffron taste on his tongue was bitter. Justin had a notion that his brother wuz annoyed, but maybe less sure of the reason. He'd merely done his best to help them. Babies wudn' all a bed of roses.

"Best be off then," said Justin a little more curtly, knowing his services were no longer needed. "I'm goin' t'parade about town in my finery like I was a-going wassailing. Remember tha' Frank, do ee? When we wuz childurn?"

His questions weren't answered. Becca gave him a look.

"Maddy say where she wuz goin' did she, when she left here?" asked Justin.

Rebecca thought about her presence. She'd been in this very room earlier on.

"Said she was going fur a walk... With the perambulator I think. Something about going out to get un some fresh air."

Suddenly, that connected. She'd talked about that a few nights ago when Luk had confessed to them his fears about the forest. She'd said that when she had need of some fresh air she'd have a word with the forest (whatever and however that discussion would go). That conversation filled him with some degree of fear but it also boded well. Ef there wuz one individual who might be able to alter the course ov events on the mountain, that was she. Ee had every confidence in her. Ut wuz why they'd made a child together. There was that trust, and whatever she did (which might well go against all the good teachings of Mr Wes-ley) ee'd have to let she crack on with ut. As ee left, he tried not to listen to the row that might, at any point, erupt in the house behind him.

As he left, with the parcels now filled with his old clawthes, he encountered Walt Chegwidden an' Howey Knucky on their way down to start their shift. They noted his change in appearance.

"A'right Cap'n?" Walt went.

"Yew boys," said Justin in response.

"Looking good there," noted Howey, tipping his cap to un.

As artificial as he felt, his brother had been right. There wuz naw malice in they. The awnly malice coming toward him right now, wuz from his brother. He'd get over ut though ee reckoned. Ef they'd had any fall-outs in the past, they'd allays make up and shake hands the next day, telling each other how damned stupid they'd been. 'Twud be the same here surely?

Right now though, he had t'turn the whim of his mind onto other matters. He urgently needed to find out what Maddy had negotiated, and whether the forest might stop threatening his Knockie with entering the jaws of a geht wolf or being mauled by a bear, or worse still maybe, being buried alive (wuz tha' so bad fur an underground creature who could bore like no others?). All ov that may seem somewhat unconnected with what was on with George Jewell that morning, but then this wuz the Keweenaw and we are talking about the Cornish on ut: so perhaps some things are knotted together more than ee d'think.

This Eleanor Prowse, who Justin passed by on his perambulation, wuz a good-looking woman. Initially, those in Mountainside had felt she was a little haughty, but in fact, that was probably more nervousness on her part. As a place, Calumet felt like the back-of-beyond in 'Merky' (she had moved over with her father who had set up a drapery concern in that town) but up here, further up the peninsula, tha' was something. Here was the *back* of the back-of-beyond. Miss Prowse had never married. She told Doctor George Jewell she'd never met the right man. She found him intriguing, a bit of a breath of fresh air, if truth be told, when he had first entered into Calumet society. Despite everything that had happened to him, George had kept his looks. Yes he was greying, but of late, he'd trimmed his beard, and invested in some expensive new clothes. She was in her late thirties: he, his early forties, so there wudn' too much difference between them. 'Course, she knew by now that he wuz a widower, an' that his wife had mysteriously wandered off into the woods and never returned. Very odd that; very odd indeed.

When George told her all that had happened, admittedly she had been worried. Perhaps it was he who drove her to do that: though her association with him first in Calumet, and now here in Mountainside, told her that he was actually a respectable figure, who never bored her. Indeed, they had a lot in common: their enthusiasm for Methodism for one thing and their complete commitment to Revival and Temperance. Due to the lack of admirers in Calumet, Eleanor Prowse had thrown herself in with the Wesleyans over here (her family came from Redruth and she had lots of tales about attending chapel there), and had made quite a name for herself as an initiator of chapel construction and other Methodist projects. Her real commitment wuz to the setting up of Sunday Schools on the peninsula, which she viewed as essential if the church was to get younger people involved. George liked that in her. It was a quality he much admired.

Jewell had arranged for Eleanor to be brought by carriage up to Mountainside from Calumet: an offer which she first needed to think about, but then accepted. A telegram arrived at Skews' post office to tell him that she was on the way. He knew that it wouldn't do for her to stay with him and so selected Rosie's saloon for her stay whilst she was there. He inspected the room himself, and made sure that Rosie put flowers in it, and that there was plenty of cologne available. He didn't want her to see or smell the miners drinking but there was really no other choice. Rosie's was all there was. At least it was close by. At least he could get to know her better. He knew too that he cudn' be too fussy. No one cud all the way up here.

In her view, Mountainside was still a mining camp. It may have had pretensions, and to an extent, George had talked it up, as if it was some woodland paradise, but it certainly was not that. She knew the risks. She knew that if she moved here with him, that the culture and social calendar of her Calumet would be much truncated. On arrival a few days ago, the first thing that she'd heard was the vibration and thunder of both of the engine bobs working, as well as the stench of steam and smoke. The Deads made her cough. If it was a kind of paradise, then ut was of a sorely twisted and somewhat sorry kind. Could she put up with that? She didn't know.

Two other things were on her mind. Obviously, George Jewell had introduced her to his housekeeper Jenny, and she'd come to meet little James, who was now toddling around his property. Did she really want to take him on? At least he was young. Maybe she could shape and mould him the way she wanted. He seemed kindly enough. But takin' on someone else's child was a big responsibility. She did not even know if she was maternal or not. For all his enlightened views on women, she feared that George might want her just to replace Jenny, and therefore save a pretty penny; but no, he had assured her that they'd keep Jenny on. This Jenny was distant to her and didn't say much when they were first introduced (Eleanor didn't knaw but of course Jenny'd never quite got over the shock of him feeling her up that day). Eleanor reckoned that was because up until now Jenny had run the house and organised things, and now her coming in from fancy Calumet might upset that. Ut was a fear she understood. See, this Eleanor had some sense about she.

The other thing that bothered her was the ghost of Clara Jewell. Could she compete, but when George talked about her, he did not do so with much affection. She was a thin-faced woman apparently, quite skeletal in form, and had never really adapted to life in America. Eleanor on the other hand, had completed that transition; she had no expectations now of ever returning to Cornwall. That was a world away. Maybe this Clara offered her no threat. She'd spoken to Rosie Koskinen about her, and curiously, Rosie was unable to describe her. The other thing apparent was that she was skinny. Eleanor Prowse looked at her own flabby body in the mirror. It was true. Her father's success had allowed her to overindulge. She had to work hard to force her white stomach's flesh into her corset, but seemingly, George Jewell had no problem with that. He was a man after all, and despite his faith and respectability, he still had needs, still had urges. What would that be like she wondered? It was a question that vexed many older maids who'd had no previous contact with men. Maybe she'd talk to Rosie. She'd know, she felt. She knew her type.

That lunchtime (dinner in Cornish parlance) she'd agreed to meet with George up in his house. He'd organised it so that Jenny had taken James out for a walk and a play up near the preaching pit, so that the pair could talk over his ideas for the establishment of a chapel at Mountainside. She already knew the gist of it: that he and the man called Trevorrow were seeking subscriptions and donations so that a proper chapel could be built. So he'd decided, he wanted it placed near to the established preaching pit, but there was still some considerable debate over its size and the materials used for its construction.

Chapels down in Calumet were now built of stone, but up here, it would need to be wooden-framed. A considerable question was over how large he thought the future community there would become. From what he'd said, it seemed expansion was on the cards, but yet again, there still no tarmacadam roads in Mountainside, whereas Calumet had a number. Something more might be needed in terms of fundraising too. Despite his Revivalist wishes, at the rate current monies were coming into the building fund, the chapel would not be erected for at least another ten years. Maybe she'd have to tell un straight. Maybe she'd need to put un right. As her father used to say to her, "'Twas time fur somethun' to be put goin'." Perhaps she was the mechanism for this.

"Put un goin'", she told herself.

She knew what to expect. George had been cooking. There was a luncheon of pork and vegetables, followed by junket. Maybe George had done it on his own, but perhaps more likely his daughter or Jenny herself would have helped. This was fair enough. She knew he had a lot on right now: the mine owners had asked him to help with a safety assessment of some God-forbidden tramway they were about to construct. More noise she reckoned – more rattling from sunrise to sunset.

On entry, she was greeted by George, who had put on his best suit. He did look rather dashing in it: she knew he'd purchased it in Calumet. He had an eye for things, that much was true. She hoped she might be in his scope too.

"Lovely to see you Eleanor," he said upon entry. "May I take your coat?"

She consented and allowed her coat to fall into his hands.

"And how is the new grandson?" she asked.

"Good. Very good, I believe."

This tuss see, he knawed nawthun' 'bout the truth of ut, not what had transpired that morning.

"And Rebecca? She alright?"

"Yes. Splendid I believe."

He liked to give her a good sense of things did this Jewell. Maybe he was trying too hard, but that is the way of love, idn't ut? Sometimes we try a little too hard.

"And her husband...?"

She had been introduced to Francis, but struggled to remember his name.

"Francis. Frank."

"That's it."

"He's well. Busy with the new tramway I believe... but loving his role as a father."

Now what do ee say 'bout that? Perhaps Francis' ears were burning. Boy Jewell wuz a bit far off the mark wudn' a, all the same?

Their luncheon conversation continued in this way for an hour or so. Eleanor had to admit, the food had been tasty. Maybe life on the mining frontier was not all bad. She was wavering was this woman. All this pretence see, just to well, you knaw... That's the way of ut idn't ut see, when we'm trying to be coy, when we'm trying to impress? But finally, when George had put away the dining items into the kitchen, he moved across to where she sat at the end of the table. Back in Calumet that would have been seen as impolite and rather forward of him, but here it seemed natural. Perhaps she was coming to like this man Jewell. There was certainly something about him.

"So, shall we chat over the proposed chapel here? I've been so looking forward to this..."

Maybe this was true and maybe ut wasn't. Perhaps it wasn't because George Jewell fancied her, but perhaps too, he wanted to draw on her guidance and advice. They chatted for some two hours. All sorts were covered. They began by recalling admirable chapels back home with their neo-classical façades and their stone workmanship. Then there was the matter of roofing. 'Course back home, it was all Delabole slate but here shingles probably, though having said that, lots of slate was now being quarried in Pennsylvania. Maybe they could order some of that. 'Twould definitely be worth ut in the long term. Ut turned out that Eleanor had a liking for the Gothic revival: that is why she liked Central Wesleyan chapel in Calumet, but Jewell was of the view that all that was a bit too High Church for him. No tower of course because Methodists never used naw bells.

What was needed was something robust. Eleanor knew that. Whatever was constructed would have to withstand some hard winters. She could tell by the way he was speaking that what George had in mind was something much simpler: perhaps more along Bible Christian lines. But she reminded him of the expected numbers at Mountainside over the next few years.

"I was thinking rectangular," protested George, "a door at the end, and say four windas. Quite simple. Suits it here, and the way we have been doing things at the preaching pit. Just like Wes-ley..."

He could tell Eleanor was unimpressed. He'd have to change tack.

"It seems to me that you really need something grander. It has to be a statement George. When emigrants walk in to Mountainside they should feel at home instantly... Some *grandeur* surely?"

He liked the way that she said that. Of late, he'd not had much cause to deal with *grandeur*. Instead, moast of his days were spent on miners' ailments, the barking lungs of the Finns and the foot ailments of the Germans. Alas, syphilis too. Grandeur was elsewhere and not in Mountainside.

"What about money then?" she asked. "I know that you are fundraising."

He liked this directness. Ut had never been there with Clara. She never called a spade a spade when needed, but this shapely woman in front of him, she was different.

"We've amassed a fair amount. Several hundred dollars."

"You'll need more than that," Eleanor advised. "Labouring and materials won't come cheap..."

"What do you suggest?" asked George.

"You need a sponsor. A big donor. Someone who's really prepared to put up most of the money. In my experience, that's what works best. You can still fundraise but without a substantial donor, you'll never get there... What about the mine?"

"They've already given. The company have been good."

"Really? Maybe they need to step up a bit. Ask for more. Have a meeting with the directors. Go through the costs. Maybe there's more money sloshing around than you think. If that boy Justin can afford the garb of a Cap'n, surely there's a bit more available?"

He knew she was right. Perhaps it was just that he was incapable of asking – of formulating a plan, like all the middle-class Cornish were: too slaw to carry a cold dinner.

"You want to be appealing to home as well?"

"How do you mean?"

"Methodist societies in Cornwall. There's nothing more they like than to donate to an institution trying to give the Christian faith to those following idolatry. Get a letter home and put somethun' in the *Royal Cornwall Gazette* newspaper about what you'm trying t'do out here."

"Play the Missionary card you mean?"

"Yes. Of course... People like it George. It gives them hope."

"Talk about the natives and what you are trying to do."

George considered this. The awnly native he really knew was Nimkii, and even now probably he'd be educating his wayward second daughter in some lore or some secret way of doing things.

"You really think so?"

He asked this because in reality he did not want to be forced to think about this.

He'd seen the merits of Indian society when Flannery's wounds got healed. He'd seen Nimkii's skill at tracking... and how he had found Clara's bonnet. Yes, he was a committed Methodist but this conquest of the world, he asked himself, was that what Mr Wes-ley really wanted? Did he really want to brush away all of that with some kind of Missionary fervour. He was never like that. He was never a zealot. He left that to others. In fact, it had been one of the push factors for their leaving of Bodmin. There'd been too many of them. He didn't necessarily want that here. He didn't want it for Rebecca, for Mabel, for James and now, not for Richard either.

Although he realised this, he liked the way that Eleanor talked. He found her inspirational. There were never hurdles. Any problems were transformed into opportunities. He could see why she had been so successful in Calumet. But at the same time, he wondered if she was truly happy. Maybe all this love of fundraising, Revival and Missionarying could be transferred onto him. Those were important, but so was what he needed. He considered this and wondered if she could be exactly what he needed. Jewell continued in this daze. He felt a similar sensation to that which he felt earlier on in the week when his eldest daughter had been so frustrated about her inability to breast-feed her son. Eleanor was continuing to do her best to enthuse him. She was gabbering on about plastering, ceiling roses and pulpits. Then he believed she progressed to patterned glass, benches and hymnals. Apparently, she knew a very good book dealer in Chicago who could get the latter at a good price. Every so often, Jewell found himself interjecting with a comment like "Wonderful" or "Yes, of course" but actually, none of this was what he really wanted to discuss with her.

He didn't know quite what it was, or what came over him. Maybe it was her enthusiasm for Revival and getting the best chapel built for Mountainside that they could muster, but then again, maybe it was the way he thought about her white belly under her corset and the intoxicating perfume that she was wearing. It perhaps was all of that: but so too, was it the fact that a long time ago, as Jenny had suggested, he also had needs and desires, that eventually, he stood up and said, "Stop!"

Eleanor seemed shocked at his. Her mouth became pursed. She thought for a second that she had bored him into action. She knew she could talk Wesleyan chapels till the cows came home, and feared that he'd had enough of her by now. She momentarily felt that he'd be sending a telegram for another carriage to come back up here from Calumet and take her down to the dull drapery world of her family. But no, that wasn't so.

"Look, I didn't mean to startle you Elly..."

Elly, he'd said. That was nice.

"...but I really want to say something..."

Her body tensed. She took a deep breath.

"I know I'm innocent about these things. You know so much more, but the reality of it, is that in the bigger scheme of things, that doesn't matter... I am confident we can build a chapel here. I really am... but..."

He paused a while. This unnerved her.

"But what?"

Jewell shifted nervously on the spot, looked out of the winda' to see the rusty galvanised panels of the mine across the way, and tried to collect himself. He couldn't remember this moment with Clara, but at some point it must have happened. Or did it happen? Maybe they'd just fused together. He couldn't recall. When he thought about this, he knew he had to do things here differently. He knelt before her.

"Elly, Eleanor Prowse, you know how I feel about you. My heart sings when I see you. I have fallen in love with you."

Bleddy hell. He'd been an' blurted ut out. No turning back now.

He saw her blush like a girl, not the woman he knew.

"Would you do me the great honour of marrying me?"

It looked like he was about to pause, but then he carried on.

"I know this place isn't much. I know Mountainside is not Calumet, but we can make it wonderful. I know we can do that... Yes... we can help each other... What do you say?"

At this point, Jewell could not even look at her. He produced from his waistcoat pocket a box which contained a ring he had bought a long time ago in Calumet should this opportunity ever arise. He opened it and presented it to her. Now fur maids like Eleanor Prowse such moments dun't happen very often: not least when you live on the Keweenaw. She might have guessed that this would come one day, but perhaps not as soon as this. On the other hand, what point was there in waiting? Ut awnly wasted time. And when she thought that, and considered what George was trying to do here, ut didn' take her very long to come to a decision, though to be fair – to the doctor himself, near prostrate before her – it seemed an eternity.

"Alright then," was her response. "Yes. I accept. I accept your offer of marriage."

At this, George Jewell took a breather, as if he had just drilled a twelve-inch hole in a geht lump ov granite. He was breathing deeply, but maybe she understood. This man had been through a lot. Finally, in her something seemed right. Something at last, clicked into place. In one moment, he pushed up with the palms of his hands and in an athletic movement that would be worthy of a man half his age, he stood up then took her hand. With his other hand he pressed the engagement ring onto the fourth finger of her left hand. Thankfully it fitted. In this instant, Methodist protocol was thrown out the winda' and he bent down to kiss her. With this accomplished, he grabbed her hand and yanked her outside. They stepped onto the front porch, and once out there, he shouted, "Wondrous news. I am to be engaged to this beautiful woman. Shout ut from the rooftops. From the head-frame!"

Now, so loud did ee shout ut that it rose above the dull, incessant clank of the engine bobs, and echoed around the town. Gourgy heard un. So did Luk. There was no doubt that the forest heard ov un too. And then, being like ee wuz – at this point in love, and properly mazed – he jumped down the steps pulling Eleanor Prowse with un. Next, he proceeded to walk down the main street in Mountainside telling the world their news. Rite on. That wuz one way of doing ut. Es. There wuz plenty who'd heard of ut, and not just they out there in the forest. In an upstairs room of Rosie's saloon, two people peered out of a bedroom winda' and looked at the sight of them. One of they wuz Rosie Koskinen; the other wuz ee with the gammy leg, but nonetheless, a fat wallet. That boy's name wuz Dicky Mint. What a heller, eh? He and she. You didn't see that comin t'all, did ee?

33

My Lord! You might say that ef you wuz a bit ov a Methodee. Ef you wuz anyone else, then maybe you'd say 'twas a right hell up. Ef you went chapel jus' fur the gossip an' to see wozzon, fur the tay an' a hot saffron bun, well, you wuz in good company, fur thaas how 'twas. Thaas how things panned out here on the mountain. An' whilst the two brothers were having a bit of a fall-out you, and Miss Prowse wuz accepting an offer ov marriage from George Jewell, not to mention also the covert liaison between Dicky Mint and Rose Koskinen (perhaps by now, she'd fully given up on ever turning the eye ov tha' Justin Nankervis), other matters were afoot on Mountainside. Let's just say fur a moment that ef everyone here had behaved a bit more according to the superior teachings of Mr Wes-ley then maybe none of this would ever have happened in the fust plaace, but life is more than jus' doctrine an' sermons, idn' ut? All ov we step out of line sometimes, dun't us? 'Tis unavoidable. We's awnly human see.

All these individuals were too busy t'nawtice other actions in the township of Mountainside. A bustling Mr Skews an' Cap'n Trevorrow had met early in the morning to discuss how they would approach their negotiation with Nimkii, and after crowst-time was done and the groushans 'eaved outside, they wandered down to where Nimkii seemingly held out his last stand against the mine: this wuz his odd labyrinthine encampment at the collar, right next to the engine house that took down the cage to the levels belaw. Dark they were, but contained ripe ore fur the plucking: copper see, wuz the apples of the earth.

They knawed what they would find. He'd be meditating in the rusted galvanised steel panels that made up the sides of his accommodation. There'd be a fire burning outside, and inside, there'd be animal skins for warmth and comfort. Around him would be other oddities of his culture, that Skews and Trevorrow would not wish t'ask about fir fear ov treading on the sacred. One thing that they had noted was a severed eagle's claw atop a stick. He'd somehow also managed to make a drum, from skin and some wood that he had brought back from the off-cuts of the carpenters. Nothing, so ut seemed, wuz wasted. The talons on the claw looked sharp and ut put a bit ov fear in boath ov they.

They knew too that they would likely find Mabel down there. Ut seemed to they that her feythur, the Doctor, had given up on she, and that he'd let her go. Ut felt like she'd become so wayward that he had no control over her anymore, and that even his housemaid, Jenny Spargo, didn't have any say in what she did, or how she behaved. Tha' wuz how ut wuz with youngsters if you didn' give un boundaries. Sometimes you needed t'be cruel to be kind. Tha' wuz the way ov things, and sometimes, humans, in their generous concern and their misguided hope, forget tha', and when tha' happens, you end up with a situation like this one. Oh es.

See ov ut. She wuz in there with un – that Nimkii. She'd started to dress differently now had this Mabel. She'd started to fuse her trousers and blouses with adornments from Nimkii's people: how mazed wuz that! Now she had leather accoutrements in the form of a belt (something which awnly emphasised her waist and shape) and a purse. She wuz wearing her hair differently too; sometimes in plaits. She even walked differently they'd nawticed ov late. Instead of planting firmly each foot on the earth (for that was allays unmoveable and solid fur the Cornish) she padded like Nimkii, as if she did not want to disturb anything, as if she were creeping into someone else's private world. Et wuz as ef she wuz trespassing and didn't want to disturb nawthun'.

Now in that, there wuz much learning fur this pair but as usual, neither of they saw tha'. Naw, they still had their mind on how to best make money, and how best to exploit the earth. In tha', they wuz naw different to the rest of the Cornish see, and therein lied the problem. In essence, thaas where ut all comed from: all this trouble. Maybe Nimkii knew it all along, and maybe by degrees, so did this Mabel.

"A'right there," said Skews surreptitiously, as they drew up to the camp.

Nimkii retained his meditative state as ef ee were far away. Nawbody knawed ut, because nawbody asked but he had been in pain for a while now.

Ut wuz Mabel who answered.

"What do *you* want?" she said curtly – and with an edge of scepticism.

This wuz she these days. Naw greeting. Naw awareness that these two men should, by rights, be respected by her, and that they wuz her betters an' elders. In this, Trevorrow saw perhaps why Jewell had given up with her. Skews, on the other hand, felt a sense of pity, but also a degree ov hurt at being snubbed and derided. In his mind, he had reckoned on them once having a connection: of him truly loving her, and of him transferring any lingering act of parenthood in him onto this Mabel. But then again, something else more sinister drove him concerning her too – and well do ee knaw that by now: all that innocence, that cuteness of her, the way that she saw the world. He wondered where that poppet was that he had once given her – that she once treasured so much? Now, ut wuz probably not important enough for her to value, or to carry forwards, not even from a sentimental point of view.

Mabel stood up. Ut looked like the two of them had definitely been sleeping together. Now, that wudn' zactly right t'all, wuz ut? 'Mean, there was the age thing, and then there was she (a white girl) cavorting with ee (a baissly Injun, in Skews' view). Skews pushed this to the back of his mind. Ee didn' even want to contemplate ut. Indeed, his mind almost refused to consider ut. Alright fur ee though, to think anything he wanted ov she, but not fur this Nimkii. Hypocrisy see. But then, tha' wuz Skewsy all over. An' her feythur a Methodist preacher too. Wha' had ut come to? Bet they wudn' go much on this back Bodmin Wesleyan.

"We'd like a word with Nimkii, if we may," stated Trevorrow.

"What about?" came Mabel's suspicious response.

Who wuz she? Wuz she now his controller, his master? His agent even? Were they, as experienced bosses, going to be forced to negotiate the entire future of the mine with a young girl? Ut looked like ut. Hell-fire, how had ut bleddy-well come t'this?

"He's meditating at present," she said assuredly. "He doesn't like to be disturbed when he's meditating."

"Right on," said a by-now truculent Trevorrow, planting his heel down on the earth. "We'll hang on fur'n then... when he've... finished..."

Mabel gave un a look. She strode past them toward where the fire was burning down to embers. She put a few more sticks onto it so that ut would glow again. In this moment, Skews nawticed how much she had changed. She wuz no longer the cute girl he had once fantasised over. She had matured and wuz now a young woman, with all the shape and form that any young woman would carry. This is what surprised him the moast. All the while since Francis had warned him off, he had kept his distance and viewed her from afar. He'd never been this close to her in a long while, and it wuz at this moment he realised he was still susceptible to her charms. She had girlish ways before. Now she had the appeal of an adult. Es, the girl had fascinated him, stimulated him, and... well, in that moment he knew she'd be a tasty catch fur any man.

Somehow, she'd become even more comely than her sister. Rebecca, he'd noted, wuz pretty but somewhat plain (too much of the school-ma'm in she). That Irish slut Maddy, he realised had everything going on at once: she was too much in the body and gob fur moast men, and maybe the reason why awnly that mazed boy Justin had been able to take she on. Mabel though, well, she lay in a sweet spot between them: enough of the pretty innocence, but also a dangerous spark in her eye: an awareness of her power. Perhaps that was why Nimkii had encouraged her, but perhaps too, she had noted the way that other miners looked at her.

"Maybe he doesn't want to speak to you," stated Mabel, purposely trying to make they pair taissy.

This again wuz surprising words coming from she.

"Why not?" asked Skewsy.

"Maybe he knows what you want..."

"Does a know?" said Trevorrow, puzzled.

"I think he does," stated Mabel, speaking very quickly. "You only come to see him when you want something. The rest of the time he doesn't exist. Ee certainly never features in your thinking."

Now, at tha', Trevorrow and Skews didn' care fur her tone very much. But at the same time, deep inside, they knawed there wuz some truth in what she wuz saying. She'd exposed them in some way and discovered their plan, and it unsettled them. They were being taken apart by this female; she could dissect them using a scalpel of words.

"He and his people get his fair share," responded Skews indignantly. "They always have done."

"It's not that though, is it?" responded Mabel.

Here she wuz then; this young woman, trying to take them on.

"How do you mean?"

"Like I say, it's more than tha'... See what you've done to this place. Why do you think he sits here?"

Skews and Trevorrow glared at her. They did not know how to answer her. Perhaps it wuz because Nimkii could obtain free off-cuts of galvanised steel.

"He is recalling what it was once like... before all this..."

She pointed to the mine complex and down to the Deads, where an oily and steaming ooze gathered in a lagoon, like the River Styx.

"He's wishing for it to return to the way it once was. He knows he has upset the balance of things. The Forest..."

It looked like she was going to continue her diatribe against the pair but she stopped short, like there was something that even she could not speak about.

"Mabel," said Skews, saying her name softly, like he always used to, "we don't mean him any harm. We don't mean to destroy things. But you have to step back and think of the importance of all of this... So many people are reliant on it now. It's not just me or Cap'n here... It's everyone. You father included... Your brother, your sister...Things aren't always black and white... You'll see that as you grow older..."

"Will I? Well, I see it clearly enough already thank you. Nimkii has taught me that. He's shown me. He sees it very clearly too..."

"We've come to negotiate..." pleaded Trevorrow.

"What? For more land? For another slice of him. The land here isn't just for taking," said this Mabel, shouting and gesticulating. "Where you see timber, I see forest. Where you see barren wilderness, I see the balance of nature. So many lives are affected by you, but you'll never get it. You can't even see what is right in front of you."

"What are we meant to see?" asked Skews. "Tell us..."

"If I told you, you'd never believe me..." she said, her voice exasperated. "What do you think happens to all the animals and creatures who live here when you encroach on them? Things living here for thousands of years – and then overnight, their world gets turned upside-down – all from your desires, your wishes."

"Nimkii freely gave us permission," argued Trevorrow. "If he wuz the custodian, then what did he expect? No one forced his hand as far as I can recall."

"I don't think he expected all of this," argued Mabel. "Neither did I. When I first arrived, this place was no more than a few shacks in the forest. Now look at the state of it. It's a hell on earth. A cesspit."

"This place has provided for you," said Skews. "You and your family..."

"I know," said Mabel, "but at what cost?"

Skews and Trevorrow could not answer her. They did not want to answer her. The problem wuz that they didn' even understand her thoughts.

Meanwhile, Mabel continued her diatribe.

"He can't cope with it. He has been exiled by his people. They know what he did here. The Forest knows. What swirls inside him is guilt, but nothing will take that guilt away from him unless you absorb some it, unless you take it from him. It is his way. Until someone does that, then he will have to live with it."

This wuz clearly a heavy burden. Ut felt like she wuz callin' fur his redemption in some way. Skews and Trevorrow were trying to come to some realisation about what she was saying. However, it wudn' like they could just reach into his heart and somehow absorb all his pain, or even share it around. All the time Trevorrow had known Nimkii, he'd allays been a willing participant.

"But the money..." he argued. "His people were given lots of copper."

"They have more than enough," said Mabel critically. "Why is it the Cornish always want more? Can't they live more frugally? More simply? Always reaching into the earth, aren't they? First tin, and now copper. I's never enough. What next, eh?"

"Because we are taking a chance," said Trevorrow. "We're trying to do our best, for our families, for our communities, for Cornwall... You really want all that to end? We've been doing it for thousands of years."

"It doesn't matter what I want," said Mabel off-handedly. "You need to think what you really want. That's what Nimkii wants you to do. If you don't... then I fear what will happen..."

Why wuz she speaking in such an apocalyptic way? Wuz this a slice of her feythur coming out in her? Bah. Chapel people see. All doom and gloom. Even though Trevorrow supported the erection of the chapel, ut wuz perhaps more out of social duty than faith. Ee'd sent faith packin' several moons ago.

"But Mabel," said Trevorrow, trying to be optimistic, "one day, believe me, this will all return to the wild... I mean, I hope we have a few more years here yet considering the investment and effort, but I've seen enough of mining to know that eventually nature reclaims everything. Look down the Cliff Mine. See how that's now all overgrown, There are places back home, that when I wuz a boy were filled with arsenic and tailings, but which nature will have colonised and made her own again. You're too young to see that..."

His argument, he realised was valid, but after he said it, he knew that his final sentence would have insulted Mabel's intelligence.

"I know that Cap'n Trevorrow. I know one day it will return to some semblance of reality, but at what cost, eh? An' if we carry on doing this eh, what will it be like? What will we hand on? What will there be for Nimkii's children?"

"I didn' knaw Nimkii had any children," said Skews intrigued by her comment.

"He doesn't. I'm talking theoretically Mr Skews."

Ut was hard to argue with she. Her wuz talking like a lawyer. All they fairy stories she used to read seemed to now be reprocessed in her mouth as she delivered her sour observations to the pair. The talk of children though made all of them think of liddle Jago and his cousin Richard, but also Skews cudn' help but wonder if Nimkii had Mabel in mind as a womb for his awn offspring as well. Ee allays saw sin in people did tha' boy but didn' think much 'bout his own actions, which were just as bad, or sometimes, even worse. This thought sent his already annoying nervous twitch into overdrive. This moment made him contemplate something that from that moment onward grew in his mind and that he would not let go ov. But such things are best not spoken of now. That will do fur later.

Mabel paused in her onslaught and once more, went inside the steel tepee to sit next to Nimkii. She put her hand on his arm and, at this, Nimkii opened his eyes. From wherever he had been, he came back to the collar of the mine. He nodded at Skews and Trevorrow as he adjusted his eyes to the morning sun in the east. He shifted his position slightly, perhaps to shake the numbness from his crossed legs.

"More land?" he asked, raising his head.

Ah, so ee wuz speaking now, wuz a? Mabel had some uses then.

"Always more."

She glared at the two of them, to see what they had to say.

Trevorrow gasped and groaned (his rheumatism hurt like buggery) as he sat down before them, but ef a negotiation was to be made, he needed to at least be on the same eye level as they were. He gestured for Skews to do the same, and creakily, Skews also followed by placing his bony frame to the ground.

"Where?" asked Mabel. This wuz a false question though because in reality, she knew what they wanted. She'd kept her ear to the ground did this Mabel. People thought she wuz away with the fairies all the time but tha' wudn so t'all. She'd heard her feythur talking. Besides his energetic desire for a purpose-built chapel, she'd known that a tramway down to Eagle Harbour was on the cards.

"Tramway?" asked Nimkii.

He knew already then. He already knew the term: understood what ut meant. He must have observed them down state in the mines around Calumet.

Skews nodded. From inside his tail-coat jacket, ee pulled out a drawing ov the design and pushed et towards Nimkii. The land for ut had been marked out in blue pencil. A cutting needed to be made right through the forest. The scar would last a long time. He genuinely felt like Nimkii and Mabel might want to study it for a while, and so sat back slightly to let them contemplate it, placing the sweaty palms of his hands on the ground. And from the earth he felt the shake and shudder of the great bob inside the engine house. But Nimkii barely looked at it. He gave ut a cursory glance only. Mabel pored over it slightly longer, but her observation was over ten seconds later.

"He knew this was coming," said Mabel. "We saw Mr Mint and you surveying it. We watched you. We saw him with the instrument on the tripod. You were holding the measuring staffs."

Fur a while, there wuz silence. Skews expected her to continue, or at least fur Nimkii to say something, but instead, nothing wuz said.

"And so?" asked Skews.

"Seems to me," said Mabel, "that it no longer matters what Nimkii says. You will enact your will anyway. What can one man do to stop you? What can you offer him? He needs no more money. He needs no more copper. He had all that he needed, and what he needs now was lost."

"We will do what he wants," said Trevorrow, though tha' wuz something ov a lie, truth be told. "I know he is reasonable..."

"If you do what he wants, then you will shut the mine and go back home to Cornwall. There, you won't ruin yet another landscape."

Skews gave a sneer. He could not help it. Professionally, he thought ov everyone here who'd have to uproot. Personally, he knew there wuz nothing left fur un now back in Cornwall. He'd lost touch with his flesh and blood: that was part of the reason why this Mabel still charmed him. He still felt it even now, despite her coldness, despite her fiery temper.

"I don't think that's possible," said Trevorrow in a low voice. Ee wuz a boy used to negotiations underground and top-side.

"So take it anyway," said Mabel. "Have it. Have all of it. Have all the bleddy forest if you want it. Nimkii doesn't mind."

She was being sarcastic and bitter, but Skews saw an opening an' wuz not about to let this go. He had to act quick. She might regret her words later on.

"You mean we can have it for free?"

Mabel gave him a sneering look. Then, she leaned to her left and whispered something unintelligible into Nimkii's ear. He nodded at what she said. He said something back to her and pointed at the drawing. Trevorrow tried to discern what passed between them but he realised that now Mabel was a better communicator with Nimkii than he had ever been. Ee'd been a colonial upstart with un. She, on the other hand, was talking to him properly in the way that all people should.

"Yes," said Mabel. "You can have it fur free. I mean, what difference does the cutting down of a small swathe of trees running to the harbour make? Nimkii here says it makes no difference."

The implication wuz that the land was wrecked already. How could any of this make a difference? Ut was a conversation that perhaps was not just happening on this tiny part of the Keweenaw, but all over the vast landscape ov 'Merky'. Ut wuz a conversation that the Cornish had once had at home; now they were having it all over the world because of their dogged instinct to dig beneath their feet. Tha' wuz the greed of they. Skews and Trevorrow didn't need to say anything to each other. Did ut really matter that Nimkii and she objected? Not really. Not in the grander scheme of things now. Nimkii seemed to be losing the plot. Besides, who cared? Who would actually know this conversation had actually taken place? Francis and Justin were otherwise engaged. The details ov ut were not relevant. They did not matter for people like Bobby Moyle or Diddy Pasca, or the Germans, Stefan Gries or Klaus Knickmeier, nor the Finns, Faas Jokinen or Roope Toivonen. All they wanted wuz work and grub – and beer. Then, every couple of months, some money t'be sent home.

"What about you?" asked Skews, his stare penetrating her soul. "Do you need anything Mabel?"

"How do you mean?"

"Well, you have helped mightily with our discussions here. How might we see you right for your services?"

"Pay me off you mean," said Mabel rolling her eyes, "to keep my gob shut."

"No, no, no." said Trevorrow gesticulating. "Not at all. But for helping us here. Clearly you and Nimkii here have a... special bond..."

These were words that twisted and turned in Skewsy's heart. What did they do at night? Wuz she enveloped by un till dawn? If this wuz back home, 'twud be in all the papers.

"We just thought..."

"I don't need anything," she said bluntly.

"Alright," said Trevorrow. "Fair 'nuff... but if there ever is, just let we knaw. We ent against you Mabel... we'm for ee really... Your feythur'll tell ee tha'."

To they though, she wudn' see sense. Mabel chose not to respond. She'd had enough of their patronising words. But it wudn' do to sustain this conversation any further. She wanted them gone, and she hoped that she wudn' have t'see either ov them in the near future.

Normally, Trevorrow and Skews might have shaken the hand of Nimkii at this moment but not on this day. This wuz different. They both knew that this had not really been a negotiation but more ov a steam-rollerin'. Whatever it had been, they had got their tacit permission, even if really it had not been given freely. They began to ease themselves up from the ground and onto their feet again: Trevorrow's arthritic joints needing Skews' helping hands. Nimkii just stared at them like they had dropped down from the sky. He knew he'd need to tell the forest about the wound that was about to be made. He'd also need to inform Yolkai: a conversation he was not looking forward to. Ee wuz in enough trouble with she already. 'Twas hard when those who you loved turned their back on ee.

As Skews and Trevorrow were leaving, Mabel briefly clutched the arm of Nimkii and he nodded at her. Her hand lingered there just a little too long fur Skews' liking, and he knew that later on, when ee wuz trying to sleep, that image would churn around his sick mind. Apparently, they did not need to say anything else. Tha' wuz the way ov they. Moast people say too much, but not these two. They realised that speakun' too much sometimes led to pain. Instead, they smiled at each other in acknowledgement that they boath felt the same way about things.

In her mind, Mabel thought back to her mother's leaving (some days it felt like she had awnly existed in a dream) and contemplated all she knew, all that learning she had gathered from the fairy stories she had consumed when she wuz younger. There were messages in them, she decided, fur every turn in life. They were true. She'd allays argued that, even when her stupid father was so dismissive of them. She knew the small people of the world. She could see them well enough, just as she could glimpse the teasing Gourgy and Luk – and the rest of them.

With this still in her mind, Mabel reached into the shadowy rear of the steel tepee that had been constructed by Nimkii. This felt like her home now. She preferred it to her father's house where he would by now, surely be entertaining that God-bothering fuss of a woman, Eleanor Prowse. She liked it here too because she could escape the clutches and dictates of Jenny Spargo. Nimkii meanwhile, said nothing to her. In fact, he had already realised wha' she wuz about to do.

From the back of the tepee she pulled out something that had stayed with her for a year or so now. Ut was the expensive poppet tha' lusty and dangerous Skews had given to her when she wuz younger. When she had been a child, she had created an aura of love around that doll but now, it felt false and a complete pretence. She had called it her piskie, and perhaps that wuz once what ut wuz. Now it seemed something parasitic, something out of place: an anachronism that needed to be got rid of. It reeked of falsity and deceit and maybe, she could sense ut.

Nimkii watched as she got up and walked down past the timbering yard and the blacksmith's shop. She could hear some row in the street over by Rosie Koskinen's but she paid it no attention. She was in the distance now, but he saw her reach the festering lagoon of the Deads then dip over the levee of the lakeside. Had he been close up, he would have seen her kneel down to the ground. At fust, she peered into the morose gloop but there was no reflection to observe. She knew the item she wuz carrying with her had to go. She took the poppet and turned it upside-down, then very slowly, she pushed it through the somewhat harder skin of the surface so that gradually, et disappeared into the clayey, liquid mass belaw.

Initially, the head, then the torso, then its pelvis went in, and momentarily, she paused to watch the two legs of the poppet sticking out into the air as if it had dived in purposefully to escape the self-destructive town of Mountainside. What lay beneath was dragging it down anyway (she could see it sinking) but then gleefully, she pressed boath of the feet of the doll, and very soon, they were consumed as well. Once it went under, she understood what she needed to do – something hopeful maybe – something Nimkii had taught her to see. She needed to escape all this industry and the incessant pressings of Cap'n Trevorrow and Samuel Skews. She needed to be a girl again, and go into the forest. That, she then did. Nimkii didn' need t'knaw this. He understood ut already. He wuz trying to commune in the same way that another wuz.

Much of wha' wuz happening elsewhere on Mountainside passed Maddy O'Donahue by that morning. Up early, the first thing she had done was to feed and dress Jago. Lovely he wuz and when he'd been fed, he seemed t'purr like a kitten. Oh, ee wuz joyful wuz tha' boy! Such soft skin and his tiny fingers would grip her thumb. Attentive ee wuz and took joy in anyone or anything he encountered. Ee wuz one ov they babies who you knaw es just glad to be here on earth. When he needed changin', he let Maddy get on with ut, and when he wuz due to be fed he took pleasure from latching on to what had become his mawthur. And this Maddy – bit evil like she wuz (but, you understand, in a way she cudn' help) – doted on un.

There wudn' anything she wudn' do fur'n, dear obm. Well, 'tiz like tha' when you find somethun you really love. You keep ut clawse and never let ut go, for you knaw you wun't find the like ov ut again. Ee wuz some precious t'she. When 'twas time to go up to Rebecca's, she settled un in the perambulator and set off. Perambulators like the one she had, and that Rebecca had, were costly items, but they'd managed to have two brought up from Calumet. They'd come even further though, from down in Houghton, where there wuz a company tha' supplied them. Now, babies – thaas a good industry t'go into. Tidn' like 'twas ever goin' to go boom and bust like mining. The ore ov infants never runned out.

Ut was in response to Doctor Jewell's urgent request that she'd gone to visit Rebecca, but of course, she didn' stay long. She didn' want to. She knawed what they'd be going through, but this was the only way. Yes, et wuz the only way. So she'd given Becca some advice, but it came out rather condescending she felt. She didn't even really want to see that Richard, even though Becca had placed un in her arms. Aw yes, ee wuz calm enough with she (that was natural for a Pooka and its creator) but she really didn't want to look too close, not that close at least. She could smell ov un, an' she could see he had that green tinge to un; that elongated and pointed nawse. She knawed where he wuz heading – and that scared her.

Nonetheless, ut did not make her want to confess her sin and swap them back, or even tell Rebecca the truth. Had she been different, then she might have, but this wuz Maddy O'Donahue of the Beara, an' she wudn' about to give up easily what had been so hard won. Ef anyone could cope with a Pooka, ut was they pair: Francis and Rebecca. They had the patience of the saints, them pair. They'd need to. She knew that. She'd observed Pookas before. She knew what they could do: what wounds they might inflict.

This Maddy though, took the perambulator deep into the forest. She and the forest needed words. She had not said anything before but now ut wuz about time she put ut straight. Ut was about time somebody told ut the truth. All the while, she wuz trying to connect with it, but also with others too, who perhaps understood ut. Not all the buggers back the mine see, but them – yes, them. Them two. Them pair. Aw es, she knawed who she meant. Taking the pram this far in wuz no easy feat. There were stumps and tussocks, rivulets and brambles all to be negotiated, but she pushed on. She wanted to be sure enough that she was far enough away from everything else in the world of the Keweenaw. She'd done this kind of thing before, high on the windswept moorland of the Beara. Ut needed to be the same here. She knawed she wuz being watched. She knawed she was being tracked. There were sprites following her. Whenever she turned around to check, she could see the traces of them, darting into cover. There they'd hide, until she trundled on again. She went past the U-shaped tree branch in which a long time ago now – with misguided hope – she had tried to force a baby into her womb.

Magic dun't always work though, and ut hadn' gone the way she planned it, but nevertheless, there was now a bouncing baby in front her. Things work out alright in the end, ef you have enough faith in the magic of the earth. Aye. That's what she told herself. That's what she tried to convince herself of, this Maddy, this woman who'd done a deed so bad that she could not even contemplate its full evil. She could not yet see the tragedy of it, because the tragedy of having her son being still-born was enough to negate it tenfold. How works the human mind! How wrong ut sometimes gets things. Es. We've all been there.

And in the earth below, tree roots retched and shuddered. Fungi helped them communicate all of this. Dull was the plod of the engine bob, and ut wuz still noticeable out here, this far from the mine; but here too, was an energy zipping through the peaty leaf litter, conducting itself through fibres and spores, all multiplying in intensity and instruction. This wuz how the forest communicated. Ut was how the trees knew what each other wuz thinking. Ut was their warning mechanism.

Already, news had come in of the proposed wound from Eagle Harbour up to Mountainside. Ut was the gossip that morning. Maddy knew ut was in the air and in the earth. She'd know what Justin and the others were planning. Not a good place to be she reckoned, since the odds were now in the forest's favour. She had very little to bargain with, and indeed, she was probably below expected currency already. The forest knawed what she'd done. They had watched. They had listened. They had seen the Pooka up at Rebecca and Francis' place. How could they not know ut wuz a Pooka? She'd been discreet with Jago, but the forest had witnessed her first birth. Ut had seen the sticky mess of a child that she had first produced. Ut knew ut had no life to it, sensed in the leaves and the twigs, the fact that ut was not breathing. Spores from mushrooms and toadstools had already travelled in that moment, and fell on the back of the dead creature she had produced. How could she have this new bright-as-a-button boy with her? Ut made no sense. The forest was smart see. Ut knew. Ut allays knew.

She stopped in a circle of trees: great long maples that stretched to the sky. Ut seemed like they could reach upwards so high so that they could touch the very hem of Yolkai's dress. These were the elders: those who had been there the longest. She wanted them to know the truth. Ut wuz important. Tell them and the whole forest would know. Ask them and they would speak for the whole forest. They'd voice the concerns of the sprites, and all those who had been made refugees, who'd had to cart baggage and bookcase all the way across the forest away from the encroachment of the mine: the churning up of the ground there, and the vicious slaughter of trees. The memory of tha' cleansing wuz still in their sap and leaves.

On these maples was old growth, gnarled runs of bark that had lost its sap an eon ago, and now housed insects and ants. There too, hung yet-to-transform chrysalises. Such old growth was wise and knowledgeable. Ut would confer with the rings of growth inside. Ut would hear her out. Time for Maddy to speak ut wuz. Ut wuz now or never. As she spoke she swirled around, projecting her voice as far as she could. This wuz naw Calumet Opera House but she would give ut a good go.

"Listen. I know you've been hurt," she began, simultaneously touching her shell necklace, imbibing the magic of an ocean away. "I know the pain you've suffered. I know you feel let down by those who should have protected you. But you cannot blame him. It is not all his fault. It is just fate: circumstance if you will. No one really plans these things. I know you have endured an apocalypse the like of which you have not seen before, but I am pleading with you now... Stop the revenge. Stop the taking. Cease with your harm."

She caught sight of the glowing eyes of some the sprites. Hellers they were, those little people. As soon as you'd look at them, they'd close up and hide again. So skittish they were; like deer, only much worse; all of them trying to make sense of the mine, her and her baby. She picked up Jago and held him high in the air.

"Bejesus I know you know who this is, but I am begging you, don't punish him or me. Don't release that knowledge. Don't tell the world, for if you do, things will collapse. I know you want things to collapse. I know that one day it will. Just not yet. I promise you. I saw it back home on the Beara. One day, when the mine halts, the humans will leave and then you can take over again. You can put your tendrils under the planchen. You can grow in the bedrooms. You can dress your brambles across the street. You may wind your vines around mechanisation so tightly that one day, no one will ever know it was there. That is what you do, oh Nature. I bet your Moon Goddess has told you that. She knows. If you don't believe me, then listen to her."

At her voice, a few crows and blue jays scattered. There was movement in the undergrowth; small tense breaths being taken under the lichen and moss. They were absorbing all that she wuz saying.

"I know you forest. I know what you can do, but I also know that you have a different view of time. The mine, I know it is a tragedy but it is temporal, you know that. Allow it to happen. Be tolerant. You share this world with humans, and yes, they are greedy... greedier than any animal alive, but things are changing. You have to see that... You have to think long term. Oh yes, this might be a helleva' century fur all of ya but doan't let that ruin things. You can ride that out. You know ut. Give them a chance to rethink... I mean, you know yourselves humans are programmed that way. They aren't like you."

After this, nothing stirred. It almost felt to Maddy like the forest was no longer listening; like ut had given up on her words. Perhaps they were too idealistic, but perhaps she did not recognise the death and the endurance that had been suffered. The truth ov ut wuz that she knew ut all too well though. She knew the graveyard of plants and trees underground. She knew the piles stacked high beside the blacksmith's forge and in the timbering yard. She knew the wood that had been cut to fire the boiler under the steam pump. But they knew that surely? They had to know that she wuz trying to be sympathetic, to recognise their side of the story. The problem wuz that they never had a voice: someone who could respond. The only change you saw were roots contracting or expanding, reaching for you or reaching for safety into the earth again. Right now, they were static. The ground wuz not moving: there came over the forest, a kind of echoing stasis. Dark bark did not stir. The light seemed to fade.

It didn' matter. She wuz in fer a penny, and in fer a pound now. She'd be cheeky and she'd ask. In fact, she'd plead. She'd explain the individual's weakness, that individual's lack of association with the mining camp: that reluctance to come across an ocean away from her people. Maybe this person knew, and could foresee the future. The forest had noted it as soon as she stepped off the boat, as soon as she had entered the old Cliff Hotel. The forest was like everything else in nature: it relied on the survival of the fittest, and those who couldn't resist, those who heard the forest calling, well, they'd be taken: an eye for an eye, a tooth for a tooth.

The forest was a predator like the rest of nature, and when it saw weakness instead of strength, it pounced. Never mind circumstance, never mind family or friends or who might be hurt; if there was need to get back, if there was need of revenge, then ut would call upon its army of workers to do so. And even though they might well be doing the enticing, the victim would never even notice. The forest wuz even so skilled that ut made ut look like the victim wuz complying willingly. She assured them that there would be no consequences, nor revenge this end. All they wanted wuz a return. In doing that, ut might even make everything alright again – though she knew herself that that might be too much to ask. Alright, she conceded, maybe it would go some way.

Cudn't it just…?

Might it perhaps…?

Maybe it could rethink and…?

Ut wuz still quiet wuz the forest; still listening to this Maddy. She could only hope ut understood. She hoped too that ut would not do anything to harm her connection to Jago, even though ut knew the truth. Best to confess all, she told herself. Nature has a way of showing the truth, more than human beings but still, was all of ut out there in the open? Had she dished up everything fur it on a plate? Maybe not. Maybe there were still some things that needed solving: that needed closure. Maddy glanced around her. The forest had gone utterly silent. She hoped that she'd done enough. She hoped that a lingering magic might work. She looked down on that bright-eyed boy of hers and smiled at him,. Fur now at least, she had done her best. Even ef others weren't interested yet she at least, had tried to make peace and engender a new relationship. Maddy undid her blouse and put Jago to her breast. She sat contemplating what she had just done.

"Ah, you were hungry weren't you, my little man…?"

Ef he could have nodded, then Jago would have done so.

The forest had gone quiet on purpose. Gradually, the elder maples had induced a migration southwards. The animals and birds, the insects and the butterflies, they were all moving to a spot in the forest that still remained untouched by human hand. There, on a cliff-face of a ravine was a secret world; that individuals like Nimkii had not been able to locate: and there, for some time, this forest had kept something alive. Each day it had been brought water and fruits, tubers and sustenance. They'd fed it edible mushrooms, and from Lake Superior, even brought her tasty lake-weed and nutritious algae. There, it had been safe from bears, and wolves, and anything else that lurked in the wood. Oh, it had aged badly but you'd expect that. A year and a half in the forest is like twenty years elsewhere. Ut had weathered like the crevassed granite back at Land's End. Zawns ran down ut's cheeks.

It wuz old now, old in a way that you cannot imagine but maybe old in a way that awnly the skin of that Gourgy and Luk wuz. Old in a way that even close up you could not tell if 'twas a boy or a maid. Dark see, had been the canopy. Snows and ice that had blown in during the last winter had expanded and levered up crinkles in its skin, and there were purple marks ov bruising upon its arms and legs where tree roots had grabbed it each night and smartly sucked it inside a cave for warmth and shelter. Roots, ut had discovered, could be tentacles ef they wanted.

Its original clawthes had long since been lost, and so the forest had woven it clawthes of lichen and moss. Although its hair had greyed from the experience, from its scalp issued forth earwigs and centipedes who managed and nourished the fine white strands still issuing from its skull. Chrysalises were found on there too. All that time, it had not seen a soul, and all that time, no one had a said a word to it; and from the start, ut had felt that it had lost its power of speech. It felt easier to ingest moss than to form words. They cudn' be formed. It had become as dumb as stone. It had lost its memory see: the forest does that to you. But maybe keeping it captive wudn' right any more? Before, ut had seemed to be the right thing to do. See, the forest cudn' kill; least not in the ways that humans do. Tha' wuz somethun' that ut could not even contemplate but holding ut here, keeping ut barely alive, well, that wuz its speciality. But that Maddy, that witch, she who had done that swap, she'd called time on ut. Fair 'nuff. 'Twas time. She knawed ov ut and the forest knawed ov ut.

With tha', you might have thought 'twas all over. But naw, see humans never learn, do um? They d'never knaw when to call ut quits, and that Cornish energy, that drive, the pushing downwards into the earth, was about t'come back and give um another slap across the faace. 'Twould be some sore you. 'Twas certainly goin' t'need someone t'draw on every bit of Methodist verve they ever had lurkin' inside ov um. What ee reckon?

34

Dunnaw you. 'Tis hard t'tell. All you'n say to anyone is dun't make too free ov themselves or they'll go backwards again. In such situations, 'tis sometimes best to keep the words of a circuit preacher in mind. Your mind then might wonder back to Sunday's drab service and be minded ov the right words in the Good Book. 'Course, ef you wuz Dicky Mint, then you didn' think 'bout tha' t'all. You wuz thinkin' 'bout getting ov your leg over they ov Rosie Koskinen half an hour ago.

All that shouting from George Jewell had levered ee and Rosie Koskinen out ov bed t'gake out the winda' at um. Ut seemed like the Minter wuz someone trying to make too free of hisself. As he got dressed, nearnly tripping over his tin-tipped cane, ee contemplated what had transpired between ee and she. Dicky see, ee'd become one of Rosie's best customers down in the bar below, and loneliness, well, tha' can sometimes force those together, who by rights, should be at the opposite end of things. He'd dallied with the other girls in Rosie's over time, but ee'd always kept his eye on she. 'Mean, ee once thought ee didn' have a hope with she, but these past few months, whilst the rest of the township seemed t'be solely focused on babies and the talk of some strange darkness in the forest (you had to have had your head in the sand not to pick up on tha'), ee'd got to knaw she a bit better.

Ee'd done nice things fur her and tried to shaw ee cared. Ee didn't expect this 'ere now, but maybe she'd like un a bit better. See, the Minter wuz a man who'd actually lived an unsettled life, ov having to hop round 'Merky' supplying head-frame gear and his h'engineering skills to they prepared t'pay. But in truth, ee'd had enough ov tha'. There's awnly so much a man can take ov being uprooted like tha', and ee'd come to the decision that whatever happened here, ee'd put his roots down in this copper country. An' when a man does tha', ee is lookin' for more than just settlement and security, ee is lookin' fur someone to share tha' with. Ut so happened, that ee an' Rosie collided on they matters.

Rosie'd knawn ee liked her fur a while now, and fust ov all, what went between them wuz a kind of teasing: playful insults an' comical comments, but that game developed a bit ov late. Though she still had Justin on her mind (ee'd have been what she really wanted in a man) this Minter might just have to do. Ee wudn' nawthun' to look at (too high a forehead and a fat belly that hid his willy), and the gammy leg didn' help. Ee wuz what, perhaps twenty years older than she too, but what wuz tha' in the run of things? Nawthun', compared t'say, the age ov the forest or the run of the seasons. Then there wuz his daft reputation to consider: the man wuz knawn amongst the miners she served every night, as a bit careless sometimes in boath his designs and ideas. They seemed to suggest tha' he never really thought through the detail ov a mechanism and tha' ut would be left to the men and women on the ground to solve that, whatever obstacle had been presented to them, and ignored by him. But she had found him different: ee'd regularly bought her flowers, when she moaned about the lack of wallpaper available in town, he'd had some high-end patterns brought up all the way from Houghton: but ut wuz not just the materialist side ov things. When Rosie needed someone to talk to, he wuz there fur she. 'Course, she never said a word 'bout she an' Justin all them moons ago, nor what groinal infection passed between them: that had all been sorted now. But the bottom line wuz tha' when she needed company, ee wuz there.

There wuz plenty ov other men who'd like to have given that Rose Koskinen their company but these days, she allays kept her distance from they. She had successfully transformed herself from a lady of the night inta somethun' very different. Minter didn' ask much 'bout tha' and she liked un fur ut. Ut wiped the slate clean. Ee might well have guessed at her past, but so what? She had knawn his predilections too. Ut wuz like-fur-like, and sometimes tha' can be a good thing. Ut bonds. The scales ov justice make balance in the thing, and fur they pair, tha' might be jus' wha' wuz needed. Besides, she rather liked the fact tha' she wuz associating herself with an h'engineer. H'engineers had status in mining societies, so if a Cap'n wudn' on offer, then maybe someone like ee wuz the next best thing.

The doctor's shoutin' brought them back t'reality. They'd been dozing after their frenzy of copulation, which had, in point of fact, been nawthun' lasting. 'Twud do though. 'Twud do.

"Whaas a saying?" asked the Minter, intrigued.

"He's saying he's getting married to Eleanor..."

"Eleanor?"

"You know, the woman from Calumet who is staying with me."

"Ah," said Dicky confirming he knawed who 'twas. "She..."

"We could do with a wedding," observed Rosie. "The last one was his daughter with Francis..."

"Es..."

"I suppose he is free to marry again now. Aren't there laws though, about how long you have to wait if someone leaves you?"

"There probably are back in Europe," said Dicky logically (ee worked like tha' see, being a man of pistons and rods, or levers and gears), "but not up here. I mean the state of Michigan has a lot of laws on its books, but I don't know the ruling on tha'."

Rosie was still at the winda' watching them.

Dicky swung his gammy leg off the bed and sat upright. He did a small fart, which he tried to hide, and then began to dress. Rosie considered the hope of marriage. Maybe now ut might come to she too. Nawthun' like tha' had been discussed with Mr Mint, an' yet had she spoke to him bout ut, she might well have been surprised, because unlike moast men, the Minter may well have been receptive to ut. She didn' turn around to look at un, gruntin' and heavin' like a stuck boar. 'Twudn' pleasant. She saw the run of hair up his back from his ass crack.

Maybe in her own mind she'd spent the night and the morning in bed with someone else. He wuz a substitute: another changeling. This wuz something she knew, but she parked this thought where it would not be found. Had the Finns had confession like the Irish, then ut may have been something she'd air, but well, nawbody wuz watchin' she up here, wuz um? She doubted that even God had his nawse inta' everyone's business on the Keweenaw, so far away from the rest of the world wuz they.

"I'd best be getting back," said Dicky. "I ah... need to see Samuel and Cap'n Trevorrow. We begin the cut tomorrow..."

Rosie understood. She knew that the cut meant preparing the ground fur the tramway. Running at an incline, down the mountainside, ut somehow made her feel close to Eagle Harbour. As things become familiar, distances contract, doan't they? Whereas once upon a time, up here had seemed completely isolated, the incline showed that in fact, things were closer than she thought. The incline would negate ravines and rivers. Ut would push through difficult terrain. She knew ut. She recalled the time when that pair Francis and Justin Nankervis had first turned up at the Cliff hotel.

"When do you think you will run through my old place?"

By now, she had gathered this information. Justin hadn't told her, but the Minter had. Ee'd been direct about ut, not fully understanding the emotional connection she had had to the place. But tha' wuz all over anyway now, wudn' ut? Thaas why she asked.

"Fairly quick I d'reckon," replied Dicky. "Samuel and I reckoned on two teams of navvies; one pushing up from the bottom and one coming down from the mine. Meet in the middle see..."

She understood. She knew how ut went.

Dicky wuz 'eaving on his stockings and boots now. Outside, the Doctor and his lady-friend had walked back up the street and gone into his house again.

"What will you do now?" asked the Minter.

"Rest," said Rosie.

He kissed her goodbye and walked down the staircase, into the bar. Nawbody wuz in except a few ov the other girls. They knawed wha' wuz on though, and they wudn' say nawthun' t'nawbody. Rosie, they reckoned, deserved a bit ov happiness, and if Mr Mint could offer ut to she, then who wuz to question ut? After all, Mr Mint wuz worth a dime or two as well, wudn' a? Good on she.

Rosie tried resting but she cudn' sleep. What she'd done with Dicky Mint played on her mind. Had she stooped that low that ee wuz good enough fur she? But then, what other choices were there? The man she wanted wuz proper loved up with a bouncing baby boy. Like we all, she had t'make the moast of ut. Chances in life were few, and up here on the Keweenaw, they were fewer than ever. Sometimes you had to make do. Tha' wuz what the Cornish always did: they made do. But she was a Finn though. What kept her awake wuz that lingering feeling that it wouldn't do to make do. That wasn't the way of her people.

Not much more happened that day, which wuz a good thing t'be honest. Sometimes, time is better weighed out in cupfuls rather than tipped out on ee all at once. Skews and the Minter met and planned. Boys in the mine had been assigned roles in making the cut. The Finns would need to be fust in, to cut back the timber. Underground, Francis would keep things ticking over, so enough ore would still be mined, and on the grass end, Justin would see to ut that plenty wuz processed and trundled down to Eagle Harbour in the usual wagons. Like before, when they'd constructed the engine houses, enough stock had been brought t'grass already to keep the laker captains happy. So after the Finns, in would go the Cornish and the Germans, making sure that the land fur the incline was shaped right. Francis and Justin would have a more skeleton crew with they, an' then the rest of the Irish would pick up any other aspects of labouring that would be required: that wud likely include the heavy lengths of track that needed to be shipped up.

Now, in the normal run ov things Maddy O'Donahue would have been in there with they, making preparations and helping to co-ordinate things, but not any more.

Instead, her man Flannery would be doing all ov tha'. A hard nut ee wuz but he knew how t'manage a team ov boys. The Irish would get the job done. Maddy wudn' goin' to be there fur obvious reasons. She wuz too busy looking after her bab. That day see, she had done a precious thing and tried to negotiate with nature. She'd tried to get ut on her side. She knawed ov the tramway but ov' course, when she got back an' Justin told her tha' they wuz about to start work the next day on the cut down through the mountain, well, she wudn' best pleased. Put ut this way: 'twudn' the best ov timings, not after what she had said to the trees and the sprites.

Maybe now though, they'd understand. Maybe her persuasive powers would have made the forest rethink its actions. She had to believe this, for the reality wuz that she did fear ut. She feared exposure, and she felt ef anyone might do ut, then ut would be the forest. She dared not tell any of this t'Justin, or he'd think she might be best consigned to a downstate asylum, but in everything that she did, she kept up a pretence; yet inside, deep inside, ut unnerved her. The unnerving itself wuz strange; she had not felt that emotion before. Normally, she'd stay hard as nails. She hoped she was not cracking. So like that Rosie, she just got on an' did her best like wha' moast woman do. But men see, just mope. The awnly thing she could do wuz hope that somewhere out there, somewhere on the mountain, fur a change, something good was happening. She tried to imagine ut. She even tried to conjure ut.

Across from she, wuz her Justin. Ee wuz holdin' their Jago Ciaran in the air, and making whoopee noises to entertain him. She wuz glad fur him to momentarily take over childcare duties. Frankly, she never had much hope with that bugger, but to watch un now, well, ee wuz a different man, grawin' right inta' the role ov a decent feythur. She knew how she had changed too. She was becoming softer. Motherhood does that to ee somehow. You'n resist ut all you like but something happens. Your cells reform. They combine in different ways and send new messages to your brain. She wuz feeling ut at this point. Maybe the Doc wuz right about how the hormones kick in. Chemistry see. Metallurgy.

"Word has ut that Doctor Jewell's getting married again..." noted Justin.

"With she?"

"Es."

Justin held baby Jago high in the air so he was soaring like an eagle. He was gurgling and smiling, loving the play with his father. Maddy, he wuz forming a connection: a connection of muscle, smell and taste. They were ingesting ov each other. Maybe tha' biological connection wuz less important than people think? But then, Jago didn' knaw tha', an' neither did Justin Nankervis.

"How do you know?"

"Ee announced in the street. Walt Chegwidden heard ov un... some hollering from un apparently"

"Oh, I see."

More ground beneath Maddy fell away. Where wuz a Knockie when you needed one?

What if?

What about?

Not awnly was ut falling out from beneath her feet; it seemed t'be falling on her head too. It felt like the whole level was collapsin' in on itself. An' when she felt tha' she wondered ef it wuz come-uppance for what she'd done: the reckoning. She moved across the scullery to where Justin wuz sat. She knew he and Jago were bonding, but right at tha' moment she needed to hold Jago. Even Justin sensed ut, so he suspended his game and handed the boy back to her. Awnly when she was fully clasping him, and he smiling up at her did she feel any sense of reassurance. Magic could do good things and bad things, and at this moment, she wondered which way ut might go. When she later put Jago to bed in his cradle, he slept soundly, as did Justin beside her. And when Luk walked in, he nestled down beside the cradle, like they wuz one happy family. Luk seemed happier, and not so scared. Maybe something *had* shifted. The sprites had seemingly stopped their threats of bears, wolves and ov burying the little man alive.

But she... well she... had a restless night.

Further up the town, when the darkness came down and the moon rose, two other parents were doing their best. Sometimes, tha' is all you can do. See what nawbody had told Francis and Rebecca wuz that Pookas grow very differently to other babies. Other babies grow steady, but Pookas, well, they grow wilfully. An' they have fits and starts. Sometimes, nothing would change for days, or maybe even weeks, or months, and then sometimes too, they'd suddenly mutate and alter, like someone had re-written all the rules about how babies should grow and develop. In part, this wuz because Pooka changelings could think things and make them happen. They could will change in themselves. They didn' wait for nature. Who'd have thought ut? Not even the Knockies could do tha'. So this Richard sometimes seemed to grow much larger than the average baby, and so too, did seem to consume more milk. That day they'd runned out of milky daishals. Moast of the stock around the mine had already been used up, and when the little bugger did latch on to Rebecca's breast – an' t'be honest, he was never tha' keen – ov late, ee'd near 'bout sucked she dry. At the end of ut, she felt deflated and all out of energy and verve.

Earlier on that night, she and Francis had put Richard in the cradle for a rest, and then soon as their back wuz turned, he'd tipped over the lot. He'd used his weight to see-saw the cradle's rockers, so that eventually they went up at a ninety-degree angle. That then allowed un to scramble out an' do wha' mischief he liked. You might consider Francis and Rebecca irresponsible parents, but to see such actions as this in a baby wuz completely unexpected. Do ee knaw what he did, you? Well, fust, ee crawled over to the grate ('mean, how many babies can do tha' when them barely a week old?) an' he managed to push a poker inta' the flames t' land a hot coal on Gourgy's foot. You'n jus' imagine the row. You'n imagine wha' language comed out ov Gourgy's geht hole ov a mouth. 'Twudn' stuff you'd want t'ever say in front ov a preacher, thaas fur sure. Knockies all knawed cusses beyond cusses. But then again, t'be honest 'twudn' stuff you'd want t'say in front of anyone. At ut, Gourgy wuz up dancing round the room on one leg, grabbing his foot like as if ee wuz doing some kind ov jig down a kiddleywink.

"Wozzon?" asked Francis sardonically at fust.

"Cen't you see?" pleaded Gourgy. "Your boy here eaved a hot coal onto me foot. Ut burnt like hell."

Ee wuz right. Francis could smell the slight singe of Knockie skin. Besides tha', Gourgy's skin had turned black, which wuz never a good sign.

"Bad boy!" said Gourgy directing his anger at the baby, who even he saw had grown a lot.

But baby Richard didn' look unduly concerned. Instead, he just laughed at the Knockie and grizzled up at un, seemingly delighting in the pain ee had caused un.

"I dun't think he meant t'do ut," said Francis, trying hard to account for his son's behaviour.

"Dun't ee?"

"No. He's exploring, isn't he?"

"Well, he need to explore away from the fire and not 'eave hot coals on me feet."

The Knockie had a point. Francis was trying to defend his son, but inside, ee knawed ut wuz indefensible. But what could a do? Francis never liked hitting kids (he and his brother had had enough ov tha' off their awn feythur when he comed home beered up from the Wink), and it wudn' like ee wuz goin' to gibm a little slap over the back ov his legs. He didn' think ee'd ever need t'punish a baby. But then, the fire, tha' wuz dangerous. Perhaps boy Richard needed to knaw right from wrong. Maybe he quickly needed to learn what wuz safe and wha' wasn't. His fear wuz that one day seeing as how he wuz a bit of an escapologist he'd head down the mine itself and stick his nawse into somethun' really dangerous. Then, there really would be consequences.

"He's laughing at we," noted Gourgy. "Look."

Richard was gaking at them boath, laughing his little head off, in celebration of the chaos he'd just caused.

Ut wuz interesting how Gourgy had altered his position on the boy. When initially he had fed him the daishal milk, he'd been kindly and loving, but now ut seemed like Gourgy judged un as the Devil incarnate.

"I dun't like un," he said nonchalantly. "Look too, where the coal's burnt a mark on the planchen."

Ee wuz right. Francis picked up the coal with the fire tongs and placed it back into the grate, where ut fizzled into life once more.

He wuz still holding his foot, and pressing it, to try an' alleviate the pain ov the burn.

"Some row! Whatever's goin' on in here?" said Rebecca, coming back through from the kitchen. "What's that smeech?"

"Gourgy's burning foot..." said Francis, resigned to the situation.

"Whaas happened?"

"That psycho there..." said Gourgy pointing at the baby.

"Richard accidently moved a hot coal onto Gourgy's foot."

"My Gar! How did a do that?"

"'Twudn' naw accident," noted Gourgy. "Ee did ut on purpose, ee did."

"Naw. Ee wouldn't do that..." protested Rebecca, still thinking that a chield like ee wuz as innocent as the day wuz long.

This is how Pookas work see. They knaw how to manipulate. They work out how to cause mischief and chaos. They work out how to make those who should offer love, hate each other. They are a bit twisted like tha' but thaas the magical realm fur ee. Naw sense of Wes-ley in um t'all.

"Gourgy's right," said Francis correcting his wife. "Looks like our boy got out of the cradle."

Rebecca wuz forced to look across the room. There she saw his upturned cradle. Although she saw the evidence, that didn' stop her from gathering up Richard, checking he was aright then placing him back into his cradle. A mother's instinct see:

at that moment, ut locked in.

"I'm so sorry," apologised Rebecca. "I'll get a bandage. Some carbolic..."

Gourgy scowled at the baby and the baby scowled back.

"See," stated Gourgy, folding his arms.

This was the trick of this Pooka. Ee knawed see, that Gourgy wuz hot-blooded and could be wound up in an instant. Ee'd found his first target, though he could see that there were many more to poke fun at. You cudn' odds this: thaas the way Pookas think see. They'm awnly in ut fur the laugh. They got nawthun' to lose.

"Ef I wuz you," said Gourgy, "I would take a banjo-shovel, scoop ee up and tip un in the furnace of the boiler..."

"What?!" said Rebecca, re-entering, carrying a nest of bandages and some soothing carbolic cream. She didn't fully hear what he had said, but got the tone of ut.

"You heard," said Gourgy. "Take my advice or leave ut."

"Did you saying something about scooping him up?"

Francis gave his old underground friend a look not to say anymore but he understood his Knockie's sentiment.

"Es. Scooping un up and givin' un a bit of love. Need warming dun't ah? Properly cold he wuz... and thaas why he went to the furnace... I mean, the fire..."

Francis nodded at him. He'd done enough to extricate himself from what he had originally said. Meanwhile, Rebecca knelt down to rub soothing carbolic cream into his skin, and bandaged his foot.

"Better?" she asked, tying up a knot from the bandage ends.

"Yes. Lot better thank you." Gourgy said, but you could tell from his tone that he still wudn' happy.

Tha' wuz ut with Knockies see. 'Twas all about protection. When a miner comes to they, they have to swear an oath, t'allays protect the miner, an' ef necessary, the miner's family. But this thing here in the cradle, well, ut didn' seem part of their family at all. Instead, ut was a snake in the grass. That snake or that boy – whichever 'twas – wuz proper tickled up. He'd done zactly what he wanted. He already knawed he was a changeling see, and well, changelings knaw from the outset that they'm second-best. What more reason do ee need to understand how their minds work?

Rebecca went back into the kitchen again, returning the unused bandages and cream to a cupboard.

"You want to watch ee," said Gourgy, clambouring up Francis' leg and torso and then placing himself right in front of Francis' face. He used his gangly arms to hold on to Francis' shoulders and pressed his knees into Francis' chest. "Ee idn' right in the 'ead. An' by my reckoning you ent right in the 'ead 'anging on to ee any longer."

Francis knawed what ee wuz saying. In fact, ee'd felt ut himself. Ee'd felt ut when ee had that stain of jealousy about his brother erupt all over his body. But maybe still, ee wuz in denial. We humans are like that see. Magical creatures are more honest and upfront, but well, humans, allays like t'think they'n do better: that they dun't need tellun'. Allays too full of themselves, they are.

"We'n work on un," said Francis. "Rebecca an' I..."

"What, train un?"

"Yes. Make him better. Make un' a Methodist... We'll get un t'Sunday School..."

"Ha! What, un have un colouring in pictures of donkeys?"

"'Twill be the best way to improve un. Put un close to the Bible."

Now, Francis didn' really believe tha', but he was gettun' desperate.

"That, what you got there is a proper spriggan," said Gourgy, almost spitting the final word from his mouth. "I dun't knaw how one ov they have ended up here, but I'm tellin ov ee, he idn' something I'd want sleeping in my bedroom."

"How do you know?"

"I dunnaw. I feel ut in me loincloth. In me pick-axe."

"But she gived birth to un..."

"Maybe so, but summin' idn' right..."

"Na. You'm wrong there boy. I knaw you'm allays right underground an' tha' but thaas our Richard. A'right, so ee's a bit of a bewdie... but never mind... I mean, trust me; me an' brother wudn' naw saints when we wuz younger? How the 'ell do you think we ended up here? You knaw all that."

Gourgy considered his words and contemplated what had happened. Maybe his master wuz right. Maybe ee had over-reacted. Certainly, ee didn't really want to feed a baby inta' a furnace. What would that be like? Well, 'twudn' be proper at all. And ef there wuz one thing Knockies liked, well, tha' wuz to do things by their code. Without tha', there wudn' nawthun'.

"Maybe..." said Gourgy, but that wuz all he could manage to say in response.

The bottom line – the bottommost level of ut – was tha' ee wudn' sure.

"Ee'll grow an' mature like we all do... Mark my words."

This was this Francis trying to do the right thing. But even then, he needed to have a good gake into his own heart – somethun' none ov we like t'do. Gourgy wudn' convinced but ee didn' say naw more.

Es. Later on, the moon came up. Es. You d'knaw she: that Yolkai. Now that Mabel, well she wuz still in the forest being lit by the lunar rays. She wuz hopin' t' find somethun' and wuz searchin' hard fur ut. Somethun' inside her told her that now wuz the time. She'd felt ut with the poppet and now she felt a sensation of somethun' else: a callin' if you like – something yanking she ever onwards. Sometimes such matters as these were better in the dark. Sometimes, daylight can deceive. So on she plodded, oblivious to all these shenanigans back in the township.

The boy Jago wuz sound asleep but the boy Richard wudn'. After the incident with the hot coal Rebecca hoped he'd settle. Francis wuz less sure. Ee knawed wha' ee wuz dealing with by now, and so ee wuz a little less comfortable, a little less relaxed; but nonetheless ee managed to sleep. Ee knawed the mine had a big day ahead finally: the start of work on the tramway. Ee wanted t'be fresh and wide awake fur ut. So ee forced hisself to sleep.

But what about Gourgy? Well, the boy wudn' confident ov sleepin' there in Francis and Rebecca's property so ee went back to the old shack that had once been inhabited by his master and his brother. Es, ut felt comfortable there, not like somethun' wuz goin' t'wrap its digits around his thin throat, an' strangle un t'death. Ut wuz safe and there, ee cud burble and dream of fried hog's pudding following by clotted cream on top of jammy scones. Such thoughts allays calmed un. Maybe he'd have chanced ut ef Becca had made some saffron buns but there wuz none in the spence. That bleddy boy – that thing of theirs – was taking up all their time and naw mistake. With his dreams, he tried to forget the throbbin' ov his scorched foot.

Now Becca, as you knaw, wudn' have a bad word said about her boy. Fair 'nuff. All mawthurs are like that see. They never want t'see evil in their awn; they awnly want t'see ut in others. But all tha' wuz about to change. Becca felt that Gourgy wuz harsh about her boy and she cud tell that because of wha' had happened earlier on, ee didn' much care fur'n. Well, she'd just have to change his mind on that. As she started to drift to sleep, she resolved to make un see sense. However, in the cradle this Richard, this liddle Dicky boy wuz up to his tricks again see. His parents had kept un close, but changelings like ee, well, them sneaky see. They do what they want, and night-time is often the best time fur they. They like t'create havoc when the clock strikes midnight. He'd learnt had this bugger, how to leap out of the cradle. He was ingenious too. He knawed what he wuz on upon. So he flexed his limbs did this Pooka and did what he needed to do. Believe ut or not, the bugger could walk! Who'd have thought that ee could get upright and mozey along like tha'? Stroathing around like ee awned the plaace! He tip-toed past his snoring pap and his dozy mam. Rite on, ee told himself. This wuz the way t'do ut. He had ut all down pat. Sneaky this dink ov a fella wuz, but you knaw that by now. You knaw what ee wuz made ov.

Up he climbed then, like a spider, and with a twist ov his feet, he opened the door knob. And then, after dropping down, he went into their parlour. The fire had died down now though, and a guard was up at the grate. Naw fun there. Naw. He wuz on the search fur somethun' else. Tiny ee wuz, but still ee clicked his neck and put out his hands to feel for somethun' he might have some fun with. Pookas have good eyesight too, and in the darkness his eyes found the kitchen. The door there wuz open. He could hear the thud of the pumping bob still (ee chalked tha' up for fun on another day – they maak mental lists do they buggers) but he reckoned on there being plenty to keep un amused in the kitchen. See Pookas dun't like silence. They like noise. They like the depravity and endless scritching and screeching of the underworld: that world that lay far down in the earth, beyond the mine and its levels. Some row wuz what wuz needed. Ee knawed where he wuz heading. Fust, ee climbed onto the dresser (the chippies had made them this as a wedding gift) and there, ee found the enamel-coated tin cups and plates. Aw es – they'd be perfect for what he intended to do.

So in a couple of moves, ee skiddered across the shelving and 'eaved as many of they items of crockery he could onto the kitchen table. That made enough of a row when ee did ut but ut wudn' his end target. From a pot ee pulled out a spoon and jumped onto the table. In his view of the world, 'twas time to make some music and thaas what the wilful bugger did. He bashed every plate and cup as hard as he could with the spoon and caw d'hell, did ut clatter. Ut sounded like the stamps had started work again, or that some twenty people or so were cobbing at ore. Ee delighted in ut, ee did. An' he wuz smiling and dancing like a wild thing. He wuz dancing hard on the table like he was wearing geht hobnail boots, so ut shook and vibrated against the wooden planchen. Laughing he wuz. But ut didn' really sound like laughing. Instead, 'twas more ov a gleeful cackle. What a tuss this boy, eh? Some heller.

Ut wudn' necessarily the banging of the enamelled tin plates and cups that fust woke Rebecca Nankervis. Instead, ut wuz the vibration on the floor, which travelled up the bedpost an' inta' she. In an instant, she knawed ut wudn' Gourgy who wuz making the row. She knew ut was Richard, and when she spied his empty cradle she knew she must act fast. What did they have to do to keep un in his bed? Maybe they'd need to tie un right down in the future: straight-jacket un. She genuinely contemplated this as she pulled on her dressing-gown over her nightwear. Now, the sound wuz clearer. Someone wuz in the kitchen and had grabbed all the crockery off the dresser. She could sense ut. At the same time, she comed to realise that what Gourgy had said earlier wuz true. This boy of theirs – he wudn' just a bit naughty – aw naw, he wuz properly wayward, an' with a mean an' vicious streak to un too. Ef her feythur saw un, she feared he'd think the baby was of the Devil himself. She cudn' allow tha' to happen.

Now, in her role as a school-ma'am on Mountainside, she'd dealt with some rowdy an' temperamental individuals. She knew how destructive children could be: how disobedient they could be at times – often just so as to see her reaction. Ut seemed the same way with this thing. In making her way through to the kitchen she knew he wuz no longer something she wanted clasped to her breast. That place was reserved for niceness and love, not this. After all the attempts to feed him – and the advice of her feythur and Maddy O'Donahue – now she no longer wanted to nurse him. Ef tha' made her a bad mawthur, she didn' care. This wuz she now.

She looked around the open door, and ut wuz as she expected. The varmint was atop the table givin' ut beans with his spoon and making a veritable orchestra of noise. Richard wuz lovin' ut, but she could sense the houses around them were already wondering about the noise being made, having been woken up by the din.

"You'n stop that right away," Rebecca said, calling every inch of her old school-ma'am self into her body.

"No," said Richard and laughed at her, blowing her a huge raspberry with his lips and tongue.

That surprised her so much she almost fell over. What? Now they had a baby who could talk. Ee learnt fast. All changelings do. But then standing on the table, ut didn't look much like naw baby. Ut looked like somethun' else that she cudn' give no words to. Ef she had a thousand years devoted to the task, she wudn' have been able to describe what stood there – and hell, out ov her womb too, her skin and blood: her and Francis. She didn' care fur what stood before her. And then, as she watched, there were flashes of her baby dancing: like drops of light which flashed between his dancing, that made her look again. What wuz a? Wuz a under some kind of spell? Ut cudn' be. She'd allays been sceptical of such matters. She knawed she wuz like her father in this way: all book learning and science, not superstition and folktale.

Wha' she did knaw wuz tha' this wuz the same being who had dropped a hot coal on Gourgy's foot. Ut wuz as Francis said. Knockies allays told the truth. She hated herself now fur thinking ill ov that Gourgy. In fact, she wished he wuz here now. He'd knaw what to do widn' and make un stop the noise. Clank, clank, ut went. Clank, clank again! Aw. Harsh on the ears ut wuz. Maybe he'd been ill-wished in some way. She'd heard of such tales at home but dismissed them. That wuz the lore of the moor, and well, nawbody listened t'tha' anymore, did un? But then ef Knockies wuz true (something she'd awnly knawn of fur a relatively short while), then maybe some other aspects could be true too. Had Mabel kept all those fairy stories at home? She'd definitely need to look.

The closer Becca got to un, the more frenetic his dancing became. When she stepped closer to the table, his banging of the crockery became more intense. She reached her hand in. What she wanted to do wuz to take the spoon away from him. Fur the moment, that would help prevent some of the hubbub. She wuz aware by now, tha' she wuz not the awnly adult in the kitchen. Behind her stood an outraged Francis, also seeing with his own eyes how the uproar was being created. Ee'd been right ee told himself. Gourgy had been right. This, in front of them, wuz what they had. Why them? Why had God provided this for um? He knawed he'd need to speak to Jewell who'd need to be wearing his preacher hat, not his doctoring one.

"How did ee get in here?" he asked his wife involuntarily, but as ee said ut ee had already begun to realise that probably nothing on this earth would contain their son or prevent him from doin' zactly what he wanted. So inventive and so damned cunning wuz a that ee could transcend any restraint and in likelihood, any punishment. They realised in those moments too, that at no time ever in the future were they likely to get the kind of sleep they had obtained in the past. At the very least, one of them would have to stay up and look after him and make sure ee did not do anything violent or dangerous. Everyone said that their lives would change when they had childurn but not this much, surely? Thus wuz too much change to even contemplate or process.

The real moment of change wuz yet to come though. As Francis was thinking through all of this and, in those seconds – the jealousy he felt for his brother, Maddy and their son – Rebecca wuz gingerly moving her hand in towards the spoon. Et wuz like she wuz dealing with a wolf. Richard wuz snarling at she, making threatening noises just like he had done when Justin had been there, At that moment, the noise suddenly temporarily halted. A couple of bowls fell on the floor but these soon stopped rotating and wobbling, and came to a halt. Their neighbours would have been glad: awnly the thudding regular movement of the engine-house bob was discernable once more. The spoon now lay between Rebecca's left hand and the right hand of Richard, and thus ensued a silent tug-of-war on the table top. Fust, ut swung his way, and then back to she. But then, in an instant, the Pooka seemed to realise ee wuz beat. Ee let go of the spoon and it fell to Rebecca. But tha' wudn' the last ov ut. She may have pulled her hand back, but Richard lunged forward. In so doing, in one vicious motion, ee clamped his jaw around Rebecca's index finger and bit down hard.

"Ow!" screamed Becca in agony. "He's got teeth."

In any normal circumstances a baby only a week old having teeth would have shocked the whole of 'Merky'. Indeed, ut would have been a medical marvel, worthy of a write-up in one of George Jewell's medical journals that he always keenly subscribed to, but here now, it didn't seem so odd somehow. Ut just felt like a continuation of the very un-normal life that they had become so used to of late. All that said, their son's frankly unbelievable chomp on his mother's finger wuz the last straw fur Francis. This wuz Francis remember, the boy who wudn' hurt a soul, and who wuz as placid as they comed. But t'see tha', did something inside ov un. You could nawtice a change come over him. Yes, giving his mother a bite was hard enough – that was wha' beasts did – but to then sit back a laugh about ut, well, that infuriated him.

Maybe even this Pooka realised what he had done by now. Ee laughed a little more but then perhaps realised that in that day he'd gone too far. See, there were Pookas, and then there wuz *other* Pookas, and this one wuz definitely of the latter kind. Francis raised his hand. Ee wuz about t'bring ut crashing down on his son, so hard that ut would have scat him flying. Given his age and his form, whatever he wuz, ee wudn' a thing ov strength. Despite his violence, his biting, his noise, his sheer capacity to annoy and be malevolent, at the end of the day, he wuz still an infant. Becca wuz bleeding from the cut he had made. He could see the puncture wounds from his sharp, razor-like teeth, but because of who ee wuz, because ee had been brought up in the ways of forgiveness and peace, ee could not bring himself to lay harm to a hair on his head. And so, the Pooka went unpunished.

But Pookas knaw the minds of humans. Ee knawed he had the advantage: knawed that his smallness, his normal cuteness, his parents' wishes for him, all made sure that he'd get away with ut. And like us all, once we've got away with somethun' once, we'll do ut again and tha' wuz unashamedly the way ov this Pooka boy. Ee knawed he had them right where he wanted them, right on the end of his liddle finger. So ut seemed to ee, if ee asked they to jump that they'd ask him how high. Now such a situation wudn' naw good for the parents, nor naw good fur the chield, but thaas sadly how 'twas there, that night. Realising ov this, Becca retreated into the lowered arm of her husband. He'd take care of her: wash the wound and bandage it. The bite would make a scar though – perhaps even more lasting than the run of trees that had to be cut from the mine down to Eagle Harbour.

Despite all of this, Francis still spoke to his son and said, "You'll never ever do that again Richard. Do you understand?"

Ee didn' expect him to respond. Ut wuz the kind of discipline that adults hand out to childurn all the time, knowing all too well that ut is likely to be impossible to enforce. What came back from Richard was a seething hiss of anger. The very Devil hisself this chield! Whatever wuz a like? Possessed wuz a? Fur now, ee didn' knaw. All ee wanted to do wuz to get his wife's finger bandaged and her calmed down. All ee knawed wuz that somethun wudn' right. And as is the way with such things, ut wud come to gnaw at un on the inside.

Still, this Richard didn' seem to care. The moment he'd turned to a bowl and poured in a jug of water in order to wash Becca's hands, as if something oozing, this Pooka had climbed down the table leg and wuz now at the winda'. Ee wuz looking out the winda' and up at the moon. An' somehow, as he saw his reflection in the winda', Francis nawticed that although he wuz a baby, at times when he turned, when the moonlight caught him, he shifted into something older, something unsettling. By the time he looked across again, the boy had opened the winda' catch and gone out into the night. Now they had another problem, but fur the moment, boath ov they wuz glad to see the back obm. Now, is that any way for a pair of parents to speak about their child? Not really, but then again, as you knaw very well, this wudn' their chield. Ee wuz behaving to type see: just like all changelings do, just like they have ever done, in a thousand stories across the earth. And now this one; another one to add to the geht list of they.

The awnly thing they could do now wuz to pick up the discarded cups and plates and arrange them back on the dresser. Then they'd put his spoon back into the pot. After tha', Francis took a shaken Rebecca back into their bedroom, and they climbed into the sheets together holding each other tight for love, for compassion and for hope that things might turn around. Neither of um looked over at the cradle. They knawed all too well jus' wha' wuz missing. Right there an' then, there wuz nawthun' they could do 'bout ut. Awnly perhaps when ee wuz 'ungry would the boy come back.

35

Bolting Pookas wuz bad enough eh, but right then, at the same time that all of this wuz occurring, elsewhere on the mountain Mabel Jewell pushed on into the forest. She felt like the moonlight wuz guiding her. Each time, that momentarily her route got lost, the moon would release another shaft of incandescence that lit her path. Occasionally, breaks in the run of dark trees enabled her to be able to look down upon the seemingly infinite waters of Lake Superior. How vast ut looked from up here. She thought of all that time ago when she and her family had first arrived, and the exciting words of her father to she and her sister about how it was all going to be such an adventure. Ut had perhaps not been the adventure she thought ut might be, but nonetheless, she could still appreciate his words. Maybe it was better than Cornwall. Maybe ut wuz better than the safe life she had once had back there. Here, there lurked a certain danger, from things like the tomahawk that Nimkii had taught her to throw, the risk of industrial accident (always the case in mining zones), but also this confounded darkness about the forest. Mabel was a creature who the forest accepted though. Ut noted the empathy in her. There wuz never a conflict with she. The one had respect fur the other, and over time, a different relationship had been forged.

Nimkii had trained her well in the ways of the woods. He'd shown her how to survive, told her where to find water and food, explained what not to eat, and how, without causing long-term damage, one might utilise all that wuz on offer. If used properly the forest would offer a lasting relationship with humanity. What had been missing on Mountainside, wuz that humanity had forgotten this pact – this lasting covenant. She knew Skews had spotted ut; she knew that he had seen through the relationship she had with Nimkii. She realised too, how that must have come across to someone like him.

What she liked about Nimkii was that he cared about her in a way that she valued. Oh, her father and then Jenny Spargo, they cared about her to an extent, but awnly in ways that satisfied their needs; not hers. They had not been physical yet; Nimkii was older than she, and he respected her position and age always. Indeed, their relationship so far had been a different kind of love; a love that wuz somehow more sacred than the rest of those in the township. She knew what they were embarking on was different. She knew how ut would look, but this did not worry her. She was Mabel Jewell, and she wuz a free spirit.

She knew that one day the mine would close; that wuz the brutal inevitability of mining. What then, she wondered? She knew her father, that Miss Prowse and James would probably move down to Calumet, and maybe so too, her sister, her husband and their boy Richard. By then though, she realised that the edifice of a chapel that her father wuz trying to build would paradoxically have a short life. The moment the mine had a plan of abandonment (the way the levels were flooded and how all the gear wuz returned to grass), ut would have to shut its doors and be left. At the same time, the community there would stutter and fail, and then fall into neglect. What then would become of all these chapels the Cornish were erecting in order to stamp their faith on the earth? They'd likely become curiosities of a long-forgotten past, and people would become sentimental about them. Some might be preserved but others would fall by the way – the way of all monuments.

None of tha' mattered now. No. Here, she had a different purpose. When she got far enough away from the mine not to hear the continual judder of the bob and its connecting rods into the earth, the forest sounded different. Ut no longer cowered or hid away from her. Its sounds became vivid again. She could hear a thousand different movements which worked together so as to calm her and ready her for what wuz coming, and exactly what was to be brought to her. She thought of Maddy O'Donahue: now there wuz a woman who understood, who wudn' like the rest, who seemed, well, to know what she wuz thinking. She'd felt this about Maddy a long time ago, when she wuz younger. There wuz a connection between them but neither of them ever spoke ov ut. Somehow, there wuz never a need to. She didn't have much to do with the Knockies either. They knew she could see them, and to Mabel, they were just another layer of life that she accepted. There wuz nothing strange in they at all. Accepting then, wuz this maid, full ov openness and aware of all of the infinite opportunities of the earth, sea and sky. She'd not shut herself down like moast humans.

The forest knew all of this. Ut wuz why from the distant and hidden ravine, the roots lifted up the form of a human and pushed it upwards into the moonlight. So bright did it shine that its brightness filtered through the moss and lichen clawthes that this thing wore, and thus cast its thin body into shadow. It then got carted through the forest, reaching tree limb after reaching tree limb, bending down to clutch it and pass on the parcel. There wuz no weight to it: this thing wuz fragile as gossamer, and following the words of Maddy, the elders of the forest had decreed that it should be returned. All had been forewarned to be careful with it and not to let it be dropped. A fall might shatter it to pieces. On it passed then, between lime and oak, between maple and birch: a wave of energy carrying it forth through the forest's twists and turns, where saplings observed and noted how things could be done. Back in the ravine, at the bottom of the gully, a fairy ring formed to mark wha' had once been there. Fungi coalesced and made it so.

Somehow, Mabel knew what was coming. She could hear the whoosh and spring back of branches, the lilting and lulling motion of something being passed on. All the while, the moonlight watched: the being, the goddess, that Nimkii called Yolkai. In the end, the thing that wuz anticipated by Mabel some time ago, arrived in the quiet hand of a massive maple. The maple had collected it from a birch tree who now stood back and watched what was about to unfold. Mabel turned to see its actions, and noted the four fingers and the thumb of branches and leaves turn and twist ninety degrees so that this thing was deposited on the earth vertically, just as ut had been found in the past.

And was it?

"Yes," Mabel responded.

Is this?

"My Mother?"

What had been handed over was not how she remembered her mother, but in truth, she had never expected her to be the same. Nimkii had told her that she would have changed massively, and probably initially have the look more of the earth and tree bark than of skin and flesh. He had been right: her mother's form smelt dank and looked almost unrecognisable, and yet still, Mabel recognised her: that bond between childurn and their mawthurs see, ut es never broken. Ut allays stays strong. What her body was enveloped in was actually extremely beautiful: a dress formed fully of moss and lichen, through which poked hundreds of differently-coloured flowers.

Her mother again. Es. Her mother – still there – clad in clawthes of wonder, but still there. How odd wuz this? She had been recovered. She wuz not the same, and she never could be: not after what had happened to her. But the thing wuz, none of that mattered. This wuz because now she could go back home. Mabel knew the burden well. She tried speaking to her.

"It's you," said Mabel. "We've missed you so much..."

And Mabel knew that her mother wanted to speak but that she could not. She was trying to shape her lips and respond, but nothing came. When one is silent for so long, one loses that ability; that much was obvious. It would come again, Mabel felt. But now, no words between them were really needed. The daughter hugged her mother and kissed her face. Her skin tasted peaty damp and of the copper earth, but no matter.

"Thank you," Mabel said to the forest, "for her safe return."

But no response came. The forest stayed the same as it had always been. Maybe that was all it needed to say.

"Let me take you home, eh?"

Mabel reached for her mother's hand. When she reached for her palm and fingers she thought that her skin would feel cold to the touch, but instead, there was a warmth. Alive then. The wood had kept her incubated at least. But ut had certainly worn her down, she realised that. Her mother wuz weathered and had prematurely aged. And maybe in the pattern of all of this, ut was not the forest's method of deliverance that had shocked Mabel the moast, ut was purely this: that so many years were put on her and that they could never be given back. She was old before her time – the worst fate of all. Nonetheless, she had to be thankful. Her mother's heart wuz beating, and with that, could come repair. The hope wuz that now things might be fixed.

"You don't even know, do you? You're a grandmother now! Yes, Becca's had a baby boy named Richard. She and Francis Nankervis. Oh, you should see him. He's adorable..."

This daughter then, the wayward one, the one who her mother always worried about as being too dreamy and too far gone with the fairies, was now tightly clasping the hand of that same mother (and now grandmother) and leading her out of the forest. Mabel understood ut: this was the fairy-tale moment. She had been released from the thorns and briars, and was now heading back to the world of love and understanding. Maybe her time in the forest would have given her mother a new strength, a new resolve. She spoke of such things as they walked, but there came no response from the older woman.

At present, maybe her mother did not even realise that she was being guided by Mabel. Indeed, ut felt like maybe Clara Jewell had forgotten everything. Maybe ut would come back, once she saw familiar places and faces. She had to hope for that at least. And yet she was frail, frail as a fall leaf, whose veins held still, but whose surfaces between them were starting to turn to brown and copper dust. Any longer, she realised, and this woman would not have made it. How had she survived the winter? How had she kept warm? Somehow, the stoic innovation of the forest had managed ut. She could only barely contemplate how it had achieved this aim but at the same time she knew of the wonders of nature. Nimkii had often reminded her of it.

They pushed on in the night, returning along the route she had completed earlier, a fair few miles away now from the handover, back to the immediate forest around the camp. Dawn was breaking now. An autumnal sun lifted itself above the eastern horizon and lent morning shadows to every object in its beam. Mabel still chittered on, telling her mother about the changes that had occurred, and in so doing, she recalled the conversation she'd had with Mr Skews and Cap'n Trevorrow.

"You'd have been proud of me," Mabel said. "I set them straight."

But at the same time, she knew what was coming. She knew that as soon as the disc of morning light grew bold enough for men to work in, there would next come the sound of sawing, the shouts of "Timber!" and the breaking of new ground with Cornish shovels. She had managed to rescue her mother through a closing door that soon would be locked tight. How close ut was! How had ut all come to this?

At the edge of the township, where a long time ago, her mother had first felt the forest call, they stopped. Mabel needed to contemplate their next move. She could perhaps take her to Nimkii's camp at the collar of the mine. Maybe alternatively, she could go and see Maddy, and show her what she had found. She would know what to do. Retrospectively, that option would probably have been the moast sensible thing to have done, but you have to imagine the joy that this Mabel felt in rediscovering her mother, as well as all the lost time that needed to be made up. Thaas wha' Mabel wuz thinkin' ov, and ut motivated her to do something different. Instead, she took the most natural option; the one that felt right in her heart. The town wuz still quiet as she entered ut. All its residents were still inside, levering themselves out of bed-sheets and eiderdowns: perhaps boiling on the stove their first pot of coffee of the day. They entered the main street. No eyes greeted them. They were stealth itself these pair. Just like the Pooka boy. Es, just like ee.

"Come on," said Mabel. "It's safe. You know it here."

So she led her ever onwards, and then at the top, they climbed up some steps in order to knock upon the door of one familiar house. An oil light was already on inside so the occupants were up. There were voices inside, all of which Mabel recognised, but on her mother's face, there was no cognisance. Instead, the woman with her gave no sign of recognition of the place, and just stared blankly ahead. At this moment, Mabel saw past her premature aging. In fact, she now looked resplendent in her dress of moss and lichen, the heads of hundreds of flowers poking through, even as if she were to be married in some ceremony from long ago.

The door opened. The man who opened it asked how he might help, but was rather surprised still at the early-morning interruption to his breakfast. He was humming a tune that carried a purposeful energy, and in an instant, Mabel knew where that came from: some other process in the building of a consummate chapel for the community had obviously just fallen into place. Then he looked at them and his humming stopped. In some state they both were. In fact, many things stopped at that moment for Doctor Jewell.

"Look who I found lost in the woods," said Mabel.

Here wuz a swap – an old wife fur a new one, and yet another changeling.

36

Gah! A bigger lerraps you party had never see'd a'fore Richard the deviant Pooka scrambled out of the winda' and wildly disappeared with a geht fart and a burp out inta' the night. 'Twas a mute question whether ee knawed much about the forest, nor the shimmering of Yolkai's moonlight up there, but ee didn' come back before dawn, and ee wuz clearly intending on being out there fur the rest ov tha' next day. 'Twas true enough that in awnly a short number ov days, ee'd become a fearsome and baissly-looking ol' thing, and the toxic boy still kept on grawin' and developin', even though ee wuz far from the nurture and kindness ov his worried parents. He played with their nerves. There seemed naw stoppin' ov un. Ee wuz like a mazed thing; proper out of control. There wuz innocent changelings like Clara Jewell, and then, there wuz this un.

Ee had found the schoolhouse door locked but nonetheless, like quicksilver, ee'd squeezed hisself through a left-open gap at the bottom of a sash winda' in the schoolhouse an' had a gake at everything in there. Now Pookas are naturally intelligent see, and so wide-eyed wuz ee with his terrible vision, he'd decided to take chalk and write some rude words all over the blackboard. Then, jus' because ee cud, ee did a few drawings which likely wudn' be much liked of by any Methodist putting their spectacles on an' looking up close at they. After tha', ee took a fountain pen, dipped ov ut messily inta' an inkwell, and because he ee cud, he drewed some big willies all over the Methodist hymnals. Cock over Christ. Es. Tha' wuz just right, ee told hisself. What a little bugger ee wuz!

All that row with the pots and pans, the biting down hard on his mam's finger and now this. When ee'd done all that and proper cackled-up at hisself ee went out through the gap in the winda' again, and began to search for more mayhem. What a heller – allays acting up like there wudn' naw tomorra'. Es. Full of sauce and impertinence ee wuz – a proper bowjack.

But hang fire! Across town, George Jewell wuz still looking with horror on the ghastly figure that his daughter had brought back to his door. Es – ee jumped like a mackerel did tha' boy at the sight of she. Of course, he recognised Clara, but could not believe the fact that she had been found, and had somehow managed to survive alone in the dank forest for all this time. What ee did not know wuz that she had not really been on her own: in fact, the forest had nurtured her, even if, in point of fact, it had barely kept her alive. They'd fed her just enough. That all disturbed him, but even more so did her appearance. There was boath the shock of what she wuz wearing: a dress consisting of moss and lichen, the mesh of which was darted through with the heads of flowers; but then, there was her awful ageing. 'Twas like looking at your awn mortality seein' she.

Ut wuz this latter aspect of her appearance that disturbed him the moast. Ut was not just a layer of mud or forest mould over her either; she had definitely aged, as if some twenty years or more of her life had been lost. At first, Jewell could not even speak. An ocean of thoughts tumbled through his head. How was he meant to accept her back after all this time? Did she madly just think she could pick things up again? He also knew how rapidly his own situation had changed of late: he was now due to be married to the bounteous Eleanor Prowse, a woman who, in many ways, he had much more in common. Primarily, there was the question of why she had gone in the first place, but even if he asked that, he suspected that an answer would not be forthcoming.

In that moment, he had decided that he would not be letting down Eleanor Prowse but simultaneously, a huge pang of Wesleyan guilt ran through him. What stood before him was his wife, the mother of his children and his supposed partner for life. Before God, they had made solemn commitments, and there he wuz now thinking of breaking them and of completely ignoring them. He was his own worst enemy in this respect. On Sunday mornings and evenings he had always preached about the sacred nature of marriage (to offset rampant venereal disease there, and of course, to provide a loving home for children) and those listening in the outside pit or inside the schoolhouse, had allays been reminded of the fact that his own wife had somehow disappeared backalong. What jubilation in his mind there should be now that she had returned to him, but he was aware of the fact that this thing before him brought him absolutely no joy at all. How could he reconcile tha' with his congregation? They'd have un fur ut, good an' proper.

All the while Clara Jewell gazed through him, as if he were some kind of new, rare tree tha' had come inta' blossom. He dare not even bring out James to meet her. Considering her pallid look and the clawthes she wore, she would probably scare him. Es. She looked like death warmed up.

"Can she speak?" asked Jewell, not wishing to get too close to she.

He realised she had said nothing to him, and seemingly, no look of recognition passed over her face at either him or her old house.

"No," said Mabel. "I don't think so. I've tried talking to her but she's said nothing back. Maybe it's the shock..."

"The shock of what?"

"Being released. Being back here."

"Released from where?"

Jewell was intrigued now. He thought back to his wife's bonnet, the one that Nimkii had found: the one that held the forest mushroom and toadstool spores which had destroyed a drawer.

"The forest was looking after her. It gave her back to me. I had this feeling see; this idea of where I would find her... The trees... they handed her back..."

Mabel realised that what she was saying sounded profoundly unhinged to her more logical father. He spoke in scientific terms; not notions of activated trees who had feelings of hope and loss. Hadn't he learnt anything at all from watching Nimkii? Seemingly not.

"Nonsense," the Doctor said. He knew his daughter well enough; knew how she could be caught up in romance and fantasy. Then there wuz she and the Indian gentleman. He found that even more disturbing but knew he had no power to do anything about ut. Mr Skews and Cap'n Trevorrow had asked him, but he had no answers fur them.

"What do you mean?"

"She went into the forest freely. It was of her own will that she did so. She can't expect to come back here after all this time and fit in like she never left."

"So you aren't going to take her back then?"

"No. Why on earth should I?"

Mabel knew why. He had a new, replacement wife lined up now. There was no need of the old one. She could seemingly be tossed into the Deads for all he cared. That wuz wha' ee thought of this changeling.

"I thought you were principled. Had a set of morals."

"I do. I am," replied the Doctor, shifting a little uneasily on his feet.

"If you did, then you'd willingly accept her back. When you married her you made commitments: 'in sickness and in health'."

Jewell became exasperated with his daughter.

"You know how she was before she left. Surely you remember?" he gasped. "You can't expect me to give her a wondrous welcome. Remember she not only left me; she also left you and James, and Rebecca... She walked out on the lot of us."

"I don't think she could help it."

"Help it or not," commented Jewell angrily. "What she did was unforgiveable."

See that you. That hardness coming from the mouth of a Methodist. No levity see. Thaas the way of they sometimes you. Watch fur tha' in the future mind, when tha' chapel d'get built.

"I don't want her anywhere near me."

"I thought that..."

"You thought wrong..."

"I see."

"How many other people know?" asked Jewell. "I mean, how am I going to explain this to Eleanor?"

"Nobody," said Mabel, but then she corrected herself. "Nimkii senses it..."

"Oh well, if *he* can *sense* it," said Jewell sarcastically, "then everyone is fine... You continue to believe *his* claptrap I see..."

Mabel ignored his comment. Her father was breathing deeply now. No love was coming forth from him though. She realised why. She knew the hurt that it had caused him, and now that he was seemingly getting over it all, and moving on with his life, here wuz the frail remains of his marriage standing before him.

"Maddy knows too..."

"Maddy O'Donahue? How the hell does she know?"

"I don't know. I can tell. She talks to the forest more than I do."

"Girl, you are not making any sense."

Although he said that, Jewell was nonetheless aware of the rumours. He knew how the town perceived Maddy. In a way, he liked the woman (maybe even better now that she had become a mother) but he knew there was something odd about her: odd in the same way that he knew his own daughter was. For a moment, ut seemed like they pair were boath working against him. Now that he had reach of happiness with Eleanor, along came this pair, apparently seeking to destroy everything. With her reappearance, his plans for the chapel might be put on hold. Indeed, Clara's return might well shake everything from top to bottom, and he could do without that.

"What should I do with her?" asked Mabel, "I mean, if you don't want her..."

"Do what you want," said Jewell, his heart hardening. "Take her to Becca, or perhaps your splendid Maddy O'Donahue. Maybe they'll know what to do."

At this, Jewell turned his back on the earth ghoul and his daughter and stepped back inside of his house – or was it *their* house, once?

"Everything alright?" asked Jenny Spargo, who was at the breakfast table, feeding James some milky porridge.

Jewell gazed over at them. He saw his son. How could he inflict what was outside upon him? From the look of her anyway, she had lost all maternal feelings. She'd obviously become mentally unwell. The reality was that the asylum down in Calumet was the best place for her.

"No," he replied.

The curtness of his response jarred with Jenny, who found what he said and the tone of it very unexpected. Even James picked up on it.

"I must go down to see Eleanor," he said under his breath.

He knew that he was about to have an extraordinarily difficult conversation with Eleanor Prowse. He only hoped that he could persuade her not to catch the very next carriage back down to Calumet, telling anyone there who would listen, how mazed they wuz up in Mountainside.

People often try to cover surprise or anger. They enforce a set of platitudes: words which are meant to hide hurt or intrigue. Maybe – at another time – Mabel might well have said something like he'll come round. He's just surprised, that's all. But when she contemplated saying it, she came to realise what a travesty she had, in fact, inflicted upon her father. She realised how awful it had been for him. Clearly, he'd had a different view of events than she. Mabel had always felt there was hope, even though she could barely remember the things her mother used to say to her. James would not remember a thing. Becca would know more. But her father? Well, he had buried her a long time ago and mined any love out of his heart. The run of it had been scooped out. There'd be no return to that particular stope.

Mabel considered taking her mother to Rebecca. Surely she would be sympathetic? But when it came to it, she moved the withered mass of lichen, moss and flowers across the township down to the home of Maddy and Justin. She had timed it right. It was still early. Few in the town were outside yet, but she knew it was a big day for everyone: the start of the cut down to Eagle Harbour. This time, she'd do things differently. She left her mother sat upon the edge of their veranda and then knocked on the door of the residence. It was Justin Nankervis who answered it, looking tired but as if he was ready to go off to work.

"Mabel?" he said, sounding surprised. "You'm up an about early, aren't ee?"

"I know," she answered. "Is Maddy in?"

By now, Justin had nawticed the form of a being sat on the veranda floor.

"Who's tha' then?" he asked first, then answered her question with, "Maddy yeah? I'll get she fur ee..."

"My mother," responded Mabel.

Justin's face took a while to contemplate what she had said.

"What? She's still alive..."

He remembered all those long hours looking for her to no avail.

"Yes," said Mabel, "I found her. She's a bit different... than you'll remember her..."

Justin viewed her clawthes. He had no need to look at her face. Indeed, he didn't know if he even wanted to. From her back only, she looked haunted and frail – and what the hell wuz she wearing?

"Maddy," he shouted inside. "Someone to see you... It's Mabel... with her mother."

At this, Mabel wondered what gears and sprockets would connect in Maddy's mind. If she was right, then Maddy would already know about this: she would maybe even be expecting it. If that was not the case, then Mabel realised that she'd very much be on her own.

"I'd best be off," said Justin, tipping his hat habitually to Mabel and her mother. He had not known the woman well in the first place, and judging from what sat there, he didn' think he wanted to knaw much ov her now. When he bounded down the steps, he avoided looking too closely at what sat there. Its form unnerved him.

"Feythur knaw, do he?" he couldn't help but ask.

"He knows she's back," answered Mabel.

"I see," he said, recognising that the Doctor probably did not appreciate this interruption into his other plans.

Justin didn' look back. A few moments later, from the door slid a still-sleepy Luk. Mabel could see him, and obviously he her.

"A'right Mabel?" he said to her.

Instantly, he seemed to glean what was happening.

"That your ma?" he asked.

"Yes."

He gave a huge yawn, so vast that it exposed his tonsils.

"Well, good to see she back. She d'look a bit wisht though..."

"It's why I've come to see Maddy," said Mabel.

"'Course," said Luk. "'Course."

This Luk see. He knawed who wuz magic and who wudn'. Knockies are like tha'.

"Maddy'll sort she out," Luk said confidently.

"I hope so," responded Mabel.

"Es," he said. "Dunnee worry."

Luk's words reassured her. He seemed to think that her mother's presence could be solved – and that she could be reintegrated. Luk then ran to catch up Justin, on his way across to the headgear.

Mabel listened for Maddy. She was probably having to deal with Jago's needs. She'd understood he wuz a sweet boy that one; a brae bit different than her own nephew apparently, who had established himself as a bit of a terror. Men meanwhile, were gathering some distance away at the bottom of the town, sizing up the job ahead. Several Finns were arriving, carrying newly-sharpened axes, ready to begin the process of clearing the way. Their focus wuz on the task, not on what was going on outside the Nankervis residence. Therefore, no one saw Clara. If they did, they'd probably not even recognise her. Men went down into the woods. She noted that bastard Skews, Trevorrow and Mr Mint. Then echoing across the mountainside, she heard the first chopping smash of metal into bark.

"You'd better bring her in," came Maddy's voice. "They released her then?"

"Yes."

"Like it promised. I knew it wouldn't let me down. How is she though?"

"Not good," said Mabel.

"Let me see."

Mabel turned her around to face Maddy. This Maddy'd seen some sights in the past. She knew how magic could work but this, well, this was unsettling. The enormity of what had happened now ran through the whole of Maddy's flesh and blood. This wuz wha' ut had come to, wuz ut? Mabel and she having to deal with this ghost of a woman, and somehow turn her around.

"Your father?" she asked. "Accept her back, did he?"

"No," said Mabel.

"What I thought," said Maddy. "You'd best bring her in."

She did. They led Clara Jewell through the front door and into the living room of the property.

"Beautiful this really, isn't it? That nature made all this for her."

Maddy was eying Clara's dress of moss, lichen and flowers. She knew what minute and marvellous structures nature could build but it did not stop her from taking a pair of sharp scissors (the same pair she had used to cut the placenta of her own dead son) and cutting a tear all the way down from her shoulder to her calves. The dress disintegrated and fell onto the floor in grey and green granules. Clara's grey naked body stood before them. They could see every bone and sinew, each wasted muscle. She smelt of the earth.

Then, when this was done, Maddy carefully picked the remaining insects, invertebrates and chrysalises from her hair and dropped them outside. Some scuttled to a dark place and for a while at least, remained there. Then Maddy took a brush and tried to comb out the knots that had formed. She was careful not to do it too hard, because any more force would have pulled out the remainder of her thin hair and leave her bald. Once this was done, she grabbed two sack towzers from a hook and gestured for Mabel to put on one of the aprons. She tied the other around her waist and heated water on the stove. They positioned Clara so that she could first stand and then sit in a tin bath. There, they would clean her and try and bring her back to life. Even then, insects and multi-legged small things ran from crevices and small ravines in her skin. With their washing, the pair of them would attempt to coax her back to life.

Both of the washerwomen knew why George Jewell had rejected her: the problem was that, in the end, you have to move on with your life. Who can stay static? He had tried, but such a way was now impossible. No return meant no hope, and the nothingness had driven him mad. The bonnet that Nimkii had found was a false dawn. Indeed actually, its finding had in some ways confirmed that Clara had willingly disappeared from his life. But both of these women knew it was all a little more complex. Women often do, see.

So they carried on gently washing her. But the greyness, the blackness, the earthiness never seemed to disappear, no matter how hard they scrubbed. When they'd finished, they dried her, and clothed her afresh with old things that Maddy had. And once that was done they sat her down and tried to instigate conversation, but nothing came back. The problem then became what to do with her. Already, they felt the burden of responsibility, and how it would be if Doctor Jewell went ahead and married that Prowse woman. Maybe this Clara could not speak but she could see and watch. Another woman marrying her husband? Now, the sheer shock of that might kill her.

In the dark places lurked an individual who had now mapped this town and was finding his own feet. The insects, invertebrates and chrysalises came as a pleasant surprise and when he picked them up with his bony fingers, he wolfed them down, crunching their exoskeletons with his already sharp milk teeth. Like fangs they were.

He had taken glee from banging the floorboards of the high-set houses and dwellings of the town. Changelings tend to do this: the more they achieve mischief, the more it lurks in their hearts to cause even more. Ee was searching then, wuz this Richard, to find more targets. He could lock in on things that mattered and play with them. He'd already seen that little Knockie Luk go to work. He knew the direction he was going in: maybe he should follow. That fella might be good fun. The mine already looked like a place that would benefit from his sense of humour.

All night ee'd been out there but that didn' bother ee. See, in their world, the world that existed far below the Deads, and far even belaw the levels of this copper mine, they often worked at night: so when Francis and Rebecca tried to make him sleep, ut wuz counter to his nature. Changelings react badly to tha'. They get anxious. They do what they want. And that is what Francis and Rebecca had found. So be ut that he'd disappeared into the night. At least, they might be able to sleep before formulating a plan of how to deal with him. So having finished off the insects, invertebrates and chrysalises, he scuttled toward the mine. Growing still wuz he, this baby. But see, ee wudn' naw baby naw more. Ee wuz somethun' else that you didn' want to touch and didn't want to get too near to. No wonder Becca didn' wun't that latching onto her breast. Maybe Gourgy wuz right and that ee was some kind of spriggan.

Ee'd watched that young woman bring across the other strange woman dressed in clawthes of the forest. He knew the oddity of that. He understood that she was different: not like the rest of these humans. All of them were ripe for teasing though, and because she wuz different – and because ee had a terrible bullying streak to un – she'd soon be on his list; but for now, he knew what he must do. Now some changelings can be managed. There were people back home who had changelings for years, and kept on goin'. Such people believed to the end of their days that they'd made the creature that they shared their lives with, and tha' ut was their responsibility to keep un goin'. But my Gar, tha' wuz some job. Moast others just hoped and prayed that someone would come and return their true baby from the fairy realm and take this thing back with um. But here see, 'twuz a little more complicated ('twas after all, the twentieth century). This Pooka had been manufactured and when they're like tha', then they'm the wust in the world fur antics. You've seen wha' this liddle bugger can do, ebm ee? Ee wudn' goin' t'stop any time soon. The mine. Es. The mine had lots of potential. Ee wuz seizing all ov tha' up.

Above him the washing came to an end, and now began the drying and the powdering. They removed their towzers and tried adding perfume to Clara's skin to try to take away the smell of the damp earth. Ut would not go away though. At least they'd tried.

"You a'right with yer mother now? asked Maddy once they have finished her ablutions, trying to refashion her as a human being.

"Yes."

"Good. I'm just goin' up t'see Doctor Jewell..."

"Really?"

"About Mam?"

"Well sure enough yes, but other things too. Your father needs to take a look at me – after the birth an' tha... I promised I'd go up and see him."

"Of course – but you won't change his mind..."

"No. I don't expect so. I'll try talking to him though. You alright there looking after Jago too?"

"Yes. He'll be no trouble."

Maddy gave a last look at Clara. She empathised with the doctor really. She wudn' have wanted to spend the rest of her life with that. The hope could only be that eventually she'd recover and get back to being her normal self. Ef that didn't happen, then the reality of ut wuz tha' Maddy didn' knaw what would happen. She had not accounted for the fact that Clara Jewell would be altered. How on earth could she tell Mabel this? She had to hope that Mabel might even come to the same decision. Another death? Another arrangement? Hellfire – now would that mean another body to dispose of? She really hoped not.

She caught up with the flustered-looking doctor coming out of Rosie Koskinen's saloon. He'd explained matters clearly and fully to Miss Prowse and assured her that nothing was going to change his mind. As far as he was concerned, they were still to marry. He had no time for his wife at all, and in fact, what had turned up only seemed a very frail individual, who in fact, he actually hoped would not survive. What a thing to say you, but it was what he wished. His life was easier now without her. And then there wuz her mental health. Clearly, she'd be better off in an asylum given whatever experiences she'd had over the past year and a half.

For her part, Miss Prowse had been assured that the Doctor was genuine but nonetheless Clare Jewell's presence wuz, so to speak, a Dicky Mint-style spanner in the works. It hardly suited them as committed Methodists, but then, who'd have known she'd ever come back? It had seemed settled that she wouldn't. Her arrival had been perverse. The thing their conversation did do wuz to make Eleanor Prowse intrigued. She wanted to see what, or rather who, she was battling against. Perverse that may have been, but still, it dominated her thoughts after Doctor Jewell had left. By now, the only sound that she could hear from the bottom of the township was the continual chopping of axes and the occasional rush of foliage as another tree was toppled. What wuz ut that Jewell had said about the forest? She hadn't quite understood.

"Doctor Jewell!" shouted Maddy after him, as he stanked up the main street.

"I've come to make an appointment with you. Remember? You told me to."

He was clearly distracted by events that Maddy fully knew about, but still he managed to respond professionally with, "Hello Maddy. Yes, of course. We could do it now if you like... That is, if you've the time."

"Alright then... I'll walk with ya."

She caught up with the Doctor who had paused slightly in his forward movement to allow their conversation to take place.

"Everything fine is it?" asked Jewell, seemingly with a little edge in his voice.

"Yes. All good."

"And Jago Ciaran.. All well with him still?"

"Yes. Absolutely. Mabel's looking after him..."

"Mabel?"

This intrigued him because an hour or so before now, he had been conversing with her outside of his property.

"Yes. She ah... She brought around Clara..."

Ah. So Maddy knawed then.

"Good that she's back, eh?" stated Maddy.

"Not really," deadpanned Jewell. "Her return has rather upset my plans to be honest..."

"I see."

"I mean, I presumed her dead or not wishing to be with me any more, and now..."

"And now you have Miss Prowse?"

"Indeed."

It was time to apply some reverse psychology.

"I understand," said Maddy. "I mean, after what she did to you, why would you want to be near her? If Justin did something like that to me, I wouldn't want to speak to him at all – forever."

"Quite," said the Doctor. "I've discovered that..."

Suddenly, ee stopped what he was about to say. He cast his eye across to the mine, peering into the distance, rubbing his eyes with his two forefingers, each at the same time.

"I say, did you see that?"

"What?"

"I saw something moving... Something small... definitely moving..."

Maddy checked the horizon that he was pointing to.

"Nothing," she said. "I can't see anything..."

The Doctor checked himself. What ee'd actually seen was his grandson Richard – or rather tha Pooka version of ut – skidderin' across the exterior of the cage ov the engine house. Had he been asked to name what he had observed he would definitely have said that he saw an imp, but because he was a man of science, he put it down to something else.

"What did you see?" persisted Maddy.

"The stress," he replied in a rather more downbeat manner. "The stress of all of this is getting to me."

"How do you mean?"

They were at the surgery door by now.

"Clara's return. You've see her, I take it? I thought Mabel might take her to you."

"Yes..."

"What did you think?"

"Well, she's obviously been through a lot..."

"She looks like her grandmother now... not the Clara I once knew. Indelibly, she's not the same person at all... I swear as God is my witness."

"Probably not. I mean, I wouldn't be if I had lived in the woods for that amount of time."

This wuz a lie. Maddy knew that if she faced such a situation, she'd still come out of it in the same way as she went in. Nothing phased her and she knew it. But still, she could see the Doctor's point. Maybe she was trying to shame him into acting.

"Can you do anything for her?"

"How do you mean?"

"I mean, is there any remedy? Can she be turned around? Medicine perhaps?"

"Frankly, no. She's obviously had some kind of mental collapse. Her speech is gone – that can happen you know? The best thing for her is an institution. They'll be able to look after her. No one up here can."

Maybe he had a point. If Clara did not alter, then she'd definitely be a burden. Was Mabel willing to take her on? Not likely, considering the closeness now between she and Nimkii. And Becca? Perhaps not, because she already had her work cut out with the errant Richard.

"Let me be honest with you," said Jewell letting her inside his examining room and gesturing to a seat for her. "Things were never good between Clara and I. Oh yes, we had children... but it was never how I wanted it to be. We were forced together back home in effect. Two Methodist dynasties so to speak... You know how it is. I was younger then. Felt I should conform and do the right thing. But now, here, on the Keweenaw things are different. Everything is different. And Miss Prowse and I we... er..."

"Click?"

"Yes – that's it. We click... Clara and I never did really."

Maybe Maddy could have helped at this point. Maybe she could have told Doctor Jewell about the forest. Maybe she could have explained how the forest had selected her as someone weak, someone who could easily be called. Might she even tell him that she felt that in snatching his wife the forest was enacting a piece of revenge for what humanity had done to it, and that she'd been a kind of sacrificial victim. The Doctor was getting prepared for her. She knew that soon he was about to ask her to lie on the examining table and that he'd need to look at her, and see that everything below was fine. She knew she needed to act this out – be proper, as the Cornish might say – so there was no doubt about her having given birth. And then all of that started to dominate her thoughts, and she pulled back from even thinking about telling Jewell about the forest, and in the end, let him get on with ut.

"Please could you place yourself up there," the Doctor gestured.

Maddy wanted to be anywhere but here but she knew she had to convince him.

"If you could..." he said again.

This meant for Maddy to lift her layered dress and ease down her undergarments.

"So many women never come," said Doctor Jewell. "I mean, I understand why but you see it's in their best interests. At least you know its importance."

"You intend on going ahead with the wedding then, all the same?" Maddy asked. It was anything now to take her mind off what he was doing and seeing.

"Yes," said Jewell, looking elsewhere. "And our great plan for the chapel.."

"Ah yes..."

"How many days since the birth?"

"Nine or ten, I think..."

"Well," said Jewell, "I am pleased to see all looks well... I still can't quite believe you did all of that by yourself..."

"I've seen ut enough time with lambs and calves back on the Beara. Just the same now, isn't it?"

"Well," considered Jewell. "When you put it like that... then yes, exactly the same... All looks fine. Back to normal I believe."

"So is that it now?"

Maddy was hoping for freedom from this. Ut was the last hurdle she had to cross.

"Yes... for you... But obviously keep bringing in Jago Ciaran just to see how he's fairing. Weight checks and so on."

"I will. How's Becca getting on? I did see her."

"Thank you for that. Well, I think they're struggling a little. Babies are like people. They all have different personalities. Some take a while to settle. The world can be a shock after the warmth of the womb."

Maddy knew tha'. Oh, did she knaw tha'.

"They'll get the hang ov un soon no doubt... just like you and Justin..."

By now, Maddy had rearranged her clothing and stepped down from the examining couch.

"Look, don't say anything to Mabel, will you? But I'll be sending a telegram to Calumet today – for Clara to be transferred down there. It's fur the best... believe me... Sense will prevail."

At this, somehow Maddy felt the forest had won. But then one damaged human seemed reasonable when compared to the devastation going on right now down the incline. When she was back out of the Doctor's, she gazed down at what was happening. Despite the agreement they had made, the men were back in there again. The grinding of the engine bob told her that the mine wuz still at work and on her way back to her dwelling where this remnant of humanity (Clara Jewell) was sat, she espied Nimkii and nodded to him. He nodded back. He would know by now about everything that had transpired. He knew too about the vicious rape of the forest taking place right in front of them. They knew what would be broken and how those homes were now being trashed and burned. As voyeurs to this abuse, they saw how negligent they had become, how twisted things were, but that wuz perhaps nothing compared to what else wuz about to happen next. But let's not get too far ahead of ourselves.

Overhead, they both heard the sound of the crows and blue jays cawing incessantly, as the navvy gangs drew further down the incline.

37

Caw! Quite how the by-now quiescent forest would respond to all ov the noise being made in developing the incline, nawbody really knawed. By mid-morning though, a swathe of the lower woodland had been cleared, and they who lived there had to ship out, just like the earlier forest-dwellers, as woebegone refugees. There wuz they who minded all ov this carefully, but they wuz few in number and really had naw say in wha' went on with ut. Then, there wuz everyone else, who saw ut as just a necessary part ov the mine's progress. In their mind, progress meant removing nature, and the implementation of anything non-natural wuz their on-going jag. Maybe some too, didn' even think tha' far beyond the need to fill their bellies and send money home. Thaas solely why they wuz there.

Somethun' else unnatural was creeping around the headgear of the engine house that let down the cage into the earth. A couple of cores had gone down already that morning to carry on the work belaw. Ut wudn' the normal numbers obviously, because moast men were now working top-side, navvying the cut through the forest. Justin and Luk were making safe some small alterations to the outer casing of the engine house, where ut was discovered that on some days a cold wind came down from the north, and created a bit of a blaw inside the building. What they were doing would shore things up fur the winter ahead of them. As they worked together, in their minds, boath were intensely aware of the return of Clara Jewell to the town, as well as the fact that Justin's brother Francis, and Luk's co-worker Gourgy, were yet to put in an appearance. Wha' wuz up with they? They normally looked in by now to see wha' wuz on – before entering the cage, and being carefully lowered inta' the earth.

Unfortunately, ut wuz the case that Francis an' Rebecca were late out ov bed that morning. How could ut have been any different? What they had endured in the night had made boath of them weary, and sometimes, when you'm that tired, and that exhausted, you just have t'rest. Neither of um had anticipated that this wuz the way parenthood would be fur they. They had previously been so prepared and so committed to the project of bringing up their boy but now... well, things had altered. The fact that they had not bothered to chase Richard said ut all. Boath were worried up, and whereas before, their feelings about the being that they had made together had been suppressed, they knew now that unless they talked, their very marriage itself could potentially fail. A failed marriage wudn' the Methodist way neither.

They knew what might happen. The flawed chield would drive a wedge between them. Each would blame the other for its waywardness – this might come through a notion of their blood somehow seeping through from their line, or it might come from the particular way that each of them had brought up the baby. But what was there to say about the latter? Ee hadn' been around that long for they to have an influence on un. Ee seemed to be plain evil from the start. Maybe growing inside Francis wuz even a notion that madness ran in Becca's family – 'mean, you awnly had to see the way her mother had behaved backalong, and maybe that inherent mad streak wuz coming out in their son. Likewise, Becca knew of Justin's past – the way he'd been a bit wild as a young man (ee'd done a few things that were not spoken ov) – and maybe that strand of the Nankervis family was shining through. But to go down tha' route, as you well knaw by now, would have been a mistake, fur in fact, none ov tha' had any discernable impact on how their son behaved. Ee wuz what ee wuz.

When they woke, they checked that ee wuz not back in his cradle, and as they might have predicted, ee wuz not there. Where on earth could they begin searching for un? Maybe ee was lurking around the town still, or perhaps ee had gone into the forest. They cudn' tell. To search fur un would be like lookin' for a needle in a haystack, but at the same time, they knew they now cudn' keep his disappearance a secret. What would come with that too? People would say they were bad parents. How could um let a mite like Richard just run off inta' the might? More significantly though, they'd wondered how on earth a baby that age could be so wilful, though ut wuz true too, that many in the town commented under their breaths about how ugly and gangly their baby wuz.

Some even thought that the thing didn' look right, but, as is the way of things, they didn' say nawthun'. Well, you wudn', would ee? 'Mean, this wuz Cap'n Nankervis' baby. You wudn' want to go against ee. And 'twas Rebecca Nankervis' chield. She wuz the school-ma'am an' everyone gived she respect. She must knaw 'bout the best way of bringin' up childurn. She should knaw ut more than moast. And then he had good lineage see – brains in the family – what with his grandfer being Doctor Jewell. All this wuz thought, but not much of ut wuz said. You didn't like to think like tha' ef you wuz Cornish, but then again, you cudn' help ut. Perhaps their baby wuz disabled and not right in the head: a piece of fuggan cake withou enough dough.

What they cudn' understand the moast wuz how the liddle bugger wuz s'wilful an' wild. Ut almost felt like ee wudn' theirs: that ee had just dropped down to earth from the sky, instead on being made in Becca's belly. That morning, as she nursed her sore finger, Rebecca had a notion of this. Maybe ut wuz a mother's instinct, but there wuz in she, this feeling of absence: this feeling of non-belonging and non-ownership wuz gradually eatin' inta' she. Francis could see it too, but ee didn' even want to raise the matter with her. He couldn', fur ee wuz too filled with anger still. He wuz angry about wha' God had sent them and jealous of his brother and all tha' he had. Ee wuz worried that ov all the challenges ee'd ever faced (an' there had been a fair few) that ee wuz not ready fur this one. What cud um do to turn their boy round? Perhaps puttin' un on a strict Methodist path wuz the way. Hopefully, her feythur and tha' Miss Prowse would get on with the construction of the chapel. Ut wuz sorely needed at this point – an' though ee didn' knaw ut right there and then, ut would be in the hours an' days to come.

Francis had become frantic about all ov this. Ee could see the desolation on the face of his wife. When Gourgy arrived in the morning, he too, had had a restless night. He'd heard a row first in his dreams and then, when he woke that dream turned into a reality. Francis explained about the incident with the crockery and then told him how Richard had levered himself out of the winda' and purposefully gone missing.

"Told you," said Gourgy. "I said you had a spriggan on your hands, didn' I?"

Francis said little but inside, ee had a feeling that his old friend wuz right.

"You want me to look fur'n?"

"Please, ef you would..."

"'Course," said Gourgy. "I'll get on ut. You should have said before. You could have comed over in the night and told me ee'd gone missing."

"We'd had enough by then. I mean, ef Richard wanted to go out, there wuz no way that we could have stopped un..."

They knawed that ee wuz fiercer than a buckrat. At this, Gourgy nodded. Ee knew of the baby's will, but maybe ee wuz coming to his awn conclusion that this baby wudn' human in any way. The problem wuz ee cudn' rightly judge where ee'd come from.

"I'll go an' have a gake about fur'n."

"Thank you."

Gourgy left and stepped out into the morning light. Down bottom, he could hear the sounds of the timbering boys at work. The mine and the town were now a huge site though. Where to begin he wondered? Tha' boy Richard, ee might well be wayward, but Gourgy reckoned ee wudn' have gone tha' far. He began out the rear of the Nankervis building, seeing if he could see any tracks go in either direction, but the problem was that the boy wuz so light ov foot that he barely made a mark. He peered left and right, and out into the watching forest, but he could discern no trail.

He knew ee'd need to keep his wits about him. Ef that boy caught one snifter that Gourgy wuz out to track him, then fur zertain, there wud be hell to pay. Changelings are very independent see, and the thing they moast dislike in all ov the world is to knaw that someone wuz following they. Wha' Gourgy failed to realise is tha' at tha' very moment ee wuz being watched from on high. Es. Richard had scaled the engine house. He cud climb like naw tomorra' that boy. So he was up there see, sat on top of the chimley stack watchin' the world go by – and gettin' a sense of his bearings. Below, ee'd by-passed the work of Justin and Luk. Ee'd have some fun with they in a moment or two. Fur now though, ee felt like ee wuz king of the castle. Ee cudn' help but laugh at tha' Gourgy peerin' in everywhere lookin' fur'n. Oh, what a slave to his human ee wuz! Poor Knockie. The clot!

So thaas what Gourgy did. Ee stanked everywhere in the township and all around the timbering yard. Hell, ee even went out to the Deads, which amused this boy Richard greatly. Es, funny to see a Knockie out there you – where Richard had been formed, where ee'd been constructed (fur ee instinctively knawed all ov tha'). He comed back by the blacksmith's shop because see, to Gourgy, fire wuz maybe a place to which tha' spriggan might be drawn. But the Pooka just laughed and cackled at his antics high on the chimley stack. And because he was nimble on his feet, he danced around the lip of the stack, avoiding the smeech of smoak that comed up from the furnace below. Aw es, this changeling up there, looked like he was doing ballet atop the stack you. Nawbody seen un you. Everyone wuz too busy lookin' at the ground. Well, tha' wuz the Cornish all over see. Ut wuz tha', that caused their race to have tha' slight stoop in their back from allays looking downwards to see wha' the earth would offer.

This Richard had gone beyond being wilful now. He'd even gone beyond being wayward. Now, almost overnight, he'd become wild and anarchic. Ee knew he had a touch of the Devil in un. An' because of who ee wuz, ee liked that aspect ov hisself. He'd come to realise he actually didn' need that fool ov a feythur, Francis Nankervis, nor his mousey-lookin' wife. He laughed at his awn antics and thought back to the moment when he bit she – supposedly his mawthur. Her blood had tasted good, and when he had tasted ut, ee didn' want her milk naw more. Oh naw, ee knawed what he needed see. Proper vampires they cud be, these buggers.

Tha' stupid Gourgy wuz still out there gakin' fur un. Ee'd come up the other way now, and was having a quick nawse around the ostler's yard and the plaace where the mine kept all the ore wagons. Richard made notes. Es. Horses an' wagons could be fun.

Some day he'd have good truck with tha' lot and set they a-frighted by setting off a fuse or somethun'. Aw, tha would bugger up their plans big time. Ee knew now of course, tha' Justin wuz the top-side Cap'n and tha' his substitute 'feythur' Francis wuz in charge underground. He considered too, the fun and giggles he might have underground. Es. That seemed like a wondrous playground fur'n, but ut could wait. Es. Ut could all wait. See this Pooka could be patient. They be like tha'.

Now things were takin' a new turn. That Gourgy wuz knockin' on the door of a certain house below. He knawed the plaace right away. Ut wuz where he had lurked in the dark and feasted upon tasty forest insects, invertebrates and chrysalises. Aw, so ee knawed they then. There wuz that maid answering the door, the one who seemed a bit special, and there inside, ee could make out the movement of the odd woman – the one ee promised hisself ee would have a go on. See Pookas always prey on the weak; thaas the way ov um. He widened his eyes and looked closely at wha' wuz transpiring below over there. Gourgy seemed to have learnt somethun' important. Ee could tell that in his body language. See how they d'read ov ee, these Pookas. Clever like tha' they always have been – all throughout the centuries. Thaas the real reason you need to be wary of they. Any weakness, any notion of inferiority and they'll seize upon ut.

Before Gourgy's movements had been slow and methodical. Once ee'd met with the young woman though, his steps got faster. Now, ee wuz runnin' back up through the town to the top road, where his house could be found. Well, ut wudn' really his house – ut was just by fate an' devious placement tha' ee had found hisself there. Aw es. There wuz tha' oaf Gourgy, the one – ha, ha – whose foot he had burnt by throwing a hot coal at un, now enterin' back inside. Gourgy reckoned ee had some kind of message to tell they inside. Es, definitely somethun' important. Ee kept watching, reaching out with his arms to shoo a crow from landing on top of the stack. The crow didn' move fust ov all. 'Mean this wuz ut's realm, wasn't ut? But then Richard more aggressively swiped at the bird, and then it moved, cawing back at this infernal being who now sat at the very top of the very highest human-made tree.

Now, nothing keeps a mother awake at night more than not knowing where their child is, or if they are in danger or hurting some place. That wuz running through Rebecca as you might expect, but also, when Gourgy brought back news about her mother, the agony of the past year and a half fell away from she. Richard knew something of the conversation that had to have happened, because just a few moments later, his dullard parents – that Francis and that Rebecca – were urgently strolling back down the street, with Gourgy ahead of them gesticulating and pointing energetically. Ut wuz easy to knaw where they were headed.

Aw – so that woman – the odd woman, she must be Rebecca's mother: es, and his 'grandmother'. Ut didn' take much to work tha' out now, did ut? And from the look ov um, there wuz some concern, some degree of wonder tha' she wuz even back in this township. Richard could not see all tha' transpired from high on his perch atop the stack, but he noted the joy felt by his mawthur. Ut looked like some kind of reunion. Ut was good to knaw these things about one's adoptive parents – they could then allays be used as leverage. Damme. See how his mind worked, this evil Pooka.

38

By now, the Pooka was gettun' hungry. Now Pookas can go for a considerable time without food. They tend to overeat, so that their stomachs become distended, and awnly when everything is all passed through and the nutrients absorbed, do they seek out other food. Pookas eat things from the natural world in general, and they will follow that diet if they have to, but of course, what they moast like is stealing human food, especially human food that is spicy, warm and tasty. An' see food wuz essential to miners, fur the work boath underground and top-side wuz very physical. Miners needed a good amount of stodge to keep um happy. An' stodge, well, that wuz wha' Pookas really liked, fur in the natural world, there idn' much ov tha', so they have to take their chances when they can.

Thaas see, why this Pooka Richard slithered his way back down the outside of the chimley stack, and got drawn to where Luk an' Justin were working. Aw es. Here wuz what his nostrils had sensed. Here wuz two ripe crowst boxes that Justin and Luk had brought to work with them. Luk would normally have been pleased with a morsel of an end bit of pastry off a pasty, but considering the work he'd been doin' ov late, ee'd been packed off to work each day with a box ov his own. Naw need see placation see. Naw need fur Knockies to keep ee safe, not when you wuz working top-side, wuz there? Or perhaps so you thought...

Devilry wuz at work though. How might Maddy O'Donahue have acted ef instead ov being up there with Doctor Jewell she saw wha' wuz about to transpire here. Would she ever have made the thing ef she could see what ut would bring? See, tha' Pooka had an itch in his nawse. A smell wuz ticklin' ov his taste-buds and rightly (because he wuz from another world), ee didn' knaw what 'twuz. But ee wuz locatin' ov ut and had homed in on where ut wuz comin' from. Ee wuz inside ov the engine house now, beside the boiler and beside the steam engine producing the vapour to turn the wheels and the gears of the cage. Up they'd come with ore and down they'd go again with an empty tram ready fur the next load. The noise ov ut wuz incessant, but Pookas as you knaw, aren't bothered a bit by clamour and din. In fact, they d'delight in ut all. This wuz way better than shakin' up a bit ov kitchen crockery.

Ee couldn' be more fast and silent this boy. Sometimes, ee even seemed t'be greased up, so quick and fluid wuz a. 'Twas like he wuz there one second, and gone the next, and the engine room, well, 'twas a wondrous plaace to hide in fur any mercury-like magical creature. Shadows everywhere you, and piles of gear ready to be used in the future. All this wuz Dicky Mint's realm. He'd designed all of this paraphernalia, and although he was filled with a brae bit ov drecklyism, he'd managed to complete its grand installation, and these days, ut all worked fine. Now, what would a make of this Pooka in here, having fun: lifting levers and turning cylinder valves, playin' with stuff he clearly had naw right t'touch. Aw, there was plenty in there see, fur his pliable hands to reach for. 'Twas a veritable toy shop fur'n.

"Ha, ha," ee went to this and then, "Ha, ha," he went to somethun' else.

Some power he had see, this Pooka. Ee wuz awnly small really but they'm some strong in the arm and wrist you. Ee knawed ut too, so any disruption ee could cause ee delighted in. Fur fun, he 'eaved up a tin of grease an' smeared it all over the floor. Some bugger'd come in on a job and go ass over tit. Thaas zactly what ee liked see. Ee took delight in seeing the agony of others. Wisht, eh? But you cudn' alter un. Tha' wuz who ee wuz, and there wudn' naw stoppin' ov un. Ee wudn' naw baby. Ee wudn' naw innocent either.

These were distractions though, to his real aim. That food wuz smellin' some good and rightly, ee wanted a taste of ut. Tha' Justin an' his Knockie Luk were working on ladders on the side of the building, but they'd dropped their crowst bags and boxes down on a spare set of balance beams. This boy Richard wuz ravenous by now and ef you wuz there, you would have seen un salivating away like there wudn' naw tomorra'. Coincidentally, ut wuz Luk's bag ee picked up fust, and because ov the row of the engine working above, ee felt ut wudn' matter ef he tipped the contents out onto the floor. Tha' wuz ee all over see. Never mind about the mess. Tha' wuz fur someone else to clean up. Not ee.

Out fell a tin crowst box, which buckled at the side, and in doing so, caused the lid ov ut t'open. From ut, out tumbled his miner's jack too. The jack contained hot milky tea (sugarless see, because tha' wuz the Methodist way ov doin' things), which wuz ideal to warm ee up after working outside on a Fall day like that one. So Richard the Pooka guzzled tha' down in one go. Lovely ut wuz, but that didn't satiate un. Aw naw. From the box had spewed forth a geht pasty and so with his sharp teeth ee bit inta' tha' one. Ut tasted glorious because the warmth of the range wuz still in ut. Crazy these Cornish were, but they knawed how to eat well. They'd knawed how to satisfy their own hunger, and by doing this, ee'd shaw them how they'd satisfy the hunger ov a Pooka too. Now, Pookas dun' eat pasties end-on like moast Cornish would do, holding onto the crimping for fear ov pollutin' your food with arsenic or some other poisonous metal. Naw, the Pooka opened his up like a letter from home and devoured the interior of meat, potato and onions first before gobbling down the envelope of pastry. Ideal you. Ut tasted grand to un, did this food.

But then see, ee digged around on the floor again and pulled up a saffron bun. Good and fresh ut wuz – made yesterday – and well, when ee put that in his mouth, ut completely distracted un. 'Twas as if ee wuz flying above the whole ov the mine like one of they baissly crows ee'd seen earlier. Aw, the taste of ut wuz wondrous, and when he found a little tub of clotted cream and smeared that on the bun with one of his fingers, well that took un somewhere ee'd never been before. Momentarily, he considered staying around here, especially ef there wuz more food like this. Damme, 'twas good, and when he said tha' to hisself, ee licked his lips and pressed the last of the spicy bun down his clunker. What need wuz there of breast milk when you could have this? Now, this wuz more like ut, ee thought.

The boy Richard wuz just about to help himself t'the contents of the second bag, when from behind, someone sneaked up on un and gived un a geht whack on the side of his head with a triangular-headed Cornish shovel. Ol boy Richard wuz scat flying you. Thwack the shovel went, and the metal ov ut clanged hard on the Pooka's skull. Now someone ought to have done that to un a while ago, but here 'twas – a bit ov Knockie-style come-uppance – for the wielder of the shovel wuz none other than Luk. Luk had been up the ladder passing nails to his master when he heard a different kind ov clatter inside the engine house. See, Knockies have extraordinary hearing. They can hear small movements in the ground a mile away from where they are standun', so they'm always sensitive to sound: and despite the vibration and movement of the bob,

Luk had heard someone at play below. Damned if they wuz goin' to get a gain on his lovely crowst you. Ee'd been looking forward to ut, as well as a cup taa from his jack, and what did a find? Well, ee found this bugger munching away ov ut. Nawthun' d'wind up a Knockie like tha'. Food, well, tha' wuz a special domain. Ut wuz untouchable. Anyone takin' ut was like a crafty miner stealing another's strike. Did this bugger here knaw that?

Luk had shimmied down the ladder quicker than duckshit, when ee knawed somethun' wuz on. Now Luk, as you d'knaw wuz the shier, more retiring type of this pair of Knockies. Ef you ebm picked up on tha' by now, where 'ave ee been? An' a short while ago, when the forest sprites had threatened ee, well, ee runned a mile; but touch his crowst an' well, tha' wuz a different matter entirely. While mehty wuz still lookin' stunned, curled up on the floor like a pile ov rags, Luk wuz puttin' two and two together. Ee didn' knaw Richard had gone missin' but ee knawed enough 'bout un t'knaw wha' he looked like. He recognised his eyes see, and then Gourgy had already told un to watch out fur un – that he wudn' a nice piece ov work. So, this wuz ov un, wuz ut? Well, ee wuz goin' to give un what fer now. Luk banged his shovel on the floor when he nawticed tha' not awnly had a consumed the whole of his pasty (there wuz a brae few crumbs on the floor), but also his saffron bun, and then t'top ut all, the scrumptious scalded cream ee'd readied fur ut.

"Ebm nawbody warned you 'bout takin' a Knockie's crowst?" he spat. "You'm messin' with unknown forces here boy."

By now, the Pooka wuz getting up and rubbing his head where he'd been scat. Two or three of his spiky teeth had been bloodied too, and he spat that mass out onto the floor of the engine room, teeth an' all.

"Who are you?" the Pooka asked. "Whom am I about to kill?"

"My name's Luk," said Luk, "and you'n try if you like boy, but you ebm got a 'ope."

They wuz well matched these two. Fur a moment, ut might have shifted inta' some kind of wrasslin' match which would have been the Cornish way ov sortin' out a matter: Luk recognised he could give un a good hug and make un surrender. But naw, this wuz always goin' to be more like trial by combat. Luk had his shovel, and the Pooka had picked up a length of chain, and wuz swinging it around like some kind of Roman gladiator. Boath ov these buggers may have been liddle, but they had some sprawl on um you. They hit each other harder than hell, fust Richard whipping the chain out to knock Luk off balance, and then Luk slicing the leading edge of the shovel through the air and towards Richard's neck.

In Richard's eyes, ee wuz the unknown force. 'Mean, Knockies were two a penny, wudn' um? There were perhaps fifty more ov they probably in the runs and levels belaw. What made this one any different than the rest? But Pookas, well, Pookas allays felt they were a bit special, and thaas the sense of hisself that this Richard had. Ee wudn' 'bout to let naw upstart like Luk have his way widn'. So they scat each other again: this time the chain wrapping itself around one of Luk's legs and causing un to drop the shovel and fall right over. But then, ee wuz always quick wuz Luk in nasty situations. Ee soon had the chain untangled and although Pooka boy tried to kick away his shovel, ee was able to roll across and reach ut. In a second, ee wuz back on his feet again. Knockies be some nimble with a shovel.

"You know who I am then?" teased the Pooka.

"Reckon I do," said Luk. "You'm Francis and Becca Nankervis' son... the one who've been causing they a drop ov' trouble ov' late."

"I might be," teased the Pooka laughing. "Then again, I might not be."

Maybe Luk should have taken a bit more nawtice ov what mehty boy wuz saying, but in the heat ov the moment, ee forgot about ut.

"'Twas 'bout time someone taught you some manners," went Luk, moving the shovel rapidly from fist to fist.

"What? An' you are the fairy to do ut, are ee?" taunted Richard.

Luk made a lunge at un.

"I ent no fairy!"

The two of they collided again, this time Luk's shovel pinning Richard's neck to the galvanised metal of the shell of the engine house. One move and Luk could probably slice through mehty's neck. Ut didn' seem right though. What ee needed wuz fur this bugger to be interrogated and questioned so as to find out wha' was motivating un and where he'd come from. A question remained in Luk's mind. How come when he had been born this Richard has been so lovely, but then, in just a few days he had transformed into this vicious thing in front of him? Ut didn' make sense and Luk wanted answers. But there wuz no doubt that ee should have finished the job, because what Richard wuz observing wuz weakness. Ee knawed the way of their species. Ee knawed that something too nice percolated through them: all that knocking underground, all that saving ov lives at the slightest rumble ov movement.

So when Luk paused and reflected, Richard kneed Luk right in the unmentionables and he collapsed into hisself. Then, as he fell onto his knees on the floor of the engine house, Richard took the heavy chain he had and ran ut in spirals around Luk's neck. In his mind's eye he had a plan to hang him; the next moving up of one of the rods and he could connect the chain to it and Luk would be pulled up into the air. The chain would tighten around his throat and he'd lose the ability to breathe. His windpipe would seal and then he would kick and wriggle his way to death.

"Rite on," went the Pooka (see how they d'learn the lingo s'quick), sitting against the boiler to warm his back. Justin had a pouch of tobacco in his crowst bag, an' he then located his clay pipe, which had also fallen out of a pocket in the bag. The end of ut had been chipped a little, but tha' didn' stop the Pooka filling it with 'bacca, and then holdin' it in front of the open boiler furnace door, to catch ut alight. All this could happen because ut would take some time fur the bob and its mechanism to return. The Pooka sat down and casually watched the struggling Luk, his legs kicking out, trying to loosen the tight chains ee wuz now wrapped in.

"Told you, didn' I?" he stated, confidently blawing out a keenly circle of smoak from his mouth. Sharp teeth ee had you. Ut looked like they could bite right through copper plating.

Boy Luk knawed that his death could well be imminent. He looked at the position ov the bob and knawed that the moment it rose again, then he'd be yanked up inta' the air. Hollerin' ee wuz though, probably makin' enough noise fur even the forest out there to hear ov un. Ee had one last thought though before he closed his eyes: how terrible ut looked fur a small baby (ef you cud ever call *tha'* a real baby) to be cuffing down – ov all things – on a pipe.

Luk may have thought that his life wuz over but a couple of others didn'. Es, they comed in the form of Justin and Gourgy. Justin had been outside and observed how Luky-boy had gone inside for something. He had meant to be passing ov un another nine-inch nail but clearly, somethun' had bothered him inside. Now, with the scene that greeted him, he understood why he had come inside. He instantly saw the remnants of the crowst tins on the floor and nawticed the cheeky Pooka cuffing away on – bleddy hell – his awn pipe. He knew in an instant what his plan wuz: fur the imminent execution of his loyal friend Luk.

With un, ee'd managed to coax in Gourgy who had come back up past the mine with his brother an' Becca. Ee'd nawticed his brother's arm around his wife. Ee knew zactly why ee wuz comfortin' she. They'd obviously been down to see the remnants of her mawthur and obviously, ut had been a fair old shock fur she. Your mam turning up like that after all this time, and she lookin' wisht as a winnard – like as ef the earth had half-consumed she already. Es, ut didn' look good, but at least she wuz back. Now, because of tha', he called over Gourgy. Ef there wuz somethun on inside the engine house, then Gourgy wud be a good ally to help un sort ut. So, as Justin comed in on the lower level, Gourgy had made 'iss an' climbed in through the hole in the side of the building where the shears were set up. Ee had snuck along one of the interior access balconies to see what wuz on. 'Course, ee had found zactly the same thing that Justin had noted – that their meht Luk was about to come a cropper when the bob raised utself.

Gourgy instinctively knawed what his job would be: it wuz to swing over to where Luk wuz and to start swinging un around in an anti-clockwise direction so the chain would unravel from around his neck and loosen un up. This, Gourgy did with accomplishment, using a set of monkey-like manoeuvres to work his way across to his meht. They'd been in some situations over the years, an' Gourgy wudn' about to allow his meht to perish. Oh naw. Ee would not see that happen. Ef they had survived that huge fall-in down Botallack half a century ago, then they could survive this. That Pooka – ee might think hisself a feisty bugger – but they knawed better. This wuz hopefully awnly the start of putting ee right. So Gourgy swung across, gripped onto the rod with his hands and started to unwind the coils of chain from around Luk's neck. Gourgy had never been so black in his skin colour as ee wuz now, nor had he seen Luk become so dark in tone. Boath of they was pretty angry you.

Meanwhile, Justin wuz getting ready to deal with the Pooka. Maybe ee wuz his nephew, but so what? Maybe he wuz the son of his brother, but clearly this thing smoking away on his pipe needed sorting out. And tell ee wha' – a bit ov telling-off wudn' goin' to do ut. From what ee'd heard, that had been tried before, and now that ee had his best magical friend in the world about to be hung, ee wudn' about to mess around. So this time, curiously, just like Gourgy had suggested the other day, he picked up the banjo shovel for the boiler (the tool that wuz usually used to 'eave in coal) and in one motion, ee scooped up the Pooka (so fast wuz the motion tha' the bugger didn't knaw what hit un), and fast as he could, he opened the door to the rush of flame in the boiler, and tried to 'eave un in there.

His plan, honest you, wuz t'see un burnt to a crisp. An' in tha' action, Justin reckoned he'd be doing everyone on Mountainside a damme good favour, seeing as how this boy wudn' nothing more than a pile full of hate an' misery. Ee certainly wudn' the kind of child he'd wish on anybody, and ee didn' even knaw at this point tha' the Pooka had gone fur Rebecca, and bit at her finger. He'd have been brisker still in his actions, naw doubt, ef he'd knawn even the slightest hint of the fact that this vile Richard preferred the taste of blood to milk.

So there wuz ee with the scoop of a Pooka on a shovel ready to shove un inta' the furnace, and up on the rod, there wuz Gourgy untangling his millennial meht. All this passed see without a soul even knawing about ut. The rest of the miners wuz all underground see; Dicky Mint, Cap'n Trevorrow and Mr Skews were all still down the cut, supervising its construction, and even Nimkii – sat beside the engine house – didn't hear anything. He wuz too busy contemplating the massacre of the forest once more, knowing that there'd be consequences. No one knew then of this struggle inside: the combat of these Knockies and this Pooka, the quest for survival between the Pooka and Cap'n Nankervis.

They all could see that the bob had steadied itself but that the next pull would yank the rod upward. Ef that happened, Luk wudn' last long. So Gourgy wuz now frantic with his fingers unpicking the iron. In the stopes belaw though, for hundreds of years, such Knockies as he had reached into the attle for gems and tin and copper, and now, that dexterity wuz comin' in very handy. Ee knew that imminent release wuz coming for his Knockie brother and just before the pump rod rose once more, Gourgy unwound the last of the chain, and then scooped his meht by the rear of his loincloth, swinging un to safety back across to the interior balcony. The rod then rose high though, with Luk gasping at what might have happened to him.

"I wuz some glad to see you boy," ee said to Gourgy. "I thought my time wuz up."

"Na. You knaw I wudn' about t'see that happen. Nick your crowst did a – tha' Richard?"

"Es," said Luk. "I've never seen a baby like ut in all my born days."

"You wun't," said Gourgy. "Thaas because ee ent naw baby. I tell ee straight – what we'm dealing with here is some kind of spriggan, but 'tis a type I've never seen before. Best we get down there, and give my Justin a hand..."

The pair skedaddled along the balcony to thunder down the interior steps beside the movement of the iron bob. Belaw, they could now see the problem that Justin faced. Ee had attempted to toss the Pooka inta' the furnace but the boy had been quick, and when Justin swung un in, Richard reached out with his hands and feet to clasp the entrance. So there he wuz, boobed-up there, with his belly and willy gradually heatin' up and his pointy nawse poking further than anything else inta' the blaze. All they items wuz starting to cook and steam, and Justin wuz hopin' that by continually beatin' his back with the banjo shovel, ee would eventually be unable to resist holding on and be sucked into the flames.

"Whack!" the shovel wuz goin', as yet another blaw landed on Richard's back, but as you d'knaw, Pookas are very determined things. They'll hold on fur as long as they need to. You can never count your chickens with um because they've allays got another move planned, another counter-measure to ensure longevity and not yet put an end to their need fur chaos.

"Whack, whack!" came two more hits of the shovel. You would never have believed this, would ee, not ef I was tellin' ee of this down some 'Wink somewhere on a cool summer night with a glass ov cider in your hand. But the whacks continued onto the back of the baby or the Pooka or the baby, or whatever ut wuz, and ut wuz still holding out, still resisting being beaten. Hard ee wuz see. Ut was snarling up good and proper too now, like as if at any moment ut would bite into the metal of the shovel and tear that abroad. Vicious the thing wuz, and Justin was still doin' his best to whack un inta' the furnace and lock tight the door on un. Right then, nawthun' would have given un greater satisfaction. Justin took out every frustration of his early life on the critter but he still wudn' move. Ut wuz as if geht rivets had pinioned his hands to the outer wall of the furnace, and nawthun' could peel they back. Some job you. Justin had a sweat on un as moist as they Finns working down in the cut on the side ov the mountain.

Justin awnly relented when he heard a voice say, "What the hell's goin' on in here?"

Es. Ut wuz a voice he knawed well: his awn brother.

"We'm dealing with your boy..." said Luk.

The Pooka was still clasping on, too afraid to go inta' the furnace, an' too afraid to go anywhere else.

"What a do?"

"Nick Luk's crowst," observed Gourgy, "then tried, fur fun, to hang un..."

"Hang un?"

"Thaas right, an' thaas why we'm here now, trying to get rid ov un. You knaw ut yourself, ee's the very Devil's child..."

At tha', Richard let out a kind of guttural laugh.

Things went awful quiet fur a moment, but still the Pooka didn' move. Ee curved his back a bit though, so the heat on his body parts wudn' quite so fierce. Around them, the bob had dropped again, and the rod went back down again.

"But he's my son," said Francis.

"Es, well," said Gourgy. "We d'knaw tha' but..."

"But what?"

"I should be protecting him..."

Justin moved the banjo shovel back out of the way, realising his guilt at what he wuz doing.

"I should be stopping him from suffering... You'd be the same brother, if ut were your son. You'd do the same thing for Jago, surely?"

"'Course I would," said Justin. "Obviously."

"Es," said Luk, "but Jago is lovely, not at all like this sod..."

Richard stared meanly at the Knockie, a stare that meant, "When I get out of this situation, I'll have you!"

"Can ee just leave un alone fur a minute? Thaas all I'm asking..."

"But..." tried Gourgy, wanting to explain and wanting to reason with his master. But he was not allowed to. Francis stuck his hand out, indicating he did not want any further discussion. All three of them – Justin, Gourgy and Luk – stepped away from the furnace and allowed Francis to gather up his son in his arms. And when Francis did tha', he played his game again, and returned in an instant, to be more baby-like, opening and closing his wide eyes and sucking his thumb, like as ef butter wudn' melt in his mouth. The heller.

"Pa-pa," the thing gurgled, returning to some pretence of cuteness.

"He's deceiving you," warned Gourgy. He was the awnly one who could say such a thing. He was, after all, Francis' Knockie and his life had been dedicated to warnin' un ov danger. "I tell ee straight Master, I wudn' want that thing gettin' close to ee again..."

But the Pooka knew the game he had to play. He knew how to get out of tight situations like this. Aw yes. There ee wuz now, all shrivelled up again like a glowing infant, like he wuz the dear Christ Child himself, asleep in the manger. Francis backed away from them, like as ef they were now the danger. Luk and Gourgy glanced at each other, wondering how bizarre life now wuz – and how it had all come to this.

"'Spect all of you knaw," speculated Francis. "We awnly jus' found out tha' Rebecca's mam's comed back... She came out of the wood. Rebecca would like to shaw her her first grandchild..."

Jeez. What a move that would be? He'd probably bite her arm off; tha', or he'd be so badly behaved as to make her run back into the forest again.

"Brother," said Justin. "I d'knaw wha' you'm sayin' but you ent thinkin' straight. That thing you'm holding, it's deceiving you. Let us carry on with our work here. I knaw ut wuz some painful fur you to see tha', but that thing idn' human... You let tha' loose on Clara Jewell and I guarantee, sure as eggs is eggs, tha' she'll end up dead."

"You just hate him. You allays have," protested Francis.

"No, no," said Gourgy to his master. "You need to listen to what your brother is saying. We've seen what ee can do. All three ov us have... You have too. Stop trying to tell yourself there idn' naw problem. 'Tidn' somethun' thaas goin' to go away neither... you got to fix it today."

"How can I fix ut though?"

None of um wanted to say how, but at that point, the furnace had seemed a pretty reasonable option t'be honest.

"Think what he've done to Becca an' you so far..."

Francis was starting to break. They could see his countenance change.

"Whaas a dun? Somethun' else?" Gourgy urgently asked. "Tell um..."

They knawed tha' Francis didn' want to speak. They knawed that ee didn' want to say ut, but on the other hand, ee knawed ee needed to tell them. Ut was an unbearable situation for this Francis to be in. You remember now, ee wuz allays the sensible one, the kind one of the pair. Ee wuz crying now, great long gasps of air, in which ee seemed to cry fur all humanity at what had become of the world – at what had become of this Paradise on earth.

"He bit Rebecca's finger," he sobbed. "He drew blood."

All of they watching un, shook their heads. Still, the Pooka kept quiet. His 'feythur' wuz defending ov un, and ee knawed ut was the best thing that could happen to un right now. The others all sighed. They knawed that drawing Rebecca's blood awnly actually scratched the surface ov wha' ee cud do, this Pooka. Tha' morning they'd seen his real capacity. They all knawed ee wuz a spriggan-style killing machine. They all knawed that ee'd comed to Copper Mountain from somewhere very dark. Ef they'd awnly knawn about his origins in the Deads, then perhaps they'd instantly take him back there and force him under. But right there an' then, nawbody knew tha'.

Fur a while, everything in the engine house went silent. Maybe, just maybe things were being thought through, but then, out of nowhere Luk spoke up.

"'An' ee tried to kill me," ee said.

Perhaps, ut wuz the way ee said ut, or perhaps ut wuz now, that despite his wish to be a good feythur, Francis had reconsidered: or maybe even a combination of Luk's words and what he had done to his wife, that Francis seemed to alter his perception. Maybe he wuz not awnly thinking through what had already transpired with the

Pooka, but more worryingly, what would come in the future. Although the little bugger looked sweet as a daisy right now, Francis realised the pretence of ut: that the thing ee wuz holding wuz actually puttin' on a performance. His apparent complicity wuz just an act. He looked up at them all, and nodded, knawing what needed to be done. Right now, the thing looked half-asleep and ef they were quick, then they might be able to dispose of un.

Francis' final nod wuz a cue for his brother to open the furnace again, but when the hinges of ut squeaked open (they should have been greased regular-like according the instructions of Dicky Mint), Richard woke up seemingly able to predict his fate. He leapt out ov his notional feythur's arms an' this time ran over to where Gourgy wuz standing. Regaining the immense strength ee had had earlier, and also morphing instantaneously inta' something proper queer (somehow ooglier than before, and more lizard-like), ee grabbed hold of Gourgy, weakening him by standing on his recovering burnt foot. Now Gourgy wuz tough, but with the pain of tha' targeted stomp on his foot, he doubled up in pain. And s'fast-moving wuz this Richard, seemingly now able to work at double the speed ov before. Like lightning, ee wuz, an' ee wuz able to dart through all of they with some considerable ease.

"Jeez," went Justin, realising he should never have released him. He wuz trying to be kindly to his brother, and follow his wishes. What a grim mistake tha' wuz!

Richard had his fingers around Gourgy's neck and ee wuz dragging un along, like some scary creature from wha' they scientists d'call the prehistoric times, that wuz carrying off uts prey. Gourgy wuz tipped over at an angle now on the heels ov his feet. The boy wuz tryin' to fight back at his abduction, but ee wudn' doin' a pile ov good. What Francis wuz trying to work out wuz what wuz Richard's motivation? Why did a do this to others? What made un so angry? What made un tear at everyone around un? Ef awnly there wuz something they could do to placate un and make un happy. But then, they had tried tha'; they'd tried to give un everything ee needed as a baby, and ee'd rejected all ov tha'. Ee realised sometimes you cen't change things fur the better. Sometimes, thaas the way individuals want to be. There's naw oddsing ov ut.

The main question now wuz wha' wuz a doing with Gourgy? Where wuz a takin' ov un? Now, the Minter had set things up good an' proper at the collar of the mine, but his designs were enhanced by the observations of Doctor Jewell, who'd tried to make things a little safer. All well an' good wuz tha', but what need did Richard have to go to the collar? You cudn' really see the ground anymore there now – not the ground where Francis and Justin made their first excavation and discovered copper ore – and instead, ut was surrounded by concrete and layers of planchen. But still, they could see where he was heading with Gourgy. He wuz moving towards the cage that men went down inside of, and where ore came back up. Wha' wuz his plan then? Fur a moment, ut looked like ee wuz going to take Gourgy belaw (maybe ee had some gruesome plan fur un down in the levels), but when they got to the shaft where Richard had taken a helpless Gourgy, things became a bit clearer. The Pooka had scat Gourgy around the head a good few times, and the blaws had made the Knockie dizzy. The cage wudn' there right now. Ut was down bottom, probably filling up with men. Ut was comin' on for the end of forenoon shift now.

They'd all armed themselves with spades and spars by now, rendering them at the Pooka, but he had one of his long arms grabbing hold of the iron framework, an' wuz looking down right inta' the darkness of the shaft. There, ee reckoned ee could make out the top of the cage. He had that agility this Pooka. Like an acrobat ee wuz – and able to swing and move wherever ee liked. All the time comed his laughter – a sound that went right through ee and inta' your bones. They could all see the panic in Gourgy's eyes. His skin had already turned black with rage but now ut wuz goin' a colour that none of the brothers had seen before: a bright purple. Luk nawticed ut too.

"Tha' idn' good," ee said, trying to downplay ut but not really able to do so.

"Whaas up with un?"

"What ee think?"

"You tell me..."

"Means he's so enraged ee must burst open..."

"I didn' knaw tha' could even happen."

"Well," said Luk, "we've never had cause fur ut before... I ebm seen un like tha' for well, at least two hundred years or more..."

Francis now knew the urgency of everything. So ut seemed then Knockies will self-sacrifice ef they feel really threatened, rendering them useless fur their captive. The thought ov this enraged him. He did not want to see his Knockie explode in this way, but more to the point, perhaps ee didn' relish the prospect of cleaning up the internal juices ov un when ut wuz all over. All joking aside though, ee cudn' see his meht meet his end in that way.

The long and short ov ut wuz tha' they needed to sort this matter out. Now normally, there'd be a boy on shift here operating the mechanism, which was determined by a bell, but ut being an odd kind of a day what with the cut happening, Justin wuz on that job. The system could be shut off too, and tha' wuz a good thing because nawbody knawed what the Pooka had planned. When they looked again though and drew nearer to where he wuz standin', right on the edge of the shaft, ee'd positioned Gourgy's head right in the line of the cage coming up. Fur all intents and purposes, ut seemed like his plan wuz to severe Gourgy's head when ut comed back up, like some kind of reverse guillotine. The little bugger wuz sat on top ov Gourgy who by now, wuz so dazed from the scats Richard had given un, that ee didn' knaw what wuz even happening to un. His head and neck were over the shaft, ready to be sliced off.

"You cen't do anything," shouted over Justin. "The mechanism is off. Even ef they give a ring up from belaw, nawthun'll happen. They'll knaw somethun's up."

The Pooka looked around him for a way out of this conundrum. That wuz ee see: his mind allays workin' overtime and finding solutions. You could maybe even predict what he wuz thinkin'. Fur a moment, ut appeared like he would cut the steel cables of the cage so that would put ut out ov action, and properly bugger up the mining operation long-term, but fortunately that proved too difficult fur'n. Ee didn' have any cutting equipment and besides, clambouring out there above the shaft wuz dangerous, wudn' ut? Pookas dun't take they kind ov chances. They ent stupid.

The thing wuz though that the Pooka had been conceived by magic, and ee had a fair strand ov ut running through un. All Pookas do, and so just to shaw off his power, when the bell rang for the cage to come up, the Pooka set the motor running again. When ee did tha', there seemed no way that anyone top-side could do anything 'bout ut. Up on the headgear, the wheel started turning to pull up the cage from belaw. Ut wuz a cage full ov men, and there wuz naw tellin' what he would do next. Ef he could manipulate the lever in tha' magical way of his, then ee'd probably be able to shake they to buggery inside of the cage. They wudn' knaw their ass from their elbow, because he'd bring um up and then send um down again. Up and down all the while, so they boys inside wudn' knaw ef they wuz coming or goin'.

Plenty would end up with broken bones an' the Doctor could put off all his wedding plans. Involving others wuz makin' ut more serious. The boys down there were good men too: hard-working an' loyal. They didn' deserve tha' kind of treatment t'all. No doubt ef ee could control the mechanism from where ee wuz, ee'd also bring ut up sharpish, and with Gourgy still lying there, well, nawbody even wanted to think 'bout tha'. That Pooka wuz still gleeful in his antics, but thaas they all over see. They never have the vision to see an end to ut, and inevitably, 'tis someone else who would get to tell um their time es up.

So now, not awnly wuz there Gourgy to think ov; there wuz also the men belaw in the cage. They cudn' have this happen, not here on Mountainside. Overall, with the help of the Doctor they'd had a good safety record. That would be burnt though if the cage comed up too quick – if the Pooka moved the lever too fast. The cage would come up, not awnly sheering off Gourgy's neck and head, but then the speed ov ut would smash inta' the head frame, an' knock all ov tha' t'smithereens you. The likelihood would perhaps be that the cost of rebuilding all ov tha' would render the mine unworkable, and then, ov course, there wudn' even be any need of the mineral tramway that somewhere out there, wuz being constructed at zactly the same time as all this wuz happening. 'Twas a sobering thought, and the more Francis thought about ut, the more ee knawed ee needed to act decisively.

Ee suddenly realised tha' the Pooka had set the cage in motion. The trundle ov ut upwards could be heard. Ee could see distant, belaw, the men's faces inside. They'd be looking forward to gettin' cleaned up in the washroom, and then laying out their clawthes in the drying house. Maybe they'd have a stroll down an' see how Skewsy and the others were gettin' on. Later, they'd stroll over to Rosie's fur a beer or two, and then Sunday they'd be thankful to God above fur givin' um deliverance from the many dangers of working underground. Panicked at this, Francis did the awnly thing ee could to try an' tempt the Pooka away from his task.

He readied Luk and Justin. Inside, scattered on the floor wuz still the remnants of Justin's crowst. The pasty had been demolished in the earlier struggle, but the saffron bun remained. Francis grabbed ut up from the floor an' presented ut to Richard. Tha' put un in a muddle. Ee wuz trying to concentrate on the lever and increasing uts speed, and so too wuz a trying to keep Gourgy in a wrasslin' lock that would have been worthy of any champion ov Cornwall. Gourgy cudn' move a muscle you, and ee wuz still that awful purple colour. The trundle wuz comin'; the cage wuz making uts way up and atop the headgear, the geht wheels spun.

The bun wuz enough to make Richard lose his concentration. He'd developed a taste fur um see, and maybe Francis had worked tha' out, knawin' that he'd already scoffed the whole of Luk's crib. Justin's bun wuz larger, and had more sweet currants in ut. The Pooka wuz caught between a rock and a hard place. Ee wuz reaching out fur the bun tha' Francis had placed down in front ov un, just out of his reach, so tha' ee had to stretch slightly further than ee wanted to. Justin was counting the levels ov where the cage wuz. Ee knawed ut was getting closer, and es, the speed wuz building up. But then, who can resist a saffron bun?

Not this Pooka, for as ee wuz reaching tha' little bit further to gain it and placed its astringent yet sweet flavour inta' his mouth, he had to let go ov Gourgy. With tha' done, and Gourgy up on his feet moving away from the shaft, the Pooka lost all concentration as he reached out fur the delicious bun. Tha' allowed Justin to work the lever and slaw right down the pace of the cage comin' up. Its trajectory could now be controlled by him: and so he stopped it, allowed the men from belaw to step out. The twin cage doors got opened and out they stepped, unaware of the chaos ov events top-side.

So consumed wuz a by hunger and the wish fur that taste inside ov his mouth again, that this Francis could now make the move he had wanted to make fur a while. Luk passed un a Cornish shovel, and its triangular head slipped right under the Pooka. Ee didn't even nawtice ut; in fact, ee didn' even see ut comin' so fixated wuz a on filling his belly. Thaas when Francis pushed un across the wood planchen and he tumbled into the thin air of the shaft. At this, ee dropped the saffron bun, an' that went tumbling into the darkness. Fur a while that Pooka Richard didn't even knaw ee wuz suspended in space: that there wuz now no floor. There wuz a final reach out with one of his gangly arms to find a hold but ut wuz too late. He was too far away from the edge. Then, ee dropped.

He wud have fallen down fifty fathoms to the bottommost level ov the mine. All ov they watchin' knawed ee wudn' survive tha'. Es, finally Francis had done the right thing and got rid of the bugger. Down belaw, every bone in his body would have been broken and his brains would be turned to mush. Luk, Gourgy and Justin could draw breath but the antics of Francis had gained attention from some of the forenoon shift who had seen wha' had happened.

"You a'right Cap'n?" asked Diddy Pasca.

"No," said Francis. "Not really."

Word went up to Becca. She wuz told she'd best come down mine right away. So she did. And then the cage went down again, and they brought up the remains of the Pooka. But well, you knaw the ways of Pookas now, and so when they all looked at Richard's body, ut was just a sweet baby, like ut had been once upon a time. Changelings can do that see. And when Rebecca discerned what had actually happened, and why her son wuz dead, she then realised the awful truth: that ut wuz her dear husband who'd gone an' killed un.

39

Many a mouth went clean abroad tha' day. All they present wuz daggin' to knaw the outcome ov this. Doctor Jewell was called. Some keddle boys runned up there. None ov they was brave enough though to tell un zactly who had been killed. They just told un there'd been an incident at the collar of the mine. He made his blustering way down there (realising of course, that he might need to deal with a serious injury or even a death), with a breathless Eleanor Prowse trailing behind un. After Maddy had left his surgery, Miss Prowse had come over and they had further discussed both plans for the chapel and for their forthcoming marriage. The hard, sweaty knock on the door broke all this conviviality.

When Jewell got there, he found silence, and of course, the broken body of his grandson on a bloodied tarpaulin that had been brought up from the eighth level. Taking a sharp intake of breath, he examined the infant, but stopped midway through: to prevent himself from being sick. 'Twas clear ee needed a breather. He'd seen a few sights had boy Jewell, but nawthun' like this. He wuz clearly retching at the sight of what he thought he was dealing with, and the duplicitous Pooka, as you know, looked all divine and sweet, as if ee wuz some kind ov cherub. Now, how grates beauty with blood, bone and guts?

All the while, George Jewell wuz talking to himself, as if out of body, and as if this wudn' his awn grandson. Those around him could tell. Then, he did his pronouncement. He spoke that as he delicately covered the body of Richard with the now-folded edges of the greasy tarp. True it wuz then that Francis had killed un. Justin tried to explain to both the Doctor and Rebecca what had actually happened, though when ee told ut like it wuz, ut sounded like a fiction, like some fantastical story that was made up fur daredoing and entertainment. In fact, ut sounded like some droll from the old country. Neither Knockie said nawthun'. Ut wuz probably best that they blended in at that moment, so they camouflaged themselves amongst the machinery. They just observed an' listened. But as to what they heard and saw, perhaps boath of they knew wha' was coming round the corner.

"You d'knaw zactly what ee wuz like," said a recalcitrant Justin to Rebecca, but this Rebecca had gone into a kind of denial about the prior behaviour of her son, despite her forefinger still being sore: despite ut almost bein' chomped off.

"He was my son," wuz the only thing she could repeatedly say, and that everyone about her heard from she. Some sad ut wuz to hear she in tears. Like The Flood 'twuz. Ut didn' look very good you, for Cap'n Nankervis.

"You didn' see what ee tried to do," pleaded Justin. "The boy would have had we all dead."

"He was just a baby," responded Rebecca. "A child."

"Es, but a baby who could shift his shape and become something else, something that wuz loathsome."

The way Justin wuz talking surprised the Doctor. Had the man been drinking again? Had he relapsed from his prior Teetotalism? Maybe that wuz the case. He was aware, like everyone, of Richard being a little truculent and unsettled, but this: this was something else indeed. The Doctor was trying to deal with his awn grief, he was trying to comfort his daughter, but was still trying his best to be professional. His voice had the same tone as usual, but stuttered slightly in uts delivery.

"I will need to send a telegram... down to Calumet. For the Record Office. This is our... first death. Not something we have contemplated before, but face it we must. Ground... will... will... ah... need to be consecrated. It's a matter I cannot do. Someone will need to come up. I think perhaps the flatter ground... to the right of the preaching pit. I will consult with Mr Skews but I am sure he will be agreeable."

Jewell could hear a muttering and low cussing from Justin.

"Cap'n Nankervis. You've clearly a view on the matter?"

Justin didn' really want to speak but felt forced to; all the while, his moping brother wuz in earshot. Ever since the boy's body had come up, Francis had collapsed in on himself and had been almost unable to process the gravity of what had happened: how in a moment of rage, he had killed his own son. Ee sat with his back to the brick base ov the furnace, rocking hisself into realisation ov what an error ee'd made.

"That baby dun't warrant no Christian burial," said Justin. He told um straight.

"Why ever not?" asked Jewell. "He is an innocent. He is one of God's children."

"Well, tha' might be your view," declaimed Justin, "but 'tidn' mine, nor my brother's here too. That thing wuz about as far from being innocent as the very Devil hisself. I tell ee – a strand ov evil runned through tha' boy – an' ee hisself caused his awn death through his actions. Francis here wuz just tryin' to protect we."

A few ov the boys present who'd come up in the cage knawed precisely what ee wuz talking about. They'd seen ut all fust hand, but there wuz naw way they cud mention how the Knockies were saved. To alert the Doctor to tha' would have broken the code, and that wudn' on the cards t'all. Justin knew that Becca had a notion ov they, so perhaps 'twas a matter best left fur she later, when maybe his brother could talk to her properly and explain his actions. They who didn' need to knaw had no requirement to understand or comment upon the relationship between miners and their Knockies. All they who went underground however, knawed how important ut wuz. Hell, you'd rather save your Knockie than just 'bout anyone else.

"I'm sorry you feel that way," said Doctor Jewell, trying to hold back his awn tears.

At tha' moment, ee stared into his own heart. Ee realised that his bond with Richard had not yet been fully formed. That is the way ut is with grandparents. He had hoped ut would come later though, but really ee knew that his pain was derived from feeling for his daughter. Ut was she who was heartbroken. Ut wuz her sobbing lamentation that had scared off the blue jays pecking at the earth outside, and those birds then even dared to enter the housing to pick up the rest of the crumbs from the squashed pasty.

"I suspect I'll need to file this with the authorities too," noted Jewell.

"The police you mean?" asked Justin worriedly.

"Of course. The matter will need investigating: how the baby got down here in the first place, how it fell down the shaft and so on..."

"We've explained tha' to you," said Justin.

"Maybe, but it is a serious matter Cap'n Nankervis. Infanticide always needs to be reported. This stuff... this stuff you've told me about its abilities... I have to keep a scientific mind on it."

Francis listened a bit more intently to this. Ee'd been solemnly quiet so far. The last thing he wanted wuz an investigation and to be interviewed by the police. But ee'd realised the consequences of his actions.

"I thought we wuz doing alright up here," said Justin. "I thought we runned our community the way we like ut..."

"We do," said the Doctor, "but surely you can see man, this is a lot more serious. I would be breaking my professional code as a mine surgeon if I let this pass. Perhaps it was an accident, but if there was any foul play then it needs to be detected and scrutinized."

There wuz he then – Doctor Jewell – now talking like ee wuz boath judge and jury.

"You'd best bring the body up to the surgery," he suggested to Bobby Moyle and Jack Hocking, who happened to be standing next to him. "I'll move things on with the consecration and the funeral. By the look ov ut, his father and mother are in no fit state to do anything."

They pair gingerly bent down to scoop up the Pooka's body. 'Course, never in a million years did they knaw what they wuz carryin'. Never would they have guessed that what they lifted up had been conjured up from the Deads awnly a short while ago. As Jewell left, ee comforted his daughter and in whispers told her that ut might be best for her to come back to his place, and spend some time with Miss Prowse and him. The Doctor looked relieved to see his new love when he stepped outside of the engine house. It wuz towards Rebecca that she wuz now pulled though, and despite her barely knowing her, Miss Prowse wrapped her arms around Rebecca's shoulders and tried to comfort her. Well, she wuz in now wudn' she – an' her real mawthur didn' seem capable of makin' ut outside – let alone caring fur another human being in a time of trouble.

By now, the bob had stopped working and temporarily, the ground had stopped juddering. Because of this new peace, fur Nimkii something had altered. He had left his accommodation and strolled around to the entrance of the engine house where all of the men were still standing. He'd come past the original place where all that time ago he, Justin and Francis had landed the first kibbles of ore that comed up from the mine.

"Richard's been killed," Justin said, simplifying events for the Indian.

"I know," he said. "I sensed it."

T'be honest, tha' wuz almost the kind of thing tha' Justin expected him to say. Ee wuz like tha', wudn' a? All mystical and full ov sensory abilities. Wha' Justin didn't expect wuz fur Nimkii to look over at the floor, where the crowst boxes had been scattered. Nimkii bent down, and in his hand he picked up a few crumbs off the floor, peered at them intently, and then sniffed them deeply, as if he were tracking an animal through the forest.

He then smiled at Justin.

"Saf-fron," he said.

At first, ut was hard for Justin to make sense of him. Ee was not much accustomed to dealing with Nimkii, and maybe Nimkii felt he should say it again. Justin put his hand to his ear, encouraging him to speak again with his hand.

"Saffron," he offered, this time more loudly and more confidently.

"Yes," said Justin, and in that, he knew that at least Nimkii had understood what had happened, and why they needed to do what they did. Maybe he truly had sensed the presence of that thing. Ut was certainly the kind of thing he did. This was an important boost of confidence to Justin, who up until now, had felt he was almost a lone voice trying to defend his brother.

The boys who had comed up in the cage began to scatter now. None of they knawed what to say. 'Twas terrible what had happened you, but there wudn' nawthun' they could do 'bout ut. They was worried up 'bout Francis though. Ee was a good Cap'n and seeing ee like ee wuz didn' fill they with much confidence tha' things were goin' to return to normal any time soon. See, events like this were not good fur a mine. How you want ut to be is to gaw on steady. When things is tense, thaas just when some bugger'd make a mistake or something would end up where ut shouldn' be and tha' would have an effect on something else. A chain of consequences see, that nawbody really wanted. Es. Changelings above and changelings belaw.

Word as to what had happened spread quickly. Time ut had spread through the town, the news about Richard's death made ut down to the cut. There, ut shocked all they involved. Skews felt ut the moast perhaps. Ee, as you knaw, had that interest in childurn and didn' like to see they suffer. And when they got told that ut wuz Francis who'd had a hand in ut, well, even the bosses downed tools fur the day. Ut didn' seem right carryin' on. Methodist respect wuz due. Trevorrow thought he should best get up there and see what wuz on, but Skews dissuaded him from doin' anything. At the moment, ut would all still be very raw and private.

"Best let sleeping dogs lie," Skews noted, but see this boy, well, ee allays had a plan, and maybe when ut all fell on his ears, ee wondered ef this Francis would survive this. Maybe he'd be incarcerated, and in Skewsy's mind tha' wuz a good thing, because fur a while now, ut had always been him and Francis who'd been at loggerheads over plans fur the mine, so him having problems might open things up a bit. Maybe Skews would have the power to buy him out, and thus gain his share. Ee projected a forty-percent share. The prospect wuz tempting. Already, this passed through his mind, as news as to what had happened met the navvying team working down the slope. What a tuss, eh? Ef Justin knawed tha', he might well have comed across an' battered un t'death, and perhaps ef ee wudn' in such a bad way right now (moping an' sighing as ee wuz), Francis would have done the same thing too. What Skews also liked wuz that now Francis didn't have anything over un. He cudn' say anything t'all now that ut seemed like he'd killed his awn son, whether 'twas accidental or not. His misdemeanours eclipsed Skews' awn failings an' tha' delighted un.

The Minter who had been absent-mindedly and lustily thinking about the wide realm of Rosie's thighs, was snapped back into life again when ee 'eard tell ov events. The cage and the collar were where all his h'engineering propensities had gone, as was the furnace and the boiler. To have all of they mentioned worried him a good deal. Ee didn' want to be accused ov some sloppy piece of construction that caused a life to be taken. He and Jewell had built up a good working relationship ee thought, and ee didn't want that compromised. In his mind, the key question wuz this: wha' wuz a bleddy baby doing ov there anyway? There wuz nawbody who'd argue with un because, let's be honest you, everyone wuz thinking the same. 'Course, none of they had a clue about the unique abilities of Richard, the dead Pooka.

'Bout the awnly thing they agreed upon though wuz that there wuz goin to be a period of mourning, a time of lamentation. That thought ran down through the cut, where already root bases and stumps were being levered up and hauled out of the ground. Es. 'Twas true what they were saying: this wuz the first death t'come the way of the town. 'Twas a soberin' moment: perhaps made even more sobering by the fact that 'twuz an infant who'd been taken into the care of the Lord above.

"What have I done?" Francis wuz loudly wailing in the echoing confines of the engine house. Before, ee'd been quiet and numbed by the shock ov everything, but now he had started to think about how his life had altered so quickly.

"You done the right thing boy," Justin said, "Dun't get all angsty on me."

Nimkii wuz observing all ov this, looking sympathetic, but not knowing what to say. None of his healing wuz goin' to work here, right now. The inner wound was too deep and too serious. Ut not awnly affected Francis physically; from his actions, ee knawed he'd never have any peace in his mind again. That got him to thinking ee should end it here and now, and launch hisself off the planchen boards and tumble to his own death just like his son. Es. Suicide would do ut, and that would really see him not being buried in any consecrated ground. Perhaps such a fate wuz best.

The problem wuz tha' all of his dreams had been upended. Ever since the three of them had stood over that first dig, ee had wanted something of the life he had until now shaped fur hisself. Ef awnly Becca and ee had not abandoned Richard. What ef they'd stuck with un, and managed to alter his behaviour? This wuz wha' good parents did see, and apparently, from his actions here, ee did not have the patience. What a piss-poor feythur he had been! He weighed all ov this up in his mind, jus' like anyone would. What had pushed un this far? Wuz ut the coal on Gourgy's foot? Wuz ut the biting ov his wife's finger – or wuz ut the fact that he'd had a crack at killing two of his closest and moast valued companions? When he thought about ut, he realised that it was actually all of those factors that had pushed him into doing what he did. Richard had been cruel. That cruelty ran right through his body, and when Francis did what ee did, ee had to see that end. Justin understood, and maybe this Nimkii got ut too.

None ov that compensated though for the heartache ee had caused his wife and family. He prayed that she would think through what their boy had done, and how ee had torn them apart. Yet ee also knew that his actions would mean that ee'd perhaps have to face time in jail, or the gallows, and that Rebecca would never want to speak to him again. For him, ut wuz a bitter irony that he had dealt with what wuz pushing them apart, and breaking their marriage; and yet this very act of dealing with it, would apparently do the same thing. Ee realised ee had responded badly to a situation ee could never have won. The fact that ee had been a fool made him even more despondent.

The jealousy that had once raged inside Francis about his brother and his life had now dissipated. A long time ago, Francis had turned Justin's life around by bringing him to 'Merky'. Now, the boot wuz on the other foot. Whatever had passed between them ov late was superseded by their brotherly care for each other. Justin knew that if Francis had not done the job with Richard, then he hisself would have finished the creature off. As they had seen with Jewell, the difficulty was explaining precisely what had happened to a disbelieving audience. Their awnly true witnesses were Gourgy and Luk, who had now made themselves visible again. Nimkii barely batted an eyelid when they joined in with the conversation. Like Mabel, he could see them. He knew of their presence, as well as the rest of their species down in the levels belaw. He knew well the other land sprites out there too: the ones who hid and rustled in the forest.

"We seen ut all," said Luk.

"We knawed zactly what ee wuz like. I'd testify," said Gourgy.

"I appreciate it," said Francis, "but there's no way I'm putting you pair before a court."

"'Twould be worth ut," stated Luk.

"Not sure it would," responded Francis. "We cen't have you reveal yourselves. That would be it."

Francis feared that the magic between Knockies and humans would then forever be broken. Ut couldn' happen.

"I think tha' when you tell Becca that their lives were in danger, she'll be more understanding..." said Justin, trying to raise his spirits.

"She didn' seem that way before," noted Francis.

"Give her some time to think ut through."

"We'll have a word," said Luk to Gourgy, "wun't us boy?"

"'Course. She'll see ut... We'll make her see ut."

There was a pause. Everyone thought about what they'd said. Ut seemed the best plan they could muster for now.

"A'right then," said Justin. "You pair work your magic..."

The Knockies left. Maybe they'd creep up to the Jewell house and see what wuz on up there.

Justin looked tense. He needed to be somewhere else. Maybe he needed the comfort ov his awn boy at home.

"I'd best be getting back... I need to tell Maddy..."

"Do that" said Nimkii. "He comes with me."

Nimkii lifted up Francis and took him out of the engine house, around the remains of the kibble-landing station, and to his own steel tepee. There Nimkii planned on some restorative medicine: that for the body and also that for the soul. And what he did with Francis, ironically, probably Doctor Jewell would love to have seen, but as you know, he wuz busy elsewhere. Even now, ee' d be notifying people in Calumet. He planned to see Skews and get some telegrams urgently sent down there. He also, for the first time in a long time, took a renewed interest in his son James when they got back. Maybe he wasn't protecting him as much as he could. Maybe he'd need to make amends with his Mabel too, to try to show her how much he cared. He knew she was probably still down at Maddy's place, trying to stimulate her mother (his wife) into some kind of response. All this, and she had not even met her first grandchild when it was alive, when it hadn't been tossed down a dark shaft. He couldn't help but be saddened by that in particular.

Meanwhile, Nimkii set about calming Francis, aiming to give him the strength to cope with the death of his son, but also to consider what he had killed and why he had done it. Maybe Nimkii, via incantation and chant could make him come to understand what had happened. Maybe he could somehow explain that this child – this Richard – was never what he thought it had been, and that the world, the universe and Yolkai had predetermined his end, for Nimkii understood – and although he had only seen the child a couple of times – he knew its difference: that it wuz somehow not of this earth, and that someone or something had made ut.

If he could show Francis this via visions and projections then maybe things could heal. The first thing he did wuz to put Francis asleep. He prepared a tea made of herbs and flowers for him to drink, which lulled him into a drowsy sense of space and time, and then made him enter a deep sleep. This Nimkii decided wuz what he had stayed for. Ut had been growing and underpinning everything, and now a deed had been completed. Sometimes, such deaths were necessary. They were part of the story, for Nimkii knew well (like that Irish woman) of the grey line between reality and magic. He was hoping too, in completing this healing, that he might discern where this feeling had come from, and why it had been inflicted on this tiny part of the Keweenaw. He'd need to talk to the forest. He'd need to converse with Yolkai.

As he made preparations for Francis, he considered his relationship with Mabel. Now that her mother was back, maybe it was time soon to ask her. Maybe the moment was right. Perhaps things were in place, and they needed to be enacted. He had not yet seen Clara Jewell, but it was something he'd planned on doing that day before the disruption. For now though, there was the urgency of this. They were not that different in ages Francis and he, and yet bags were forming already under Francis' eyes and, even at his temples, his hair was greying. And now this: this infanticide. All he could do was to heal the only way he knew. So he set forth. He and this miner from Cornwall were going on an important journey.

"True is ut?" asked a puffed out Trevorrow, walking back up the slope from working the cut. "Whatever happened?"

He asked that latter question in the high-pitched way that the Cornish do sometimes when something needed to be faced. Justin shook his head, agonised over what he should say.

"All I'n say is tha' Francis did what he needed to do," wuz what ee eventually mouthed.

"So ee did kill un then?"

"Yes."

"Hell-fire," said Trevorrow. "'Tis true then... a murder here."

"No, not a murder..."

They stared at each other, waiting for the other to break. These men went back a long way. They'd been through much.

"Nawthun' to do with the gear or equipment then?"

"Naw... Thaas all fine..."

"Minter'll be pleased. I think ee wuz worried."

"Ee had no need. Naw, this was all man-made... this... incident..."

"Es. How's brother?"

"Not so good. Ee's with Nimkii."

Trevorrow nodded. Ee had naw idea what Nimkii might do with un, but at the same time, ee realised that the Indian's care might well be what he needed.

"And Becca?"

"With her feythur..."

"Good... Well, 'spect we shall learn more soon, eh?"

Trevorrow wuz right. They'd all knaw soon and they'd decide who wuz right and who wuz wrong. Lurking Methodism saw Trevorrow feel pity for the boy.

"Some sad," he said, "about the liddle boy..."

And he knew the moment he told Mrs Cap'n, she'd burst into tears. He had that to come.

There was another pause between them, as they contemplated the grim significance of what had happened. Justin knawed the truth inside, but felt he best live up to what wuz expected. Other boys wuz coming up now, giving respectful nods to Justin; they knew then. So too, were Skews and Minter, who at this point in time, just kept their distance, not yet knawing the full truth. Minter would be going to Rosie's and Skewsy well, ee'd get home and scheme.

"S'pause this is the time we really need a chapel," said Trevorrow.

"Yes," said Justin. "Would be very handy if we did. I gather Doctor Jewell is sorting out some consecrated ground..."

"Es, well we should have done that time or two ago... but ut's something we never got round to."

Another pause.

"I'll leave ee to ut then boy," said Trevorrow, which is what all Cornish say when really they ought to grab somethun' by the horns.

"Rite on," said Justin.

Trevorrow continued up the slope and Justin sidled across to his own residence.

"Aw... I near forgot," ee enquired. "How's the cut going?"

"Making good progress boy. Good progress."

They doffed their bowlers (by now, Justin's wuz straddled with grease, coal dust and bun crumbs, but Trevorrow's wuz still, after all those years, neat and tidy) and walked on.

Inside the Nankervis and O'Donahue property, Justin returned to see Mabel reading to her mother. Ut was neither a romantic story nor a fairy tale, but instead, a work on practical animal husbandry – one ov the few books they had in the house.

"Any change in your mam?" Justin enquired.

"Nothing," said Mabel. "Not that I can see anyway..."

Clara just sat there upon a straight-backed chair, staring forward. She did not make eye contact with either of them.

"I expect she'd have liked to have see'd her grandson," said Justin nervously.

"Perhaps," said Mabel, "but when I gave her Jago there she didn't know what to do with him, so I don't think she's ready..."

In his cradle, Jago grinned up at his feythur, reaching out his stubby arms for him.

"Look... Maybe thaas a good thing," said Justin, which for Mabel sounded a slightly perverse thing to say.

"Why?" she asked anxiously.

"You've not heard?"

"Heard what? I've been here all day with my mother."

"Jus' tha' somethun bad's happened. You see... tha' boy..."

He wuz about to explain matters to Mabel, when Maddy entered, strolling in from taking a bath in the kitchen. She had felt like it after that awful examination from Doctor Jewell.

"What's happened?" she asked, vigorously towelling her hair.

Justin sat down at the table and put his head in his hands. Then he explained. He told them the full story. He told them how Richard got killed and what had happened next to Francis and Becca. Mabel listened urgently to the full run of the narrative, interrupting him with questions that anyone might have. Maddy's skin turned white and she remained quiet: just listening to what her man wuz tellin' ov them.

"The poor thing," said Mabel, but she knew what he was like. She had heard tell ov un being a bit of a bewdie.

Justin didn' respond. Ed cudn'. Ee had his mind set already.

"Poor Becca... You say Francis pushed un off an' inta' the shaft?"

"Es... Well, you should have seen un..." said Justin, and he expanded his account of events.

Maddy wuz by now ashen-faced. Her response surprised him.

"I need to see his body," she said.

"Why's that?"

"I just need to..."

She began to put on an overcoat.

"You cen't go now..."

"Why not?"

"It's up at the surgery... What's your interest anyway?"

"Just want to see the boy. That's all. I mean, technically he's my nephew... Now, surely I can if I want to?"

"You'll have a hard job..."

"Why's that?"

"There idn' much left ov un. The eighth level's a good way down."

Maddy paused. She realised how what she had said so far sounded too urgent. She had shown too great an interest. She knew she had to be careful. She knew precisely why Francis had acted as he did, but too little interest in events could show an all too casual and almost knowing response to things, whereas too much might also be damning in the sense of an overenthusiastic interest in her 'relatives' and her now dead nephew.

She knew she would need to play this just right. Justin wudn' naw ordinary fool either and she realised that if she got any of this wrong, she might raise some suspicions. Sure, he would never find out because no one could even begin to tell him of the substitution, but here indeed was something she had feared. Maybe she should have toned down the Pooka, made it easier to handle, and not made it so vile and aggressive, but that wuz the way of things with they. Ut wuz pot luck always, and at the time, and resolutely right then at this moment, she still did not regret what she had done. That Francis and that Becca; they'd get over this. There wuz time for they to have another chield. She wudn' in that position. Ut wuz why she had acted the way she did. The venereal disease had given them naw choice.

So she asked about the details of what had happened, and Justin told her more precisely what transpired up mine. And at appropriate moments she shed the right amount of tears and made the right sounds of surprise and comfort from her mouth, which she hoped would convince the very earth itself. As Justin told ut though, she could almost predict precisely what would happen. Of course, he'd climbed high on the chimley stack. Of course, he'd gone for their crowst. Of course he had dropped everything for a taste of a bit of saffron bun. Tha' wuz the way of they things. She knew ut from home. This one, she admitted though, sounded particularly vile.

Was ut her fault? No, she kept trying to tell herself. There'd have been no need of a swap, no need for a changeling... if... well, things had been different. She told herself she had not engendered that. Fate, circumstance and others had determined it. See how we are so quick to blame others for our own selfishness and our own frailties. When those thoughts emergent in her heart, she took a sharp needle and thick thread and sewed it right back up again. They would be kept inside her no matter what: no matter even if her man, Justin, felt this heightened sense of doom from it, and no matter that this being, this Pooka boy, had been sacrificed along the way. It was a price worth paying she told herself. Good see, this Maddy was, at telling herself the right tale, and never deviating from the trail.

All she had to do was to keep quiet and not flinch at anything put her way. She'd only have to survive that for a while. Had she anticipated this moment? Well, perhaps inside she had, but she'd told not a soul. Her mammy had taught her that see. Stay hard. It's the only way. Move any, and they'll take the piss. Once all this present heartbreak was over, it would return to normal. Aye, it surely would. The thing wuz though that whilst Justin slept that night (despite the horrors of the day, he had been exhausted), Maddy could not. She got up and paced around the planchen, holding tight her little Jago Ciaran in her arms. And the moonlight streamed in on the floorboards, marking out the wood where she had strewn her own blood – her own blood you – to make it look like this one in her arms had been born here.

As she paced, she hoped all would be well. But that didn' stop her thinking of brewing another changeling that might perhaps become a foundling – that could be put in the forest, and be timed exactly so that Becca might find him or her. But no, she was thinking crazily, wildly now. That could not be enacted. Changelings, you see, were one-shot deals. You had one chance with they. Any woman of her kind knew tha'. Ut took every power you had to make just one, and all the magic in the world wudn' about to give ya a second chance. She put Jago to her breast and fed him. Such moments as this were worth everything. Thaas how she saw the world, this Maddy. Deep inside ov her evil coating, there wuz something soft and vulnerable. Maybe you'll understand ut and maybe you won't, but that was the way ov she.

From what Justin had said, ut looked like there would be a funeral then. She'd have to stand firm. She steeled herself for the ordeal.

"Doan't you be cracking Madelaine O'Donahue. I'm telling you. You'll have me to answer to if you do."

She could hear her mother's toughened voice.

Jago got put back into his cradle and she got into bed with Justin. He was warm and she moved herself close to him. She was going to need him.

In the morning, when Nimkii awoke, he found that to his great surprise, Francis had gone. In that instant, ut felt like all of his healing had somehow failed. His pain had been too great. Straight away, she went across and notified Justin first, and then they searched the mine itself. Naw trace ov un underground you. Naw Knockie had seen un. After tha', they went and hurried to Francis and Becca's residence. There, matters became a bit clearer. Ut wuz what Justin had feared: his knapsack wuz gone and moast ov Francis' clawthes had been taken from the cupboard, where ee usually kept them. They went on to the Jewell residence but when Jenny Spargo answered the door, she said that they'd not seen un either. Becca, and the Doc, were still asleep.

The thing wuz Francis didn' want to be found guilty by anyone investigating the death of his son. That said, ee knawed ee couldn' stay for he had a very deep vein of guilt running through un. Nimkii had tried his best with all his mumbo-jumbo new world magic – he understood tha' – but at the same time, ee needed to get away. Ee wanted to return to Cornwall, but fur now, somewhere else would have to do.

Waking up at Nimkii's residence in the pre-dawn, ee had collected his things from home and then written a brief note to Becca. Then, he'd made his way down through the planned cut to Eagle Harbour. Ut took un an hour or so. A Captain named Nathaniel who he knawed said that as a favour he'd give un free passage an' take un down state. This particular laker normally put in to Port Huron, but later that week, they'd make ut all the way down to Detroit: a vessel now laden with copper ore from the mine that had once meant everything to Francis. But if anything, all Nimkii's attempts to calm and soothe him, had had the opposite effect. In Detroit, he knew he might find his fortune. There, the streets might be paved with gold. Everything else needed to be left behind. This wuz another shift; another migration. Ee'd have to become something different.

40

Some time passed you. How long passed is now hard to recall. We think we d'knaw the minutes an' the hours but the memory is always fallible. A good deal happened though. For a long while, nearly everyone (maybe you' knaw who wudn' though) spent their hours and days grieving. Foremost, there wuz Becca Nankervis, who in a few hours, had lost boath her chield and her husband. Ground wuz consecrated (an elderly minister by the name of Revered Josiah Davies came up from Calumet, and before Richard's burial, the ground was blessed). The funeral service wuz conducted by him too (Jewell wudn' in naw fit state to orate or manage proceedings, as he wuz mourning alongside Rebecca), and wuz held in the schoolhouse, and afterwards, a small, wooden coffin (the fust the carpenters had made at Mountainside) was carried out to the newly-formed cemetery. He wuz laid in the ground at the top of the run of land: perhaps the first of many to come. All present considered Richard's fate, but as is the way at all funerals, also their own: the likelihood that one day too, their remains would end up here – lonely and unremembered – but at least looking down over Lake Superior. They imagined their own future graves: no longer any flowers left by respectful and loving mourners, fast brambles growing and headstones toppling.

All they in the community were present for the service (as many at least who could squeeze inta' the schoolhouse, whilst others remained in respectful silence outside). Anyone who wuz anyone in Mountainside attended. News had travelled fast in the Knockie community too (and they knawed what they wuz dealing with here), so all they (least the ones who wuz young enough to go top-side) were all boobed up, looking at the interment though out ov respect, hidden from view. They camouflaged themselves against the backdrop of the dark forest an' looked on with mouths abroad. Nawbody'd heard from Cap'n Frank, but they still felt they'd better be there, despite wha' Gourgy and Luk had said about this boy who wuz being buried.

Bit ov a bugger ee wuz and naw mistake.

Perhaps Cap'n had done the right thing.

Cap'ns knaw see.

At the service, Rebecca stood beside her father, and slightly behind him wuz Miss Prowse. Jenny Spargo wuz there, looking after an inattentive James, though Mabel could not attend. She wuz, of course, looking after her needy mawthur, and since the unexpected leaving of Francis, Clara had moved into the Nankervis residence with her daughter. Well, ut wudn' like she could continue to be with Justin and Maddy. That wudn' right. Tha' pair were there too though; boath ov they with very different thoughts going on inside their minds. Justin wuz there under duress: everyone knawed how ee felt, not least Jewell and Rebecca, but out of respect (in that frosty way of the Cornish) he comed anyway. Despite his inner turmoil, ee knawed he had to front this one out. It wuz the case too tha' a man in his kind of position should be there.

With Maddy, ut wuz different. Despite wha' she had told herself about her conduct over this next period of time, she had withdrawn herself from the community. Perhaps this wuz her awnly way of dealing with ut. At least, all of her Irish companions were there too (treading on a very different part of the cemetery, for a Catholic part of ut had also been consecrated of late). Behind she, stood Flannery, Cillian and the rest of her boys, fresh from navvying the lower section of the cut.

Maddy's withdrawal allowed her to forget what had been done. She focused on Jago Ciaran, who even still a nursling, wuz grawin' fast, and wuz as bonny a boy as anyone could hope. By naw, ee wuz into everything, and had an inquiring mind. She knew why that wuz, but she tried not to think too much about ut. Instead, all her energies went into talking to him and telling him stories from her past – and others than she made up on the spot. Besides, ut wudn' like she wuz goin' to spend any time with Rebecca, wuz ut now? A woman who've lost a chield dun't particularly want to spend any time with those tha' do have one. Maddy reckoned ut wud have been insensitive of she to turn up at her property anyway, regardless of the deeper and more malign reason ov her wish for limited contact.

What Maddy came to learn about however, was something she had not contemplated – and tha' wuz Francis' leaving. Him picking up and goin' wuz somethun' new to the mix. There wuz something about tha' that didn' sit right with she. She seem to knaw ut would have ramifications. 'Course, she understood well why ee'd gone. Jewell had stood by his word, and asked the limited and somewhat pathetic constabulary from Calumet to come up and investigate Richard's death. Now, you can imagine what lengths Justin had to go to in order to defend his brother. Ut wudn' naw easy story to put across, but the police did take a bit more nawtice when he told um that he believed the baby to have been possessed by some bad spirit. Nimkii had weighed in at tha' point and spun some tail about this part of the forest being evil (maybe ee really believed tha' at this point) but his simple sentences seemed to confirm wha' this Justin Nankervis had said to them. The miners from the cage gived their side of ut too, which wuz one hundred percent supportive, telling the police about the strange power of the chield. A few of um mentioned ut's evil intent too.

As part of the investigation, they'd politely asked to see Rebecca's finger, and whilst the wound and the severing of her skin were perhaps healing a little (ut would fester fur many months yet), all ov that did add extra evidence to the tale they were told. 'Course, who they really needed to speak to, wuz Francis Nankervis, but now that ee'd disappeared, the trail went cold. Certainly, his name would be circulated across Michigan though and other surrounding states. Maybe someone wud knaw of un. The other thing they faaced wuz the very real possibility tha' he'd made his way across the country, and even now wuz catching some vessel bound fur Cornwall. Becca'd shown them the note he'd written but ut told um nawthun' really; awnly tha' he couldn't stand to live in Mountainside anymore an' that ee had to go. And after all ov tha' nonsense, the Police filed the case under the category ov 'unresolved'. There wudn' nawthun' more they could do. Maybe at this time infanticide wudn' given the full attention it should have had. But tha' wuz ut. See, a lot ov childurn died back then and such deaths went unreported. Still, the police marked Mountainside as maybe a plaace to keep an eye on. An' they Cornish up there, well, they were some weird, wudn' um?

Maddy's heart did jump a few beats though when Justin told her tha' he'd spoken to the police, but she still knew at this stage, tha' nawbody could pin anything on she. She wuz at a good distance to the whole killing of Richard. She reviewed events in her mind's eye. She'd been with Doctor Jewell, and then she'd strolled back to her residence fur a soothing bath. She'd spent time with Clara and Mabel. Aye. There wuz nawthun' for her to worry about. She realised that her sin had gone undetected and had taken place so long in the past now that ut could be from time immemorial. She kept telling herself not to worry. Like her mother had told her to be, she kept hard. Maybe you can see ut, but perhaps some gads and wedges were being driven into her heart though: and tha' was a direct result of Francis' leaving. That action had altered fate. Her plan had been fur he an' Rebecca to cope with the changeling, and then once they killed un, well, there wuz plenty of time for they to have other children. She awnly wanted one, and if she hadn' acted the way she had, then she'd be childless. Preserving self wuz all tha' mattered to she. And the bond between she and liddle Jago – that lovely baby boy – wuz some tight. She'd filled un brimful ov love.

Funerals are a test of allegiances, en't um? Allays, there are the vagaries ov remembrance. That morning, ut looked t'anyone watchin' tha' Rosie Koskinen and Dicky Mint were standin' a bit closer together than usual. Nawthun' had been made formal yet, but a few eyes nawticed the looks they wuz givin' each other. One who did nawtice they pair wuz Justin Nankervis. He'd wondered why she and Dicker Mint seemed to allays be in each other's pockets, and now, well, ut seemed clear to him what wuz on. Ee didn' say nawthun' though. 'Twudn' the time nor the place. But ee did note how they wuz in the service: they had the same look about um as Doctor Jewell and his ladyfriend, tha' Miss Prowse. Ee knawed tha' currently at least, Maddy and ee didn' give across tha' appearance of being all loved up. Ee felt she'd been distant with un fur a while now: maybe ever since ee'd comed home with the news ov Richard's death. Still, tha' wuz how relationships go sometimes: ups and downs and turns and twists. You cudn' odds ut. What you had to do wuz stay there fur the ride and the final destination ov things.

Aw, there wuz some singing in the schoolhouse you, fur the baby. 'Twas tha' which even in his grieving ignited the heart ov Doctor Jewell, fur in tha' brief moment ut felt like a proper chapel, and tha' the crescendo ov miner's voices were really praising the Lord. Bewdie hymns were sung. See, nawbody could sing quite like the Cornish on such occasions, and the baritonal resonance of ut all near shook the walls ov the schoolhouse. Ee cud feel ut in his chest cavity. Ee didn' want another funeral but he accepted that this was a feeling he wanted again and again. Fur the first time maybe, ut had felt like home.

In the service and at the grave, wuz Mr Skews too. He had been very helpful to Doctor Jewell in arranging everything. The moment he had learnt about the death of Cap'n Nankervis's boy, he had done his level best to help with arrangements over the body and even coordinated the making of the coffin. He never neglected any telegram messages that needed to be sent, and liaised with the authorities. Ee rushed over with anything that comed back on the wire. Ee wuz good at all tha' wuz this Skewser. Knawing the mechanisms wuz his speciality. Ee put a grease on everything so ut would slide forward with ease. In all of this, people admired un fur wha' he'd done. The Doctor publically praised un up good an' proper, and in those days after the incident, well, a fair few people looked at un in a different light. Maybe ee wudn' such a geht tuss as they'd all thought. Maybe there wuz a whiff of kindness in the man's heart.

'Twas a front though. You knaw tha'.

Ee'd been 'oping tha' at the funeral ee might spy Mabel, fur ee hadn' seen she fur a while now. Ee still had they urges see. Then again, ee knawed the reason behind ut: ut wuz she who wuz now caring fur her weird mother. He'd briefly seen the state of Clara Jewell, and on seeing she, he'd immediately gone back home to check his own appearance in the mirror above his washbowl, just to double-check there wuz not the same wear and tear on he as there wuz with she. His tick wuz still there, but hell, she looked like a ghost. But then, thaas' what a year and a half in the forest could do to anyone on their own. His Mabel though, the Mabel tha' he craved, was allays distant now. If she wudn' with her mawthur, then she wuz with Nimkii – an' sadly fur ee, ee cud tell where tha' wuz going.

Once all the procedures of burial had taken plaace, people drifted off. There'd be hot tay es, an' a bite of saffron bun, back in the schoolhouse, but the Reverend Davies and Doctor Jewell stayed a while, affixing a wooden cross with Richard Nankervis' name on ut. Eventually, at some future point, they'd pay a mason to put up a more permanent memorial. Right now though, they tidied the passel ov flowers (moast ov which had been collected the day before from the forest) and then agreed, as a pair, that they'd done the baby boy justice, howsoever ee had ended up being deaded.

Jewell had been alarmed tha' Francis had done what he had. His running away felt like a sign of guilt. The fact that he had done this to his own daughter made him taissy as a snake. Ef ee ever laid his eyes on that boy again, ee give un what fur. He realised he needed to be careful though, Right now, despite his cool Methodist exterior, inside him a bitter fire wuz burning. Es. He wanted to see that bugger Nankervis caught and brought to book. Ef he wuz innocent, then surely ee would have stayed, wudn' a? What did a have to hide? Ut must have been somethun'. An' ee an' his brother: now thick as thieves – es, fur the thieving of a life.

This doddery Reverend Davies wuz a goodly old soul (who knawed the Prowse family) and ee wuz jabbering on about the planned construction of their new chapel here, but Jewell's mind, see, wuz elsewhere. He even wondered ef Rebecca wud ever forgive her husband fur wha' ee had dun. The unspoken element ov all ov this wuz tha' awnly ef wha' he and his brother said wuz true, then maybe they could begin to rebuild their family. But now, as well as losing her chield, his daughter wuz also near 'nuff a widow. To take off, in the way tha' ee'd dun', well, 'twudn' proper t'all. He knew the thought of this would give un restless nights for years to come.

On top ov this, of course, ee now also had to deal with Clara. He knawed she'd moved in with his daughter, which in an unconventional way, wuz a good thing. She cudn' carry on stayin' with that Justin and Maddy, but in reality, ee wanted her off the scene. Ee knawed what she'd become – and from what ee could diagnose – there wudn' goin' to be any immediate change. This Doctor wuz good see, at sterilising his past. He wanted to take a disinfectant-infused cloth, and wipe ut all clean. There wuz his former wife right in front of un all the time, like some festering mass of forest fungi, and all he wanted was for her to be removed. He felt a pang of guilt though, that rubbed him up the wrong way: that Francis had wanted something cleansed, and now he wanted exactly the same thing too. Perhaps they were more alike than he thought. This unnerved him completely, and back at the schoolhouse, he had to put on a kindly pretence. Ut wuz enough to fool Miss Prowse, who held his arm tightly – and maybe even lovingly. Meanwhile, back at the Nankervis house, Mabel levered up another spoonful of a thin vegetable soup into Clara Jewell's unreceptive mouth. As usual, some ov ut oozed out beyond her lips, and Mabel had to dab her jaw with a napkin.

Nimkii watched the comings and goings ov all in the community in the lead-up to Richard's funeral. He knawed well what went inta' the earth there. Ut had never been his plan to have put something ov that order into the ground here, but he knew their reasoning. The consecrated ground wuz necessary so it seemed, in order for they and their god to conduct the passage of the soul into the afterlife. But this thing tha' went in – from what Justin had said – in life, ut didn have much ov a soul, fur ef ut did, then ut would have acted very differently. He'd seen the state of uts body when they'd brought ut up from belaw, but even then, after the funeral, and after everyone had departed, Nimkii went up to the ground and stamped down even more firmly on the wave of earth. Like several others he knew, they dun't want anything coming back, crawling out of the earth again.

As he did so, the forest watched, as it had done all day. Of late, it had seen the former land of itself being given over to the name ov some strange human god, and then a small lozenge of a box placed in the ground. How odd these humans were, and there now, wuz this Nimkii, flattening ut all down with his feet. Maybe it should have said something to that Nimkii about his actions, and maybe too, it should have been more willing to talk, for it knew all about Maddy and the Pooka. It knew why that Cap'n Frank had to dispose ov ut. It had seen what the thing could do. As a stealthy voyeur, it had been watching all the way through, but surely, some of the forest sprites thought, there ought to be some reckoning: some new negotiation for what had been done: why this man had done what he needed to do, and why others judged him. Maybe this Nimkii wuz picking up on this – and sensing ut – but who could tell? The forest worked slowly: did things its own way and at its own pace. When he was younger, Nimkii could tell what it was thinking, but perhaps not so much now. He and it had come apart.

It had watched that women, that witch (for she was tha', it knew) negotiate with it. It had seen her a long time ago sit in its trees and mark them with chalk, it had seen her give birth to a dead creature; and of late, that same woman had negotiated – or rather pleaded – for the return of Clara Jewell. It knew the confederation it had with this woman (she was as close to it as any human could be), but on the other hand, the forest deplored deceit. Deceit was why it had taken vengeance in the first place. The rest of the humans were untrustworthy. Now there was this swathe of clearance going down to the shoreline of the lake. Although out of respect, work had ceased the day after the incident at the collar, ut started right up again the next day. Fur the greedy Cornish see, time wuz money.

It had been cut and timbered ten days before the funeral, and when the navvying began again, once more, the forest felt pain. This woman had promised it future promulgation and power, but right now, it did not feel that way. As the team working up from the harbour met the team working their way down, the raw assault on it seemed complete. A crime was certainly being committed because no one had asked for consent. It knew of the conversation that went on between Skews and Trevorrow, and Nimkii. Nimkii had let it down in its view. Could the man ever be forgiven, or was he now just another servant of them? He was supposed to be part of it – in union with it – but now, that had somehow dissolved and fragmented.

Nimkii knew he was being watched. He'd felt it for some time. Maybe what he planned with Mabel wuz a good thing, for ut would take him away from all of this. America was vast: the north of ut here, still unexplored. There'd be other places to go, and where lessons from here might be learned. He wuz resolved to ask her, tell her how he felt. There was though, the problem ov her mother; a difficulty that would be hard to solve. Maybe she could go with them, but maybe she would not cope with the transient life he had planned. He knew though, that Mabel would embrace it. Perhaps the Doctor's plan could work towards his benefit too. Corrupted now see, wuz this Nimkii: tainted by the Cornish. In the cool autumnal air, Yolkai wuz rising. It seemed that a stance had been taken towards him for his indiscretion, for letting this happen in the first place, and it was to the goddess Yolkai that he would need to speak. Death always prompted ritual, and so he prepared himself to later have dialogue with the moon woman. Oh yes, now he could hear it. The ruptured landscape of the mountain was groaning. Ut would need fixing.

The fabric of reality had become unravelled for Rebecca Nankervis. Each day, she picked up the note that her husband had left her and considered it again.

"Dearest Rebecca," ut read. "I am so sorry but you know that I have to leave. I did what was necessary. Only when people see the truth can I return. I will take care of you. Much love, your Frank x."

Rebecca did not often see her husband's writing but she knew it well enough to know the speed at which he had written those words. He'd obviously dipped his pen into ink that would be enough for the scrawl, because a blob tainted the page just before he formed the letter D of Dearest. She knew handwriting and its cursive intricacies because she had taught it to the youngsters of the township. Some of Francis' letters were slightly malformed as if the energy of making them wuz too great. She smelt the note for any sense of him. She re-read the sentences morning and night to see if any further meaning could be derived from them. It became clear however, that the message wuz stark; she wuz unlikely to see him. The one saving grace of the note was that he said he would continue to take care of her. What that meant, and how that would be, she daily puzzled over.

She'd showed the note to her father and the police when they came to talk to her. She explained to the police that they had struggled with Richard's behaviour and that he had been difficult. And when they questioned her on the fact that he was a new-born baby (What could it *really* do? they'd asked themselves), she did try to explain that it had unnatural powers. But she knew that when she said ut, the police looked at her funny; as if she'd lost her mind a bit. Well, she was onto a loser with tha' she realised, for the police awnly had to look at her mother – an' well, they did, didn' un? She realised they saw a trait. Maybe all of this had come from mental weakness. She did not like the way the police questioned her about her marriage though. Their questions got too intrusive. She responded by telling them that they were gloriously happy when their baby arrived, but that soon after its birth, their son altered. In the end, she was forced to say that someone had put a curse on them and the baby. She knew ut sounded outrageous, but ut seemed the awnly feasible explanation. As she said ut, she nawticed the police gave up taking notes. The case here on Mountainside just got stranger every day.

During that phase, she realised her awn insecurities. She felt the pain in her finger which daily needed re-bandaging and which daily festered. Her heart wuz filled with conflicting feelings. Outwardly, she wuz still tha' grieving mawthur whose baby wuz now in the earth. Ut wuz why people gave her a wide birth. Inwardly though, although she had protested, and been shocked from the death, she had more than an inkling of why Francis had done what he had done. She began to hate the way she had treated him when she had first gone down to the mine that day. They ought to have comforted each other, but more importantly, she needed to have been there for him. Ut was he who had ridded them of the thing in their midst; ut wuz ee who had taken on that guilt for the rest of his life, and at that crucial moment, she had denied him her affection. As time went on, she came to realise the mistake that she had made. Right now, there didn't seem naw way ov correcting ov ut either.

Ut ate away at her. The stope of her heart got mined daily, and the ore that comed out wuz a longing fur Francis' return. She prayed fur un daily. She knew that she wuz moving to a position of forgiveness. Well, perhaps ut wudn' even that. Forgiveness wudn' even the right word. What Francis had done wuz to confront his wust fears. Ee had done it on his own, out of care for both her and others in the community, and having done that for everyone, the community then seemingly rejected Frank. She understood more and more why he had to go.

Part ov the reason for her alteration came in the form of her conversations with Gourgy and Luk. They pair had actually moved back into their old accommodation: Gourgy because Becca had enough on her hands coping with Clara, and because 'ee didn' want to scare she. Ee wuz afraid that her time in the woods would have given her some degree of magical insight, so ut wudn' do fur ee to be around. Luk had moved because ee felt Maddy and Justin needed the space. Ee didn' knaw quite how to put ut, but relations between they'd been somewhat frosty ov late. Perhaps ee'd considered, ut wuz his presence there, so ee felt like 'twas best to leave they fur a while. Ee knawed Justin wuz tryin' hard: to be honest you, ut wuz Maddy who wuz offish. Es, there wuz somethun' tha' lurked in her mind. She never had time fur anyone except the liddle boy Jago.

But Gourgy and Luk did speak to Becca. They told her straight how 'twas tha' day and what had happened. Ef she didn't believe Justin, then at least listen to they. 'Mean, there wuz no way they could talk to the police. The prospect of they turning up to talk to the law would have sent um flying back down to Calumet in an instant. Talking creatures, as well as a weird baby! 'Twud be enough t' put they in an institution, let alone anyone else. At least Becca listened to they. She showed them the note tha' Francis had left her. Ef their master wuz to come back, ut seemed like something had t' change and shift, but how could they engender tha'? There an' then, tha' seemed impossible.

The three of them pondered where he'd gone. Had a made ut down the peninsula perhaps to Calumet or Houghton? The former seemed unlikely because tha' wuz where the police were based. Houghton would give un more of a chance, but surely someone would have seen him? Canada wuz an option, but thinking about tha' wuz more scary because the territory wuz so vast. There, ee really could disappear, an' never be found. Maybe he'd make his way inta' Minnesota or Wisconsin. There were iron mines in boath. Work could be found. Boath states would have welcomed him as an experienced miner. Minter wuz allays chatting to un about plaaces there, so perhaps that wuz where he had headed. Down below got spoken of too, since the lakers now daily moved between here and Detroit. Wha' they feared the moast though wuz that he'd already gone back 'ome? That would have been the wust of outcomes fur everyone.

Gourgy and Luk promised they'd put word out. Their kind have an incredible way of communicating with the earth. A lot can be sensed from the vibrations in the ground. 'Twas all about feeling tremors ov they who worked ut. Knockies can feel things happening hundred of miles away, and so, ef Frank was at work in the ground, someone would spot un, an' a message would come back. They did jus' tha', but nawthun' comed back you. You'd have reckoned on a man ov Francis' worth soon stepping inta' a mine again, but so ut seemed, ut didn' happen. Ee'd elected for somethun' different. When Francis fust went they'd seen Nimkii an' asked ef ee could do anything. Wuz there any trail ee could pick up on? Ee looked fur one but comed back with nawthun'. Ee'd tracked un back to his own plaace, and then after tha', nawthun'. Gourgy and Luk mourned un too though, especially tha' Gourgy for Francis wuz his master, and now tha' ee'd gone, well, things just didn' feel right. Being masterless once more, wuz proper strange.

Gourgy and Luk still worked hard though, boath underground, and upon the mineral tramway. And as Becca mourned, lower on the mountain, the navvying of the tramway had begun proper. Now tha' the trees had been felled and the stumps lifted, a laker putting inta' Eagle Harbour had delivered the fust of the rails. So the sleepers were positioned and the lengths ov rail were manhandled into place. 'Twas a bit ov a job you, but 'twas comin' on. An' tha' wuz a good thing you, because the tonnage of ore coming out from underground each day wuz gettun' better and better.

Now that all ov this wuz on the cards, in order to distract hisself from the death of his grandson, Doctor Jewell had had detailed plans drawn up fur the chapel. He'd been shawing everyone and anyone who would listen to un about wha' wuz planned and how the chapel would become the centre of life in the town. Richard's passing had given un renewed energy. Ut wuz clear tha' the schoolhouse and the preaching pit were no longer fit fur purpose. The funeral had proven tha'. Naw doubt the Catholics would want somethun' constructed too (ee realised tha') but getting a Methodist chapel in plaace initially would still be somethun' to shout about. Ee an' Miss Prowse had set a date too. Jus' like his daughter an' tha' loser Francis once did, they'd planned on somethun' in the New Year. Even ef there wudn' a chapel in plaace, then old Reverend Davies would come up and officiate.

Now see, Minter and Jewell had spoken to the police too, and fur a while, they'd examined every single aspect of the collar under the head-frame. Everything wuz sized up and measured, and Jewell tried hard t'instigate new safety procedures. Now tha' may well have been one of the inconsequential benefits ov Richard's death, for the running of the cages up and down got a whole new load of rules and ways ov operating that initially drove they who used um mad: but even though they moaned, they knawed tha' 'twas all about keeping they as safe as possible.

A whole load of new guarding went in t'make sure no body part could possibly be ripped off. Fur Jewell, all of this felt like ee wuz doin' God's work on a daily basis. Now that his son James wuz grawin' up, ee tried to involve him a little more. Some day, he'd inherit all of this. Perhaps he'd failed with Mabel, and Rebecca, well, she wuz goin' to need some time, and maybe even then, she wudn' get over ut (Francis wudn' even there to help offer she another baby, which might have helped), but James wuz someone who ee could ground. There wuz a medical college now in Houghton, and tha' wuz were ee aimed to send his son. There were better times ahead, he told hisself. Es. There had to be.

There were some days in the immediate aftermath of the death of Richard where Becca barely found the time to think about her son. Her time had become consumed with looking after her mother: the responsibility of which wuz being shared between her and her sister. She tended to look after her in the days (what else wuz there to do?) whilst Mabel covered the nights. Mabel herself now seemed to lead this inverted life with Nimkii, and so ut suited the pair of them. They had boath come to accept the fact that their father wanted nothing more to do with her. He neither enquired after his wife nor made attempts to see her. So ut seemed he had written her off as a loss.

Perhaps boath Becca and Mabel had hoped that their mother might pick up a bit after being released from the forest, but as time went on, little change wuz seen. In fact, ef anything, Clara wuz becoming worse. She'd got thinner, which was hard, as she wuz stick-like already. All femininity had been removed from her. Her hips (tiny anyway) no longer existed. A straight line ran down the side of her, and her breasts (already small) had now become negligible. They had hoped that by recalling elements of their childhood with her (tea-treats, chapel anniversaries and days out at the coast) maybe something would connect. From her father, Becca had learnt about the so-called synapses in the brain, those threads of life which allow things to connect, but as wuz his original diagnosis with her, these were not re-growing or re-connecting. Oh, they tried hard the pair of them. But all humans have limits. In the end, they stopped the storytelling and they kept things very simple. They got her out of bed, tried to force her into ablutions and washing, clawthed her and fed her when need be. Later, they put her to bed, whether she wanted ut or not. Caring fur she got some hard.

The forest, who had caused all of this, gave no help. It didn' even look on. It said nawthun'. 'Mean they'd even tried walking her back into nature to see if that would light a fire in her mind, but nothing occurred. The blank stare remained, as if the forest had sucked life from her; as if some proboscis had pierced her skin and drained her dry of emotion and feeling. Although neither Becca nor Mabel said anything, perhaps on reflection ut would have been best ef the forest had kept her. At least out in it, there might have been some connection, some coalition between her and what held her. Here now, there wuz no syncopation and no joy. Ef she had dared to look, then the awnly one who'd have truly knawn tha', wuz Maddy O'Donahue. Perhaps ef she comed to visit Clara, she could instil some response (Mabel had said tha' she'd been good with her) but ut seemed clear tha' Maddy wudn' about to pay naw visit. They boath understood. She'd have been preoccupied with Jago Ciaran, and this, this mother of theirs, was undeniably their responsibility. Hard the work wuz see, and still Rebecca's finger festered.

The vagaries of memory indeed. One day turned into another, and Becca cudn' remember zactly when, but there wuz one day in December when there wuz a knock at the door, and when she opened ut, who was standin' there but tha' Miss Eleanor Prowse. Of all people, she! She wuz cordial this woman; diplomatic to a tee – but wha' did she want?

"I thought I'd pay a visit to Clara," she expressed, with due concern.

She wuz carrying a basket with something in ut.

"I know all of this is rather unconventional – and hard for us all – but I was sitting at home – well, I mean, at your father's... and I simply felt I should come and introduce myself."

Rebecca did not know what to say. She had not conceived of this moment. The likelihood was tha' ef her mother had any cogency about her, never in her life would she have wanted a visit from her husband's new partner, but here was she, trying to make amends, trying to do the right thing. But even though that thought passed through her mind, she couldn't help but think ef there was some darker intention about her?

"You know me well enough by now, Rebecca... I'm not the schemer some people judge me as being... I do care for your father, and of course, I see the... ah... difficulties..."

By this, she presumably meant that the Doctor still had one wife, even though he was gearing up for another. The issue of bigamy maybe underlined her visit.

"How is Clara?" came the direct question. "Maybe I can see her?"

Whatever intentions Miss Prowse had, Rebecca allowed her to enter. Days of non-companionship had made her feel lonely and isolated. At least, here wuz someone who was trying to do something for her and her mother: whatever covert intentions were afoot.

"She won't say anything," Rebecca observed, as she led Miss Prowse into the living room, and to the spot where Clara was sitting.

"He-llo Clar-a," Miss Prowse said, in that way people do, when someone is old or infirm.

She had expected a response but nawthun' came back, not even a blink of eyes.

"See what I mean," said Becca. "You can try... Feel free... I'll make us some tay."

"I've these for you boath," said Miss Prowse.

She lifted the tea towel off her basket and inside wuz a clutch of warm saffron buns.

"It's her recipe. I hope you don't mind, but Jenny showed ut to me... I thought the taste might remind her..."

Although quite shocked that she and Jenny had delved into her mother's private recipe book, at the same time, she entirely understood what this woman wuz trying to do. Despite the intrusion, ut wuz moast definitely an act of kindness. The recipe wuz a family one and it had been handed down to Rebecca as well.

"Thank you," said Rebecca. "That's very kind of you."

Becca made tay and plated up the buns, hopeful of her mother partaking of them. Meanwhile, Miss Prowse tried to communicate. She began enthusiastically at first, offering comments about the weather, what she wuz wearing, and the progress of the marvel that wuz the mineral tramway but no response came. And when that happens, ut is hard for a person to continue. They find themselves acting a kind of soliloquy that no one is actually bothered about. Like Rebecca and Mabel had found, ut wuz actually best to give up and say nawthun'. So instead, Becca and Miss Prowse sat and drank tay and each ate one of her buns.

"Nice flavour ent um?" said Rebecca.

"Yes. Lovely," said Miss Prowse. "Your Mam knew – I mean *knows* – how to make them obviously..."

"I use her recipe too,"

There was almost a moment where Miss Prowse felt she should ask how Becca wuz doin' and whether she had heard anything from Francis, but she held back and clamped her mouth tightly shut when that urge of her tongue came. Instead, they talked over Clara about her condition, and then there wuz a little about the forthcoming wedding, but ut was a topic that Miss Prowse, despite her best intentions, did not much want to discuss. Becca pulled back and instead, moved on to she and father's plans for the chapel. All wuz ready apparently. All they needed wuz the first tranche ov money.

As you might expect, there were many awkward pauses that afternoon, but at least Eleanor Prowse felt she had done what she needed to. She had tried to make peace, to allay some fears and to show that she did care.

But when she left, ut wuz obvious to Rebecca why her feythur had fallen for her. She would offer him everything tha' her mother couldn'. Becca wuz about to remove the plate on which the saffron bun sat (her mother hadn' touched it) but then, on a whim, she left ut there and later forgot about it.

"How is she?" asked Doctor Jewell when Eleanor got back.

"Not good," said Eleanor. "Not good at all..."

"Hmmm," said Jewell.

"I think I'll go and lie down fur a bit," she said.

The visit had been hard for her, and the effort of being polite and kind had drained her. George wudn' understand, but she felt wholesome and good because she'd done something that she considered to be the Methodist way.

Back below, beside the engine house, Mabel wuz still asleep. The challenge of her mother had made her tired and she'd fallen inta' a deep slumber during the day. She wuz awakened by the arrival of Nimkii, who had for the past few days gone into the forest. He'd apparently needed discussion with Yolkai and the trees, and Mabel already knew of this. But what he seemed to want in that moment of her waking, wuz something different. When she sat up beside him, he leaned in slowly and gently, breaking many taboos, but seemingly, in this moment, he very much wanted to kiss Mabel.

She welcomed his affection. She had wanted this to happen for some time, and perhaps even had tempted him with her manners and playfulness. The taste of him wuz as she had dreamed ov: warm, and somehow of the forest: that rising heat from the leaf litter on a summer day. She cared now not what anyone thought of her, and when they had finished that initial moment of passion, there were many more. Yes, she wuz younger but so what? Between these signals of affection, Nimkii explained that he wanted them to leave Mountainside, and travel. He would make her a member of his tribe, and then they would proceed in whatever direction that they wanted. Surely they'd find somewhere better, a new Paradise, and there, well, tha' would be the place for them to have their own children. It would mean leaving Mountainside, and perhaps an opening up of the whole of the continent for they. Mabel knew well the stories they would find together. Ut wuz what she wanted. An unexpected turn fur she then, but what else would she have wanted? She'd grown bored of the mine and its claustrophobia. She wanted action and adventure. Rebecca would cope; es, Rebecca would cope. An' she realised tha' ef she never see'd her feythur an' brother again, ut wudn' bother she t'all.

They'd look to leave as soon as possible. She knew now that ultimately, she would reject her past – all tha' stupid culture of home – and embrace something different. The cloying aspect of her Cornishness would be shed and she'd become something new. She'd evolve. And when Nimkii told her this, in all of his broken English, and all her use of his language (whatever ut wuz named), she knew she'd awnly have perhaps a few more nightshifts at the Nankervis residence in order to look after her mother.

However, nawthun' works out the way we plan ut, do ut? Some things never change. See, when she got up to her sister's place, just as dark wuz falling, there wuz a good deal ov commotion at the front door. Rebecca though, wuz standing back from ut all, like as ef she knawed wha' wuz happening already, and had fully accepted ut. Mabel did her best to intervene and to ask questions, but ut soon becomed clear wha' wuz happening: their mother Clara wuz being forcibly loaded onto a covered wagon. The men who drove the wagon, and who were assisting her up into ut had come up from the asylum in Calumet.

"She'll be given good care," one of the men said.

'Twas hard to believe un, since another wuz wrapping her mother up in a straight-jacket.

"Thass jus' so she dun't injure herself or try to run off on the way down."

They tied a leash onto the straight-jacket, and this was clipped and locked on to the frame of the wagon.

"She'll be assessed, and then Doctor Jewell will be sent the results... we can see about some treatment then."

At this, Mabel feared battery electrodes put to her head, or pills that would make her even more distant. But she could do nothing. The men were strong and powerful, and seemed used to such 'collections'. Rebecca wuz in tears, but looked as if she could now only accept the fate of their mother. Maybe, she considered, she would be better off there. Perhaps they really could help her to recover herself. But ut didn' look good you, when the wagon trundled out of Mountainside for an overnight journey down into Calumet. Losing her like this, wuz perhaps worse than losing her to the forest. And she lookin' out of the back of the wagon, staring back at they.

Boath sisters sobbed and hugged each other. Loss, all the time, wudn' ut? At least Mabel had something to look forward to: a new life ahead of she.

When they went inside – a curious thing – an empty plate. Ov her awn accord, Clara Jewell had eaten ov the saffron bun tha' had sat there before she.

41

Talk ov saffron see. Well, ut do put ee off.

Now, where wuz us to?

Aw es. We'm back when Clara Jewell got taken away. You'll understand see, 'twas fur the good ov she. They could better take care of her down there in Calumet. Ut comed out tha' her husband Doctor Jewell had arranged ut all. 'Mean, ee knawed wha' wuz goin' on with Rebecca an' Mabel, and ee knew how tired an' taissy they were boath getting. Ut wudn' a situation tha' could continue in the long term. Their angst over their mawthur though, wuz helpful to his cause see, because put simply, ee wanted she gone. She wuz a vestigial and painful reminder of his old life, and her insanity wuz convenient to un. Es, the forest had done good there. Word comed up from the asylum tha' she wuz doin' well, though there wuz still naw speech and little change. She still had tha' blank look to she, as ef all prior memory had been completely gone. They didn' have t'worry you, because ef there wuz any improvement, they'd let um knaw up in Mountainside. To be honest weth ee though, ut didn' look good. Ut wudn' like she wuz about to be released any time soon.

So now, Rebecca had to faace the fact that she had lost her son, her husband and now her dear mawthur too. She cudn' help but think that her mawthur beginning to eat of that bun that day wuz a sign ov her recovery – that she'd remembered a smell and a taste – and tha' wuz why she wolfed ut down s'quick. Ut wudn' like there'd been any Knockies around tha' day to ingest ut. Rebecca knew they would ov eaten ut, ef they were present, fur Knockies can never resist a warm bun like tha', but she knawed they wudn' even there tha' day. They'd been down mine. Perhaps then, ut connected. Perhaps more taste and smell wuz the way to bring she back. But 'twudn' likely she'd be fed any more saffron buns down the asylum, wuz ut? 'Twas more likely to be just bread and soup. Each day, Rebecca thought over her, but her thoughts about her mawthur intertwined with her feelings over dead Richard and missing Francis too. All of them tumbled about her head, like as if she cudn' escape from them. Wuz this all her life wuz goin' t'be from now on? Ut felt like ut. Still naw word from Francis neither. What wuz a doin' ov? Another broken promise, so ut seemed.

Because she had no other purpose, she started once more to keep school. Sal Clemo stepped back t'the running ov the bal-maidens again. With this, ut felt like her life had reached a stasis and tha' every day became a dull repetition of the previous one. 'Twudn' naw life, and ut certainly 'twudn' the life she had imagined fur herself. Each day she prayed hard and deep to the Lord God above fur the safe return ov her husband, and fur the care ov her mawthur. She cudn' decide wha' wuz worse: to have her mawthur lost deep in the forest, or for her to be shut away in a dark institution. Becca had had difficult conversations with her feythur over ut. He'd tried to show his loving side in incarcerating her, and was sympathetic to the fact that boath Rebecca and Mabel had been worn down by her. This wuz the best thing fur her, he had said, and maybe ut wuz – but somehow ut didn' feel right my 'andsomes, did ut?

That year, the winter comed in early. Hard ut wuz too, with high drifts beginning in mid-December. Fortunately, the navvying had continued apace, and by the time they had appeared, the construction of the tramway wuz almost complete. Minter, Skews and Trevorrow were very pleased with this, but felt forced to hunker down and hibernate when the bleak snow came. The awnly thing that needed to go in now were the cables, but tha' might have to wait until the spring or until the weather cleared. All they running the mine were glad that they hadn't chosen the water propulsion system. Tha' would have been naw good at all in such a hard winter as this.

When the sky emptied its white ore onto the land below, the focus went back to being underground once more. Level Nine was beginning to be excavated belaw, and the higher levels like two and three got forgotten. All that could be excavated from they had been taken: the best runs of metal were now goin' further below according to Mr Skews' latest survey, and they were still tracing a line that took them back to the swathe of mineral that ran back down to the old Cliff Mine. That place now, wuz almost all overgrown with trees and vurze, and ov course, the old hotel had long since gone. From down state, a series ov lakers had brought in the tram wagons themselves, and they were all sat pristine in Eagle Harbour ready to be used.

Because of the weather, several people's plans got thwarted. The Doctor's wish to marry Eleanor Prowse got halted because they'd planned on an event presided over by Reverend Josiah Davies, and with the weather s'harsh around Christmas time, nawthun' wuz goin' t'happen. They'd have to wait until the spring, something tha' frustrated the Doctor enormously. Miss Prowse wuz overtly still living at Rosie's to keep face, but covertly, she wuz staying at the Doctor's. They wudn' in the same bed, aw naw, fur that would break every Methodist code there ever wuz, but 'twas true that they had become ever closer since the placement of Clara elsewhere. This move had certainly allowed Eleanor to feel more comfortable, and that she would not be sent packing back to Calumet with her tail between her legs, and labelled a fool for her crush on some doctor from Mountainside. For all intents and purposes, the Doctor and she were already married. Ut just had to be formalised in the eyes of the Lord. Jewell had a plan though. As soon, as the winter broke, they'd head down to Calumet and conduct their marriage down there. He kept a close eye on the weather each day.

Work on Mountainside Chapel had begun though. Before the weather comed in bad, between the Doctor, Minter, Skews and Trevorrow, the foundation for the building had begun. The site had been cleared, and the bowl of the old preaching pit had been removed. Tha' had taken some diggun' out you, but whilst the men were in navvy mode, ut seemed a good time to utilise their skills. The curvature of the space, which in prior summers had hosted all of Jewell's best sermons, was taken away and the peaty earth from that, was brought further down the slope to level ut out. In this way, the proposed dimensions of the chapel could be put in. The work had required a lot of ripping out of roots and tubers, but when ut was levelled, ut was clear to see where the chapel would fit, and how it would all look when ut wuz finished.

The snows were gathering in the sky above, and coming down from the north, when Trevorrow set the charges and blasted away the preaching rock: that old, natural pulpit which had now been worn away of any lichen and moss through Jewell repeatedly stepping upon ut. A lot of people in the community were there to observe the drilling into the core ov ut, and then the setting of the charges. When ut comed, the blast echoed amongst the forest and out over Lake Superior. Ut scattered crows and blue jays, and made all the childurn hold their breaths and muffle their ears. To the men who enacted the drilling – Diddy Pasca and Bobby Moyle – 'twudn' naw different from what they experienced on a normal working day belaw ground, but fur Jewell and the soon-to-become new Mrs Jewell, ut wuz a tremendous occasion.

The time-worn pulpit rock got split into two, and the top half tumbled down the rise, and came to land in the middle of the old bowl. From there, further drilling took place and the rock was broken into sections which could be processed in the stamps mill and by they who still cobbed ore. Es, 'twuz some moment. There wuz singing of hymns, an' Jewell did a major speech about how important a step this wuz to the 'cleaning up' ov the community. He still had that reformist zeal in un see, like as ef a new Revival might begin right there on the Keweenaw and spread across the continent. He hoped in some measure, to be a new Wesley, and put men and women on the right track, emulating what had gone on down in Calumet a few years earlier. Finally, he told hisself, ut wuz happening.

"Looks like you got what you wanted," said Mr Skews to the Doctor.

"Yes, it's coming on now," replied Jewell enthusiastically.

What Jewell didn' say wuz tha' the money for construction of the chapel was still not fully in place. They'd gained enough for the ground works, and a few days later, for the foundations to be completed, but there wuz still some way to go in terms of fundraising. Still, the fact that the foundations wuz in wuz somethun' to be celebrated. This time, next year, the chapel really would be in place, Jewell told hisself, though perhaps even then, ee wuz realising tha' to achieve his aim, a good deal of his awn money wuz goin' to have to go inta' the project. Perhaps though, Minter could be tapped. He could chip in, surely? Now that he wuz sweet with Rosie, surely sometime soon they'd want to marry. Jewell would continue his fund-raising unabated. He knawed his vision wuz in sight ov un right now, and ee didn' want anything t'stop ut.

'Course, they further down the camp wuz awnly too aware of wha' wuz happening, but they wudn' there to celebrate ut, not like everyone else. See, Mabel had let go ov any residual Methodism in she a long time ago. She realised tha' in fact, she'd let ut all loose when she wuz still a girl. Although she had turned up for anniversaries and services at home, and when younger, had continued to support her father's Christian views when they arrived here, by now, that had altered markedly. Nimkii had shown her that this one Christian God was a load of nonsense, and that other more interesting and less judgemental deities were worth considering. She knew of Yolkai but there were other gods and goddesses within Nimkii's spiritual system that appealed to her. They were more magical somehow, and certainly less judgemental. There were goddesses too; not one patriarch looking over everyone's morality. She'd always detested the concept of sin. Who wuz this Lord God above to do all the judging anyway? In her time with Nimkii, he'd taught her another way, and it appealed to she. She knew her father had given up on her. She knew that he now regarded her as a pure heathen, especially since she wuz still comparatively young and Nimkii wuz a brae bit older. Tha' didn' make naw difference to she though.

All this wuz why they didn' talk now, but ut had been compounded by her relaying her plans to him (through Rebecca), that she and Nimkii planned on a union, and leaving Mountainside. In effect, she wuz to shed her original skin and become something else. She wuz undergoing a metamorphosis. Her father found ut hard to deal with this. He felt his way wuz the awnly way, but now, he had to confront his daughter's chosen path. When this wuz known to Jewell, full communication ended.

Before, he had realised what wuz goin' on with she and Nimkii, but now ut had to be put out of mind.

See, ut wuz hard to question she and he. Nimkii still had the respect of just about everyone in the community, and although ut wudn' the normal way of carryin' on an' tha', who wuz they to contest their union? They wuz obviously happy together, so ut wudn' like anyone wuz goin to march on down to his steel tepee and put um right using a stiff word or fisticuffs. Moast Cornish might be Methodists but in fact, they wuz pretty easy goin' when ut comed t'such matters. There wuz also tha' view that you didn' want to meddle much in Indian affairs. Tha' wuz best kept out of, as wuz shown with all that discussion ov the bad spirits surrounding baby Richard. Live and let live wuz wha' moast ov they underground said. They said tha' because they knawed each day wuz special and tha' ut should be savoured. Besides, when they looked inta' their awn hearts, 'twudn' allays very pretty. So there wuz never goin' to be any mass protest, or any sense tha' wha' Nimkii wuz doin' wuz wrong.

But the weather that had frustrated the completion of the tramway, and thwarted the wedding of Jewell and Miss Prowse, also played ut's hand here. Nimkii and Mabel had intended to leave the mining town and begin their travels that year, but as they were preparing to leave, ut soon became clear that a full winter wuz coming in earlier than usual, so any hope of escape had to be put on hold. Now Nimkii see, wudn' afraid of the snow. But now that ee intended to take Mabel with him, then perhaps they would be better waiting until the spring unfolded. That would then give them the whole year to wander. Ut wuz not what either of them wanted, but maybe spending one last winter here would be for the best. He could teach her more of his ways, and boath of them would learn more of each other's language. At present, they'd ended up with a hybrid way of communication which worked, but perhaps could be improved further. Trevorrow got to knaw ov their plans, and as ee and Nimkii went back a goodly way, to the old Cliff Mine, Nimkii was able to better communicate to the old Cap'n his intentions with the girl. His role as a go-between came back into play, especially when information got passed on to her father. Of course, there wuz no way ov telling her mawthur her intentions.

Mabel supposed that she might not ever see her again, and so perhaps just like her father, had put her mother into a locked box, sealing her away from anything that might hurt her. If she could have communicated with her though, maybe, Mabel felt she would understand: how she had been drawn to the natural world just like her mother had been. She had told her mother her thoughts when she had sat with her on those long days of tortuous attempts at communication. Maybe some of it had gone in. To her regret, maybe she should have persisted: to try to engender memory in her, just the same way that eating that final bun had. But a decision had been taken and she could not alter it. She realised fully, of course, that her mother's incarceration would paradoxically lead to her own freedom. In that came some guilt, but she wuz dealing with it, and coming to understand more and more what the way life truly wuz.

Justin had shifted his role after his brother's disappearance. He had gone back down in the mine to become the Cap'n there, rather than remain as the Grass Cap'n above. Walt Chegwidden had taken over up there for the time being, with maybe the hope in Justin, at least, that his brother might one day return. Good tonnage wuz coming out you, and they wuz making brae in-roads on developing the ninth level. Whenever a mine opened up a new level, tha' wuz allays a dangerous time, because nawbody knawed zactly wha' ut would look like, so there wuz a fair bit of Knockie activity with all of they on high alert, in case there wuz anything tha' might go wrong, or if they felt anything in the earth. 'Course, this far down, they wuz now away from the old roots of some of the tallest trees, and that had a calming influence. Where there wuz roots, as in the upper levels, then there wuz potential movement, but down in the slimy mine bottoms, well, in some ways, 'twas much more stable. Hard rock now, you.

Now although Justin's work belaw ground wuz goin' well, fur some time now, things between ee an' Maddy wudn' quite right. Ee didn' knaw how ut had gone wrong though. Ut wudn' like ee could put his finger on wha' wuz wrong with she. Prior to the baby's arrival, and even in the immediate aftermath ov Jago's presence, they still made ·love madly and gloriously, but thinking back on these past few months, ever since the death of Richard, things hadn' been right. Ee cudn' understand why because he tried to be the best feythur he could, yet 'twuz as if whatever ee did wudn' naw longer good enough fur she. Perhaps she wuz bored with un, he considered. Perhaps now that she had the boy, his plaace in her life wudn' significant anymore. The wust ov ut wuz ee could feel her slipping away from un, and tha', he knawed deep down, wuz something he never wanted. Every day on core, ee weighed ut up. But ee still cudn' understand she. Ut wuz like as if something had altered inside of her – some kind of transformation.

He'd tried talkin'. Women want tha' he felt. Men dun't always need ut but women do, see. He tried talkin' to her about marriage because fust of all, ee thought tha' wuz the problem, what with Nimkii and Mabel pairing up, and then all the talk of the Doctor's marriage. Perhaps she wanted un to make her an honest woman, but tha' wudn' ut. Naw, she wudn' be bothered about that. So when tha' had been gone through, he tried to do more things for she. Ee picked she flowers, they went on walks in the forest, they had picnics together, but all the time she wuz offish with un. Finally, like these things allays do, ut comed out.

"Have I dun something wrong to you?" he asked.

She wuz inside the scullery, sortin' out Jago's clawthes.

"No. Why would you say that now?"

"Because I'm feeling ov ut Maddy... like you ent my Maddy anymore..."

"I'm just tired. That's all. Take no notice."

But they'd been here before.

"No," said Justin, and this time her grabbed her arm, making her nearnly drop all of the clawthes she'd folded. "There's something wrong, isn't there?"

Maddy didn't like being interrogated in this way. Ut wuz enough to raise the bile in she.

"No. Nothing wrong. Now, just fook off and leave me alone won'tcha?"

"No," said Justin, "I won't. Unless you tell me wha' this is all about, I'm leaving... I'll go, just like my brother."

"Go on then," she said, her voice uncaring in its pretence.

This exasperated Justin, though he tried to control his frustration with her.

"Confide in me," pleaded Justin. "What's troubling you? I knaw there's something. I can feel ut. I've felt ut for a long time now."

"It's nothing," she responded. "Maybe just the winter... I hate it when it's like this."

But she wuz lying to him.

"Stop behaving like this," argued Justin. "Let me into that mind of yours."

"You know my mind," she said in response.

"Do I though?" contested Justin. "Ut feels like you've something secretive in there, that you're not telling me. And that hurts me Maddy. In the beginning, you and me, we wuz always so open... Ut felt like we could tell each other anything. But now... it's like stepping on egg shells living with you..."

"You finished?"

"No. I haven't finished," said Justin, his voice now louder. "I just wish you'd let me in. Whatever 'tis, we can solve it together."

She felt his pleading. She knew she had to alter. She could not work out why she had been so hard on him. In that instant, she wanted to confess. She wanted to share with him everything that had happened, and let it out. She knew that what wuz happening inside of her was making her into a crone. It was hunching her back, pulling at her skin and giving it lines and crevices. She knew that the bags under her eyes came from when she could not sleep. She sometimes thought that the light had gone out of her pupils, her eyes now dull and devoid of life – like the very Deads themselves had entered her. Maybe she cudn' see anything anymore. Maybe the polluted lake had given her cataracts.

She briefly considered ut. What a relief that would be: to share some of the burden. To split it in half. To tell him the truth about the Pooka. To explain how terrible she felt about Francis' leaving and what she had done to harm him and Rebecca. Even to involve Justin in all of this, tore at her and made her curse herself. This wuz the reason for her quietness. Ut wuz why she removed herself from the society of Mountainside: why, for example, she had not attended the marking-out ceremony of the chapel, and why she hated going up to see Rebecca.

He saw her become distant with him, even as they spoke,

"You go too far," said Justin. "Luk's worried about you."

"Do you think I care what your Knockie thinks ov me?"

"You know the magic there," retorted Justin. "You know you have that too, so don't deny it. Stop suppressing it."

Here, he was driving an iron spar into her heart. He was right, of course, but she had to stay strong.

"Just stop ut Maddy. Stop playing the hard-faced bitch and tell me what's wrong..."

When he said that, momentarily, she did want to speak. There wuz a flood of hurt and repentance that she wanted to let out, but if she did ut, where would that leave her? The momentum wuz now too great. She could not let ut drop. The moment he found weakness, he would wheedle his way in. She feared he was doing it now. That is why she had removed intimacy from their lives. Ef ut was just she and Jago, then she could stand ut. But ut wuz hard already. What wuz ut going to be like over the next few years? She feared herself, and when tha' happens to a person, then watch out. That's when you push things to the limits, and burst open like the guts ov a purple-skinned Knockie who knows there is no other way out. She genuinely feared that the same thing wuz happening to her.

Unbeknown to Justin, she'd even gone around to see Flannery, to see ef he could somehow help but the moment she saw him, she became reminded of what had happened at home, and how different her life wuz here. She had this liddle boy now, and tha' had been all that she wanted. So although she went there with the intention of talking to him, and maybe even telling him all that she'd done, and all that she'd conjured, she couldn' say anything, for although they'd been through a lot together, swooping up someone else's baby wuz not something he'd ever approve of. And then Justin, her Justin, he never deserved this, or so she told herself; but there wuz in she, still that latent feeling that ut wuz his actions, his contagious disease which had wrecked her chances and which had caused her true son – the nameless one – to be still-born.

As Justin went on at her, she could only think of the moment she stepped outside of Flannery's and horror-upon-horror, when, for the fust time since the funeral she had bumped into Becca, returning home from a day's teaching at the schoolhouse. This was a meeting she had done her best to avoid: to put off until when the memory of the real identity of Jago had faded so dimly that she could cope with ut. She knew the power of time with such matters. Ut wuz such proximity of the moment of the swap that now gave her pain, and even more came when Rebecca asked to pick up her true son. She had no choice but allow her to do ut, but in every loving caress offered by the woman (in effect remember, her sister-in-law), pain heaped itself upon pain, so that she could no longer speak, nor even look at the pair of them together.

"May I hold him?" she'd asked. "It's alright. I mean, I'm alright to do so. I won't become a gibbering wreck."

Maddy had barely been able to respond. She wanted to be protective and say no, but by this point, Rebecca'd already lifted him up. He was no longer a baby. What stared at her wuz a little man. And Maddy knew precisely why he seemed so happy with her, and when she held him, why they looked right together. How sharp a knife wuz tha' into every part of her soul? Such moments drained her and made her realise the evil. The guilt crippled her.

"You alright Maddy?" enquired Rebecca. "You look white as a sheet."

"It's nothing," Maddy said. "I... I... just need to get him home. It's tiring... you know, motherhood."

Was there a worse thing she might have said? Probably not. How could Becca know? Her own baby had been abducted and the changeling put in its place was now buried under a snow-coated mound.

Involuntarily, like as if she wuz being controlled by some other force, Maddy held her hands out, waiting for Rebecca to release Jago. But she delayed just a little too long, and again, something made Maddy say something harsh.

"I need him back."

Rebecca wuz somewhat surprised at her tone, and this comed across in her facial expression. Desperately, Maddy tried to counter what she had said.

"Sorry Bec... It's just that I said I'd be back home. Justin will wonder where we've gone."

"Of course," said Becca handing him back across, small visible breaths coming from Jago's mouth in the cold air.

Now that her boy wuz back with her again, Maddy began to feel more comfortable. She couldn' allow that to happen again. This was the reason she'd become overprotective, why in Justin's view she wuz wrapping him in cotton wool too much and too often. But she knew precisely why she did it. She wuz afraid of anyone taking away what had been so hard to have gained. And when Rebecca handled him, well, ut wuz fur Maddy, like the Devil himself had picked un up. She knew that wudn' right at all, but the power ov women and babies is untold. You knaw tha' by now, dun' ee?

And in this moment, Justin wuz now on to her. She might have known ut would come to this. The storm had been brewing for months. She wuz trying to change, she really wuz, but the instinct and the magic were so strong that she could not counter ut. At his slew of comments, she became worried as to whether she could last out. Could she keep up this façade? If her plan wuz to work, she would have to maintain it. Despite all the accusations thrown at her, somehow, she would have to comply. That's why later, when she was fully assured that Jago was tucked in safe, she acquiesced: and as a front, let Justin enter her like he used to. She realised that ef she didn't do this, something would have to give; and that movement was not something she wanted. Maybe he'd relent fur a while, and think that they were close once more, and that all wuz hunky-dory between them. She realised she had two long-term choices: she could either tell Justin the truth about what had happened, or she could do a Francis, and leave Copper Mountain completely. Either way, she knew that she was utterly fucked.

Moast people hunkered down during the winter. Jago grew, and Justin grew more suspicious of Maddy. She still wudn' let un in. Rebecca's fears grew because she still hadn' heard anything from Francis. The passion between Rosie and Dicky Mint grew, because, well, 'twas cold outside – and what else wuz there to do? Although their marriage could not take place yet, the love between George Jewell and Eleanor Prowse also grew as they worked on organising the next phase of the chapel, which was getting the four walls upright. Just how tha' wuz goin' to be paid fur, they didn' quite knaw but the fund fur the chapel wuz grawing bit by bit.

Mr Skews meanwhile, tried to distract hisself in any way possible from the love that was growing between Nimkii and Mabel. He'd picked up on their plans that they wished to leave Mountainside and go travelling. Time wuz running out. He found hisself down in some ov the bunkhouses with other miners, playin' cards, singing dirty songs and tellin' ov a good few Jacker-style drolls. Ee wuz drinking a brave bit too. Ee edn actually been teetotal fur years, even though ee pretended to be. Anything fur a distraction ut wuz with ee. Gourgy's worries grew since ee hadn' heard from his master, and that worry got transferred onto Luk too, who wuz already worried-up enough about his awn master, who seemed melancholy allays these days. Outside though, the forest didn' graw much. All ut did wuz watch in the way that ut always did. Spring would knock it on again and cause it to blossom and spurt. The butterflies would be back.

Some saving grace came in the form ov a break in the weather in January. Ut went that way on the Keweenaw sometimes when the warming effect of the waters of Lake Superior seemed to have some impact on the cold from the north, and slow ut down fur a bit. 'Twudn' long, but it was a winda' t'get the cable systems in place. That wuz the last job to do really, an' when there was a bright day, the navvying team went down through the cut, checking the cables and shovelling off any excess snow. There wuz a big moment when the first wagon rumbled down to the shore, emptied its load of copper ore, and wuz then turned around again on the turntable t'be pulled back up by those goin' down.

"Grand," went Minter.

Drecklyism seemed over with ee these days.

He wuz right. The system worked like a treat, though everyone recognised that snow clearance on the tracks would need to be a priority fur a while. They down bottomside loved the new system. Ut meant tha' when loads comed down there wuz naw more shovelling. The wagons dropped their loads right into the holds of the lakers. Their bottoms opened up automatically to release their ore. Ideal you. Some man hours were saved by the process. 'Course ut did mean that the ostlers and the drivers had to be redeployed on the new part of the mine, but like Skews told um, this wuz the way forward. In a short while, there wudn' be naw oss and carts naw more. 'Twould all be these new vehicles there wuz talk ov. They wuz full ov tha' see down in Detroit. Skews hoped he had tried to keep the mine ahead ov the game in this way.

The tramway wuz a source ov great amusement to the miners. One day, Howey Knucky and Stefan Gries, decided – fur larks – t'see if they could ride the tramway down to Eagle Harbour. 'Twudn' somethun' tha' they wuz meant to do, for the Doctor had warned them ov the dangers, but this pair were witty see, and thought 'twould be fun to ride the wagons down. Aw es. They wuz like childurn on a rollercoaster they wuz, as ut trundled down the mountain.

"Naw problem you," observed Howey. "'Twuz comfortable enough, wudn' ut Stefan?"

"Ja," replied Gries, "but I ground my teeth a little when we reach the bottom!"

Now, when they two found ut could work as a transportation system, well, you should have seen ut. Just about every miner enjoyed a ride, and they got pretty casual about ut. You knaw how 'tis. Everybody d'want t'be a part ov ut, and the tramway not awnly facilitated an increase in output for the harbour and the quantity of lakers puttin' in there, but also offered much amusement for they who dared to ride ut. 'Course when the mine's management heard of the larks they wuz havin' with ut, they wuz some unhappy. Jewell reckoned ut could be a real danger, and observed that if they treated ut like a fairground ride, somebody wuz goin' to get hurted. A rule went down tha' no man or boy wuz to ride the tramway. But when the Cap'ns, Skewsy and Jewell wudn' lookin', they did ut anyway. Ut would save some walkin' to go down with the wagon, so they carried on, when the management ov the mine wuz lookin' the other way. Like the sayin', as soon as the cat wuz away, the mice would play.

Backalong, the boy Justin would've tried ut. This was just the kind of diversion ee used to love at home, but these days, ee wudn' the same. Ef anyone got injured or deaded, then 'twould be his responsibility. Now ee had this to worry 'bout too, as well as his brother and the mood of Maddy. How had ut come t'this? Only a few years ago his brother an' he had been carefree, just trying to make a bit ov a strike. Now look at um, and where they were. He questioned whether 'twas all worth ut, but ut wudn' like ee could walk away now (not like what his brother had done), fur he had responsibilities. He had to step up and be the sensible one. Besides tha', ee loved his boy Jago, and deep down still, his Maddy.

"Dun't let me see ee be doin' ov tha'" ee told Jack Hocking and Diddy Pasca when ee caught boath ov um ridin' the wagon down one morning. The thing wuz they felt they knawed the Cap'n well enough t'do ut anyway. Anger burned in Justin at their response. He felt like ee wuz losing control: boath of his professional life and his personal life. This see, wuz the way he had t'carry on and ee didn' see naw way out ov ut. Ut ate away at un.

A quiet change comed one day though. A young boy by the name of Tommy Carkeek was sent on shore by the Captain of the laker ee served on. Tommy wuz nearnly fourteen, and had never been up this far on the Lakes, and although he'd heard of Mountainside before, he'd never actually been there. When he got on shore, he asked fur the best way to get up to the mine, and he wuz put right, wudn' a? They told un he'd be a'right t'travel the tramway.

"You sure 'tis safe?" he asked ov um, his faace all worried lookin'.

"'Course 'tis boy," they said. "We d'use ut all the time."

So inta' the wagon got this Tommy Carkeek, sweating like a poultice, and wondered if, in following their suggestion, ee'd actually bought a one way ticket to Hell. But naw, despite his fear, and despite un keeping his eyes tightly shut as he ascended the rise, ee arrived up top in one piece. Tha' wuz a'right, ee told hisself. The awnly thing wuz ee knawed he'd have to go back down in ut again, and that prop'ly filled un with fear. Jiddery and juddery then wuz this young man who'd arrived there at Mountainside. Ee, see, wuz on a bit ov a mission. He'd been given instructions from his laker captain. The boy Tommy made enquiries, an' a few of they who overheard his questions, wondered wha' wuz on with un, ee being a stranger an' that. But turn up ee did, at the front door ov the Nankervis property.

'Twas still early in the morning, an' Rebecca wuz gloomily getting ready for another dull day of teaching. She wuz pinning back her hair into a bun when the knock comed. She wuz puzzled to answer the door to a stranger. Not many arrived in Mountainside.

"Can I help you?" she asked.

"Are you Rebecca Nankervis?" the boy asked.

"Yes..." Becca answered, somewhat puzzled at what he wanted.

"I've been told to give you this."

He handed her a somewhat crushed and worn manila envelope that had her name on ut. Ut was sealed. Rebecca tried to make sense of his actions.

"Who's it from? What is it?"

"I don't knaw tha' ma'am," said Tommy. "I was just told by my Captain to give it to you. Ee put a lot ov trust in me."

She realised he had come up from Eagle Harbour. He wuz wearing the typical woollens of the mariners who worked the lakes.

"Do you know who it's from?"

"I dun't ma'am. Sorry."

"And you've come from?"

"Port Huron. We've comed up these past few days. I've only just joined our vessel..."

"I see."

Becca felt the weight of the envelope.

"Well, thank you," she said, and went inside to fetch a coin to give to the boy. She tipped him and he doffed his cap. He went on his way, going north along the road back around the mine.

When inside, Rebecca feverishly opened the envelope. To her surprise when she pulled out its contents, she found two hundred dollar bills. When the last note tumbled out onto the table where she sat, she found a note which she instantly read.

"Dear Rebecca, I said I would look after you. Love, Frank x"

His message and the money left her breathless. So much money was released that ut left her puzzling over how he had gained ut, but also there wuz a sensation that he wuz still close, and that seemingly, he had not gone back to Cornwall. She smelled the notes, and tried to feel his energy whilst counting them. Whatever Francis wuz doin ov, whatever he had become, he wuz doing well at ut. A thrilled shiver ran through her body too, with the notion that he wuz still alive somewhere, and still thinking ov her. School, she decided would have to start late tha' day, and grabbing the money and the note, she went down to Justin and Maddy's place to tell them. There, they all hugged. Aw, the relief ov ut. But 'course, one ov they there thought different. One ov they didn' carry the same kind of love, or feel the same relief as the other two.

The boy Tommy wudn' finished in his delivery duties though. In the inside pocket of his jacket wuz another envelope, and when he found out where a man called Doctor George Jewell lived, he handed that over to the surgeon. This wudn' bad this delivery lark. Ee got another large tip from the Doctor. Tommy recognised he wuz talking to a man ov importance but could awnly convey the same information as ee had offered to the woman. What he did knaw wuz tha' this envelope wuz thicker an' fuller than the previous one. He had guessed tha' ut contained money.

Now back inside, George Jewell piped up to Eleanor.

"The oddest thing," he said. "A boy just delivered this... He came up from the harbour."

"Open it," suggested Eleanor.

Jewell did just that and a flurry of dollar bills fell out onto the floor, many of which she had to pick up. A quick count showed there were three hundred dollars.

"An enormous amount of money," said the Doctor.

Ut wuz. Even by the mine's standards this was some lot of greenbacks.

Just the same as in his daughter's passel, there wuz a scrawled note. The Doctor read it aloud.

"Dear Doctor. Some money for the chapel fund. Maybe you will now think better of me. Francis N."

"Francis?"

"Seems so... but why?"

Jewell began to contemplate why this arrived. He knew that Francis had been aware of their struggle to get the chapel built. And prior to his apparent accidental killing of his grandson, he had been a chapel-man. This then, seemed to be his son-in-law trying to offset what he had done in the eyes of God. He understood. The Doctor realised he had said some terrible things about him, so both guilt and remorse filled him. A sin might have been committed but now Francis was trying to do the right thing in terms of his faith, in terms of his admiration for the teachings of Wesley. And here ut wuz: spend a bit, save a bit and give a bit. Here, in his hands, were boath the saving and the giving. In his mind, Jewell thanked the Lord. Such money wuz a godsend for he had feared what might happen. The projected costs for the next stage of the chapel's construction would, without this generous donation, have forced the Doctor himself into debt.

"Eleanor," Jewell said smiling. "You know what this means. We can carry on. This money is glorious. And righteous. It will fund God's love here on Mountainside. We can begin the walls, and we can follow precisely what Mr Mint has drawn. All that we wanted and planned for! You remember those style of benches we saw? We can have those made now... and that pulpit design... we can go ahead with all of this now... thanks to Francis."

"I told you to have feyth," articulated Eleanor. "And you kept feyth George. You wudn' have got this far without it."

"You're right, yes. What a moment! I must tell Rebecca. I wonder if she has heard from him. This will be the most glorious chapel ever built on the Keweenaw. It's everything I hoped for."

Jewell paced excitedly around the living room of his home.

"I'll get Mr Skews to get the carpenter and joiners straight on it. The weather's getting better, isn't it? We might have it up for a summer opening. Imagine that my dear Eleanor. Just imagine... And then, well, then we can appoint a full-time minister..."

"Wonderful," said Eleanor. "The Lord has blessed us. He knows we are doing the right thing. We are doing His work on the earth."

"Well, He sometimes does work in mysterious ways indeed..."

At this, they moved close together and kissed. All this joy see, had been brought on by a man in exile, a man who miles away, could awnly imagine the joy he might have brought. And fur now, there didn' seem any way of changin' tha'.

Later tha' day, when he'd consumed his crowst, the miners 'eaved the boy Tommy inta a wagon and set un goin' back down the mountain. The boy nearnly shat hisself by the time ee'd reached the bottom. The speed ov the wagon wuz some fast you. But he'd do ut again ef he needed, and thaas wha' happened you. Each time tha' particular laker put in, more envelopes of money were delivered up to Rebecca Nankervis and Doctor Jewell. Over time, when the weather broke, and there were sunny bright days at the end ov winter 1902, the chapel rose from its foundations. The framework went in and then the corner boards and panelling went up. Frieze-boards and a run of coping were to be added before the addition of the roof. The horizontal clapboards were painted sparkling white and already the four cornices were levered into place. Ut soon looked grand.

Some of the money was spent on a splendid doorway which had a plinth held up by two fine transoms. Above the plinth sat an impressive pediment. By the time the days grew longer, trimming wood had been added to the windows and at the bottom of the rectangular structure ran a fine exterior skirting board. Now that all of this wuz in place, finally, the inside would be fitted out in the way that the Doctor and Miss Prowse wished things to be. Aw – ut did look some 'andsome, this new Mountainside chapel, even though at present, tarpaulins over a temporary wooden frame kept the snow and rain from entering the interior. Tha' would soon change though, when Jewell and Miss Prowse spent the next lot of money sent to they from Francis.

As the building came together, two other things happened. George Jewell and Eleanor Prowse could wait no longer. On a whim, they caught a coach down to Calumet, and got married there. Rebecca and James went to the ceremony, alongside others such as Skews and Trevorrow. Mabel never went though. Her father could do what he wanted with the chapel and the money being sent to him by Francis Nankervis. She wudn' interested in the least. The other thing that happened, wuz that brought on by all this romance in the air, and because ov his success in designing the tramway an' the chapel, Dicky Mint proposed to Rosie Koskinen. 'Course, Justin heard tell ov ut, but what could a do? He wuz loved up anyway, so people thought, with tha' Maddy

O'Donahue. Eh, an' wudn' ut 'bout time they got married too? Tell ee truth, Justin wudn' feelin' ut, and neither wuz Maddy, but let tha' go fur now. They had more than enough on their plates bringing up that Jago, who wuz a tacker by now. Some boy ee wuz too.

Despite all the money coming into Mountainside, nawbody much spoke about Francis. Maybe he'd found a new life and wuz happy with ut. Ee wuz clearly doin' well by the cash coming back this way, but all of this annoyed Justin, for he now felt the lesser brother once more: and when he didn' knaw what to do about ut, he went to the cemetery up near the chapel and pulled up the memorial cross tha' had been placed there last year by Revered Josiah Davies and George Jewell, and snapped it into pieces. He placed the shards of wood inta' his pocket: and later on, down mine, he'd 'eave ut inta' the furnace. He might not have burnt the creature tha' he felt had caused all ov this back then, but symbolically, ee wud do ut now.

All the while, the growing chapel looked on, like a beacon of light in the dark forest, high above the mine. Ut wuz comin' to life he realised, though ut felt like he hisself wuz heading for the Deads. The forest saw its own soul being re-made as planking boards and panelling were nailed into place: wood drawn from the cut sent down to the harbour. How 'twas all goin' to pan out, it truly didn' knaw anymore.

An' Maddy, well, she felt like she wuz hurtling downward on one ov they hairy-assed wagons of the mineral tramway, only without sight, or use of a brake.

42

Ut comed in proper dirty. The snows lasted a goodly while. Between breaks in the weather, other parts of the chapel got constructed. A scaffold had been put around the structure, and then, when the days weren't windy, the roof framework got put in. Beams and rafters were levered into place, supported up there by a set of struts and props. When a glimmering of spring came, the carpenters shaped and crafted the shingles, and after battens had been nailed into place, those shingles got laid on the roof. Launders and drainpipes were added. Es. 'Twas takin' shape and everyone admired ut's look. Ut seemed to suit the community ut had been built for, an' no one wuz more proud of its erection than George Jewell; well, ee and his new wife, Mrs Eleanor Jewell. As the structure became evermore watertight, this pair approved the inside fittings and instructed the carpenters over the construction and carving ov the benches and pulpit. Some work there wuz you, and it wud keep they busy fur months to come. Then there wuz the geht ceiling rose itself which had come up from a plaster company in Chicago, and wuz shipped up on a laker. Aw, 'twud look lovely that, right in the middle of the ceiling, like some gaze at the forthcoming Heaven. They'd ordered the best they could find. Well, the plaace should have the best in their view.

All this comed at a cost, but you knaw who wuz paying fur ut by now. The monies didn' stop either. Every fortnight there wuz an envelope. A puzzle fur sure how Francis wuz gaining the money, but on the other hand, the Jewells tried not to think about tha' too much (Becca too, wuz getting monies, so much she hardly knawed wha' t'spend ut on). Ef it wuz his redemption money, then so be ut. There were wust things ee could spend his money on. The question now wuz whether ee'd one day make ut back to see what his money had funded. At the moment, tha' looked highly unlikely. Still, Jewell had had a foundation stone installed, near to the main door, and on un were the names of himself, Mrs Jewell, John Trevorrow, Justin Nankervis (who'd donated a fair bit o'money hisself) but also Francis Nankervis. There they were then, those two pards' names on the stone with the rest ov the great an' the good ov Mountainside. Maybe Francis wuz working off his moral debt.

'Twudn' all heavenly light though around the plaace. Aw naw. Ut certainly wudn' like tha' t'all. The hollerin' between Maddy an' Justin increased and he becomed worried up proper. Ee wudn' sure they wuz goin' to survive the next few months together, tell about the next year or the rest of their born days. The main problem had become tha' Maddy wudn' goin' out. She wudn' takin' Jago out either. She started to prefer just she and he in the home, not seein' ov anyone else. The boy needed sun and dirt to play in and explore, but so closeted had she become tha' she wudn' let un do nawthun'. Justin didn' knaw ut, but 'course, t'she, now everything wuz a threat. Her biggest fear wuz tha' somethun' wuz goin' to swoop down an' take un away from she. 'Twas like she imagined a geht dragon pulling at un and grabbing un hold ov by its claws, and then carryin' un off. She stopped speakun' to other women about their babies, and the name ov Francis Nankervis clearly wudn' to be mentioned. And when she heard about the monies comin' up, well, that seemed to make ut even worse. Justin cudn' work out why, but 'twas all gettun' stranger and stranger, and ee knawed ut.

See, Maddy should have been better at disguising that you. She should have welcomed the money fur the chapel and fur Becca, and told everyone how joyous ut wuz that he was still alive, an' makin' good. But the fact that he'd upset her plan, niggled away at her so she cudn' disguise tha' as well as she wanted. An' when that failure happened, there were sure to be others. Es, a geht fissure had formed inside ov she, and t'be honest you, she didn' knaw where t'turn. Ut wudn' like the Deads could offer a solution, and neither now could the forest, because she knew that it knawed her secrets. She feared it to be honest. Despite her time with Jago, which was the only time on Mountainside that she did love at present, fur the fust time in her life she felt alone.

There wuz nawthun' Justin could do though. Ee just had to get on weth ut. So ut seemed, she even didn' like ut much when ee had time with Jago. 'Twuz like ut suddenly wudn' his son any more, and tha' his access to un wuz restricted. Ee wuz daggin' t'take the boy belaw ground t'see his reaction. Well, there wuz nawthun' like startin' ov um young, but she didn' go a pile on ut. She even said – hark at this – tha' she didn't want the boy to go inta' mining. Adamant 'bout ut, she wuz too. Justin reckoned she wuz watchin' closely the evolution of Doctor Jewell's boy James, and wanted tha' kind ov a life fur'n. 'Twas almost as though she wuz dismissing their collective past. She didn' even allow him any time with the Irish. Ut wudn' like she wuz teachin' un any of his background either. Perhaps she had different hopes fur the mite. Justin cudn' work ut out, howsoever he tried to think ut through. Odd, she wuz in the fust plaace, this Maddy, but she wuz becomin' odder – tha' much wuz sure. Maybe too much ov tha' magic had possessed she in some way. Ut had become dark. Thaas wha' ut felt like. E'd been up to the chapel time or two and prayed to the Lord God above fur a bit of guidance, but nawthun' presented utself, so ee had to carry on the best way ee could. At present though, 'twas like a geht fuse. Somethun' wuz goin' t'blaw. 'Twas in the air you. Take cover boy.

The mine utself wuz goin' on steady. The ninth level wuz yielding good ore, an' as long as the tracks were kept clear of snaw, then the tramway kept on runnin'. Now tha' winter wuz ending, nawbody expected any problems with ut. The system had heightened production, and everyone associated with the mine wuz happy with ut. One ov the two jobs at the moment wuz to sort out the piles of quartzite tailings which were sweeping down the hill. This wuz rock from which the copper ore had been extracted, and the quartzite was a by-product. The problem wuz tha' the tailings were gettin' out of hand. You dun't realise just how much waste d'come out ov a mine when you get goin' on ut. These were nearnly 'bout takin' over these days and somethun' needed to be done about um. What wuz really needed wuz t'see if they could sell off some of the waste, perhaps fur road-building or somethun' like tha', but a solution wudn' easy to come across. Daily, Mr Skews an' Justin had meetings about ut, and right then, this wuz Skews' next big job: to see ef they could find a way of gettun' rid of ut, and make a bit on ut too. There wuz naw reason why the tramway cudn' carry that down the harbour too. Tha' wud give um more room fur the new attle still comin' up from belaw. Rite on.

The other issue affecting Justin that spring wuz that some of the water launders needed re-directing. When the mine had fust gone in, well, they'd been 'eaved in piecemeal to be honest you. The triangular-framed gutters carried water all over the mine for the processes of washing and cleaning ore, but improvised runs of ut wuz going' everywhere an' ut wuz startin' to look a mess. Aw, you needed ut you, to run water-wheels, fly-wheels and the stamps and all tha', but it appeared some oogly. There wuz a view that ut ought to be sorted out a bit, and maybe have one main launder shute coming down from the river, then splitting off to various locations. Bit more ordered like. Right now though, lengths ran off the river in all directions, like gangly wooden spider's legs running all over the camp. Ut wuz an eyesore really, and whilst ut had served ut's purpose, somethun' better wuz needed. Skews and Justin, surveyed ut alongside Walt Chegwidden, who wuz still in charge grass-end these days, and Minter drawed up some plans. Now the Minter these days, was puffed up like a bladder ov lard about ee gettin' hitched to Rosie Koskinen, but whenever that got mentioned in passing, Justin allays steered the conversation back to the matter in hand, which wuz how the launders should best work. Men see, they'm some jealous like tha'. An' ee, tha' Justin, already with a maid an' boy at home!

All the while, the sprites of the forest looked on. The trees watched, and the animals, birds and insects watched. They knew now what had become of Clara Jewell. They knew something of their power over humans. But their efforts wudn' last. Ef awnly they'd waited a while and let Clara re-adjust then things would have been fine. She wuz starting to come back, wudn' she? She communicated with the forest when she'd been taken away. As always, the forest never said much, but it knew all the secrets of Mountainside. Maybe it knew what wuz coming. That wuz because it could see beyond the present. It was attuned to those small steps, those small changes that alter the world slightly, but then, if there are enough of them, things alter full scale and prompt too radical a change: change that led to destruction and extinction. It knew those words all too well, and it knew too that parts of itself were now sacrilegiously being used to erect an edifice up in the bowl of land which had stood untouched for centuries. It had seen it all crafted: the timber frame, panels, and the skirting boards. The shingles too: all pieces of itself. Body parts. Using they now as a temple for their god. What right had they to alter this place? What right had they to bury their dead inside the land here? How come it had been blessed in the name of a god they did not know or understand? As the days became longer, and flowers and leaves began to bud and sprout, it contemplated all of it.

Taking note of these spring changes wuz Mabel Jewell. The winter had been hard for her, because she had wanted to leave with Nimkii: and finally commit to their travelling together, and she becoming his wife. The hard winter had delayed their plans but every day now, they were taking fruition. She was pleased at the shift in the season: for the moment the snows fully left they planned on leaving. There would be no looking back and there would be no lament. She didn' want to end up here, buried in some plot at Mountainside. She wanted to be ever-moving and when the day of death came, she swore she would be burnt and her ashes put to being part of the wind. This wuz this Mabel all over. She'd been like ut since she'd been a child. Those fairy stories had set her on this route a long time ago. Gah – everyone at Mountainside knawed tha'.

She was beautiful now wuz this young woman. She was more beautiful than her sister. She knew that. It was as if she had inherited more of her father's bloodline than her mother's. That plainness of her mawthur wudn' in she. This spring would be her time. It would be when she would blossom and come of age. Back at the mine, she knew what was going on. The management were fussing over the tailings and the water courses. Nothing could ever be left alone with they. They were always looking for improvements and developments, and would never be satisfied. Why, she considered, couldn't they just leave things be? Down in the cut where the tramway ran, Mabel was out collecting herbs and flowers. She and Nimkii were making bottles of healing, in case on their journey some event happened that merited this knowledge. He'd told her what to collect (chiefly thyme, sage and a local balm that awnly Nimkii could pronounce), and she wuz enjoying the morning light cutting in across the elevation and causing the surviving trees to cast shadows of their form across the tracks. It was still, aside from the rumble of the wagons. One had just gone down laden with new copper ore, and somewhere below, another was on its way up. They would clatter noisily at they went past her, but she had the presence of mind to ignore them.

With Mabel, the sprites were not scared. They opened their bunkers and their hidey holes that little bit wider. After all, it was almost spring, and after the hibernation what better thing to look at than a beautiful human girl, a girl who was not like the rest – and who was sympathetic to their needs. She oozed that, and the sprites picked up on it. They ran before her, placing the right herbs in front of her that she needed. Oh see, the forest could be kind to those who cared. To those it trusted, it gave total affection. This one was Clara Jewell's daughter as well. She needed to be looked after. And now she was with that Nimkii. Of late, Nimkii had expressed his sorrow. He had explained how he had let the mine slip in, and expand too greatly. Ut had not been what he had wanted and he regretted his actions. He'd told Yolkai that.

One day, he had said, the forest would gain control again. It liked Nimkii and it wanted to believe him. Perhaps there was still good in him – and maybe this Mabel with him – well, that was a good combination. It never judged them like others did. Ut wuz a combination that should be celebrated, and although it knew their intention to leave this place, the wider earth would sustain and support them wherever they went on their travels. Maybe one day, when they came back here, they'd find things repaired. They'd find the cut gone and the scar on the landscape from the mine removed – the forest back in control. The blue jays were calling that morning and the butterflies were fluttering from early flower to early flower, drawing sweet nectar wherever they could. Es. The forest was entering a new phase of its cycle; it was renewing and reproducing. It was re-inventing itself once more, and this burst of nature was something Mabel delighted in. So the forest watched her, and she watched the forest, and the mine and its pollution felt a world away, despite the immediate rattle and rumble of the wagons going up and down the tramway.

The forest was not the only thing watching this Mabel though. That morning, frustrated and perverted as he wuz in his ways, that boy Skews had been out inspecting the tailings, and out of the corner of his shifty eye, he'd see Mabel go down the path beside the incline. Now ee, being ee, couldn't help but be intrigued by she, and like the forest, ee initially nawticed not what she was doing, but her sheer beauty. The winter had meant that he had not spied her much ov late, and his mind had outwardly been taken up with other matters, but inwardly with ee, there wuz still that perversion, that sense of him wanting something he couldn't have. That wuz in un, but so too, wuz this sense that ef ee couldn' have ut, then ee would destroy ut fur anyone else. An' thaas zactly how he thought, this boy Skews. 'Twudn' pleasant at all, and 'twuz somethun' that moast God-fearing and -abiding people wudn' even consider. But then, this wuz Samuel Skews we wuz talkin' 'bout here; a bugger who didn' knaw any better, an' although ee could be seen nodding and affirming at the chapel's erection, actually ee didn' give a flying fart about following any true Christian way of living.

Then see, well, ee reckoned upon that Christian God failing ee good an' proper, what with a probably never about to see his wife and daughters back in Cornwall, and ee thinking that ee'd been cursed in this plaace called Mountainside. Loneliness see, ut can kill a man, and ut can also drive un insane, and do things that in the normal run of things, he would never ever consider. Therefore he'd decided a while ago that he'd soil it. He'd soil she and thereby hurt tha' Nimkii – ee who shouldn' even be close to she. They might think ee perverted, but nawthun' could compare to that Nimkii and she. The thought ov ut: his inferior blood corrupting she – and one day soon – them producing some kind of half-breed. See, Skews cudn' contemplate tha'; he could see naw sense in ut, an' from dawn to dusk, ut irked un.

Aw, ee occupied hisself did this Skews with this and tha' concerning the mine. His great achievement had been the tramway. See how overnight, that had doubled profit. See how ut had made the mine the foremost copper producer on the Upper Peninsula. Aw, ut was ee alone really who'd instigated tha'. Others had had their say you, but ee'd been the driving force behind ut. The thing wuz no one really appreciated ut. They just assumed. No wonder ut was his right to cream off a bit more of the profit, like he'd been doing from the outset. Nawbody cared. Nawbody even nawticed. Tha' wuz the kind of fools ee wuz working with, and hell, if ut wudn' fur ee and his skills in assaying and surveying, this plaace would still just be a small, untouched clearing in the forest.

Ee being ee, wuz glad of all the clamour about Francis and Rebecca's boy. Ee didn' really knaw the ins and outs ov ut, and neither did he want or need to. While they wuz busying themselves with tha', Skews could concentrate on other matters: making a bit more here and there. They didn' have the eye fur detail like ee did. Of late, ov course, ee'd been spending more time with some of the other miners. One or two of they wondered ef he was the kind ov man who liked other men a bit too much, and tha' actually helped his cause a bit. 'Mean, ef ut come to anything, with wha' ee wuz about to do now, ut wudn' be pinned on ee; and well, that Francis still being away (fur ee did knaw the truth), well, that suited un proper. Ut made un seem incapable ov such an act. Actually, ee'd hated his time sat with them and their plods and drolls, and their cakey way of leading their lives. Backwards they were, compared to his sophistication. Sometimes, he wished his Cornishness could be pulled out ov un and tossed inta' the Deads like every other piece of waste.

So this wuz ov ee at this time, and he'd spotted Mabel alone. Time, ee told hisself, to make a move. There probably wudn' be naw other chance. His mind wuz full of what he used to do on his own when he'd follow her, and that made un hard belaw. 'Twudn' nice, aw naw, t' think ov that, but this wuz the way this bugger wuz. The forest seen ut you. Maybe others should have too, but they wuz too busy, too ignorant ov un. Not like tha' Francis. Ee knawed.

Padding then, wuz this Skewser, goin' down the side of the tramway, on the edge of the forest. Ee wuz stalking she see, like a mountain lion, and on the air ee could smell her. He knew that fresh virginal smell of she from old, and it was a smell tha' he craved. When you find a man like Skews, then nawthun's goin' to stop ee from doin' something sinful. With a man like ee, well, ee d' think 'tis his God-given right t'behave in the way tha' ee wanted to, and fur Trevorrow and Jewell, all wantin' ov this plaace to be ordered and following lawful Christian practice, right there and then, tha' wuz not what ee had in mind at all. What a bastard, eh? Sometimes see, you have to call a spade a spade. And ee might have been Cornish you, and ee might well have done some good things, but the bottom line, the bottommost level ov ut, was that ee was a wrong un. The forest knew ut. The crows cawed, and the blue jays scattered; and fur now, the emerging butterflies kept their distance. They all could tell what ee wuz goin' to do and wha' ee wuz about to enact. Maybe he'd be successful they felt, but there'd be a reckoning. There allays wuz.

The wagon coming up the tramway hit the spots in the track where there were slight gaps between each rail, giving a rhythm which suited Skews. The noise gave him cover as he made his approach. Where wuz Mabel? Well, she wuz away with the fairies, just like she used to be. Now that, that had been his twisted fantasy with her a couple of years ago, but perhaps now his aim was straighter. The arrowhead of his need was sharper and more defined: a shaping defined by her present form and beauty. In this moment, so convulsed with desire was he that he did not care about what became of him. Why should he? He had nothing beyond her to care for. That is why such events happen. They happen because men like him are lacking. He never believed that though – not even for one moment. Rancid and rotten ee wuz, this boy Skews. The mine had made un corrupt and selfish. His mind wuz putrefied an' full ov slimes.

When he finally made his move, the forest went silent. The sprites who had emerged jumped out of their skins and retreated below ground, so aggressive was this man's movement on Mabel. They knawed ov un though: saw what ee wuz doing, saw him use his force on she. He came at her from behind, and pulled out a length of sharp quartzite on she. He'd gathered ut from the tailings and recognised that ut would act as a nice threat to her beauty: the beauty tha' he wanted to make solely his own, that he imagined wuz his right.

"Do as I say," said Skews.

She knawed who ut was right away. She recognised the look of his clawthes, the stench of his breath. She'd grown up with this man. What wuz this? Some kind of revenge fur what she'd done with the poppet he'd given her, now deep in the Deads. But ut wuz genuinely hard to resist un. He was strong, and she instantly knew what he wanted. Her breath quickened as he waved the shard at her throat and began tearing at her clawthes. The layers he hated the moast were the Indian ones; these he torn at wildly, but when he got under that layer, he took more time, taking pleasure in the unwrapping ov her. Yes – this wuz the fairy tale she deserved, and he no longer cared ef he was the Big Bad Wolf. His cock wuz hard and he wanted her. She wuz, all the while, struggling and fighting him, but he was good at holding her down. There was that awful sensation of him pinning down her legs onto the forest floor with his own. There wuz her resistance, but his ever harder pushing of her into the earth. She could feel the leaf litter's spiky hardness on her flesh. What had a mutated into? How had a transformed? But maybe he hadn' changed one bit.

You knaw Mabel by now though. You knaw she wudn' just goin' to let un have his wicked way. Aw naw. Although she wuz struggling, she fought un back hard. She used her teeth to bite at his hands. Any time they came close she gaped open her mouth and tried to latch onto him. Further hurt was caused by her trying to knee him hard in the bollocks in any way that she could. She was screaming too, hoping that someone would hear her. In her mind, she was thinking already ov what Nimkii would do to him, when she finally told him. And then, the horror: what would ut be like ef he got his fluid inside of her? Ut was that she feared the moast. She knew she could be fertile at this point in her monthly cycle and to have his child? That was unthinkable. She could not let that happen.

As well as this though, wuz his utter infringement of her right as a woman to exist here, without such attack: for she knew his attempt to now rape her was very real. And in those moments, the more she thought back to knowing Skews when she had been younger, the more the thought of him repelled her. Her sister had told her, hadn't she, all that time ago? Rebecca'd sensed the evil in him. Looking back, she'd felt it too, only she didn' knaw what it wuz. There he wuz now, on top ov she, this pillar ov the community, drooling at the whiteness ov her body and letting saliva from his mouth drip onto her skin.

"Bastard!" she kept shouting at him. It wuz the awnly thing she could say, and the more she said that, the more ut motivated Skews to do what he had long since wanted. Potentially, he knew that what he was doing would wreck the relationship she had with the Indian. Fair enough, Skews told hisself. He deserved ut completely and utterly: geht primitive ape ov a man tha' he wuz.

These moments were frantic fur Skews. You cudn' say that ut was something enjoyable or even pleasurable fur him though, because none ov ut wuz. Pleasure didn't really come inta' ut in that way though. Ut was more about stating his power: making her respect him; making her have to deal with him; getting his needs met. He could now smell the perfume of her body, his face next to her breasts and he was kicking down his own trousers and underwear. No, she told herself. This cudn' happen. Not here. Not now. Ee'd pulled her underwear aside though and now ee wuz touching her with his thing. 'Twas enough to make she wretch, and she did so: bringing up phlegm which she spat at him. Skews liked the fight though. He was enjoying the struggle. When the phlegm hit his face, he unleashed his long tongue and licked it into his mouth. That act though, sent a shudder of energy through Mabel, and with it, she wuz able to summon the power to push him off her. She screamed again in the hope that someone would come. She called out at the forest, asking for help but Skews would have had no understanding of that dialogue.

"They'll kill you for this," she managed to say. "When my father hears about it, the whole town will track you down."

"I hope they do," said Skews calmly. "They'll hang me fur zertain."

She understood the measure of him. All care had left him. If that had gone, then an atrocity like this wuz something he was quite capable of.

"I thought you were Methodist," she said.

"I thought you were too," he managed to say in response, twisting her words at first, but then again, his knowledge of the real her caused her palpitations. "You're hardly chapel material now, are you?"

Bastard. Ee wuz now seemingly using her heathen beliefs against her. In fact, that sense of Christian conquest over her seemed to excite him further. The quartzite shard was soon back at her throat. She looked up and down the tramway. Where wuz one ov those miners who rode the wagons now? They'd amused her before with their fairground antics. Now, she needed someone to arrive, but as another wagon trundled downwards, ut didn' look like anyone was about to come any time soon. Skews wudn' made of much really she realised. In many respects he was a mere weevil of a man, but right now, the drive in him was motivating an unexpected strength. She considered running into the forest, but what good would that do? If he followed her in there, she might not ever come out. Maybe he'd do his business and then dispose ov her. She'd be found with her windpipe sliced. No, she had to steer him into the open ov the cut. At least there, there would be a chance of them being spotted. In the forest, her screams would be muffled. In the open, someone might hear. Where were those idiot Knockies when you needed them? Perhaps, of course, they were underground, in the deep levels right belaw where they were standing.

The anger welled in her. It sluiced around in her heart and travelled the launders of her veins. He was too close now; too close to getting what he wanted. She would resist him though, and suddenly, she found the core strength to lever him off her again. When that had been accomplished, he started laughing, cruelly and evil-mindedly. To ee, this wuz a game. To she though, things had shifted. Ut wuz now a matter ov life and death. Mabel covered herself again, and let down her skirt which he had hoiked up but seconds ago. She knew she needed to get to the bag where she had been collecting the herbs. In there, wuz something she now needed: something that she had been trained in fur a while; something that wuz now a key part ov her, and who she considered herself to be. The bastard Skews wuz still laughing though, as if this were some prologue to something more lasting and even more nightmarish. A tuss ov the first order then. Na, worse than that. There were many condemnatory Indian words that she called him under her breath. There were plenty of ripe miners' cusses too, despite the shock she was in.

He wuz stood in front of she now, with his milky-white cock still exposed and twitching, like ut was still waiting to be satisfied. This couldn't happen, she told herself. At least she wuz free ov un now. Ee wuz philosophising by the sound of un: talking to hisself about all that he had achieved. Ee'd become distracted by his ego and small cock. She'd 'ave un now. She told herself she could do ut. She'd been trained. They'd practised it a thousand times out in the forest, when nawbody else was watching. Awnly the forest saw. Perhaps that wuz what it was waiting for now.

In her bag was a copper-inlaid tomahawk. Nimkii had crafted it for her, and whilst he was orating about his glory, she pulled ut close. Her hand found the plush blue ore of the handle, and she already knew the sharpness ov the blade. The blade had been made from that same attle that he wuz holding, and had been bound into place. Hard and tough it wuz: the same as it had been for a thousand years, and used by Nimkii's ancestors. Spin around, go on, Mabel wuz saying to herself.

"Tell me about the tramway. Your idea wasn't it? You said so. Just now... I mean, the mine should celebrate you more shouldn't it... Mr Skews?"

She held her nerve as she said this, hoping he would gaze over his empire. For a while he stood facing her still, maybe even realising that half-dressed he looked ludicrous: his shirt-tails whipping around his milky white ass.

"By rights," he went on, turning around slightly, "I should be one of the founders of that chapel... I put enough money into it, only they don't see it..."

He wuz almost there now. Only few more degrees and then she'd act.

"But you know that, don't you my dearest Mabel? Don't you? Eh?"

She didn't hear what he said. As soon as she lost eye contact with him, and his turning movement reached another few more degrees in the right direction, she launched the spinning tomahawk into his back, and it landed there with a thud. Ut wuz a deep sound; one she had heard before, like when a collapse happened underground. And when the blade went in between his shoulders just like Nimkii had long taught her, initially, ut had no discernable effect. He didn't topple or fall right away at all. Seemingly, ut was almost as ef he had expected some retort; some missile to be launched at him. He even turned around to she, smiling at her.

"Bye poppet," he said eventually.

At this, he started to topple, and in instant fell onto the outer track of the tramway. Mabel could not ever have planned this, and neither could have Skews as a piece of suicide, but just as his head and neck clumped onto the metal of the track, up comed a wagon from the harbour below. The bone and flesh ov Skews' neck wudn' nawthun' to the rapidly turning wheels of the wagon; as ut passed, ut sliced clean through his head and torso like a knife goin' straight through butter. This wuz what Justin and Doctor Jewell had been worried about all along, but ut didn' bother the wagon none. Aw naw. Tha' just trundled on up the incline nice an' easy, whilst Skews' severed head dropped inta' the gap between them on the track, near to where a fair few daishals were grawin'. Ee wudn' be touching she naw more, even though his body wuz still jerking. The nerve endings were still responding to his fate.

Mabel looked around to see ef anyone had seen this action. She looked to the forest for response, but none came. Although she couldn't see ut, all this scared the sprites mightily, but the thing wuz, they knawed Skews, an' so were glad. Mabel quickly got dressed the best that she could, even though her blouse and undergarments were torn. They would have to do for now. Her Indian accessories had been torn apart by Skews, but nonetheless she picked them up the best she could. Last of all she went over to the body, and pulled out the axe from between his shoulder-blades. It seemed to have precisely connected with his spine and released itself with a squelch of blood and tissue. There was a small cut in the rear of his jacket where it had cut the material, but otherwise, there wuz not much blood. Elsewhere though, where the slice through the head and torso had occurred, a glistening red lake gathered. Another Deads. She avoided looking at the bone and gristle of the man.

43

What happened next seemed like a dream – or perversely, a real fairy story. Mabel rushed back to the tepee that was now her home. Inside, she found a calm Nimkii and asked him to come with her urgently. He could barely understand what she was saying but saw the urgency in her. He also noted that her clawthes had been torn.

"The forest," she said. "I got all the herbs though."

She led him speedily around the mine, past Rosie's and past her father's surgery right up to where the new chapel was being built. There wuz a minor occasion taking place. Apparently, all of the roof shingles had gone on, and the carpenter boys were stepping back, admiring their work, alongside a proud George and Eleanor Jewell. As the job had been completed ahead of schedule, the new Mrs Jewell had taken it upon herself to make a round of saffron buns and hot tay fur they men just comin' down off the scaffold and ladders. This cessation coincided with Mabel and Nimkii's arrival. 'Course the bun recipe wudn Eleanor's awn you, but ut went down very well amongst they present. Mr and Mrs Jewell noted with interest the arrival of this pair: ut wudn' like they ever comed up here normally. What wuz on with they? What had altered? How had things shifted?

"Is it open?" Mabel asked them, her heart beating fast.

"Not officially," said her father, "but you'n go on in if you like."

He noted the urgency in her: a wish to commune.

Mabel did that. She entered its fresh surrounds and could smell the new varnish and paint. Above were the expensive glass chandeliers for lighting the place. She plonked herself on a bench initially, then for a while, knelt in prayer. In those few moments, she clearly had some things to tell the Lord God above. She wuz hoping that He'd still be amenable to listening to her after all this time.

Outside, Nimkii stood with George and Eleanor Jewell,

"What's up with her?" asked George.

"I have no idea," said Nimkii in broken English, shrugging his shoulders at the same time. "She wants God maybe."

This surprised George Jewell. Maybe he felt that she wuz finally returning home. Maybe she was having second thoughts. Perhaps she'd come back to chapel once more. This pleased him, and so courteously, he offered Nimkii one of the buns that Mrs Jewell had baked earlier that day. By now (and having lived with the Cornish for some years) he knew their flavour and he liked them. He readily partook of one of the buns, and had eaten a couple before Mabel emerged from the chapel: now looking serene and calm. Jewell felt it best not to say anything. He knew, by now, that ut was best not to upset his daughter. Instead, his conversation with Nimkii continued.

"What do you think of our chapel then?" he asked the native.

"Good," Nimkii responded, nodding with somewhat mock enthusiasm.

"Mountainside Chapel," said Jewell proudly, gesturing towards it.

Nimkii looked the building up and down, and saw the Cornish who had worked on it having their crowst and tay.

"No," said Nimkii sternly, looking intently at George Jewell. "Not the right name."

"How do you mean?" asked the Doctor.

"This not the right name. This place... This is Saffron-Bun Chapel," Nimkii smiled, looking at what he wuz eatin'. "That, the right name... You Cornish... always with the buns, yes?"

George Jewell didn' knaw what to say. He mulled ut over.

"Well, I see your thinking... But I'm not sure whether we can call it that – can we?" He looked around at his new wife.

"Can we?" he asked her once more.

"We can call it what we like..."

"That's right. More relevant than Mountainside," chipped in Mabel. "It's got a nice sound to it. Rolls off the tongue. What do you reckon boys?"

Those working on the church affirmed the new name; their gobs already full of bun, but with broad smiles on their faces. Ut seemed like God might say rite on then. A bewdie name fur'n.

"Fit fur purpose I s'pause," thought Jewell.

"And a name nawbody's likely to forget," said Eleanor. "More lasting... People will hear tell ov ut back in Cornwall with a name like tha'."

"Well," said George Jewell with some degree of ceremony. "Seems Nimkii here has found us a new name. Mountainside Chapel – now otherwise officially known as Saffron-Bun Chapel."

Those there clapped, and those who wuzn't, would later have to make sense of ut's new name. They'd find that out soon enough when the body of Samuel Skews got remembered at the next service. That wudn' right though – or at least some ov those there thought. When the chapel had been re-named, then Nimkii and Mabel left. They went back to his steel tepee, and she finally told un what had happened and what fate Skews had suffered. She told un about what he'd tried to do to her and her use of the tomahawk. Whilst he wuz glad all his training given to her had paid off, he was angry with himself for not being there to protect her. He questioned how she was and how she now felt after Skews' actions, and promised to fetch her anything she needed. After the attempted rape, was she really still ready to leave? Yes, she wuz. He also asked her what she had done in the chapel.

She told un. She told un she had prayed to God for forgiveness.

When she had washed herself clean in the river, they boath knew ut was time to go. The axe wound in the back of Skews would surely link Nimkii with Skews' killing, and then so too, Mabel. Nimkii knawed that had she not completed the task of killing him, then he would have taken it upon himself to do so. No man could dishonour him, nor his woman, in this way. At least the evil had been defeated: that wuz the main thing. Nimkii then realised that he could do no more. By the time any investigation had happened, they would be long gone into the dark forest. Ut wuz fur the best. Once away, they could marry and live their lives as they wanted. Out there, they could forget about Skews and a number of other things. They could even forget about Saffron-Bun Chapel too. Out there, they'd find new stories together.

Nawbody knawed what had happened to the Skewser until about a week later. Up until then, he'd disappeared off the face of the earth. On the prior Tuesday, he'd been present in the morning there with Justin looking at the quartzite tailings and wondering what to with them fur the best, but after tha', nawbody'd seemed t'knaw where he'd got to. Ee wudn' in his residence fur zertain. Fur a while, some people even wondered ef he'd fallen down the shaft, or had wandered off, like Clara Jewell, inta' the forest. The boys sought hard fur'n and they cudn' find naw trace of un.

Trevorrow and Minter got worried up because they knawed ut wudn' like un. 'Mean, ee wuz regular as clockwork was the Skewser. You could count on un doin' the same thing every day at precisely the same time. And ef he disappeared, in the short term, he'd be some loss to the mine you. Not tha' Justin cared much, nor Maddy either, because they had some measure ov un, just the same as Rebecca Nankervis. 'Twas actually she tha' sensed he'd come to a bad end, and 'course, she couldn' help but think about tha', and the simultaneous disappearance of her sister and Nimkii. Maybe Francis would be glad not to see un again too. She just prayed to God tha' her Francis didn't have anything to do with ut.

How they found his body wuz some simple really though. See, the boy Tommy Carkeek was making one of his envelope deliveries again, and as usual, he comed up the incline in a wagon, and gaking out the front, saw the body beside the tracks. Once he got up top, he nervously told everyone what he'd see'd. That wuz ut then. Up top, they knawed what to expect, and so Trevorrow, Justin, Minter and Doctor Jewell made their way down the slope to where the boy had said he'd seen a body. What they'd expected to find wudn' the way they'd imagined ut. In their heads they'd foresaw a lone body, and from what the boy had said, he reckoned ut didn't have naw head. Grim 'twuz goin' to be.

Now, instead of tha', what they saw wuz something orange-and-black covered, all of ut moving in motion like some gigantic seal-shaped form over the tracks of the tramway. Fust ov all, you cudn' make out zactly what 'twas, but the closer you got, you saw the individual nature of ut. 'Twas a moving mass of butterflies, what they d'call a kaleidoscope of they, and each of the orange and veiny black wings were fluttering together, the luminescent feel of they shimmering all at once. These were Monarch butterflies: what the Cornish called Tigers. That fust name had been given they a long time ago, so ut was said, because they represented King William III, the Prince of Orange. A few days before, these winged bewdies had emerged from their chrysalises, having undergone a transformation from caterpillars into vibrant flitterers. More changelings see.

There was something about their fragmentary movement that fascinated the four men who had found this writhing mass. They spoke something to them about the ephemerality of human life: about the way it can turn on a whim, how something can so soon, morph into something else. These Tigers had come off the nectar and were now engaged in feeding on the pooled blood and licking the already decaying flesh of Skews.

"Ugh," went Minter. "Ut d'make me urge. I've never seen that a'fore now..."

Neither had anyone else, but there wuz some knowledge in Trevorrow that sometimes butterflies fed on rotten fish and meat, knowing that it gave them a different kind of sustenance, and that sometimes they'd seek ut out, particularly when opportunity arose. When they got up close, they seened that the boy wuz right: tha' the body had been decapitated. Their presence forced the orange kaleidoscope to move, and most flittered off in hundreds of different directions back into the forest. Only a few remained, still feeding on the goo.

"Wha' wuz a doin' ov with his trousers down?" asked Trevorrow.

Nawbody could answer tha'. It did seem odd though. What had a been doin' ov' here? 'Mean, wuz this purposeful, or did someone put un there? Whatever 'twas, somebody would have to let the police knaw down in Calumet, and there, they'd again be investigating they weird Cornish up on Mountainside, and even weirder if this boy had committed suicide with his trousers and underwear down to his ankles, and his flaccid penis hanging over the daishal-infused ballast.

"Dun't say anything 'bout tha' fur now," insisted Jewell, trying to snap everyone there out of embarrassed pondering. "Pull his trousers up and let's get the body up to the surgery so I'n investigate."

Nawbody wanted t'touch any ov ut but thaas wha' they did you. A couple of tarpaulins were brought down: one fur the body and one fur Skews' head. Gingerly, they moved the two parts of the corpse. His face looked serene whatever had happened to un. Like an angel, accordin' t' tha' Dicky Mint.

"But surely 'tis the site of a crime," commented Trevorrow.

"Ut might be," said Doctor Jewell, "but if we don't get ut inside, time the flitterbies have had their day, there wun't be much left ov un."

On reflection, Trevorrow knawed the Doctor wuz right and so they began the process of moving both parts of Skews' body up to the surgery.

On the way up, Justin leaned in to the Doctor and asked un straight.

"What ee reckon? Suicide?"

"Reckon so," whispered back the Doctor, his eyes still looking straight ahead.

"Some wisht then."

"Yes. 'Tis. I thought he was goin' on well enough..."

"Apparently not," said Justin.

"Reckon we'll chalk ut up as an accident, don't you? He'n be buried up cemetery then."

The last of the butterflies had left. Their food had been wrapped up and was no longer there for feasting upon.

Later, Doctor Jewell realised that the opening of his chapel for the fust time wudn' goin' to be fur naw great ceremony, but actually for a funeral. This disappointed him personally: but professionally, he still carried on his duties as an impromptu coroner trying to find the cause of death. 'Course, ut looked obvious didn't ut, when ee fust scrutinized the body? 'Twas the severing of the spinal cord which would have caused instant death. Thaas what he wrote down fust, but then, when he turned the body over and laid it on ut's stomach, he saw the strange cut in the jacket. Nawbody else would even have nawticed, but now intrigued, he took off the jacket and the shirt and traced the wound. The incision had been precise and accurate and deep. The size of the wound matched precisely the weapon he'd seen Nimkii use. So that is why he had gone. And there he'd been, recalcitrant, indulging in a bit ov saffron bun after committing a crime. But then he knew Nimkii, and despite his loathing of the association between he and his daughter, ee wudn' ever have direct cause to do anything to Skews, would a? Naw, surely not.

The Doctor contemplated this all evening and wondered what he should do. He'd already gleaned that Nimkii and Mabel had left. And then he came to realise who wuz last seen out practising with the tomahawk. 'Twas his daughter. On his mind also weighed something that he'd remembered about his elder daughter: that she had said to him some time ago, that she didn't really approve of the relationship Mr Skews had with Mabel. He'd sensed that she felt there wuz something not right about it: something ethereal, dangerous and elusive. Maybe what she had seen had in some way, been acted out on the tramway's incline. When he thought through the matter, there wuz also that urgent need of hers to get into the chapel. Ut wudn' Nimkii t'all.

After considering this carefully, he thought he knew what might have happened, what with Mr Skews half-dressed. The man had been odd, and in knowing this, he knew something of his possible perversions: something sick in his mind. Even though she was now far enough away, he did not want to implicate his youngest daughter in any of this, and so when he came to write his post-mortem report, as mine surgeon, he classified, just as he had observed it to Justin Nankervis, that Skews' unravelling was an accidental death. Whatever he put on the form, Skews would, in the end, have to face God's judgement. He prayed that Mabel's prayer for forgiveness would some day save her too.

When he'd finished writing up his findings, he put the head of Skews back on his mortuary table, next to the rest of his tortured body and covered it with a sheet. The next time he'd see it, the remains would be shovelled into a coffin, with his funeral service taking place at the newly-named Saffron-Bun Chapel.

"Oh Samuel," Jewell said in a soft voice. "What on earth did you do?"

He turned off the gas lighting and shut the surgery door. Under the shroud was caught a single butterfly.

44

'The bugger flipped, didn' a?'

Tha' wuz what everyone said at his funeral. 'Mean, in the forced solemnity ov the service, in hushed tones Jewell said ut wuz an unfortunate accident, but ut didn' feel like that, did ut? Na. Moast people had concluded that basically, Skews had topped hisself, an' fur whatever reason, ee wanted out. Perhaps 'twas the isolation. Perhaps 'twas the fact that he had no hope ov ever seeing his wife and childurn again. Perhaps ee'd just had enough. People didn' say ut, but maybe they wondered if the forest – that especial darkness of the forest that moast people there were aware of by now – had somethun' to do with ut, the same way ut had flipped the fust Mrs Jewell. 'Course, nawbody even contemplated that Mabel Jewell had a major hand in ut. All tha' wuz except fur Doctor Jewell hisself, who felt he knawed the full truth 'bout ut. And es, there wuz the forest too. Well, ut had seen the whole thing, hadn' ut? Good job trees cudn' speak. Handy that fungi and mushrooms graw, but dun't say very much.

Still, a service wuz held. Skews' body wuz scooped up by the carpenters who had to double as the undertakers, and his broken body wuz placed in the earth. Ironic you might say, fur a man who'd spent moast of his time above ground with the mining operation; he wuz at last about to get close to the smell of soil. Minter said he'd have a word with the masons about eventually sculpting a memorial that would be appropriate fur a man of Skews' status. Ee'd talk ut over with his Rosie, he said. Somehow too, they'd have to get some sort of note back home, but where to begin? Then there wuz all ov his property and considerable savings to be sorted out.

Having more time on his hands than moast, and knawing Skews' situation better than moast, Trevorrow agreed to take on the job. To be honest, there wudn' nawbody else more fittun'. A message wuz sent down to Calumet to inform the police there of his death, but since ut wuz accidental, nawbody comed up. Well, they Cornish wuz mad enough up there anyway. Why bother? Ef 'twuz accidental, then 'twuz a mines matter anyway. Time an' effort an' manpower fur nawthun'; jus' like the las' time. Anything else comin' out of there, they'd let go. They could sort ut out amongst their selves.

The shock of his passing though amplified utself throughout the community. Ut shawed just how bleddy dangerous some bits ov kit could be. You'll knaw what happened as a consequence then. There was another safety briefing fur all they that worked the tramway, up top and down bottom. Absolutely naw one to ride ut, alright? An' when walking ut, always do so with a pard. All the workers gathered around fur ut, but even though Jewell wuz leadin' ov ut, ee fully knawed the farce ov ut. Ee wudn' about to admit anything different though. Actually, the internal dilemma had gived un a lack ov sleep, an' 'course, the new Mrs Jewell had nawticed tha' ee wudn' quite settled. She wondered ef 'twuz her presence in the bed (ee did seem t'like grabbing her rolls of fat fur pleasure), but maybe 'twuz best not t'say anything. Skews had been a long-standing companion of her husband's. They'd done a lot together. Perhaps her husband wuz spending a bit more time up there in prayer before God than ee should have done. But she knawed tha' she cudn' say anything. Part of the reason she'd married un wuz because of his deep feyth. 'S'pause the awnly other thing that worried she is that her husband hadn' said much ov late about the legality of the position with Clara, but Jewell had said t'trust un, because 'twuz all sorted. Tha' wuz all she could do. Clara had long stopped being a threat.

Now all the while, Rebecca Nankervis had some notion ov what might have happened, because deep down, she knawed wha' Skews wuz like; but again, ut wudn' like she wuz goin' to say anything. She wanted her husband there to discuss ut with, but as ee wudn' there, she had to put ut to the back ov her mind. Right then anyway, she had enough swirling around her brain. The fust thing she contemplated wuz how she could trace her husband, and try somehow to get un back here. She prayed he hadn' found another love, and tha' he still ached fur she. She concluded that he must do in some way, since the money comin' up to she never stopped.

But the thing tha' hurt her the moast – an' you'll understand this – wuz that she longed fur another chield. Now, as you knaw already, that can drive a woman to do the maddest and moast dangerous ov things, and perhaps there wuz a touch ov tha' goin' on with she. Ut wudn' like she wuz goin' t'grab the nearest man and let he get a bit close t'she. Aw naw. This wuz Rebecca see, and in fact, she still loved her Francis. Still, ut wuz making she jittery in the way tha' ut does with all women. Like another you d'knaw well enough by now, she formulated a plan. Somethun' had t'change. Somethun' had to give. Because ov this, she cudn' much concentrate on her teachin'. She forced the childurn to read in silence, an' work through dull textbooks because she wanted peace an' quiet. She needed t'think.

All this wuz compounded by the fact that when she visited Richard's grave, she discovered that the temporary cross set there by Reverend Josiah Davies and her father had clean disappeared. An' whilst ut shocked her to see ut – ut's disappearance making her cry – she perhaps knawed why ut had gone, and even perhaps who'd got rid ov ut. The awnly thing that would've seen ut being taken wuz the forest, but ut wudn' like she could ask it anyway now, wuz ut? At least the flowers hadn' been removed, and when she visited, she made sure the old ones were replaced, the grave tidied, and new ones plaaced down instead. Despite wha' Richard had become, despite wha' ee'd turned into, there wuz still tha' motherly love ov hers there. Despite whatever monsters people become, at the end ov the day, they'm still some mawthur's chield. They wuz once innocent, and once loved.

She wished she'd had someone to talk to a bit more about all ov this. She'd tried with Maddy, but seemingly, these days, she didn' want to knaw. Some women go like tha' once they've had a chield: all self-absorbed and wishing to be alone with their baby. She recognised that in Maddy, and hoped that one day soon ut might pass, and the two ov them could spend time together. She could take ut. In fact, she'd love to see her Jago a bit more often. She'd picked up on the fact too, that things wudn' tha' sweet between she an' Justin. But wha' could she do? Ut wudn' like she could interfere. For now, she spent a few evenings a week with young James. Well, ee really wudn' wanted that much by her father and Eleanor. He wuz noticeably bright tha' boy and she knawed what her feythur wanted fur'n in the future. So she gave un further lessons on elementary biology and chemistry in order to set un the right path. She knew the irony ov this. Ut was she who a long time ago had hoped to attend medical college. Now look at her. But she did the task regardless, fur she loved her brother and wanted him to do well. Selfless, she wuz, this Becca Nankervis, but you d'knaw tha', dun't ee?

Time wuz moving on fast you. They were already at the end of March and the full spring swept over the whole ov Copper Mountain. You could feel the energy of the earth bursting forth. In quiet moments, Rebecca thought 'bout her sister and Nimkii travelling far and wide, and wished them well wherever they'd got to. She'd allays known Mabel had been a bit different, a bit special in her awn way and again: when in Saffron-Bun Chapel, she allays prayed for her protection. Fortunately, she knew the worth of Nimkii (even though others sometimes thought bad ov ee) and she knew he'd be looking after she. In her mind she sent them blessings of fertility too, for she knawed tha' as she'd matured, ut wuz Mabel's intention to begin a family with un. She'd dismissed ut when she wuz a maid, but well, maybe things had shifted. What would tha' be like, she wondered, travelling the true north with a band ov tackers? But then, ef anyone could do ut, then Mabel could.

So in her awn way Rebecca planned and contemplated. She knew what she needed to do. She'd worked ut out. She hadn't told anyone else but she'd organised time off work. The Easter break would be a good opportunity to enact her plan. Well, 'twudn' easy fur a young woman such as she. There wuz lots to be taken into account. But in all ov this, there had t'somehow be a way forward. Somethun' had t'give she told herself. If fixed things like Skews could change overnight, then surely other things could do. Like her feythur, so ut seemed, she did a lot of praying in the chapel. An' in tha' maybe she knawed truly what such plaaces were fur. Ut wudn' just all that praise to the Lord God above. Aw naw. 'Twuz actually fur moments like this, fur when ee needed stillness and contemplation and nawthun' else. She didn' rightly knaw ef 'twas God's universe or anyone else's, but sometimes, when alone, Rebecca knawed 'twuz good to talk to it.

Talk had come up from Calumet that a grand new theatre had opened there, which delighted Rebecca. That wuz somewhere she'd like to go, but then Methodists like her feythur wudn' be keen. Theatres were immoral plaaces in his view, but Rebecca realised their function and importance. So ut wuz said too, down there, there were now automobiles to be seen. Who'd have thought that, eh? Give ut a while, she contemplated, and they'd soon be up here on the mountain. Aw es, the world wuz rapidly shifting, and she knawed she had to do the same thing. 'Course, there wuz a considerable fly in the ointment still, and tha' wuz her mawthur. In vying to go see such wonders as the theatre and automobiles in Calumet, she would surely have to go visit her mawthur at the asylum. But ut wuz a plaace she didn' want to go. She didn' even really want to contemplate her incarceration, but there 'twuz.

Before now, her feythur had gotten reports each week but as time went on, these seemed to cease. What wuz obvious then, wuz tha' there wudn' much change in she at all. Facing tha' wuz hard, especially when there been a last minute hope ov recovery. So even though she contemplated time down there to view the excitement of drama and invention, perhaps 'twuz better she didn' go. Naw one said anything to James. Ut seemed to be felt easier not to say anything to ee. So Clara Jewell, slowly and gradually, got wiped off the map of the Keweenaw. Daily then, Rebecca told herself – convinced herself – that her other plans needed to happen.

One day, Justin Nankervis wuz belaw ground checking progress on the ninth (with a later notion of having another gake at level two), when a puffed-out boy comed along the level and told un that Trevorrow wanted t'see un up the Assay Office.

"What, now?" Justin asked. "Cen't you see I'm lagged?"

Ee wuz pretty dabbered up with mud and slimes.

"I'n see tha'."

"Got to be right now 'ave ut?"

"Es," said the boy. "Reckon so. Cap'n Trevorrow said 'twuz urgent."

Justin cleaned hisself up the best he could and worked his way back along the level to where the cage wuz. Ut made un laugh because even down here a few of the Tigers tended to fly. They comed down the ventilation shaft he reckoned, but poor buggers, he thought, they wudn' find much nectar down here.

When up grass, he trudged up to the Assay office, and inside found a resigned Trevorrow at work. In Skews' office, his main desk wuz now surrounded by piles of paper, and account books, listings and receipts.

"Wozzon?" asked Justin, making sure that his muddy clawthes didn' drop dirt on the planchen.

"You need to have a good ol' gake at all this," said Trevorrow, a concerned look on his faace.

"Why?"

"Well, as instructed, I've been goin' through things here. Seems our meht Mr Skews wudn' zactly honest with we. We all knawed he had his moments yes, but this, well this, is on a new scale."

"How do ee mean?"

"Well, he'd been creaming things off fur a long time now... By rights, we should be a good deal richer than we are, and so should everyone else here on Mountainside. But ee, well ee 'ave been leading we up the garden path. He've been proper cooking the books boy. Look here see..."

Those words allowed Justin to have a look over his findings. In the long and dry columns of the account books, ut soon became clear that many a time Skews had made up costings and receipts just so ut would be an extra expense for the copy. Those monies were creamed off because there wuz another book in which Skews kept his awn finances. The dates of they entries compared precisely to the ones in the mine's accounts.

"So you'm sayin' he've been siphoning off the profits then?"

"Es, by my reckoning, he have been. Clever though see. He knawed the tricks ov fleecing we good an' proper. Knawed how to adjust the figures too, so each time we produced more ore, he adapted the figures. Thaas why we never spotted ut..."

"Jeez," said Justin. "Well, what did a spend ut on?"

"Well, see, thaas the biggest puzzle. I mean ee wudn' zactly knawn fur splashing out, wuz a? Quite the h'opposite really. Ee wuz a proper tight-ass."

"So, there's a good deal of money swilling around here somewhere then?"

"Thaas right. You got ut."

"We just got to find ut. Seems ut idn' in the safe. I got the combination of the lock of tha'. You and I have knawn tha' fur a while. Needed ut for to pay the men and women see. But, es, from the look ov ut there's some slush fund here somewhere..."

"Wha' do ee reckon he wanted ut fur?"

"Well. Dunnaw. I mean, ee wuz doing well enough on his wages anyway, wudn' a? What he'd want more fur I really dun' knaw."

"Passage perhaps? Buy hisself a fust-class ticket 'ome?"

"Maybe, but ee never said to me anything about goin' back. I mean, I thought ee wuz fixed here... 'Mean, there's an address fur his family, but did a ever say anything 'bout goin' back 'ome?"

"Nope. Not that I ever heard."

"Well," said Trevorrow sharply, "'Tis a mystery then... But leave ut with me. No doubt we shall get to the bottom ov ut. And ef we find the money, then I think we d'owe everyone here a bit of a bonus, I should say..."

That would be good, Justin considered. The winter had been hard. The men and women who had worked the mine had slogged their guts out. 'Twas awnly right that they should get rewarded. Before now, such monies might have funded the chapel but that had already been taken care of in small measure by hisself: but also in guilt money by way ov his missing brother, who wuz now trying to absolve hisself. Now perhaps, as well as offering a dividend to they who'd worked hard in the mine fur years, the money could be used as a civic fund. 'Twuz something tha' he and his brother had talked about fur a long time: the erection of an institute to improve the miners' literacy and skills, tarmacadam on the streets, the installation of gas lighting and running water, like what they had down in Calumet and Houghton. Es, at least then, something good might come out of Skews' fraudulent activity. Es, and 'course Trevorrow and Justin resoundingly kicked themselves fur not spottun' ov ut sooner when Skews wuz alive. And when they thought about ut some more, perhaps the pair of they here realised that this wuz perhaps the very reason why Skews had flipped. Now, 'twuz all beginning to make sense. Ee knawed his guilt too well an' cudn' live with ut.

"I'll investigate more," assured Trevorrow. "Dun't ee worry. I shen't let ut go until I get to the bottom ov ut."

Discoveries then, coming at Mountainside from all angles see. Dussn't ee worry 'bout ut though. 'Twill all sort utself. Es.

The forest didn' knaw nawthun' 'bout tha' yet, but 'course, it had a memory of Mr Skews and what he used to do: what he would sow and scatter. Right now though, it wudn' very happy about the blood that had been spilled on its ground from the 'accident' involving this Mr Skews. Although they'd extracted the two parts of Skews' body from the scene of the incident, the blood that had formed into a pool in the tracks gradually seeped out onto the forest floor.

Blood wudn' a thing that it much liked, and it talked to Yolkai about it. But because Yolkai said the blood letting had been just, the forest had to deal with it. Normally see, when blood wuz spilled, there'd need to be some kind of payment back to the earth in recompense for what had been done, but as Yolkai advised, it was best to be forgiving. These humans see, she said, they kept on making silly mistakes. The advice wuz to be patient, for one day soon, the forest's time would come again. The sprites would be able to return to their ancestral homes. The forest would regain control. Mark my words, she said to it – and to all the beings of the forest who had felt betrayed.

Yolkai too, had seen the completed chapel, and the sprites and the trees had moaned to her about that. How could it be right, they'd questioned. It wuz an intrusion, they'd stated. An abomination. She understood, she said, but now her mediator had gone. He'd long since left and was travelling lightly through other forests and woods, not touching them at all. What about it though? What was the answer? The forest demanded this of Yolkai but the only answer that she could give was that one day soon: the forest would come to feast upon the human's feyth.

Feasting upon their feyth. None of the trees and spites knew precisely what that really meant.

"Trust me," Yolkai said. "One day, it will come to pass."

And one day it would – when this bal became good an' knacked – but fur now, at this time, they'd just have to be patient. The need wuz to watch and wait.

But what about...? the forest asked.

And when it asked that, everyone knew what it meant. They didn' like to mention ut because ut wuz one of those disturbing elements of human life, that made forests shiver and wish that the gods had not populated the world with selfish humanity.

"It is coming," Yolkai said, and with that, the dawn broke and she disappeared again.

'Twuz by now, mid-morning, an' after seeing Trevorrow up at Skews' Assay office, who did Justin stumble upon but Rosie Koskinen? Thaas all I needed, he said to hisself under his breath

"A'right *pupu*?" she said, still teasin' ov un after all this time.

"Es. You?"

"Ya. All good..."

"Good."

"I haven't seen you and Maddy of late. Not at the chapel and not out and about. Is she alright?"

"Fine," said Justin, a little awkwardly.

"Heard you rowing the other day," she tipped into the conversation just to wind him up. "I was just walking past. Sounded bad. Sounded like she wudn' very happy..."

Bitch.

"Really? Somethun' and nawthun' I 'spect."

She looked around to see if anyone else had noticed this coincidental meeting.

"Maybe you should come over fur a drink sometime?" Rosie smiled.

See, she still liked un.

"Maybe not" said Justin. "You knaw I'm trying to be teetotal again. I d'go to all the Temperance events up chapel..."

"Shame," said Rosie.

"Perhaps not. Maybe you ought to be home with Dicky..."

"Oh, well I don't get much of that these days..."

"Shame," said Justin, half-smiling to hisself. At least, ee and Maddy still made love, even ef she wudn' very responsive.

"Thought you an' he wuz ready to marry?"

"We are. We've booked it at the chapel with Doctor Jewell..."

"Sorted then..."

"Yes..."

"Dicker alright is a? Ebm seen un much of late..."

"Well, you know..."

"Do I?"

"Ya. His heart. Jewell told un to take ut easy. Things aren't working like they should, if you know what I mean."

She wuz frustrated then. Well, there wuz a heap of men out there who'd still like to be on top ov she.

"I see," said Justin. "Well, wish un well from me."

"I will."

"Best get on. Got a job down on the second level... we're thinking ov reworking ut."

She ignored that. Mines bored her, like moast women.

"Say hello to Maddy fur me."

"I will."

An' tha' wuz ut. He knawed she liked to toy with un in this way. He didn' knaw that the Minter wudn' doin' s'well though. That might have implications – on the mine, ov course. An' tha' from she to Maddy! 'Course ee wudn' be saying anything. Maddy hated she more than anyone else in the world. Rosie went on her way. She cudn' resist lookin' back at un flirtatiously though, an' givin' un a wry smile. He didn' glance at she though. Ee wudn' about to give she the satisfaction.

Down in the darkness of the mine, the Knockies Gourgy and Luk were working. Gourgy had at least become aware that his master was still sending up monies to Rebecca and fur the chapel. They also become aware of the fact that the chapel had got named after their most favourite food stuff, and they rather liked it. Moast chapels had stuffy names, but this one didn'. Ut felt right, just like Nimkii had said apparently. They knawed too of Nimkii and Mabel's leaving, and much as they would have preferred them to stay, sometimes you have to leave and begin again. They'd done the very same thing when they'd packed up in Cornwall and travelled across the Atlantic Ocean to come to 'Merky'. Jus' like Knockies, allays moving people were. 'Twuz right and proper. 'Twuz the way ov things. At least they'd been able to have some fun with Mabel. At least she recognised their magic and respected them. She'd do a'right, she wud.

Skews' death had shocked them. 'Mean, nawbody can go on forever, can um? But ee. Mr Skews. Well, though miserable as ee wuz, ee seemed indestructible. They s'paused everyone d'have their limits. Skews knawed about Knockies. He had heard the conversations all miners have about safety and how things wuz proceeding underground. 'Mean, ee wuz from Cornwall, but ee wuz a sceptic. There wuz naw doubt about tha'. The forest didn' like un; they knawed tha' – but then, nawbody in the world wished un to end up like tha'. An' course, seeing ov his head all sliced off like that runned geht shivers through Gourgy because ov what that Pooka Richard had tried to do with un backalong.

These pair had just had crowst, and these days, Rebecca Nankervis wuz makin they a goodly lot of saffron buns. To be honest you, they'd got a bit piggish ov late, and instead of ends and crusts of such buns, they wuz wolfing down two or three whole at once. Well, 'twudn' naw good. See, they wuz some tasty though, but there's nawthun' like saffron buns every day fur spreadin' yer girth, and boath of they knawed they wuz gettin' big. Tha' wudn' naw use to a Knockie you, for underground. They wuz meant to be lithe and sylphlike, moving between spaces in the rock. But fair old tummies on um, they had. 'Twas as ef they wuz still gettin' over some kind of winter hibernation: awnly there hadn' been one. There had jus' been a lot of extra tonnage ov bunnage fur they. Honest you, ut looked like Gourgy hisself had gorged on um s'much that ee wuz fit to burst. At least the bugger wudn' yet turning purple!

Gazing at his gut, Gourgy realised what they had to do and said, "Reckon 'tis time fur we to cut back a bit..."

He gave a belch at this, and then closed his crowst box.

"You'm right here pard. We'd better, else we shall be like Dicky Mint!"

These fairy pards then, this pair ov underground mehts, knawed well then that the best way to work off a meal, wuz a bit ov labouring at the earth. 'Twas allays the best way to make muscle, and perhaps, ov late, they become a bit too lazy. You cudn' afford for the flab to set in now, cud ee?

Now ut so happened that they wuz back in the second level. This hadn't been touched in a while but on a recent survey ov ut, their master Justin had asked um to 'ave a look again, and see if there wuz any more high grade copper in there. See, at the time, more had been found on the third, and ut being easier to extract, they hadn' gone much further along level two. Some muck in there you. And some water too, dripping in somehow from the river system up top. Perhaps tha' wuz the reason ut had been abandoned, and not worked s'fully along as the other level.

There'd been some goodly stopes in here though. They remembered ut. See, Knockies have a way of instantly processing the layout of a mine. Their brains ent good fur that much, but knawing mines inside out, well, tha' wuz their thing, wudn' ut? So es, they were in there recalling the tonnage pulled out, and who had worked ut. Ut smelt some old in there you. Musty as y'like and, as the pair walked ut, ut gived they a bit ov a shiver. There was no oddsing of ut. You allays had parts of a mine like tha'. Thaas just the way 'twuz. But ut did make um cautious you. See Knockies knaw a lot but sometimes askin' ov a human Cap'n whether they felt the same way, wuz jus' wha' a Knockie needed. They were interdependent see. Symbiotic. Es. Tha' wuz the posh word fur ut.

'Twas some dark on this level. Sometimes, even down in the depths, you'n see a'right, but not this level. Luk struck a match and lit the candle on his own helmet and on Gourgy's. Now with a bit of illumination, they could carry on. By their reckoning, along here, there wuz one or two stopes that might benefit from being looked at again. You could see the blue of the copper in there, especially as they proceeded along. Skewsy would normally be here looking at this kind of thing, but neither of they needed to be naw surveyor to knaw that there was a goodly run ov ore going east, but that might necessitate a right angle of the level in order to exploit ut. 'Twudn' be naw problem, the pards considered. A bit of a blast here and they could turn the shaft easy, to follow the ore. Perhaps thaas why they'd stopped before, especially when level three had given up a good yield. But es, there wuz plenty more in here to be had.

Then, somethun odd happened. Well, you d'knaw how moths get attracted to flames. Well, what flittered around Luk's candle wuz naw moth but instead one of they black and orange butterflies that seemed to be everywhere at the moment.

"*Tikkydew* look," said Gourgy.

A *tikkydew* wuz what all Knockies called butterflies. Ut was a word drawn from the depths of their old language of the underground.

"Whaas that bugger doing down here?" asked Luk.

"He be a bit lost."

"Like all of we," returned Luk. "It's annoying me though."

Ee wuz right. The thing kept flitting around Luk's head. Although pretty, Gourgy could see how the thing could rapidly become a pest. Butterflies are comparatively small to humans, but to Knockies, they'm that much bigger. They got much more flitter close up: and down here in the level, they could hear the thing's wings buzzing aplenty.

"Get rid of un for me, will ee?" asked Luk.

"Rite on boy."

Gourgy did his best to rid Luk of the flitterer but ee wudn' doin' a good job. See being big round the waist these days, and currently filled with saffron bun, ee cudn' jump very high t'all. Awnly eventually using his pick-axe, did a manage to shoo the thing on along the level, almost accidentally braining Luk in the process.

"There," said Gourgy. "Ee's gone on now..."

Luk wudn' convinced though.

"Naw ee hasn't. Ee've nestled in there see. I worry 'bout un gettin' out. 'Mean, bit grim fur'n stuck down here, idn' ut?"

Gourgy agreed. 'Twas grim. Knockies love all living things and they were hopeful they could get un to go back along the shaft. In time, then the thing might find ut's way up the ventilation shaft, the same way as ut had comed in.

But the bugger wudn' move. In fact, ut had nestled near a crack in the next stope along. Nawbody'd been in here fur a while. Despite Gourgy swishing at ut, now ut didn' want to move. He stopped moving his arm because ee didn' wanted ut to be hurted, or even worse, deaded. At that moment, both of these pards, these pards, who'd allays knawn each other, seened something tha' they didn't much like the look ov. 'Twas something that had obviously been pressed inta' the crack an' had been filled in backwards with a few bits of attle to try an' hide ut. Of late though, some of these had gradually fallen away and exposed the surface of a piece of tarpaulin. There wuz somethun' 'bout ut see, that didn' look right. Naw miner nor Knockie would have left this where 'twuz. The butterfly remained next to ut, still twitching; the orange glow of ut's wings being illuminated in the candlelight.

Knockies have a way of sensing fear, and ut wuz fear they felt. Ef ut wuz an imminent rockfall, then they have knocked to high Heaven to warn people of what was forthcoming, so averting disaster, but this – well this – wuz very different.

"What ee reckon?" asked Luk.

"Dun't knaw," said Gourgy.

"Dun't look good, do ut?"

"Naw... Somethun wrong I d'think."

They can sense tha' see. Thaas the way ov they. Thaas why you allays want one next to ee.

Ut took um a brae while to reach into the crack and discover what had been tucked in there. They found a parcel, wrapped in a dull, grey tarp bound with twine. So well hidden wuz ut, tha' ef the *tikkydew* hadn't settled next to ut, then they'd never have even nawticed ut, but somethun', somethun' in the universe had told um to have a gake in there and see wha' 'twas. Whatever wuz inside ut had some kind ov form and density. Gourgy felt the weight ov ut. Ut felt odd, but inside ut, ee knew there wuz something organic in there. 'Twudn' naw set of gads or tools. Aw naw.

To get into ut, they had to untie the twine and that had been bound very tight. Ut wudn' like you wanted to use your teeth – and Knockies had good teeth you – but they didn' want to get too close to ut. So Luk bent down and helped Gourgy untie ut. Whatever ut wuz the tarp contained, wuz now on the slimes ov the floor, but to be honest, neither ov this pair ov pards wanted to hold ut anymore. There wuz a definite sense in they that they were finding something disturbing: something that unfortunately, would come to haunt they fur the next few centuries.

When they unravelled the tarp, what they found inside was like a mass of clayey silica. 'Twas obviously a dead baby: new-born by the look an' size ov ut. Ut's skin had turned grey, but in the cold atmosphere below ground, the form of the thing had been preserved. In effect, ut had been mummified. 'Twas a boy, or had once been a boy, and because of the size of ut, not long out of the lady's belly. The wust of ut wuz ut's eyes. There wuz no colour to um you. They'd gone white, as ef whatever this mite had suffered, twuz not ever to be seen. But there he wuz. Definitely a baby and definitely stuffed secretly down here so nawbody'd find ut. Someone had put ut there who knawed the mine – that much wuz true – because they'd have to knaw which levels were abandoned; and prior to Justin's instructions ov late, to consider ut, they'd have to have known that this part wuz abandoned and unlikely to be used again. 'Twudn' like the liddle gray thing had crawled in here wuz ut, not like the Pooka Richard? Na. Ut had definitely been placed there, and placed in the crack not be found by any Knockie, and certainly to be hidden from God. But who would do such a thing? The shock of the sight ov ut nearnly made both these pards keel over. Es. 'Twas brae an' sickening, and some sad to see. Why place ut here?

At least that bugger Richard had got a grave. He'd got blessed before God an' sent on his way, even though he wuz a Devilish thing. This boy here hadn't even had tha'. He'd been abandoned to the mica slimes, and the feel and touch of quartzite, for the afterlife. Honest you: 'twuz pitiable t'even glimpse at. Never in all their centuries ov workin' underground, had they comed across something s'poignant. What could um do though? There seemed like naw way of discovering who'd placed ut there. Because of this, they cudn' help but squall for a bit. Aw, the tenderness of the thing! Its poor position in the rocks, not even handed over proper-like to the afterlife. Ut seemed tha' Death wuz everywhere right now, with his sharp scythe an' his quest fur souls. Fust, Mr Skews, and now this un. 'Twas goin' to need some sortin' out, this would. Someone knawed the truth ov ut fur zertain.

Along the level came the stank of someone walking towards them. Whoever 'twas, had one of they new carbide lights on his helmet, and the light bobbed in time with his steps. Ut took un a while to find them, but their candles were bright enough for that person t'locate them. In fact, they anticipated 'twould be Justin, and 'twuz ee there, now standing behind them. His day so far has been stressful and awkward. Not awnly had a had to deal with the dubious accounting ov Samuel Skews, ee'd also had to put up with the jibes ov Rosie Koskinen. Ee was hopeful ov some better news belaw ground.

"Whaas she like? Found anything 'ave ee?"

His voice echoed loudly in the cavernous stope.

They didn' answer (which wuz highly unusual for any Knockie). Then they shawed un. Mazed ut wuz. When they looked, the *tikkydew* had gone.

An' in tha' moment, the world becomed unhinged.

45

Ass 'bout faace the stupid world had gone. In some state they wuz. They wuz dabbered up good an' proper, and lampered in mud as they carried the cold body of the baby along the level, an' inta' the cage, in order to take un up t'grass. When they reached light, up on the collar of the mine, all they could think about wuz this mite, who in the daylight, now appeared even more scat to scudmo than he did in the half-light belaw ground. Babies shouldn' be like this. They should be in the fresh air, thrivin' and grawin'. Walt Chegwidden wuz there to greet they. He saw their grim faaces and took note.

"Wha'f ee got there?" he asked the three ov them when he saw the tarp.

"You dun't want t'knaw Sos..." began Justin.

"Naw," said the Knockies in unison. "'Tidn' very nice."

But they shawed un anyway. Direct the Cornish allays were. Walt had seen some sights. He'd be able to handle this well 'nuff.

"Dead baby, eh? How long do ee reckon a been down there then?"

"Naw idea. Cen't be longer than when the level wuz opened up..."

"Es, but we'm a good few fathoms down now. Someone must've knawn that level wouldn' be visited much more."

"Whoever 'twas," said Justin, "didn' want anyone to find un. Tucked in good and proper, ee wuz. Hidden fur eternity, wudn' a boys?"

"Es," said Gourgy.

"Es," said Luk. "Nawbody wuz meant to find un."

"So whoever put un there knawed the mine then," noted Walt.

Ee wuz right. Naw ordinary fool had plaaced the infant there. The person who'd done ut knawed their operations intimately. Walt and they chatted precisely about the crack where the baby's body had been located. Ee knawed the spot well, but ee didn' think anyone had been along there fur months; perhaps even fur a year or so.

"Can I tell people?" asked Walt.

Justin considered ut.

"Well, es. People need t'knaw. It'll come out soon 'nuff."

Walt nodded.

"You might get some information that way," ee said.

Walt had a point. Someone knawed somethun', true 'nuff.

"I'll put word around."

"Thanks Walt."

A good ol' boy wuz Walt.

"Up the docs now, are ee Sos?"

"Best had," said Justin. "Another body fur'n to examine."

Walt nodded and watched they head across the mine site to Doctor Jewell. Some wisht you. An' even Walt knew that somethun' serious wuz goin' to come from this find. 'Twas awnly a matter ov time.

See, already, the minds of Justin, Gourgy and Luk wuz workin' overtime. Once the shock had dissipated, they wuz thinking back to wha' had happened ov late. Neither ov they could rightly put their fingers on ut, but they wuz wonderin' ef this find wuz somehow connected to the evil Pooka named Richard. Es. There wuz somethun' in tha' – tha' wuz zertain. Justin wuz already thinkin' along the lines that somehow the dead baby they'd found wuz, in no small measure, connected with Richard, and that somehow, a swap had been made, new fur old, and tha' what ee wuz carryin' wuz a direct result of ut. He could even feel ut in his bones. He knawed ut all along: that the right Devilish thing he wished he'd been able to push clean inta' the oven, must be connected to this. An' that led un thinkin' then t'the fact tha' this thing he wuz carryin' must be connected to his brother's leaving, an' all the pain he'd gone through. He cudn' quite work ut out, but he knawed there wuz some link. The earth wuz speakin' to un, and ee wuz listenin' to wha' ut was sayin'. Yippin' up at un 'twuz.

Es. His Knockie Luk wuz thinkin' on the same lines. 'Mean, the baby had to have come from somewhere, hadn' ut? Some woman must knaw the answer. Aw es, ee knawed that some Knockie women didn' protrude out much when they wuz pregnant, so maybe they just needed to find out who had been pregnant a while back. So Luk, ee wuz goin' through his mind, an' ee wuz thinkin' ov they who'd had a chield ov late. 'Mean, there were other women, but foremost on his mind – an' ee didn' like to admit ut – were Maddy and Rebecca. But how could a even think tha', let alone say ut'? Ass 'bout faace ut had gone right enough. All ee needed t'do wuz turn ut round again, and then ee might find the answer.

Gourgy wuz thinkin' through all ov this too. Now, because of who ee wuz, his liddle brain had gone in a different direction. Ee didn' knaw who'd put ut there. Ee didn' knaw ef 'twas a man or a women who had secretly gone down inta' the mine and plaaced the poor thing in there, but ee reckoned on callin' a meeting zertainly ov all they magical creatures who worked belaw ground to find out whether they'd seen anything unusual. 'Twas a brae while ago, but Knockies had good memories see. There wudn' much they didn' note that went on underground. But his mind wuz goin' in another direction too, and ee cudn' help but think ov the forest. Ef ee could speak to it and ask ut straight up, who'd put ut there, ee reckoned he'd glean an answer. The forest saw ut all – ee'd knawn tha' fur a goodly while.

Justin knawed they were doin' the same as ee. Ee could tell that in the silent pattern in which they walked. Normally, the three ov they would be jabberin' on 'bout this an' that, but in this moment, they wuz all silent. Each of they wuz trying to solve the puzzle and work out wha' had happened. Each ov they wuz thinking about yet another funeral, up the chapel. But this un, this one who Justin wuz carrying: ee looked some sweet – angelic even – and they three knawed ee wudn' ever naw mazed Pooka.

Up the Doctors, they handed over their shocking find to George Jewell. They gived un details ov how they'd come across un and where precisely the mite had been found in the mine. To say tha' Jewell wuz flabbergasted wuz an understatement. He wuz surprised because ee thought he genuinely knawed all the women ov the camp who had been pregnant. Ee could list them on one hand: two of which were Maddy and Becca. Now either they wudn' bein' honest, or one of the other three had done somethun' devious. But then maybe too, there wuz someone who'd had a baby secretly. Such things did happen. There wuz a girl (underage you) back home in Bodmin, who'd looked thin as a rake, but one day, gave birth to a beautiful baby daughter. Ut ud happened tha' she got a bit too friendly with a boy from up Lower Kernick. So perhaps there wuz something like tha' at play here. Rumour wuz prob'ly goin' inta' overdrive.

Jewell cudn' see the Knockies, but they wuz in there with Justin while the doctor examined the body. T'be honest now, they didn' want to look, but they did want to hear wha' the Doc had to say.

"Well," said Jewell both to hisself an' Justin. "Fully formed. No wounds.. Looks healthy enough, but I can tell it's a new born. The belly button, you see. Not quite healed. The cut of the placenta looks somewhat rushed in my considered medical view. Perhaps given birth to in haste. That's what I'd say..."

"How did a die though?" asked Justin.

Now see, when Justin said this, ee had naw idea he was actually askin' 'bout his awn poor son. Tha' wuz the terrible thing 'bout ut, but right there and then, no one knawed as such, so nothun' could be said ov ut. But still, you felt fur'n.

"Childbirth. Well, I say tha', but ut seems to me that he wuz still-born. Someone had this boy and then, when he came out dead, the parents wanted ut hidden... Maybe didn't want to face up to ut. Maybe though, the best thing to do wuz to hide it... forget it ever existed."

"But how can anyone ever think tha' way?" asked Justin.

"Aw, you'd be surprised... you'd be surprised... The things I've heard tell about babies would make your skin crawl. We had ut all back on Bodmin Moor... scrofula... ill wishin'... you name ut. Superstition see. People do all sorts..."

"Do um?"

"Always, Cap'n Nankervis... in my experience... That's why the Lord God gived we Mr Wesley..."

Jewell stood back from his investigations. The baby wuz now on the table, at which only a while ago, the split body of Mr Skews had been placed. Here wuz another soul who'd come to an untimely end.

"Ent there anything you can do?" asked Justin.

"What do you mean?"

"Well, like a test or somethun'..."

Jewell took a sharp intake of breath and weighed up the options.

"I mean, there are these new blood tests you can do... Complex though. I mean, we'd have to collect blood from everyone, and then that would need to be compared. Some big deal though. I couldn' possibly do it. We'd probably have to bring someone in who wuz an expert. Up from Houghton, or maybe even Detroit."

"That would be difficult then?"

"We can do it, but the cost would be horrendous..."

Justin wuz thinking about Skews' money. There wuz also the money from his brother. Maybe the chapel or Becca would grant some of ut fur this purpose. He knawed she would, especially ef ut might lead to some clarification about Francis' killing of the Pooka.

"We don't seem to have a very good record with babies up here do we, Cap'n Nankervis?"

'Course, this wuz in reference to his awn dear grandson, who wuz already lying in the cemetery, next to Saffron-Bun Chapel.

"Will you be informing the police?" asked Justin.

"I'll have to. It's my duty to do so. I did it with Richard, and I shall do it with this one..."

"I see," said Justin interrupting him.

"... But they're unlikely to do anything. Babies don't interest them. An' well, they weren't even much interested in Mr Skews' passing..."

Jewell felt ut safe enough to say that now that the Assayer's body was six-foot under.

"You know the police think we're mazed up here, don't you?" stated Jewell.

"Really?"

"Oh yes..."

Justin knew he'd been part of the problem, but ee didn' like to think the police in Calumet were so unconcerned as to think of this community as barbarous and unworthy of investigation. On the other hand though, ut did allow them to sort things out in their awn way, just like the Cornish did back 'ome. Justin turned things over in his mind. He looked at the Knockies and knew what they were thinking. He'd have to say it. He didn't want to, but he knew they pair were edging him to do so.

"Doctor Jewell, I honestly dun't mean to be rude, but should we consider your daughter... Mabel..."

"Mabel?"

"Es. Well, she an' Nimkii. They were close. Nimkii said that their plan wuz to get married... and after all, as you knaw, they left in some geht hurry... Do you think? I mean, could there...?"

Jewell paused for a bit. He quickly contemplated what Justin was asking. At first, he felt the man rude and insensitive, but then he realised the speculation and the man's reasoning. .

"No," responded Jewell. "I mean, my dear boy, you only have to look. The baby's Caucasian..."

"Caucasian?" asked Justin, confused as to what he meant.

"White," affirmed Jewell. "I can tell. Both of this boy's parents were white. I mean, I could tell if..."

He didn' need to say anymore. The evidence wuz there. Justin sneaked another guarded look at the boy. Gourgy and Luk had, by now, placed themselves under the mortuary table, and sat quiet, still thinking through events, putting two an' two together but every time, comin' up with a total ov five.

Jewell again asked for confirmation about the circumstances of finding the baby belaw ground. Yes, ut would be fine fur the Doctor to see the exact plaace. Justin understood the need. He could do ut any time ee wished.

"I'm thinking through all those who were pregnant on Mountainside Cap'n Nankervis. I'm thinking if there wuz any chance that anyone of those women could have had another baby somehow. But do you know what? I was there for all of the most recent births. Not one of those women could have possibly had another child and got rid of it. I see all the entrances and exits of life on Copper Mountain."

"I know," said Justin.

"But there was one I didn't see, as you know..."

"How do you mean?"

"Come on man. Think... Remember the night of your Jago being born?"

"Es..."

"Well I wasn't there. Neither were you as I recall. Maddy had your Jago at home on her own. A quick birth, so far as I can remember. Jago just slid out... Maddy told me so... The bloodstain on the planchen and so on."

"Yes, you're right," said Justin, not wanting to have this conversation. "No one was with her."

"No," said Jewell. "We'll need to talk to her... you and I..."

Shit. Justin didn' want this. Ee didn't need this. How on earth could Maddy be in the frame? No, ut did not make sense. What ee wuz saying wuz nonsense. Thankfully, the Doctor then confirmed ut.

"But no, thinking through it... it could not possibly have been Maddy. I mean, she had Jago, but there was no way on earth that she wuz having twins. I mean, I know her pregnancy was low and so on, but she was never big enough to be carrying twins. You *can* tell Cap'n Nankervis..."

The Knockies mopped their brows because fur a moment there, 'twudn' looking very good fur she, tha' Maddy. Besides, the boy on the table didn' much look like Jago, did a?

"Sorry," said Doctor Jewell. "I was just thinking aloud. I didn' mean to worry you..."

"Naw problem," said Justin. "'Tis awny right you consider everything..."

"Well, 'tidn' she clearly... we need to think differently."

Jewell wuz pacing up and down his surgery. In the window wuz another one of they butterflies flittering to get out. Whilst Jewell wuz contemplating things, Justin took the opportunity to open the winda' and swoosh the flitterer into the outside air. There, ut headed toward the edge of the forest.

"We have, I believe," said Jewell magnimoniously, "awnly one option..."

Justin turned to the doctor to listen more intently.

"I shall need to speak to all the women of the town. We need to gather them together and ask them."

"When?"

"The sooner the better..."

"Where?"

"The schoolhouse perhaps..." but then Jewell rethought ut. He wuz still in the old world of Mountainside. They had another, better option now.

"The Chapel I think," he said. "Before God. In my experience, the truth often comes out then."

Justin wondered who he might be thinkin' ov. In his mind, Jewell had, in fact, been thinking of his own daughter Mabel and her prayer for forgiveness for her killing of Samuel Skews.

"Do other people know yet?" asked Jewell.

"Yes. Walt's putting it about as to what we found..."

"Well, good. My view is that we get all the women up there as soon as possible..."

"All the women?"

"Yes... girl and maids too. We can't be too careful. Young *and* old will be needed."

"You sure?" asked Justin. The thought of this round-up disturbed him somewhat. Here was the patriarchy of the township making their mark once more.

"What ef uts a man?"

"How do you mean?"

"Who put the baby in there... I mean, not all women like ut belaw ground..."

But then the mine had kept expanding. There wuz actually a brae few women who now laboured belaw. Tutwork mainly.

"Yes. Well, I take your point Cap'n Nankervis, but in this case we need to be cruel to be kind. If it was a man who plaaced it there, then the baby clearly came from a woman. Last time I looked, God made only women capable of such delivery, eh?"

Justin didn' like where this wuz going, with some awful corralling of the female population; but still, as much as he did not like ut, he realised the sense in what Doctor Jewell wuz saying.

"An hour should be enough, shouldn' ut?"

Justin nodded in a knowing Mine Cap'n kind of way. Ee didn' knaw ut but the biggest test ov his life wuz about to be mined out ov un. 'Twas an ore he'd never felt before or even put on a cobbing table.

The town snapped inta' energy ov a kind tha' hadn' been seen in a while. The call went out for all women and maids to head up to the chapel, where apparently, they wuz needed. Some already knawed wha' 'twuz all 'bout. Others were clueless, but they that knawed nothun', would soon find out wha' wuz on. Moast ov the women were willing. Not all though. Rosie and her girls wudn' tha' keen. 'Mean, they wudn' zactly motherhood material, wuz um? One other too, wudn' impressed with the call.

"Comus on Maddy. You have t'go," said Justin to her.

"Thought this place was the land ov freedom; not the land of servants..."

"You need to be there. Every other woman is going. Rebecca. Eleanor Jewell. Maid Spargo. Walt's missus..."

"Good for them. What's this fookin' nonsense about anyway?"

"Ebm you heard?"

"Na. Should I have?"

"Moast people d'knaw by now..."

"Knaw wha'?"

"Well, 'tis some upsetting. A body. A body ov a baby's been found. In the mine. "

This Maddy, well, she didn' even flinch at tha'. She'd convinced herself see, that all tha' wuz someone else's doing, so convinced wuz she of her present life. Naw emotion didn' even cross her face. Well, see Justin wudn' expectun' anything, wuz a? By his reckonin', she wuz still innocent, but still, she'd have to go and sit in the chapel like all the other women. Inside ov she though, a kind of horror tumbled out, but she'd been good at not lettun' ut out so far. This would be a challenge, but she'd deal with ut. She would have to.

"Where to?"

"Second level."

How could anyone knaw? Ut wudn' like she'd been tracked wuz ut? How the hell had ut been found now anyway? She knawed she wuz goin' t'have to be hard again. Maybe once 'twuz over, and they stopped being s'taissy, then she could breathe a sigh of relief. 'Twuz true she'd had nightmares about the baby: the one that wuz properly hers, not this Jago that she wuz carryin' with her up to the chapel. Miners, see, she cussed, always pokin' around where they shouldn', the fookers. An' Cussies, they wuz the wust ov the lot. Maybe she should have just buried the thing in the forest, but then, could she trust the forest anymore? Maybe she cudn'.

Her prayer wuz tha' she didn' have t' see the thing. She knawed that would be the one thing that might turn she, and make she change. Anything else wudn' do ut. Nawbody on earth could make she confess ut. Her mind even raced to considering the fact that perhaps some other unfortunate maid might have had another baby stillborn and hid ut down in the mine too, but wha' were the chances ov tha'? Beyond minimal. Na, this wuz hers – hers an' Justin's. She knawed too, what power she used to offset ut, what she had conjured in the Deads, and where now tha' was hiding – deep in the earth too. She told herself tha' wuz all that wuz happening: the body they'd found had already been in the ground. And afterwards, ut would be put back in the ground again; awnly this time, with God's approval, up near the newly-named Saffron-Bun chapel.

So all the women and maids went in there see. And 'twuz proper strange to see all they women who lived their lives in the town: they who'd somehow drifted to this random point in time and space on Copper Mountain. All ov they had drifted there in some way, to make a new life fur themselves, and had left comfort and stability fur this new environment. To shaw she wudn' afraid, she sat up front with her little Jago. Rebecca wuz already in there, an' Maddy nodded at she. Aw, the front on she you. Some pushie see. But tha' wuz this Maddy.

Up front wuz her Justin, this time performing the role of Cap'n; his bowler clasped in his hands. There too, wuz Doctor Jewell pacin' 'bout, like he had a geht tick up his ass. A few of the women present were muttering. They didn' like the call tha' had been made fur they. Ut has disrupted their work. Bakin' had t'stop and washin' and cleanin' be put on hold. Some had comed over from the cobbin' tables. Others from up belaw. The childurn who cudn' look after theirselves also had to be inside the chapel. The smell of the varnish and new paint made um cry, an' they didn' much like being contained in the newly-carved benches.

"Ef you got somethun' t'say to we, then get on with ut," stated Maddy loudly, brash as ever: and although a lot of the other women steered clear ov her (well, there wuz somethun' odd about she, beyond her Irishness), they agreed with her.

'Course, in good time, Doctor Jewell yipped up to all they gathered an' told un zactly wha' had been found. He told the story a bit different an' explained to um 'twuz Walt and Justin who'd found ut; thaas because Justin didn' mention naw Knockies when he first arrived at the surgery. Some there knawed already but when ee actually said wha' had been discovered, a fair few present erupted inta' tears. This wuz wha' Jewell seemed to want, see. Maybe tha' would make someone who knawed somethun' come forward, or raise their hand. But ut didn't look like 'twuz goin' t'happen. In fact, they were hushed by ut and what the good Doctor had to say. Well, 'twuz understood why they'd have to investigate. 'Twuz hardly an everyday occurrence now, wuz ut?

"How come no men are here?" shouted out Maddy. "Why is it we women are being castigated? A man could have put the baby down there. Haven't you stupid pair thought ov that?"

Tha' got lots of affirmation from the other women. She wuz awnly speakin' for the rest of they. She wuz just expressing what all of they felt. But once she'd said that, she let her anger subside. Maybe her feistiness would betray her. She let others do the gabbling about ut. She'd done just right, she reckoned. She'd set the men up to be attacked by all the other women present. She now just kept quiet on the front bench and the rest told Jewell wha' they thought ov un. He responded with more detail about the infant, but she could handle this. She put herself somewhere. Where did she go? Back to the Beara, back to being down Ballydonegan Beach.

All the while, the women gaked at each other and wondered about their awn biology. Who wuz menstruating? Who wuz past their time? What maids might have had a baby in secret? Wuz there some old maid keepin' a secret fur a youngster who'd made a mistake? But you cudn' fathom ut; not all of ut at least. 'Mean, there were some of child-bearing age, but moast of they had never even comed across a boy, let alone slept with one. An' the others? Well naw. In such an intimate community, everyone knawed each other's business: everyone else's biology. Nawthun' went unnawticed, except the magic ov she – or so she thought.

"I'll leave you contemplate for a while," said Jewell, and he let the women sit there for a bit, hoping inside his heart, that someone would reveal somethun'. Just to put pressure on, Jewell slowly and deliberately went up the pulpit and in silence, read the Bible to hisself. But 'course, ee could have kept there all day and all night, an' naw more information would be gleaned. In the end, then, the women could go.

Maddy wanted to tell them that she didn' need naw man to tell her when to come or go, and many women felt the same, but see, ut wudn' have done good to say anything more would ut? Any remonstration awnly made she look more guilty. Maddy knew tha' now. Despite wha' wuz goin' on around her, publically, 'twuz best to let ut go. A day or two, and 'twud pass. Some other distraction would re-focus the town and that baby (her son) would be just put in the ground where, at this point, ee belonged.

When they'd gone, Justin asked Jewell wha' ee'd nawticed.

"Nawthun'," he said.

"Nawthun'?"

"That's right. At least we tried..."

He took a disparaging gulp of air.

"Women see..."

Whilst all this wuz goin' on, Gourgy and Luk headed down to the seventh level. Down there, there wuz a cavernous space where all the Knockies and other magical species from other countries beyond Cornwall comed to meet. Such meetings were rare, but this one wuz of major importance. There wuz a knocking code they used to summon they from all the levels wherever they were at work: an' awnly then, did they knaw they had to leave their masters and come fur convocation. When the special knock comed, then their ears all pricked up, and they knawed in an instant where they must be. To tempt um, Gourgy and Luk had brought along a passel of saffron buns – allays good Knockie food – to reward an' relax these boys underground. They'd – ah – liberated they hot off the kitchen table of the new Mrs Jewell. She'd discover their disappearance later on an' blame some baissly keddle-boy.

They soon comed, extricating themselves from stope holes and from sollar platforms, from stinkun' rises and baissly dips ov lodes, all t'see wha' this pair wanted. The thing wuz that Gourgy and Luk demanded tha' kind of respect. When things were tough for the Knockie population, 'twuz allays they pair who sorted matters out, and had a word with the humans. They wuz good fur the mine, and 'twould be a sad day whenever they had to move on. So then, amongst the munchin' of the morsels of saffron bun, Gourgy and Luk explained wha' wuz on, an' told um wha' they'd found on the second level.

Nawbody said much. 'Mean, the buns wuz good, wudn' um?

Then again see, there wuz nowhere like mines fur hidin' things people didn't want others to see. Thaas wha' many ov um said at once. All throughout existence, mines had been places where things could be hidden an' stored without anyone nawticing. Moast of they present had seen tha', with awnly some of the younger ov their species yet to nawtice ut. But es, 'twas the way of things. Ut didn' matter ef 'twas a dead baby or an' old perambulator. They'd seen ut all tipped down shafts an' stored on levels.

This wudn' goin' the way Gourgy and Luk wanted. They needed information. Someone must have seen somethun'. But na, nothun' comed back from um. Ut seemed like whoever'd done ut, moved with some degree of swerve and magic.

"Must have been," said the boy Branek, an ancient bugger from St Agnes, "otherwise we would have sensed um."

He wuz right. That boy wuz half-blind hisself near 'bout, and could sense things s'much ee could tell 'bout um afore they even happened. But ef ee didn' have a clue, then what hope wuz there for the rest ov um?

"Someone made we blind," Branek observed, and every other Knockie nodded in agreement.

That sealed ut then. They wudn' goin' to get any more out of they. And maybe there wuz some truth in ut. Maybe someone had made they blind, just like they'd done top-side too. Whoever 'twuz, wuz some pushie you. An' they deserved a big slice of scolding tongue pie when their identity wuz finally discovered.

"Eh" went Branek. "Never mind all tha', got any more ov they buns, 'ave ee?"

Jeez. The needs and selfishness of Knockies. An' now this bugger gakin' up fur more. Well, they had none.

Gourgy and Luk let um go back to work .They grumbled and gabbled on, but the solution wudn' goin' t'be with they this time around. They 'oped that they wuz havin' better luck top-side, up chapel.

When moast of they had left, there wuz this one pair of Kobolds remaining. Kobolds see, were the German equivalent ov they. They'd come over with Gries and Knickmeier, but by now had almost fully become absorbed into the Knockie world. Indeed, ef anything, they wuz just Knockies with a German accent.

"Wozzon boys?" went Luk.

"We ebm got naw buns left," observed Gourgy shawing them the empty tea-towel they'd put them in, back in the Jewell kitchen.

"Nein. Not buns," said the fust ov they. Ee 'ad an unpronounceable name that they pair always forgot. Somethun' like Hansgogen.

"Long time ago now, but there wast, I think, ein frau inst level zwei."

At this, he held up two ov his fingers.

"A woman?"

"Ja."

"Can you describe her?"

"Ja. But you will not like it much think I."

"How come?" asked Luk.

"She is yours. Your masters..." the kobold named Hansgogen said.

Luk looked at Gourgy. Naw, ut cudn' be, could ut? Not after what Doctor Jewell had said. They boath feared wha' wuz comin' next.

"Die Irish frau. You know her, ja?"

Luk collapsed inta' a ball. He knawed precisely wha' he meant.

"You sure?" asked Gourgy. "I mean, really sure."

"Ja, as I see you now. I swear it. Ist that what you want?"

"Ut es," said Gourgy. "You did right to tell we..."

"Gut. Then we go back to work."

The other kobold nodded at them.

"We are sorry," he said. "Sometimes the truth ist not so nice to see."

"I know," said Gourgy. "You have our eternal respect good friends."

The Kobolds politely nodded and strammelled back along the level. They then slid down a rise to where Stefan Gries and Klaus Knickmeier were at work that morning on the level belaw.

"Christ," went Gourgy. "Didn' expect tha'..."

"So what we sayin' then?" asked Luk, crying his eyes out. "We sayin' Maddy did have another boy then, but ee didn' survive?"

"Looks like ut," said Gourgy, but somethun' didn' sit right with un, not after wha' the Doctor said.

"Why didn' she say?" asked Luk, worried now fur his master.

"Now that, tha', my pard," replied Gourgy, "is zactly the right question someone d'need t'ask... I tell ee wha' though. 'Tidn' goin' to be me. Best leave ut to others I reckon."

"Es," said Luk, looking like his whole world wuz about to fall in on his faace. "I'd best tell Justin."

Es. 'Twuz best. But then he remembered: there wuz tha' time they'd argued about the venereal disease (ee fully knawed what tha' wuz): that which Maddy had caught off Justin. That wuz when his master scat at un, and then somethun' in Luk told un that this wuz behind all ov ut. At the mere thought of tha', some wisht he looked. Luk may have looked tha' way, but Gourgy was now wearin' a mask. He knawed how sad an' how serious this wuz about to get. Hellfire man, ut could even lead to the ruination ov the mine. Their new chapel might be abandoned before its first anniversary. However 'twas goin' to go, some serious questions needed to be asked though. At the same time, Gourgy was back thinkin' again about everything ov late. His mind turned to the *tikkydew*, the Pooka and the odd disappearance of his old master. Up grass-side, Luk would need a word with Justin, and ee hisself, would need a word with the forest.

Later on, back home, not much wuz said. But Justin wuz watchin' Maddy close fur any sign, any signal that might confirm what ee wuz comin' to believe. Ee knawed 'twud take some doing ov, somethun' extraordinary to break she. So ee considered hard what he wanted to say. Aw, dun' ee worry – 'course they'd gone over what happened up chapel – and 'course Maddy wuz still enraged at how the women had been assembled together and branded murderers. 'Twas just the sort ov thing that made she mad, and Justin knawed ut. But ee had new information now, and even though last night, they'd made love together, and even though ee cared fur she very deeply – an' in all honesty, loved she t'death, all of this had to come out in the open. 'Twas the awnly way. Ut cudn' carry on. Ee needed t'get t' the bottom ov ut; and he felt sure that ef ee did, then a good many things here on the mountain might be solved.

"That eejit Jewell bringing us all up there to stand trial before God. Who does he think he is? The balls on the man are bigger than the gob on his mouth. I can't stand him Jus, I can't stand him."

"Why's that?"

"T'accuse we of what he said. I notice no man had been called in there. If he did that back where I come from, his testicles would be severed off and shoved down his throat. Everyone thought it, even if they didn't say it."

Justin didn' say much. He just listened. Ee'd gone a Cornish kind ov quiet, which is t'say 'twuz better fur'n not to open his mouth at tha' point. He could tell she wuz riled. But then, she'd been riled for some reason, for months now. He wuz perhaps now awnly beginning t'understand why. He'd thought about his awn plaace in all of this. Ee knawed rightly wha' ut meant, He'd seen the sorrow too, on his meht's faaces, on the visages of they pair ov Knockies, who'd been there with ee an' his brother all the way through. Wha' must this be like fur they? Terrible, ee reckoned, and when he'd asked ov um where they wuz goin' that evening, they said they wuz heading up Saffron-Bun Chapel in order to pray. Now, tha' wuz unheard ov. When Knockies start praying, well, you knaw then, that you'm in the shit. Now God seemed to be the awnly one they could turn to. As Maddy raged, ee wondered if God would take nawtice ov they. 'Mean, their kind wudn' especially knawn fur being God-fearin' or -abiding, but perhaps there'd been a shift. Perhaps now things could go face about ass, instead of the other way round.

"Put us up there to try and make us confess. Now there's a fookin' joke if ever there was one. It's not even my kind of church. That's a Cussie place – not fur the likes of we off the Beara. Do you think that's right? Tell me Justin. Is that right now?"

"No," said Justin. "It's never right, but 'twuz what ut wuz. I mean, no one said anything anyway, did um? – so it didn' work..."

"Bullied we are by you men, and I mean tha'... Always the same. It never alters. Look at me now here in this brand new country, and still I am getting the same shite as ever... just like my own mammy."

He knew what she wuz referring to there. But this: this wuz different. Justin had considered what to do fur the best. Perhaps ef she could tell ee what she'd done – the full truth ov the matter – he could deal weth ut. Maybe if she could tell un zactly what had happened up grass and belaw, then she could confide in un. However sinful ut wuz what she had done, maybe he could help. Maybe he could make ut gaw away, but he needed to knaw now. That wuz what wuz driving un. Everything else was secondary: the mine, that Rosie, his Knockie, his past, all of ut could be forgotten. But this woman next to un, the woman who ee knawed wuz a witch of some power, wuz still acting up, acting up like as if she was performing in that grand new theatre down in Calumet. She wuz good see. She'd always been good. She knawed how to turn ut on, but also how to keep things hidden. So beautiful, so engaging wuz she, that she'd made un blind, and ee knawed ut. But ee wudn' goin' t'follow naw siren song any more.

She wuz up now, playing hide and seek with Jago, and his eyes were trailing she. And in they ee could see the love. He could see how ut had been fashioned. But ee realised at this point at least, tha' what wuz in front of him was some kind ov deceitful vision; that 'twuz not true an' honest – that ut had somehow been falsified. Somehow, ee had quickly come to knaw that day that the thing laid out on Jewell's mortuary table wuz in some way related to the beautiful ball of energy that she wuz now playing with. Ut was starting to all make sense to him: her reluctance to go out, the way she kept the boy to herself, the fear that anyone wud take him. Justin knawed nothing about what

Doctor Jewell called the new psychology but he knawed how people worked. They might try an' hide ut, like some kind of fool's gold, but 'twud come out in the end. Tha' wuz allays the way ov things.

He carried on watching them play together: his dear Jago and she. Es, like butter wudn' melt in her mouth. After his time up in the chapel, ee knawed what Gourgy would bring back from the forest. Previously, ee hadn' put much mark in all that claptrap about the forest being angry with they for what they'd done to this place, but this time – right in the there and then – ut sounded convincing. The forest saw much and maybe ut saw she too. Maybe ut had seen she and her ways. He'd seen what she could do. Maybe she'd just been put off her guard of late.

"You putting him to bed now?" he asked of she.

"Reckon so, doan't you? The little man's tired. We went for a walk today didn't we, my sweetheart?"

"Where did you go?"

"Oh, out beyond the Deads..."

She liked ut there, did Maddy. Tha' place, tha' place where nawbody else much went.

"Es," said Justin, "well, put un down ef he's tired an' taissy."

She gathered him up and took him into the cot in the bedroom. He could hear of she settlin' un down, and singing a small rhyme in Irish to un, which he allays liked. Justin wuz imagining ut in his mind; but he was also imagining what he'd say to she when she comed back in. When she did, Justin spoke slowly and carefully.

"I want... or rather, I need... to tell you something," said Justin. "Something I should have told you a long time ago..."

"Go on then," said Maddy, much intrigued. "This some kind of confession?"

"Maybe," said Justin.

She gestured for him to continue. All the while, he wondered how she kept up that pretence. How could she just continue like nawthun' had happened. Maybe this wuz the way ut would work. Ef he could scratch her back, maybe she could scratch his. Tit fur tat. The best way, wuz to come right out with ut.

"You knaw I once killed a man, dun't ee Maddy?" Justin said.

She didn' answer. She just gaked at un, like she knawed un, but didn't knaw un.

"'Twuz like this. Before we comed out here. Down Penzance. There wuz a bit ov a card game on... and I swear to God, this boy wuz cheatin' and I could see un doin' ut... and well, he won all the money... everyone's hard-earned money... and well, I wuz good and beered up, and so when I seened un outside in the street, taking a piss, I grabbed un see..."

"What did you do?"

"I broke his neck. I twisted ut so hard, he fell to the floor like a dishrag."

She nodded. His story wuz purposeful and controlled. He wanted she t'see that she could tell un whatever she wanted. Ef ee could do this, then so could she.

"Anyone see ee?"

"Awnly brother. He comed outside to touch pipe, an' happened to see ut."

"Jeez. What did you do?"

"Well, he set me right. Told me my gambling and drinking days wuz over, and tha' ef we wuz ever found in 'Zance again, we'd be the fust to be accused, for the others in the game, well, they knawed how I felt."

"Sounds like the fella deserved it."

"Na, not really my lover. Ee wuz just havin' a bit of fun with me, but the younger me, took ut to be serious see, and thaas why I comed to twist his head off, near 'nuff."

"I mean, I always knew there was something in you," Maddy said. "There's a lot about me that you don't know, that I'm not so proud ov. I only really started to change when I got here, and found you... That's when I found myself see, really discovered who I was. I'm not judging you on ut Jus. We'm tough, you an' I. We've had to be."

She wuz right. Tha' much wuz true.

"Francis saved me see. He turned me round. See, ef I'd carried on the way I had done, well, I dare say I'd now be in a cell in Bodmin Gaol. That, or put to a hanging. But see, after I'd done that, ee said the best thing we could do wuz to migrate see. Transform... Disappear. Go to 'Merky' like, fur thaas where we'd make our fortunes. Thaas what brought me here, up to the Keweenaw, and how then I comed to meet you. But see Maddy, I ent a bad man... I made one mistake, and every day, I cuss myself for ut. Every day, I pray to God fur redemption. But 'tis very hard you... idn' ut? To turn back time?"

"Aye," she said. "It is."

But there was no budging she. Even when he asked her straight.

"Anything you've ever done, that you regret? I mean, something big. Something life changing. Something that affected not awnly you, but many others?"

"No, not really," she said.

Hard see.

Bleddy hard.

There was the act: but by the time they went to bed, ee reckoned that he'd placed her in such a dilemma that she'd now have to tell un the truth. He'd made such a bargain with she that she'd have to confess. He hoped that by doing so, ut would make them closer and, in realising the union of sin between them, their shared wrongs would diminish. A balance might then be achieved.

'Awnly ut didn't quite turn out tha' way though. Aw naw. In fact, their awn tragedy got multiplied in ways that neither of they expected. Ut begun with Maddy getting out of bed to make use ov the piss-pot at three in the morning. After she'd finished, she leaned over to un, and gived un a kiss on his cheek.

"I need to tell you something," she said. "Now, you promise d'you, that you won't be mad at me?"

"Promise," he said sleepily, but even then ee didn' knaw quite what was goin' to come out of her mouth.

"Prepare yourself then, y'Cussie," she said.

Surely now, could come relief.

And then, confident as y'like, as ef the mask of the past year or so wuz now free to fall away, she told un the tale, leaving naw stone – and naw changeling – unturned. The whole story got unleashed. Bewdie fur some, but not really fur she. An' in all ov tha, despite ut's wonder and ut's horror, Justin knawed ee'd been right to listen to the earth.

46

The way Maddy put ut made her evil seem s'normal. Any woman would do ut, wudn' um? Thaas wha' she said. 'Mean ut worked, did Justin's strategy – a shock fur a shock, a sin fur a sin – because ee wuz never sure ef ut would work. He never had complete feyth that ee could break she, but in the end, ut all tumbled out. Ee had tha' edge now see; the extra information tha' made un think ee wuz right about she. An' when she told un, she didn' squall or plead any. Naw. She just went through how ut happened, and wha' she did. 'Course, there were some things tha' Justin could never have guessed. When she said tha' she wanted to speak to un and confess wha' she'd done, ee wuz expectun' ov she to explain that, in spite of wha' the Doc had said, she'd had twins; awnly, one of they didn' survive and so she'd hidden ut. But naw, tha' wudn' ut at all, so when the revelation comed tha' in fact, she'd already had their son in the forest, and then hidden ee in the second level of the mine, he wuz quite speechless. But as you d'knaw, tha' wudn' ut, wuz ut? Aw naw. See, there wuz then her creation of the Pooka (she called ut tha' fur the first time) an' at tha', ee wuz amazed. 'Mean, ee knawed she had power, but not tha' kind ov power. She did explain. She tried to explain how she couldn' handle the loss ov their boy and wha' tha' had done t'she, and why she had to make tha' thing.

And tha' Justin, you had to feel fur ee, because all this comed as some shock to ee; but ee didn' respond none or say much. Ee just kept quiet and listened. And so she manufactured that thing – and es – there wuz naw other word for ut, because it really wuz a changeling: and God help she, for then what she did wuz t'swap ut fur the real Richard, and pretend that he wuz their son, their Jago. An' ut took un a brae while to think ut through, but to come t'the realisation that the being who ee thought wuz their son and who ee loved s'dearly: wudn' their son at all and in fact, belonged to Francis and Rebecca. By right, ee wuz his nephew and not his son. And tha' thing buried up in the ground by the chapel wuz somethun' malevolent, just as ee had argued all along. Es, ee remembered the night well, when she had stolen the mite and brought un down here. Aw, the deceit of ut, the heartbreaking, awful deceit ov ut!

An' all the while, whilst she told un about just how she'd done ut, and what she had t'go through, his mind wudn' s'much fixated on tha', but on Francis and Becca, an' what they'd had to endure. Naw wonder the boy behaved like ee did. Naw wonder he wuz s'naughty and truculent. Naw wonder the Knockies didn' go much on un. Small wonder then, that he'd wanted to beat un with the banjo shovel and 'eave un into a furnace. Ee'd been right all along. An' the sin he'd committed all that time ago, seemed to pale inta' insignificance compared t'wha' she had done here on the mountain. Es, she'd used witchcraft to make the thing, and she carried on using ut to deceive; awnly last night, he'd managed, by hook or by crook, to hoik ut out of she, and make she confess. She said ut. She told un. These last few months ut had got to her. Ut wuz why she kept their Jago s'closeted. Ut wuz why she kept herself to herself and not much wanted to go out. Now, ut all made sense.

'Course, where she'd placed the body of their real son made sense too. Maddy wuz one the few women who worked underground with they. Maybe ef Justin and Jewell had been smarter, they'd have called all they in anyway. She though, knawed all the levels. Ut wuz the whole reason she'd gained the respect of men like Trevorrow. She knawed which ones were to be worked, and which ones were abandoned. She'd have knawn precisely the spot where she pushed their son into the ground. But then (due to her pregnancy), she hadn' been in the mine much ov late. Es, and ef ut wudn' for the butterfly and the wisdom of Gourgy and Luk, their dead son would still be in there. But thanks to they and their Kobold friends from underground, they'd considered who'd have been there a while ago. She might have used her magic but underground: the magic ov their people wuz stronger. She clearly hadn' thought tha' through enough. Maybe her confession occurred because she knawed that ef ut hadn' unravelled yet, 'twuz about to. Someone wuz bound to think of she and connect ut all. She realised tha' tha' wuz what her Justin had already done. Ee'd been ahead ov the game all along.

And then see, there wuz the forest, because she spoke about it. Next time, Justin seened Gourgy, Gourgy would tell Justin what he'd discerned, tha' the forest told un precisely what had happened in a clearing some while ago, and tha' ut had seen a baby arrive, but that ut arrived dead as a stone. But Maddy told un tha' anyway. She explained in grim detail wha' happened and wha' she'd had to do. Ut wuz never somethun' she wanted, but there 'twuz. Perhaps, she said, the forest wuz takin' revenge on she and had deaded the babe inside ov she, just like ut had deaded the mind of Clara Jewell, but Justin wudn' s'sure 'bout tha'. Perhaps instead, she'd just been plain evil.

She pleaded with un though. She explained tha' she'd wanted to tell un. She needed un really, but she didn' knaw ef she could tell un, especially not after his brother wuz sitting pretty there with the real Richard. Something in her mind flipped, she said. She couldn' rightly control ut, and thaas why she acted in the way she did. She'd done ut fur they because she knawed their baby would unify they, an' make they complete. But maybe tha' wuz just twaddle. Maybe tha' wuz this Maddy puttin' her guilt on him, makin' un feel complicit with her act. But 'twuz true, ee wudn' have wanted this to have happened. He'd rather have faced up to her having a stillborn baby than wha' she'd gone an' done. Ee wuz picturing she at the Deads makin' the thing an' twuz an image that would stay with un fur a long time. Perhaps people wuz right about this Maddy of his. Perhaps tha' wuz why they gived she distance. Aw, es, there wuz many a man who fancied she, but somehow, they knawed her power. They'd seen perhaps wha' he hadn', and that she had this thread inside of she. He reckoned he'd been blind. But sometimes, thaas the way 'tis with love. You cen't odds ut. 'Tis what ut es.

Ee asked her whether anyone else knew. 'Mean, did she tell Flannery and the rest of her crew? Naw, she said. They wudn' understand. Ee even wondered why she didn' tell Doctor Jewell, but as she explained, he realised why she took such a dislike to un. Tha' wuz because he'd asked she too many difficult questions tha' morning. Ut wuz he she'd been moast worried about. An' when Justin thought all this through, he asked she straight: had she knawn ov these confounded Pookas before? 'Mean, had anyone else conjured up one ov they back home. An' well, sadly, she had t'confess. She knawed of they being made a time or two back home – but awnly when things were desperate – when 'twuz the last rescort. 'Least then, ee wudn' the fust to face one ov they buggers. Apparently, this bugger though, had been especially evil. Moast ov they were a bit more mild.

Then ut became an issue ov blame. Ee knawed where this wuz goin'. And this perhaps wuz where ee wuz more sympathetic. When she told un, he knawed part of ut wuz his fault. This see, wuz the venereal disease he'd caught off tha' slag Rosie Koskinen, and which he'd passed on to Maddy. He knawed what she wuz goin' to say. Once tha' had taken hold, like the Doctor had told she, there wuz that chance; that chance of deformation, or just as ut rightly turned out, death. Es. Infant mortality. Somethun' people knawed well here now on the mountain. She told un about her pregnancy; how all the time she had tha' fear of loss: ut went through she and consumed her on the inside. An' well, when ut happened, tha' wuz ut. She felt she had naw choice but to act. She pleaded her age. She pleaded her lack ov fertility. Tha' wuz again, supposedly one of they things to affect women after catchin' ut. She couldn' conceive of a world without her havin' a baby; and when she considered ut, well, Richard wuz ripe fur plucking, wudn' a? He wuz the perfectly-formed apple in the orchard an' when opportunity arose, she gathered un in.

She could plead all she liked. Fur Justin, nawthun' could change his mind. Stealing ov another mawthur's chield wuz the wust thing you could ever do, an' she shouldn' have done ut. Es, there were reasons why she'd done wha' she had, and maybe even he felt culpable for wha' he'd passed on to she, but tha' wuz one thing. This, wuz somethun' else. But guilt see, ut did rage through un, because after tha' incident in Penzance, he knawed precisely wha' gambling and alcohol could bring: and yet here in 'Merky' he'd been an' broken that, down in the old Cliff Hotel, and yet again, one thing had led to another. He did tell she tha'. At least, maybe 'twudn' all Maddy's fault. Ef he'd acted a bit better, and been a bit more Wesleyan, then maybe none of this would have happened in the fust place.

"You knaw what you got to do now, dun't ee?" he said to she.

She shook her head. She didn't want to hear ov ut.

"'Tidn' naw good being like tha'."

"I can't give un up. You promised..."

"I promised I wudn' judge ee," ee said, even though he had. "I didn' say anything else."

All the while, their liddle Jago had been sleeping; all the way through wha' she'd told un.

"Ee idn' ours Maddy."

"He is."

"Naw, my lover, ee idn'... He've never been ours. He, well, he be just a changeling, and 'tis time fur ee to hand un back."

"To who?"

"You knaw who..."

"But how do I tell them?"

"I dun't knaw. You just have to. You have to make this right. Ef you dun't, well, me an' you shall be cursed fur life. Just like you have been... you told me... ut's been a curse on you. This is the awnly way you'n get your freedom back. You can break ut. I knaw you can."

"They'll kill me."

"Naw. They wun't. Not ef we explain. Not ef we tell um what happened and how ut comed to happen."

"But there's only Rebecca... What about Frank?"

"Well, we'll start with she... and then, when she d'knaw the truth, we'll see ef we can find Francis. 'Mean, ef anything will bring un back, then his son will."

"I can't do ut Justin."

"What ee mean?"

"I can't face them... I've done something terrible. I'll never be able to look them in the eye again. And then everyone will come to know... I can't. What say you, we leave here? Plenty of other places to work in America... We could leave now..."

The way she wuz saying ov ut still sounded like she had no intention of handing Jago back.

"We cen't just leave," said Justin. "Our lives are here..."

"Ireland then? Back on the Beara. Plenty of mines still there. Enough of you Jackers left. Plenty ov opportunities for you."

"No Maddy," said Justin.

"But you ran, when you did something wrong?"

"I know. I should have faced up to ut, but I didn'. I learnt from tha' though. I knaw better now..."

He knew she still didn' want to let Jago go. She'd stepped over to hold him. He knawed how hard 'twuz goin' to be. He didn' want to make ut difficult, but ee knawed wha' wuz right.

"Look. I've thought about this. You doan't have to tell anyone 'bout the Pooka. Just say you had a boy – an' tha' ee died. Say 'twuz grief tha' made ee do ut. In time, people will understand. But you understand me; you put an end t'all this magic Maddy. Ut ends now."

"You've always known I was a witch though..."

"Es, but not a bad one. A good one I thought. A wise woman, not one filled with hate and bile."

She thought through what he'd said to she. She wuz still peering down at Jago, knowing that he wuz about to be severed and sliced from her.

"He knows us though. It'll be hard for him to move somewhere else..."

"Maddy," Justin said more snappily. "That *somewhere else* is his real mother and father. They are who he should be with. Not us."

She wuz crying more now. Great volumes of tears ran from her eyes onto the boy below: the boy who she'd reckoned on being her son, the boy who she'd appropriated and made her own. Aw hell. Some sad to see 'twuz.

"It idn' like you'll never see un again Maddy. He's your nephew. He'll still love you. We'll still be here fur'n..."

"Aye. And me childless."

Ut still hadn' gone from her; whatever 'twuz.

So far, Justin reckoned he'd been tolerant. He'd listened and understood, but now 'twuz out there, there wuz no point in prolonging ut. The return had to be made. He'd need to be cruel to be kind. There wudn' naw other way. Now that he knawed the truth, Jago had to go to his rightful home.

"You can either come with me, or stay here, but I'm takin' un back Maddy. It's the right thing to do. You know that, deep inside your heart, dun't ee?"

She wuz pleading with un now, but Justin, God help un, had runned out of all patience. Es, she'd confessed, but there wuz naw point in such a confession unless reparation could be made. Maybe she'd felt that their deal, their exchange of secrets, would have allowed Jago to remain. But that wasn't the case. Aw naw. Part of that exchange for Justin, wuz that she, having admitted her sin, would have to acquiesce, and let the boy return to his natural parents. Perhaps she hadn' realised that. Perhaps the old her wuz still inside, and couldn' get out. Perhaps there would be naw change.

"I cen't let you do tha," she said.

She started to move. See, her love fur the boy wuz still strong as ever.

"An' I cen't let you carry on this way," said Justin. "Ee idn' ours."

Maddy wuz trying to leave. She'd take her chances with the boy. She'd do wha' wuz necessary. See, she loved Justin, but she loved the boy more. An' this wuz still motivating her. But Justin wudn' having' none ov ut. Es, he'd had his aggressive moments, like in Penzance, and when he'd tried stoppin' ov the Pooka, but now he'd have to employ they t'stop she. A bit ov a tussle commenced you. See, ee snatched Jago from she, an' placed un on the bed. And she responded by pushin' ov un out ov her way. So ut had come t' this had ut, with this pair, now arguing like a pair of gulls over a tiny chad?

See, a woman's love fur a child d'give they superhuman strength, and this Maddy, she had plenty ov tha' you. She went fur ut, scatting Justin in the faace with her fists. Hard punches they were. Well, you knaw she can fight. But then, so could he, and in order to return the mite home, he gived as good as he got. What wuz this like, eh? This pair fighting over a baby, but each see, had their reason. Neither didn' want to give up. Back an' forth they went. Aw, terrible 'twuz to see a woman an' a man fighting like this. An' all the while, poor Jago there – innocent as the day he wuz born – watching ov um. Plenty ov furniture got scat over in the struggle, and in the end, the awnly thing fur Justin t'do, wuz to knock she clean out. Es, ee gived she a geht right hook which scat she flying. An' t' be honest you, tha' wuz the end of ut. How can ee recover from such a calamity? Fur a minute though, until she comed round, Maddy wudn' be doin' ov naw more magic. Not fur now, at least.

Justin checked to see she wuz still breathing. She wuz. Ee didn't want naw repeat ov Penzance. He turned she over so she could breathe. Then he went over to his nephew and took one last close look at un, to see what the pair of they had helped to shape. Naw, they hadn' made un, but they'd helped to shape un, and despite she there on the ground, they'd helped make something special. In a moment, he was out the door and in the bright sunshine of the morning, carrying ov Jago up to where Rebecca lived. Outside, over on a bench, were sat Gourgy and Luk. They'd been up early and heard the row. They'd listened as the furniture got scat over, and with all this, they knawed the truth wuz out. There was Luk's master carrying the boy Jago back. Justin could see the upset in Luk's eyes, but in Gourgy's he saw something different. Clearly, that Knockie had conversed with the forest and the forest had confirmed to him all that ut knew. Gourgy gave Justin a reassuring nod. They'd been right, an' wha' he wuz doing wuz the right thing to do. Luk knawed a lot ov the truth ov ut, an' wanted to run over an' see how Maddy wuz, but Gourgy told un to hold fire. Instead, they followed Justin up to Rebecca's place.

When she opened the door, she wuz surprised to see Justin there with Jago. She wuz still in her nightgown. She hadn't planned to teach that day. Ut was the time she had booked off, as part of the Easter Holiday. She had other plans, and her brother-in-law and her nephew turning up wudn' zactly ideal.

"Can we come in?" asked Justin urgently.

"Well, it's not perfect. I've got something on today. I have to be somewhere..."

"I need to tell you something," said Justin, some brae force in his voice. "And you'll want to hear ut."

"Sounds very important," she said, a bit worried up.

"Ut es," said Justin. "And you'll definitely want to hear ut."

And then, Becca nawticed Gourgy and Luk standing there, and because of who she wuz, she invited they in too.

"Es," said Justin. "Good that they'm here. They'll back up everything I need to tell ee."

He began by saying, "There's been a mistake. Some confusion. This un here idn' Jago t'all."

He handed the toddler across to Becca. She allays delighted in un, but didn' expect what wuz comin' next t'all.

"He there, be your Richard."

"Thaas right," went Luk.

"Correct," said Gourgy. "We got to the bottom ov ut."

"Bottom of what?" asked Rebecca, with she still havin' no idea ov what wuz about to be revealed to she. And so they told her, and in tha' moment, the world went face about ass once more. And from hereon in, the wound on Becca's finger would fast heal. Magic see.

Meanwhile, in the other Nankervis house, Maddy recovered an' comed out of her doze on the floor after being scat flyin'. The anger she'd felt before consumed her again, but the violence inflicted on she by Justin, shawed how strongly he felt about the issue, but ut also confirmed to she, that in the cold light ov day, she had to finally accept wha' had happened. Jago had gone. In fact, she didn' knaw if there would ever be any more Jago. Her plan to abscond with un had failed, and now he'd be up there with Rebecca. Soon after that, Jewell would knaw, and then 'twud be on the tongues ov all they in town. A day later and 'twould be all over the Keweenaw. She longed fur her boy. She really did, but she knawed she cudn' have un. How might tha' feel? The last couple of years ov her life then had been somethun' ov a dream; as big a piece ov unreality as you could imagine. Suddenly, ut had comed to an end.

She realised Justin had played her. He'd played her well. That niggling feeling she'd always had about un, that there wuz somethun' lurking in his past, and caused she to confess what she'd done. An' when that finally tumbled out, she had naw choice. The game wuz up. She hated, in that instance her awn mother, who told she to stay hard. She hadn't. She hadn't been hard enough. He'd coaxed ut out of she. One sin for another. If I tell you, you tell me. Tha' wuz ut then. There wuz nawthun' more now fur she on Mountainside. How could there be after what would come out? She'd be a pariah, and likely burnt at the stake. Either tha', or she'd be pushed into the very Deads tha' had been her cauldron. Maybe they'd toss she inta' the furnace now. Prob'ly the forest would betray her. Perhaps it had done so already – or perhaps it would do sometime soon. Nature see, you cudn' trust it. She'd learnt tha'.

Maddy knew what she needed to do. She didn't bother re-arranging the broken furniture from their fight. He could do tha'; he who'd sold her out – he who had promised tha' he would forgive her, and the he who'd gived her the new shiner on her face. She still felt the power of his fist when ut scat her over. 'Twas like he had embedded his knuckles with a horseshoe. Still, that would go. What she needed to do now was pack. She was leaving. She needed to. Ut wuz the only way that anything good could come from this. She filled a kit-bag. Ut wuz the same one she'd used when she had first come over across the Atlantic. She never expected that she'd ever have to use ut again, but good job she'd kept ut. She rammed things into ut the best way she could. She knew she didn' have long. By now, Justin would be explaining zactly what she did in the forest and zactly what she did in the mine. Then he'd tell she about the Deads. Then she'd knaw that 'twas utterly Maddy's fault that Francis had left.

There wudn' naw time to reflect, or to consider the good times she had had here on the mountain. No, that would have to come later. That could come when she wuz a long way away. Stayin' with Justin wudn' really no option now, wuz ut? 'Mean, she'd shafted un. She'd utterly shafted his family. He'd hate her. Allays. Best to make a clean break ov ut. But she had one more thing t'do. With her bag on her shoulder, she left her home fur the last time, walking straight past the mine that she'd been instrumental in makin'. She went straight past the Irish bunkhouses. Any other time and she'd have said goodbye, but not this day. No, there were bigger things on her mind. She went past Rosie's and hurled a big mouthful of gob at ut. She stanked on then, powerful as ever. Liked she knawed zactly where she wuz goin'. Like when Justin had first seen she. Even then, she wuz being watched and noted, but tha' didn' bother she now. They could say what they wanted, the bastards, and aye, that forest out there, ut could do what it wanted to. Before, she courted it, tried to appease it, but not any more.

Maddy was heading up to Saffron-Bun Chapel. She saw the mounds of earth where the Pooka and that Skews had gone in the earth. In all honesty, there wudn' much difference in they pair, in terms of evil. And then she thought of herself? Aye, evil incarnate she wuz. Did she give the Pooka a thought? Not really. He wuz best off in the ground where he'd come from. Inta' the chapel though, she strammelled (ut wuz never locked), and stood breathing heavily in the aisle. Only a few hours ago, she'd been in here with all the other women, accused of doing something wrong. Now the truth wuz out, and now 'twuz awnly she, standing there before God. She saw the irony in ut. This wudn' her Catholic God. This wuz the Protestant one, and come to think ov ut, she usually didn't have much time fur any kind of Christian God. Her gods had allays been older, but right now, this one would have t' do. Perhaps this Methodist God might have some vestigial Catholicism in un, and perhaps, in the stillness of this place, she could confess what she needed to. She could make repair and atone.

She knelt down and clutched a Bible: a new one that had been pulled off the storage shelf. She saw that it had been published by the Methodist Tract Society of America, but it was the same Bible she'd always known. Ut would be her talisman here, and so she pressed ut to her breast and began to speak to God. What comed out, she didn' quite knaw, because when she told the story ov what she'd done, ut comed out in a gabbled an' tearful way, that would have made no sense to anyone else but only made sense to she. Geht waves ov ut comed out of she before this God, and she hoped that ee could somehow find a way to forgive she fur all the hurt and pain that she'd caused. Aw, es. Ut tumbled out of she like a geht spring tide hitting the cliffs over in Coulagh Bay.

Thank heaven this chapel wuz here; otherwise she'd have to carry tha' fur a very long time. 'Mean, she'd carry ut to her death anyway, but this just made ut easier. Perhaps she'd been too disparaging of they Cussies and their Methodism. In the morning light, the plaace was still and beautiful. Ut wuz at peace with utself, and momentarily, so wuz she. There wuz awnly one place more she could go and tha' wuz to make her way down to Eagle Harbour. She wudn' go with the mineral tramway. No, she'd take the old road down; the one that she'd come up all tha' time ago. She put the Bible back, crossed herself once more and stood up. Out of habit perhaps, she bowed to the pulpit and turned around.

"I heard what you said," came a voice at the open door of the chapel.

The voice was male and in silhouette at the eastern sun rising behind him.

"I seen you goin' along earlier with your kitbag, and wondered wozzon. Ebm seen you much of late maid..."

She now knew who 'twuz. Ut wuz Cap'n Trevorrow. He had a soft spot fur she. Aw, he'd hated her at fust, but when she shawed un what she cud do underground, well, then he allays found time fur she.

"Been busy," she said.

"Es. Busy doing wrong, by the sound of ut."

"Does it matter to you?"

"Naw. Not really. Ut d'just sadden me."

"How come?"

"To see you here, like this... and well, you a-parting from your Justin..."

"Had to be done. If you heard me, then you'll know why."

"We all do stupid things," said Trevorrow.

"Aye, and some ov us do more stupid things than others. What I did, wasn't just stupid. It was plain evil."

"Maybe," said the Cap'n. "God'll understand."

"Will he though?"

"Reckon so."

Maddy smiled to herself.

"Best get on," she said.

"Where ee making fur? Calumet? Headin' west, eh? I hear California es good."

"No. 'Course not. Heading home."

"Allihies then?"

She nodded.

"Well, I'n see you've made your decision... I want you to have this... to see you on your way."

He pulled an envelope out of his pocket and handed it out to her.

"What is it?"

"Some money."

"I got money."

"I knaw tha' my 'andsome."

"This is money that nawbody d'knaw 'bout. Not really. Found ut see, in Samuel Skews' office. Tucked away, fur a rainy day."

"Skews?"

"Es."

"Really?"

"Well, ee wun't be needin' ov ut, an' I dare say, this, is perhaps your rainy day. Have ut Maddy, and have ut with my love. This'll set ee up a bit, eh?"

She accepted the envelope and brushed past him in the aisle.

"Take care of yourself, eh?"

"You too," she said.

Out the chapel she went, and picked up the old wagon road down the harbour. Trevorrow took a pew, and lowered his head. He now wanted his awn word with the Man above.

Justin had a mind to what he might find at home. He realised that their final fight had made their continuance impossible. She'd never accept the need to return Richard back to his mother. He knawed that sometime soon, he'd think ov Maddy and smile, but not right now. Not fur a bit. Time needed to pass. Time needed to heal.

Time though, wuz not wha' Rebecca Nankervis had. When Gourgy, Luk and Justin left, she wuz still in a state of amazement, but also gradually, she moved to a state ov anger. Now she understood zactly why Maddy had behaved in the way tha' she had with her. She understood why this past year had been such a hell for she. She had just gained back her son which wuz joyous and incredible. Ut wuz as if the dead had comed alive again. An' although 'twuz wondrous to see un again, she had made plans. Her plans were important because they were all about making her family complete again. She'd questioned that Tommy Carkeek. He'd knawed when the next laker to Detroit would pull in. Tha' day wuz today. This wuz why she had been initially so annoyed about the arrival of early-morning visitors. Now, there wuz the baby to be accounted for. She couldn' take un with her, much as she wished to. What she had in mind, wudn' work if he travelled with her.

She went round to her stepmother's. She would have to do. She relayed the story to her in a garbled way.

"No," she said. "She wudn' goin' to change his name back to Richard. He'd stay Jago, but yes, he wuz their son: her feythur's true grandson. She'd explain further when she got back."

"Alright," said Eleanor. "But...?"

She knawed there wuz lots to explain.

"Speak to Justin," Rebecca said.

He'd put um right.

Ut wuz hard to leave the boy the moment she'd got un back. But unless she did this now, she'd never be able to put everything else right. See, despite the advice, many miners still used the tramway to ride up and down on. The slice made between Skews' body an' head didn' put um off none. She'd anticipated the by-now usual fortnightly arrival of the boy Tommy with her money and the money for the chapel too; but this time, she'd be returning with him, so she could speak to the laker captain. If she could awnly talk to him, then she wuz sure she could locate her husband. An' although she feared ut in the bottom ov her stomach, the boy Carkeek said 'twould be alright, and eventually, they'd make ut down bottom safe an' sound. Thaas zactly wha' they did then. She got in behind un in one of the wagons and she roller-coasted down the mountain, hoping and praying to God that the ride would reunite she with her husband.

Eagle Harbour wudn' somewhere she'd been in a while. When she'd come in on that laker all that time ago, 'twudn' much more than a jetty. Now, 'twuz a bustling harbour, and one ov the main in-roads inta' the Keweenaw. The mineral tramway had done tha' see. Ut had made the plaace, and 'twuz now a thriving community of ut's own, dedicated to serving the mine above. This was all part of what her husband and her brother-in-law had made. Ef ut wudn' fer they, then none of this would be there. There wudn' be naw tramway nor no crowd of dockers who looked after the transfer ov ore and the bringing in of coal. One day, this might all be Jago's. She cudn' call un Richard. Whatever tha' wuz, ut wuz now buried up in the ground beside Saffron-Bun Chapel.

She stuck with Tommy. He wuz the touchstone she reckoned to her finding her husband, and to bring un back home. He'd be her compass. She knew ut would take a while fur this vessel to get down t'Detroit. Detroit wuz a big city, but even in that maze of a troy town, she'd find un. She reckoned she'd locate him zactly the same way that miners could smell copper. As she stepped up the gangway onto the laker's deck, she looked back an' saw the smoke rising from the mine's chimley in the middle of the forest. She knew she'd have to clasp that image close to her heart, as well as the wondrous faace of her true son, with whom she had miraculously been reunited. Es. This wuz the right thing to do. Nawbody else could do this: awnly she. She'd find un an' bring un back. She made herself at home in her cabin and settled in fur the journey.

Just as they wuz about to cast off the ropes that tied the laker to the jetty, someone else stepped up the gangway, and negotiated her passage down to Detroit. One thing fur sure: she wudn' Cornish.

47

Pop an' towse you! Pop and towse. As Justin sat in pitiable isolation hearin' ov the crows and the blue jays cawing and chattering, the usual, yet slightly misshapen ball of constructive energy tha' wuz Dicky Mint had a heart attack – an' fell down dead. Call tha' Divine intervention ef you like. Or call ut wha' you want, but the plain fact ov ut wuz that the boy had popped his hob-nailers. Now, you d'see how God arranges all. The Minter was attempting a half-hearted feel of Rosie's ample boobage in her upstairs boudoir, when he felt a severe pain in his chest. Ee eased back on his fondling, and very briefly, sat up straight on the bed, revealing all his hairy flab, then, after makin' a few groaning noises (as ef coming t'some kind ov an orgasm) ee keeled over and dropped t'the planchen of Rosie's room. Fur a second, Rosie didn' quite knaw ef ee wuz dead or whether ee wuz in some kind ov ecstasy, but when she turned un over and felt fur his breath, 'twuz clear the poor bugger wudn' be doin' any more h'engineering at Mountainside Mine. Ee wudn' be doing naw fondling ov she neither.

The Doc had warned un a few months ago tha' he needed to ease up on the over-eating (fur ee loved his saffron buns with scalded cream as well as a couple of pasties per day), and to draw back on the amount ov hard liquor he wuz consuming. Of late, he'd spent even more time than usual steadying his stance with his tin-tipped cane. Jewell told un straight tha' ef ee carried on like ee wuz, ee wuz liable to 'go on ahead' (fur tha' wuz what Cornish people called dying) and hell, there ee wuz, flat out on the floor ov Rosie's bedroom, laid out there like a geht pile of white quartzite attle. Now, tha' Rosie Koskinen wudn' silly. She gived un mouth-to-mouth, an' pumped his chest fur almost quarter ov an hour but there wudn' naw response from the Minter. All she could do wuz look at his small, flaccid willy and his puss-filled gammy leg, and realised that the dream ov their planned life together wudn' ever goin' to happen.

Jewell got called, didn' a? What wuz ut ov late up here on Mountainside? Fust, there wuz Maddy and Justin's baby (ee'd learnt the full truth of tha' now from Justin hisself) and tha' babe's small body wuz still lying on his mortuary table. Now, there wuz this body to be examined too, an' 'eaved in the earth. Apparently, the very las' thing the Minter had done wuz to approve the final design of the memorial fur Samuel Skews, so the masons could start work on ut. Ut didn' look like ee'd be there fur the unveiling of tha'. Naw. Instead, ee hisself would be tipped inta' the ground too, and not ever get to be the official wedded husband ov Rosie Koskinen, a fact tha' in the last few seconds ov his life, he prob'ly would have realised. Although the bugger had had a bit of a reputation fur drecklyism and fur piss-poor design before ee got to Mountainside, actually here, ee seemed to have made a good name fur hisself: even though he gained a new an' more dubious reputation with the ladies of the night, and fur likin' a drop ov hard liquor ov an evening. Rosie'd been appalled by un in the beginning, but as you knaw, they'd grawn close and they'd then moved towards each other like scattered mushroom spores.

'Twudn' goin' to be naw fairy-tale romance, thaas fur sure. Still, Rosie had wanted somethun' ov tha' though. She knew their marriage wuz the first official one to be booked at Saffron-Bun Chapel, and now, tha' wuz in tatters. She got dressed and the call went out fur Jewell to come down. Jewell had had enough shocks of late – what with ee learning that this Jago (originally his grandson Richard) wuz still alive, and he near-cursing the very bones of Maddy O'Donahue (his wish wuz to be a Christian, but ee wuz findin' ov ut hard) – and now, there wuz this discovery in Rosie's bedroom.

In walking in, he couldn' help but ingest Rosie's perfume and air-bound powder, and then, got down on his knees to examine the Minter. Ee wudn' down there long and quickly pronounced un dead. There wudn' naw investigation needed, not like the body of the baby tha' had come out of the mine. Jewell enquired about his last minutes. Rosie didn' quite tell Jewell the truth ov wha' had been goin' on. She just said he'd been restin'. Obviously, the sight of Rosie's breasts had got the Minter over-excited and that had pumped the blood a bit too lively through his heart. His heart couldn' take ut and thaas' why he wuz now sprawled out on the floor.

"I warned him," said Doctor Jewell. "You were there when I said it."

"I know," said Rosie. "Ya. I know."

Now Rosie's fust thought here wuz about the Minter's fortune. He'd amassed a goodly amount see, and had a fair size plaace up the top of the town. Well, when he'd got the news off the Doc a while back, he'd already made provision so, well, Rosie would be set fur life. At least tha' ud come out ov ut. But see, when ut got spread about that Minter had passed on, people's minds turned to the notion that ut wudn' that good fur the mine really now, wuz ut? Fur see, despite their deviations and distractions, Skews and the Minter had made themselves instrumental in the running of the plaace. Good assayers wudn' easy to come across, and nor were decent h'engineers. Some duo would be needed to replace that pair, and perhaps 'twuz up t'Cap'n Justin now to put word out that they needed two bloaks with they kinds of skills. Perhaps someone would be interested down in the iron grounds ov Minnesota or Wisconsin, but more likely, they'd try to recruit back home again. Apparently, there'd been a dip in the fortunes of many a mine back home, so maybe there'd be an assayer an' an h'engineer chomping at the bit to utilise their skills over in 'Merky': still the next parish after Land's End.

'Course, the problem, as everyone knawed by now, wuz tha' the boy Justin wudn' in much ov a fit state t'do anything. People didn' knaw all the ins and outs ov ut you, but so ut seemed, his Maddy had gone on an' left un, an' in the meantime, their Jago wuz now t'be looked after by Rebecca Nankervis, but she, well, she'd also headed off somewhere of late, and right now, the boy Jago wuz being looked after by Mr and Mrs George an' Eleanor Jewell. Nothun s'weird as folk, an' thaas allays true. Some men and women hoped that Justin might get a second wind, and carry on as before, whilst others hoped that somehow, Cap'n Frank might come back, and pull the mine out ov the doldrums, fur thaas what ut felt like they were in: without an assayer and without an h'engineer. Still, as yet, ut didn' affect any outcomes. There wuz still enough quality ore being lifted, an' sent on ut's way down to Detroit.

Over the next week, fust, Justin's boy went inta' the earth. There wudn' many there at the funeral. 'Twas a quiet one, but the service inside the chapel wuz lovely. Fitting 'twuz, for the death of a baby, and there wuz some lovely readings from George Jewell, Eleanor Jewell and Cap'n Trevorrow. The latter seemed to be speaking a lot ov truth tha' day. Not much wuz said you, 'bout Maddy O'Donahue. Even the Irish remained quiet, but Flannery and a few other Irish boys shawed their faces. Well, the mite wuz partly one of their kin, wudn' a? The crotchety Reverend Josiah Davies had come up from Calumet and stayed the next few days so that ee could officiate too, when secondly, Dicky Mint's coffin wuz brought in to Saffron-Bun Chapel. There were some good hymns sung tha' day and Dicky's body must have felt the vibration ov all they bass and baritone voices singin' un on into a Heavenly future. Some tall coffin you, well, in order to fit his geht gut in the box.

Justin sat at the back of the chapel and partook of the singing. There wuz the Minter then, all boxed up in the middle of the aisle, and under the posh ceiling rose that had been made in Chicago. Justin doubted that Dicky wanted to be in there this soon. He'd designed the plaace but 'twuz doubtful he'd reckoned on meeting his Maker quite s'soon. Prob'ly he'd wanted a bit more of a feel ov the crevices and gunnies of Rosie Koskinen, an' a few more glasses of high-strength whiskey, but this you, this wuz his fate on Copper Mountain. So inta' the ground he went, an' the dark forest again looked on, as yet another human tumbled inta' peat and earth. Maybe Yolkai wuz right. His funeral wuz bang on time you. Nawthun' dreckly 'bout ut at all.

"Grand," a few ov the boys said, in imitation of the great man hisself. Tha' wuz the way the Cornish did things. They were never afraid to poke fun at one another – even in death. Ut was their way of makin' ut palatable, and they hoped that somewhere on High, the Minter wuz looking down on they, and smiling, still clasping hold ov a set-square and gnawing down on a bun.

Now, all tha' prompted Justin to do two things: the fust wuz to make ee think back to tha' moment when everyone had been all-hands-to-the-pump underground: the day the Knockies foresaw that cave-in. He should have knawn before now that Maddy had been the one who'd been in the second level; she knew the workings of the mine well enough. Perhaps deep in his heart, he didn' need naw confirmation from the Kobolds via the Knockies. Perhaps too, he didn' need the forest telling ov Gourgy, tha' ut had seen Maddy have their baby in the middle of the forest.

He realised he'd actually knawed ut all along, and that just like she'd done, he'd repressed ut. A lot might have altered ef he'd said something before; but you cudn' change the past, could ee? All you could do wuz learn from ut. The other thing that happened wuz tha' as the coffin proceeded past Justin, trailing on behind ut wuz Rosie Koskinen. In Justin's mind, she wuz the one who'd started all this mess. She wuz the one he should never have gone with, and had he had a committed Temperance mind that night back in the Cliff Hotel, then none of what happened would have even occurred. But there she wuz now, and instead of lookin' at Rosie, Justin kept his eyes forward facing. She wuz wearing a black veil ov course, but even behind tha', he could see she givin' un a good gake up an' down.

Before these funerals took place, Justin had, of course, gone up to see George an' Eleanor, fur 'twuz now they who were lookin' after Jago. He knawed by then wha' Rebecca wuz on upon, an' he realised the necessity of her doin' it. She'd planned ut, and he turning up with Jago wudn' zactly wha' she wuz looking fur. He understood fully her need to locate Francis. Ut would be up to him to inform the Jewells ov precisely wha' went on and how Maddy had deceived the Doctor: how in fact, she'd deceived all ov they. And es, boath George an' Eleanor were incredulous as to how they'd missed ut. Justin's response publically wuz tha' Maddy had been very good at deceit and that she wuz a liar beyond all liars, but even then, he felt his awn guilt. He felt like he should have seen ut comin' sooner; that she'd made un take his guard down.

There wuz probably more he could have said about the changeling – an' about how she'd manufactured the Pooka – but none of tha' would have done any good.

Ee didn' say she wuz a witch. 'Mean, they pair wuz obsessed enough with the Lord God above and the redemption offered to the world by Jesus Christ: there'd be too much chatter about forming something evil in the Deads. Jewell wuz reluctant to see the magic in ut though. His brain didn' work like tha' see. Every time Justin seen they, they managed to extract some further information from un, and zactly what happened at different stages, and after extracting this knowledge, they'd boath go back up the chapel to pray, taking liddle Jago along with um. Divinity, so ut seemed, would protect they from such a fate ever happening again.

Now Justin had seened Jago – an' at times, ee even thought he recognised un – but fur now, 'twuz perhaps best he kept his distance. After all that had happened, maybe the boy should be with his awn side of the family. Maybe when Rebecca returned (perhaps with Francis in tow) 'twould be better. Ut broke his heart though, not to see un all the time. An' in such moments, his sympathy fur his Maddy comed back to un in waves. The awnly thing wuz, she wuz naw longer *his* Maddy. *His* Maddy had gone on a long time ago. Now boath of they wuz destined to be alone, and ut didn't feel very good, did ut?

Luk and Gourgy tried in vain to cheer un up, but they knawed full well that nothun' on earth could do ut. He'd just have to plod on. That ee did you; awnly when ee went chapel, he prayed harder, thought more, and weighed up the wider pattern of good and evil. He thought not awnly ov sin on the mountain, but also too, ov that old sin of his back in Penzance: so long ago now, that ut seemed ut had happened not to him, but to another person. So ut seemed, awnly the chapel could give un comfort these days, and in tha', he realised why Doctor Jewell had pushed hard fur ut. In times like these, you needed ut. Ut served up boath feyth and hope.

Now, any thought of Saffron-Bun Chapel wuz a long way away in the mind of Rebecca Nankervis as she rode the laker back across Lake Superior and down through Huron towards Detroit. She kept herself to herself, in her cabin, only going out a few times a day on the deck to take in some air. Anything else she needed wuz brought to her by Tommy Carkeek. She didn't see who else wuz travelling on tha' vessel: not least because Maddy had opted fur a cheaper fare that saw she in steerage, the same way tha' Justin and Francis Nankervis once made ut up through the Lake System. An' Maddy, well, she kept herself to herself too, and resorted to being hard and mean again to anyone who spoke t'she. She liked ut tha' way. Then there'd be no hassle off other men, who might want a piece ov she. Right there and then, she'd had enough ov they fur a lifetime. She didn't need naw more. 'Course, neither had any notion that the other wuz on the same vessel, but thaas how 'tis sometimes. Life d'fling ee apart, but ut d'also push ee together. In fact, boath of they wuz tryin' t'erase the memory of each other. 'Twuz hard though, especially when they boath thought 'bout Jago's liddle smiling faace.

Maddy's business wuz to plan and forget. Rebecca's business wuz to plan and remember. The boy Tommy had been a bit vague about where the money came from each fortnight, but ut matched exactly the movement of the laker up and down the lakes. He'd already told her tha' the captain of the ship wuz the man who she needed to talk to, and on the first couple of days of her route down, she tried to engage him in conversation. Ut didn't go well though. Fust off, she wuz told by a deckhand not to be up near the wheel-house, and then, when she initially attempted to have a word with un, he considered her just a fussing middle-class women, who should return to her cabin and stay down there fur the duration of the journey. Any problems she had might be sorted out by his First Officer, and not him. He had enough to do, bringing the copper ore down through the System and could not be bothered by females like she.

The awnly way forward wuz to utilise Tommy Carkeek. Apparently, his father had comed over from a ship-building family in Fowey an' had based hisself at Port Huron. If the boy wuz to make ut in the world, then ee needed experience, an' thaas wha' ee wuz gettin' on this particular laker. She wrote the Captain a note and paid Tommy to take ut to un. She explained in the note that she was the wife ov Francis Nankervis and that she needed to speak to un about the whereabouts of her husband. If ee didn' tell her, she threatened to call the Police in Detroit, for them to make enquiries.

'Twas a brave move on her part, an' it might backfire. He might be the one who would come to report she; but fortunately, just as they got through the gap of St Mary's River, there wuz a knock on the door of the cabin. She opened ut to find the Captain standing there. There wuz no greeting.

"You Rebecca Nankervis?" he asked her, straight to the point.

Working the lakes had made un tha' way.

"Yes."

"The boy gived me your note. Police, eh?"

"Well, if need be."

The Captain thought fur a while, then began his own investigation ov she.

"How do I knaw you'm Frank's wife?"

"Tommy's been bringing me the money and the other money for the chapel has gone to my father, Doctor George Jewell."

"Well, Frank dun't want to be found. He made me swear not to tell anyone his whereabouts."

"But he's clearly in Detroit..."

The Captain said nothing.

"Tommy said so."

"I told the boy to say nothing. The instructions were clear. Just give you the money – well, you and the Doctor. Nothing else..."

"But you've seen him? You must meet him every fortnight..."

"I cen't say. Maybe he dun't want to see you again. Maybe he've had enough ov ee. I d'get paid well fur wha' I do... I dun't want nothun' to mess tha' up, not for me see, or the boy..."

"What's he paying you?" asked Rebecca.

"Enough."

"I'll double it. I'll double all the money you've been paid so far... if you tell me where I can find him."

"You'n do all you like," the Captain said truculently. "Me and he go back a bit. I wun't be betrayin' un."

"You have too," said Rebecca now in desperation. "I dun't knaw what he's said to you... but he've got a baby boy waiting for un back on the Keweenaw."

"He told me he'd been accused of killing a boy... and tha' he needed to leave."

"That's true, but ut wasn't what he thought ... We know the truth now. He's innocent. He has to come back."

"An' what ef ee dun't want to?"

Rebecca hated the Captain. The way he said that sounded like he had found another woman.

"Is he with someone else then?" she enquired, suddenly a little green with jealousy.

"Not that I knaw ov. As you know, he's doing alright fur himself..."

"I'm begging you," said Rebecca. "Just give me an area. An address. Where he works..."

The Captain gaked at she good an' proper. He wuz trying to work all ov this out, an' what he'd stupidly committed to. Frank had told un there wudn' be naw problem but here wuz one, staring ov un in the faace.

"You'm Cornish, ent ee?" the Captain asked.

"Yes."

"Well, you knaw we Cornish then. Once we d'make a promise, we stick to ut. We ent fly-by-nights like some. By rights, I dun't have to tell you nawthun' maid."

She knew he wuz right. She knawed all Cussies were tight. A promise wuz a promise. Deep down, this Captain wuz a good man: a just man. But then again, he could see her desperation. He knawed she wuz his wife: the wife of the man he'd made a deal with. She wuz wishing she'd brought Justin with her. She'd been fool-hardy to come on her own. How did she expect leverage? Her brother-in-law would have added weight to her case. She backed off. She knew that any more pleading would likely result in him sticking to his guns even more.

"It wun't stop me," said Rebecca. "I'll search every street if I need to."

"Detroit's a big city," said the Captain. "Rough too."

Maybe this would steer him right. Maybe he'd think about her and what she might face. The Captain eased hisself back into the corridor.

"We've a few days journeying ahead on Huron. I need to contemplate what you've said. Let me think on ut."

Rebecca thanked him. She shut the door and moved to her bed. She knelt and prayed to God that he would change his mind. In her imagination, she wuz back at Saffron-Bun Chapel, praying fur His help. Every hour, for the next few days, she kept up this petitioning, hoping this Captain would change his mind. She hoped that a bright of run of copper ore would run up the Divine and dazzle Him into action. Mad eh, but tha' wuz the way it wuz with the Cornish and their prayer. She knew that ef God didn't answer her prayers then long-term, ut would make she as mazed as her mawthur. Tha' wuz the fear that drove her.

So, down this pair went then – this pair of women who'd known the very soul of existence on Copper Mountain – who now should be bitter, bitter enemies. Es. The Easter weather wuz good to boath of they, an' the waters of Huron were calm. Awnly when they got down to the bottom of Huron did the lake become so contained again, that you could see the shore of the lower peninsula ov Michigan and the coast of Ontario. There, they'd have the run down the St Clair River and into the harbour at Detroit. Some close now they wuz: one to finding her husband, the other to finding her way home. Being on a ship tha' long, 'course, you get to knaw all that are sailing upon her, and 'twuz down there on the lower half ov the Huron, tha' the vessel revealed ut's secret.

Neither of they rightly knawed how ut happened, but they stumbled upon each other. One minute, they'd been watching the shoreline on the starboard side and the next minute, there wuz a look of recognition. Rebecca recognised Maddy's hood, and the jewellery she wore: that predominant necklace of shells. On her feet, her decorated boots. Maddy noted Rebecca's pristine school-ma'am look, the slight wisps of grey now at her temples. She saw the starched white Methodism of her. First, came the nomenclature of old. Sisters again.

"Maddy? That you?"

"Becca!"

Then, came the surprise fur Rebecca at least, that they'd both ended up on this vessel. Maddy knawed different.

"I didn't see you get on," said Becca.

"You weren't meant to," responded Maddy. "I saw you, with the boy... down the tramway... I came down the old path through the forest."

A pause.

"I know," said Rebecca, her tone serious. "I know what happened..."

"I should go," said Maddy, turning away. "I know exactly what you must think of me."

"No," said Rebecca. "Don't go."

Maddy turned back.

"You sure?"

"Let's talk."

"Alright then... if you insist... Not sure I got the answers you want."

"Please."

Rebecca penetrated Maddy's eyes in a way she didn' like. 'Twuz almost like she wuz trying to see into her soul. If tha' persisted, she'd go anyway. Fook her and fook the lot of them back on Mountainside. But then, she re-thought. Perhaps there was hope here.

"Back with you then, is he?"

"With my father and Eleanor..."

"I see."

"Bet your father, the Doctor, hasn't a good word for me right now?"

But Rebecca did not answer.

Instead, she said. "My finger's healed now."

She held up her forefinger for Maddy to observe.

"See, look..."

"Sorry about tha'. I didn't knaw the thing would be s'powerful. Tha', I didn' plan for..."

"It doesn't matter."

Both were afraid to speak, but again, it was Rebecca who broke the silence.

"You leaving then? Forever, I mean."

"I've no choice. I know what I did... Me an' Justin. We're over. We're done. We weren't right. We weren't part of the pattern... the right pattern. We had a fight see. A massive one."

She showed Rebecca her shiner.

"Sorry to hear that."

"He's better off without me..."

"Don't say that..."

"It's true. He will be."

There wuz another pause. They could feel the vibration of the laker's engine. At the rear of the ship, there wuz the constant noise of churning water.

"He loved you. I know that."

"You think so?" asked Maddy. "Not much now... not after he found out about what I'd done."

"I don't think it was the swap Maddy. I think ut was your baby. His baby. The one you hid in the mine..."

"Aye. Maybe so..."

More thought.

More recollection.

More of the future too.

"Where are you making for?"

Maddy told her. Rebecca was shocked that all this had transpired.

"Back to where I'm from. Back to where the magic began... Not good, eh? Not really. I swore that I'd never go back."

"Well, we boath know the magic of the world. We know Pookas and Knockies, and we know the magic of the forest up there."

"Ut won't ever let up," said Maddy.

"How do you mean?"

"You know. The forest might have been pushed back fur now... but it'll come back... stronger and fuller, when Mountainside's nothing more than a memory... when the mine eventually gets abandoned."

"I dare say..."

That pause again. The almost unbearable unspoken; the knowingness of women.

"We boath helped shape tha' place..."

"... and we both fell in love with two eejits..." she laughed.

For minutes, nothing. Only them and the lake. Only them and God. Them and the chapel.

"I knaw why you did it," said Rebecca looking out over the expanse of water.

"How come?"

"I've felt it myself. I was feeling it lately. That craving. That awful desire that you can't control. That need for a child. You lost – and I lost, and when that happens, something inside of you ignites. It's a fuse you can't control. You know that Maddy. You've felt it – and I've felt it. I mean, when Francis left, and then I had to go back to school-teaching, ut was an itch I couldn't scratch. You think of any way, don't you? Any reason. Any path. I know I did. I understand what you did. I understand why you had to do it."

"Can you ever forgive me then?" asked Maddy, embarrassedly looking down at her feet.

Rebecca turned to face this woman: this woman who had made her life a Hell, but had somehow given her a new connection to the Divine in everything. Maddy stayed stock-still and Rebecca touched her face: her cheeks, her forehead and her lips. These were those very lips that had deceived her and so many others.

"I can Maddy. Of course, I can."

"Thank you," said Maddy. "I never meant..."

"I know."

And tha' wuz the last time Rebecca ever saw tha' Maddy O'Donahue. She walked away from her – and didn' look back, not once. She wuz now absolved. 'Twas as if she oozed down through the cracks in the decking, disappeared into the steam coming out of the funnel. However, Rebecca had been glad ov that conversation. Aw, you could keep something bitter tight in your heart, but 'twud awnly ever eat at ee. You had t'let ut go, and by doing tha', she felt she'd given Maddy back her freedom. Chapel see, had taught her tha'.

They'd be in Detroit by the early morning. There'd still be nothing from the Captain, she conceded. She again said her prayers before she went to bed that night: wishing for providence in finding her husband, but so too, praying for Maddy's safe return to the Beara. They were more alike than she'd thought.

When daylight streamed through the porthole of her cabin, she observed a small note had been pushed under her door. Hand-written on it was the number and the name of a street. God had done His work. The copper rod had conducted His energy through the Captain and now to her. She had a lead, and that wuz all that she needed. Perhaps too, prayers back at Saffron-Bun Chapel had worked.

The boy Tommy seemed sad to see her go.

"You coming back Lady?" he asked dolefully.

"Hopefully," Rebecca replied.

"What shall I do with the money if there's any more ov ut?"

"Well, keep it," said Rebecca, "but I have a hope that there won't be any more..."

The boy pulled a face, because he knew his income would drop.

"Don't worry," said Rebecca, "We'll see you right on our return."

Our return?

She wuz confident then, ov bringing back her husband.

"How long?"

"A few days maybe... but perhaps we'll be ready to sail when you're back down here. I'm sure our paths will cross again."

Already, geht cranes with buckets were scooping the copper ore from Mountainside out of the vast hold of the laker she'd travelled down on. Time wuz money. Once coal had been loaded in, the vessel would make ut's way up the Lake System again. A few moments later, and Rebecca wuz down the gangplank, and found herself on the grand structure of the foremost Detroit jetty. She looked back, but there wudn' naw sign of Maddy's departure. Perhaps tha' wuz best. Purposeful even. That final split of the two changeling mams.

Rebecca went one way, taking, for this first time in her life, one of they new automobiles all the way to the address she'd been given: 450 Amsterdam Street, and when Maddy eventually stanked down the gangplank, she went the other way. Her intricately painted boots were taking her back to where they'd been made. So far apart these women were about to become, and yet, not long ago, they had been tightly bonded by two babies: two babies that had altered everything: two swaps (good for bad, and then bad for good), two changelings who had defined them.

Ah, the blessed relief ov ut Maddy thought, as she went on her way to the steamer office. There, she wuz goin' to book a ticket (with the crisp money ov Skews tha' Trevorrow had given she) to travel down the Detroit River to Lake Erie. At the northern end of Erie, she'd make for shore at Buffalo and then head by railroad across to New York. From that vast port, she'd take a liner back to Ireland and eventually, arrive at her Allihies. All seemed clear. All seemed well, but then the damndest thing...

She went to a newly-built public convenience and checked. She had rags ready. 'Twuz time fur her monthly bleed, but ut had been a few days now, and ut wudn' happening, wuz ut? A laden womb again? No. Could it be? 'Mean, could it really be?

That fooker God, ee truly did work in mysterious ways.

48

Some gallivanting and gabbling there wuz to be had in Detroit. Es. Despite having an address, looking for Francis still felt somewhat like she wuz looking for a tiny needle in a geht haystack.

"Where's a to?"

Ut made Becca poor-tempered. She barely remembered the city from when she'd passed through here a few years ago. It hadn't left an indelible impression on her because the Jewell family had stayed only one night at a hotel near the harbour. She remembered that her mother didn' care fur it much, but then, she hadn' liked the Cliff Hotel either. Tha' wuz she see.

Now though, the city about Rebecca was going places: it had become the main manufacturing hub for the Mid-West, and everyone she saw, seemed to be working towards some new way of earning a buck or two. The sprawl ov the city reminded her of just how small her life was back on the Keweenaw, and whilst this urban experience thrilled her, actually, she longed even now, to be back up there. She knew too, that out there in the midst of everything, was some of that copper that her community had mined. It was being used right now for something important. It had been raised up from the earth, and then sent (like she and Tommy) down the wagons of the tramway to Eagle Harbour.

Modernity commanded everything in the city. Whilst Mountainside still had remnants of the old century about ut – in its way of doing things (perhaps even in its adherence to the old creed of Wesleyanism) – here, all seemed new. She imagined Francis within it. She thought of him here: hopefully, in her mind at least, him thinking about her. She knew he'd still be reeling from what people had said of him backalong, that they called him a 'baby-killer': that he couldn' take the guilt of what he'd done, and that he'd wrecked what they had together. She told herself that she would reassure him. She'd tell him the truth and communicate that he was very much wanted. Now the full story wuz known, it wuz, in fact, he who wuz the victim. He had nothing to feel guilty about. He had acted to protect her. She looked at her forefinger again. Yes, it was now all healed. She hoped that she could now heal him. Maddy had told her that she hoped she could find him. She hoped too, that Rebecca and Francis could repair what they had.

Detroit's streets these days were an admixture of mainly horse and carts or carriages, and some automobiles of the kind that she was currently riding in. She'd never been in one before, and its speed and solidity much impressed her. So this wuz what people now had in Calumet too? She felt moneyed as she rode through the streets, with the novelty of the vehicle enough for her to gain admiring glances from those still walking the sidewalks.

"Now lady, you know where you're going right?" asked her driver.

"Well, not entirely..."

"You sure about that address you handed me?"

"Yes. Very sure. You know it?"

"'Course I do ma'am. Everyone in Detroit knows that address."

"Why?"

"That there place lies on the intersection of Cass Avenue and Amsterdam Street. It's just tha' I don't carry many ladies of your kind down tha' way. That's why I asked about the address."

"Is it rough then?"

"No Lady. It ain't rough. That location is the hub of Detroit these days. But it's a kind of... male-dominated place."

"Oh don't worry. I come from a male-dominated place. I come from a mining community up north..."

"What – on the Upper Peninsula?"

"That's right. On the Keweenaw. Copper."

"The Keweenaw, eh? Now say, that accent of yours... You are one of those Cousin Jennies, aren't you?"

"Yes, I'm Cornish."

"Plenty of them here in Detroit these days... Heading to Wisconsin for the iron mines... And boy, does Detroit need iron and copper."

All of this seemed to be giving Rebecca clues as to what Francis wuz involved in.

"See that address you gave me. Plenty of iron and copper taken there..."

"Why's that then?"

"Lady, that's the home of the Cadillac Motor Company. It produces the ten horsepower Cadillac, the automobile you're riding in right now. Same really as the Ford Model A, only it's got a Leland and Faulconer engine in it. In my view, much better than Ford's design. See, well, a year ago now Henry Ford had a dispute with his bankers and he moved on. Leland see, carried on making the same design but put a new engine in. You look around. Most of the cars here right now are Caddys. Ford's finished, I reckon."

This was more than enough information for Rebecca. In some way then, Francis had got to Detroit, and then applied himself in the automobile industry. With the quantity of these vehicles expanding daily on the streets of Detroit, perhaps there wuz understanding on her behalf now, as to why he'd been able to send money to her, and for both the founding and erection of Saffron-Bun Chapel.

"You know a man named Francis Nankervis?" she asked the driver.

"No ma'am. Can't say I do..."

"He's my husband. He... ah... came down here to work."

The cabby thought for a while.

"Well, ef he knows metals like copper and iron, he'll be in demand. All you Jackies know that kind of stuff, don't you? Look up there see. That's the plant ahead ov us."

Rebecca saw a vast building in front of her, part of ut five stories high, and on its roof were two massive, conical-topped water towers painted with the word 'Cadillac' on them. At the rear, several chimleys heaved black smoke into the atmosphere above Detroit. Already, she noted a revolving door and a bustle of men were going in and out. Everywhere around the plant, moved humanity. The man wuz right. This wuz the very centrepoint of Detroit. Ut wuz this that was putting it on the map. Maybe ut made men money, but she didn' care much for the look of ut. It reminded her ov some kind of Hell. When the mine engine at home wuz goin' full pelt, like everyone else, she felt the earth shake and ut vomited smoke into the air high above Lake Superior, but that wuz nothing compared to this. This wuz industrial activity on an epic scale, and in that, momentarily, she saw the future. She couldn' help but gasp at the immensity of it.

"Amazing, huh? Most folks have never seen anything like it. 275000 feet of automobile production line. That place has got multiple forges, several machine shops, a textile department and two foundries; one for iron and one for brass."

Now she understood the growing need for copper and iron. This place would have eaten through it. She knew what that meant. It meant more places like Mountainside. It meant less forest. It meant a decline in the natural environment; all fur this intense demand. She also realised that if she were to find Francis, then maybe he'd have something to do with the manufacture of brass. 'Mean, she only had to look around her on the automobile: all the fittings were of brass. Brass alloys allays needed copper. But then, she also knew that copper would be needed in new electrics, and her driver seemed fond of they. She could see ut coming, where thousands of miles of copper wire would be needed for such vehicles, and here wuz her Frank, in it right at the start. This further explained the good money he was making.

"What do you think?" the cabby asked.

"It's vast."

"Only going to grow I believe. The invention of the internal combustion engine is going to change the world ma'am. Fifty years from now, and everyone in the world will have one. If your husband's in that, then he's definitely in the right business."

She couldn't respond. All the while she'd known Francis, he'd not been in the automobile business; he'd been in mining. Maybe this wuz the result of things. Maybe he now had everything he needed: some posh apartment on the river and some new lady-friend. Why on earth would he want to come back up to the primitive north with she when he had all of this? Then perhaps, if she found un, he'd want her and Jago to move down here, but to she, this was no place for childurn.

Perhaps then, the Pooka wudn' be the thing that drove them apart, but in fact, 'twould be this plaace right in front ov her. She felt palpitations at the thought ov ut. She didn' want to grow old with him here. This wuz no place to raise a child. She wanted the Keweenaw's simplicity and its connection to nature. But so too, did she know the paradox. She knew that such development was what the Cornish wanted. It wuz such use of metals that had set up hard-rock mining for centuries. And now, they were mining the materials that built automobiles. That seemed a new zenith of achievement. She braced herself for the task. She realised tha' her husband wuz no longer an adventurer in copper, but wuz now an adventurer in automobiles: all this, within a comparatively short matter of time.

"You know where your husband is based?"

"No. No idea. Sorry..."

"No apology needed Lady. I'll just drop you at reception there. If you head in there, they'll be able to tell you..."

The cabby halted outside of the Cadillac building, and she paid him the fare. A quarter apparently for the ride over from the harbour but she tipped him a dime extra. for the conversation.

"Thanks," he said. "I appreciate that. You take care now."

Rebecca found herself standing in front of the edifice. He was right. This was a male world. Men seemed to move everywhere, either finishing one shift or starting another. Apparently, the plant ran twenty-four hours, producing forty new Cadillac vehicles a day. For a while, she stood in the street, not quite knowing what to do. Because there wuz such a high density of men there, oftentimes, as she turned, she accidentally bumped into those emerging from or entering the building. Like a fool, she kept saying sorry to them, but most ov they weren't bothered. They were used to the rough and tumble of life here in the city.

"Where wuz a?" she asked herself.

She thought back to when she'd first seen Francis that morning in the old Cliff Hotel. That now seemed an awfully long time ago. So much water had passed under so many bridges. She considered too, the possibility that he'd not much thank her for turning up at his work unexpected. Back on the Keweenaw, ut had never been a problem, but here? Well, here, ut was different.

Yet she realised in those few moments, that she had no choice. Him being somewhere in this complex wuz all that she had to go on. She delved deep and pressed onwards through the main revolving door of the building: itself made of polished brass and thick glass, stencilled with the plant's name. Inside the building, ut smelt of oil and male sweat. She knew what it would be like inside here in one of those oppressive mid-continental summers. She saw her husband standing here, his armpits drenched in sweat, and the whorls on the skin of his fingertips lagged in grease. This wuz the smell of the future then.

"Can I help you?" a man behind a desk asked her.

He'd seen her spinning, and recognised from her clothes that she was from out of town. She looked old-style religious to him, wearing the fashion of a decade ago. She hadn't heard him though.

"Ma'am, may I help you?"

He tried again, and this time, Rebecca realised he was talking to her.

"Sorry," she said. "I've just got into town. What a place this is!"

"Certainly is. Home of the Cadillac Empire."

He paused for a moment to watch her.

"You looking for someone?"

"Yes. I've travelled a long way. I'm seeking my husband. I believe he works here."

"You got a name for him?" the man asked.

"Yes. Francis Nankervis."

"Francis Nan-ker-vis?" he checked.

"That's it. That's right."

"Lotta' men work here," the man said. "You know which department?"

"No. Sorry I don't."

"I'll have to check down through some lists. Excuse me for a moment."

The man behind the desk pulled out two vast books from a low-set cupboard which seemingly, held lists of the names of everyone employed there.

"Now, would he be contracted or hourly?"

"Contracted, I think."

She didn't know. But she guessed that given the money coming back to her, he'd not be on an hourly rate.

The desk man put down one book and levered the other one open. She saw him go for somewhere in the middle of the book. He ran his finger down through the list.

"Got a lot of names here," he said. "But I don't see no Nankervis."

"Can you look again?"

"Look yourself. Here's everyone under the N category."

He turned the book so she could see. She gazed at the names under the letter N. The man wuz right. His name wasn't there. She panicked at this. Had he changed his name perhaps? How could she possibly track him down ef he'd done that? Maybe the laker Captain had been right. Perhaps he really did not want to be found.

"Can you look in the hourly book, just to check?"

The man gave a sigh.

"Sure," he said.

He repeated the same process as before but shook his head. He handed her the book, so that she could see he was right.

"Nothing there. Sorry ma'am. You *sure* he works here?"

"I was told that he did..."

"Ma'am, it ain't really my place to say but you've seen the company's lists of employees. You need to check your source."

"I know," said Rebecca distractedly. "I will."

Baffled, she moved away from the desk and the man gave her a comforting smile to try and help offset the news that he'd given her. He realised that she'd travelled a long way and the disappointment on her face and in her whole body was very visible. Deep inside the factory, she could hear the sound of riveting and welding, the knocks of hammers and chisels, the occasional shout and laughter. All that seemed to now poke fun at her. It laughed at her naïvety. How on earth did she think that an address was enough? She'd been utterly duped. Maybe ut was time for her to get back into the less industrialised part of the city and seek out accommodation. She'd begun to realise that a woman like her travelling alone wuz no way of carrying on in somewhere like Detroit. Maddy had warned her. She even now understood why Maddy had developed that hard, outer shell. It protected her from the kind of disappointment that presumably the Irish woman had experienced a few times in her life. She saw the sense in it.

And then, if she cudn' find un, there'd be that long, lonely haul back up through the lakes, and then, they up there, disappointed that she'd not tracked un down, and failed to bring the father back to the son; that she'd failed to reunite two brothers, that she'd failed Gourgy, and so too, even more desperately, herself. The awnly thing she could really do wuz to pray. Beyond the desk was a bench where some of those at the plant congregated. Her clear desire was to sit. Nawbody wanted to engage she in conversation. She knawed she looked weird t'they, but her presence soon moved the men on, and she was able to rest. Here then, she'd pray to God once more, and ask for the Lord to give her direction. She tried to evoke all the energy ov Saffron-Bun Chapel. Es, 'twuz a long way away, but she imagined it right in front ov she. She imagined the smell of ut, the pride of her father at its forthcoming opening ceremony, and the joyous hymns sung. Even then, she thought of the geht revel buns being brought out. She imagined a time when her Jago and other childurn of Mountainside would run freely, and that their shouts, whines and yelps would act as a bright chorus for the world.

But she knew that what she'd have to do here might just go beyond normal prayer. Es, ut would have to call on the Divine in everything, in the natural world, but also this new world of smoak, grease, dirt and sidewalks. She didn't care who wuz watching or those who considered her prayer strange or bizarre. Matter like tha' wuz just fur out in the sticks, wudn' ut? Not fur the here an' now in modern Detroit. Throughout her life, nothing like this fazed she. She hadn't been fazed when on that night, the Pooka was loudly bashing their crockery with a spoon, and she hadn't been phased either when the thing had bitten she. She cudn' be phased here now either. She would not let ut happen. She'd learnt see. After talking to Maddy, she realised that you have to follow your heart. If you need to conjure something, then do ut. If you need to make it from nothing, then do it. There is no point in wasting time, or of thinking you cannot do ut. All humans have the power to do ut. Believe in magic then. Es. Believe. There wuz nothun' more she could do beyond tha'. Maybe, even now, in some distant plaace, Maddy'd be proud of she.

She stayed on the seat all morning. Maybe prayer to God and maybe prayer to all other things were just the same? Maybe in that moment, conjuring and prayer were identical. There were the Deads es, an' then there wuz Saffron-Bun Chapel, and although they wuz apart, they wuz all part of the same pattern. She realised tha' when she'd spoken to Maddy that echoed right in the here and now, in the lobby of the Cadillac Plant. Es, you'n make judgements and write labels, but at the end of the day, 'twuz all the same. 'Merky' proved that. A melting pot ut wuz: zactly the same as she wuz doing now in her own mind's melting pot. All those gods ov Nimkii were the same thing, just given a different name. How could one be right, above another? The answer wuz that they couldn't be. What all this had taught she wuz that all ov ut wuz the same: the inherent hope and feyth of humanity and respect for the natural world. This wudn' naw new epiphany fur Rebecca Nankervis. Aw naw. All that had happened wuz that her time spent there tha' morning had crystallised it for her.

Above the bench wuz a small, somewhat indistinct plaque. She ignored ut fust ov all. Now, ut spoke to her. The conjuring had worked. The prayer had worked. She glanced at ut briefly, but then, as she read down, she noted a name. It was not just any name. Ut wuz her name. And the plaque wudn' there fur fun either. Naw, the plaque listed the current directors of the Cadillac Motor Company, and at the bottom of the list, below the names William Murphy, Lemuel Bowen, Henry Leland, Robert Faulconer, was her husband's: Francis Nankervis. Now, she understood. Now, she realised why his name had not been on the list of employees. No wonder the man at the desk had been unable to find his name. She rushed over to him once more.

"My husband Francis, he's one of the directors... Look, his name's there on the plaque. See."

"Aw. You mean Frank then?"

"Yes."

"You didn' say he wuz no director. You said employee... I didn't even think you meant Mr Nankervis. I should have worked that out for you, shouldn't I?"

"Sorry. My fault. I mean, I didn't know he was a director."

"Oh well, Mr Nankervis has revolutionised things here for Cadillac. I don't know where we'd be without un..."

"Why? What did he do?"

"Don't you know?"

"No."

"You and he ain't much married then..."

"We've been apart for a while."

"I see. A good while then..."

"See, Frank revolutionised the way we made brass. Made ut harder and firmer but more durable. For the instruments on the car see. He d'knaw alloys like naw other. Mining see. Brought some experience with un. A 'Cap'n of the Mines' once, they do say."

"That's right. That's him."

"And now see, well, he be looking at copper. Very soon, Cadillac will have electrics on board their cars. Copper wire all over the shop. Even Henry Ford hasn't got that far. He's the man, your Frank. He'll keep we ahead..."

She'd been right about him. Rebecca considered what she knew about her husband. A long time ago, before he'd come out to the Keweenaw, apparently he'd taken up an apprenticeship in Metallurgy. He knew the properties of minerals. He knew how they could work together. An' he wudn' no fool. He had that time at night-school in Camborne School of Mines too. He wudn' just a Jacker underground. Ultimately, she knew all that, but she'd forgotten ut. Her husband had a scientific brain, and somehow, he'd put ut to good use down here in a relatively short space of time.

"I need to see him," Rebecca pleaded.

"I can see that. Who shall I say is here for him?"

"His wife. Mrs Rebecca Nankervis."

"I'll phone up for him. His office is on the fifth floor."

On the desk was a new telephone device. They had everything down here in Detroit. He wound the handle and then picked up the receiver. Then, he dialled in a number. Eventually, someone picked up the other end.

"Reception here. Message for Mr Nankervis. Someone to see him at the front desk. A lady by the name of Mrs Rebecca Nankervis. His wife. "

A voice came back at him, which she could awnly just hear.

"Alright. Ideal. She'll be waiting for him down here."

He put the phone down.

"They'll tell un. He'll be down shortly."

"Thank you."

"I'm just glad we found him for you," said the man.

"Me too," responded Becca, but in her mind, maybe they hadn't found un at all. In fact, ut wuz she who'd conjured un. Maybe out of thin air. Maybe out of the Deads. She'd go tha' far if she needed to. She'd been pushed to the limit here.

There was an interminable wait. Probably, in real time it was no more than five minutes, but to Rebecca, ut felt longer: perhaps almost half-an-hour. She wuz dreaming of running towards him, and he catching her, spinning her around like some scene from a melodrama down at the Calumet theatre. Ut wudn' quite as she expected though. How could it be? He hadn' wanted to be found, and she'd managed to track him down. She adjusted her expectations and she was right to.

The Francis who entered the lobby wuz transformed. He'd changed markedly. He'd grown a moustache which gave him a stately air, and his former Cap'n's clothing had seemingly been abandoned. Now, he wore a fashionable Detroit-style suit. His hair had altered. Greyer yes, but now with a centre-parting, and patted down with oil. He wore an aftershave too; something he had never done before. When he first saw her, he wuz incredulous that she wuz even standing before him. He could barely speak and only just managed to stutter a few words to her. There wuz no great hug or spin around the lobby.

"Becca," he managed to say, but the way he said her name sounded different. "You're here. How... how... did you find me?"

"The money you sent up. I traced it. Talked to the Captain. Made my way down here."

"Nathaniel?"

"Is tha' his name?"

"Yes. The Captain on the laker, right?"

"Thaas him..."

"I go back with him a long way. He brought Jus and I up all that time ago. A good man. I knew I could trust him to get the money to you... and your father."

"We got ut. We got all of ut."

But Francis looked angry.

"Confound the man! He gave me his word," he blustered, turning from her.

Frank's accent had altered. Maybe 'twuz put on. Maybe here he needed to speak proper.

"I know. He was a hard nut to break Frank. But I did it. He gave me this address but nothing else. I thought you worked here. I didn' realise that you were a director... How come? What happened?"

"I'll fill you in," said Francis, glancing around him. "But not here. Come on. There's a café a little way down Cass Avenue. Let's go there. Ha – they do pasties. Are you hungry?"

She was. A pasty would go down very well. She watched him as he walked. He had the same mannerism of gait, but she couldn't believe his clothes and hair. And there she wuz, looking nawthun' special.

"You met anyone else?" she asked. She had to get that out.

"No," he said. "My love for you has been constant."

Some comfort fur she at last.

"How's the mine?" he asked, switching the subject. "Seems to be goin' on good. Still plenty comin' down. We use it all here now. Cen't get enough of it. I mean, I should contact Skews, shouldn't I?"

Rebecca shook her head.

"I don't think so."

"Why not? What happened?"

"He met with an accident. He's buried in the ground now."

"Where?"

"On the tramway..."

Francis said, "All the while he wanted tha' bleddy thing, an' look wha' happened to un. But then, you knaw how I felt about un..."

"Me too. Good riddance I say."

She informed him of the grim details.

"So who's assaying now then?"

"No one... Trevorrow's putting a turn in, but he's naw expert as you knaw..."

"And brother?"

"Well, that's why I'm here. There's so much to tell you. It's why I came to find you..."

Francis barely heard that. Instead, he sought other news.

"You got all the monies then?"

"Yes. I saved them."

"What for?"

"For a rainy day. I haven't really needed to spend much, apart from my trip down here."

"But what about your father? Did he get the money for the chapel? That wuz so important to me."

"Yes. It's all built. Your name's on the foundation stone."

"What? Finished?"

"Yes. It's gorgeous. They've gived ut a funny name... I think you'll like ut somehow."

"What then?"

"Saffron-Bun Chapel."

He laughed.

"Really?"

"Yes... Good name isn't ut?"

"The right name, yes... I can see that. I'm glad it's built. That eases my conscience."

By now, they'd reached the café. He opened the door for her to step inside, and soon they were seated.

"What'll you have?"

"You know what I'll have..."

When the waitress came over, Francis ordered two pasties and a pot of tay. This wuz all froth though, compared to wha' they really needed to talk about.

"I hear you're doing well. They tell me you're quite the inventor now."

"Not really," said Francis. "I got lucky, like we all do sometimes. When I arrived, I didn' know what I wuz going to do, but when I saw in the newspaper tha' Cadillac needed a metallurgist I put my name forward. I mean, you know I've got experience of smelting. If brother wudn' such an idiot, I'd still be doing that back home, but there 'tis."

"You've done well though, and so quickly..."

"I dun't like to drag my heels. See, when Ford left, this crowd didn' knaw their ass from their elbow, but I helped sort um out a bit. Our brass is the best goin' see and now, the amazing thing is that we've a team of people developing electrics in cars... All through copper wire. Copper see. That'll be the driving force of the automobile industry over the next few years..."

"I heard," said Becca. "I was put right by my cabdriver and the man at the desk. Does that mean you're never coming back to Mountainside then?"

Francis looked down at the table. He knawed tha' question wuz comin' but ut seemed like ee didn' want to answer ut.

"I wanted to make a bit... For you and me. So we wudn' have to work hard ever again..."

"Weren't you coming back then?" Rebecca asked, now a bitter tone in her voice.

"No. I was goin' to send for you down here. Then you and me could start again."

"I don't want to live in Detroit though. Did you ever think of that?"

"Yes," said Francis. "Yes, I did, but it wasn't like I could ever go back. My name is mud up there. All they think I did was t'kill my awn son. How can I ever go back?"

"That why you left then, wuz ut, without even a parting word?"

"Tha' wuz wrong of me I know. But surely you can see why I left? Nimkii tried but even he cudn' pacify or console me."

Rebecca didn't answer. She didn't rightly know how he could think like that. The pasties arrived and they began to eat. Francis poured out a cup of tay for Rebecca. Like all good Methodists, she wanted no sugar. He asked her anyway, but he knew the answer. They ate in silence, each carefully thinking through their actions and what they needed to say. She shouldn't have to say what she wanted to say, but she said ut anyway.

"You were selfish Francis. You awnly thought of yourself. Not me."

"I cared for you. I sent you money."

"I didn't want your money. I wanted you. I wanted you more than anything else. Cen't you see that?"

"Yes," he admitted. "I see it – and I'm sorry. I acted too rashly, I realise. But I wasn't thinking straight. Not after what happened at the collar of the shaft."

"You should have stayed."

"Why's that?"

"Then you'd have found out the truth."

"What truth?"

He was looking at his wife intently now.

"The truth about our son."

That flummoxed un. He seemed to be more back to being the old Francis now: the pretence of his Detroit life dropping away.

"Go on," he said, but rightly, ee never had an inkling of what she wuz about t'tell un. The whole story took half-an-hour, by which time Francis had left half his pasty. None of ut seemed digestible in the way that she wuz tellun ov ut. Ut sounded too outlandish, too bizarre and too mazed ever to have happened. 'Twuz as ef ut had come out of one of they old drolls they used to tell childurn at home to maake ov um go sleep ov an evening. Thus wuz a tale 'bout a dark forest, dark happenings and deception on such a scale that he could barely believe ut. An' when she told un that their Richard (now liddle Jago) had been handed back, well, he didn' knaw wha' to do with hisself.

"How could we have been s'blind?" he asked.

"Easy," said Rebecca, "when you got a master – or rather mistress – of conjuring playing with ee."

"Maddy?"

She nodded, and told un what becomed of she an' Justin, and also how she'd informed her she was heading back to Ireland to begin again. At fust, Francis wanted revenge on she and his brother (fur he knawed now what boath ov they wuz like) but Rebecca dissuaded un from action. Justin, she explained, wuz just as in the dark as they were, and right now wuz in the doldrums all the way up Copper Mountain, and Maddy, well: Rebecca put ut so maybe Francis could see where she was coming from an' why she'd swapped a Pooka for their boy. She told un just how she had felt when he'd left her at Mountainside to come down here. Nawthun' wuz cut and dried like ut seemed. In fact, the world wuz a good deal more complex – allays and forever.

By now, ut had started to sink in that their boy wuz still alive and tha' there wuz much to celebrate. She told un all the other news too, such as the leaving of Mabel and Nimkii (a fact tha' didn' surprise un), the forthcomin' marriage of Dicky Mint and

Rosie Koskinen (good on um), and the jubilant activities too about her father and the new Mrs Eleanor Jewell.

"An' what ov your mawthur?"

She told un, and maybe he understood. Maybe he knew what a plaace that forest wuz – an' just how it could change a man or woman. Perhaps the asylum wuz best fer she. There wudn' nawthun' he could do fur she now anyway which hurted un a bit. He remembered seekin' fur she in the geht forest.

And then see, there wuz the Knockies.

"They'm alright," Becca said. "But Gourgy d'miss his master some. Luk longs fur you too."

Francis nodded. He missed his meht Gourgy – and loyal Luk too. 'Mean, a man an' his Knockie were a powerful duo. A man an' his Knockie could take on the world, and well, down here, there wudn' naw magic. Seemingly, ut had all been either machined or forged away. Tha' wuz progress fur ee. Automobiles es, and telephones es, but not much magic you.

"I need t'gaw back," said Francis. "'Mean, I reckon I can still work fur Cadillac. Maybe I can convert Skews' old lab, eh? Come down every whip and wan. Still keep an eye on the mine, but come down here too. Keep boath goin', ef I can."

"Good," said Becca. "Brae an' good. You've a plaace here?"

"An apartment that I rent. Nothun' special, but roomy enough... I can keep tha' going."

"And may I come back tonight?"

"Es. Of course. There'll be a brae bit to sort out," said Francis. "But nawthun's impossible, is ut?"

"No," said Rebecca. "Nothun's impossible."

"There are things I need to see," said Francis.

"What are they then?"

"Firstly, this Saffron-Bun Chapel... I need to see what your feythur's been doing with all tha' money..."

"What else?"

"Then I need to see you and Jago and me in our house up on the mountain. There's a lot of time t'be made up. He with you and me, but also me and you."

Tha' pleased she. Finally, her wuz able to smile.

"You forgot Justin..."

"Es. Well, he too..."

"An' wha' about Gourgy and Luk?"

"They little buggers too, I d'reckon... Aw, an' one of your saffron buns... fresh out the oven..."

An' so, he set to ut.

49

"Boy Frank did a'right, didn' a? They d'say he be some director now, down Detroit way, with they new horseless ve-*hic*-les being built. Dun a'right, ebm a?"

Tha' wuz wha' wuz coming, she and ee 'oped.

They that knawed ov ut, had wished Rebecca well in her quest to locate her husband, and prayed that she and ee would come back safe. She had stayed with Francis in Detroit for almost a fortnight, whilst the weather in May made everything back on the mountain bloom. There had been much to sort out, of course, with Francis going to the Board and expressing his wish to take on a slightly different role with the company. Some eyebrows were raised. He'd been wise though, and registered all his patents, and the other directors wanted him to stay. They viewed the man as ingenious and wanted to accommodate him. Yes, well enough; he could devote some of his time to work back on the Keweenaw, as long as every so often he got down to Detroit. A telephone might be installed too, and they would agree to funding a well-equipped laboratory up there for un, so he could continue his experiments and research for Cadillac. The main thing wuz that they didn' want to lose him and when he tried explaining that his son, who he thought wuz lost, in fact, wuz alive, they were sympathetic.

These Cornish though. Bit weird, wudn' um? But they had the brains and the know-how.

Ut took a while for things to be arranged, and in the meantime, Becca decided she rather liked his apartment in the city. Compared to their basic property up at Mountainside, this wuz much grander. Maybe she could even get to like Detroit. A life spent between the two locations sounded appealing. Since her arrival she had noted her own dull clothing and, upon seeing the new fashions in the city, succumbed to spending some of the money she had. She bought gifts for everyone – and, of course, toys for young Jago. In the meantime, Francis negotiated his future with the Plant.

There wuz a period too, in the city, where they came to know each other again. This came mentally at first (where they could now, at distance, properly reflect on what had happened to them), but then, physically too, and when they entwined their bodies around each other again, all seemed well. That closeness: ut hadn' gone. She'd been worried, but naw, ut wuz still there; just as passionate and just as loving as before. She observed one day that Francis had shaved off his moustache, and started once more, to part his hair to the side. There wuz still his traditional Mining Cap'n's clobber in a wardrobe at his apartment. Some hobnail boots too: the ones he'd worn to come down there. Maybe she came to understand that he had not ever totally abandoned the idea of going back.

They discussed much, as, in early evenings, they sauntered through the city's parks. Becca explained to him more about the situation with Mabel and Nimkii, and that although she felt like she might never see her sister again, she was glad that she was doing something that she liked doing, and was with someone she loved. At first, she explained, her feythur hadn' been accepting at all, but later, this altered when George Jewell married Eleanor. She'd been sceptical of this woman at first, but Rebecca explained that she'd had a positive effect on her father, and that she'd been instrumental in getting the chapel constructed.

In the light of this, Skews' replacement got talked about. Yes, they'd need someone, and Francis knew of a young man from Devon, who'd found his way over to Detroit, and was employed in the foundry. He knew his skills in assaying, and felt he might be a good fit for them on the Keweenaw. The young man, an Algy Luscombe, liked the work at Cadillac, but longed for a more rural existence. He wuz someone who he felt Justin and he might be able to work with.

"Skews' shares will need sorting," said Francis worriedly. "Has Justin done anything about that? Either we get another shareholder to come onboard and purchase Skews' portion, or effectively, we buy him out retrospectively. Not sure where the money would go though."

"I think," said Rebecca, pondering what he'd asked, "they were talking about a community fund, to develop the town. I know they were investigating it."

This sounded promising. Perhaps some good could come of Skews' passing. But then, they didn't knaw the full story.

"Again, there's Nimkii," argued Francis. "He had a fifth in the original deal. When he left, did anyone buy him out? Was an agreement decided?"

"That wasn't possible," responded Becca. "They left in such a hurry. I mean, I think he and Mabel, they came to despise money. They saw what it brought."

"How do you mean?"

"Oh, well, you know, the way the mountain got abused. The stripping back of the forest. Mabel told me. Nimkii felt guilty. He felt he'd started the whole thing by giving you permission. I don't know ef anything more went back to his people."

"That will need redress," said Francis. "That'll be one of the first things I'll do when I get back. To my eternal regret, that's a thing we should have done more sensitively. I've no idea how, but although we acted in good feyth widn', we didn't act well enough. We let un down... We let the landscape down. Ut got lost in all ov our getting and makin'"

"The Deads are still growing, and the attle pile grows every day."

"We need to sort tha' out too. We really do. Unless we do, we shall be cursed with ut fur the rest of our lives."

Francis sounded altered when he spoke like this. Ut seemed he'd realised which way the world wuz goin'. Mad ut wuz, but maybe he wuz right.

"I'n see ut comin'," he said. "All those interminable cars and vehicles. Guilt see Becca. It's altered me... Not just guilt over Richard, but guilt as to what else I've done."

She tried to understand. When he spoke this way, she found herself thinking of her mawthur, and she being snatched by the forest: an eye for an eye see; a tooth for a tooth. They took from the forest, and the forest took from they. Maybe, in all that Francis wuz saying a peace could be negotiated. There might be a new way of thinking. Hard though. Such a view wudn' zactly in the Cornish mindset now, wuz ut? She knew the thousands ov acres of upturned and dishevelled earth back 'ome: that seemingly got abandoned without repair or restoration. She knew the woodland that got removed for the want of timbering an' props underground. Some job you, to change minds. Perhaps her Francis could do ut. Perhaps though, 'twas too big fur ee alone. In reality, ut needed everyone. 'Twould take some doin'.

When they were set, and nearnly a fortnight had passed, they made their way over to the harbour jetty.

"Hey Nathaniel," Francis said to the Captain of their return laker. "You got some gob on you, ebm ee boy? And there I wuz, thinkin' I could trust of ee."

"You have a very persuasive wife," laughed Nathaniel.

"I wuz reckoning you wudn' let anything slip," argued Francis jokingly. "And there you are with a mouth on ee as big at the shaft up Mountainside."

Nathaniel now looked a lot more accommodating than when Rebecca had first encountered un. Then, he'd comed across as some fierce.

"You took after this one," the Captain said. "She've got a touch of magic about she. Must have! To make me blurt out where you wuz."

"Old friend." said Francis. "By doin' so, you saved me some good deal ov heartache so, in fact, I am thankful to you. Whatever rumour you heard about me, none of ut wuz true. Not a bit ov ut."

"Glad to hear that boy. I never take naw notice ov tittle-tattle anyway... You should knaw tha'."

"Listen boy, I reckon I might be sailing down with you a good deal in the near future."

"How's that then?"

Francis explained.

Watching all ov this at distance, wuz the enthusiastic boy, tha' Tommy Carkeek.

"And this," Becca said knowingly. "is the young man who brought the money up to Mountainside. Tommy, this is my husband, Francis. He's the one who you've really been working for."

"A'right?" said Tommy, his Cornishness not yet scat out obm.

"He've been a grand help to me... We rode down the tramway together, didn' us, eh?"

"That we did Lady," said Tommy shyly.

"I am more than grateful to you young man. Time for a pay rise, eh?"

Francis handed Tommy a couple of dollar bills for his work. He looked proper tickled up ass at tha'.

"Thank ee sir," he said. "Anything else you need sir, let me know..."

The boy took their cases to their cabin and smiled at Rebecca.

Nathaniel and Francis discussed un. Rebecca looked to see what they were saying.

"When I retire, that boy will make a good Captain," offered Nathaniel. "Ee's coming to knaw the Lake System well you. Water and shipping see, 'tis in the blood."

"I know," commented Francis. "I know."

The trip back on the laker wuz much better for Rebecca now that Francis wuz with her. Nonetheless, she chose to relay to him the detail of the conversation that she'd had with Maddy. Francis wuz rightly still angry about what she'd done and what she'd put them through, but she wanted that anger inside of him to dissipate. By telling him of the truth, she hoped that he could come to forgive her. There wuz no point in keeping that in his heart.

"When you get back up there, I pray that you leave ut alone. I pray that every day you try to forgive her."

He listened intently to what she wuz sayin' ov.

"If you do tha', then one day, it will be gone. It will be snapped out of you. It's the only way we can progress Frank. There is no other way."

"I know."

"By Divine intervention, we have our boy back... Think of tha'. Always."

"I will."

"Promise?"

"Yes. I promise."

She let him contemplate what she'd said. Then, she spoke again.

"As soon as we get back, I want you, me and Jago to go to the chapel and thank God for what he has given us – or rather, what he has given back to us?"

"Alright, yes." said Francis, with no tone of scepticism or distrust in his voice.

"I know you think I'm mad. You think I'm becoming like my father, but you have to understand Frank, every day, these past few months, I have been praying for this moment. You do see that, don't you?"

"Of course I do. I know exactly what you are saying. We faced Devilry once and got through it. It's important we celebrate. We should be joyous. I mean, I feel joyous. Don't you?"

She nodded and kissed him.

She needed to hear it at this moment in time. The healing would come she hoped, when they might wander the woods again, when they'd give Jago the toys she'd bought him, and when they could be a complete family again: not a changeling's one.

"How do you think they'll react when I show up?" Francis asked.

"Why? Are you worried?"

"A brae bit actually. I'm not sure how they'll respond."

"You'll be welcomed back like a hero. I guarantee ut."

When they fust got back though, the news comin' out of they around them wudn' zactly good. So ut seemed, the boy Dicky Mint had suddenly left this world and had gone on inta' the next. Ut felt like Minter wuz the kind of boy who wuz dead, but wudn', as the Cornish would say, prop'ly lay down. Everyone wuz gabblin' on 'bout ut. Rosie wuz devastated obviously, but she wuz comforted – as anyone would be – by what the Minter had left she in his will. So ut seemed, she wudn' goin' to be the fust bride at Saffron-Bun Chapel. Not yet at least. Becky and Francis gived her their collective condolences.

"We'm some sorry," said Rebecca.

"Es. Dicky will be hard to replace. I knaw he and I had a few set-tos to begin with but the truth ov ut wuz that ee knawed ov h'engineerin' like no one else. A proper Trevithick ee wuz you."

"Thank you both," she said. "He thought much of you Francis. You know that, yes?"

Francis nodded in response. They left her to it at his graveside. What next fur she wuz a moot question now tha' things had gone somewhat backsyvore fur she ov late. Happenstance, there lurked a bit ov an idea inside her mind. Too soon, wuz ut? Her *pupu*? Na. Not really. Not up here on the mining frontier. Not ef they knawed the whole truth.

They were almost up to the chapel see. They'd arrived late in the day, and the town wuz quiet. Gear still rumbled on. The tramway thundered up and down, and the bob still moved back an' forth. But ut wuz up there that they needed to go. Before anything else though, they'd stopped by her father's, and told them the good news: that they wuz back. There, they could pick up Jago too. Out comed Doctor and Mrs Jewell. The Doctor looked some sheepish.

"Knaw wha' happened then, do ee Frank?" said Jewell, trying to be down to earth widn'.

Francis nodded.

"I'm some sorry," said Jewell. "I misjudged you boy, and fur tha' I truly apologise. I didn' knaw nothun. I didn' wha' you wuz dealing with, but you did, and you knawed zactly what you needed to do with ut."

"Thanks fur your apology," said Francis. "It's appreciated. You'll know now why I felt had no choice but to leave..."

"Curse the day," mumbled Jewell, "and curse tha' Irish maid..."

The Doctor raised his hands in the air, unable to say anything else. In truth, ee knawed he shouldn' think tha' way but sometimes a spade needed to be called a spade.

"Never mind she. You've done very well fur yerself I hear..."

"Not too bad," said Francis, self-deprecating in tone.

"Well, I knaw Becca will be some pleased to find you and see you home here."

"It's joyous to be back," said the Cap'n. "You... ah... got the money then?"

Jewell raised an eyebrow, wondering momentarily what he meant.

"Fur the chapel?"

"Aw, tha'! That wuz so kind of you boy. We d'appreciate ut. I mean, everyone here on Mountainside appreciated ut. What you did wuz wondrous. An utterly selfless act. An act of a true Christian. We shall forever be in your debt, ent that' right Eleanor?"

"Completely," she said. "You'll see the foundation stone up there... Your name's on it. We always kept feyth Francis. An' by the look ov ut, so did you."

Another plaque with his name on ut. What had a become ov late?

"I'm grateful," said Francis. "Really grateful. But let's move on from ut, eh? Now, where's that fine boy of mine? The liddle changeling..."

At this, out toddled the boy Jago. Aw, well, what can ee say? There wudn' nawthun' on earth like that fust cuddle he had with ee.

"Does he look the same?" asked Eleanor, intrigued at how he felt.

"I honestly don't know," said Francis. "Ee d'look like he's meant to, as far as I'm concerned. Whatever look God got planned fur'n, then ut do suit me."

He held his son high in the air and gaked at un intently, making un smile and giggle. Then he held un close to his faace, and smelt that incredible smell of the young and all the hope that that contained. Aw es. Ee ingested ut deep, and felt, at that moment at least, like ee never wanted un out of his arms again. An' with tha', he looked over at his wife and nodded. Es, he could forgive those who'd deceived them; those that had separated them. As Rebecca had said to un, there wuz no other way. Forgiveness wuz now all tha' mattered.

There wuz much to catch up on. Jewell wanted to know all that he'd been doing at Cadillac, and Eleanor wanted all the gossip from Detroit. But they boath realised wha' wuz needed. Es, that wuz tha' the three of they – the proper Nankervis family – went up to Saffron-Bun Chapel and gave their thanks to God.

"Who named ut tha' then? Must've been someone?" asked Francis when they got up there, past where Rosie had been sat ov late, half-mourning her Dicker, half-thinking what she could do next.

"You'll never guess..."

"Stop teasing me..."

Rebecca took an intake of breath.

"It wuz Nimkii... He told my feythur what ut should be called, an' he liked ut. Apparently, he said ut, all because ut was our favourite food stuff. 'Mean, there's nawth do un' more suitable really, is there?"

"I do like ut," said Frank.

"Me too," said his wife. "I hope you like what you funded. Shall we step inside?"

That, they did, and spent around half-an-hour inside, admiring their design and the decor.

"It's Dicky's design..."

"Ha," said Francis. "I'd never have believed it."

Once again, the Minter had triumphed.

"Quite something, isn't it?" asserted Rebecca.

"Yes," said Francis. "Quite something..."

"Did you hear my father? Now that you're back, he wants an opening ceremony. A brass band. Tea-treats. Revel buns. Games and dancing... And after tha', every year, an Anniversary."

"I bet," said Francis, nodding his head in affirmation. "So, this is where we give thanks, eh?"

"Yes."

And holding hands and cradling liddle Jago together, before God, thaas wha' they did. In silence they raised a copper conduit to the Lord and gave un proper thanks. Es, in reuniting they, He'd done a 'andsome job.

Boy Justin wudn' doin' s'well though, wuz a? They d'say he'd been drinking a brae bit ov liquor ov late. Frank heard all the gossip, an' went to see un. The plaace wuz in some state you. Despite the weeks tha' had passed by, ee hadn' even picked up the scat over furniture, and when Francis found un, he wuz in the same clawthes he'd been wearing fur over a week. The bugger hadn' shaved and looked like he'd been 'eaved through a hedge backwards.

"You've come back then?" wuz the fust thing Justin said to un.

"Es. Looks like I wuz just in time too."

"I'm allowed to be like this if I want," he protested.

"True 'nuff," said Francis. "'Tis your call alright. An' I cen't odds ut."

"Word is you'm made ov money these days. Surprised you didn' drive back up here in one of they posh new automobiles..."

Francis laughed.

"'Course not, y'tusser," ee said. "Went on the laker like everyone else..."

Justin took another swig ov whiskey.

"That idn' goin' to do ee naw good. Look where that got ee back Penzance."

"What do you care anyway? You'm set. Look at me. I've lost everything. My son... Well, not my son... but you d'knaw who I mean... and Maddy, she's gone... I ebm got nawthun'."

"Must feel tha' way right now," said Francis. "But none of ut wuz your fault... Not from wha' I'n gather. You wuz there with me brother, tryin' to kill the thing."

"Es. So I wuz."

"Why s'down-hearted then?"

"I loved tha' boy, and ee wudn' even mine... Mine's dead in the ground up the cemetery. Cold as clay."

"Es. I knaw. But 'tidn' like you'm givin' up Jago. He'll allays be a part of your life. You'm his uncle. Nawthun' can change tha'."

"Maybe," Justin grunted.

"An' regarding Maddy, well, me and Becca talked. We've boath forgiven her. Becca saw her on the laker. She explained."

"Well I cen't."

"What ee mean?"

"I mean, forgive she... All she did wuz t'deceive me. Why do you think I'm like this, eh?"

"Sometimes deceit is well-intentioned," offered Francis. "Thaas wha' I've learnt."

"Naw 'tidn'," replied his bother, "not when 'tis a bleddy taissy changeling..."

"You got to move on," suggested Francis.

"The Mine's gone to pot. Skews is dead. We ebm got naw assayer, nor agent."

"I got a solution to tha'," offered Francis.

He explained his idea.

"Dun't matter. Dicker's gone on too. We still need a skilled h'engineer."

"Do us? Mean, do us really? Me an' you, we still got a bit goin' on up here."

He pointed to his brain.

"I reckon we'n get by. An' Walt Chegwidden, he' idn' naw fool. He's got handy with designs and instruments."

"But what do you care anyway? You dun't need this place. Like I say, you'm set fur life."

"I plan on spending half my time here, and half down in Detroit. Ef we keep that link goin', we'll have enough work here fur the next twenty, perhaps thirty years. Honest Jus. 'Tidn' just me who's set. 'Tis boath ov us. I went to Detroit fur boath ov we."

Francis could see Justin thinking through ut.

"'Tidn' just that though, es ut? 'Tis me. I'm a useless bugger. All tha' work I've put in, an' I got nawthun'."

"I thought tha' when I left. When I got on tha' bleddy laker, I thought I had nothun', but time proved me wrong see. You got to think tha' way a bit more Jus. You'm the Mine Manager here now: the main man. An' I knaw Maddy's gone, but so what? Let tha' go. You have to."

"But I wanted another chield with she. A daughter maybe... We tried, but ut comed t'nawthun'."

Francis could see the pity in un. 'Twuz something ee didn' like t'see in anyone, let alone in his awn brother.

"You'm sat there all s'righteous," Justin went, his voice now angry and bitter, "but you dun't knaw the half ov ut, not the real truth ov ut."

"Tell me then."

An' in tha' droll tellin', then Francis finally understood wha' Justin had to be bitter about. Now he knawed why Maddy's baby wuz stillborn: the startin' point fur all ov this agony of late. His brother put ut down to tha' fust encounter with Rosie Koskinen and wha' ee'd caught off she. Hell. Es. 'Twudn' naw childurn's picture book to hear tell ov tha'.

Perhaps ut needed new life. New for old and old fur new.

"You knaw she still like ee, dun't ee?" Francis stated. "I see ut. I see the way she d'look at ee."

"Who do ee mean?"

"Are you mazed? Rosie. She didn' want Dicky Mint. Never did. Tha' wuz all show in my view."

"Na 'twudn'. Dicky told me ee loved her."

"No brother. The awnly one she ever really wanted wuz you. She set up with the Minter to make you jealous. Thaas how I d'see ut. And then, well, when you wudn' leave Maddy – despite how she wuz to ee, from what you've told me – when Rosie cudn' get a rise from you, she wuz forced to marry un. Naw better offers comin' her way, wuz there?"

"You reckon?" said Justin, perking up slightly.

"'Course Sos," said his brother. "You and she... There's still time."

"Gah! I ent s'sure. Ef 'twudn fur she... then..."

But then suddenly, he stopped.

"Look boy. Clean yerself up... I need t'find our Knockies. Where be um?"

"Prob'ly down on the ninth level I 'spect."

"Think on," said Francis and left Justin to overhaul hisself.

This would be ut then, seeing ov Gourgy and Luk again, after all this time. By now, Francis wuz back in his Cap'n's gear, and needed to view the state of the mine fur hisself again. He'd have they pair, he reckoned. Some playful ricks wuz in order. Inta' the cage he went, and that got lowered to the ninth level. All wuz familiar. This wuz his true 'ome. He knawed tha'. From one of the tool stores belaw ground, ee took a hammer. He tried to catch the sound of they along the level. See, Knockies usually sing while they'm at work, and faintly, along the level, he could hear their song. Their song wuz a work chant. 'Twuz in their old language, and they tended awnly to sing such songs when they reckoned humans wudn' around. That wuz the way of they see.

Fur a while, he stood still, to hear ov um: Luk's higher voice an' Gourgy's lower tone. They sounded like a pair of angels, down there in their underground Heaven. Underscoring their chant wuz the rhythmical 'clink, clink' ov their pick-axes at work. He realised they didn' knaw nothun' of his return. In such songs, Knockies took comfort. When times wuz rough, thaas when they tended to sing the moast: deep down in the levels. They did ut back home and they did ut here.

He pondered how they'd be. He considered the fact that not much would have changed with um. Considering the total spans of their lives (which could last several millennia) ee prob'ly wudn' nawtice any big changes. Ut wuz comfortin' to hear ov they though. Ut was now like he wuz home. There wuz Rebecca es, and now Jago too, and whilst they wuz wondrous, ut ud be this pair that would reinforce how far he'd come. Ee contemplated they, he and his brother all that time ago, traipsing through the forest, and they moaning on. The thought ov ut made un smile. Ut made the hair on the back of his neck stand up.

Fur fun, ee gived a knock against the level's wall. There wuz no pause in their song. He did ut again; this time harder. Tha' wuz enough to make they stop singing. He could hear the echo of their little voices.

"Hang fire. Hear tha' did ee?" went Luk. "'Tis either a knocking or someone givin' ut bell tink."

"What?" responded Gourgy.

"A knocking. Es. A knocking."

"Naw. Didn' hear nawthun'."

But then Francis made a knock again.

"I heard ut then," said Gourgy. "You wuz right boy."

"But whose a-doin' the knocking? There wudn' nawbody else down here with we," noted Luk.

"Maybe 'tis the earth talking. Y'knaw, like ut does sometimes."

Francis then made an even greater knock with the hammer, which this time, made they jump. You could sense their movement up from the floor an' inta' the air, then down again.

"Dun't like the sound ov tha' boy," said Luk.

"Me neither," said Gourgy. "Time fur we to skedaddle."

"Rite on. Dunnee forget your crowst box. We'll need to tell Master Justin 'bout this..."

"Es... Well, we'n try."

By now, Francis had turned off his carbide lamp and stood there in the shaft. Along they comed, moaning an' grumblin' like they allays did. He laughed at the hurry tha' they pair wuz in to get out the shaft, almost falling over themselves to make their way from the stope along the level. As soon as their shadows emerged, caused by their own lit tallow atop their helmets, Francis turned his carbide light on full. Ut near blinded them, and they pulled up straight, shocked at the form in front of them. Luk nearnly turned on his heels.

"A buccaboo," he yelped.

Francis laughed. A buccaboo wuz a ghost in their tongue.

"Na, that ent naw bucca," observed Gourgy. He was already recognising the form that stood in front of him.

Momentarily, Francis turned off his light again, which allowed for the light on Gourgy's helmet to see who ut truly wuz.

"Master?" he enquired nervously. "Is that truly you? Or is this some kind ov illusion?"

"What ee think?" said Francis – but the way he said ut echoed the thousands of times underground he had asked tha' question before.

Luk, who'd recovered his awn wits by now, wuz gakin' at the form in the level too.

"'Tis," he said. "Gourgy, that be Master Francis... He's back."

As Francis stepped forward into their light, they could now see who ut truly wuz. Es, 'twuz Francis; their Francis.

"I had you pair then, didn' I?" he said, laughing. "You thought there wuz a knocking..."

"We did," said Luk. "Oh master, we'm some glad to see ee. Wherever have ee been?"

Gourgy had been made speechless, and tears were streaming forth from his wide eyes. Normally, ee allays had a lot to say, but not now, not at this moment. Ee'd come to write off his Master as one who might never return, and now here ee wuz: back from the dead.

"We thought you never wanted to see we again," said Luk.

By now, Gourgy was claspin' at Francis' leg, holdin' ov un s'tight that ut didn' seem like he'd ever let go. He wuz near restricting the blood flow down to his foot.

"I wudn' goin' to let down you pair now, wuz I?"

"We wuz s'worried," blabbed Gourgy.

"I knaw," said Francis. "See, I had to go... after wha' happened... but Rebecca found me, and told me the truth."

By now, ov course, boath they knawed zactly what had happened on the mountain. Finally, now reassured, Gourgy released his grip.

"You two been alright?" Francis asked.

"Es," said Luk. "Goin' on steady. Goin' on steady."

"Come on. Let's go up t'grass. I got nicies fur ee boath, bought down in Detroit."

"Hear tha' boy?" stated Luk.

"Es," said Gourgy.

"He got nicies fur we."

"Proper," went Gourgy, but he wuz still squalling like a chield at the return to normality.

"Comus you on," shouted back Francis. "Make 'iss..."

They looked at each other and then followed un along the level. They'd follow that boy anywhere in the world. And when Justin wuz sober again, they'd do the same with he too. All good then. Es. All good.

"Rite on," said a still sniffly Gourgy. "We'm a-comin'."

Francis put the hammer back in the tool store and they rode the cage up t'grass.

May seemed an apt time for the ceremony to mark the grand opening of Saffron-Bun Chapel. It wuz fittin' too, because ut all seemed to coincide with the return of Francis and Rebecca, and their reunification with their son. Some geht spread wuz put on you, and from down Calumet, George Jewell had organised the arrival of a ten-piece brass band, as well as a cartload of revel buns which were issued out to everyone present. There wuz the formal ceremony es, and the proper unveiling of the stone, marking they who'd founded the chapel. Then, there wuz a brae deal ov good old Methodist revival and jaunty hymns sung to praise the Lord. The whole thing wuz infectious, and ut caused every Knockie and magical creature underground to come up and watch. They stowed in the woods amd gathered covertly at the edge of the forest, and watched wha' wuz on. The laughter and music spread up to the highest fells of the mountain.

Boy Justin wuz there, now dressed dapper in his newly-cleaned Cap'n's clawthes. He'd had a shave by now, and had dressed up good an' proper. He'd even borrowed some of his brother's fine new aftershave. Aw es. Some celebration you. There wuz readings, and poems, and dedications. 'Course, there wuz some geht oration by George Jewell as his Eleanor an' James gazed at un admirably. An' the Reverend Josiah Davies gived as joyous a sermon as he possibly could. Ut honestly took what seemed like an eternity to endure but at least, at the end, there wuz the thought of saffron, clotted cream and hot tay. There wuz soda an' nicies brought in too, fur the childurn, an' they danced and played like there wuz naw tomorra'. Eleanor had even organised ut so there wuz a parade down around the mine an' back. Es. 'Twuz some grand. Dicky Mint would have been proud. Maybe in the ground, maybe somewhere else, Mr Skews looked on too. Maybe this would have gived ee the kind of joy ee cudn' ever find on earth when ee wuz on ut.

All they important wuz here. Walt Chegwidden had a geht smile on un. Howey Knucky had a belly full of bun and wuz laughin' like a piskie at ut all. Flannery, Cillian and the rest'ov the Irish boys turned up too. They wudn' there fur the religion in quite the same way everyone else wuz, but they joined in with the food and the dancing. Well, in living 'mongst the Cornish these past few years, half ov they had developed the same tastes. Then see, there wuz Jenny Spargo (temporarily relieved ov her duties with James by Eleanor), and she wuz getting some admiring glances from Cillian. So too, was a brae few of Rosie's maids gaining a good deal of admiration from the male members of the community. The German boys, Gries an' Knickmeier wuz in there too, alongside the Finns, Faas Jokinen an' Roope Toivonen. All they wuz hiding their bottles ov beer from George Jewell and the Reverend Davies. Sat near to they, wuz the stickler Malcolm Edyvean who'd struck up a bit of a liking fur Sal Clemo. Aw es. Everyone in the town wuz there, and a brae few had arrived from Calumet. Even Nathaniel and Tommy had come up from Eagle Harbour. Hellfire you. They'd took their chances an' ridden up there on one of the tramway wagons. Later, when the moon comed up, Yolkai sat above all they celebrating the erection of this fine new chapel. All she could do fur now wuz to watch.

That evening, Diddy Pasca pulled out a fiddle that he'd been learnin' on in the bunkhouse, and Jack Hocking had made a bit of a drum out of a barrel. The boy Moyle wudn' bad on the groaning keys and wheeze of the accordion, and so ut wuz agreed that later on, there'd be a bit of a dance ov sorts. 'Twudn' the kind ov thing that the Reverend Davies and George Jewell would normally approve ov, but today, well, today wuz the opening ov Saffron-Bun Chapel, so who wuz goin' to argue with tha'? In fact, maybe God hisself might even approve – after wha' they had all been through.

Es. Francis would dance later with Rebecca, but in a pause in the activities, he went over to see the two small graves of two infants. One he knawed well; the other he'd never met. There they were; safe in the earth. After he'd said a prayer to they boath, he went back to the crowd.

"A'right?" asked Rebecca.

"Es. A'right." Francis said back to she.

At that, they joined in the bizarre furry dance tha' wuz now takin' place. When they boath glanced over, they seened a stream of Knockies, all paired up and in procession, goin' down the street. Gabbling and laughing they were. Leading ov' um wuz Gourgy and Luk. When his eyes turned back t'the humans, there behind they, wuz John Trevorrow and Mrs Cap'n, sprightly see, as ef they wuz but twenty-one again. Francis then nawticed his brother gaking at Rosie Koskinen whilst she wuz dancing. Ee wuz watchin' the fall and rise ov her breasts, as she bobbed up an' down to the tune of the fiddle.

Somehow, a smile passed between them; a trifling thing, but Francis seen ut. Ut could all still be well.

So ut seemed, thanks to the Chapel, everyone wuz now free ov obligation. Es. There wudn' be naw begritchin' ov anyone naw more.

50

Hark now, will ee! We'm nearnly there...

Once upon a time, there were two brothers who made ut big in 'Merky'. Es. So ut turned out, there wuz the good one – and then, well, come to end up – there wuz the other good one too. They had helped to found a geht mine and a Methodist chapel, in the middle of a dark forest, high on the Keweenaw Peninsula. Not bad fur a pair ov cakey ol' pards like they, eh? Not bad either fur one ov they to be on the board of Cadillac Motors 'til his dying day, an' fur the other t'carry on managing the mine. A helleva' lot got forgotten an' neglected from tha' time, but so too did a lot get remembered and recalled, just as I've told you here. Thaas the way of these people see, and the way ov their story. Thaas truly the way they d'belong t'be.

On Copper Mountain, a lot got absolved. The souls of a fair few also got redeemed. Saffron-Bun Chapel had done its job. Some fitty then.

One day, a long time after the day of the opening ceremony of the chapel, in the morning mail arriving at the Jewell household, there wuz a photograph taken somewhere out West (Montana or Idaho maybe?) – an image of two people – a Native-American man and woman, proudly standing there with their three children. Why on earth had um been sent tha'? Awnly a few days later, did um realise that the woman wuz their Mabel: the man, Nimkii. In the end, 'twuz Eleanor who nawticed ut. Some contented Mabel looked though, didn' she? And now too, Eleanor's step-son James through medical school at Houghton: making a name fur hisself in researching natural medications an' remedies. Some proud George and she were.

An' then, some short while later, comin' up from Calumet, an apologetic and grovelling note from the Asylum Governor that somehow, beggaring belief, Clara Jewell had gone missing. Es. Escaped. They cudn' tell how zactly. In her room (though in truth, ut wuz more like a cell), some lengthy scrawled jottings in a journal she'd requested, detailing all manner ov strangeness. He didn' say anything about the crazy writing or the drawings. Best not too. He glanced at ut. What ut described wuz roots cradling she an' then trees carrying her through a forest. On another page, a drawing of a tall stag with crows sat in its antlers. One look at ut all wuz enough: the psychosis remained. Ut would awnly disturb the family, so he tossed it inta' the waste-paper bin in his office. He got a lot ov this kind of thing from the insane.

One morning too, a goodly while after all that, a long time too, after the fust Great War that consumed the century, when aged twenty or so, on a whim, this Jago Ciaran Nankervis decided that he'd like a geek at his awn true country. Not tellun' ov anyone (fur they'd surely put un off), ee secretly got on board a laker (well, tha' habit d'run in his family see), captained by one Tommy Carkeek no less, through the Lakes to Buffalo, rode the railroad to New York City, and from there, caught a liner to Falmouth back in Cornwall. He had skills see, and now tha' the copper mine at Mountainside wuz in decline (all the lodes had been worked out good an' proper), he decided tha' goin' back there might just be the best option fur'n. Ee didn' tell no one; not even they magical pair who might've travelled with un. They belonged to his feythur and uncle see. They were their Knockies; not his. His parents an' family kept utterly secret what had once happened to un, when ee wuz no more than a mite. Allays and forever, ee knawed nothun' 'bout ut, and perhaps, all told, tha' really wuz fur the best.

Across that same Atlantic tha' Jago Nankervis crossed, on the storm-strewn beach at Ballydonegan, a young woman gazed out at the ocean like she'd done for the past seventeen years of her life. High on the cliff, above the attle waste from the old Pengelly Budehaven mine, her mother waved at her. An' naw, despite all the coaxing she tried, this young woman never found out the name of her father, who instead, was at that moment being put in the earth on the Keweenaw: replacing some ov the ore tha' there, he'd once dug out and sold. The storm had brought in fresh shells on the tide, an' she wuz gathering them, to make a necklace. Such a necklace would act as a charm – and protect she – or so her mother told her. She never did say much 'bout her time spent in America.

There wuz, a long way from the Beara, tucked away, in a clearing, once a small field where the women an' girls ov Mountainside had planted crocus flowers: and from them, gathered golden stigma. Old Mrs Cap'n Trevorrow had laid that out originally. Ut didn' take long fur that to be subsumed by moss and bramble. Naw comforting buns now you.

A few years later, a map ov the mine's abandonment wuz handed in t'the State Department, an' although a few people lived on there (fur sentimental reasons), moast had, by now, moved to Calumet or Detroit. The doors of Saffron-Bun Chapel had allays been kept open, but this time, they got locked shut. 'Twas zactly like wha' the moon goddess Yolkai had said. People soon forgot the mine and chapel ever existed: and gradually, the forest encroached, daily extending its fronds and roots, claiming back what wuz once its awn. Even that finest of constructions, Skews' mineral tramway, became consumed: made indistinguishable from the rest of the growth. The land sprites regained their homes. Moss grew on the skirting board of the chapel and in time, damp lichen and mould attached itself to the pulpit.

Es. There 'tis then.

Well, not quite see. You'm by now prob'ly wondering who I am? I ent nothun' really. I'm just the spice of this tale, found in the gap between the ground and God. And I d'reckon thaas all you really need t'knaw.

Coda

That mouldering smell of time. The forest had been in here a long time you see: and for a century or more had its own wicked way with the chapel. That was until recently when volunteers from the Eagle Harbour Historical Society had decided to recover the chapel and the remains of the copper town of Mountainside, which apparently was once just known as New Diggings.

Twelve months before, the Society had formally agreed to bring the chapel back to life and use it once more. They'd spent weeks cutting back the bracken and the brambles, repaired the planchen and roofing, put in electricity and water, and made the building serviceable again. They'd felled trees that had sprouted too close to its foundations: ash, oaks and firs. One maple had grown up on the inside of the overgrown chapel, pushing up through the ceiling and roof. When that had been done, they'd tidied the cemetery and strimmed down decades of growth to discover long-hidden tombs and markers. They'd reopened paths and mapped what was there. Today's re-dedication was splendid. Before they partook of the revel buns, they'd got a young minister up from Calumet, fresh out of training college, but apparently with Cornish heritage (hard not to, in a town like that).

This is where her family had been all those years ago. She had traced the line back, using on-line censi and the help of the Cornwall Family History Society. Then there had been correspondence across the Atlantic (especially when she set out to discover the full extent of her family tree), and an official letter: an invitation for Ms Cecilia Nankervis to attend the formal reopening of Mountainside Chapel (what everyone still knew locally as 'Saffron-Bun Chapel'). To have a relative of one of the founders present: what an honour for her, and what an honour for the Historical Society – a direct link to the past. She got a special welcome by the trustees. There were photographs and handshakes, interviews with the local press, and earlier that week, a spot on Radio Keweenaw. It was clear that they valued her presence. Then, the drive up here, in a swish, air-conditioned Cadillac.

So this was where it had all happened. This was where her grandfather Jago Ciaran Nankervis had been born. Originally, in her researches, she had thought he was the son of one Justin Nankervis (her great uncle) and another individual with Irish origins (apparently from the Beara peninsula), who went by the name of Madelaine O'Donahue. The O'Donahues had been hard to trace, seemingly disappearing off the face of the earth, and then, according to her folders of notes, there had been some past connection with the Pengellys (a big Cornish copper-mining family) who had been working over in the Beara. That was something she still had to sort out – to fill in all the gaps – and at the moment, there were still many. But getting this far back pleased her very much. To think her line had had something to do with all of this. Well, it was wonderful.

So it seemed there was some confusion (something she could not quite get to the bottom of, despite her best efforts) for later on, mysteriously, Jago Ciaran ended up being with her great-grandfather Franciṣ Nankervis and his wife Rebecca. She was the daughter of one George and Clara Jewell (the mine's surgeon and his wife), who had originally come over from Bodmin. She'd discovered that Jewell had been a part-time preacher too, and the trustees had shown her his name on the foundation stone, alongside that of her relatives Justin and Francis, and one other individual by the name of John Trevorrow – all of them Cap'ns of the old copper mine there.

It looked like Justin married a Finnish woman by the name of Rosie Koskinnen, and after that, Jago somehow became his nephew. Her grandfather could just remember un. There was some scandal she knew, because later on, so it seemed, that George Jewell got married to another woman named Eleanor, and her name too, was on the foundation stone. All very odd admittedly, but there was no one to ask and no one could answer her questions anyway. She could only speculate and even then, how could you wade through time and rumour? It was always a gloopy kind of treacle, and just when you thought you had solved it, another problem came along to disrupt your theories again.

"Cecie," called Jean Kenitzer, the organiser of this gathering, "let's take a stroll shall we, and go on down through the cemetery?"

Jean was a lovely woman, now in her late seventies, who was part of the enthusiastic driving force behind the chapel's restoration. Cecilia admired her greatly and had been thankful for the invite to the event. Cecilia was mid-way through a slice of revel bun, but acquiesced so that her host could show her around. She clunked down the part of the bun in her mouth already, and took one last sip of tay to wash it down.

"It's really so lovely to have you here," said Jean, gently grabbing Cecie's arm at the elbow.

"It's been incredible," Cecilia said back. "I never thought I'd see the mine... and this chapel..."

"Well, the mine's not much to look at now, but we think the State might give us some grant money to do it up. I mean, the forest is wrapped around it right now, but so I'm told, the inside of it is still in pretty good shape... More or less just as the last core of miners abandoned it. Be nice, wouldn't it? We think a lot of people would make their way up here and see what went on. We want to make it part of the Copper County trail. Now wouldn't that be real fine?"

"Looks like there's a lot to do..." observed Cecilia.

"We're ready for that but the mine buildings are comparatively easy. It's that area over there, that's going to be the biggest problem..."

She was pointing to the north-east.

"What am I looking at?"

At present, it just looked like a mass of ragged trees and bushes.

"Hard to see now I know.... but that area used to be called the Deads. It was where the mine put all its waste. It used to be a kind of lake apparently, but it's all hardened over now. The State Environmental team need to make a full assessment of it and then plan its removal. All sorts of awful chemicals in there still apparently. That'll be costly to get rid of..."

"I know that kind of thing is expensive. We have the same problems at home..."

For a while, their conversation returned to opportunities for Jean to visit Cornwall. She'd never been over apparently, but she'd read some Daphne du Maurier, and felt a connection. Of course, Cecilia said she would be welcome to stay with her.

They were in the cemetery now. Although the growth had been cut back and the incursion of the forest halted, many of the graves still needed individual work. They needed love and attention to restore them to their former glory.

"Each community had a segment... the way it is in a lot of American cemeteries. So here see... we've got the Finns, and across the way there, the Germans..."

Cecilia wandered over to the Finnish end and saw names like Jokinen and Toivonen. Then, there were memorials for the Gries and Knickmeier families.

"Fascinating, isn't it?" observed Jean. "These men would have known your great-grandfather and your great-uncle. They'd probably have worked for them..."

"Amazing."

"Yup."

They got down to the bottom of the small cemetery. From where they were standing, they could gaze into the far distance of Lake Superior, and see the large freighters travelling its length and expanse.

"This was the Irish section," said Jean. "You can tell. The graves are a bit different... They needed to be a bit separate from the Protestant ones."

Cecilia glanced at them. One she noted in passing was the name Flannery.

"So they say, the Irish and the Cornish got on pretty well up here. It wasn't the same everywhere. Oh yeah. Big fights between them apparently down Calumet way."

Cecilia took it all in. If there was one thing she had learnt from her visits, it was that Americans loved their family history. It was that whole 'finding yourself in the midst of globalization' thing with them. She'd already learnt in her few days on the Keweenaw not to say too much sometimes, or she'd enter yet another dull conversation about family history and their possible origins in obscure parishes in Cornwall and whether she knew anyone by that name still there.

"Let's head back up top," said Jean.

She was telling her about the original preacher's pit they had once had here; in fact, where the chapel was eventually constructed. They'd had to blast away a piece of rock that had once been the natural pulpit to allow room for the chapel's construction. Up until that point, services had been held in the outside there, only apparently shifting inside to a schoolhouse during the winter. That was all before the chapel got constructed.

"See this lot," said Jean. "These are all the Cornish... Funny names aren't they?"

Maybe they were to Jean, but not to Cecilia. She read them carefully and noted their intricacies: Spargo, Clemo, Edyvean, Pascoe, Snell, Hocking, Moyle, Knucky and Chegwidden. Finally, a lop-sided headstone for a man named Richard Mint: perhaps a little older than the rest. Some had been married; others not. She thought not about them though, but instead, about who they'd had to leave behind. No doubt many of them had wanted to be buried back in their homeland, but death had caught up with them here and they were unable to make it. Perhaps too, they had no memory of Cornwall. Perhaps more likely, this was their world and all that was important to them was here.

Further graves followed.

"You'll know him," said Jean.

Cecilia peered at the headstone, and saw it was devoted to Cap'n John and Mrs Edna Trevorrow. Jean waited for her to make the connection but it seemed Cecilia was so overwhelmed with everything that she could not do it.

"You know... John Trevorrow... one of the founders of the chapel... along with your Francis and Justin..."

"Oh... yes. Of course..."

Cecilia looked at their memorial edifice. He was clearly a man of some means.

"He would have to have made a good bit to afford that... but look at this one..."

Jean showed him an ornate memorial to a man named Samuel Skews. Atop a plinth on the monument was the figure of an angel, which was beautifully carved. The lettering below was highly ornate, with lots of flourishes.

"He was the Mine Agent and their Assayer from what I can gather... Bit different to the others, eh? But see that, look..."

She pointed to the detail of the inscription.

"Says he was killed in an accident..."

"Really?"

"Must have been a hard life for they. I must look into that in the future."

Cecilia took some photographs of these graves and then the pair of them carried on. Back at the chapel, they could hear the sound of singing. Apparently, some old miner's songs and hymns had been dug out and the plan was for them to, later on, launch a new local soda, to be named Knockie, after the legendary quaint creatures who supposedly could be found in the bottom of mines and who protected miners from rock falls. It seemed to fit the occasion. Cecilia had heard of similar creatures back home.

"See that, look..." pointed out Jean.

She pointed to the largest edifice in the Methodist section of the cemetery. The tomb was high and ornate, and covered by a frieze around its sides. Rising from it was a large Celtic cross, at least as tall as some of those she had seen back home.

"Looks like someone who knew his past," commented Cecilia.

"Well, yes. See that's the Jewell memorial. I think it's lovely. All that knotwork done by the mason. Must have taken days..."

"Jewell?"

"Yes, that's your great-grandmother's father. Rebecca was his daughter, wasn't she? And there look, is Doctor George Jewell. He was some chap as you can see. The mine surgeon... and a preacher. Now, if you look closely, you'll see the wife buried with un here is Eleanor. She was his second wife. A Prowse I believe from down Calumet. His first wife was Clara: that's your great-grandmother, but there's no record of she. She wuz here at one point though. The shipping lists say she came across. Disappeared clean off the earth. Odd, isn't it?"

"Very," said Cecilia.

"He must have done away with her," Jean joked. "Perhaps she wuz a nag."

"Maybe," acknowledged Cecilia, "But I'd read they had three children... Rebecca (who you know), then there was Mabel and then a James. He was the youngest."

"No record of them either," said Jean. "But like you say, Clara and he were the parents... Not Eleanor. We know where Rebecca's buried, but if you say from your research that there were two more, well, there's no clue here."

"Must have disappeared. Left for new climes then."

"Quite," said Jean. "Or maybe they went back home..."

There were no answers to be found. Go back far enough and everything becomes a void. Information collapses. It falls in like rock in old levels below ground where damp timbers rot.

They wandered on. It was hot now: another mid-continental, muggy day.

"Now," said Jean with great relish. "This is your set here I believe..."

She pointed to a series of graves.

"I'll wander back. You take your time my dear... You've come a long way to see these."

That's when Cecilia saw her origins. There was the grave of her great-grandfather (miner and automobile engineer ut said) and with him, dying a few years later, was his wife: the eventual parents of Jago Ciaran Nankervis, her grandfather who, when the mine became a knacked bal, had made his way back to Cornwall. That Irish middle name of his though? Puzzling. Very puzzling. She had her own take on that. Just along, she found her great-uncle and auntie: Justin; his wife Rosie dying a few years before him. No children though. She spent perhaps fifteen minutes there contemplating and thinking over their time here. She took detailed photographs and cried a few tears, not perhaps for those dead, but more in thanks for this final connection with her ancestors. Here they were, lined up for inspection.

Her mind ran to the next few days: the drive of her hire car back down the peninsula. The flight from Houghton back to O'Hare airport in Chicago, and then the night flight Atlantic crossing, back to Heathrow; then the morning train back down another peninsula to home. But as she wandered around her line in the earth, she observed two other graves close by. Maybe others had not even caught sight of them because of the former incursion of the forest. Their mounds were not high, nor long: and so she knew they were children, possibly not even yet children because they were so tiny. She realised they were probably infants. At some point, one of them had had a wooden marker – the stem of it was still there, but the other part of it had been worn away by time. The other, set further away, was unmarked. But by the way the cemetery was organised, ut looked like these had gone in first.

When she found Jean back outside the chapel, she had to ask her about them.

"You okay?" she asked, noting perhaps a change in her expression.

"Yes," said Cecilia. "I wanted to ask you. Back at my family plot, there were two graves... of infants... one closer, but one apart from them... had you seen them before?"

"Oh yes," said Jean. "I've seen them. Probably those who died in childbirth. A lot of infant mortality back then."

"There's no details... they've worn away..."

"I know... we mapped everything else... it's all on the website... Those two are still a bit of a puzzle though."

"My family, do you think? Maybe Justin and Rosie perhaps? Maybe they tried but they didn't survive."

"Maybe so. Hard to tell, isn't it?"

"Yes," said Cecilia. "It is. So sad... for them."

And on her mind still wuz that Maddy O'Donahue. How did she fit in to all of this? But there was no more anyone could do. She could only go back inside 'Saffron-Bun Chapel' and hear more of the celebratory music. There, she'd finish her revel bun and later be handed a bottle of Knockie-themed soda.

Belaw ground at the knacked bal, in the deepest part of the mine's levels that had not flooded, two beings suddenly awoke from a long hibernation – a hibernation that had lasted nigh on a century (but a momentary pause for they). Others had moved on – heading for California and Nevada – but they'd remained here for a bit of a breather, knawing that one day soon, time would come and catch up with they.

"Wozzon?" said one, yawning and brushing the sleep away from his eyes.

"They'm a-singing up chapel again," said the other, stretching.

"Really?"

"Es."

"She've finally come fur we then?"

"Reckon so..."

"And a Nankervis?"

Vibrations see, goin' round the earth. They'd heard of she. Stories too, ov lithium mining opening in Cornwall.

"Es. Finally, we'n tell our tale then..."

"... an' put she right."

They made plans and climbed up some rickety ladders to the surface. After a hundred years belaw ground, the fresh air above tasted some sweet. But when they met the collar, all that they had remembered had been subsumed by forest. Ut took a while fur they to get their bearings.

"I'n smell saffron buns," said Luk.

"Me too," noted Gourgy.

They mozeyed up there to have a gake at she. Cecilia Nankervis didn' knaw ut, but up chapel, she wuz about to have the shock of her life – and gain two new pint-size companions. It wuz about to get... brave an' magical. Es. Another cycle wuz beginning.

Crows cawed, blue jays sang and caterpillars transformed into butterflies: emerging into the Keweenaw afternoon light from a thousand chrysalises.